Still Waters

JUDITH SAXTON

Still Waters

ST. MARTIN'S PRESS NEW YORK

Library of Congress Cataloging-in-Publication Data

Saxton, Judith.
Still waters / by Judith Saxton.—1st U.S. ed.
p.   cm.
ISBN 0-312-18185-X
I. Title.
PR6069.A97S75   1998
823'.914—dc21   97-48356   CIP

First published in Great Britain by William Heinemann, an
imprint of Reed International Books Ltd.

First U.S. Edition: April 1998

10 9 8 7 6 5 4 3 2 1

For my cousin Gloria and her
husband, Alan Collinson, who made
our stay in Melbourne so
memorable – see you soon!

Acknowledgements

My thanks go once again to all the people who helped me to sort out both ends of the story, in particular the library staff of the Great Yarmouth Branch, who sorted out all the material available on Barton, both Broad and villages, in the twenties and thirties, and particularly to Cassie Turner, whose father fished Barton Broad at weekends – her memories of the beauty and richness of the Broad then made it all come to life for me.

The staff of the Castle Museum, Norwich, were very helpful in finding me details of the war years, and Angela Wootton, of the Imperial War Museum, helped me out over Rhodesia and the training camps for Air Force personnel in the early forties.

And many thanks to Tony Winser of Buxton, Norfolk, who I met quite by chance and saw that he was wearing a Lancaster bomber tie – he very kindly answered all my questions, gave me a delightful wartime song much sung in the mess, and explained the complexities of the aircraft which I needed for my story. As usual any mistakes are mine, but the bits I got right are his!

And in Australia, Gloria and Alan Collinson took me all over Melbourne and told me where to find old street plans and the sort of information I needed, my son Tony Turner did the same for Sydney, and Cass Gardiner, the Cairns librarian, was absolutely invaluable – without her wonderful book list I should have been sunk indeed when it came to Queensland in the twenties.

And as always, many thanks to the staff of the International Library in Liverpool, who found the books that I couldn't buy in Australia, and to Marina Thomas and the staff of the Wrexham Branch Library, who did likewise.

Prologue

Melbourne, November 1918

It was a hot night. High in the dark sky above Melbourne the stars twinkled down on the motley crowds surging back and forth across streets and pavements, but Malcolm Chandler, clutching his mother's skirt, never even looked up, though a few months before his mother had told him about the stars and pointed out the Southern Cross blazing above them, explaining that he was lucky to be able to see it at all.

'Your grandparents, in England, have never seen those special stars,' she had said. 'They have the Plough, instead. It's – it's kind o' small, made out of small little stars, but then England's quite small, too.'

It was odd, Mal had thought, how when Mammy said England was kind of small she sounded wistful, as though in her book small was best. But when his father said the same thing, the words held a sneer. Small is rotten, his voice said. Small is measly, something to despise and look down on. And Mal suspected that Bill Chandler really did think small was rotten, because Mal was small himself and sometimes Mal caught Bill looking at him with dislike, as though he wished him far away. And to be so regarded is frightening, especially when you are only five and the person who dislikes you is a grown man, and your father into the bargain.

'You all right, son?'

Kath's voice brought Mal's thoughts back to the present, but though he tried to pause, to look up and answer Kath properly, he was unable to do so. Even as she spoke they rounded the corner

1

of Queen Street and burst on to Little Collins Street and the noise and the crowds were such that Mal found himself being pulled away from his mother by the press of people. He whimpered, tugged desperately at her skirt, and Kath stopped, stuck a sharp elbow into the face of a man who had somehow managed to get between them, then kicked out in a manner which Mal knew she would consider unladylike later, when she thought about it, and forced her way back to her small son.

The man who had been elbowed yelped but shouldered his way past them and Kath bent and picked Mal up, settling him firmly on her left hip.

'Hang on, son, this is no time to be separated and I can see something going on ahead . . . Oh my word!'

An explosion, accompanied by a thousand brilliantly coloured stars, split the night. Mal, from his higher position, saw that someone was letting off firecrackers. Right near them a small shop, its shutters erected, a barricade of stout wooden planks nailed across them, seemed to be swaying as though it was about to fall . . . he had no idea what was happening but a skinny young man with a shock of black, frizzy hair, turned and grinned at him.

'The bloody chinks nailed their shutters up but we've broke into them any old how,' he shouted above the din. 'Them's firecrackers a-goin' off, what the chinks save for their New Year. Jeez, how the old feller's screechin'!'

The movement of the crowd now surged Kath and Mal up on to the pavement and within a couple of feet of the small Chinese shops and Mal found himself with a ringside seat at the lively proceedings. He could see a tall Chinese in a long robe with a funny little silk cap on his head, trying to drive people away from the front of his shop. He had a long stick with a silver knob on the end and he was using it to good effect, but even so the shutters had given way at one end and people were shoving and wriggling through the gap and coming out with their arms laden with gaily coloured cylinders, things which looked like blue and orange wheels, other things shaped like cones . . . and one man had what looked like a sack laden with something heavy over one shoulder.

'Look, Mammy!' Mal squeaked. 'The chinky whacked that fel-

2

ler's head, *wham, wham*, but he didn't drop nothing, he didn't even blink! Crikey, there's a lady with a stick too.'

A tiny Chinese woman, laughing and shouting, was hitting out at the crowd with a large umbrella. Her hair had come down from the tight little bun on top of her head and hung in feathery strands round her face and her skin, more ivory than yellow, gleamed in the gaslight's glow. Mal thought she was very pretty and waved to her, but she was too busy whacking with her umbrella to wave back, though she acknowledged him with a tight little smile.

'My God . . . that isn't just high spirits and celebrations, that feller's looting,' Kath shouted, her eyes following her son's pointing finger. 'That's thieving, that's not just taking a few firecrackers to make a good loud noise. Where's the police? Someone's going to get hurt . . . Hang on, Mal, we'd best get out o' this.'

But even Mal could see that getting out was now impossible. In the relative quiet of Queen Street they could have gone their own way but here, packed into the crowd as sardines are packed into a tin, choice was denied them. They would be carried forward at the crowd's whim whether they would or no.

Kath tried to turn and realised at once that it was not going to be possible. She sighed and hugged Mal tight, then bent her head and spoke into his ear.

'Sorry, feller, we're going up to Swanston Street whether we want to or not! Just hold tight!'

Mal would have liked to remind his mother that they had been heading for Swanston Street anyway, that they had promised Bill they would meet him outside the Town Hall at ten, but he realised it wasn't the moment. She would never hear him, and besides, he was getting caught up in the excitement of the crowd and had no wish to go tamely home. Someone near him was starting up a chorus and he raised his small, piping voice in the same tune, though the words he knew didn't seem to be quite the same as the men were singing.

> *I don't want to be a soldier,*
> *I don't want to go to war,*
> *I'd rather stay at home,*

3

Around the streets to roam,
And live on the earnings of a high-born whore . . .

Another firecracker went off, turning the sky above them momentarily incandescent, and Kath squeaked and then laughed.

'Well, this is a night you'll never forget, Mal! The war's over, your daddy's home, and all Melbourne is celebrating – all Australia, very like. Any moment now we'll be on Swanston Street, and then I bet we'll see a lot of folk all giving thanks for the Armistice.'

Mal wanted to say he couldn't imagine more people than there were here, but whilst he was struggling to make himself heard, the crowd surged out of the confines of Little Collins Street and on to Swanston, almost opposite the Town Hall, which was decorated with enough bunting to hide its normally solid stone façade.

The street was wide here, and Kath managed to cross it, still with Mal on her hip, and to take up her station on the broad pavement right outside the Town Hall. There, she stood Mal down and rubbed her arms ruefully.

'You're quite a weight, old feller,' she told him. 'Reckon we'll have to ask your daddy to carry you home, eh?'

Tactful for once, Mal said nothing. This was such a good evening, he didn't want to spoil it by having to think about Bill – and as for his father carrying him home, why on earth should he? The two of them seldom exchanged a word, far less a touch. *I hate him*, Mal thought automatically now. Coming back from – from wherever it was he'd been, saying now he's home we must have what he wants for dinner, getting into *my* bed with *my* mammy and making me sleep on the horrible, hard sofa, telling Mammy she's making a nancy-boy out of her son . . . The list went on and on, though Bill had only been home four or five days.

'Can you see Daddy, Mal? He's not an easy man to miss . . . what colour would you say his hair was, son?'

'Yaller,' Mal muttered. That was another sore point. Bill had looked at Mal's dark, straight hair and then at his own blond curls and at Mammy's beautiful, light-brown fall of hair and had said, resentfully, that the kid must be a changeling, with colouring which favoured neither his mother nor father.

4

'He's a sulky little brute, what's more,' he had growled, not bothering to keep his voice down, though he knew full well that Mal was only feet away, in the living-room, lying on the crude bed of sofa cushions which Kath had made up for her deposed son. 'Looks at me under his brows, don't answer when I speak to him . . . I can't abide a sulky kid.'

'He's not sulky, Bill,' his mother had said. 'But he doesn't know you very well, yet. He's – he's shy. After all, you're a stranger, really.'

'A stranger? I'm his pa, Goddammit!'

'Yes, but he wasn't quite a year old when you went away, love. You don't expect him to remember you, do you?'

There had been a laugh in her voice, a sort of soft, teasing sweetness which made Mal grip both hands into fists and then bite the knuckles. How *dared* she push him out of her bed and put that – that yellow-haired man in his place? How dared she laugh and tease him . . . no doubt presently she would curl round him as, until five nights ago, she had curled round Mal. Then, he supposed wistfully, she would kiss that Bill on the tickly back of the neck and laugh when he giggled and say 'Night-night, sleep tight', just as she always had with Mal.

There was a short pause, then Bill had spoken again. 'He was a bonza kid then, Kath; what went wrong?'

There was a smooth, snuggling sound which Mal could not interpret, then his mother spoke again; soothingly, sweet and soft as honey dripping from the comb.

'The war happened, my love, and Mal had to learn to grow up with only me for company. Oh, he's been to kindergarten, has friends, plays out when he can, but he's become a bit of a loner. And I couldn't provide him with a playmate with you away now, could I?'

Mal had sat up in bed, all the hairs on the back of his neck prickling erect. She had spoken in an almost pleading tone, yet the laugh was there, the tease. He heard more rustling, then the creak of bedsprings, and then his father said, 'Oh Kath, Kath – dear Lord, I've missed this!'

This? What did he mean by 'this'?

'Me too, dearest. Oh, Bill, when you do that . . .'

5

The laughter had gone from his mother's voice and reappeared now, as if by magic, in his father's.

'D'you like it, girlie? Shall I do it again?'

'Oh Bill, Bill! Oh dear God . . . oh Bill!'

Mal knelt up. The beast was hurting her, he would go and fetch a knife out of the kitchen and then run into the bedroom and tell Bill to leave her alone or he'd stab him to death! That would teach him that Mal was neither a changeling nor that other thing he had been called – a nancy-boy, that was it – but a person who could look after Kath perfectly well without any help from *him*, thank you very much.

Only he hadn't moved, of course. And presently, he had pulled his blanket up, shame flooding over him in a great wave. It was no use, he was just a little boy and Bill was a big man. He couldn't do anything to save Kath, and in his heart he knew she didn't want to be saved. So he had lain down again, and presently, slept.

But right now, with the seething, chattering crowd all about him and firecrackers going off at intervals, with a long line of people with their hands clasping each other's waists so that they looked like a snake weaving up and down the middle of the road, he was in charge. His mother would look to him for protection and companionship, at least until the hated Bill turned up. Perhaps he's gone away again, Mal thought hopefully, as he scanned the crowd and didn't see a yellow head anywhere. Perhaps he's gone back to the war. Perhaps we won't ever see him again, and I can go back and sleep in my big bed tonight, and cuddle Mammy and make her laugh.

But he didn't believe it would happen, not really. His father would turn up, like the bad penny he was, and start boasting and shouting and trying to pretend he was important, when Mal knew very well that Bill was nothing.

'What does your dad do?' one of the kids in the kindergarten had asked him only the previous day. 'My dad's a tram-driver. *Ting-a-ling, ting-a-ling, move farther down the car, please.*'

Mal had mumbled that his father had been a soldier, that very soon he would . . . he would . . . but the kid wasn't interested. He moved off, pretending to turn the handle of an imaginary ticket-

6

machine, shouting to imaginary passengers to climb aboard, or mind the step, or show us your season ticket then, sport.

So Bill wasn't even any good to boast about. Fathers were supposed to go out to work and bring home presents and exciting food, they weren't supposed to hang around the flat all day and grumble about somewhere called Civvy Street where a decent bloke wasn't wanted no more. They took their sons to the beach, or to the park to play cricket or football, they didn't lounge on the sofa drinking warm beer, or go mysteriously off somewhere and return late at night, singing rude songs which made Mammy cry out to him to 'Hush, before you get us thrown out!'

'There he is! There's your daddy, Mal – see his fair head above the crowd?'

Mal pretended to look but he didn't, not really. He stared at waist-level, because all men looked the same to him then and he could pretend for a little longer that his father had gone off once more and wouldn't be returning for absolutely ages. Weeks, months – years!

Kath gave an impatient little cluck and swung him off his feet. She pointed. Coming down the road towards them was an untidy group of men, most of whom gripped a beer-bottle in one fist. They were singing, shouting, cat-calling. Half-way down the line Bill's blond head shone, unmistakable.

'See him, love? Give him a wave and a cheer . . . go on, call him – it'll please him no end.'

Obedient to the pleading in her voice Mal called, but kept his voice low; he didn't want to give the intruder into his life any false hopes, not he! War had been declared from the first moment his father had ordered him to do something – *Git your bleedin' fingers off that bleedin' cake, sport, or I'll teach you a lesson you won't forgit!* – and Mal did not intend to go weakly giving in and making friends, just because it was Armistice Day and people were letting off firecrackers.

But Kath, who had hoisted him up so that he could see over the heads of the crowd, didn't know any of this. 'Can you see him, Mal?' she asked rather breathlessly, for her son was heavy. 'Go on, shout!'

And then it happened. A tram came down Swanston Street,

ringing its bell. It was almost empty, but the driver had slowed down, presumably because of the press of people. Mal expected the men to get out of the way but suddenly someone shouted something and men who had begun shambling towards the pavement turned round again and began to charge unsteadily towards the oncoming vehicle. The tram-driver rang his bell more furiously than ever . . . then stopped, and Mal watched, awed, as the men, his father well in the lead, clambered on to the tram, pulled the conductor and the few passengers out of their seats, and lastly evicted the driver, who stood uncertainly beside his vehicle, apparently attempting to reason with Bill, who was nearest.

'Mal? What's happening, son?'

'They've stopped the tram,' Mal announced. 'Oh! Oh!'

For his father was now completely in command. He issued orders, pointing to this man, to that, and then barked a further command, bending down as he did so to grip the tram just behind its front wheels. Everyone followed suit and before Mal had done more than take in a breath the tram was lifted bodily off the rails and was crossing the width of the road, the pavement . . . people screamed, cheered, shouted, but the tram-carriers ignored advice and recriminations alike. Using the tram like a gigantic spear, with Bill at their head, the men thundered towards the huge plate-glass window of the Electricity Company's office.

The crash was incredible, unbelievable. A thousand firecrackers could not have made such a marvellous sound and the shards of glass, erupting into the store, caught the light and twinkled like a thousand stars. Mal, in his mother's arms, screamed at the top of his voice, his hair on end, his eyes bright with excitement and pride.

'Daddy! Daddy Chandler! Bill Chandler's my daddy, he's the best man in the whole world!'

Giddy with excitement and reflected glory, he found himself on the pavement once more whilst beside him, Kath was saying flatly: 'He's drunk, the stupid wallaby! Dear God, what've we done to deserve this? What've we done? They'll make him pay, Mal, they'll make your daddy pay – don't say a word now, we've got to get out of this.'

'I'm going to wait for my dad,' Mal said in a hard, grown-up voice. 'I won't go away from here without my dad. Leave off tugging at my hand, Mammy – I'm going home with my dad.'

And presently, when Bill joined them, Mal let go of Kath and attached himself, limpet-like, to his father. Bill shouted with laughter and hoisted his small son up on to one broad shoulder and told him to 'hang on!' and then put his arm round Kath's waist and marched her off down the middle of the road to see 'What me an' the lads have done to make today a *real* night to remember!'

'They'll crucify you for this, Bill,' Kath whispered, trying to pull away. 'Don't you want a decent job, a place of our own? You won't get it by acting in that wild way – half Melbourne must have seen what you did tonight.'

But Mal held on to his father's blond hair and felt the muscles in his father's broad shoulders move as he strode out and knew only a blinding, dizzying happiness. His father was a real man, a man who could pick up a tram and ram it through a plate-glass window and then walk down the middle of the road like a king! And when they reached home and Bill lost patience with what he called Kath's whingeing and slapped her across the face and pushed her into their bedroom, Mal quite saw that a man who could pick up a tram mustn't take any heed of a silly woman. He got into his own makeshift bed and cuddled down, planning how, when he was a man, he, too, would pick up a tram and hurl it through a window. And when he heard his mother begin to weep he thought what a pity it was that she couldn't enjoy things like he and his father could.

He did have a moment's doubt because Mammy had wept, but presently she stopped crying and gave a watery chuckle and he relaxed. It was all right, she admired his dad too, women had to pretend to disapprove of tram-throwing.

Soon, he slept and dreamed of fireworks, and fizzy lemonade, and the Southern Cross blazing down on him as he, single-handed, hurled a tram through the biggest plate-glass window in Melbourne.

One

August 1927

Tess was dreaming of the sea. She dreamed that she was running unsteadily across a long, dark-gold strand where, beyond the gentle slope of the beach, were the white horses, the tumbled grey waters, the darker line of the horizon where sea and sky met.

She was running unsteadily because in the dream she was small, very small. She had come down on to the sands by herself and she knew it was naughty, in the back of her mind the tiny voice of conscience told her she'd be sorry when They found out, but the young Tess loved the sea and the shore, was prepared to take the consequences.

She reached the breakwater and collapsed on the smooth, downward-sloping bank where the sand around the bottom had been eaten away by the restless waves. Here, the breakwater rose out of a long, deep pool, the sea-water in the pool now rising, now sinking, its reflections of the scudding grey clouds barely beginning to settle down before another wave shattered their peace. When Tess looked towards the sea she could see the waves surging into the long pool, so she must not go too close – it was dangerous. If she slid down the sand and into that water it would close over her head without a sound and she would be drowned-dead in a very short time. Someone was always reminding her that the sea was never to be taken lightly, that though she loved to play in it, the waves were not truly her friends, and she took heed. She had been knocked over by a monstrous wave when she was even smaller than she was now, because she had run away from her daddy and paddled out, never realising the monster was lurking, waiting for someone to come within its range. It had hurt quite badly. It had pelted her with small stones and sand, as well as crushing her with the sheer weight of its water, and her gasp of outrage – for until that moment she had always thought of the sea as her friend – had nearly been her last. Water rushed into her lungs . . . then she was snatched from the wave, tipped upside down, squeezed like her bath-time sponge until all the water ran out . . . and she had laughed down into the worried face of the person who held her, and tried to kick the naughty sea.

But she had learned her lesson. Never turn your back on the sea, never let it trick you, beware of even the stillest, most tempting water when it was deeper than your small fingers. So now she sat on the hard wet sand and stared down at the goings-on of the sea-creatures in the long pool. A tiny crab scuttled, then disappeared into the sand. Transparent shrimps skated along the bottom, making little clouds rise up where they settled. Barnacles waved tiny filaments from their places on the wooden groin which stretched from the top of the beach right down to the low-water mark, so that now it was half hidden by the restless, choppy caress of the waves.

Tess looked away from the tempting water, down at her own small person. She was wearing a candy-striped dress, white on pink, and frilly pink knickers. She couldn't see the knickers of course, but they went with the dress; Mummy would never have dreamed of putting her into the candy-striped dress without the matching knickers. And because it was a mild and windy day her short, fat legs were bare though she had white ankle socks on, and new bright-red strap shoes. Sitting on the sand, she admired them for a moment, then looked hopefully back at the water. It was no shallower, indeed it seemed to be deeper. Such cool, splashy, beautiful water! Tessie wants to paddle, her small self said suddenly. Mustn't paddle here, too dangerous, but further down, where the low-water lies . . .

She got to her feet and began to trundle down towards the sea. There should have been a low-water for paddling, but when she reached the edge of the waves she realised that the huge, shallow pools hadn't yet formed so the tide must be coming in, not going out. She had heard the remark enough times to understand its meaning vaguely. It meant she would probably not get a paddle today, because presently the waves would creep higher still up the shore, and she would have to retreat to the dry sand and the dunes above the beach.

Small Tess stood for a moment where the low-waters should have been, and pondered. She would not paddle here. If she tried, the sea would undoubtedly knock her down and probably hit her with its stones, too. But if she went up the beach again, alongside the breakwater, right up to the very top, then surely she might find a pool?

She turned round and faced up the beach once more. She trudged up the shingle bank, uncomfortably aware that her new shoes were chock-full of sand and tiny pebbles and that her feet were uncomfortably hot, so when she reached the top of the bank it seemed only sensible to sit down on the pebbles and remove her shoes and socks. She put the socks in the shoes, feeling proud of her achievement in doing this, and stood up again, shoes in hand. Oh, the lovely feeling of the sand between her toes, the glorious coolness of bare, bare feet!

She reached the breakwater, with its dangerously deep, current-induced pool. She kept clear, but walked close enough to look into the water. At this level the water was really very deep, and it was dark and mysterious, too, the groin sewn thickly with marvellous seaweed, barnacles, limpets, and the long blue shells of mussels. She stopped and slid to a halt, sitting down so suddenly that the hard sand met her pink-clad bottom rather sharply; she chuckled, then resumed her scrutiny of the watery depths before her. All that seaweed, differently coloured, differently textured, some fat and dark, some pale and fine as hair, all moving gently and in perfect unison as, on the shoreline, the waves advanced and retreated.

And it wasn't only weed in the water, there was . . .

A voice, a cry no louder than that of a seabird, caught her attention. She turned her head and stared the way she had come earlier. She screwed up her eyes the better to see, then scowled. It was that boy! Oh, he was horrible, she really hated him, he would come running up, scatter sand all over her, tell her off, perhaps he might even smack her as Mummy wasn't there to see . . . she really hated him!

She got to her feet and as she did so the shoes and socks seemed to leap from her hand and duck-dived neatly into the deep water. Immediately she forgot all about the hated boy and moaned aloud. Her new shoes! They would be so cross, they had left her in the garden, snoozing in the hammock, they didn't know she had learned how to jump out of it without hurting herself . . . she had meant to be back before anyone returned . . . They would be so cross!

The boy shouted from behind her, his voice high, breathless.

'Hey, get away from there! The water's deep, get away . . .'

She ignored him, squatting above the water, staring down at her shoes which were moving up and down, up and down, the socks trailing from them, as though they had a life of their own. The boy could be useful – he could fish them out for her, if she kept her eyes on them and was able to tell him exactly where they were! But even as she watched the shoes she saw, out the corner of her eye, that there was something else in the long, deep pool. Something different. Not a little crab, nor a shrimp, something very much bigger, something strangely sinister . . .

She was staring at it, forgetting the shoes, when the boy grabbed her. He lifted her off her feet and turned her into his shirt front. She could feel, against her face, his heart hammering away, and she could smell the horrible flat black Pontefract cakes he was always eating. He said they were too strong for babies, only *men* could eat them – as if she were a baby! As if he were a man, come to that! She wriggled in his arms, trying to escape, trying to explain about the shoes, trying to point . . .

He said in an oddly muffled voice, 'Don't look. You mustn't look, it's – it's awful naughty to peep. Come with me now, there's a good girl.'

'But I dropped my shoes in the water – my new shoes,' Tess wailed, and gave one last, determined wiggle. The boy teetered and half turned and Tess looked down into the water. She strained to see her shoes, but saw, instead . . .

Moving, moving, with the water. Something terrible, something horrible . . .

The small Tess clutched the boy hard, hard. The scene in front of her began to sway and dissolve and waver before her eyes. And she screamed, and screamed, and *screamed* . . .

Tess woke. Pale early sunshine flooded into her bedroom, dappling the wall by her nose with a moving picture of leaf-shadow, but she was too hot and bothered to notice. She sat up, a hand to her thundering heart. It was that beastly dream again, always pouncing on her when she least wanted or expected it – and it wasn't as though she could ever remember the bloomin' ending of it, either. At first, it was always such fun; transported back to being a very small girl again, probably aged around two or three, finding herself on a beautiful beach, and then . . .

The word 'beach' however, pushed the dream right into the very back of her mind. Tess felt a broad, contented smile spread across her face. Today was Saturday, it was the school holidays, and Daddy had said she might go with the Throwers to Sea Palling, where they would stay for a whole glorious week in Mrs Sutcliffe's beach-bungalow.

'We'll go shrimpin', come low-tide, so bring you a flour-bag on a split cane,' Ned Thrower had instructed her. Ned was twelve, four years older than she and Janet, who were both eight and had been friends for as long as Tess could remember. But she and Janet liked Ned all right, thinking him more fun than the twins, who were always together and had no time for kids two years younger than they. 'An' bring a spade an' a bucket,' Ned had continued. 'Acos you'll need 'em, one way and t'other.'

Tess had promised to do so and now she scrambled out of bed and padded, in her striped pyjamas, on to the small, square landing. Her father slept in the room opposite her own. Tess bent and listened outside her father's door. No sound. He was, she guessed, still asleep, for she had known from the angle at which the sunshine fell on her wall that it was still very early. But today was Sea Palling day, so no time should be wasted. She had packed last night, helped – and hindered – by Janet, who was terrified that her friend might bring best clothes and ruin them, so all she had to do was wash, dress, and get some breakfast inside her. Then she could run down the lane to where the Throwers' tumbledown cottage crouched on the staithe, and make sure that Janet, too, was ready for the great adventure.

She went back into her room and poured water from the ewer into the basin with the poppies around the rim. The water gushed cold, but who cared? She was off on holiday with her best friend and that best friend's family . . . she simply couldn't wait!

Ten minutes later, Tess let herself out of the creaking back door, ran round the house, out of the front gate and along the lane. She adored the Throwers, from tall Bert, who was eighteen, to the baby, Podge, who was going on three, and Mr and Mrs Thrower were grand. Mr Thrower was a reed-cutter, and could be seen on icy winter mornings in his flat-bottomed boat, sculling out on to the Broad with Bert to harvest the reeds which, he was fond of telling anyone who would listen, was the only crop he knew which needed no husbanding yet repaid the harvester well.

Of course Mr Thrower did other things to make ends meet; in summer he harvested the marsh hay from the low-lying water meadows, he trudged from farm to farm doing labouring work, and he had fish traps in the Broad and snares in the woods. What was more the Thrower cottage had a very large garden which always bristled with vegetables, as well as with apple trees and fruit bushes, a rhubarb patch and a veritable forest of raspberry canes. As she ran up the path and skirted the cottage to go round the back, Tess thought of the way the boys and Janet helped with the garden. Indeed, they had been working feverishly of late to make sure that it could survive without them for the week's holiday . . . only two evenings ago she and Janet had hoed patiently between the vegetable rows and then laid cut reeds down, to keep the soil moist in the unlikely event of a rain-free week.

Tess reached the back of the cottage and saw various Throwers engaged in various pursuits. Two boys were filling a soft cloth bag with peas, another was helping Mr Thrower, who was pulling his boat ashore, and Ned was digging potatoes and dropping them into a sack. No one took the slightest notice of Tess as she ran round to the back door, which was open, and tumbled into the huge, earth-floored room which was kitchen and living-room for a dozen lively, quarrelsome Throwers. Podge was sitting on the rag rug in a pair of trousers which were much too big for him, eating a round of bread and jam, whilst Mrs Thrower fried something in a big black pan.

'Tess, Tess!' Podge squeaked. 'We're goin' to the seaside!'

Mrs Thrower turned and grinned. 'Marnin', lovie. Hev you had breakfuss?'

'No, not yet, but it's all right,' Tess said quickly. 'I'll have brekker at home, with Daddy, when he gets up.'

'Let's save your dad the trouble, hey, since I'm a-cookin',' Mrs Thrower said amiably. 'There's fried eggs, my last year's pig-bacon, and a mess o' spuds. Here, mek yourself useful; wet the tea, my woman.'

Tess was gratified, for at home her father made alarmed noises when she suggested helping in the kitchen, though the size and blackness of the Thrower kettle, sitting on the side of the rickety range, was a trifle daunting. Nevertheless she moved the teapot as near as she could, stood on tiptoe and began to pour. It comforted her that Mrs Thrower made no move to help her, though doubtless she was keeping an eye.

Tess filled the pot, replaced the lid, then turned to the older woman. 'Done it! Where's the milk?'

'There's some in a jug, in the bucket o' water under the table,' Mrs Thrower said, beginning to dish up. 'Just enough for all, I reckon.' She raised her voice. 'Come an' get it.'

Throwers began to materialise inside the kitchen, queuing to wash their hands at the old stone sink which was so low you had to bend to it. Some clattered down the stairs, others came in from the garden. Janet, emerging from the front room with her arms full of clothing, beamed at Tess.

'Tess! I'm puttin' my clo'es in this here sack . . . Gi's a hand!'

Tess began to help whilst, behind her, the family settled themselves at the big wooden table and watched closely as their mother served the food on to cracked pottery plates. Mrs Thrower was always fair; Mr Thrower and Bert got the most, and helpings gradually diminished down to Podge, who ate his small portion from a chipped fruit dish.

Tess finished shovelling clothing into the sack and she and

Janet joined the rest of the family at the table. Because the two of them were the same age, they got identical helpings; Mrs Thrower would never have under- or over-fed a guest simply because she was a guest. Besides, Tess spent so much time with Janet that Mrs Thrower had more than once remarked she was family, or as good as.

As she began to tuck into the fry-up, Tess reflected that she admired Janet's mum more than anyone else she knew; she worked incredibly hard yet she was always cheerful and always had time for her family. Mrs Thrower made willow baskets from the osiers which overhung the Broad, and she cleaned for the only two big houses within cycling distance – the Sutcliffes, who lives at Horning and had lent the seaside bungalow, and the Hunts, who lived rather nearer, at Neatishead. She cleaned for the Delameres, too, but they scarcely counted since their house was small and compact. It didn't take her above a couple of hours a couple of times a week to 'whisk round' as she called it.

And cleaning wasn't all Mrs Thrower did; in her search for paid employment she cycled long distances, doing any work available from cooking and serving meals when the farmer's wife was away, to minding beasts grazing on the common, and people from miles around agreed that no one worked harder than Mrs Thrower. In addition she preserved and bottled quantities of the fruit and vegetables raised by her husband and made jelly from the blackberries which grew in abundance around the Broad. Most of these delicacies she sold to a grocer in North Walsham, though the Delameres often enjoyed Thrower jams and bottled raspberries in wintertime, and Tess knew that the Hunts and the Sutcliffes bought her produce, too.

'More spuds, gal Tess?' Mrs Thrower's voice broke in upon Tess's reflections and Tess, blushing, realised that she had cleared her plate in record time.

'No thanks, Mrs Thrower, that was delicious. Umm . . . if you don't mind, I think I ought to get back, I expect Daddy's up and . . .'

'You'll be wantin' your brekker,' Mr Thrower said, grinning at her. 'What a gal you are for your grub, my woman! Well, if you can get outside another meal like that, I'll tek my cap off to you!'

17

That made them all laugh, because Mr Thrower never removed his flat cap, not in company, at any rate. Tess suspected that he wore it in bed, though she had never been cheeky enough to ask. Certainly, his face was burned red-brown by wind and weather and when he pushed his cap to the back of his head – as he did occasionally, when puzzled – his forehead was white as driven snow.

'No, I couldn't eat another thing, honestly,' Tess said now, wriggling on her chair. She knew better than to get down until she was told she might do so, for the Throwers, though casual in many ways, believed that children should remain at the table until given leave to go. 'Only Daddy doesn't know where I am, and . . .'

'Oh, go on with you; you can git down,' Mrs Thrower said, seeing her dilemma. 'Janet, you go along wi' Tess, see if you can help. But be back here in half an hour, no later. The carrier'll be along be then.'

'Don't forgit your bucket an' flour bag, gal,' shouted Ned as they scampered out of the back door. 'Do you'll never hev nothin' to put your shrimps in.'

Tess paused long enough to yell back, 'They're packed already, bor Ned!' before Janet had squealed 'Race you!' and they had set off, skidding on the cinder path, then erupting into the lane and pelting along it until they reached the gate of the Old House.

Peter Delamere was sitting at the kitchen table when they came in through the back door, placidly eating toast and reading a book propped against the marmalade jar. Tess thought he was the best-looking father any girl could have with his browny-gold hair and goldy-brown eyes and the neat golden moustache which tickled when he kissed her. She adored his chin, which had a deep cleft, and his neat ears and his beautifully kept hands with the golden hairs on the backs. He wasn't as tall as Uncle Phil, but he was tall enough, and today he wore a brown-and-white checked shirt and brown corduroys, which meant he wasn't going to go into the city to work, nor was he going to play golf. He would be at home, gardening, working in the house, having his dinner out on the daisy-studded lawn, picking an apple and sharing it with the blackbird which sometimes came right into the kitchen, it was so tame.

Tess went round behind him, put her arms round his neck and squeezed, and Peter grunted, removed her arms, pulled her round and gave her a hug. Then he took another big bite out of his toast.

'Wretched child,' he said fondly. 'What sort of an hour did you get up this morning? I hope you haven't been making a nuisance of yourself down at the Throwers'. Oh, good morning, Janet.'

'Marnin',' Janet said. 'She in't never a nuisance, Mr Delamere. Mum told her to mek the tea an' she did!'

'Well done, Mrs Thrower,' Peter said abscntly. 'Now I suppose you'll want some breakfast kids. Well, there's toast and coffee . . .'

'We're had a fry-up down ours,' Janet said briefly. 'We come to fetch Tess's truck an' do her jobs, if she've got any today.'

'No jobs . . . well, unless you've not made your bed, sweetheart?'

Tess, shamefaced, admitted she'd not made her bed. Peter shook his head at her, but he was laughing behind the sternness, she knew.

'Do that then, like a good girl. And tidy your room. I brought your bag down, and I've got some money for you.'

'Money? Oh Daddy, thanks . . . but what'll I want money for?'

'Ice-creams? Gingerbeer? I don't know, but I gave Mrs Thrower a bit for the boys, only I thought I'd hand you and Janet yours this morning . . .' He grinned at them both. 'Give you less time to lose it, I thought. It's two bob each, so don't spend it all at once!'

Two shillings! It sounded a great deal to both girls, Tess guessed, since she usually got tuppence on Saturday mornings and Janet, to the best of her knowledge, never received pocket money at all.

'Daddy! Thanks ever so . . . we'll be really careful, won't we, Jan? And now we'll go up and do my room.'

'Good. And Tess . . .?'

'Yes, Daddy?' Tess paused, already through the kitchen door and standing in the hall. 'What?'

'Take care of yourself. You can't swim, so don't go taking

19

chances. The sea's a tricky old beast, though it can be great fun, of course.'

'I know,' Tess said tolerantly. 'I've been before, Daddy.'

Her father snorted. 'Once, with Uncle Phil and the cousins. But there's no one I'd rather trust you with than Bessie and Reggie Thrower. They'll keep you out of mischief.'

Tess agreed that they would and she and Janet hurried up the stairs and into her room, but her father's remark had brought the dream back to her mind – the dream and its ending which always happened off-stage, so to speak.

Now she strained after recollection, but it would not come; it never did. The dream was in some weird way secret, private, a little glimpse into the hell a very small child can uncover for itself and then never share. And anyway, it was over. Whatever the young Tess had seen in the water, the older Tess – for was she not eight years old, now? – knew it meant nothing, was nothing to worry about. She had diffidently mentioned it once to her father, and Peter had stared at her rather blankly for a moment and had then asked her, in an oddly thin voice, just what it was she thought she'd seen in this sea-pool or whatever?

'I don't know,' Tess had admitted. 'That's what's so silly, Daddy. I never do see whatever it is I'm screaming about.'

Peter had lifted her up in the air and then lowered her into a close hug. It was a very different hug from the dream-boy's hug; there was warmth in it, and comfort, and a solid, protective strength. 'Sweetheart mine,' Peter had crooned. 'That's what's known as a nightmare; nightmares come when we've eaten the wrong sort of things or had a worrying day, but they don't have any roots in reality, none at all. Think about it. Where do you live?'

Tess had been six at the time, still very conscious of identity, time and place. She had said in a sing-song: 'I'm Teresa Annabel Delamere and I live at the Old House, Deeping Lane, Barton Common, Norfolk.'

'That's it. And have I ever taken you to the seaside?'

'No, never,' Tess had said, but even as she said it a tiny shadow of doubt flitted across her mind. Never? It was easy to say, but did she really know such a thing to be true? Could she know it? In the time before memory . . .

'There you are, then. So the only time you've been to the seaside was last year, when Uncle Phil took you and the cousins. So the nightmare has to come from that.'

'Ye-es, only the beach in the dream wasn't the same as the Yarmouth beach,' Tess said uncertainly. 'It's a darker sort of colour, and the sea's different.'

'Ah, but that's how dreams work, darling. They muddle up reality with fantasy and sometimes good people become bad and bad become good. I imagine, darling, that something in your mind remembers that trip to the seaside and muddles it up with . . . oh well, with something like everyone telling you never to play near the Broad alone, that water, any water, can be dangerous . . . that sort of thing. Does that make it clearer?'

'I don't know,' Tess had said, unhappy not to be able to assure her beloved father that she now understood perfectly what the dream – or nightmare – was all about. 'I'm not miserable in my dream, it's nice right up to the end. And Yarmouth beach was white, and steep when you got near the water, and full of people, absolutely full. But the dream-beach is empty. Almost empty.'

'Darling Tess, a beach is a beach! There's sand, sea, shingle . . . honestly, sweetheart, there's nothing real about a dream. It's just like a game of pretend, do you see? Only it's a game we can't always control, which is how nightmares happen.'

The six-year-old Tess had looked into her father's worried, loving face, and had simply wanted to take the anxiety out of his eyes. After all, she'd been dreaming the dream for a long while now, she could cope with it.

'Oh, is *that* all it is,' she had said, with a big sigh of mock relief. 'Oh well, then, I shan't worry about it. If I dream it again I'll just make myself wake up!'

But she never mentioned the boy, because somehow it was he who made it so extremely real to her. The fact that she had recognised him, disliked him even, seemed to set the dream firmly in reality, as though it was in truth something remembered rather than something imagined.

'You take that side, gal Tess, an' I'll take this,' Janet said, bringing Tess sharply back to the present, to her sunny but dishevelled bedroom and the excitements of the day ahead. 'We'll hev it made an' the room tidy in no time, do you'll git wrong, an' Mr Delamere might stop you a-comin' alonga us.'

'He wouldn't,' Tess said stoutly, but she began to tug at the bedclothes, nevertheless. 'Once he's given his word he won't take it back.'

'Well, good,' Janet said encouragingly. 'Where's your bag?'

'Downstairs, by the front door. I'd better put my fawn dress down for washing, though it won't get done until your mum is back.'

'Your dad might get someone else in,' Janet said. 'He wou'n't do that, though, would he? My mum need the work.'

'Course he wouldn't; he's going to manage, he said he could,' Tess assured her friend. 'Good, that's done . . . let's go down and watch for the carrier!'

The carrier's cart was painted brown with a gold line round it and it was pulled by two horses, both huge beasts with polished conker-brown sides and long, flaxen tails. The cart, which was a large one, comfortably held all the Throwers and their personal possessions, though Mr Leggatt, who owned the cart, pulled a doubtful face when he saw the mountain awaiting his attention.

'Will that all goo in, along o' all them yonkers?' he said mournfully. Janet whispered to Tess that Mr Leggatt did funerals as well as trips, and left Tess to work out just what she meant for herself.

'Course, it 'ull,' Mr Thrower said heartily. 'Come on, lads, get all this here truck aboard.'

'Well, I dunno . . .' Mr Leggatt began, but was speedily forced to agree that it was possible when the boys had loaded the cart, leaving just about room for the family to squeeze in somehow.

'Up you go, mother,' Mr Thrower said encouragingly, when the children had managed to stow themselves away amongst the luggage like so many sparrows in a granary. 'I'll sit by the driver, but the kids'll find room for a littl'un in the back.'

More laughter. Reggie Thrower was a small, whippet-like man with very large hands and feet and though immensely strong, he wasn't really a match for Bessie Thrower, who was tall, broad and golden-haired, with the bluest eyes you could imagine and skin like milk. Now, she squeezed good-humouredly into the tiny space the boys budged up to make and beamed at Janet and Tess, who were perched on a cardboard box stuffed with vegetables and taking great pleasure in calling each other's attention to everything they could see from their new vantage point.

'There, off at last, eh, gals?' Mrs Thrower said. 'You comfy?'

Both girls assured her that the cardboard box was a delightful seat, and then Mrs Thrower got out a bag of small, early red apples and handed them round, to ensure some peace, she said. Certainly there was quiet whilst they munched, but then Henry kicked Ozzie and presently, Mr Thrower, who had been talking animatedly to their driver, swivelled in his seat.

'You all right at the back, there? Now what do I allus say now? Podge, he don't know nothin', he's too tiddly, but Hal, you should 'member.'

'You say *Penny to the first one to see the sea!*' the five-year-old Henry said triumphantly. 'An' you let me stand on the seat so it was all fair, an' I was fust an' all.'

'That's it. Now no talkin' nor chatterin', just you put your minds to bein' fust to see the sea.'

Tess pretended to keep a look-out over the tops of the hedges – the cart was a high one – but really she was so happy that she could not concentrate on anything for long. The sweet sunshine, the marvellous scents of summer, Janet's smooth, tanned leg pressing against hers, was a dream come true for Tess. She had been hearing about Palling and the Thrower exploits there ever since she could remember – now she was going to see for herself.

And presently Mrs Thrower delved into the blue cloth bag which shared her lap with Podge, and produced a rustling bag of sweets.

'Here y'are, kids, I brung a foo cushies. Hand 'em round and no cheatin'. It's one each an' no more; savvy?'

Tess's fingers delved into the bag as eagerly as anyone's, because Peter thought sweets were bad for her teeth so she did not see many of them. She tucked a striped humbug into her cheek and sucked ecstatically. What a wonderful day this was going to be – what a wonderful week! Despite the dream, or perhaps because of it, she loved the sea and longed to know it better. She and Janet had found an old book, beautifully bound in dark-blue leather, on her father's study shelves, called *Flora and fauna of an East Anglian shore*, and had familiarised themselves thoroughly with the contents in anticipation of this trip. Nothing they might find would fox them, they told each other, studying the illustrations of birds, fish and beasts, all of which managed to have a Victorian look about them, which fascinated Tess almost as much as the text.

'It's like cats,' she told Janet. 'You know the cat in *Alice*? Well, it doesn't look like our cats, but it looks just like the cats in that illustrated Dickens, and like the ones in *Simple Susan* and other old books. I always wonder whether it was the cats or the artists that have changed, but this person, the one who illustrated this book, has managed to give even birds and crabs that sort of old-fashioned look.'

Janet had laughed. 'I niver noticed afore, but you're right, mor. Only I reckon we'll recognise 'em from this, even if their 'spressions are different.'

So now, perched on the cardboard box with a gentle breeze lifting her dark hair and tangling it with Janet's long, golden locks, Tess knew perfect happiness. She just knew everything was going to be wonderful – and she hoped that by the time she got back to Barton again, she would be able to swim. That, she thought, would be the best thing of all.

Because her father refused adamantly to let her go boating or sailing on the Broad until she could swim. And when the Thrower boys said they would teach her, Peter said at once that the Broad was no place for a beginner, it was far too dangerous.

'When I can spare the time to teach you, that's another matter, and once you can swim . . . well, you can have a boat, swim from one side to the other for all I care. But until then, sweetheart, you'll stay on the bank. Is that clear?'

It had been. Now and then Tess had fretted over it, moaned to herself that it wasn't fair, and indeed until the previous summer it hadn't worried her all that much since Janet did not swim either. But last August, when the Throwers had returned from Palling, Janet had announced that she could swim.

'I'll teach you, Tess,' she had promised. 'We'll go somewhere quiet, where the water isn't too deep, and I'll teach you.'

But they'd never got round to it somehow, and besides, Peter's edict was not to be lightly disobeyed. Only it became clearer and clearer that he wasn't going to find the time to teach her.

'He's working all week, at weekends there's the garden, and things like cooking a Sunday dinner, and then there's his horrid golf . . . oh, Jan, I'm never going to get to learn,' Tess had moaned as the two of them sat astride an ancient willow which dipped down over the water and watched wistfully as the row-boat, laden with Throwers, bobbed past. 'If only I could come with you to Palling! You learned there, so perhaps I could, as well. Beaches go slower into the water than the Broad does, don't they?'

'Tha's true; I'll ask Mum,' Janet had said, and next thing Tess knew, Mrs Thrower had come visiting one evening, all dressed up in a clean cotton dress with her hair tied back and a dash of powder on her nose, and bearded Peter in his study where he was sitting at the big desk doing sums in ledgers, or that was what Tess believed he did in there. Invited to take a seat, Mrs Thrower had made herself comfortable, cleared her throat, then told Peter straight out that it wasn't right for a child to live so near the Broad yet be unable to swim. Tess, shamelessly eavesdropping in the hall outside, had actually stopped breathing for a moment when she heard what Mrs Thrower was saying. If only her father would agree!

'You know, Mr Peter, as how I allus speaks my mind,' Mrs Thrower started. 'My Reg, he wanted to tek the girls on the water last year, but they could neither of 'em swim so he wou'n't. But now Janet swim and your Tess don't, so they still can't go reed-cuttin' wi' Reggie, nor they can't set the fish-traps, nor go babbin' for eels, and wha's more, they can't learn to sail nor to row, and they're things they should know about, livin' where we do.'

'There is a good deal in what you say, Mrs Thrower, but I'm so busy . . .' Peter began, and got no further.

'Of course, Mr Peter, but there's them as do have time. We're orf to Pallin' again come August; what's to stop us takin' Tess along? We're there a week and she's a bright 'un, your Tess. She'll come home swimmin', believe me.'

Peter laughed. It was a laugh which said Mrs Thrower was talking nonsense. Tess hissed her breath in through her teeth. She could have told her father that Mrs Thrower would not like to be laughed at, though she was always happy to be laughed with.

'In a *week*?' Peter said incredulously. 'I doubt that, but in any case . . .'

'You doubt it, do you? Would you care to put money on it?'

There was an astounded silence. Tess recognised it because Mrs Thrower's forthrightness had once more reduced her parent to speechlessness. She did hope that her friend had not gone too far, annoyed Peter. After all, it would not help if Peter decided she had better not spend so much time with the Throwers in future.

'Put money on it? I don't think . . .'

'Two bob, Mr Peter? My two bob say she'll be swimmin' in a week, your two bob say she won't.'

Peter laughed again. 'Mrs Thrower, you never fail to amaze me! But . . . do you know, you have a point? I know Tess should swim, I've felt guilty for a long while that I've not made the time to teach her . . . if you would be good enough to take her with you when you to go Sea Palling then, I'd be happy to pay for her keep – and her swimming lessons, of course. And to pay up, if you really can teach her in that time.'

From that moment, Tess knew they had won. She would go to Sea Palling, learn to swim, and the Broad would open up before her, the Promised Land.

'The sea! It's the sea, the sea, the sea! Oh, an' I want my penny, Dad!' Henry was pointing to their left to where a deep-blue line had appeared above the golden corn and Tess and Janet, jumping to their feet at the same moment, knocked into each other and overbalanced on to the assorted luggage – and also on to the assorted legs of young Throwers. There were shouts and a good deal of mild cussing, whilst Mr Thrower solemnly went through his pockets and tried to palm young Henry off with a bent ha'penny and Mrs Thrower laughed and handed round more humbugs and told Tess that 'It won't be long now – fifteen, mebbe twenty minutes and we'll be there!'

And it wasn't even that long before they were bowling along between banks, with the gap ahead – most self-respecting Norfolk

26

seaside places have a gap – and to each side of it the mighty, white-gold dunes tantalisingly hiding the sea.

'Yonder's the Sutcliffe place,' Ben said, pointing. 'Awright, in't it, young'uns? D'you know, Tess, there's *beds*?'

Tess opened her mouth to say of course there were, and remembered. The young Throwers did not sleep in beds, they had mattresses on the floor, big ones to be sure, and the oddest assortment of blankets, old coats and even curtains to keep them warm in winter. She supposed that Mr and Mrs Thrower had a bed, but Janet had only a thin flock mattress which was rolled up under the sofa in the front room in the daytime and produced at nights.

'And there's a bathroom,' Ben continued impressively. 'A bathroom, Tess, with a real bath!'

'Ben, Tess knows . . .' Janet said uncomfortably, but Tess leaned forward and addressed Ben directly. Ben was only seven, he didn't know that most modern houses had bathrooms. Indeed, Peter was always promising that he'd have a bath installed one day but for now they used the big tin bath before the kitchen fire.

'Gosh, a proper bathroom, in a holiday bungalow? The Sutcliffes must be very rich!'

It was the right thing to say. Mrs Thrower, who cleaned at a couple of large houses where bathrooms were the norm, beamed at her.

'Tha's true, my woman, they're rare rich,' she said. 'Cor, I wou'n't mind livin' in this place for the rest of my days – eh, Reggie?'

'Too near the blummen sea,' Reggie said. 'That might flood.'

'Our cottage floods,' Ned pointed out truthfully. 'Many a winter flood we've had at Barton.'

'Aye, but it's good clean Broads water, not that salt stuff,' Mr Thrower said, and was howled down by the rest of the family who reminded him of the mud which the 'good, clean Broads water' brought into their home, and the stinking carcass of a dead sheep which had once come in on the flood and made their mother tearful and jumpy for days.

'Well, you may be right,' Mr Thrower conceded majestically. 'But better dead sheep than dead sailors, tha's what I say.'

'Reggie!' 'Dad!' 'Mr Thrower!' The objections came from a good

27

few throats but before Reggie Thrower had to answer the implied criticisms, the cart jerked to a stop outside a pretty, pebble-dash-and-tile bungalow with a red-painted front door and a well-kept front garden. Mr Leggatt went to his horses' heads, Mr Thrower came round to help his wife to alight, and everyone else began to seize the baggage and hand it over the side.

'The key's in my pocket,' Mrs Thrower said, as the boys started to drag assorted boxes, bags and bundles up the garden path. 'We'll go in the back door; most of the grub's goin' to live in the kitchen, I dessay.'

'Wait'll you see our room, Tess,' Janet said, panting up the path behind her mother with a sack over one shoulder. 'It's beautiful – there's pink curtains!'

And presently, Tess saw the room for herself and agreed with her friend that it was both beautiful and pink-curtained. There were two small beds with pink-and-white-checked counterpanes, a couple of easy chairs, even a square of carpet on the floor.

'We have to be awful careful, an' keep everythin' awful clean,' Janet warned. 'We scrub everythin' before we leave, an' Dad do the garden an' clip the hedge an' mow the lawn. One year Mum had to paint a door, 'cos one o' the boys banged into it wi' a bucket an' took the paint off. Dear Lor', but ain't it just beautiful?'

'It is beautiful, and it's bigger than our house,' Tess agreed. 'I bet your mum loves the kitchen.'

The kitchen was all fitted cupboards and a sink at waist height and shiny taps, and there was an oil stove to cook on and an enclosed stove which you lit for hot water. There was a dining-room, a living-room and a conservatory, as well as four wonderful bedrooms – they were wonderful to Janet and the boys, so Tess thought them wonderful too – and of course the bathroom.

Exploring the house, however, was not a lengthy procedure, and presently Mrs Thrower called through that dinner was ready and they hurried into the kitchen – the dining-room was for the evening meal, Janet told Tess.

Dinner was cheese sandwiches, home-made pickles and a cup of tea, with an apple to follow. As soon as the table was cleared and the plates and cutlery washed and put away, Mrs Thrower took one of the kitchen chairs out into the sunny garden and announced that she intended to have a nap.

'No swimmin' till an hour after your grub have gone down,' she decreed. 'And then only when your dad and I are around. Off with you!'

It was the sort of command which everyone wanted to obey. Out into the sunshine, with the breeze wafting the seaside smells to their nostrils, sand underfoot, the blue sky arching above. They tore down to the gap and, amidst the sand dunes, scattered, the boys roaring as boys will, Janet and Tess stopping as soon as they reached the beach itself to shed shoes and socks, to tuck their skirts into their knickers . . . and then to run on. Tess ran with all her might, though as they neared the sea the wet, ridged sand hurt her bare feet and sent shock-waves up through her spine. But she didn't care, and as they ran full-tilt into the little waves she was conscious of a joy and a sense of well-being greater than she could remember experiencing before.

'In't it good, gal Tess?' Janet shrieked, well ahead of Tess now with the waves at knee-height, her skirt escaping from wobbly knicker elastic and dangling in the restless water. 'Isn't it the best thing you ever done?'

'Yeah, yeah, *yeah!*' Tess shouted back. She kicked spray in a dazzling, diamond arc between herself and the great yellow eye of the sun. 'I wanna swim, I wanna swim, I wanna swim!'

'We will, later, when our dinner hev gone down,' Janet said. She came back to her friend's side and suggested digging a castle or searching the shallows for sea-life – crabs, shrimps, anemones.

'We'll dig a castle,' Tess said. 'My spade's up at the bungalow, but it doesn't matter; I can dig with my hands, like a dog.'

Both girls fell to their knees and began to excavate. And Tess glanced round the beach whenever she thought herself unobserved, and tried to see whether it was anything like the beach of her dream. It had the long wooden breakwaters all right, with deep pools beside them where the tide had gobbled the sand away. And there were dunes, which weren't in her dream, but no pebble ridge, which was. A different place, then. And she remembered Yarmouth as being very different both from this beach and from the dream-beach.

But what did it matter, after all? Tess returned all her concentration to castle manufacture and to the creation of a really deep moat and a drawbridge made out of driftwood, to a shell decoration, to battlements . . .

That night, Tess could not sleep. She was too excited. Her first swimming lesson had been a wonderful experience – Mrs Thrower, vast in a garment which she swore was a swimsuit, though it seemed every bit as voluminous as her day-dresses to Tess, had held her chin whilst Ned had told her to pretend to be a frog and Janet had sculled up and down beside her doing first one stroke and then another and begging her to 'Look at me, look at me, gal Tess!' until even her placid mother told her to 'goo tek a runnin' jump, you irritatin' little mawther!'

The lesson had ended with Mrs Thrower releasing her chin and Ned holding on to the straps of her swimsuit and saying that though she wasn't breathing right they'd soon have her frogging it up and down, every bit as good as young Jan, there.

Tess still didn't quite understand why breathing was important, and Janet said impatiently that 'the breathin' kinda *came*, when you stopped thinkin' about it', but she felt in her bones that swimming was something she could master – and would.

Sleep, however, was another matter. This was her first night away from home, and she couldn't help worrying about her father, and missing him, too. Of course they'd been parted for a night before – often. Peter was a partner with a firm of accountants in Norwich and as such, frequently got invited to functions which, he explained, he could not refuse. Then, nice widowed Mrs Rawlings from Catfield would be fetched home with Peter in his car, and would stay with Tess until Peter returned. Once, her father had gone skiing in Scotland for a whole ten days; another time he went to Oulton Broad for their Regatta week and crewed for Uncle Phil. Tess would have liked to go along, but Peter said not yet; another year perhaps, when she was older.

'When I'm older you said I could have Janet to stay, instead of dear Rawlplug,' Tess reminded him. 'Am I older this year?' But Peter only laughed and said there was plenty of time for that.

Peter would be all right really, she knew that. He would probably enjoy a week at home without her – though he would miss her, that went without saying. Tess tried to turn over and bumped into Janet, which was something else she wasn't used to – sharing a bed. And it was only a single bed, and Janet kicked in her sleep. But I'll drop off presently, Tess assured herself. I always do at home.

But she had not realised what a noisy family the Throwers were, come bedtime. Podge and Henry, sharing the second bed in the girls' room, weren't too bad, but when the older boys came to bed they made a terrible din, and Tess lay there listening to their top-volume conversations and chuckling to herself. Boys boast and shout, but they're no better than us, really, she told herself.

And scarcely had the boys stopped thumping and calling than Mr and Mrs Thrower came along the corridor. They were noisy too, in their way. They washed in the bathroom, loudly admiring various gadgets – the real toilet-roll holder on the wall, the wrinkled glass in the window so no one could see you in your bare skin, the bright taps which gushed water when you turned them on. And they were loud in their praise for the flush lavatory. Tess agreed with them that it was a great improvement on the earth closet at home. Peter kept saying he was going to have one installed at the Old House when he had a bath put in, but he had not got round to it yet. Tess knew that Uncle Phil had two – one upstairs and one down – but she only visited the big, ugly house in Unthank Road a couple of times a year, so flushing the lavatory was still very much a novelty.

When the Throwers vacated the bathroom at last Mrs Thrower said: 'I'm just a-goin' to have a peep at the gals,' so, forewarned, Tess closed her eyes and tried to look as though she had been asleep for hours. She obviously succeeded, too, since Mrs Thrower tiptoed back to her own room and then said loudly, as though the walls were at least two foot thick, 'Fast off, the pair of 'em! They'd sleep the clock round, no error, if we 'lowed it.'

'I wou'n't mind sleepin' the clock round,' Mr Thrower said wistfully. 'Still, we'll hev a bit of a lie-in, hey old gal?'

'I'll see,' Mrs Thrower said. The bedsprings creaked. Any minute now everyone will be asleep, me as well, Tess thought hopefully, and sure enough presently echoing snores began to

31

sound. Mr Thrower was plainly in the land of Nod, though his wife said his name crossly a couple of times before succumbing as well.

Mrs Thrower snores ladylike, Tess told herself, still awake and listening. I wonder if all ladies snore higher than men? And then Janet turned on to her back, kicking Tess in the knee as she did so, and proved that girls, too, can snore almost as deeply as men.

I'll never get to sleep, poor Tess thought, as Janet's snores, and those of the elder Throwers, began to compete for her attention. And when morning comes I'll be all stupid and dopey, and they'll think I'm ill and send me home! Oh, I must go to sleep, I must! She turned on her side, her knees caught Janet a well-deserved wallop, and Janet moaned something and turned too.

Miraculously, silence descended. The rhythmic roars which Tess had likened, in her own mind, to that of a pig being strangled, ceased. With a sigh of real thankfulness, Tess curled up, put her thumb in her mouth, and was immediately asleep.

And at some point in the night she found herself on her dream-beach in a pink-and-white-striped dress and frilly knickers, looking down into the cradling sea-water and worrying about her drowning shoes.

Tess awoke suddenly, as she always did from the dream, and immediately, as though she had lain here for hours working things out, she realised what she must always have known, even when she was trying to agree with Daddy that the dream simply must be pretend. She had dreamed the dream long before that first trip to the seaside with Uncle Phil. She was absolutely sure of it, now that she thought. Time, when you still aren't into double figures, takes such an age to move that you can remember what happened and when very accurately and she just knew she had been dreaming the dream long before her fifth birthday. Because it was on the day following her fifth birthday that Uncle Phil had called round, shoved her into the back of his old Morris Minor with four or five of her dreadful cousins, and driven the whole crowd of them down to Great Yarmouth, to have a day on the beach and a picnic, and afterwards to go up to the funfair and enjoy a few of the rides.

'She want the company of other kids, bor,' Uncle Phil had bawled at Peter, putting on a Norfolk accent to try to make his brother smile. 'Do my kids eat her, I'll pay you compensation, that I 'ull!'

Daddy had laughed, then, and leaned into the car and kissed Tess on the nose and told her to have a good day or he'd tan her backside for her. And, knowing she was watching, he had walked back into the house doing his Charlie Chaplin walk to make her laugh, and Uncle Phil had said that Pete had always been a card and did she, Tess, like fish and chips?

So now, Tess lay on her back with Janet's warm bulk pressed against her side and told herself that she would find out, one day, just why she dreamed the dream. I'll find the boy, she decided, and he can tell me. Daddy won't, but that boy would.

And it was the first time, ever, that she had admitted to herself that she believed Peter knew more about her dream than he was prepared to tell.

Very early that morning Marianne Dupré had ridden her bicycle down Deeping Lane, not hurrying but enjoying the peace and quiet. She knew the lane wound down from the main road – well, as main as roads got round here – until it stopped when it met the Broad, and there were only four houses down it. One was a tied cottage where the Ropes' ploughman and his family lived, another was the Throwers' waterside cottage and the third belonged to the Beaumonts. They were brother and sister, both in their seventies. Mr William Beaumont was a botanist and Miss Ethel Beaumont was an artist, and together they wrote and illustrated books on the wildlife to be found on the Broads.

But Marianne was only interested in the fourth dwelling. She had come down Deeping Lane before the sun was up, when the Broad was covered with a gentle white mist and a gold line on the eastern horizon was the only sign that the sun was about to rise. On reaching the first dwelling she dismounted and walked slowly along, pushing her bicycle, pretending to herself that she was just admiring the countryside. When she got to the Old House she pushed her bicycle deep into the woods opposite – for all the dwellings on Deeping Lane were on the right side of the road as you came down towards the Broad; the left side was woods which gradually gave way to marsh, to reed beds and finally to the Broad itself – and hid it in a copse of young willow trees. Then she took off her waterproof jacket, folded it and laid it on the mossy ground, sat down on it, and produced from the bag at the back of her bicycle a flask and some sandwiches.

I'm a holidaymaker who has just happened to find this remote spot, Marianne told herself. Presently, when the sun comes up, I may stroll down to the water, chat to anyone I happen to meet . . .

But she knew she wouldn't, not really. Because that might easily ruin everything.

She unscrewed the lid of her flask and was pouring herself some coffee when the child came running down the path from the Old House, then dashed down the lane towards the gleam of water which Marianne could just see through the trees. A small, dark girl, skinny and plain. Not a bit like . . . Marianne cut the thought off short; she was a stranger, a holidaymaker, she didn't know anyone here – remember?

She had drunk the first cup of coffee by the time the child came back and when the carrier's cart arrived she was cross, uncomfortable, and beginning to regret the impulse which had caused her to get up literally at the crack of dawn and arrive here so very early. After all, what had she gained? She felt like a spy, an intruder, and what was more the damp was beginning to seep insidiously through her waterproof jacket and, by the feel of it, into her very bones. No good would come of catching a chill . . . but she was stuck here, now. There were too many people about to allow her to move, because she knew very well that, if she was spotted by the child or the neighbours, she would have a great deal of explaining to do.

Peter had never pretended, he had always made his feelings clear.

'You are my Hickling Water Frolic, my shooting trip to Scotland, my fishing weekend in Wales,' he had told her. 'My darling, darling Marianne, that is all I can offer you. Is it enough?'

'It's enough,' she had whispered throatily, that first time. 'Oh my darling, darling Peter, it's enough!'

But it wasn't, of course. It hadn't been enough once she'd really

34

fallen in love with Peter. The hunger to be with him always, to be acknowledged, had almost driven her crazy. She had plotted, planned, persuaded . . . but she had not thought of the obvious.

Until now. And because she felt that the battle was all but won, she had come extra early to the Old House, as a spy admittedly, to see the child who was so precious to her lover that he would not risk allowing her to meet his mistress. So precious, in fact, that he would not remarry, simply dismissed such an idea out of hand. Yet he loves me, Marianne told herself petulantly, as the laden carrier's cart passed her, the peasants on board laughing and shouting out as though they were unaware of their lowly status. Marianne, an aristocratic Frenchwoman to the tips of her fingers, knew peasants when she saw them and wondered, fleetingly, why Peter, who was so careful of his daughter, should let her go away for a whole week with such people. But then self-interest reasserted itself; I'm glad he's sent her away, Marianne thought, so what does it matter what these Throwers are like? I am grateful to them, peasants or no, because Peter and I have a whole week together – as well as the rest of our lives.

Marianne had not seen Tess until that morning, never clapped eyes on so much as a photograph, because Tess was always at home, so she and Peter had to meet away from the house and village. In fact she had never set foot inside the Old House. Instead, Peter arranged to meet her in pubs, small hotels, holiday cottages, cafés. Because of a plain little girl we've been forced to skulk, Marianne told herself as she packed up her picnic and prepared to wheel her bicycle across the road and up the path to the Old House. How absurd it has been, as though he were a married man with a jealous wife, instead of a widower with a small daughter who would probably love a stepmother.

And although she was sure that the farce was just about over, that her new life was about to begin, she still pretended to herself that she was a holidaymaker, approaching a house to ask the owner whether there were any hire-craft on this part of the Broad. She wheeled her bicycle across the muddy, rutted lane, up the short gravel path and round to the back door, reminding herself that it would not do to break cover now. All must be respectable, for everyone's sake. Even the child's.

Marianne propped her bicycle up against a rabbit hutch, then knocked on the back door. She desired most urgently simply to walk inside, but caution forbade it. Suppose he had a friend staying, or a housekeeper? He had never mentioned such a thing, but . . .

The door opened. Peter stood there, his light-brown hair on end, a pair of tortoiseshell spectacles perched on his nose. He was wearing an open-necked shirt and corduroy trousers and tartan bedroom slippers and he had a book in one hand, one long finger marking his place. He looked at her almost uncomprehendingly for a moment, then said, sharply: 'Marianne! What on earth . . .?'

'My darling, are you alone?'

He nodded uncertainly, then moved aside as Marianne, seizing the opportunity, stepped into the kitchen. My kitchen, she thought wonderingly, looking round. Goodness, it needs redecorating, smartening up. But I'll do it – I'll have all the time in the world once we've sorted things out.

'Yes, I'm alone. Tess left about ten minutes ago. But I've told you never to come here, you know very well . . .'

'Peter darling, I had to come.' She kept her voice low, throbbing with passion. She put her arms round him and then stood on tiptoe to kiss the only part of his face she could reach – his strong, cleft chin – and pressed the length of her body against him in a manner she would once have considered wanton in the extreme. Only . . . she had to be wanton, if that was the only way to make him see sense! 'Why are you cross with your Marianne?'

'You know our agreement! Right from the start . . .'

'Darling, I'm having a baby.'

He stood very still. Sensing shock, fearing rejection, she pressed her cheek against his chest and kept her arms round him, but he jerked himself free and held her at arm's length, staring down into her face.

'A . . . a *what*?'

'A baby, Peter. Your baby.'

'But that's not possible! I've always taken precautions . . . we both agreed we didn't want any sort of complications. Marianne, you must be mistaken, you must!'

She had not expected this, but she should have done so. Peter's feelings exactly mirrored her own, last week, when she had first wondered if she might be pregnant. She knew that Peter had taken precautions, but accidents do happen. She had been horrified – the very last thing she wanted was a child – but then she had realised that a baby might well be her trump card. Peter was, above everything else, a true English gentleman. He would never desert her, and judging by the ridiculous, obsessive way he loved his daughter, he would be sure to love a child which he and Marianne had made together at least as much he loved Tess.

'There's no mistake. I went and saw the doctor, he says I'm *enceinte*. Peter, I know it isn't what we wanted, what we'd planned, but – don't you think that perhaps it's for the best? You need a woman in your life, so why should that woman not be your wife, the mother of your child – children, I mean? Peter, you've told me you are a widower, it isn't as if you've a wife, living . . . you wouldn't cast me off?'

It sounded melodramatic and Marianne flinched internally, but she knew she could not bear to lose Peter. She had thought herself to be, if anything, cold, because she had come to England with one purpose in mind; to marry a rich Englishman and to make her life here, as far away from France as she could envisage going. Only a marriage such as that could make up to her for the pain of seeing her younger, plainer sister wed before her.

Because, rather later in her life than she had expected, Marianne had met and become engaged to a rich, languid young man with a château in the Dordogne, a seaside house in the South of France and a little *pied-à-terre* in Paris. Armand Nouvel's family owned famous racehorses, made famous wines, mixed with the upper five thousand. Proud as a peacock of her conquest, Marianne had taken Armand home, introduced him to her family . . . and watched, helpless, as her plain but brilliantly clever sister, Dédé, had made it clear that she really liked the gentle, rather spineless young man. And Armand, who had seemed dazed by Marianne's beauty and wit, had simply ditched her for her wretched, wretched sister Dédé.

Even now, Marianne could remember her pain, her fury. She hadn't loved Armand, but she had wanted him! And she had not even considered Peter as a possible man-friend when they had first been introduced. He wasn't rich, or stunningly handsome, or titled, even. He was just a not-so-young man at a rather boring party who had been introduced to her, and who had made her laugh. So she eyed him covertly whilst waiting for something better to come along, and finally allowed him to dance with her because one glance at the assembled company had told her that this was a wasted evening. There were a couple of rich young men but they were with boring, po-faced English girls. She would wait until she knew rather more people before casting out any lures. She intended to make use of her advantages – her beauty, her intriguing French accent and her sharp wit. A rich, possibly titled, Englishman would show Armand that he wasn't the only pebble on the beach and would prove to that cat, Dédé, that there were better fish in the sea than ever came out of it. But she was at the party, and she was bored, and Peter was bending his head to speak conspiratorially into her ear. The least she could do was listen.

'Why don't we go for a walk along the river bank?' Peter had said. 'I'm sure the air in here is at least twenty degrees hotter than the air outside, to say nothing of being full of cigarette smoke. Or don't you trust me?'

He had smiled lazily down at her, as though the question of any woman not trusting him was totally absurd, and indeed she had looked up at his open, friendly countenance and thought that both of them were safe enough. He's likelier to bore me than bed me, she thought. But it would be nice to get out of this hot room.

So she had smiled back and gone with him, down their host's long lawn to the river which wound its way through reeds and willow copses and meadows, where the scent of wild roses and honeysuckle was brought to them on the breeze, where the milky moonlight cast long black shadows behind them as they walked. And in the darkness beneath the willows, with starshine and moonshine and a gentle breeze their only audience, he had taken her in his arms and kissed her very nicely and just as she was about to suggest that they make their way back to the party he had begun to make love to her with such heat, such passion, that cool, self-assured, rather calculating Marianne Dupré had found herself responding – and responding with ardour and appetite, what was more.

Afterwards, she could scarcely believe the things she had done, the way she had behaved! All her plans had been whistled down the wind because a man had been sweet to her when she was unhappy, and had taken advantage of her, and stolen her most precious possession – for Marianne prized her virginity as a highly saleable item in the marriage stakes. Armand had never come within a mile of intimacy, he had been content with her occasional kisses, and now Peter had simply taken her, as though . . . as though . . .

But her thoughts had broken down in confusion at that point, for she had lain in Peter's arms, under those willow trees, and begged him to love her, to hold her, never to let her go. And Peter had made love to her so enchantingly, and promised that they would meet often, as often as possible, and helped her to dress, and taken her back to the party as calmly as though nothing at all had happened out there in the windy darkness, far less something as world-stopping as the experience he and Marianne had shared.

He had not tried to meet her again, either. It had been Marianne who had found out where he worked, bumped into him 'by accident' in the city, suggested they might meet that evening for a meal. She had named a small hotel, he had agreed – and afterwards, when he took her up to the room he had booked, he had actually had the nerve to say he'd assumed that was what she wanted!

It was not only what she wanted, it was what she had planned, but she had no intention of admitting it. No decent man, she told Peter tearfully, would have assumed any such thing.

'I am a stranger in your land,' she said piteously, exaggerating her accent and fixing her huge, dark eyes on his face. 'I do not zeenk what you say is gentlemanly. I am nineteen . . . I know nozzing about men, only zat I badly need a friend.'

She was a good deal older than nineteen and she had nearly snookered herself with that particular lie because he had promptly apologised and said that he was a bounder and had misread the situation. Of course he wouldn't dream of taking advantage of her – he was almost twenty years her senior, dammit – and would see her home at once, would cancel the room . . .

Afterwards, she realised that they had both been playing a part, and playing it with considerable aplomb what was more, but at the time she simply burst into tears, threw herself into his arms, and told him that she was in his hands.

'And zey are gentle, kind hands,' she said soulfully. 'You will not harm me, Peter, zat much I do know.'

He hadn't harmed her, he had given her much pleasure. But he hadn't wanted to marry her, either, and had made it clear that she could never be anything other than his mistress. And for many months, being his mistress had been so wonderful that she hadn't wanted anything more. His love-making was tender, but so satisfying that she thought about it all the time they were apart, yet when they were together, she found that she simply enjoyed his company, his sense of humour, his occasional bouts of wanting to explain something to her, even the way he drove the car. I like him as well as loving him, she realised after time had passed and her affection for him had simply deepened and strengthened. There won't ever be anyone for me but Peter, it no longer matters that he's neither rich nor handsome. He's Peter, and that's enough.

When they had sorted out their relationship into that of two people who enjoyed both each other's company and each other's love-making, they had laughed at their early, ingenuous efforts to take control of the situation. Marianne, who had not always found it possible to laugh at herself, knew that she had Peter to thank for a new-found gift which gave her a lot of pleasure. He had told her, gently, that she must try not to take herself so seriously, and she had studied her past and realised that most of her unhappiness could have been avoided had she done just that – laughed, shrugged, moved on – instead of turning everything into a tragedy.

Yet now . . . how could she laugh if he truly meant to cast her off? But the ice which had seemed to turn Peter into a figure of stone was melting, she could see it. He stood there, staring down at her, and suddenly he took her hands and held them up, just beneath his chin.

'A baby? You're sure, Mari?'

'I'm sure,' Marianne said tremulously. She did not have to act a part now, she was truly terrified that he might continue to insist that marriage was out of the question, that a baby made no difference. 'The baby will be born in the spring, all being well.'

Peter nodded, then carried her hands to his mouth, uncurled her fingers, and kissed both her palms. Then he folded her fingers round his kisses and tilted her chin until they were looking straight into each other's faces.

'Would you like us to marry, then, Marianne? You know I can't offer you much, but what I have I'll share with you. And you must love Tess, because she's been my life now for eight years. But she needs a mother, even though she's not aware of it yet. Could you be that mother, sweetheart?'

He meant it. He would marry her, share his life with her, but if she didn't play fair, if she was a wicked stepmother rather than a loving mother to his small daughter, then he would contrive to get rid of her. She didn't know how she knew, but she was certain she was right. He wouldn't threaten, he was telling her plainly the terms on which he would marry her, and she would tell him, equally plainly, that she would do her best by the child.

'I'll try. I'll really try, Peter,' she said earnestly. 'When can I meet her?'

'When she comes back from the seaside,' Peter said unhesitatingly. 'As soon as possible, in other words. Look, Marianne, are you sure marriage is what you want?'

She could have sung for joy but she assured him, sedately, that in the circumstances marriage had to be what she wanted. He shook his head at her, pulling a rueful face.

'I know that, but is it truly what you want? If circumstances had been different . . .'

She hesitated, thinking about it. Should she tell him that the sum of all her desires was marriage to him? It might be unwise to put all her cards so plainly on the table, to give herself no possibility of an orderly and dignified retreat. Yet if she was not honest with him he might not think her commitment sufficient.

'Oh, Peter, doesn't every girl want to marry the man in her life?'

Compromise of a sort; would it be sufficient, or would he

41

demand total capitulation, would he expect her to plead for marriage, for respectability?

They were still standing in the kitchen, with the kettle steaming on the range behind Peter and the back door slightly ajar behind Marianne. Peter sighed and carefully took off his spectacles. He produced a small leather case and pushed the glasses down into it, then slid them into his pocket. Then he smoothed back his hair, including the lock that had dangled over his forehead. Then he took her hand and led her across the kitchen and into the small, square hallway.

'I shouldn't have asked you that, should I? After all, circumstances aren't different. You're having a baby, that's not something which can be discounted.'

'It could,' Marianne said slowly. 'There are ways . . .'

She hated saying it, feared suddenly, with a cold, deathly fear, that he would swing round, offer to pay . . . He did not. Instead he shook his head and flung open the nearest door, gesturing into the room before him.

'Living-room. Looks nice when the fire's lit, but we don't spend much time in here in summer, Tess and myself.'

Marianne looked around the large, well-proportioned room with french windows leading on to a small terrace, a huge fireplace which took up most of one wall, and comfortable, rather shabby furnishings. 'It's nice,' she said, and heard the breathlessness in her own voice and knew it was because he was showing her his home without holding anything back, without saying 'if you behave, this could be yours', even if that was what he meant.

He crossed the hall in a couple of strides and threw open another door.

'Dining-room. Used half a dozen times a year at the most, I suppose. Tess and I eat in the kitchen, as a rule.'

Another room, as large as the first, but with two ordinary windows, curtained in red velvet. A long, dark dining-table, gleaming like still water, with a silver candelabra in the centre and a number of long-backed chairs drawn up to it.

'Not cosy,' Peter said. 'But functional.'

'Marvellous,' Marianne breathed. 'Stately, impressive – oh, Peter!'

But Peter was shutting the door, leading her across the hallway again, opening another door.

'My study.'

A smaller room this time, dominated by a large desk, the walls lined with shelving upon which stood innumerable books.

Marianne nodded. 'Not cosy, but functional,' she said. She grinned up at Peter. 'Bedrooms?'

He took the stairs two at a time, leaving her to follow more sedately. The upper landing had four doors leading off, as had the lower hall. They must be very large bedrooms, Marianne thought, but then the first door was opening and she saw that the room revealed wasn't very large at all, was, in fact, cosy.

'Tess's room,' Peter said briefly. 'Good thing she tidied round before she left.'

Marianne thought the room untidy and rather ill-planned, but dared not say so. She also saw that it was pretty, with honeysuckle wallpaper, dark-yellow curtains and a square of fudge-brown carpet on the linoleumed floor. She moved forward, to take a peep round the door, but Peter was already on his way out. He closed the door firmly, opened the next.

'Spare room. The bath's in here. I keep meaning to make it official, but you know how it is. Tess and I manage.'

'Oh! No lavatory, either?' The words were out before she could prevent it and Marianne could have kicked herself for the implied criticism, but Peter just said, 'Been meaning to have one installed as well as a bath. I'll do it if you'd like it. Otherwise it's a chamberpot during the night and a run down to the end of the garden during the day.'

'I'd like it,' Marianne said feelingly. She had no urge for the simple life, not as regards plumbing, at any rate. 'But I could manage, I suppose.'

He nodded, then opened the third door.

'Spare room. We don't have many visitors, but when I'm away Mrs Rawlings sleeps here.'

It was a pleasant room, though it seemed chillier than the rest of the house, possibly because the walls were ice-white and the curtains and bedspread a very pale blue. But Marianne nodded approvingly. It was fine for visitors. And what she wanted to see was where Peter had slept – alone – for the last few years. She realised as the thought entered her head that she had no idea when the first Mrs Delamere had died, but there were some things, she decided, that you simply didn't ask Peter. It wasn't that he was secretive, exactly, simply that he was rather a private sort of person. He would tell you things in his own time, you couldn't hurry him.

'My room.'

He opened the door and Marianne looked almost furtively through the doorway, then heaved a sigh of relief. She did not know what she had expected, but it certainly wasn't what she saw. A beautiful room with low windows set into the thick old walls overlooking the land and the woods beyond, a very large double bed spread with a warm, gold-coloured counterpane and curtains, a dressing-table and matching wardrobe in some very pale wood . . .

'Like it?' Peter sounded almost embarrassed, Marianne thought, as she turned to smile up at him.

'I love it! It's a beautiful room and tastefully furnished, too. I love the colour scheme, the view . . . everything, in fact.'

Peter walked into the room. He sat down on the bed and patted the counterpane beside him, inviting Marianne to follow suit. She came, and perched. He put an arm round her.

'What about this bed? Cosy, would you say?'

'I can't judge without trying it,' Marianne said demurely. 'Oh, Peter . . . no, Peter! What if . . .'

'We're alone. We're going to get married.' He put a hand around the nape of her neck, caressing the soft skin with a gentle, hypnotic movement. 'You're sure you can cope with a little girl of eight, as well as with a new baby?'

Honesty, as well as caution, forbade over-confidence here. 'I *think* I can,' Marianne said. 'I *hope* I can. But no one can foretell the future, Peter. Tess may not like me.'

'Liking has to be earned,' Peter said. 'Just as love has to be. She's a good, sensible girl, my Tess; she won't dislike you on sight, but she'll stand back a little, give you space to prove yourself. All you have to do is show her you're prepared to be a proper mother to her.'

'I'll try,' Marianne said earnestly. 'I really will try, Peter.'

'Good. Then in that case, why don't we have a kiss and a cuddle, just to show willing?'

Marianne left the house late that evening. She was extremely happy and very relieved, and she sang little French songs as she cycled along the flat country roads. She was going to be Mrs Peter Delamere, she was going to be very good indeed to her little stepdaughter, and she would be the best mother in the world to her new baby when it was born. Already she loved the house, its garden, the location. She would make changes, of course she would, starting with a bathroom. She would divide the room in two, so that the lavatory would be separate, paper the walls with suitable paper, enjoy buying the various fixtures and fittings. And then there was the kitchen. Shining cream paintwork would help and lots more working surfaces and an Aga instead of the old range. Then she would get some bright linoleum for the floor and light-coloured curtains for the windows. She had no intention of trying to run a house from a kitchen which resembled something from the dark ages!

It wasn't until she was back in Norwich, in her digs on Clarence Road overlooking the marshalling yard, that something occurred to Marianne. Peter had not once said he loved her, in fact his main preoccupation had been that she and his daughter should get on. She brooded over this for a little, but then her practical side took over. Poor Peter had been totally bowled over by the news of her pregnancy, she could scarcely expect him to behave like a love-lorn swain when bluntly told that he was about to become a father. Naturally, he had thought at once of the feelings of his small daughter. Any decent man would have behaved just as Peter had.

Marianne had a bath, enjoying the fact that her landlady's displeasure over anyone running water after nine p.m. was no longer of any importance to her. She tipped the best part of a jar of bathsalts into the hot water and lay there, day-dreaming. A white wedding dress with lilies of the valley in her hair was essential, as was an official photographer – she would send the photographs home, the best one to Dédé – with Peter's Tess as one bridesmaid and her landlady's daughter Bertha for the other. She thought a deep, rose-pink would be nice for the bridesmaids . . . or possibly a misty blue. When the water was cold she got out, dried herself and put on her nightgown, then made herself cocoa and cut a slice of cake, and got into bed. I'm going to be a married woman, she told herself happily, snuggling down. I'm going to make Peter the happiest man on earth, and that will make me happy.

But she wished he had said, just once, that he loved her.

Two

In the carrier's cart coming home, they sang all the songs they could think of, at the tops of their voices. War songs, love songs, sentimental songs, funny songs, the Throwers knew them all.

Though perhaps 'knew them' was a slight exaggeration, Tess thought, since Mr Thrower la-la-laed to everything, Mrs Thrower got most of the words in the wrong order and the little ones only knew the choruses; but it didn't matter, because they were all so happy. The week had simply flown, and when they had locked up the bungalow for the last time and lined up for the carrier's cart, you might have expected gloom, a few tears, even. But that wasn't the Thrower way.

'What've we had?' roared Reggie Thrower as they began to sling their small belongings into the cart. It was clearly a family tradition, for the answer came at once from a dozen throats.

'A luverly time!'

'What've we sin?' shouted Reggie, heaving Podge up into the cart.

'We're sin the sea!' answered assorted Throwers at the tops of their excellent lungs.

'What did we do?'

'We swam an' we fished!' came the answer.

'And how do we feel?' asked Reggie, stowing his wife aboard in the space left by luggage and offspring.

'We feel rare happy!'

Tess, sitting in splendour on one of the wooden benches which ran round the sides of the cart, could only add her voice to theirs, for it was true, wonderfully true! They had seen the sea, swum and fished, and though it was over, though it was back to

47

ordinary life now, she still felt extraordinarily, exceedingly happy. What was more, she could swim. Not just the dog-paddle, not even just the breast-stroke, which was the real name, Janet said, for what Ned called 'froggin' it', but a splashy, breathless but recognisable back-stroke as well!

Maybe it wasn't the best back-stroke in the world, maybe she didn't progress as far or as fast as she would have liked, but if flung into the water on her back, she would have been able to save herself without turning on to her front. Indeed, the thought of telling Daddy that she could swim quite made up for the misery of leaving the seaside behind. And besides, as Janet pointed out, they still had several weeks of the summer holidays left, in the course of which they could now do all sorts – they would have to learn to row, for a start, and there was a boy who lived on the other side of the Broad who owned a neat little sailing dinghy – they might prevail upon him to let them have a go: after all, they could both swim now.

So the journey home was undertaken in excellent spirits and when the cart turned into Deeping Lane and Tess saw the familiar shape of the Old House through the trees, she felt a deep surge of pleasure and contentment. Home! It was a good place to come back to, even though the holiday had been magical, and she had missed Peter. She found she could scarcely prevent herself from leaping off the cart and tearing into the Old House, shouting for him, bursting to tell him everything she had done. Her life had revolved round her father for as long as she could remember, and now that she was back from her wonderful holiday she could not wait to tell him all about it.

But wait she would have to, because she intended to help the Throwers to unload before running back along the lane to her home. It was only polite, after all they had done for her, and Peter set great store by politeness.

'It costs nothing, but it smooths many a path,' he was fond of saying. 'Just a word of thanks or a helping hand can make some-one's day brighter, sweetheart.'

So now she stayed in the cart and jumped down when Janet did, seizing the nearest cardboard box in her arms and staggering up the path with it. It contained a great many jars of bottled shrimps – Mrs Thrower had not been idle during her holiday – and was extremely heavy, but just as Tess's knees were beginning to buckle Luke overtook her and grabbed the box, so that was all right.

Tess returned to the cart, but Mrs Thrower, turning round and catching sight of her, immediately ordered her off.

'Off you goo, gal Tess,' she said. 'We're enjoyed havin' you, but fair's fair. Go an' see your dad, now. My lazy lot can manage here.'

Tess didn't need telling twice. She snatched up her bag and shouted her thanks, then ran along the dusty lane as fast as her legs could carry her, banging open the wooden gate of the Old House, scattering gravel as she skidded on the corner and arrived by the back door breathless, pink-cheeked.

She pushed the door open and entered the kitchen, throwing her bag down on the kitchen floor, opening her mouth to shout 'Dad! I'm home!' and then stopping short.

Peter was standing by the kitchen table with his hands resting on the shoulders of a strange young woman who was sitting at the table, with a recipe book open before her. Peter looked up as she entered, starting to smile, taking his hands quickly from the woman's shoulders. He crossed the room to her in a couple of strides, enveloping her in a huge hug.

'Darling! You're early, how marvellous! What a good job I'd not started luncheon . . . oh, by the way, I've brought a friend to meet you.' He turned Tess in his arm so that she was facing the strange woman. Tess saw that she had dark, fashionably bobbed hair, quite a lot of dark-red lipstick and powder and stuff on her pointy-chinned face, and very large black eyes. She was wearing a green, open-necked blouse and she had small gold studs in her ears. She wasn't looking at Tess but at Peter, which Tess thought rather strange, especially when her father said: 'Marianne, this is my daughter, Tess. Tess, Mademoiselle Marianne Dupré.'

The woman stood up. She did this slowly and carefully – gracefully, Tess thought, rather puzzled. Why should one want to stand up gracefully, for goodness sake? But she didn't say so, of course, she just said, politely, 'How do you do, Mademoiselle?' and held out a hand which, she immediately realised, was extremely dirty and also rather sticky; humbugs had been handed round with great prodigality during the return journey.

'How d'you do, Tess? Your father often speaks of you.' Mlle Dupré said, and took Tess's sticky paw in hers. A rather odd expression flitted across her face as she did so, but she managed to extract herself without actually exclaiming aloud, to Tess's relief. As she turned away, however, Tess saw, with shame and glee mixed, that mademoiselle was wiping her palm surreptitiously across the seat of her short navy-blue skirt.

'Tess has been on holiday with friends for a week, Marianne,' Peter said. He spoke a shade too loudly, Tess thought. 'I'm sure she's longing to tell us all about it, but she'll have to do so whilst I start the lunch, or we shan't eat until dinner time.' He turned to Tess. 'Are you going to take your bag upstairs, darling? And – and freshen up?'

Tess felt most peculiar, as though she was seeing everything through glass; she heard the words, but the meaning somehow eluded her. But she agreed that she would like to freshen up, picked up her bag and walked across the kitchen, opened the door, went into the hall, closed the door . . .

Stood by it, her head a little bent. Listening. Heard her father's much-loved voice, lowered, worried.

'My God, I handled that badly! But it was such a shock . . . I could have sworn the Throwers said they'd ordered the carrier for three this afternoon . . . I really am sorry . . . the poor little soul was so confused . . . Oh, if only I'd taken you home earlier, Marianne, when I'd meant to, this would never have happened.'

'Why apologise, Peter? And what harm has it done? She is a good little girl, polite even when surprised. And she was just as surprised as we were, but she didn't lose her composure.'

'No, she took it well, considering, but it won't help her relationship with either of us to have walked in on us like that. I'd planned it so nicely, too – she and I fetching you in the car, chatting on the journey . . . now all I feel is guilty,' Peter said morosely. 'What a fool I am – now it will be twice as difficult to tell her our news.'

'Difficult, perhaps. But essential, my dear.' The Frenchwoman's voice was soft and purring, like cream, but there was an under-tone to it which was neither soft nor creamy.

So that's what they mean when they say *an iron hand in a velvet glove*, Tess thought, surprising herself with her perspicacity. Because she had sensed the steel beneath Miss Dupré's light tone. And what is it they're going to tell me? It sounds as though I shan't like it one bit.

'Yes, of course,' Peter said. 'Look, we'd better get luncheon, act normally. If I scrape some potatoes, could you pod some peas? There's a brown paper bag of 'em in the pantry. And if you could just rinse the chops – they were intended for dinner but I'll get something else – then at least we can eat when Tess comes down.'

'I'll scrape the potatoes,' the Frenchwoman said. She sounded happy now, as though she were smiling. 'And I'll rinse the chops and pod the peas . . . I am the woman of the house, after all.'

'Oh, are you?' There was the sound of a soft scuffle, during which the Frenchwoman giggled and Peter breathed rather heav-ily, then Tess thought she heard someone approaching the door and belted, on tiptoe, for the stairs.

She was up them and had her hand on her bedroom doorknob when the kitchen door opened softly, then, seconds later, closed again. She was trying to catch me spying, Tess thought tri-umphantly, slinging her bag on to the bed and following it. Well, she didn't – as if I would! She lay on her stomach for a moment, then sat up and reached for her hairbrush, beginning to brush out her tangled locks. It occurred to her, belatedly, that if 'mad-emoiselle' had been a bit faster she really would have caught Tess listening . . . only I wasn't spying, exactly, Tess told herself. What I was doing was simply trying to find out what on *earth* is going on. Why should Daddy bring a young woman home to meet me? He's never brought anyone home before that I can remember.

Still, it was no use standing here, hairbrush poised, worrying. She finished brushing her hair, poured water into her poppy basin, washed, then selected a clean blue cotton dress and white socks from her chest of drawers. She dressed, added new brown sandals, then looked long and hard at herself in the mirror. A pattern-child looked back – face tanned from the sun and shiny from the vigorous application of soap and water, tidy blue dress, nice white socks.

Good. Daddy would approve, and hopefully, once the French lady had gone he would tell her just what had been going on in her absence. Tess licked her finger and smoothed down her eyebrows – a trick she had seen someone do once, long ago – and turned towards the stairs.

In the kitchen, Peter watched as Marianne scraped potatoes for lunch. Dully, the refrain: *How could I have been such an idiot?* echoed through his head. The very first meeting between Marianne and his daughter should have been carefully stage-managed, should have taken place on neutral ground, preceded by kind and careful explanations. He had *told* Marianne that Tess was returning that day, had said he would drive into the city that night and tell her how the explanations had gone; he had taken it for granted that she would not come over to the Old House. But she had come and he had reasoned that since Tess wasn't being picked up by the carrier until three . . .

'It could have been worse,' Marianne said over her shoulder, whilst continuing to scrape potatoes. She sounded gay; carefree, even. 'We could have been in bed.'

Peter gulped. Worse? My God, that was the stuff of nightmares . . . come to think of it, they could easily have been indulging in some pretty heavy canoodling . . . but so far as he could recall they'd simply been studying a recipe book . . .

'You're right,' he said hollowly. 'I wonder if you ought to go, Marianne? I can finish the luncheon.'

'That would look very odd indeed,' Marianne said primly, continuing to scrape. 'What on earth would the child think? Well, she'd begin to wonder whether there was more to this than met the eye, that's what.'

'She's wondering that already,' Peter said heavily. 'She's a bright kid, my Tess. But you're right, of course. You can leave after luncheon. Then we'll talk, Tess and myself.'

'You can run me home,' Marianne said. Firmly. 'I'm not catching buses in my condition.'

This was too much for Peter. He gave a derisive laugh. 'Not

catching buses? A week ago you cycled all the way from Norwich to Barton, woman, so don't give me that.'

Marianne finished the last potato, popped it into the pan and turned towards him, going over to the roller towel on the back of the door to wipe her hands. Then she looked over her shoulder at him and grinned. Peter's heart gave a double bump. She was so pretty when she looked at him like that, pretty and naughty, and as tempting as a ripe strawberry to a blackbird.

'Last week was last week, Peter. This week we're engaged to be married.'

Peter laughed again and walked over to her, putting his arms round her, resting his chin on the top of her dark head. 'All right, sweetheart, I'll . . .'

The opening of the door saw them shooting guiltily apart, Peter to hurry over to the table where the peas waited, still in their pods, for attention, Marianne to the stove with her pan of potatoes. Tess strolled into the room and gave Peter a distinctly knowing glance. But she's only eight, she can't know anything, not really, Peter found himself thinking. I expect she thinks . . . oh God, I've no idea at all what she thinks!

'Am I tidy enough for luncheon, Daddy?' Limpid blue eyes gazed up into his. 'I've washed and put on another dress. Can I lay the table or something?'

Marianne put the heavy pan of potatoes down on the stove and turned to smile at the child. 'You do look nice and spruce, dear! Would you lay the table? That would be very kind.'

Tess continued to look at her father and he saw the pink flush darken her face and read the message there. She had addressed him, not his friend, she was waiting for an answer from him. And he saw the justice of it, what was more. Nothing annoyed him more than to ask a child a question and get the answer from an adult. Besides, Marianne was a guest in this house whatever she might think, and if she didn't make more effort there was no hope at all of a good relationship between her and Tess. And I made myself clear, Peter told himself. It's a good relationship or good-bye Marianne, baby or no baby. So he spoke directly to Marianne this time, and did not bother to hide his annoyance.

'Tess was speaking to me, Marianne. Kindly allow me to answer for myself.'

He saw the pink steal up in Marianne's cheeks, saw her suddenly hang her head and begin to pull out the cutlery drawer in the table, fumbling with the knives and forks to cover her embarrassment.

'I'm sorry, Peter, I'm sorry, Tess,' she said. 'I didn't mean to interfere. I'm really sorry.'

She's not much more than a child herself, Peter thought, horrified by his own cruelty. But then Tess went over to Marianne and took the assorted knives, forks and spoons from her grasp, beginning to lay them on the table as she did so.

'It's all right, Miss Dupré, it doesn't matter,' she said kindly. 'It's just that Daddy and I spend so much time together, with no one else, that I've got used to him giving all the orders.' She looked straight at Marianne for a moment, then smiled her own particular sweet, three-cornered smile. 'Shall we both lay the table, mademoiselle?'

'Then that's all right,' Peter said heartily. He could have hugged them both, particularly Tess. Perhaps things were going to work out, after all. 'Now Tess, Marianne's going to have luncheon with us, and then I'm running her back to the city. Would you like to go down to the Throwers' place for the afternoon? I'll be back no later than four o'clock. Or you can come with me, of course.'

'I'll go and muck around with Jan, then,' Tess said. 'Or do you want to talk to me, Daddy?'

Peter was caught out. He floundered, not knowing quite what to say for the best. 'Oh, well . . . I certainly do want . . . only if you'd rather play with Janet . . . naturally, I've masses to tell you . . . ask you . . .'

'We've got all evening,' Tess said, helping him out. 'You take Mademoiselle home then, Daddy, and I'll go and play with Jan. What's for dinner tonight? D'you want me to start anything cooking?'

'Oh, I thought . . . I thought we'd have fish and chips,' Peter said wildly. 'As – as a treat, you know.'

Tess finished laying the table and leaned across it to pat his hand. 'That would be lovely,' she said. 'I think it's time the water for the peas was put on to boil, though. And the chops had better go under the grill at the same time, don't you think?'

Chastened, Peter agreed, and hastened out of the room to fetch the celebratory gingerbeer and the bottle of wine which he had meant to drink at dinner time. But fish and chips were celebration enough, he knew, without adding bought drinks.

The meal was a quiet one, though Peter tried to draw Tess out. But she answered in monosyllables and he suddenly realised that she had news to impart which she would save until they were alone, and stopped questioning her. Instead, he tried to chat naturally to Marianne, but all her earlier bounce and optimism seem to have disappeared and she was so clearly watching ever word she spoke that conversation of any sort was difficult to sustain.

It was a relief when the meal was over and Peter could pack Tess off to the Throwers, bundle Marianne into the car, and drive sedately along Deeping Lane, bound for Norwich and Clarence Road.

'Phew,' he said as he turned out of the lane on to the main road. 'That was sticky! I'm sorry I snubbed you, love, but you've simply got to appreciate that as Tess said, she and I have been alone together for most of our lives. You must not try to change our relationship.'

'I wasn't,' Marianne said tearfully. 'I was trying to be sweet to her.'

'No. You were trying to assert yourself. And it won't do, my dear. That way breeds resentment, believe me.'

'Then what must I do?' Marianne asked, sounding sulky, now. She's as changeable as the Norfolk weather, Peter thought despairingly as a cloud sent a shower of rain down on them. She can't suddenly become sensible, motherly, it isn't in her. This isn't going to work, I should tell her right here and now.

He took a deep breath, then exhaled it in a long whistle. 'Do? Treat Tess like a child, not a possible rival,' he said, intentionally sharp this time. 'Or I'm warning you, Mari, the wedding's off.'

'You wouldn't! I've already asked my landlady's little girl to be a bridesmaid . . . and I want Tess to be one, too,' Marianne said wildly, as though this was a clincher. 'I thought they'd look rather nice in rose-pink taffeta.'

'Marianne, you're *pregnant*, for God's sake! You don't intend to wear white lace, do you?'

'No, not white lace,' Marianne said, and just as Peter was beginning to say, with relief, that he was glad of it, she added: 'Ivory satin, actually.'

'You can't! People will feel cheated when they realise we had to marry. No, my dear, it's a register office and a nice dark suit and a couple of witnesses, not ivory satin and a couple of rose-pink bridesmaids.'

'But I want a nice wedding! I've dreamed about being a bride ever since I was a small child! Oh, Peter, don't take that away from me!'

'Don't *whine*, Marianne,' Peter said with cruel crispness. 'You gave up your right to a white wedding the first time you slept with me. Or didn't sleep, rather.'

'That wasn't my fault! How dare you pretend it was my fault – you seduced me, you know you did.'

'I dare say I did, but . . .' Peter broke off and steered the car into a convenient gateway, braked, and switched off the engine. He turned to Marianne. 'Look, darling, what I'm trying to say is that people will forgive us for jumping the gun, but they won't forgive us for making fools of them. Jokes about all our troubles being little ones, you wearing the white of purity, honeymoon gags . . . they just aren't on when the bride and groom have already had the honeymoon . . . d'you see? I promise you that if we go away and get wed quietly you won't have people saying things, even if they have added up on their fingers and realised that two and two make five.'

'So not being married in white is . . . is a face-saver? Is that it?'

'More or less. A white wedding still means something, here.'

'Oh. Well, suppose we got married in France?'

'Can't do it. No time, not on the spot . . . Marianne, if you want to marry me then it's a register office as soon as possible and no honeymoon, just a knuckling down to getting to know one another and making a home for the new baby and for Tess. Got it?'

She turned and stared up at him, the dark eyes calculating. He knew she was examining every word he had spoken, wondering whether she could twist things to suit herself or whether it might be best simply to take his words at face value and give up her white wedding. He was sorry for her obvious disappointment but could not wholly understand it. She must know that there would be talk, that when she gave birth a bare six months after a big wedding people would talk about her behind their hands. But the expressive dark eyes were full of love now, brimming over with it. She threw herself into his arms and banged her elbow on the steering wheel, spat a curse in French, then rubbed her arm ruefully, still smiling at him.

'Darling Peter, you're right, of course. People would be just as disapproving in France – worse, probably. Very well, it will be a small, quiet wedding and no honeymoon . . . well, perhaps just a few days, a week . . . and then down to work.'

'No honeymoon.'

'Oh, Peter . . . all right then, no honeymoon.'

Peter kissed her, then started the car. He drove carefully out of the gateway and continued along the road to Norwich.

Marianne sat quietly beside him in the car as it ate up the miles. Now and then she glanced at his profile, wondering whether to come clean or whether to keep her own counsel. If she admitted that the doctor had merely said it was possible that she was pregnant, that he could not be certain yet, would Peter let her have her big wedding, or would he call the whole thing off? She didn't know, of course, but she had a horrid feeling that he might give a sigh of relief and say the wedding could wait. He would mean indefinitely, or for ever, though he wouldn't admit to that, of course.

Besides, they had been making love all week without Peter disappearing to don his beastly little rubber things, which meant that she was almost certainly pregnant, that her half-truth had become the whole truth. She sincerely hoped it had! She was sure she could bluff her way round an eleven-month pregnancy somehow, but she dared not even imagine what would happen if she did not become pregnant at all.

She had planned for it, of course. If, in six weeks, she was still having her periods, she would stage a miscarriage. She would do it when Peter was at work, acquire some animal-blood from somewhere and chuck it around, take to her bed in great pain, call the doctor . . .

But she wouldn't have to do any of those things because she must be pregnant by now, of course she must. She was being extremely careful, she didn't run up and down stairs or eat deliciously indigestible food or jump off the bus which brought her home from work. And if by some horrible unfairness of fate she actually was not expecting a baby she would go to the doctor and tell him that her periods had stopped for three months and had suddenly started again and he would say it was wedding nerves and explain to Peter . . .

It isn't fair, Marianne's inside self said pathetically. No lovely white wedding if you are pregnant, and no end of trouble and unpleasantness if you aren't. It seemed that whatever she did she was going to lose out.

But then she glanced at Peter's strong, square hands on the wheel, with the fair hairs covering the backs of them, and gave a little wriggle. He was all she wanted. Damn the wedding, the baby, everything. Just let her have Peter and all the rest could go hang.

Bessie Thrower was washing up. Dinner had been a cheerful affair, but with an undertone of seriousness. The holiday had been prime, but now reality was staring them in the face again. Bessie and Reg never discussed their overriding problem – how to feed and clothe a dozen souls – but that was because discussion would not have helped. Instead, they simply got on with things, so now Reg finished his meal and scraped back his chair.

'Goin' to tell Mr Rope I'm 'vailable again,' he said. 'Shan't be long. Bert, you an' Ben might check over the boat. Luke, Matt, there's weeds almost as high as the blummen runner beans out th'end, an' I see a foo late raspberries could do wi' pickin'.'

He went, followed by the older boys, and presently the others trickled away too, leaving Janet and the twins to clear the table and tidy round, whilst Ned fetched water and Bessie humped the big old kettle off the fire and filled the bowl for washing up.

'I'll dry, Mum,' Janet had offered, but Bessie told her she'd do

58

better to put the boys' dirty clothing in to soak and then to unpack her stuff, and Janet had done that and then disappeared into the front room.

Bessie, alone in the kitchen, waited. She had heard the car drive away from the Delameres' house and though not a nosy neighbour, she guessed that Tess would be in presently, fizzing like a dose of salts. Mrs Sutcliffe had had a word, so Bessie knew all about the little madam who'd stayed over several nights whilst Tess had been out of the road. She didn't approve, but human nature being what it was, she could scarcely blame Mr Delamere for seeking a bit of companionship. Mrs Sutcliffe had said, almost reluctantly, that the girl seemed a little lady, not some trollop from the city, bein' paid for her services, which was a good thing. Except that in Bessie's experience, little ladies didn't lie down for a feller one moment and then take theirselves conveniently out of his life when his daughter come home. Not them! The Frenchy would be after something, and Mr Delamere was a nice-lookin' feller, with nice manners and a decent home. Good job, too . . . and only him and Tess. Mr Delamere, Bessie concluded, was a Catch, and from what she'd heard, Frenchies knew a Catch when they saw one.

So when Tess burst in through the back door, Bessie was not at all surprised, and Tess's first words were no surprise, either.

'Mrs Thrower, Mrs Thrower, there was a *lady* at our house when I got home, a French lady! What's going on?'

'How d'you mean, my woman?' Bessie asked placidly, taking the big potato saucepan and beginning to scour its interior with a handful of sharp sand. 'Why d'you think there's anythin' goin' on?'

'Because Daddy's never asked anyone back before. And because they were *whispering*, I heard them. She scraped the spuds, too – that's my job!'

'You hate it,' Bessie observed. 'You said you'd rather peel 'em any day.'

'Oh well, yes, but I don't want some French person doing it in our house! And Daddy said I was back early, as though if I'd not been, I wouldn't have seen the woman.'

'Likely you wouldn't,' Bessie said placidly, but inwardly her

59

mind was racing. What could you say to a jealous child to ease the pain of rejection? She guessed that Tess, used to being the centre of her adored father's life, had sensed that this was no longer so. Even in an hour, confidence could be sapped, well she knew it. When she and Reg had been courting he'd gone off on the sly one night with Pussy Bradfield, a little slut known for her generosity to anyone who wanted a quick roll in the grass. Give her a ha'penny and she'd have her knickers off before you could ask for your change, the village girls said scornfully. Bessie, determined to save herself for her wedding night, had been told how Reggie had gone off with Pussy after the weekly hop and had known, for two whole days, the awful, gnawing pain of jealousy. Reggie wanted to marry her, but he couldn't wait for the wedding night, like she could. He had to have a bit, afore, and if she weren't willin' – and she weren't – then Pussy would do the necessary.

Next day, she'd faced him out.

'You went wi' Pussy,' she said. 'An' we were s'posed to be gettin' wed.'

'That's right,' Reg said. 'I took her home on the back of my bike, 'cos she felled out wi' that feller from Stalham way what's been eyein' her up. Wha's wrong wi' that?'

'Pussy's what's wrong. I know what you done, Reg, so don't you try to pull no wool over my eyes. I can read you like a book, that I can!'

'Well, if you know what I done, you should be happy enough, so why are you glarin' at me?' Reg had said reasonably. 'Do you'd got doubts, that 'ud be different.'

Oh, he was smooth-tongued was Reg, in those days! And handsome, too, Bessie thought with a reminiscent glow. Bronzed from working on the Broad and in the fields all year, his dark hair had a gold sheen to it in summer . . . oh, all the girls were after Reggie, that they were.

'I don't have no doubts, Reggie,' she said ominously, however. 'You're been with that – that tart, in't you?'

'I took her home on the back of my bike, I told you once,' Reg had said. 'Wha's wrong wi' that, gal Bessie? Or did I oughter ha' let her walk?'

'Did you kiss her?' Bessie had demanded at last, goaded into saying what was on her mind. 'Did you tell her good-night in that shed at the bottom of her Pa's garden?'

Reg had grinned wickedly, but shaken his head. 'What kinda bloke d'you think I am? Aren't we promised to one another?'

And of course she had believed him, and been right to do so. But the remembered pain could be conjured up right now, after all those years, after nine sons and a daughter, after getting on for two dozen years of scrimping and saving . . . and loving in the old brass bedstead. Jealousy is a powerful thing, Bessie thought, and turned to speak to Tess, for inwardly reliving that terrible time all those years ago had not taken more than two blinks of an eyelash. And Tess was staring at her with the hurt writ plain on her face and bewilderment in her dark-blue eyes. I've got to put it real careful, Bessie realised, or there's goin' to be trouble at the Old House.

Accordingly, she took a deep breath and crossed the room, to take Tess's small hands in her own water-softened ones.

'Tess, my woman, there's the love between a man and a woman and the love between a man an' his daughter, and they're different. Your father, he need a woman. I know he're got you, but that in't the same.'

Tess pulled away, began to shake her head vehemently, but Bessie hung on, and pulled the child closer yet.

'No, don't shake your hid, just you listen to me first! How d'you think I'd hev managed down at Pallin' without Mr Thrower, hey? How d'you think he'd hev managed without *me*?'

She saw Tess's mouth open, then close again, whilst a thoughtful expression crossed the small face. Tess was listening now, taking her seriously.

'We-ell,' she said at last. 'It wouldn't have been the same, Mrs Thrower. I don't think Mr Thrower could have managed on his own, do you?'

'No, my woman, I don't think he could. But your dad's been managin' on his own for a good few years, and I reckon he thinks it's time someone give him a hand, like. You're gettin' to be a big gal, soon you're goin' to need all sort o' things which your dad can't give you. Women's things. Advice, explainings . . . them sort o' things.'

61

'But couldn't you...' Tess began, but stopped when Mrs Thrower shook her head.

'Not rightly, I couldn't, love. That in't my place, for a start off. And I in't always around, not like a mother would be. So will you give this here mademoiselle a chance, my woman? You'll mebbe find she in't so bad at that.'

'I'll give her a chance,' Tess said, after a moment. 'But... Daddy *is* going to marry her, isn't he? That's what all the whispering was about?'

'You'll ha' to ask your dad,' Mrs Thrower said. 'He'll tell you. And I'll tell you somethin, young 'un. You and your dad have always been good pals; that's more than many a child can say. So remember, it in't only the mademoiselle you're givin' a chance to. It's your dad, as well.'

When Peter got back from taking Marianne home, he found that Tess had made paste sandwiches, brewed a pot of tea, set a fruit-cake on a dish, and was sitting demurely on the terrace, waiting for him.

'It's afternoon tea,' she said, when he asked her whether this was instead of the promised fish and chips. 'You said we'd talk, Daddy, so I thought we could have afternoon tea and talk out here, on the lawn. Mrs Thrower sent the cake.'

Peter nodded approvingly. The sun was still warm enough to be pleasant and the tea-table was shaded by the boughs of an elderly laburnum tree. Furthermore, he recognised the cake as Mrs Thrower's famous date and walnut, a rare treat. 'All right, darling, we'll talk,' he promised. 'But would you pour me a cuppa, first? I'll cut us both some cake.'

'Sandwiches first,' Tess reminded him. 'It's not ordinary paste either, Daddy, it's Mrs Thrower's home-made. It's crab.'

'It's delicious,' Peter said, through a large mouthful. 'Ah, tea – nice and strong, just as I like it. I'm longing to hear about the holiday, but I imagine you want to ask me some questions, first.'

'Yes, please,' Tess said. 'Tell me about the lady.'

Peter took a deep breath. He'd known what she would ask of course, but this was not going to be easy. 'I've known Marianne for a couple of years,' he said. 'We've gone out a bit together, been friendly, that sort of thing.'

'You never brought her home,' his daughter observed, eating crab paste sandwiches with gusto. 'You never even said her name.'

'No. Because she seemed to be just a friend, no more. But lately, I've found myself wishing . . . wishing that we could be – well, closer. More than friends.'

'Married, d'you mean?' Tess said. She took a sip of her milk – she did not like tea – and cocked a bright and knowing eye at her parent. 'Like you were with my mummy, years ago?'

Peter swallowed; she was making it easy for him, there must be a snag. He had seen the way she had looked at Marianne earlier in the day, he could not kid himself that this was going to be a simple matter of intention divulged and acceptance handed over on a plate.

'Umm . . . yes. Married. And – and perhaps you might have a little brother or sister . . .'

He got no further. Tess's whole face lit up. She bounced in her cane garden seat, waving her sandwich vaguely in the direction of her mouth without attempting to bite into it, beaming at her father as though he had promised to give her her heart's desire – and perhaps I have, Peter thought humbly. Perhaps I really have.

'Daddy!' Tess squeaked, cheeks turning pink. 'Oh, Daddy, I'd love not to be an only child! It would be wonderful to have a baby of our own! When will it come?'

'My darling, I don't know when . . . people have to be married first, you see . . . but probably – probably quite soon. You'd like that, would you?'

'Oh, yes – so much! Of course I'd like the baby right away, but I know it takes time. I believe Podge took *years* coming, and Mr and Mrs Thrower were married hundreds of years ago, so ours is bound to take time. Well, of course, now I see why you want to marry . . . I mean . . .'

'I like Marianne very much and I think you'll like her too, when you get to know her,' Peter said gently. 'She told me she's longing to be a mother to you and I believe she means it. She was dreadfully sorry we gave you such a shock earlier. Look, darling, I do think we ought to have a chat about Marianne as well as about a little brother or sister. Shall I tell you about her?'

Tess stopped bouncing and looked attentive. 'Yes, tell me, but I know I'm going to like her. You like her, so I shall. It isn't as though I could feel she was taking my own mother's place, because I can't remember Mummy at all, can I? And there aren't any photographs.'

'Well, not of you with Mummy, because she died . . .'

'No, I mean none of your wedding, anything like that. Nor of when you were just being friends, like you are with Marianne.'

Peter leaned across the table and took Tess's hands in his. He smiled into her innocently enquiring face. 'Darling, I've not talked about Mummy because it hurts me to remember she's dead. I don't have photographs about for the same reason, because when I lost her I didn't want to be reminded of what I'd lost. But there weren't many photographs, in fact I've only one left, which was taken on our wedding day . . . look, wait here.'

He hurried indoors, up to his room. He unlocked a small Victorian writing desk which stood on his tallboy, extracted a photograph and returned to his daughter and the garden. He sat down, pulling his chair alongside hers.

'Here . . . your mother. On her wedding day.'

Tess took the photograph and stared and stared. Peter, watching her face, saw the puzzlement on it. He looked at the photograph himself, realising as he did so that he hadn't looked at it, not properly, for years. Truth to tell you couldn't see much of Leonora because of the long, voluminous white dress which reached to just above her ankles, and the circlet of white roses worn rather low on her brow, and the veil. He hadn't looked critically at the photo before, and suddenly he was sorry he had produced it. The camera, he thought, had robbed Leonora of her fey, elfin beauty and made her look prosaic, whilst the veil hid her mass of glorious hair and made her face seem too thin.

Tess, however, was studying the picture with close attention. Then she looked up and smiled uncertainly at him. 'She looks so sad, Daddy.'

It could not have surprised him more, nor taken the wind so completely out of his sails. He started to say that his wife must have been nervous, then found his voice suspended by a lump in his throat. Sad? How could she have been sad, on her wedding day? And what had made Tess say that, of all things? He looked at the photograph again. Leonora's smooth young face looked back at him. Staring at the photograph, he could feel again the touch of her as she pressed against him at the photographer's request, feel the sunshine warming his hair after the cold inside the church, the hard brim of the unfamiliar top hat in his left hand, Leonora's cool fingers in his right. Had she been sad then as they stood close, heads together, after the ceremony that had made them man and wife?

'But you look happy as happy,' Tess said quickly, sensing she had said the wrong thing. 'And you look so proud, Daddy!'

'I was proud,' Peter muttered. 'Leonora was a beautiful thing. The photograph doesn't show how lovely she was.'

'Leonora? Oh Daddy, what a pretty name!'

Peter stared at Tess. 'You must have known her name! I must have mentioned it a hundred times . . .'

Tess shook her head. 'You always call her "Mummy", or "your mother",' she said. 'Only you don't talk about her much, do you, Daddy? Hardly ever, really.'

Peter swallowed. 'No, darling, I don't,' he said. 'And I want you to ask me as many questions as you like now, and I'll do my best to answer them. But it wouldn't be fair on Marianne if we talked about your mother after she and I are married. So . . . ask away.'

'How old was she, when she had me?'

Peter smiled. 'She wasn't twenty, darling. We married very young.'

Tess nodded. She took another sandwich but did not bite into it. Instead, she stared at it thoughtfully, as though she might find the questions she wanted – needed – to ask printed upon its white surface.

'Where did she live? Not just with you, but with her own mother and father.'

'She lived in a village called Blofield, which is on the road between Norwich and Yarmouth. Her parents were old and they didn't approve of Leonora and me getting married, so they never saw you at all. But they died years ago.'

'I see. So you met, and fell in love . . . where did you meet her, Daddy? Can you tell me things like that, or doesn't that count?'

'Anything I can tell you, I will,' Peter said. 'I'd known her for some while, but when we first met she had another boyfriend, a chap called Ziggy Freeman. Then he died and I asked if she'd come out with me. She said she would so I took her to a dance, and I knew immediately that she was the one for me. I think she knew, too, because we were married quite soon after that first date.'

'And where did you live then?'

'We didn't have a house of our own, just a rented one, because we had very little money. You and I moved to Barton after . . . after she died.'

Tess stared at him. She frowned, started to speak, then stopped short. 'Directly after she died? You and I came to the Old House?'

'Yes, right here, to this very house. Anything else?'

Tess stared at him for a moment, then began to eat her sandwich. She bit, chewed, swallowed, then shook her head. 'Nothing else,' she said. 'Because . . . no, nothing else.'

'Right. Then pass me a sandwich, pet – and can you pour me another cup of tea?'

Tess poured the tea carefully into the cup and handed it to her father. No more questions, she thought to herself. Because what was the point, once you knew you weren't being answered truthfully? Daddy had *fibbed*, because Mrs Thrower had told her many times how she had watched Mr Delamere moving in, and him with a child of Janet's age – around three years old – and not so much as a housekeeper or a maid to give an eye to the kid.

''Cos you and your dad was strangers to us,' she had said, telling the tale. 'You'd come from the city, I s'pose. That was a week afore I spoke out, axed your dad if I could give a hand, like. He were glad to say "yes", and since then, my woman, we're been good neighbours an' good friends. He told me your ma had passed on, said he were goin' to try to manage for hisself, and I said we'd stand by the two of you. An' we have, wouldn't you say?'

'Oh yes,' Tess had assured her friend. 'Daddy often says he doesn't know what he'd do without you.'

So now she knew Peter had fibbed when he'd said he had moved to Barton directly after his wife's death. Her mother had died soon after Tess's own birth, Daddy had told her so a couple of times. But why had he fibbed? It seemed such a strange thing to tell untruths about! She helped herself to another sandwich, then put it down. She did have another question and she didn't see why she shouldn't ask it, and hope for truthfulness.

'Daddy, I've thought of something else. Can I have another go?'

He laughed. But she could see unease lurking.

'Course you can. Fire away.'

'Was my mother an only child and do I have relatives from her as well as from you?'

'Is that all? I thought . . . but anyway, it's easily answered. Leonora was an only child and since her parents were both only children too, so far as I'm aware, there were no other relatives. Or if there were, I never met them.'

'Didn't they come to the wedding? People come to weddings, don't they? Relatives, I mean.'

'They do as a rule, of course. But Mr and Mrs Meadowes didn't want their daughter to marry me, so they didn't come to the wedding themselves. Sorry, love, I'm not very helpful, am I?'

'And the church . . . what church is it in the picture?'

'St Andrew's church, love, in Blofield. That's the rule, you marry in the bride's parish, not the bridegroom's.'

Tess stared down at her sandwich. Something wasn't right, but she couldn't put her finger on it, and all her questioning seemed to be doing was upsetting her father. Only she had to know! She looked up, then down at her hands once more.

'That first boyfriend, Daddy, was he a friend of yours? Did he die in the war?'

Peter's eyebrows rose and he smiled. At least that question, which could have been tricky, seemed to be acceptable, Tess thought thankfully.

'I liked and admired Ziggy, but he wasn't a close friend. We were all members of the Yacht Club, and wild about sailing. But I loved Leonora right from the first, even when I thought I didn't have a chance. Actually, it was after Ziggy's funeral that I asked Leonora to come out with me.'

'I see. Where's my mother buried, then, Daddy?' Tess said the words without looking up from her intent perusal of the sandwich she was about to eat, but she could feel the tension in the lengthening pause. She didn't know why she had asked it, either. It had simply popped into her mind and out of her mouth. She had always assumed that one of the graves in the church of St Michael and All the Angels in Barton belonged to her mother, but now she doubted it. She looked across at him and he was staring down at his clasped hands. There were, she thought, tears in his lowered eyes.

'Daddy? I'm sorry if . . .'

He spoke quietly, but didn't look up, didn't look across and meet her anxious, apologetic eyes.

'Darling, it's not something I can talk about easily. One day, when you're older, I'll take you to see her grave. There's a simple headstone . . . it's a quiet spot, I think you'll like it. But not now, not yet.'

'Thank you,' Tess said, in a subdued little voice. 'I just wanted to know where . . . I'm sorry if I upset you.'

He looked up then, and forced a smile.

'It's all right, pet. Only it was a sad time and I hate remembering it. And now, if you're ready, we could have our cake.' He smiled at her, but the tears still stood in his golden-brown eyes. 'We are honoured to have Mrs Thrower's date and walnut loaf, aren't we? She's told me often that she only makes it for very special occasions, and I can't remember ever seeing it outside her cottage before.'

'Yes, she only serves it at theirs, usually,' Tess said. 'But this one's to celebrate you getting married. More tea?'

Three

Mal came out of the school gates and began to slouch along the pavement, heading home. It hadn't been his home long, but he was used to that – used to going to different schools, moving from town to town, making new friends.

'It's your father,' Kath had said once. 'He just can't seem to get along with folks, and sooner or later the bosses realise who's causing the aggro, and they give Bill the push. But there you are, I married him. For better for worse, the preacher said – who'd ha' thought it 'ud be this much worse?'

At the time, Mal had been angry, because he'd known very well that his father was the most wonderful person in the whole world, the strongest, the best. He and Petey adored their father . . . though Petey liked his mammy best. But he'd learn better one day, Mal thought tolerantly. He was just a kid, so you couldn't expect him to understand that a feller looked up to his father. Petey, Mal thought, was scared of Bill and he was too young to hide it. That was not good. It annoyed Bill, and annoying Bill could be dangerous.

Bill had no patience with young kids, he said so often, which was strange when you thought how patient he had been with Mal. The two had been big pals even when Mal himself had only been five or so, because he'd looked up to Bill, turned to him for advice, taken his side in disputes, even when reason, common sense, everything, told him that Kath was right and Bill wrong. Dad was a man and men, Mal felt, were always right. Weren't they the stronger sex, the dominant one? So naturally, Bill would be right and Kath wrong, even if, at first glance, it looked the opposite. Besides, Bill understood what a boy wanted and needed. Kath only understood clean necks and decent shirts and socks.

And Bill had never failed Mal, though he sometimes failed others. 'C'mon, son,' he used to say. 'I'll get you out of your mammy's hair for an hour,' and off they'd go for the whole day very likely. Fishing, hunting, playing beach cricket, picking berries in the bush . . . it all depended where they were, but whatever they did it was always fun, and Bill always made sure that from each experience Mal learned something. Sometimes the lessons were hard and hurt, but Mal gritted his teeth and endured, because his father's praise was music in his ears.

Bill wanted to be proud of his son, so he didn't like you to cry or make a fuss even if you were hurt bad. When Mal had broken his leg falling in a fast-running river whilst he and Bill had been collecting fresh-water mussels, Mal hadn't shed a tear though he'd gone awful white and felt sick and swimmy. Bill had been pleased, had praised his pluck loudly, had carried him three miles to civilisation and had held his hand during the bumpy car ride to hospital.

But Petey wasn't like that. He was puny, for a start, with a twisted leg, a lumpy forehead and eyes which were always screwed up against the light – until the doc realised that Petey was short-sighted and needed specs, that was. Mal knew that Petey wasn't really a sissy or a little yeller skink – one of the many things Bill called his youngest son – but he understood in a way why Bill got so impatient with him. Petey bumped into things because he didn't see so good, and he walked slow, because if he tried to hurry his twisted leg turned under him and he fell down. But none of it was Petey's fault and if Mal could see it, why couldn't Bill?

So busy was Mal with his thoughts that he walked straight past their new street, then remembered and turned back, diving past the shop on the corner and along Loftus Street. The Chandler mansion consisted of a couple of rooms in a tall, dirty house near Circular Quay and Bill worked on the docks, loading and unloading cargo. It was tough work but quite well paid so Bill, with his usual easy optimism, had told Mal that it wouldn't be long before they moved out of the city and into one of the leafy suburbs, close to the ocean.

'Life'll be different here to what it was in Melbourne,' he promised them. 'Folk took agin me in Melbourne; they won't do that here. This is a big city, Mal!'

When he had sauntered out to have a jar or two Kath muttered, 'What does he mean, different from Melbourne? That was what he said when we went to Broken Hill, Narromine, Dubbo, Port Macquarie . . . it's always goin' to be different. And is it? Like fun it is! When will poor old Bill realise that nothin' won't change until he does?'

But that was defeatist talk. 'It will be different this time, Ma,' Mal assured her. 'Dad's goin' to make it different. Honest, Ma – he told Petey an' me.'

So now, sauntering along the pavement, enjoying the smells of fish, oil, salt sea-water, Mal considered this latest move. Dad got more money than he'd got for driving big waggons in Dubbo, or for road-making up around Port Macquarie. What was more, he was a city man who didn't think much of the outback. So, Mal thought, there was a good chance, this time, that they really would settle down, that folk would take to them instead of agin them, that they would move into a proper house instead of rooms . . .

But that was for the future; right now it was Friday, which meant the end of the school week and tomorrow, Saturday, Bill had promised to take Mal sea-fishing. Mal hugged himself at the prospect. Ma would put them up a picnic and they'd set off, first on a train, then on foot, until they reached the perfect spot. And there they would stay all day, until they'd hauled enough fish out of the ocean to keep Ma cooking all week, because Dad said the place he would take them to was that sort of place.

'It ain't the same as fishin' in some creek, or stream,' he said expansively. 'Sea-fishin' like this means takin' your rod out on the rocks which run along into deep water. We'll catch real fish there, Mal my boy – big 'uns.'

'D'you mean eatin' fish, Dad?' Mal had asked eagerly. When they moved house things were always tight for a bit and they'd not been in the Loftus Street house a week, yet. 'I'd really like to catch fish that're good eatin'.'

'Sharks, rays, whales,' Bill had promised, grinning like a shark himself. 'Shrimps, jellies, stings . . . they'll all come swimmin' past us tomorrow. We'll just take our pick, son.'

But now, Mal reached the house and pushed open the heavy front door. They were on the top floor, which meant a powerful lot of stairs to climb, but Bill said stairs strengthened your thigh muscles and a feller had to have good thigh muscles to hump cargo. A real man, he said, would deliberately climb steep stairs at a run if it strengthened him. Mal, gritting his teeth, began to mount the stairs at a run. By the time he got to the top the leg that he'd broke two years ago would be aching dully . . . but he'd be stronger, which was what mattered. A bit of pain, Bill said, was the price you paid for fitness.

Half-way up, however, he met Petey, coming down. Petey stopped and grinned. 'Hey, Mal,' he said in his rather high little voice. 'I'm goin' to buy taters an' Ma said if I saw you could you carry 'em for me? An' there's money for an apple each.'

Mal turned back with a statutory grumble, though in fact he wasn't sorry not to have to face the rest of the flight. No one, he reasoned, would expect a feller to run up all those stairs whilst carrying a bag of taters.

'All right, tiddler,' he said. 'What've you been doin' today, eh?'

'Oh, I helped Ma to set the beds to rights. Then she took me to the little school and I played with this girl . . . Fanny, she was called. I liked her. Ma came for me, dinner time, and after we'd et we went into them gardens, the ones with the palm trees an' the cannon. We saw the sea, only we din't have time to paddle, and we bought some meat from an abo . . . only Ma said not to tell, I forgot . . . an' . . . an' . . .'

'Aw, c'mon, Petey,' Mal growled, turning on the stairs. 'Let's get these bloody taters, then we can have our grub.'

All the way to the greengrocer's, Petey and Mal exchanged news. Despite the seven years' difference in their ages, Mal seldom got bored with Petey and was secretly astonished at Bill's impatient indifference to his younger son. Petey was fun, bright and amusing. He was affectionate, too, and would, Kath was fond of remarking, give you his last. She never said exactly what she meant by this, but Mal took it to mean his last sweetie, or his last cent – and he knew it was true. Petey was only a little kid, but he always thought of others first.

So the two brothers walked and talked, and Mal told Petey about the fishing trip he and his father were going to take tomorrow.

'Wish I could go too,' Petey said wistfully. 'I ain't been on a fishin' trip, Dad said I was too small. But I'm bigger now, Mal, as big as anything.'

He tried to stretch and did a sort of swagger, and then his bad leg turned him and he landed on his bottom on the pavement, the grin much in evidence. 'I'm a drongo, ain't I, Mal?' he said, getting to his feet. 'You reckon Dad'll take me, this time?'

'I'll ask him,' Mal promised. 'Here's Evans. What weight of taters did Ma tell you to get?'

It was early when the three of them set off, Petey so excited that he hopped along beside Mal, chattering nineteen to the dozen, now and then tugging off his short tweed coat, because although it was the end of June, and beginning to be cold and blustery, excitement had warmed him to a point where a coat did not seem necessary.

'We'll catch an omnibus, which will take us further along the coast,' Bill said as he hustled them across a wide road, normally humming but now, two hours before breakfast, quiet under the cool grey sky. 'There's good rocks at the bay I've got in mind.'

They stood at the stop, Mal shivering a bit in the cutting wind, even Bill looking a bit blue. Only Petey was warm, hopping from foot to foot, chattering. Mal noticed that Bill was looking bored, scowling, and told Petey brusquely to shut up. 'We've got to plan our campaign, Petey,' he said when Petey stopped talking and looked a little hurt, instead. 'Do we need to dig bait, Dad, or is there enough in the tin?'

Mollified by this attention, Bill said they could start off with what was in the bait tin, anyway, and then, if they caught some small fry, cut them up for bait. Petey winced, but the two real men in the party decided not to notice and went on talking until the omnibus came along when the boys tore up to the front of the vehicle, leaving Bill to take the last seat right at the back.

The two boys leaned on the grab-bar across the front window and gazed out; they didn't need to sit down to enjoy an omnibus ride and anyway, the vehicle was crowded, with every seat now taken. It was a working man's bus, conveying men to their various places of work, but because it was Saturday a good few of the passengers were, like the Chandlers, going fishing. Mal saw a lot of rods, reels of line, catch-baskets, and he also saw, out of the corner of his eye, that Bill had settled down quite happily to chat to the man next to him, so he took advantage of the distance which separated them to hiss a word of advice in Petey's ear. 'Don't keep natterin', Petey,' he said. 'Dad likes to be the one to talk. You're makin' him feel left out, kinda.'

Petey nodded, but Mal realised even as he said the words that he had made his father sound like a spoilt kid, instead of the hero-figure he knew him to be. But he had seen the look in Bill's eyes and had had no trouble in interpreting it. Bill wanted to be the centre of attention when he took his sons out, he didn't want Mal fussing round Petey all the time.

'Yes, all right, Mal. Only – only if I don't ask you things, I'll never learn how to fish, will I? Dad's too busy to teach me.'

'When we get down to the rocks, you watch Dad like a hawk,' Mal said, visited by inspiration. 'He's always tellin' me you learn from watchin', so you can see how he does things and then try to copy him. And ask him just what he's doing and why, it doesn't matter how often you ask him, you see – it's me you mustn't ask.'

'Oh! But Dad don't like me askin' him questions, Mal, truly he don't. He gets awful cross . . . and I get skeered.'

'I think he'd rather you asked him than me,' Mal said, but it was a sticky point, he could quite see that. Bill did tend to shout and shove Petey away when Petey tried to be friendly. But perhaps now that they were three men together, going fishing, things would be different. 'Have a try anyway, Petey. And now shut up and let's look out of the window.'

The bus was still full; as fast as one lot of men deserted the vehicle, another lot climbed aboard, and the conductor's ticket-machine was constantly rattling. The bus ran along close to the coast, so that Mal, looking to his right, could see the sea most of the time, and every time a group of would-be fishermen climbed down he checked with a glance at his father that their stop had not yet arrived. But Bill sat tight, so he and Petey continued to stare out at the road, unwinding before them, and at the trees, bent sideways by the fret of the wind.

'Ter-min-us!' shouted the conductor, making the word into three, and Mal caught hold of Petey's small and dirty paw.

'Come on, Petey, we're there,' he said. But half-way down the aisle he realised that Bill and the conductor were arguing.

'. . . I meant to go further, I was told this bus went right along the coast,' Bill was saying crossly. 'I paid up, cobber, but this ain't where I want to go.'

'Everyone knows this bus stops here,' the conductor said obstinately. 'It hasn't never gone no further to my knowledge, and I've lived here for twenty-two years. But if you tek that there path . . .'

'Then you shouldn't have charged me full fare,' Bill said. His neck was flushing, Mal saw apprehensively; a bad sign. 'I want my money back and you'll bloody hand over! They told me at the bus station yesterday, when I enquired . . .'

The conductor turned away and the driver got down from his cab and came towards them. He was a very big man, huge and hairy, like the picture of a gorilla in Mal's *Denizens of the Dark Continent* book. When he spoke his voice came out in a treacly rumble.

'Trouble, Des?'

'No, no trouble, sport, just a bit of a misunderstanding,' Bill said quickly, before the conductor could reply. 'The lads an' me are goin' fishin' – we meant to go further, but this feller says your bus don't go that far.'

'It's a five-minute walk along the cliff-path,' the conductor interrupted. 'If you want to fish in this weather, best get walkin'.'

Mal waited for Bill to square up to him, to start shouting about his rights, his money, but Bill just thanked the conductor rather gruffly and turned towards the path the man had indicated.

'C'mon, lads,' he said over his shoulder. 'Quicker we set out the quicker we'll be fishin'.'

Mal and Petey ran after him, but they still heard the driver and conductor laughing, though Bill apparently heard nothing. Anyway he walked, if anything, faster, calling impatiently to them to try to keep up.

Following behind, Mal quickly forgot the argument, partly because he was so used to Bill's aggressive attitude. Indeed, the only memorable thing about the recent confrontation was that it had not ended in more abuse, or violence, even. And besides, this was strange country to him and there was much to see. On his right the rocky coast formed small, bite-shaped bays, golden sand sloping smoothly down to meet the huge, crashing grey and white of the breakers. On either side of each bay the rocks stretched, black against the water, and the flung spume from the bigger waves reached the top of the cliffs along which they walked. Despite the coldness of the day there was warmth from the hidden sun coming from the thick bush on either side of the narrow, sandy path and Mal's eyes were everywhere, taking it in. A brilliant blue flash proved to be a fairy wren, and a very large bird which was standing on a rock with its wings held out to dry was a great black cormorant . . . Petey asked about the birds in a low voice and Mal, who had done a lot about local birds in school, whispered his answers so that Bill, striding ahead, should not hear.

And presently, Bill swerved off the path and plunged across the bush, pushing his way between gorse, broom, heather. Mal followed with more caution – he knew you could find snakes in country such as this – and Petey, clinging to his hand, followed too. Then they were on the black rocks and hurrying down on to the beach.

'Can I make a sandcastle?' Petey asked hopefully, but Mal shook his head. Bill would not be best pleased if one of his apprentice fishermen was seen to be engaged in the childish game of building sandcastles!

'Not now,' he said, however. 'Later, perhaps. When we've caught some fish.'

Bill turned to them.

'We'll go right out of the bay,' he said. 'Because we want deep water. It won't be calm, of course, but if we can get beyond the breakers we'll stand more chance of catchin' the big fellers. Come on!'

It sounded simple, but it wasn't. First they had to scale the great rocks, then they had to scramble over them, moving always further out to sea. And when Mal looked down into the restless depths, he was afraid. It was real deep here and though he'd not swum since arriving in Sydney he just knew a kid like him couldn't survive in that water. You could see the swirl and drag of the currents, the crash of the surf, the way a body would be first sucked under and then crushed against the rocks . . . this was dangerous country, his father should not have brought them here.

He looked back, towards the safe sands of the bay. Sandcastles might be childish, but at least one needed sand, and right now, sand spelled safety to Mal. He longed to be back there with his little brother, paddling in the pools, digging in the sand, doing the things kids did. This sort of fishing, Mal thought, was for grown men, not for boys. What was more, the beach, the sea, were deserted, not a figure sat on the sand or on the rocks, not a fisherman tried his luck. Even the cormorant, drying his wings, had left. If something happened . . .

But Bill was stopping at last, on a great, whale-backed ridge of rock. He was grinning at them encouragingly and Mal, who knew his father very well indeed, realised that Bill hadn't meant to come right out here, that he'd been driven by the shame of losing the encounter with the busmen. And now that they were here, of course, he couldn't admit it was dangerous and go back. They would have to fish for a while, at least.

'All right, fellers? You've done good,' Bill said. Mal saw Petey start to smile, saw the pink warm his brother's pale cheeks. 'Now come on, there's a bit of a hollow here, we'll get into it and I'll set up the rods.'

Bill carried the rods in a canvas hold-all. Now, he put it down and began to assemble them. Whilst he did so, Mal sat Petey down in what he considered a safe place, with a great deal of rock between him and the ocean.

'Stay here, Petey,' he instructed. 'I shan't be far away. We'll keep up high, or as high as we can.'

And presently Bill came over to them, handed them each a

baited line, and threw it out for them. 'Hang on to the end and shout if you get a bite,' he instructed. 'And if it's somethin' real big, if it tugs harder than you want, let go the line. Got it?'

The boys assured him that they would do just as he said and Mal watched a trifle enviously as Bill set up his rod and went to within a couple of feet of the sea-surge. Not that he wanted to be down there, but if Petey hadn't been along his father would have instructed him how to throw the line, how to bait the hooks . . . still, he would stick by Petey at least until his brother knew what he was doing.

By the time Bill decided they should eat their picnic the weather had worsened. The sea grew rougher and the wind began to shriek. Occasionally a squall of rain swept over rocks, beach, shore, and they were forced to put their backs against it and to cling to the rocks.

'Is it time to go, Dad?' Mal asked. Petey's small face was pale, his eyes had what looked like blue bruises under them and there was a blue line round his mouth. 'Petey's awful cold.'

'We'll hang on till I catch something,' Bill growled crossly. 'Just one decent fish, Mal, then we'll make tracks.'

And you had to hand it to Petey, not a word of complaint passed his lips. He clung grimly on to his line and was, in fact, the first to get a bite. He shrieked, jerked . . . and Mal and Bill were at his side, grappling with the wet, slippery line, Bill actually following it down to the water's edge, playing the fish skilfully, not heeding the sea-surge when it washed over his feet . . .

The fish was huge, they could see him surfacing, sounding, despite the surging of the sea, but he was clever, too. He came roaring up to the surface so that the line went loose, then he turned suddenly, the line snagged round a tooth of rock and the fish was free.

'Never mind, Dad,' Petey said. 'How would we have got it home?'

Mal laughed; it was true, they could never have carried a fish that size back over the rocks, slippery with the salt sea.

'One more cast,' Bill said then. 'Just the one, fellers.'

He hated to be beaten, Mal knew it, so he shrugged himself

down into a hollow in the rock and wedged his reel between his icy feet and endured. But he knew Petey had had enough, knew he should offer to take his little brother back to the beach, where they could dry out, move freely, relax. Only . . . if he did, Bill would despise him for a sissy and it had taken Mal much effort to be regarded, by his father, as someone who was tough and independent and would, one day, be a real man, like his dad.

So he stayed. And Petey, with his line broken and what remained too short to reach the restless waves, wandered between them, infuriating Bill by singing, because Bill said he'd drive the fish away. It was silly, Mal knew it, but he shook his head at Petey and frowned, and prayed for Dad to get a bite so they could leave this cold and inhospitable shore and go home.

He wasn't watching when the accident happened. He was crouching on the edge of his hollow, gazing with hatred at his line; come on fish, bite my bloody bait, he was saying inside his head. Give us a chance, I don't mind if you get away, I'd *rather* you got away, just bite at the bait so I can say you're there, and then we can leave, the three of us.

But his line still swelled with the surge and moved lightly, weightlessly, so that he knew no fish was nibbling at the bait. He saw Petey stagger over to his father, presumably to ask, for the twentieth time in the hour, whether Bill had yet had a bite, and then he saw, behind Petey, behind his father, the wave.

It was huge, a monster, the biggest wave Mal had ever seen or imagined, and it was bearing down on their shore like a great lumbering express train, coming on and coming on and coming on . . .

It would take them, Mal had no doubt of that. It would sweep right over the rocky barrier to which they clung and when it ebbed, there would be no one standing on the rock. He was cold and stiff, but he jumped to his feet, screamed . . . and ran, crab-like, as far up the rock as he could reach. He could *hear* the wave above all the other sea-sounds, it was loud, louder than thunder, and infinitely more frightening.

Mal clawed his way up a pinnacle of rock and turned . . . and saw Petey. In the sea. A white, terrified face, eyes wide, mouth gaping, actually in the curve of the great wave as it hung, for one frightful moment, above them.

Then it was curling downward and Mal saw Bill dive. Straight as an arrow, he dived into the wicked green heart of the wave . . . and the water snatched him down in a tumble of white foam and it curled and hissed up over the rocks and Mal was clinging to his pinnacle in earnest now, as the water tried, with the power and strength of a madman, to tug him down into its boiling white depths.

He caught one more glimpse of Petey, being rolled over and over, deep, deep down. And one more glimpse of Bill, hair flattened to his head, clothing black with water, a pair of desperate hands reaching for a fang of rock as the water hurled him past. Then, nothing but tumbled foam, and wind, and absolute loneliness.

He was running. Running and slipping and falling, clouting his knees on the rock, blood trickling, pain clawing . . . running on. He came to the cliff; he had no breath left, his chest was a fireball of pain, his heart was hammering so hard he feared it would presently jump out of his chest. Yet he flew . . . along the cliff path, every breath a scream though a silent one, his eyes flickering hither and thither. Help me, help me, he shouted, only no sound came out. My brother and my father are drowning, help me, help me!

He had been tempted to jump in, but cowardice, or common sense, stopped him. Useless, to pit himself against an element which had treated his father like a little rag doll. Get help, get help!

'Whoa, whoa! What's up, sonny Jim?'

A tall, heavily built man in a red shirt and grey flannels with a tanned face, broad shoulders, and a smile. A man whose strength and goodness seemed to shine out of him. Yet for a second or two Mal went on running, though the man held him captive easily enough. Then he said, 'They're in the sea! Help me!' and the man glanced at the sea and said: 'Where?' and Mal pointed to the rocks.

The man wasted no time, no breath. He began to jog back along the cliff top the way Mal had come. He said, over his shoulder, 'How many?'

'Two,' Mal said breathlessly, one hand clutching the stitch of pain in his side. 'Dad and Petey. The wave . . . the wave took my little brother and my Dad jumped in . . . he was too near the rocks.'

The man went on jogging and when they came to the rocks he told Mal to wait on the sand and climbed up with the agility of a monkey. Mal didn't wait. He followed, scrambling up with aching chest and sore knees, stiff legs, but he wasn't far behind the man.

'They'll be in the long pool if we're lucky,' the man said when he saw Mal had followed him. 'Stay out of trouble, sonny. I'm going to have enough on my hands as it is.'

'I will,' Mal promised. But he followed.

The man rounded a pile of rocks and instead of going on out to the end of the reef he doubled back, and there it was, a great, deep fissure in the rocks. It was full of water, rocking, surging. And not only water. Bill was there. Washed up, half in the water and half out of it. Not moving.

There was no Petey. No Petey.

The nightmares didn't start for ten days and that was because for ten days after the accident Mal couldn't sleep. He lay in the darkness, wide-eyed, dry-mouthed, and he waited. Out there, somewhere, was whatever had come for Petey and any moment now it would come for him.

Was it death that he feared? Drowning? The terrible violence of the ocean? He could not have said, he would simply have said that he feared. Out in the darkness roamed a terrible, faceless something which had snatched his little brother away and almost taken his father, too. Why should it not take him? Why should not Malcolm Chandler be snatched up, taken away? He was not nearly such a nice person as Petey, nor anywhere near as brave as Bill Chandler. Mal hadn't dived into that boiling, terrible sea as Bill had, he had just run and run and fetched help – too late for Petey, though the big man in the red shirt had managed to get

Bill's unconscious body out of the water and had resuscitated him after great labour.

Mal had done as he was told, that was all. The red-shirted one had yelled at him to go to the nearest house, fetch blankets, another grown man, get someone to find a doctor. Mal had obeyed. Breath sobbing in his throat, chest aching with effort, he had run back along the beach, up the cliff path, on to the sandy, meandering lane . . . and found a wooden bungalow, with a woman who provided blankets and two grown men who came back with him, to that terrible shore.

They had brought Bill back and had, with great difficulty, fished Petey's body out of the water. Tiny, blue-faced, Petey, yet not Petey. They had crossed his little blue hands on his chest and carried him up the beach and when they put him down outside the bungalow on the rough strip of grass his head had fallen to one side and water had rushed from his mouth and a terrible groaning sound had come from somewhere within his tiny, ghastly corpse.

Bill had sobbed, had wanted to take the body in his arms, but had been prevented by the kindly men, by the doctor, by the motherly woman who had lent the blankets. Mal hadn't sobbed. He had been sick into a flower-bed and then he had gone into a sort of daze, in which he vaguely remembered drinking a cup of hot, sweet tea and submitting to being wrapped in someone's huge, hairy overcoat.

At home, he had been given a horrible, sickly drink in a beaker and had been packed off to bed at once, and that first night, had slept in a jerky, dreadful sort of way.

But since then, there had been only wakefulness. During the hours of daylight he went to school, came home, ate his meals like an automaton. His mother and father wept at the funeral, at odd moments during the day, at mealtimes. Mal didn't weep; not outside, that was. Not where it could be seen. Only inside himself were painful tears shed, during the hours of darkness when he could no longer escape from his thoughts. Then he wrestled with his fears, longed for morning, and sobbed dry, secret sobs in his lonely mind.

Kath, he knew, found comfort in telling everyone that Bill was a hero; that he had nearly died trying to rescue his son. But that only made Mal feel worse, because what had he done? Screamed a warning about the wave, but not loud enough. Run fast to get help, but not fast enough. Bill had tried, had done his best, but Mal, who was a good swimmer for his age, had been too afraid of the violence of the waves, the wicked surge of the currents around the rocks, to do anything but run for help.

But he could not continue to blame himself for ever, any more than he could remain awake for the rest of his life. So one night sleep came at last, and with it, the nightmares. Most nights, at some time or other, Mal dreamed that he was sitting again on the rocks with half an eye on his line, rubbing his icy hands, hating the cold, the wet, his companions. And once again he saw the great wave, screamed his soundless warning, watched his little brother snatched from the rock, cradled for a moment in the curve of the wave, then crash down, down, down, into the spiralling depths.

And his father was odd, moody and strange. Mal never saw him take a drink now, but he couldn't help suspecting that Bill was drinking secretly. And the affection between them had thinned and paled until it scarcely seemed to exist. Indeed, Mal sometimes caught his father giving him the self-same look which he had suffered from as a small child, when Bill first returned from the army. *I don't trust you,* the look said, *One day you'll do me harm.*

He didn't seem to want to go out much, either. Oh, he went to work, came home, ate his food, went to bed, but if Kath suggested a walk down to the shops at the weekend or a bus trip, he always found an excuse not to accompany them. As the weeks since Petey's death turned into months Mal realised that he and Kath could laugh again sometimes, tease each other, fool around. But not when Bill was present. When his father was there, both Mal and Kath watched what they said.

Then sudden, violent eruptions of temper, accompanied by a brutally swung fist, began to be normal behaviour from Bill when he was crossed in any way. He started to drink again openly, coming home later and later, sometimes not coming home at all. Once, Mal found his father at the bottom of the stairway, snoring, as he made his way to school. Once he found Kath crying in the cramped little kitchenette, with a black eye and a lower lip cut and swollen until it was the size of a half-orange.

'Your father's under a lot of strain,' Kath said thickly, touching her lip with trembling fingers. 'He'll come round, learn to deal with it.'

He didn't.

Four

August 1931

It was a breathlessly hot day. Tess had been looking after her little sister, rather grandly christened Avril Mignonette though known to all and sundry as Cherie, but then Marianne had come in from a shopping trip to Norwich, rather hot and cross, and had said that Tess could make herself scarce; she would keep an eye on Cherie until tea-time. Since Cherie was sleeping soundly, sprawled out on her neat little bed with its Easter Bunny counterpane, keeping an eye on her would not be an onerous task, but Tess was simply longing to get outside and did not intend to say anything which might be taken the wrong way. It was so easy, alas, to turn Marianne from lazy good temper in spiteful antagonism with a thoughtless word. Or at least it's easy for me, Tess thought ruefully. Daddy and other people don't seem to annoy her nearly so much.

'I've had an exhausting day,' Marianne said now, turning towards the stairs. 'I shall have a rest until Cherie wakes. As for you, it's about time you did something useful,' she added, not bothering to keep the fretful peevishness from her tone since Peter was not around to hear. 'Tidy your room and dust the spare room and the stairs and landing, the dressing-room. After that you can go out.'

Because it was easier for her, Marianne had moved Cherie into the small dressing-room which was between the master bedroom and Tess's room as soon as the child was old enough to climb out of her bed in the mornings. She had also decreed that their bedroom door-handle be moved up so that it was out of Cherie's reach, thus ensuring that it was Tess who was woken early rather than herself and Peter. What was more, because Tess's room was large and the dressing-room small, Cherie's clothing and books were all kept in her sister's room. Tess didn't mind; Cherie was company, she rather enjoyed reading her little sister stories and helping her to dress.

But of course one day, Tess told herself, Cherie would doubtless be given a proper bedroom rather than the tiny dressing-room and when that happened they wouldn't have a spare room any longer. Not that they really needed it now; Marianne did not like entertaining. However, Tess hurried into the spare room where she flicked a duster around everything, checked that the sheets on the second bed were clean – they were – and then hung about just inside the pink-and-white boudoir which the room had become until she heard Marianne shut her bedroom door. It was terribly hot; she guessed that her stepmother and the baby would sleep the afternoon away in the comparative cool of the house, so she waited a few moments, then ran lightly down the stairs. Once in the lower hall she stood for a moment, listening. No point in courting disaster by going out before Marianne had settled. But there was no sound from upstairs. Satisfied, she slid out of the front door, stopping for a moment in surprise as the heat hit her, then hurrying down the garden path.

She opened the gate quietly, swung it shut behind her, and felt the smile start. Freedom! She set off at a canter along the lane, but turned off before she reached the staithe. Once, she would have gone straight to the Throwers' cottage, but things were different now. Silently, she slipped into the woods, taking the paths she knew well, not straying into the boggy patches, nor into the tangle of rhododendrons which would give her away with the cracking of their dead and cast-off branches underfoot.

The woods were beautiful, and she paid them the compliment of noticing their beauty; the greens of foliage, the tall stands of iris, the flowers over now, which crowded the boggy patches, the reeds which framed the Broad. Wild roses, pink, white, blush-red, bushed out between the willows. Honeysuckle twined round trunks and cascaded over branches. Tall foxgloves nodded their purple heads, held out their freckled faces for her inspection and delight whilst meadowsweet scented the air with its delicate sweetness.

Glancing around her with love and contentment, Tess slowed to a wander, moving in and out of hot sun and cool shade and enjoying both. She saw butterflies in abundance – Meadow Browns, Red Admirals, Tortoiseshells, and a pair of exotic Swallowtails – as well as a huge, furry bumble-bee forcing its way into a foxglove's bell and, less welcome, a column of gnats dancing above a pool of tepid brown water. My place, Tess thought contentedly. My heritage. Of course one day it will be Cherie's, too, but that won't stop it being mine. *How* I love it!

But it behoved her to tread carefully now for the Broad was only just beyond the reed-bed and she didn't want to sink up to her knees in the rich, black mud. She padded silently along in her sandshoes, sticking to the narrow path between the reeds, and there was her boat, tied to a stake, pulled up into the rushes and hidden from passers-by, as she had left it the previous day.

Tess had not known she was holding her breath but she released it in a long whistle of relief. Her boat and her bicycle were her dearest, most cherished possessions, the things which made her life perfect despite Marianne's occasional bouts of ill-humoured antagonism, and she had got them, she knew, because of Marianne. Daddy had bought the dinghy whilst he and Marianne went off to France for a week, after their wedding almost four years ago.

'It'll give you and Janet something to do whilst we're away,' he had said. 'Ned will show you how to use it safely – you aren't to go out without him until we come back – savvy?'

She had agreed, of course, and she and Janet had spent most of that summer in the boat, christened *The Jolly Roger* by its enthusiastic owners, for Janet had had shares, then, or as good as.

The bicycle had come with boarding school. 'Your dad won't never send you away,' Mrs Thrower had said comfortably when Tess, weeping, had run down the staithe to tell her that she had heard Peter and Marianne discussing boarding school. 'I've heared him say time and again that that ain't right to send gals away to school. Boys now, that might be diff'rent. But never gals.'

She had started boarding school a short while after that conversation, though at first she had only been what they called a weekly boarder. Every Friday afternoon when school had finished for the day Daddy had called for her and taken her home and for two days life returned to normal. She slept in her own bed, ate at her own table, played with her friend Janet. And on Monday morning she climbed into the car beside Daddy, with her school uniform on, her homework in her satchel and her little green purse full of her shilling pocket money in pennies, and lived in Norwich until Friday.

That went on for a year, but then Marianne announced that it was not a good thing, that in her opinion Tess was simply unsettled by all the toing and froing. And Tess saw the point, because her best friend at school, Sara, was a term-boarder and missed her at weekends. So when Peter suggested she might like to board termly, she agreed placidly enough.

But that didn't mean she hadn't recognised it for what it was; dismissal. Oh, Daddy wasn't dismissing her, but Marianne was. Her stepmother was wrapped up in Peter and in Cherie, and Tess's continual on-and-off presence was a distraction, a disturbance to an otherwise smooth routine. What was more, Tess hadn't really minded. Her school was a first-rate one, she found her work interesting, her friends delightful, and she certainly did not miss all the little digs and unpleasantnesses which were her lot whenever Marianne was cross or out of sorts. And oddly, she never had the dream at school. She dreamed most nights of course, and sometimes the dreams were nightmares; Miss Pryce, the physics teacher, chased her through an endless laboratory with a hissing test-tube of deadly poison in her hand, the dormitory was invaded by crocodiles which squiggled beneath her bed and tried to worm their way through the mattress to get at her, the lavatory block was infested by giant octopuses which waved their tentacles out of the toilet bowls. But whilst she was at school, she never found herself on that stretch of lonely beach, shoes and socks in hand, walking beside the breakwater and seeing a horror there.

So school had many good points and when she came home for the holidays Daddy insisted that she did more or less as she liked, provided she gave Marianne some help in the house and took her turn at looking after Cherie. Janet, who had been such a good friend, had her own life to lead now in the holidays so Tess was often alone, but she could take off in her dinghy, catch the bus to Wroxham and wander round Roys, or watch the boats ducking their masts to get under the bridge. Or she could go for a long bicycle ride, with her lunch in a bag, pushing the boundaries of her knowledge of the country surrounding her home wider with each excursion.

The bicycle was wonderful. It enlarged her horizons – it gave her wings! She could set off early in the morning and stay out until late when the summer evenings were long and light. Marianne encouraged this and so did Daddy, though they had different reasons. Marianne liked her home, husband and child to herself. Daddy simply wanted Tess to be happy and free, as he had been as a boy.

'Cherie will have to fight free of Marianne one day,' he told his daughter once, as he drove her back to school on the first day of the new term. 'She's a very possessive woman and she won't want to let Cherie go even a little bit. But you, my poor darling, you'll never have to do that. I'm sorry.'

'Don't be sorry, Daddy,' Tess had assured him. 'I'm much happier going my own way just like you did when you were a boy. Cherie will be a dear little indoor girl, but I'm not like that. I like the outdoors best.'

But she was lonely. She missed Janet's companionship horribly, having taken it for granted for so long, and even Sara's newer friendship would have been welcome as she pedalled along the dusty country lanes or rowed along by the reed beds, spotting bird-life.

'Marianne loves you, you know,' Daddy said cautiously. 'It's just that you were eight when she first met you, so she can't think of you in quite the same way that she thinks of Cherie. And you've never felt you could call her Mummy, have you?'

'No,' Tess said decidedly. 'She's too young, Daddy. And anyway, I do have my own mother . . . I mean, there's the photograph.'

She had the photograph in her room now. It was in a heavy silver frame richly decorated with vine-leaves and swags of grapes and she loved it and, on the rare occasions when she felt sad and unwanted, she talked to her mother's photograph, quietly and secretly, before she turned off the light.

'Yes . . . but a photograph isn't the same thing as a real, live mother, darling,' Peter said. He never took his eyes from the road ahead but Tess knew he was unhappy with the situation and hastened to reassure him. She understood that her father had needed a wife, she thought it a pity he had chosen Marianne, but Marianne was pretty, a good cook, she kept the house immaculate and managed her housekeeping money well. Tess knew, without understanding it, that Marianne made her father happy. That, for her, was enough. But as always, she felt she must make her father see that no blame attached to either himself or his wife because she could not think of Marianne as her mother.

'I know a photograph isn't like a real person, Daddy,' she assured him. 'But it would be awfully hard for me to call Marianne anything but that, because as you said, I was eight when I first met her. And besides, she doesn't really want me to call her Mummy, honestly she doesn't. She said the other day she wouldn't mind Cherie calling her Marianne, as well. It makes her feel young, she said.'

'Oh,' Daddy said rather blankly. 'Well, I'd never try to persuade you one way or the other, you know that.'

She did know it. And valued more than ever the light touch which could run the household smoothly, for she knew who really ran the household, whatever Marianne might think. Peter kept everyone in the place he had chosen for them. She was his beloved daughter, Cherie his beloved baby, Marianne his beloved wife. Because he showed, plainly, how he thought things should be, most of the time all three of them did their best to play the parts that had been assigned to them. Tess tried not to resent Marianne's bouts of jealousy, Marianne, she knew, tried to hide that same jealousy, and Cherie, lucky little thing, simply adored her older sister, her mother and her father indiscriminately – and was adored in return.

She was a pretty child, placid and sweet-tempered and perhaps not terribly bright. She always did as she was told and was content to be around the house and garden, never trying to wander further afield, happy to play alone or with a doting parent, asking no other company. She was delighted to see Tess at the end of each term, yet she waved her off at the beginning of the next with perfect aplomb. She clambered all over Peter when he came home after work, but if Peter gently put her down and told her to go to her mummy she went at once, sweet and docile, her light curls clustered around the white or pink or blue bows which perched like butterflies on top of her head, her clothing always in place, her strap shoes always on her feet. Sometimes Tess wondered if her baby sister was not a little too obliging and good, but she wouldn't have dreamed of saying so. Marianne was apt to boast that Cherie was the perfect child and who was she, Tess, to disagree? But she knew that other three-year-olds were not like that. Podge Thrower had been a little beast when the fancy took him and the present baby Thrower, Dickie, was always ambling off after mischief and seldom clean, let alone neat.

But still, I'm no expert, Tess told herself now, skilfully untangling the *Roger* from the reeds and wiping impatiently at the perspiration running down the sides of her face and neck. Perhaps Marianne is right, perhaps little girls are better behaved than little boys. But she could never forget that in her dream she had run down the beach, where she was not supposed to be, and taken off her shoes and socks . . .

It was only a dream, though. Perhaps, in reality, the small Tess had been as good as the small Cherie. Tess untied the painter, pushed the *Roger* into open water and jumped aboard, causing the dinghy to rock alarmingly for a moment, until she dropped on to the seat and unshipped the oars. A couple of strokes cleared the reeds and she was on the great, silver expanse of water.

It was mid-afternoon and breathlessly hot still, though there was more air here than on land. A tiny breezelet, so slight that only the very tips of the feathery reeds moved under its caress, touched Tess's hot brow. Tess sighed deeply and pushed her hair back behind her ears, than glanced around her. It was too hot to exert oneself; what should she do? Scull gently across the Broad to the Atkins' house? Go round to the staithe to see if Janet was in a coming-out mood? Or just get the boat in the shade of a willow and dream a little?

She and Janet were still friends, but boarding school had

spoiled their closeness and now that they were old – twelve – Janet had changed. She'd made friends with three girls from her school, girls who were older than she, girls Tess neither knew nor wanted to know. Violet, Elsie and Ruby were in the top class and in their last year of school. They wore make-up, talked – and thought – about nothing but boys, and made Tess feel gawky and young. And Janet copied them. She wore her skirts long, sometimes did her hair in a bun at the back, rubbed her cheeks with geranium petals and talked about boys. Not all the time, of course, but a good deal of the time. Now and again Tess persuaded her to take a trip in the *Roger*, but the new Janet screamed when she was splashed, fussed about the sun giving her freckles, had no desire to lie on the bottom boards and talk, or put out a line in the hope of a fish, or go round Mr Thrower's eel-traps to see what he'd caught.

'It was you goin' to boardin' school, my woman,' Mrs Thrower said heavily, when Tess asked why Janet had changed so much. 'She din't have no one to do things with, see? She were lonely for another gal. Then Vi took her up and she began to imitate, like. Whass more, Tess, she'll be workin' in another couple o' years. That's bound to make a difference to the pair of you.' She paused, eyeing Tess thoughtfully. 'And there was suffin' else, too – Mrs Delamere weren't too welcomin' to Janet, were she?'

Marianne had been beastly to Janet as soon as she had settled into the house in Deeping Lane. She had chased the pair of them out of the kitchen, had talked to Janet in a sneering sort of voice and had finally told Tess bluntly that her friend was a common little village girl and, as such, was not welcome in her home.

'But Mrs Thrower comes here,' Tess had said. At eight, she had scarcely understood what Marianne was saying, though she realised that her stepmother was deliberately being nasty to Janet to keep them apart. 'You have Mrs Thrower here three mornings a week, sometimes more.'

'She's my charwoman,' Marianne said at once. 'She scrubs my floors and cleans the lavatory. She is not a friend.'

It was tempting to tell Peter and demand that he make Marianne polite to her friend, but Tess could see that it wouldn't work, or not for long. So she said nothing and for that first year, when

92

school holidays came round, she and Janet played outside or in the Throwers' cramped cottage. But then she became a term-boarder and Janet met Violet, Elsie and Ruby . . . and Tess became, perforce, a loner. Janet still liked her, she knew, but she couldn't simply drop the others, it wouldn't have been fair.

So Tess tried to understand, tried not to hang around when the four girls came whispering and giggling down to the staithe, and though it had been difficult at first, she really did see Janet's point of view. After all, at boarding school she had heaps and heaps of friends. If Janet had suddenly been slung into that school would she, Tess, have been able to ditch her school friends for the other girl?

She would have liked to have a school friend to stay from time to time, though. Quiet Vanessa, noisy Vera, sweet, funny little Hilary. She had actually arranged to have Vanessa for a week once, but Marianne had put a stop to that.

'I can't entertain in a house which has no sitting-room for the children,' she had said sulkily. 'I can't have two great girls underfoot all day long.'

Peter had done his best, and then Marianne had played her trump card, though Tess had not recognised it for what it was at first.

'There is another reason,' Marianne had said, looking at Peter under her lashes. 'Come upstairs for a moment, darling, and I'll explain.'

Secrets aren't nice, the eleven-year-old Tess had thought resentfully, as the time stretched and stretched and still she waited. Marianne wouldn't like it if I said I wanted to speak to Daddy alone and went off with him for almost an hour.

But then they came downstairs again, Marianne looking sleepy and smug and something else, though Tess could not put a name to it, and Peter looking hot and rather furtive.

'Darling, Marianne can't cope this time,' he had said, patting her shoulder in a rather perfunctory way. 'Later in the year, perhaps.'

This meant that Tess couldn't accept invitations to stay with friends either, since there could be no reciprocal visits, but she didn't mind that, particularly. She loved her own home too much to want to swap it for someone else's, even for a few days. But it would have been nice to show a friend the Broad. In early summer, when the water lilies bloomed, the surface of the Broad was carpeted with yellow, gold and white, whilst every shade of pink, from pastel to deepest rose, abounded. And in the clear water sleak, red-finned rudd, pale green roach and pink-eyed tench swam, feeding on the facinating insect life which was supported by the green reed beds. Yes it would have been nice to take a friend out in the boat, for the two of them to bicycle off along the quiet country lanes, to have a friend to giggle at with breakfast, or to share a midnight feast.

Still. With the *Roger* for company, she was better off than most, Tess told herself, sculling lazily across the polished pewter of the Broad. She headed for the further bank because of the willows; shade was a pleasure on such a day.

When she reached the further bank, Tess lowered the anchor overboard – the anchor was an old paint tin, which filled with water as it sank – and looked thoughtfully about her. Nothing stirred. In the drooping branches above her head and even in the great reed beds which ringed the Broad there was silence, for the birds were too hot to sing or call. A dragonfly, thin as a needle and a vivid electric blue, hovered near the prow of the boat for a moment, and Tess stared at it, fascinated as always by the transparent blur of its wings, the great round eyes, the movements which were so quick that the onlooker could not follow them. She put a finger near the insect but it took no notice, suddenly darting over to a clump of water forget-me-not where it clung for a moment, blending in beautifully with the flowers' ethereal blue.

'There's no one but you and me about,' Tess told the dragonfly. 'Everyone's either sleeping or lying in the shade, because it's too hot for anything else. Even the birds are asleep; why don't you go somewhere quiet and sleep, too?'

As though it had heard her the dragonfly rose from the water forget-me-nots, hovered for a moment, then darted sideways into the nearest reed bed and disappeared. Tess turned and stared out across the Broad once more. Should she go over to the Atkins' place? But it was far too hot for sculling all that way – far too hot for any activity, now that she came to think. The whole world was resting, waiting for the sun to begin to sink in the heavens.

Near at hand, a fish jumped, then fell back into the water with a splosh and a widening spread of ripples. Tess put her face near the water, breathing in the exciting smell of it, the peaty richness. She could see her own reflection, gazing back at her; the pale triangle of her face, the wide-apart dark-blue eyes, the straggle of coal-black hair, so different from her little sister's smooth fair locks. She pulled a face at herself, then turned her head sideways; on the surface water boatmen skated, a leaf rocked as she moved in the boat, and a tiny moth skimmed the water, to land triumphantly on a burr-reed.

Tess sat up. The only people to feel really comfortable today were the fish, so why not follow their excellent example and go for a swim? She tugged her shirt over her head, then undid the buttons on the side of her navy-blue pleated skirt. It was, of course, rude to go swimming without any clothes on, but Marianne would not be pleased if she went home with a burden of wet clothing. She might as well swim in the buff, as Daddy called it. There wasn't a soul about.

She shed everything and giggled at herself, sitting pink and naked on the bottomboards in the shade of the willows and gazing out across the burning silver water. What a clown she would look if Ned or Bert or even little Podge were suddenly to appear – but there was small chance of that. No one fished in the heat of the day and besides, the whole family were probably helping with a harvest, or digging in the allotment, or simply resting, conserving their energy for later, when the heat had faded into the cool of evening.

She perched on the side of the boat for a moment, then slid into the Broad, neat as a fish, and immediately the water welcomed her, deliciously cool and fresh against her hot skin. She duck-dived and saw, through the peaty brownness of it, the mysterious underwater world which she loved so much. The shoals of tiny fish, the rich weed growth, a water-vole, going quietly about its business, its fur covered with silver air bubbles. She saw a frog, heading for the bank, its long hind legs kicking it along in smooth, swift motion whilst its short little arms hung harmlessly and did nothing. I can swim like that, Tess told herself, and was trying when her breath began to run out so she broke the surface and shook her head to get the water out of her eyes and then, revitalised by the coolness, began to swim with a steady, smooth breast-stroke, out into the Broad.

It was a magical, almost dreamlike experience. Her arms, cleaving the water, looked very white and clean, and the water felt warm, like fresh milk. She swam steadily for ten minutes or so, then flipped on to her back and floated, gazing mindlessly up at the burning blue of the sky above. How happy she was, how endlessly fortunate, how wonderful it was to be Tess Delamere, to own a boat and a bicycle and to have the freedom to enjoy them!

In the centre of the Broad, when her happiness and content-ment was at its height, she saw the boat. Quite a small boat, the single oarsman heading in her direction. Too good to last, Tess told herself and flipped around in the water. If she'd been wear-ing a swimsuit she might have gone over to the boat for a chat, but in the circumstances a tactful retreat was best.

She put her head down and went into a fast crawl and was back by her boat and heaving her skirt and blouse on before the oarsman could have realised she was bare. Not that he would have minded, she guessed. Most of the kids swam naked in the Broad when they swam at all, a boy would probably have jeered at her swimsuit had she been wearing one.

The boat drew nearer. The oarsman was a lone boy with dark hair, big spectacles and grey, water-splashed shorts. He wore no shirt and his feet were bare and he looked around the same age as Tess herself. He was rowing faster now, but splashily, and not progressing fast. At a guess, Tess thought he'd probably not used the boat much. A nephew of someone living on the further shore? Or a visiting friend, perhaps.

'Hey . . .' the boy's voice rang out across the water. 'Is it safe?'

'Safe?' Tess called back. 'What d'you mean?'

'The water, you fool . . . oh!' The boy was near enough, now, to see Tess properly, even through the screening willows. 'Oh . . . I thought you were a feller.'

Tess stiffened. What difference did it make, for goodness sake? 'I'm not,' she said unnecessarily, however. 'Can you swim?'

'With one foot on the bottom,' the boy said. 'Why? Is it deep? I thought the Broads were never deep.'

'They aren't terribly deep,' Tess admitted. 'But the bottom's soggy, mud and peat and that. You can't stand on it. You'd sink in.'

'Oh.' The boy scowled at her. 'But I want to bathe. I'm bloody hot.'

'Well,' Tess said, considering the problem. 'There is a bit further round the corner where the bottom's sort of sandy and gravelly. It's where my friend and I went when we didn't swim too well. Want me to show you?'

'Sure,' the boy said eagerly. 'Come in my dinghy; I'll row you back again, after.'

Tess shook her head. 'I'll go ahead of you. Only the water's quite shallow, you won't be able to get wet all over unless you lie down.'

'I'll lie down,' the boy said briefly. He watched whilst she pulled up her anchor, emptied it over the side and fitted her oars in the rowlocks. 'You can swim, I suppose?'

'What d'you suppose I was doing just now?' Tess asked rather scornfully. 'I was in the middle – it's deep enough there.'

'I thought you had one foot on the bottom,' the boy said, sounding sheepish. 'Especially when I saw you were a girl. Girls don't often swim, do they?'

'They do if they live by the Broad,' Tess said. 'It's dangerous, else.' She began to bring the boat out of the shade and as soon as she did so the hammer blows of the sun hit her and perspiration began to run down her back despite her recent ducking. 'Look, I'm baking,' she said crossly. 'I'll take you there and leave you; okay?'

'Oh! But I thought you might show me how to swim,' the boy said forlornly. 'I'm staying with my great-aunt for the summer and I'm bored to tears. That's why I stole the boat . . . she says I can't go on the water until I can swim, d'you see? So I'm keen to learn.'

'Well, I could try,' Tess said doubtfully. How did one teach another person to swim if the other person was taller and heavier than you? She could scarcely hold on the straps of his swimsuit,

as various Throwers had clung to hers until she could go it alone
– so far as she knew, he didn't have a swimsuit, only the patched
shorts – but she supposed that, once in the water, it might be
possible to show him how to do a dog-paddle.

'Grand,' the boy said as Tess brought her boat as close as she
dared to the gently sloping shore. 'I'm Herbert Anderson, but my
friends call me Andy.'

'Oh . . . I'm Tess Delamere,' Tess said. She filled her paint tin
with water and sank it, then hopped on to the bank. 'D'you have
a swimsuit?'

The boy shook his head. 'No, but I can swim in these shorts.
They're old. What about you?'

'Knickers,' Tess said practically. 'Do you have an anchor?'

'Dunno,' Andy said. 'There's a lot of old clutter on the floor-
boards – is any of that an anchor?'

Tess sighed but splashed out to the dinghy and pulled it in,
then rooted in the pile of rope and bits of wood in the bottom and
produced a paint-tin on a rope, very similar to her own.

'Put it overboard so it fills,' she instructed him. 'There's no
wind, she'll wait for you. And then we'll have a bit of a splash.'

An hour later, the two of them heaved themselves out of the
water, sat on the bank and grinned at one another.

'Well?' Andy asked, pushing his fingers up through his short,
soaked hair. 'How many strokes did I do that time?'

'Three,' Tess said with cruel practicality. 'Your legs *will* sink. If
we could find a way to keep them up . . . but you will arch your
back, you've got to keep it straight, I think. Want to watch me
again?

'All the watching in the world isn't going to keep my back
straight,' Andy observed. 'Give us a moment, then I'll have
another go.'

'If the water were deeper, you could do the dog-paddle,' Tess
said thoughtfully. 'But in the shallows it pretty well has to be
the breast-stroke. I wonder how you'd go on your back? I was
swimming quite well on my front, back took me longer, I don't
know why.'

'How long did it take you?' Andy asked wistfully. 'I'm here

for five more weeks – imagine, five weeks stuck in Great-aunt Hannah's house, not being allowed out in case I drown!'

'I learned in a week, but I learned in the sea, and Dad says the sea is salty, which makes it more buoyant,' Tess told him. 'Don't they teach you at school? Some boys' boarding schools do, I know.'

'Mine doesn't,' Andy said. 'I say, I'm starving! You wouldn't like to ask me to tea, would you?'

Tess took the question seriously. She stared thoughtfully at him, trying to see him through Marianne's eyes. Dark hair spiked with water, thin, freckled face, serious grey eyes. That would be all right, but the wet grey shorts, grass-stained across the seat part, and the bare, scratched legs and feet . . .

'I'd like to,' she said. 'But would she like me to?'

'She?'

'Marianne. She's my stepmother. She's French.'

'It was damned cheeky of me to ask,' Andy said. 'Only Aunt has dinner at eight, and I'm used to high tea, at five. Never mind, though. I wouldn't want to put your stepmother out.'

It occurred to Tess then that Andy didn't speak with the local accent; he referred to dinner at eight, not supper at six. Would this make him acceptable to Marianne, make up for the wet shorts and – gracious! – the sticky tape holding his spectacles together? But Peter would be home soon, and Peter was a different kettle of fish; Tess could not imagine her father turning any friend of hers away. She jumped to her feet.

'Come back with me now and we'll see if we can wheedle some lemonade and cake out of Marianne,' she suggested. 'You won't mind if she's rather nasty to you? It's – it's being French, you know.'

'I won't mind,' Andy said solemnly, but she saw his grey eyes were twinkling behind his specs. 'What'll we do with the dinghies, though?'

'We'll tow yours behind the *Roger*,' Tess decided. 'I've a stake amongst the reeds – I'll show you.'

And very soon the two children had moored the boats and were pushing their way back along the narrow path towards the woods. Once in the trees, Tess stopped and glanced down at herself. The Aertex shirt stuck to her damp skin, the navy skirt was blotched with wet and her old sandshoes were soaked and dirty. A glance at Andy confirmed that he was not much better. But in Tess's experience, tidy hair and clean fingernails calmed a lot of rage, so she produced a stub of comb from her shirt pocket, dragged it through her hair and then handed it to Andy.

'We're clean, because of swimming, even if our clothes are a bit mucky,' she explained. 'But Marianne hates untidy hair.'

Andy hastily combed his hair, then slicked it back with both hands. He looked quite different now, Tess saw; older, more responsible. His spectacles helped, she supposed, but he didn't look like a boy who could be crushed by rudeness.

'All right?' Andy said, seeing her looking. 'Tidy enough for Mrs Delamere?'

'Yes, I'm sure,' Tess said. 'How old are you, Andy?'

He smiled teasingly down at her. 'As old as my tongue and a little bit older than my teeth, as Aunt always says. Why?'

Tess shrugged. 'Dunno. I thought you were twelve, like me – you're taller than I am, but boys often are – only now I'm not so sure. You looked younger with a fringe, you see.'

'I see. Well, I'm a bit older than you – thirteen. Satisfied, Mademoiselle?'

Tess laughed. 'Yes, that's fine. Come on, then.'

She led the way out of the trees, across the dusty lane, up the garden path and round the corner to the back door. Someone was clattering dishes in the kitchen; it must be later than I thought, Tess realised, and Marianne's getting our tea. She and Cherie, despite the difference in their ages, were given high tea and then packed off to their rooms so that Peter and Marianne might dine together without distraction. Peter kept saying that Tess was too old to be sent to bed at eight, but he never said it loud enough or crossly enough and so far, Marianne had just murmured agreement and continued with her insistence that Tess should share her baby sister's bedtime.

But now Tess pushed open the kitchen door and called through it, for all the world as though Marianne would be delighted to see her, 'Hello, Marianne, I've brought a friend home – any chance of some food and a glass of your delicious lemonade?'

100

She stepped into the room, closely followed by Andy, and found her stepmother putting the finishing touches to a large bowl of salad. Marianne looked up, began to speak, and then saw Andy, hovering.

'Oh . . . Tess, if I've told you once I've told you a dozen times, if you want to bring a friend home you ask, first.' She put down the knife she was holding and frowned reprovingly at Tess. 'I'm trying to get high tea for you and your sister, so that I can concentrate on preparing Peter's dinner when it gets cooler; you should be more thoughtful . . . I simply won't have you or your friends underfoot when I'm so busy.'

Tess shrank, horrified by her stepmother's sharp tone, but Andy walked round the table and held out his hand.

'I'm so sorry if I seem a nuisance, Mrs Delamere,' he said politely. 'My name's Herbert Anderson – I simply came in for a glass of water since my great-aunt, Lady Salter, generally has a nap after luncheon and doesn't much like being disturbed. But it's all right, I can go round by the side entrance and get one of the servants to fetch me a drink without waking Great-aunt Hannah. I didn't intend to trespass on your hospitality.'

Tess's eyes widened. He sounded quite different – very much in command of the situation, not at all like a boy who has just been snubbed by a grown-up. And Marianne, instead of coming right back at him with another similar remark, was walking round the table towards them and taking his hand, a smile on her lips.

'Lady Salter's nephew . . . why, my dear boy, that makes you a neighbour! There's no question of your trespassing on our hospitality – I'm so sorry if I seemed sharp, but Tess is so thoughtless, she has no conception of the dangers of bringing total strangers into . . . I mean, you could have been anyone . . .' Marianne's voice died away but the smile remained, more brilliant than ever.

Tess, fascinated, looked from one face to the other and saw that Andy not only sounded different, he looked different. He was smiling, too, but it wasn't the casual grin he'd been giving her, on and off, all afternoon. It was . . . well, she didn't know what it was, but it might have been designed, she thought gratefully, to soothe bad-tempered stepmothers. She could almost see Marianne beginning to purr and hoped that Andy could keep it up, wouldn't giggle, turn away. But she underestimated her new friend. His eyes remained fixed on Marianne's face, his expression remained serious.

'Naturally you must be careful; daughters are precious,' Andy said. He shook Marianne's hand, still smiling. 'How do you do, Mrs Delamere? And please call me Andy; everyone does.'

'I'm very well thank you, er, Andy, though I find this hot weather difficult. You'll stay to tea, of course? Tess is about to get her little sister up, so if you would like to accompany her upstairs she'll show you where the bathroom is and so on. Lady Salter won't grudge you to us for an hour or so, I dare say?'

'I'm sure my great-aunt would be most grateful,' Andy said graciously. 'If I might borrow your telephone I could let her know where I am. Aunt Hannah dines at eight,' he added, 'and I've a good way to go.'

'Of course, of course,' Marianne said. 'Tess, show, er, Andy where the telephone is. And then take him up to the bathroom.'

The bathroom and indoor toilet were still a novelty to Tess and she was grateful to Marianne for them since it was her stepmother who had insisted that the fourth bedroom be converted before her child was born. But because the only remaining spare bedroom was officially for grown-up visitors until Cherie claimed it, Marianne insisted that Tess could not have overnight guests. Vainly had Tess pleaded that a friend of hers could share their room, that she and Cherie would not mind at all . . . Marianne simply said that until they either built on or moved somewhere larger, overnight guests for the children were not possible.

'This way,' Tess said briefly now, jerking her head at Andy. 'I'll show you the bathroom and go and get Cherie up whilst you wash, then I'll tidy myself.' They were crossing the cool, dark hallway and she pointed to the hall stand. 'The phone's there, you can use it now, if you like, or when you come down afterwards.'

'Afterwards,' Andy said, following her up the stairs. 'D'you know your feet are black? Hell, mine are too . . . fancy having to wash after all that swimming!'

'I know,' Tess said. She hadn't intended to do much washing, but she had noticed how dusty her feet had got. She thundered up the stairs, hoping to wake Cherie, showed Andy the bathroom and waited, politely, until he'd closed the door, then went along to the dressing-room.

Cherie was awake. She lay sideways across her counterpane, sucking her thumb, but struggled into a sitting position and smiled cherubically at her sister as soon as the door opened. "Lo, Tess,' she said. 'Is tea ready?'

'Almost,' Tess said. It was as well not to say anything too definite, since if Cherie bounced downstairs demanding her tea, the chances were that Marianne would blame Tess for raising the child's hopes before time. And if she said tea wasn't ready, and Cherie bounced downstairs and demanded to know why not, then she would also be blamed, for disappointing her sister. All in all, almost was best.

'Oh, good,' Cherie said, then plonked down on the floor and began to straighten her white socks and don her sandals. That task finished, both girls went into Tess's room where Cherie looked critically at her fair curls in the square of mirror on top of Tess's chest of drawers, tweaked her butterfly bow straight and smoothed down her pink-and-white smock dress with both hands. Marianne still dressed Cherie like a baby, in silky little dresses with embroidery on them, though she was more than three years old now.

'Am I all right, Tess?' Cherie said, having admired herself in the mirror for a moment. It wouldn't have mattered if she were covered in chocolate, or muddy from top to toe, her mother would think her perfect, Tess knew, but she nodded anyway, because it was true, Cherie was all right. 'Is Maman home from the city? Did she bring me anything?'

Peter disapproved of Cherie's assumption that her mother would always bring her presents, but Tess didn't see that it mattered since Cherie was absolutely right: Marianne always brought her baby daughter some small gift. But she had seen nothing, so she just told Cherie she didn't know and watched her small sister trot from the room and begin to descend the flight, right foot first on each stair.

Having dealt with her sister, Tess hovered outside the bathroom, wondering whether she should knock or not, but before

103

she had made up her mind the door opened a short way and Andy's face appeared.

'Tess! Look, you couldn't lend me some bags, could you? D'you have a brother or anything? These . . .' he gestured to his shorts '. . . are a mess.'

'Sorry, I don't have a brother or anything,' Tess said. 'It's the top of you that'll worry my stepmother, though. I mean eating tea with a bare chest is probably just the sort of thing no Frenchman would dream of doing.' She spoke a little sharply. She was well used to the pronouncement: 'No Frenchman would dream of doing a thing like that!' over the most innocent of pastimes, and sometimes it made her want to scream . . . and be more difficult than ever, of course.

Andy must have guessed how she felt, for he pulled a sympathetic face. 'Like that is it? I thought so . . . what about an Aertex shirt, though? They look pretty much alike, the boys' and the girls', I don't suppose Mrs Delamere would notice.'

'I'm sure I can find a clean shirt,' Tess said. 'I've got some shorts, too. They're a bit baggy, but they might do . . . want to try 'em?'

'Try anything once,' Andy said cheerfully. 'Can I see your room?'

'You can come and choose a shirt,' Tess said, leading the way. She threw open the door. Her room was very hot and there were flies clustered on the window panes despite the fact that both windows were flung wide, but the view of the Broad made up for any trifling annoyance such as flies. The water was smooth and still as pewter, the trees massed on the margins, the reeds scarcely stirred in the light breeze. Tess smiled proudly around her. She adored her bedroom. Marianne rarely followed her in here, it was her refuge, unchanged from the days she and Peter had lived here alone, before the marriage. Her pictures and posters adorned the walls, her books were stacked on the two sets of deep bookshelves, her cupboards had home-made calendars, school timetables and favourite poems pinned upon them. No one, not even Cherie, was allowed to interfere with this room. She turned to Andy. 'What d'you think?'

'Nice,' Andy said at once. 'Cor, what a view!'

'I'm used to it,' Tess said, but she wasn't. I never will be, she thought, going over to her chest of drawers and pulling out a white Aertex shirt and a pair of rather baggy khaki shorts. She had worn the shorts a lot before Marianne came, because they had been her father's once, when he had been young. With a belt round the waist and the legs turned up they were all right, cooler and more practical than a skirt. But Marianne didn't approve of girls wearing shorts, especially shorts with fly-buttons in front. Now, Tess held the clothing out. 'Would that do?'

He took the shirt, held it against his chest, then took the shorts. 'I'll try 'em on,' he said. 'Here or the bathroom?'

'Here. I'll go and clean my teeth and spend a penny,' Tess said happily. 'Er, Andy . . .'

They both laughed. 'Your stepmum has difficulty,' Andy observed. 'Perhaps she thinks the great-nephew of Lady Salter should be titled . . . you know, Little Lord Salter sort of thing.'

They laughed again. Comfortably. Companionably.

'Well, she is French,' Tess said.

'True. Allowances must be made. The French are so – so – '

'Stiff? Starchy? Stuck up?'

Andy flicked her with the Aertex shirt and Tess left him to change and went and cleaned her teeth, brushed her hair and then changed into her own clean clothing which she had selected, after some thought, before leaving her bedroom. She had decided to be tactful, for once, and has chosen a cotton dress with a full skirt and short sleeves. It was blue gingham with a white peter pan collar and Peter had once said he liked it. Marianne will approve, anyway, Tess thought, then remembered that Marianne didn't always act consistently. A neat dress would please her one day, annoy her the next. But at least I'm trying, she told herself, combing her hair. It'll be easier to be friends with Andy if I try with Marianne.

'Aunt Hannah? It's me, Herbert. I'm having tea with friends, is that all right? No, don't keep dinner, I won't be hungry twice in one evening! Yes, I'll be home before dark. Oh . . . they're called Delamere. I don't know if you know them, but they live four or five miles from the Hall. Yes, quite a big family. Very nice, really. Yes, of course. Thanks, Aunt. Bye.'

Tess knew it was rude to listen, but she listened anyway, because it would have been ruder to walk away and leave Andy in the hall. And when Andy put the receiver down he sighed and grinned ruefully at her, and she thought to herself, *it isn't only me who has funny relatives: that aunt of his can be funny, too.* And this comforted her, because anyone could see that Andy was all right, which might mean that she was all right, too.

Tea was lovely. Andy told them stories about his school and Marianne was fascinated and amused, and then he told them stories about life at the Hall which intrigued Marianne and interested Tess, too. And when tea was over he insisted that since Marianne had worked so hard to make them a delicious meal and would presently have to get her husband's dinner, he and Tess would clear away, wash and wipe up. He proved adept with the little mop thing and rinsed everything under the cold tap so that there were no bits of cress or fragments of egg left on the plates, and he waited until Marianne had gone into the garden to pick some parsley for a sauce before instigating a mop-and-tea-towel fight, so that was all right. He won the fight by a narrow margin and when he heard Marianne approaching he seized the big mop and began vigorously attacking the wet floor, assuring his hostess that he believed in finishing a job properly, so had decided to clean the floor for her.

Some people might have disbelieved him, but so candid was his bespectacled gaze, so manfully frank his tone, that Tess almost believed him herself – and she had been the recipient of a good deal of the flung water.

'My husband will be home quite soon now,' Marianne said as the two of them headed towards the back door. 'Won't you stay, Andy, and meet him? He probably knows your great-aunt.'

Andy, however, explained that he wasn't used to boats and had a long scull ahead of him if he wasn't to get home late and be in trouble with his great-aunt, and Marianne accepted this explanation and said that it was Cherie's bedtime, so they had best say good-night to her.

Cherie came and kissed Tess, then kissed Andy, and asked innocently why she must go to bed earlier than Tess tonight.

'Tess always comes to bed when I do,' she said plaintively. 'I like to know she's in her room, then I aren't alone upstairs.'

Andy looked shocked and Marianne angry.

'How absurd you are, chick,' she said to her spoilt little daughter. 'When you were smaller, of course Tess shared your bedtime, but she's a big girl now. She'll be up for an hour or two yet.'

'But Maman . . .' Cherie began, and found herself whisked up in her mother's arms and carried determinedly towards the stairs.

'Good-night, Andy, good-night Tess,' Marianne called over her shoulder. 'Be in before dark please, Tess.'

Outside and under the trees, with the sun at last beginning to lose its heat, the two young people turned to each other.

'Phew!' Tess said. 'I bet your great-aunt isn't as bad as that!'

'That's what you think,' Andy assured her. 'Anyway, I quite like your stepmum. Once you can see how she is, she's manageable.'

'Not for me she isn't,' Tess said gloomily. 'Besides, I don't think I can see how she is. She's a mystery, I never know what's going to annoy her next.'

Andy smiled a trifle smugly. 'You haven't had my experience,' he said. 'You going to be on the Broad tomorrow?'

'Yes,' Tess said at once. 'D'you have a bike?'

'Nope. But the gardener has. I might be able to borrow it.'

'You might be able to borrow Mr Thrower's, if you come over by boat again,' Tess said eagerly. 'Andy, how long are you staying with your great-aunt?'

They had reached the boats now and she was squatting down and untying the painter, pulling Andy's little dinghy away from her own. Andy leaned over and began to push the boat out from the reeds.

'Until school starts again, which is 22nd September. So I'll come over by boat tomorrow then, shall I? I could bring a picnic, perhaps.'

'That would be lovely,' Tess said joyfully. 'Tell you what, why don't we pretend your aunt has asked me to luncheon? Marianne

107

would be tickled pink, I'm sure of it, and that would make it easier for me to ask you to tea, next time.'

'That's a *good* wheeze,' Andy said approvingly. 'We'll say you're coming to the Hall for luncheon tomorrow . . . only not really, it's too soon . . . and I'll come to your place for tea. And I want another swimming lesson tomorrow, because I'd be stuck if my boat turned over, right now. And you might show me how to use the oars without splashing, and how to steer the bloody thing,' he added.

'Right,' Tess said. 'Do you know, I don't usually like the summer holidays all that much – well, I do, because I love this place – but I get awfully lonely, here by myself for ten whole weeks. But with two of us . . . well, it'll be grand.'

Five

By the end of August Andy was swimming well. Tess was proud of his progress, and proud, too, of the way he now handled a boat.

'There used to be a boy over on the other side of the Broad who had a sailing dinghy,' she told Andy. 'He taught me and Jan to handle it, I'm sure he'd teach you, as well, if you wanted to learn.'

But the boy didn't seem to be around much any more, and besides, Andy said he didn't want to learn to sail, not yet.

'Learning to ride a bike was bad enough,' he reminded her. 'My arse was black and blue – my knees, as well.'

'Shouldn't say arse,' Tess said absently. 'Daddy says btm.'

'My father says arse,' Andy said firmly. 'So I do. See?'

Tess saw. She was beginning to learn quite a lot about Andy. His father was a diplomat and lived abroad; right now he was in Russia somewhere, with Andy's mother. When Andy had been small he had gone abroad with them, but not any more. Now he stayed at school in term-time and with relatives in the holidays. His elder brother, Charles, travelled out to see his parents during his vacs from Cambridge and his younger brother, James, was actually living with Sir Robert and Lady Anderson; it was only Andy who seemed cut off from his parents.

'I don't mind,' he told Tess airily. 'It's something that seems to happen in families like mine. It happened to my older brother, too, between thirteen and sixteen, when he was getting his education. Besides, I'd rather be with Aunt Hannah, foreign embassies aren't that much fun, and she's not a bad old bird.'

But she was, of course. Putting two and two together, Tess suspected that Lady Salter resented having Andy dumped on her and made him toe the line and keep out of her way whenever possible. One of the maids, who lived in the village, told Tess that old Lady Salter had told Andy, in her presence, that she thought him plain.

'Odd, when you've a handsome father and a pretty mother,' she had said. 'You'll never turn the girls' heads. Hope you're clever, young man; you'll need to be.'

Andy was not particularly clever, and he wasn't athletic, either, which was why his father, Sir Robert, had sent him to Lady Salter rather than to people with a family of boys. It wasn't that he was ashamed of Andy, he simply knew that his younger son would rather spend time alone than find himself expected to join in. Swimming would not be judged an athletic achievement by the family, Andy told Tess, nor boating. His father had played rugger and cricket, with a sideswipe at badminton and squash. Spectacles were a danger in rugger and a nuisance in other sports, but Andy was blind as a bat without them, so he tended to keep off the games field whenever possible.

'But you don't swim in specs,' Tess said, and Andy told her that when you had water in your eyes or were actually under the surface, specs didn't matter.

'I can see as well as you under water,' he explained. 'And when you're churning your way along the surface you don't need to see especially well. So it suits me, you see. And I can bike like anything with specs on.'

He could, but it had been a near thing. He had no natural sense of balance, Tess had concluded despairingly at one point, when Andy simply fell off left, right or over the handlebars, and could not keep Mr Thrower's old machine rolling for more than six feet. But one day it came to him, a bolt from the blue, and he was soon expert, able to make the old bicycle do all sorts of tricks and beating Tess whenever they had a race.

So when Andy suggested, one morning at the end of August, three weeks after they had first met, that they should undertake a bicycle ride to the seaside, Tess was all for it.

'I'd like to go to Palling. I went there, once, with the Throwers,' she told him. 'That was before Janet got so grown-up, of course. Is it far on a bike?'

'Probably about ten miles; nothing, really,' Andy assured her. 'We'll take a picnic – luncheon and tea – then we can be away all day. Can you square it with your stepmother?'

He knew, none better, that 'squaring it' with Tess's father instead of her stepmother could mean trouble for his friend. Marianne always got her own back if Tess went to Peter instead of her with a request, by being particularly difficult for weeks and by refusing, on principle, any request which her stepdaughter might make.

But now, Tess saw no reason to tell Marianne where they were going. 'I'll just say we're playing at the Hall,' she said. 'No need to mention Sea Palling.'

'All right. But why shouldn't we cycle to the seaside? We can both swim . . . oh, bring your bathers.'

'And a bucket and spade, I suppose,' Tess said, giggling. 'Can one towel do for both of us, do you suppose? And are you sure you want to provide all the food? I expect Marianne would give me something if I said it was luncheon at yours, tea on the Broad, or in the hay meadow.'

'No need; Jane likes spoiling me,' Andy said loftily. 'She takes all the best grub for me, and tells Auntie that it's gone bad in the heat. But you can bring the drinks if you like. Mrs Delamere makes the best lemonade ever.' He looked at her affectionately. 'And whilst we bike along, you can tell me the story of your life: I'm sure it's full of surprises.'

They set out as they had planned, before eight o'clock, and Andy rode, not Mr Thrower's battered old bone-shaker, but a much superior machine which his aunt had borrowed for him when she realised it would, as she termed it, keep him out of mischief for hours together.

Tess had woken early, full of excitement over the proposed expedition, but a glance from her window confirmed that it was both chilly and overcast, a disappointment after such glorious weather. However, it would make the long cycle ride pleasanter if they weren't baking under the sun, so she got up, went downstairs and cut herself bread and jam, them made a tray of tea and carried it upstairs to her parents' room.

Peter was in the bathroom, she could hear the taps running, but Marianne was pleased by the tea and lay back on her pillows, sipping the hot, sweet liquid and asking Tess quite pleasantly what plans she had for the day ahead.

'Oh, just a bike ride over to the Hall; Andy's calling for me early,' Tess said. 'Lady Salter says we can have our lunch and tea there, today. Gibson – he's the head gardener – thinks we might give him a hand to pick some plums, if they're ripe enough.'

'I wonder what sort they are?' Marianne said thoughtfully. 'If they're Victorias you might perhaps bring some home, d'you think? I'd like to make plum conserve – your father loves it.'

'I shouldn't think they'll be picking their Victorias quite yet; they'll probably be Early Rivers,' Tess observed, wondering just how she would get round this one. 'But if it is the Vics, I'll ask if I can bring some home.'

'I wouldn't mind some Early Rivers,' Marianne said. 'They're more work, but on the whole I think they make better jam.'

'There's a plum tree in the orchard, right down by the back hedge,' Tess said, crossing her fingers behind her back. 'You could pick some yourself . . . or Andy and I will do it tomorrow,' she added hastily, seeing Marianne's frown begin. Her stepmother did not look on fruit picking as a suitable occupation for one such as herself.

'Oh. Well, perhaps that would be best. I don't want Lady Salter to think we're taking advantage of your friendship with Andy to try to wheedle some plums out of her! You'll pick me ten pounds or so tomorrow, then?'

'All right,' Tess said recklessly. 'If they're ripe, that is. See you this evening, then.' She wondered what she would have to do to acquire some Early Rivers plums to assuage Marianne's sudden hunger for them, because getting some was now a necessity. Tell one lie, she thought sorrowfully as she ran down the stairs, and before you know it you're up to your ears in a positive sea of the things. To the best of her knowledge the only plum tree in the orchard was a greengage, and that fruited sparsely every other year. The Throwers had some plum trees, though, and dear Mrs Thrower was still very much her friend. I'll go down and dig their garden, or help harvest their blackcurrants, or – or *buy* the

112

damned plums, but I'll get hold of some somehow, Tess vowed as she went out the back door and began to wheel her bicycle down the garden path. Oh why didn't I think of a better reason than picking plums for going over to the Hall all day?

And later, when she and Andy were cycling side by side along a pleasant country road, she told him about the plums and shared his astonishment as the lengths to which she had gone rather than admit that she was going to the seaside.

'Why couldn't you just say?' Andy said when she'd finished explaining. 'Why pretend?'

'If I tell you, do you promise you won't tease on about it, or say anything to anyone else?' Tess said at last, having thought it over. 'Because I've never told anyone what I'm now going to tell you, Andy. You wouldn't let me down?'

'Course not. Fire away.'

And thus encouraged, Tess told Andy about her dream, and her father's reaction to it.

When the story was told Andy whistled under his breath, then turned to stare at her for a moment.

'And you still don't know what you see in the water? Not after dreaming it dozens of times?'

'Hundreds of times, more like,' Tess told him. 'But each time it seems like the first time, if you understand me. It's fresh, exciting . . . the beach is lovely, the sea smells so good, the sand feels cool and nice on my hot feet . . .'

'Hmm. Aren't you curious, though, Tess? I bet if you asked the boy, he'd tell you.'

'How can he? It's only a dream,' Tess protested. 'He's only a dream, too, I suppose.'

Andy shook his head. 'No, you don't believe that,' he said. 'If you did, you wouldn't have told me about it, for a start. And if you thought it was only a dream you wouldn't mind telling your father you were off to the seaside. What do you really believe, Tess?'

Tess stared at him, then smiled and turned her eyes forward once more. 'You're right, of course. I don't really think it's just a dream, I think it's something that happened to me when I was very small. I think it was something bad, because Daddy doesn't want to talk about it, he wants me to forget it. I asked him once, when I was just a kid, and he said dreams were dreams and shouldn't be taken seriously. But to my knowledge he's never been to the seaside since we've lived in the Old House, and I can't remember anything before that. I've been twice; once when my uncle from Norwich took me and the cousins to Yarmouth, and once when I went with the Throwers to Palling for a week. Other than that, we just don't go down to the coast. Not even Marianne, not even Cherie, though Daddy says he'll take us to Devonshire for a seaside holiday when Cherie's a bit bigger.'

'And the boy?'

'I think he's a real person,' Tess said slowly. 'And you're right, of course. He would know what it's all about. Whenever I meet a boy a few years older than me I take a long, hard look at him, because I'm sure I'd recognise him if we met. But no luck so far.'

'Fascinating,' Andy said slowly. 'Abso-bloody-lutely fascinating. What does the boy look like, then?'

'Ordinary,' Tess said ruefully. 'He's got brown hair and eyes, and he wears a blue shirt and grey shorts. If I was three, I'd think he was about seven. I think he must have lived near us, or been staying near us, because when I turn to see him coming along the beach I'm not at all pleased. He bosses me about, you see, and tells me what to do and what not to do.'

'A bit like me,' Andy said, grinning. 'I try to boss you about, but I don't have a lot of luck, you're far too strong-minded.'

'You're too young,' Tess said at once. 'And too nice as well, Andy. I really don't think that boy was very nice, not to little kids, anyway. But he's the clue, isn't he? If I could find him I'd know what was in the water.'

'If it was something nasty, perhaps you're better off not knowing,' Andy said cautiously. 'Have you ever thought of that, Teasle?'

'Of course I have . . . but I really feel I *must* know,' Tess said. 'I can't help wondering where my mother was, what she was doing, to let me wander off by myself like that. If only Daddy would say a bit more . . . but he warned me when he and Marianne were about to be married that he wouldn't want to talk about "before" once that happened. He said it wasn't fair to Marianne – but I don't think it's fair to me never to tell me anything about my mother. It didn't matter when it was just Dad and I, but now, what with Marianne and everything, I think about my mother a lot. And I'm sure I must have relatives from her side, people who knew her, would like to tell me about her, even if Dad won't. Only I can't ask because of what Dad said.'

'But what would you ask these relatives if you met them? You know how your mother died, don't you? And where she's buried, and so on? Besides, she died soon after you were born, I remember you telling me that when we first met.'

'I don't know how she died, or where she's buried, or anything,' Tess protested. 'Daddy said I was only a baby at the time, but sometimes I feel I knew her – at any rate I remember a lovely woman, a cuddly, warm person, who loved me. Sometimes, Andy, I think perhaps Dad may be holding something back. He wouldn't tell me a fib, but that doesn't mean he's told me the whole truth.'

'You don't know where your own mother is buried?' Andy said incredulously. 'Isn't she buried in the churchyard at Barton, then?'

'No, she isn't,' Tess said shortly. For a long time she had simply assumed that her mother's grave was the big one by St Michael's gate with the hovering angel; she could still remember her shame and embarrassment when Janet Thrower had told her that this monument belonged to a gentleman who had died in 1840. 'Sometimes I've wondered . . .'

'What? You've wondered what?'

'Well, whether she's dead at all. I've wondered if she just left my father . . . only I don't think he'd tell a huge fib over something as important as that, do you? And anyway, it's the sort of thing that happens in books, not in real life.'

'Hmm. It certainly is a mystery, and I like mysteries. Shall we solve it, Tess? The great Sherlock Anderson and his companion, Tess Watson, will Reveal All. How about it? There must be clues in your house – how about that photograph you showed me? There must be more pictures of her . . . incidentally, she's most awfully like you – did you know?'

'Like *me*?' Tess turned to stare incredulously at her companion, their front wheels locked and the pair of them fell heavily on to the dust roadway. Andy swore, Tess followed suit, then they began to giggle as the humour of the situation struck them.

'What a pair of fools . . . are you all right, though, Teasle?' Andy said. He helped Tess to her feet, then began trying to untangle their bicycles, only to discover that his front wheel was out of alignment with the back one. 'Oh damn, look at this! *And* I've skinned my knees.'

'I've done my hands no good at all,' Tess said sadly, squinting at her palms, which were deeply grazed. 'And my knees are bloody . . . much worse than yours. Oh, and my elbow's got a huge bruise . . . But my bicycle seems to be fairly undamaged.'

'This one's okay too,' Andy agreed, having straightened the wheel. 'Are you fit? Then let's remount. Now! What were we talking about?'

'Whether there were any other pictures of my mother, and there aren't,' Tess said with conviction. 'I've looked, and there's nothing. And asking Daddy questions is so hard, Andy, because it makes him sad, and I can tell by his eyes that it's true. He says she was very beautiful, and everyone who knew her loved her. When I was little I heard him telling people that she'd died of a fever, but I don't know what sort. And that's about it, except that her name was Leonora. I wish I were called Leonora, it's such a lovely, graceful sort of name.'

'Maiden name?'

'Uh?'

'Maiden name, silly. That's a married woman's name before she married . . . oh, I'm making a poor go of this, what I mean is, your maiden name is Delamere, but when you marry you'll change it to – to Anderson. Get it?'

'Yes, I think so. But I'm afraid I don't know what my mother's maiden name was,' Tess admitted. 'Daddy may have mentioned it, but I don't remember it. I didn't think things like that were important when I asked Daddy about her. Oh, Andy, if only I could find that boy! He would be bound to know.'

'Well, you might,' Andy said. 'Hey-up, we're almost there! See the sand dunes? Oh what luck, what luck! We're going to have a grand time, there's not another soul on the beach!'

'Because it's starting to rain, that's why there's no one else here,' Tess said as the first heavy drops assaulted them. 'Now why didn't we think of rain?'

But they pushed their bicycles between the dunes, ignoring the rain which the wind swept against their faces, and indeed, it seemed to ease a little as they reached the beach itself. Tess stood between the last two sand dunes, with the Marram grass pricking her legs and the sand slithering downhill, and stared out at the long, golden beach, the low-waters, and beyond them, the sea itself, white-topped, beckoning.

'Leave the bikes here,' Andy said. 'D'you realise, I've never swum in the sea? Grab your bathers and let's go, let's go, let's go!'

'The sea, the sea!' Tess screamed, fishing her bathing suit out of her bicycle bag and throwing her bicycle down against the nearest dune. 'Race you, Andy, race you!' She set off at a gallop, knowing Andy was close on her heels. Together they splashed through the low-waters, with Tess's skirt getting soaked, and raced across the hard sand, to stop short, hearts thundering, on the very edge of the sea.

'It's rough,' Andy observed against her ear. 'Does it get deep quickly?'

'Sure to,' Tess said. She kicked off her sandals, then sat down and heaved off her socks, removed her knickers and began to struggle into her bathing suit whilst holding her skirt primly round her knees.

Tess's modesty was unnecessary, with an empty beach and Andy changing as rapidly as she, but moments later the two of them stood up, he in his suit, she in hers, and ran down the beach and splashed into the creaming surf.

It was still raining, but what did rain matter when you were about to get wet all over anyway? Tess launched herself into the water, not caring whether the sandy bottom lay a foot below her or a hundred fathoms. She saw Andy, a little less precipitately, take to the water, and then forgot everything except the wonder of the sea. It wasn't like the Broad, which simply allowed you to swim in it, the sea encouraged you, helped you, supported you. It enabled you to perform miracles, like treading water, floating, forcing your way deep and then coming up with a rush, like a cork out of a bottle. Tess did most of these things, and then heard

Andy calling to her. She looked around; he looked cross, and he was standing upright, not swimming or anything, with the water no deeper than his chest though when the waves broke round him he was temporarily obscured by the foaming crest. It wasn't a good place to stop, she knew, but since this was Andy's first time in the sea he probably didn't realise that it got calmer the deeper you went.

'What?' she shrieked. She had to shriek because he was a long way behind her, very much nearer the shore than she. 'What is it?'

'You're too deep,' he shouted. 'Come back, come back!'

Tess laughed and trod water, slicking her hair back with both hands, rubbing the salt from her eyes.

'Why should I? I can swim, can't I? You come out to me – it's much calmer out here, much more fun.'

'What? I can't hear you properly. Oh, Tess, come back. I'm not coming out that far. This is my first time, remember?'

She laughed again, full of the confidence of one totally at ease with the element in which she played, but there was a sizeable wave coming, so she duck-dived under it and saw that she was really very deep, that if she had been with the Throwers someone would have called her back ages ago. Though I was eight then, not twelve, she reminded herself as her head broke the surface once more. Still, it wasn't much fun for Andy, hanging about miles behind her, probably beginning to feel the cold and not understanding how safe she was, how secure.

'All right, I'm coming,' she shouted, and set off for the beach.

The moment she got within a foot of him she realised that she'd given him a bad scare. His face was paper white and he was shivering.

'Tess! Oh, Tess, you scared me. It's too rough for me, it keeps knocking the feet from under me. Shall we play in the lows for a bit? The rain's lessening.'

'The lows? But they're no better than the Broad ... look, if I hold your hand ...'

It was the wrong thing to say. He stiffened.

'I'm not a baby, you know, I'm older than you and a whole lot tougher, despite my specs. I'll come out with you.'

Tess hesitated. She turned back towards the tumultuous waves.

The rain had stopped now, but she was cold about the shoulders, beginning to shiver. Suddenly, she remembered the neat packs of sandwiches in their greaseproof paper wrappings, the ripe tomatoes with the tiny screws of salt, the packets of crisps. It seemed a long while since breakfast.

'We-ell, I'm rather cold now I come to think of it – and desperately hungry. Shall we get dry and have something to eat, first? We've got all day to swim, after all.'

Thankfully, they both turned their back on the suddenly cold, suddenly uninviting North sea, and headed up the beach.

They had a good day. At noon the rain stopped altogether and a watery sun appeared, and the beach filled up with families from the bungalows which lined the road beyond the dunes. Secure in their nest amongst the sand and burgeoning Marram grass, with their bicycles hidden from the eyes of all but the most curious, Tess and Andy ate, watched from their eyrie as the beach slowly became peopled, and then went back down to the sands and played. They built a huge castle, taller than both of them, and dug out a deep moat which then had to be filled with bucket after bucket of sea water. Despite Tess's teasing, they had neither of them brought bucket or spade and were forced to borrow from a family with a great many small children and a plethora of beach equipment. The buckets were good, strong tin, but the spades were wooden ones and made digging difficult. Nevertheless they did the job and in return for the loan, Tess and Andy built a stout sand-car, in which the young males of the family drove desperately round an imaginary race-track, honking and shouting.

'We bring them to the beach and they spend all their time pretending they're somewhere else,' the children's mother sighed. She was quite young, a tanned, yellow-haired creature who looked more like an elder sister to her three small boys and two small girls than a parent. Her husband, who had come down earlier and played with vigour, had suddenly decided to go back to their holiday bungalow for a book, and hadn't returned. 'But that's life, I suppose. At home they carry water out to the sandpit and slosh it about and say they're at the seaside!'

'We'll build them a sand-boat, shall we?' Tess suggested, but at that point a Stop-me-and-buy-one, on an elderly tricycle, came and rang his bell at the gap and the children's attention left the beach completely. Their mother, who told Tess and Andy that she was Mrs Underwood, gave them some money to buy ices for her children, herself and themselves, and after the ices she produced a bottle of lemonade which they all shared and after that it was time to take the kiddies off the beach and back to their bungalow for high tea, baths and bed.

'We'll be leaving soon, anyway,' Tess assured the Underwood children when they whined that it wasn't fair, Tess and Andy weren't being forced to go indoors before dark. 'Thanks for the loan of the buckets and spades, kids.'

The two of them didn't go at once, of course. They had a last swim, in a sea which was calmer now though the sky overhead was threatening, then changed, tied their wet bathers to their handlebars so that they might dry as they rode, and wheeled their bicycles down from the dunes and out on to the sandy road, pleasantly tired but still quite capable of getting home before dark.

Despite the rain, Tess thought as they rode, they had had a marvellous day. It was only on the ride back that they began to regret their rashness in not telling the truth about where they were going. The rain was pelting down in earnest, long rods of rain which flattened the grass on the verges and bounced off the children's heads with painful force.

'Why didn't we bring our oilies?' Andy groaned, trying to keep his head down and see where he was going at the same time. 'We really should have thought of rain.'

'I think we ought to shelter for a bit,' Tess said. 'It can't keep on like this or there'll be another flood.'

'We'll shelter,' Andy decided. 'If we can find somewhere, that is.' He slowed his bicycle and Tess followed suit, looking around her as she did so. The landscape was bare, rain-drenched. There were thick, wild hedges, copses, growing crops. No shelter as far as the eye could see.

'There's nothing here, so we'd better press on for a bit,' Andy said. 'We're bound to find somewhere soon.'

120

They pressed on, riding side by side, so wet now that it no longer mattered. They didn't talk much though, because they were concentrating on pedalling. So when Andy, who had forged ahead, spotted something coming up and stopped, Tess, following behind him with head down against the driving rain, didn't realise quickly enough. Her front wheel collided with his pedal, and the hiss of escaping air could be heard even above the constant patter of the rain on the grey, cloud-reflecting road.

'Oh God!' Andy's dismay was real. 'That's torn it. We're walking from now on. And I've just seen a barn, too, which was why I stopped.'

'If we can reach it, we could mend the puncture,' Tess said hopefully. 'I've got my puncture outfit with me.'

'Yes, that's true,' Andy said, cheering up. 'And it'll stop soon; bound to. Let's go, then. It's only a field away.'

They swung the gate open, went into the field, and shut the gate behind them. Then they pushed their cycles along a furrow between the rows of mangold worzels until they reached the further hedge. The barn was just on the other side of it.

'Gate's miles away,' Andy groaned. 'But the hedge is a bit thinner here . . .'

'We shouldn't,' Tess said, at the same time shoving her bike at the thin spot. 'Oh, I don't suppose it matters, there's no stock in the field to escape. I just hope the barn's full of something nice, like hay.'

It wasn't, it was full of dusty farm machinery and implements such as hay forks, but there was a loft full of hay above.

'We'll dry ourselves on the hay first, then do the puncture,' Andy decreed. 'Come on, up that ladder!'

Tess giggled and bounded up the ladder ahead of him. She was so relieved to be out of the rain, so delighted at the mere prospect of being dry again, that she would have agreed to most things. And when, presently, they were indeed beginning to dry off, she descended from the loft with confidence, turned her bike upside down, and reached for the tool which would enable her to pull out the inner tube without ruining it. She had a couple of tyre levers which she inserted, and was about to spin the wheel to find the puncture when Andy gave a moan.

'What's up?' she said, starting to turn the wheel. 'It's all right, I've got plenty of patches.'

'Have you seen the size of the split, Teasle? There's no way we can mend it, you'll have to have a new inner tube, and they don't grow on trees . . . nor in barns, unfortunately.'

Tess stared as the damage came into view. There was an immense slit in the tyre through which she could see the inner tube protruding like a pink, flabby intestine. And through the slit she could see a jagged tear right across the inner tube which must be about six inches long.

'Oh!' Tess said blankly. 'It makes the patches look silly, doesn't it?'

'It does. So we'll be walking the rest of the way, I'm afraid.'

'And we've got no bicycle lamps,' Tess said, really dismayed now. 'And we won't get home before dark – oh, Andy, we're going to be in such trouble!'

'I don't see why,' Andy said stoutly, but he watched rather glumly as Tess took the tyre levers out, did her best to shove the inner tube back, and then righted her machine. 'After all, my great-aunt thinks I'm at your place and your people think you're at the Hall. We're safe enough.'

'But only until it's dark,' Tess wailed. 'We're both supposed to be home by dark, you know we are. When we aren't, Daddy will ring your aunt and ask if he should call for me, and your aunt will say she thought you were with us . . . oh Andy, you know that bit about tangled webs? Well, we've both practised to deceive, and now we're going to be found out. Everyone will be absolutely furious!'

'We'll ring up from the nearest call box,' Andy said, visited by inspiration. 'My aunt won't mind all that much, she may not even notice I'm late, but your people will, so we'll ring them. We'll say we went for a bike ride and you've got a puncture and we're going to be very late. Won't that do?'

'We-ell, if they find out I've gone to the seaside, when I said I was going over to the Hall to pick plums, I'll catch it,' Tess said. 'Daddy will be terribly hurt and Marianne will be plain furious. And they won't let me out to play with you for ages,' she added miserably.

'I don't see why they should be cross because we've come down to the coast,' Andy said. They pushed their bicycles along the furrow to the further hedge, becoming bogged down a couple of times in the clayey soil. 'Everyone goes to the seaside – you said you'd been with the Throwers a few years ago.'

'Ye-es, but Daddy never takes us. Marianne suggests it often, in the summer, but Daddy usually comes up with some excuse. I don't think he likes the sea much.'

'I can understand him not liking the sea, because my pater doesn't like it much, either. But why doesn't he want you to go to it with me? Or rather, why do you think he doesn't want you to go?'

Tess sighed. 'It's got something to do with the dream I told you about, or at least, I think it has,' she said. 'But I'm guessing, really. It's just that I can't imagine why Daddy won't take us to the coast if my dream doesn't mean anything. And if it does . . . well, I think I should know, don't you?'

'I'm inclined to agree,' Andy said. They reached the thin part of the hedge and shoved their machines through, then followed them on to the soaked, thigh-high grass of the verge. 'Look, there's a call box; let's see if we can get through to your people first.'

They put in their pennies, waited until the telephone was answered the other end and pressed button A, only to be disappointed.

'It's what they call one way transmission,' Andy said. 'We could hear your stepmama clear as clear but she couldn't hear us. Damn and blast! And I don't have any more pennies, do you?'

'I never had any to start with,' Tess told him. 'Can we reverse the charges, perhaps? I know people do that, sometimes.'

But the telephone was clearly faulty, for though they rang the operator and she answered she could not hear their voices either so they were forced to turn away without having got their message through.

'Never mind,' Andy said consolingly as they pushed their bikes on to the shiny wet tarmac. 'We did try – that means we aren't all bad. Look, you know what I said this morning about me being Sherlock Anderson and you being Tess Watson – why don't we have a go? Try to find out what the mystery is all about? We've another five weeks of the hols left, pretty well, we could do a lot of digging around in that time.'

'Could we?' Tess said. She fell into step beside him, keeping her bicycle well clear of his, and began to plod, and to take her mind off the trouble they would be in when they did reach home, began to chatter as well. 'I'd like to find out about my mother more than almost anything – and I'd really love to find out about that beach, and the boy. Only . . . I don't want to upset my father, so we'll have to do it on the quiet.'

'Fair enough,' Andy said. 'Now let's go over your dream again. We've a long walk ahead of us, no point in wasting time.'

'Right,' Andy said when Tess had told her story. 'Now what have we got to go on? A boy who chews liquorice sweets and bosses little girls and not much else, but I'm going to solve the mystery and you're going to help me! We'll start first thing tomorrow morning, by finding your mother's grave. We know her name's Leonora Delamere, we know she died when you were born, or soon after, so we'll track her down easily, once we start. We'll catch a train into Norwich and find out who keeps registers of births and deaths and we'll go and visit the grave, see what it says on the headstone. Are you game?'

'Oh, yes,' Tess breathed. 'You don't know how much it would mean to me, Andy, to find my mother's grave. I'd feel – oh, more *real*, somehow, if I could put some flowers on her grave now and then.'

'Right. Then I'll come round to the Old House first thing tomor- row and we'll go detecting. I'll wheedle some train-money out of the old girl, because your bike won't be put right in a minute, and we'll start our search at once!'

At the Old House, Peter began to worry when Tess didn't turn up as it grew dusk, though as he said to Marianne, it was a good bicycle ride from the Hall to Deeping Lane. Marianne, clearly not worrying at all, said that Tess had promised to bring some plums back if she could and was doubtless heavily burdened. Then she turned to the task of putting Cherie to bed, having already prepared guinea fowl in red wine and a raspberry mousse for their dinner.

Peter went and sat in his study and tried to read the *Eastern Daily Press*, but he found it difficult to concentrate. It was such a foul evening, that was the trouble. Tess was going to be half-drowned . . . he cut the thought off short. What a fool he was even to think such a thing! He had meant soaked, he didn't worry about her falling into the Broad, not when she was with the reliable Andy, and besides, the kids could both swim and anyway, they were on bicycles, and over at the Hall. If you want to worry, he chided himself, worry about road accidents, not about . . . about other things.

He read the paper for a bit, then Marianne called that dinner was on the table and he went through to the dining-room, pausing in the front hall to swing open the door and glance up and down the lane. Immediately, he felt reassured. It was not really dark, it was just heavily overcast, and though it was raining, the rain wasn't too heavy. Knowing those two, they were probably deep in some game and weren't even thinking about the weather, let alone the encroaching dark. And Lady Salter wasn't a bad old stick; if the rain continued she would probably get her chauffeur to run Tess home rather than see her guest turned out in such weather.

He ate his dinner with a good appetite therefore, and congratulated Marianne on the guinea fowl, which was delicious, and on the new potatoes, which were from the Throwers' garden and had a flavour all their own.

But, dinner over, his worries reasserted themselves. It was full dark now, and there was still no sign of Tess. He went outside and walked up and down the lane in both directions, under the pretence of having a cigarette, and came home really disturbed. The rain had stopped and the moon was out, but it was no night for a couple of kids to be abroad. He had best ring Lady Salter, just in case she expected him to get the motor car out and go and fetch his girl.

He rang. Lady Salter, very surprised, said she understood the children had gone off on a bicycle ride, taking their luncheon and tea with them. They had promised to be home before dark, she added, so she had concluded that Herbert must have accompanied Tess home and stayed with the Delameres for dinner.

'We thought they were with you,' Peter said. Fear, cold and heavy, clutched at his heart. 'Where had they meant to go, do you suppose?'

'I have no idea,' Lady Salter said rather impatiently. 'My nephew does not confide in me. He's a sensible young feller, however, I don't think he would lead your gel into mischief.'

'I'm sure he wouldn't, but I'm beginning to fear they might have had an accident,' Peter said. 'The Broad, you know . . . the lonely lanes . . . then there's the common . . . they could have gone miles!'

'Ring the police,' Lady Salter said. 'I shall send my chauffeur out to see if he can find them. But they'll not have been on the Broad today, Mr Delamere; the boat is still in the boatshed, I got Aggie to check earlier, when the boy wasn't back for dinner.'

She pretends she doesn't care for Andy, but she does, really, Peter told himself, putting down the receiver and then picking it up again to ask the girl on the exchange if she would connect him to the nearest policeman. Lady Salter wouldn't have got the maid to check the boathouse if she didn't worry a bit. But then he realised that she had done nothing, even knowing the boy hadn't returned from his jaunt, and decided she was just a nasty old lady who didn't appreciate the Anderson boy.

Accordingly, Peter got through to the local policeman and told his story. Constable Peddar was tolerant of fatherly fears but said he would keep a look-out for the truants and would warn neighbouring colleagues that there were two youngsters overdue.

Meanwhile Lady Salter, alerted to the fact that her great-nephew had effectively disappeared, decided that she should telephone the authorities too, and chose to inform the Chief Constable, a friend of hers, that her nephew and a young friend had gone for a jaunt on their bicycles and had failed to return home. This had a much more galvanising effect than Peter Delamere's call; Peter was not a member of the aristocracy, nor did he employ twenty local people. After Lady Salter's call policemen on bicycles began to tour the neighbourhood and local farmers were asked if they had seen a couple of benighted youngsters in their area.

But the real fear in everyone's mind was the Broad. Peter Delamere got Tess's dinghy out, greatly relieved to find that it was safely moored in the reeds and not upside down in the middle of Barton Broad. He shed a few tears as he pushed it out from its nest, jumped in and began his search, because he was realising that he hadn't been fair to Tess. Marianne was a wonderful wife and a good mother to Cherie, but she never gave Tess credit for anything, and Peter never made her do so. Marianne had stopped his daughter from seeing Janet – and on the thought Peter rowed round to the Throwers' staithe. He moored his tiny craft and went and banged on the door.

Mrs Thrower answered his knock.

'Evenin', Mr Delamere,' she said placidly, as though it was a common thing to open her door and find her neighbour standing there, wet to the skin and shivering, at well past ten in the evening. 'What can I do for you?'

Peter told her, in a few words, what had happened and Mrs Thrower turned and shouted.

'Fellers! Young Tess an' young Andy ha' gone missin'. They was bicycling; any point gettin' the boats out?'

Peter felt sick; the fear which had been hovering in the back of his mind had also entered Bessie Thrower's, then. But Mr Thrower said, nonchalantly, that he would get his craft out anyway, 'in case', but thought Peter would do better to get into his motor and search the lanes.

'Doubtless she've had a puncture, and they're tryin' to mend it,' Mrs Thrower said placidly. 'She's a good gal, your Tess. She wouldn't worry you for the world, Mr Delamere.'

Peter read reproach into the words and muttered that he knew it; Tess was worth her weight in gold, that was why he couldn't rest until he found her.

'And you're right, I'll get the car out,' he said. 'You wouldn't have any idea where they might have gone, I suppose?'

Mrs Thrower shook her head. 'No; she in't been here much, not this summer,' she observed. 'She in't been around the same since she were sent off to boardin' school. Take Ned with you, Mr

127

Delamere; you drive an' he'll keep an eye out for 'em. Keep your pecker up, you'll find her because she still want to be found; thass the ones what don't want to get found you should worry about.'

Peter thanked her, got the car out and was backing it down the drive to where Ned obediently waited when it occurred to him to wonder why Mrs Thrower had said that about Tess. *You'll find her because she still want to be found.* He knew of course that girls did run away from home, go missing, but . . . his Tess? Surely she would never be one of those girls?

Ned opened the passenger door and got in, slamming it behind him. He said, 'Orf we goo, then, Mus' Delamere,' and Peter realised that the boy was looking forward to a ride in the car. It wasn't something which often came Ned's way, of course, and he'd not taken young Janet out much of late, either.

Come to that, you haven't taken Tess out much for a while, Peter reminded himself, beginning to drive up Deeping Lane. You've been so busy with Marianne and Cherie that you haven't given Tess nearly as much of your time as you did once. Perhaps that's why she went off with the Anderson boy today. Perhaps that's why she told Marianne they were going to the Hall, to pick plums. Because she knew Marianne would agree to a visit to the Hall because she wants to get on good terms with Lady Salter, but a mere expedition of pleasure . . .

She could have asked me, though. I'd have told her to go off, have fun. But she couldn't ask me, of course, because I'm hardly ever there and when I am, I'm always busy with Marianne and the baby. Marianne sees that I am. She makes a point of it. She bundles Tess off to her room so we can have dinner alone and I've never objected, never said it wasn't fair.

'Try the low road, sir. That might be easier for a cyclist. Next right.'

That was Ned; Peter had forgotten his companion completely, was simply driving, with his mind too busy with thoughts of Tess to wonder where he was going.

'Oh . . . thanks,' he said, and relapsed into thought once more.

He had always vowed never to send Tess to boarding school. He had agreed to her being a weekly boarder because Marianne was expecting the baby and was having a sick pregnancy. It seemed only fair when she explained she could not give Tess the attention she needed until after the baby was born. Only then she had been so busy with Cherie, and the house, and she'd said it wasn't fair to Tess, going backwards and forwards to Norwich, and Tess had seemed keen enough . . .

Marianne has pushed Tess out, Peter saw now, as the car bumped down from the main road on to the lower one, and I've done nothing to stop her, nothing to help. Dear God, what have I done? What would Leonora say if she knew? Suppose she does know? Suppose she's grieving her heart out somewhere because of what I'm doing to our daughter? I'll make amends, he promised God, all His angels, and Leonora. I'll keep Marianne in check, see more of Tess, show her how much, how very much, I love her. Because I see, now, what Mrs Thrower meant; if I don't I'll lose her. She'll run away as soon as she's old enough and I'll spend the rest of my life worrying about her and blaming myself.

'Turn right again now, sir, an' you'll be back on track for Barton,' Ned said quietly. 'They in't along here I don't reckon. Unless . . .'

'Unless what?' Peter slowed, almost stopped.

'Unless they'd been to Palling,' Ned said slowly. 'It in't that far, an' Tess were always mortal fond o' Palling.'

Sea Palling! He had never taken her to the sea because there were some memories which were best forgotten, but she'd loved the sea, once. Would she, could she, have made for the coast?

'We'll take a look,' he said. The rain had stopped and the moon was silvering the countryside as though it didn't know the meaning of the word cloud. The car purred quietly along and somehow, as they rounded the next bend, it was no surprise to see two small figures, both pushing bicycles, approaching them.

'They in't got no lamps,' Ned said almost excusingly. 'I reckon they dussen't bike without lamps. Cops can be hard on kids.'

'They're safe!' Peter said exultantly. 'Daft . . . but safe!' He leaned over and shook Ned's hand hard. 'That was a brainwave of yours, to try the Palling road,' he said. 'Well the little devils!'

But he said it admiringly, and when he drew the car alongside the truants and saw their faces he could only jump out of the car and envelop first his daughter and then her friend in a hard bear hug.

'Thank God you're safe,' he said. 'What happened? Puncture? Or just no lights?'

'A huge split in the tyre and a ruined inner tube,' the Anderson boy said. 'We tried to ring you twice . . .'member the call where no one spoke? It was one-way transmission, we could hear Mrs Delamere but she couldn't hear us.'

Peter, with his arms still about their shoulders, stiffened. 'You rang? You actually telephoned? But my wife said nothing about a call.'

'She couldn't hear us, there was something wrong with the line,' Tess said, speaking for the first time. 'It wasn't her fault, Daddy, but it wasn't ours, either. I say, could you drive home now and ring Lady Salter? Andy isn't sure whether she'll be worried or cross, but whichever . . .'

'I'll push the bikes, you two go home in the car,' Ned said, emerging from the front passenger seat. 'I'm fresh, you're fair worn out. Go on, nippers, get in the motor.'

'Ned, you're an angel!' 'Ned you're a sport!' came simultaneously from two pairs of lips, and then Peter watched indulgently as his daughter and her friend tumbled into the back seat. Once, Tess might have got in the front . . . what a *nice* child she was! He was proud of her, and in future he meant to show it. Marianne would just have to put up with it. For the first time he acknowledged that his wife was jealous of his child and, also for the first time, resolved to conquer it.

There was a reckoning, of course there was, they both knew there would be, but it wasn't anywhere near as bad as either had feared and, in fact, it actually enabled Tess to talk to her father with a frankness which had been impossible ever since his marriage.

'Why did you fib about it, pet?' he said next day, sitting on the end of her bed at an early hour of the morning, whilst Marianne was still trying to get herself into a getting-up mood. 'Lying really isn't like you, so why did you spin that rigmarole about plums and the Hall and Lady Salter?'

'Because I couldn't risk Marianne telling you we meant to go to the seaside; you've never liked the coast much, have you? And Marianne, of course, agrees to anything if it seems like Lady Salter's idea,' Tess said frankly. 'But it was daft; I see that now.'

'What makes you think I don't like the coast?' Peter said cautiously. He had always steered clear of discussing the seaside with Tess ever since she'd told him about her dream. 'As a matter of fact, I was once very fond of the seaside.'

'Were you, Daddy? But you never take us there,' Tess pointed out. 'And you kept telling me my dream was just a dream. But I'm still having it, Daddy, and I don't think it's only a dream. It's too real for that.'

'Yes . . . but a dream's no reason for taking off without telling anyone where you were going,' Peter pointed out. 'What were you trying to prove?'

'Nothing, we just wanted to go. Andy's never swum in the sea, and it is different, isn't it? It – it holds you up much better than the water in the Broad.'

'True.' Peter hesitated, looking into his daughter's small, open face. If he simply skated round it he knew that she would not try to force his confidence, but she was twelve years old, he could not go on lying to her for ever, there was no sense in it. 'Look, sweetheart, it's a long and rather a sad story which I decided years ago not to tell you until you were grown up. But I can see that if I don't it'll lead to trouble. So . . . come down to the kitchen with me and help me make the breakfast and I'll tell you why I think you dream about the sea.'

'Right,' Tess said. She jumped out of bed, put on her school dressing-gown and thundered, barefoot, down the stairs in front of him. In the kitchen she got eggs out of the pantry, bacon out of the meat-safe, and began to slice the big brown loaf.

'I'll do brekker, you talk,' she said briskly. 'Start at the beginning, Daddy, because I'd like to get things clear. It's – it's my mother, isn't it? Something to do with her?'

Peter nodded and began to lay the table, speaking as he did so.

'Yes, it is something to do with your mother. I've always let you believe that she died soon after you were born, but in fact you were almost three when she died. And she didn't die of a fever, though she had been very ill. She – she was drowned.'

'Drowned?'

'That's right. We were living down at Walcott at that time, because property was cheaper there, though it meant I had a long journey in to the city each day to work. But it was worth it, to live somewhere so pleasant. We rented a tiny bungalow, rather inconvenient and dark, but we were happy there, the three of us.'

'You lived at *Walcott*? But Daddy, didn't you say . . .'

'Look, don't interrupt, love, or I'll never get through,' Peter said gently. He turned from the table and began to put slices of bread under the grill. 'As I said, we were living at Walcott but I was working in the city, in the same offices that I work in now, and one day I had a telephone call at work, asking me to go back to Walcott straight away; there had been an accident, the caller said. I rushed back, in a terrible state as you can imagine, and found – oh Tess, love, I found that your mother had drowned after a boating accident.'

'Oh Daddy, poor Mummy! Poor you, too. And – and where was I?'

'You? Oh, you were with a neighbour. And next day I packed you off to stay with Uncle Phil and Auntie May. You weren't neglected darling, truly, but there was so much to cope with in Walcott . . . it wouldn't have been fair to keep you with me.'

'I don't remember any of it, after the beach,' Tess murmured after a pause. 'A boating accident?'

'Yes, a boating accident. A squall, the boat overturned . . . please, darling, I can't bear to think about it, not even after all these years.'

'I'm sorry. It must have been awful, of course. But Daddy, why didn't you tell me? Especially after I'd explained about the dream.'

'It was a bad time,' Peter said. He pulled out the grill-pan and turned the toast before it needed turning, then pushed it back under the heat once more. 'There was an inquest . . . they weren't absolutely sure, at first, what had happened, you see. Unfortunately the boat didn't come ashore for quite a while and there was no one around to say just what went wrong. After a shock like that I hated the Walcott bungalow and didn't want to clap eyes on it ever again, so you and I moved out and stayed with Phil and

132

May until I bought the Old House. And then I thought about it and decided that you were young enough to put it right out of your mind, provided no one talked about it. People in Barton knew nothing; to them we were just a widower and his child, they didn't connect us with the drowning down on the coast. So I simply never mentioned it to you.'

'I see,' Tess said slowly. 'But if the seaside made you think of what happened to my mother, why choose the Broads? Why not live inland?'

'Because I've always lived near the water and I didn't want to move away from it altogether,' Peter said truthfully. 'I lived at Horning until I was about five, then we moved to a house down by the river at Brundall. Uncle Phil and I were always boating, swimming, fishing. You knew that, didn't you?'

'Vaguely,' Tess said. 'So my dream's real, then?'

'I'm not sure,' Peter said. 'You might have been on the beach, you might have seen something . . . darling, it takes a good hour to get from the city to Walcott when you're in an old banger, like I was. And they didn't contact me immediately, they had to find the number and so on. I was horrified when you first told me about that wretched dream. I'd done my damnedest to keep it all from you but apparently it wasn't going to work.'

'But *why*, Daddy?' Tess almost shouted. 'Why? You're still not telling me the whole of it, are you?'

Peter stared at her. She was beginning to look heartwrenchingly like Leonora, he saw, she even had the same mannerisms. Many a time he had seen Leonora standing just as Tess was standing now, hands behind her back, pointed chin well up, mouth firm, whilst the eyes pleaded for understanding.

'Right,' Peter said, suddenly making up his mind. He owed it to her, having lived a lie for so long, to tell her at least a part of the truth. 'Right. There was a – a rumour that the boat had sunk too quickly because it had been neglected. But it was just foolish talk, love. The sort of talk that's best forgotten.'

'But wouldn't my mother have known if the boat wasn't safe?' Tess asked. 'I don't understand, Daddy.'

'Leonora loved going on the water, she really knew very little about boats. She didn't swim well, either. So you see I don't know if she would have noticed had the boat been leaking or unsafe in some way. I'm convinced that her death was a horrible accident, but at the time there *was* talk. Folk blamed me, or her, and I didn't want you hurt by it. I didn't want to stir up all that. Darling, can you understand?'

Tess was mixing eggs in a blue bowl, gently adding milk, then slowly whisking the mixture with her fork. She said nothing, her eyes on her work, but Peter thought he saw a slow tear form and overflow. He put out a hand and rubbed her cheek gently.

'Poor love!'

'Why did they blame you? You weren't even there,' Tess said, her voice no more than a whisper. 'I don't understand, Daddy.'

'They said that it was I who should have kept the boat in good condition, made sure it was seaworthy,' Peter said gently. 'I'd been around boats all my life, whereas Leonora was new to it. But I promise you, sweetheart, that the boat was safe as houses. I often went fishing in it and always cleaned it down and kept it watertight. So when the talk started, I was hurt and astonished at what people were saying; I was very young and I took things to heart, even wondered whether I'd been careful enough. So you can see why I didn't want you to hear about it.'

'I can see . . . but Daddy, how dared anyone say such things! As if you'd not be careful as careful!' Tess said, her cheeks pink, her eyes sparkling with wrath. 'Why, I know you'd never have a boat that wasn't seaworthy, and so does anyone who knows you!'

'It was only gossip,' Peter said again. 'I knew the boat was sound so I was sure then and I'm sure now that it was a freak accident which killed Leonora.'

It hurt, dreadging up such memories, and Peter found he was dreading that the child might want more detail, might expect him to reveal the stuff of supposition which he had kept to himself now for years and years. What had happened, out there on that rough and stormy sea? Why had Leonora left her little daughter alone and gone out, in rough weather, in the cockleshell craft? No one would ever now precisely how she had died, there was no proof, one way or the other, of accident or design – how could there be?

As if she could read his thoughts, Tess said: 'If the boat was sound, then my mother must have done something to tip it over – isn't that right?'

'That's it, darling. In fact an old fellow on the shore said he saw her stand up for a moment. It made me wonder if she'd lost an oar, and was trying to get it back. She was a sensible girl, she wouldn't have done something as dangerous as that without a good reason.'

'Oh. Right. So if she lost an oar . . . but when the boat came ashore, surely that would have stopped the rumours that it wasn't sound?'

Peter sighed. 'Unfortunately, when the boat eventually came ashore, it was in bits. There was a terrible storm that night, our poor little craft didn't stand a chance. But of course stupid folk simply said it had broken apart because it had been tampered with.'

'I see,' Tess said. 'Tampered with! They couldn't have thought you . . .'

'No, they didn't think I'd tampered with it,' Peter said hastily. 'I was only accused of carelessness, and of course no one ever said even that to my face. But that was enough. I wanted to get away from Walcott and the horror of it. I wanted to start life afresh.'

'Yes, I would have wanted it, too,' Tess said earnestly. 'Daddy, I'm so sorry I asked you to talk about it. I won't ever ask you again . . . except I would like to know about the boy.'

'The boy? What boy?' Peter got out plates, fetched butter from the cool box, buttered four rounds of toast. 'Andy, d'you mean?'

'Oh Daddy . . . no, the one who brought me up off the beach, the one in my dream!'

'I suppose he was just some kid who happened to be playing on the beach at the time,' Peter said slowly. 'I'm afraid I didn't ask any questions when I arrived, I just hugged you and thanked God Leonora hadn't taken you with her. You often did play with the children next door, you see, so I took it for granted that was what had happened on the day in question. But if your dream is a – a memory, then I suppose the boy could be real, too.'

'I'm sure he is,' Tess said eagerly. 'If I knew who he was perhaps I could meet him! He could tell me . . . things.'

'I've told you all I can, darling,' Peter said, unable to keep the

135

reproach out of his tone. 'It hurts me to talk about those days, but it is your right to know. Only – now that you do know, can we keep it just between ourselves? It's past, it's more painful than you could possibly understand, and now there's Marianne, Cherie . . .'

'It's all right, Daddy,' Tess said quickly. 'I won't ask you about any of it ever again. Not now I know.'

'Thank you, darling. And now let's change the subject, shall we? Are you going to make enough scrambled egg for both of us, or would you prefer fried?'

Eating his breakfast, trying to listen and answer sensibly when Tess talked, Peter found himself hoping devoutly that his daughter would be content with what he had told her. He had tried hard not to lie, but he could not bear the child to suffer as he had suffered. All the whisperings, the conjecture, the awful, painful doubts, came back whenever Leonora's death was mentioned. What *had* happened exactly, out there on the rough and windy sea? A lot had been said, people who should have known better had drawn conclusions, but he hadn't believed any of it. He hadn't wanted to believe, and he most certainly didn't want Tess thinking that her mother had cared so little for her that she had deliberately jumped into the sea and drowned herself. It wasn't true, he knew it wasn't true, but children had vivid imaginations and God knew what she might make of it if he had said too much.

When she's older, perhaps I'll tell her a bit more, he decided, reaching for the toast. Or perhaps I won't. But for now, it's sufficient that she knows the bare bones. Quite sufficient.

Tess phoned Andy that afternoon to tell him what she had discovered and they decided to meet the following day. And that night she dreamed the dream again. She found herself on the beach, pattering along, enjoying the sand and the prospect, presently, of a paddle in the sea. She reached the breakwater with its burden of seaweed, and plonked herself down on the wet sand to remove her shoes and socks. She was in the dreamy, delightful mood of one who has recently woken from a satisfying sleep. Everything around her looked crystal clear and even the simplest action seemed filled with a strange significance.

Once more, she turned her head and saw the boy running along the beach. He grabbed her, turned her into his chest, bade her not to look . . . and for the first time ever, Tess struggled in his arms and turned her face up to his.

'Why?' she said baldly. 'Why mustn't I look, boy?'

And for the first time the boy spoke to her, really spoke. 'She didn't do it,' he said fiercely. 'She didn't understand . . . it's a tricky beast, the sea.'

And then she looked . . . and began to scream, and in screaming, woke.

Six

Queensland, 1932

It was three in the morning and the sun still wasn't up. Mal came quietly out of the bedroom which he shared with two other young men, paused for a moment on the verandah, then went as silently as he could down the three long wooden steps and on to the yard. He had a travelling swag over one shoulder and he was going. He wasn't staying here, to watch his mother make a complete fool of herself. And when he'd gone they'd be sorry, and Kath would remember what a good husband Bill had been to her, and realise that she should have been content to let her son keep her, instead of taking up with Royce Malone.

On the yard, in the grey light of early dawn, his feet stirred dust. It was the dry, which was a good thing, because in the wet he wouldn't have been able to get very far. He'd lived here three years now, and knew enough about Queensland to be grateful that Kath had done her dreadful deed during the dry. Yet though he was glad to be leaving he still looked around him almost wistfully as he crossed the yard; to the house itself, where his mother, Royce and the younger children still slept, to the outbuildings – meat house, store house, harness room and workshop, laundry and blacksmith's forge – and behind them and almost into the bush to the humpies of the aborigines, their gins and piccaninnies, who did most of the rough work on the station.

Mal was friendly with several of the young men – Tink, Soljer, Canny – and would miss them, but they were used to people moving on. They did it themselves from time to time. They wouldn't miss him; they would just say 'He done gone walka-bout' and leave it at that.

He had decided last night, when Kath and Royce had got back from their honeymoon, that he would take one of the horses, because that wasn't stealing – when he got to civilisation he'd send it back to the Magellan – and head for the nearest railway station, which wasn't all that near, either. The inland railhead of Mungana must be sixty or seventy miles away, but on horseback that wasn't impossible. Once he got to a city, he would think again about what he should do to earn his living. The only thing he knew, right now, was that he couldn't remain at the Magellan homestead. Not now that Kath was Mrs Royce Malone. Even thinking of her in Royce's bed made him feel sick . . . she might have a *baby* by him, for God's sake, a child in Royce's image, and she an elderly woman – she must be thirty-seven at the very least! That made him feel worse, because he remembered Petey, and Petey's death, and just for a moment he wanted to go to his mother and smack her about a bit, like his father had, and watch her cry and beg . . . and then he thought how nice it would be to kill Royce for his cheek in marrying Kath . . . and then he realised he was crying and began to hurry, because bad though it would be if someone came out and caught him, it would be unbearable to be caught crying. They would think he didn't want to leave, for God's sake, when leaving had been in his mind now for months and months.

The Magellan had a lot of horses because it was a cattle station and cattle could not be rounded up on foot. And Magellan land went from the Palmer River to the Little Mitchell, a distance of many miles, so the men out mustering the cattle needed more than one mount. Because the constant galloping over rough ter-rain to cut off the herd and bring them back to water meant that horses could not go on, day after day, as men could; they needed a rest. So there were more horses on the Magellan than they would probably ever need.

I'll take Sandy, because I'm the one who mostly rides him, and I don't believe he'll go good for anyone else, Mal told himself, going over to the horse yard. The animals were awake and quietly grazing and he leaned on the top post of the wooden ranch fencing and regarded them. They were beautiful creatures for the most part, because Royce had once bred horses and knew what made a good one for the muster, but they were also strong; goers, every one. Royce selected his stallions with care and his brood mares, too, and he cherished the foals. Other stations simply castrated most of the colts at six months and let the others breed, but Royce picked out the best to remain stallions, and as a result people were always willing to buy any stock which the homestead did not need.

So they wouldn't miss one horse, Mal concluded. He could pick out Sandy's shape easily in the half-light and saw the horse had turned towards him, ears pricked. 'Sandy,' Mal called softly. 'Come on over.' He unwound a length of rope from the fence post – he had wound it round the previous evening in anticipation of this moment – and looped it over the gelding's head. Sandy was a light chestnut, with dramatic dark eyes and a golden-brown mane and tail. He bent his head and snuffled Mal's pockets as Mal led him out of the paddock, then stood still to let Mal leap easily on to his back. Mal laid his swag across the horse's withers and nudged him with his heel.

'Good boy, good feller. Gently now, gently,' Mal said softly, and turned the horse's head towards the bush . . . and the railhead seventy miles away.

Kath woke and lay on her back, listening. Beside her, Royce's broad back moved gently to the rhythm of his breathing. Last night, when they lay quiet after making love, she had told him she feared Mal was preparing to leave.

'He keeps saying enigmatic things like will I remember to water the veggies, and not to mind borrowing his gramophone if he's not around to lend it to me,' she told Royce. 'And he's going for all the wrong reasons, because he loves it here, I know damn well he does. He's been happier – and easier – these past three years than in all of the rest of his life, pretty near.'

'Why was I okay as a boss but no good as your husband and his stepfather?' Royce asked plaintively. 'The only difference is that you and me's wed now, with everythin' all legal. Why should a young feller mind that?'

'Royce! That ain't the only difference – we never slept together until after the wedding!'

'No-oo, but we did most other things,' Royce said, incurably truthful as always. 'I should've asked you to marry me years ago, but I couldn't believe my luck in gettin' you in the first place and I didn't want to risk you refusin', movin' out on me. I'd ha' kept you as my housekeeper for ever rather'n lose you for good.'

'I wasn't ready for marrying anyone,' Kath reminded him. 'Not after being wed to Bill for fifteen years. And after Petey's death he took to the bottle worse'n ever, and hit me more'n he kissed me. And Mal did his best to protect me then, without making Bill sore, of course. So why should he behave the way he has just 'cos I've married again?'

'I reckon he's jealous,' Royce said. 'He'd sensed you didn't love Bill no more, so that was all right. Now he knows you love me, and that ain't all right. He'll git over it; he'll find a gal of his own soon enough and then he'll be too busy worritin' over his own affairs to worrit over ours.'

'But he'll go, I sort of know it,' Kath said worriedly. 'There's Bart and Sam, too. He likes 'em, but they're the boss's sons, I suppose.'

'I wouldn't mek no difference between 'em,' Royce protested sleepily. 'Mal's your lad, the twins are mine. They'll all have a share in the station, if they all share the work. As yet, my boys are jest little fellers an' Mal's had all the work. But one day they'll pull their weight – if they want a livin' out o' the place, that is. But they ain't five until next month.'

'Mebbe you should have told Mal that,' Kath said. 'He's not had good experience of fathers, Roy. Bill adored him for years, but when he got big enough to tell Bill no and mean it, Bill kinda resented him. It 'ud be nice for him to know you'll think of him in the same breath as Bart and Sam.'

'Well, I'll tell him tomorrow,' Royce said drowsily. 'Now let's go to sleep.'

'But Roy, if he leaves tomorrow he'll never know. Oughtn't we to tell him now? I'm real uneasy about him, I tell you.'

'If he leaves, it won't be long before he comes back,' Royce mumbled. 'The only thing he knows is cattle musterin'. And there's a Depression on – or hadn't you realised?'

'Realised! Oh dear God, Roy, you can be *infuriating*, sometimes! Go to sleep then, if you must.'

But now it was early morning – too early for the light to be more than a gentle grey, and Kath lay listening because she had heard the soft tread of feet crossing the yard. Then, with ears sharpened by love and fear, she heard Mal call the horse, heard Sandy – for it would be Sandy, he always rode the chestnut if he could – clopping across to the paddock rails. Heard the murmuring voice in the early morning stillness, then the soft sound of shod hooves crossing the yard, going on to the hard ruts of the drive, getting fainter . . . fainter . . .

'Wake up, Roy! He's goin', my boy's leavin' us!' Roy mumbled a protest as Kath's sharp knuckles dug into his back. 'Oh God, I can't bear it – he's only a kid when all's said and done, scarce eighteen!'

She got out of bed and ran to the window. The house was built of timber and corrugated iron and there were fly-screens at window and door. She pushed the screen to one side and leaned out. The yard was empty. Hurriedly she ran back to her bed and pulled on a cotton nightdress, for she was naked, and pushed her bare feet into an old pair of sandals. Then she ran out of the room, along the short corridor and through the living-room on to the wide verandah which ran the length of the house. She could see a cloud of dust coming from the drive – he wasn't long gone, he wouldn't be in a big hurry, if she could just get one of the men to follow him . . .

She ran back to her room, desperately wanting to ask Royce what to do, but he was already up, his trousers on, pushing his shirt impatiently into the waistband. She said, breathlessly: 'He's gone. Taken a horse and rid out of here.'

Royce nodded. 'Guessed it. I'll follow. He's probably headin' for the railhead so he's got a long journey. He won't be such a fool as to push the horse, he'll take it nice 'n' easy.'

'Oh, Roy,' Kath said. 'You're the best – know that?'

He was sitting on the bed now, pulling on the long leather

riding boots which he wore for the musters. He grinned at her, a flash of white teeth in his deeply tanned face, then stood up.

'Oh, sure, I'm the real McCoy. Why'd you have married me, else? I'll be back before nightfall.'

'Oh Roy, I love you! You'll bring him back?'

'I'll do what's best,' Royce said. 'Tell Jim he's in charge.'

He strode from the room. Kath followed him at a trot, only stopping to pick up her rain jacket. For decency's sake she'd best slip it round her shoulders. The two of them crossed the yard and dived into the tack-room. Royce took his saddle and bridle from the wooden pole and went with his long, unhurried stride across to the horse paddock. His favourite mount was a quiet, canny 16–hand mare called Gypsy; he whistled and Gypsy came across the paddock at a canter. Royce grinned at his wife.

'Knows me better'n I know myself,' he said. 'Come on, girl.'

The mare came out, walking delicately, neck stretched, nostrils quivering. Royce tacked her up quickly, putting the saddle blanket neatly across Gypsy's brown-and-white back, slipping the bridle over her long, dark-brown nose, tightening girths and checking that nothing was rubbing or uncomfortable. He worked unhurriedly, as though he had all the time in the world, yet no one, Kath knew, could have done it more quickly and neatly.

When the horse was ready Roy swung up into the saddle.

'Wait!' Kath cried, suddenly guilt-ridden. 'You've had nothing to eat . . . I'll get you a sandwich . . . a bottle of something.'

'Bread an' cheese for two, an' a big bottle,' Royce said. Kath guessed that he would realise Mal wouldn't have thought about food or drink. 'No hurry . . . see the dust?'

Kath followed the gaze of his shrewd, dark eyes. Sure enough, she could see a small dust cloud not a mile away, for the ground here was flat. She smiled, then ran across the courtyard and into the kitchen annexe. Here, my expertise will come in handy, she thought, whipping a new loaf out of the bread crock, cheese out of the dairy safe, and a handful of dried apricots out of the jar by the window. The men usually took cold tea on musters but yesterday she had made a great deal of lemon barley water and Royce had drunk some at supper the previous night and said it was refreshing. She made up two big bottles of the stuff, then picked up the bread and cheese and ran. Royce had just mounted and took the provisions with a word of thanks, stuffing the food into his saddlebag, then doing the same with the bottles.

'If I have to do some persuadin', likely I'll be real late,' he called back, clearly suddenly smitten by an idea. 'I could be a day or two – you'll not worry?'

She could only say she would be fine, that he was the one who must not worry. 'I know Mal can be difficult,' she called after him. 'If there's nothing you can do, I'll understand.'

He raised a hand in acknowledgement, then set off along the dusty track, Gypsy breaking into a trot. Kath stood and watched them until they were out of sight, then returned to her room. She began to prepare for the day ahead. Royce was right of course; he usually was. If the boy was determined to go then all they could do was wish him well and pray for his safety. If he came back, then all they could do was welcome him and show him they cared. It was odd, though. Bill had been a hero, and his son had accordingly hero-worshipped him, but it had become apparent, in Bill's later years, that he was no longer particularly interested in Mal. Towards the end all he cared about was the drink; without it he was mean-mouthed, mumbling. With it he was dangerous. Kath stripped off her coat and nightgown and poured water from the tall jug into the basin. I bet Royce was glad he had no time to wash, she thought, smiling to herself as she dunked her flannel in the water. Men! They're all boys at heart – any excuse not to come into contact with water, except when bathing, fishing, or simply mucking about with the stuff! But water and the way men feel about it brought other thoughts thronging; the fact that neither Mal nor Bill had ever wanted to go to the shore after Petey's death, the awful nightmares which Mal had suffered from for years after that dreadful event . . . for all she knew, she realised, he might suffer from them still. He was too old, now, to admit to such a childish affliction.

And, fool that the boy was, he had almost thrown away the most precious things in the world – his mother's love, his step-father's concern, and his home. As she started carefully to soap herself all over, she began to think about those last, dreadful days before Bill's death.

They'd been in Melbourne the first time Bill got what the doc called dts. He told her it was short for *delirium tremens*, which meant Bill saw things, and the things he saw were so real that he attacked them with fists, feet, a knife, anything. By that time they were miserably poor; they rented a small room over a hardware store and because Bill was no longer able to hold down a job, Kath had taken in washing, scrubbed offices, walked miles across the city to buy stale bread from a particular baker who sold the stuff off cheap at the end of the week.

Mal had worked, too. Selling newspapers, running errands, carrying shopping . . . you name it, he did it. The day Bill, under the impression that Kath was a member of the government come to harass him, attacked her with a kitchen knife, Mal had got the knife off his father and chucked it out of the window.

'Leave her alone, you bastard,' he had ground between clenched teeth. 'Or I'll bloody swing for you!'

It was language Bill understood. He tried to menace his son but he didn't really have the strength, not without the knife. He swayed, glaring at them both with red-eyed hatred, mumbled something, lurched out through the doorway – and fell down the flight of stairs, breaking his arm and temporarily incapacitating himself.

Then came the long struggle to drink until oblivion no matter what the cost. It had ended in liver failure, hospitalisation, and eventually, death. By then he had been a monster, Kath thought with a shudder, a far cry from the blue-eyed, swaggering young man she'd married so eagerly fifteen years before.

And his death had freed them. After the funeral, Kath applied for a job as cook general to a station owner just outside Cooktown and though she didn't keep the first job long – she was too young and too pretty for the boss's wife to stomach – it got them away from the cities and into the Northern Territories.

The second job came because the boss of the Magellan had lost his wife to tuberculosis.

'She couldn't take the climate, or the work, or his long absences,' friends told Kath later. 'She was a dear, dainty little thing from Sydney – she never should have left the city.'

But Kath was different. Older, tougher. And when she heard

the station boss had twin sons not yet two, her heart had been touched.

'They need a woman's hand,' Royce had explained. 'My wife was ill from the moment they was born, jest about. There's an aboriginal girl – Annie – lookin' after 'em, but she's too soft with 'em sometimes an' she don't understand our ways. Will you come back to the Magellan with me?'

'I've got a boy of my own,' Kath had warned him. 'I'll come willingly, but whether I'll be able to bring 'em up like you want . . .'

Royce's first wife, Lily, had been a promising pianist, a delicate, pretty creature who had spent her entire life in Sydney city centre. She fell in love with Royce's tanned independence and jaunty spirits but never with his life-style, which she didn't begin to understand. She could not come to terms with the harshness of Queensland, and the weather conditions, the animals and insects, brought her to her knees. Unhappy, and ill at ease, she longed for home yet did not want to face the folk there with the failure of her marriage. The twins, Kath guessed, had been the final straw. Bringing up children when you were ailing yourself was no sinecure, and it had proved too much for the first Mrs Malone. She had died of tuberculosis in her twenty-third year despite everything Royce could do to help her.

It was different for Kath. She was thirty-four years old and a tough and self-reliant woman. She'd brought up her son alone, with more hindrance than help from Bill, and had kept them both alive under the assault of an embittered and drunken husband. She had been making good, wholesome meals out of almost nothing and patching and mending every stitch they wore for years. The things which had brought Lily Malone to her deathbed didn't faze Kath one bit. In the wet she used citronella to keep the 'skeeters off before she went outside and slung a towel around her neck to soak up the sweat. In the dry she and Mal carted water from the nearest creek to 'fresh up' her precious garden and planted, tended and harvested huge fruit and vegetable crops. She cooked, cleaned and coped without complaint. She did most of the work in her jealously hoarded garden and orchard, fished from the old punt which the aboriginals used as a means of crossing the great river, cooked in the open in the dry and fed her household on the verandah, because she said it was healthier. She loved the twins but disciplined them too, and kept the wives and children of the homestead workers in their place, whilst seeing that they got a fair deal. The climate was terribly hard on a white woman born and reared on the East coast, but Kath was used to hardship. And there was plenty of food, and plenty of money for material and the luxury of a treadle sewing machine instead of needle and thread. Without thinking twice about it she made all the clothing for herself, the kids and the workers and she preserved, bottled and dried everything she could harvest. When she arrived at the Magellan she had been a good plain cook; by the time she had been there twelve months she had taught herself how to make all manner of fancy dishes, and enjoyed her new expertise.

Some folk might think it a harsh, hard life, she reflected sometimes, but it was a bed of roses compared to her life with Bill. And she, who had never grown so much as mustard and cress on a flannel before, discovered that she had green fingers; seeds and cuttings planted by her flourished. She very quickly came to love gardening, enjoyed watering because the plants seemed so grateful, vigorously hoed the weeds which would have smothered her darlings, and very soon, little by little, she fell in love with Queensland and knew she would never willingly live elsewhere.

Aware, now, of the brightening daylight beyond the screens and shutters, she reminded herself that she wasn't the only one to love their home. Mal loved it too, and he was carelessly fond of the twins and had seemed, until she and Roy had announced that they meant to get married, to be fond of Royce, as well. Why oh why couldn't he simply accept that marriage had made no difference to her relationship with him? Why couldn't he see that it wasn't a disloyalty to Bill, either? She guessed that, in time, she might remember Bill more gently because of her happy and contented life with Royce.

She wasn't marrying Roy to get herself a place for life, either, the way Mal had seemed to think, and Roy wasn't marrying her to get a free housekeeper, as Mal had insultingly suggested. Roy, she knew, had fallen in love with her, not for her efficiency, her effortless running of his house, but for her sense of humour, her placid acceptance of the hard work and harsh conditions at the homestead, and for her long mane of chestnut-brown hair, her white skin with the band of freckles across her nose, her long, pale body with its deep breasts and slim hips.

And for her part, Kath loved Royce with a depth and passion she had never felt before. He was a good man, hard-working, uncomplaining. He fed and clothed his workers well, paid his staff more than most, took anxious care of his two small sons – and appreciated everything she did for him. So far as Kath was concerned, she had been in hell with Bill and now she was in heaven with Royce. So Mal, she decided, would have to paddle his own canoe; she had found her happiness and she did not intend to let her grown son spoil it.

Royce trotted Gypsy for a bit to get the itches out of her legs, but then he slowed her to a walk. The boy would have taken Sandy, he knew it, and Sandy, though a spunky gelding, didn't have Gypsy's long stride. He would catch the boy up, with a bit of luck, when the sun was beginning to make itself felt, when Mal would be wishing he'd stopped by the kitchen for some tucker before running out on them.

And then I'll ride up beside him . . . Royce planned busily, and we'll have a talk, and I'll make a suggestion or two.

He liked Mal, liked him very much. He was a hard worker, and Royce had always admired hard workers, but more than that, he'd taken to the life. He was a natural, appreciating the country, the harshness of the life, the sheer impossibility of successfully living out here without complete dedication.

And, in a way, Royce could even understand the boy's leaving. Jealousy was a potent emotion, as he knew well. He could still remember the agonies he had suffered when, six months after he'd first employed Kath, she'd had a friend call round, a feller she'd met whilst working in Cooktown.

'This is Bruce, Royce,' she had said sunnily. 'He's on his way to the coast, thought he'd pop in to see how me and Mal are doin'.'

Still. Understanding the boy's jealousy didn't mean he could go along with it. I'm not stealing Kath from him, any more than he could steal her from me, because mother and son and husband and wife are quite different relationships, he told himself. But mebbe – just mebbe – he's better away from us for a while. Until we've settled, like. He had never voiced aloud his secret hope that Kath might bear him a child. He'd got the twins and Mal, but to have a little daughter would be something else, something which would bind him and Kath even closer, if that were possible.

They hadn't been married two minutes but he knew they were going to be happy because they'd been happy just sharing a house, so sharing a bed as well . . . he felt the little hairs on the back of his neck stand up at the remembered pleasures of their honeymoon. A whole week to themselves whilst Mal and Jim ran the station between them and he and Kath got to know one another! They had stayed at the Imperial Hotel in Cairns for three days after the wedding itself, enjoying a theatrical performance, a cinema show, and all the pleasures of the pleasant coastal town. Then, for the remainder of their short holiday, they had gone on to Karunda by train.

It had been a marvellous honeymoon, but there was always something a mite unnatural about a honeymoon, even when the two people involved knew one another as well as he and Kath did. Because of course she was right, they'd not slept together nor made love until after their wedding, and for both of them, he guessed, it had been a pretty memorable experience. He had been used to Lily's passive response to his love-making and now to find a tigress in his arms was both enjoyable and a trifle alarming. Everything he did brought a response – and Kath was not like Lily. She did not lie beneath him, quiet and good, waiting until he moved away. She raked his back with her fingernails, kissed any bits of him she could reach and used her body to maximum effect. Kath believed in participation and revelled in their loving . . . and of course she made Royce realise what he'd been missing all these years, until he was as eager as any other bridegroom to get his new wife to bed.

But now, riding along savouring the cool morning air, Royce told himself that you had to pay for everything in this life; perhaps Mal's attitude was what he had to pay for Kath's warm and exciting loving. And if so, it was worth it, worth every scowl and every black look. You couldn't say 'every disobeyed order', because so far Mal had done his job with his usual efficiency, but Royce was realistic enough to see that, sooner or later, because of his attitude Mal's work would suffer.

So this meeting was important and must not under any circumstances become a wrangle or even an argument. There must be a right way of tackling a jealous boy in his late teens, Royce told himself, and I've gotta find it.

And rode slower, planning his strategy. And with every passing mile he felt more sure of himself, with firmer ground beneath his feet.

Kath, preparing for the day ahead, was also remembering their honeymoon, from the moment they had arrived in Cairns to the moment they had left it, on the little train which would take them up to Karunda, and the quiet aloneness of their borrowed bungalow.

That train! Chugging up the incredible gradients, with incredible views, Kath had enjoyed every minute of the journey. She worried a little because of the rocking motion as the train slogged on and on, up increasingly steep stretches of line, or carried them into dark and echoing tunnels, but it was worth it. On one particular curve they crossed a great gorge and could see the Barron River Falls, set amidst the brilliant greenery of the bush, as the river hurried from the high mountains to the sea far below. And in Karunda they had spent a further three days in the luxuriously furnished bungalow. Royce had told her the names of the trees and plants, shown her the wildlife of the bush, stalked birds with her, did all the things which, as a busy station owner, he hadn't had time to do since he was a kid.

And then, home to the station, to find Mal edgy, sullen, difficult. And now, this.

Kath rinsed off the soap, dried herself, brushed out her hair, coiled it up in a neat knot on top of her head and began to dress. Royce knew what he was doing, she told herself, he understood the boy better than Mal had any right to expect. He would either say sufficient to send Mal on his way, knowing that he would be welcomed without question if he chose to return, or he would bring him back home, which was what she wanted.

Or did she? A sulky, suspicious face at breakfast, a grumbler, someone who criticised, by look or gesture, if not in words, everything that she and Roy did? But if Royce explained, spoke to him, perhaps Mal would see sense, behave better.

Kath checked her appearance in the mirror before remembering that Royce would not be back before nightfall, if then. She was used to his being away from the station for weeks at a time at musters, but she always missed him. But even so . . . food had to be prepared, hands fed, orders given.

Kath went swiftly along the corridor and out into the yard. In the aboriginals' quarters the workers were stirring. Someone had lit a fire in the kitchen – probably Lin Ho, the Chinese cook – and the pleasant smell of woodsmoke came to her nostrils.

Kath went into the kitchen and took her big white apron off the hook on the back of the door. She put it on, tied the strings in a big bow behind, and smiled at the cook, who was slicing ham with a wicked-looking knife.

'Mornin', Lin Ho,' she said. 'The Boss has gone out for an early ride, with Mal. They may be some time, but we'll get breakfast for everyone else. Can you slice some bacon off the joint whilst I cut bread?'

'Sure, Missie Kath,' Lin Ho said readily. 'Heered Mal go off, I did, t'ought the Boss 'ud foller. They take tucker?'

'Sure. Bread and cheese and lemon barley water,' Kath said. Trust Lin Ho to know how things really stood. 'Oh . . . when Jim comes in, I'd like a word.'

Mal rode on into the morning, only remembering the tucker he could have taken when the morning was well advanced, the sun beaming down from a blue and cloudless sky. Still, he'd gone without food before – often. And though a drink would have been welcome, he knew how to wait – he always had. So he rode on, now and then leaning forward to pat Sandy's neck, coming to terms with the fact that he would have to sell the horse in order to pay for a train ticket to – to wherever he decided to go.

He was actually pretty thirsty when he heard the horse behind him. Or rather, Sandy did. For a mile or two now, Sandy had kept glancing back and now, for the first time, Mal followed suit, to see, in a small cloud of dust, a rider following him.

Someone from the Magellan? But it seemed unlikely, because if there had been any pursuit – and I am stealing a horse, in a way, Mal reminded himself guiltily – they could have caught him up at any time. And the rider, unidentifiable in the cloud of smoky dust which hung around him and his mount as it hung around Mal and Sandy, was making no attempt to overtake.

I wonder if he's got water? Mal asked himself, and reined in his mount. It seemed silly, in country as vast and unpeopled as this, to ride along the same trail in single file when they could so easily ride two abreast. He raised a hand and the man behind acknowledged his greeting, then kicked his horse into a trot.

It was Royce, dusty but smiling.

'Mal! G'day,' he said, for all the world as though they had met by chance in the street . . . as indeed they had, in a way. 'Goin' far?'

It sounded silly saying 'Yes, as far as I can – I'm running away', so Mal didn't say it. Instead he just muttered, 'You know, I guess,' and continued to stare along the track ahead between Sandy's pricked chestnut ears.

'We-ell, your mother seemed to think you was leavin', takin' time away. Goin' walkabout, in fact.'

Now why didn't I think of that? That makes it sound perfectly natural and right, Mal thought crossly. Lots of people go walkabout, why not me? Except you're leaving people in the lurch, his conscience reminded him meanly. You didn't tell anyone – even the wildest aborigine would announce his intentions, tell the Boss!

'That right, Mal?' Royce asked gently. 'You goin' walkabout?'

'Kinda,' Mal growled. 'I – I should've said, I guess. But I don't reckon Mam'll worry. Not now.'

It was said more nastily than he had meant it, but Royce merely shook his head.

'No, Mal, your mother isn't small-minded enough to discount your feelings just because she's happy. And she is happy, feller. As I am. You wouldn't want it different?'

'We-ell, no . . . but it's time I left,' Mal said. His voice cracked and he hastened on. 'I'm eighteen years old; I shouldn't be livin' at home still.'

'Your work's at home,' Royce said gently after a moment. 'You're a good worker, Mal. We'll miss you.'

It was acceptance, acknowledgement of his right to do as he pleased, and it was as welcome, suddenly, as a fist in the face. Mal blinked and felt the colour rush into his cheeks. They would miss him – not half as much as he would miss them. Not just Mam and the twins but Tink, Soljer, Canny, even Lin Ho, the cook. It's about time I said what I feel, he thought, trying to swallow the great lump which had risen up in his throat. A picture of the homestead at sunset had come into his head. The sky, streaked with red and gold, the roofs black against the flaming colours, the horses moving quietly into the paddock and his mother, the twins at her skirt, standing in the kitchen doorway, ready to serve the evening meal as soon as the last man had dismounted and cleaned himself up.

'Yeah. But Mam used to turn to me, Roy. She needed me. She don't need me no more.'

It was out, the truth. The reason, which he hadn't even acknow-ledged to himself, why he was running away. Because running away it was, not the adult, sensible, thought-out walkabout which Royce had called it. He was fleeing blindly from a situation which he could no longer control, from the woman he loved but wanted to keep as just his mother, denying her femininity, her prettiness and charm. She should be celibate, content with his company, deny all her natural urges. She was a mother, not a woman!

'That ain't so, Mal. She does need you – but not in quite the same way. Still, if you feel it's time you moved on . . . least I can do is ride to the railroad with you, buy your ticket to – to wher-ever you're bound. And take Sandy home with me, of course.' He paused, then turned and began to fiddle around in his saddle bag. Speaking without looking up, he added, 'What were you goin' to do with Sandy, by the way?'

'I ain't got no money.' Mal tried to sound neither sulky nor apologetic but suspected that he sounded both. 'I – I meant to sell him to buy me a ticket to . . . to wherever I wanted to go.'

'I see.' Royce turned in his saddle and held out a chunk of bread and some cheese. 'Feel like some tucker? Or would you rather drink first?'

The bottle was sticking up out of the saddlebag. Mal's mouth had been dry for what felt like hours but at the mere sight of the bottle saliva rushed to his mouth. He swallowed. 'Umm . . . I could do with a wet.'

Royce handed the bottle over and pulled out another. He uncorked it and took a couple of big swallows. Mal followed suit eagerly, then wiped the sweat from his brow with the back of a hand.

'Phew . . . that was good – thanks, Royce. I didn't stop for tucker. Tell the truth I was just anxious to get away before – before I began to think better of it.'

'Put the bottle in your saddlebag . . .' Royce began, then realised that Mal was riding bareback. '. . . Oh, sorry. Hand it over and tell me when you could do with another gargle. Now look, old feller, I've been thinkin' as I rode, and I believe I've a solution, of sorts. Bread an' cheese?'

Mal thanked him and sank his teeth into freshly baked bread and a ripe piece of cheese. It was good! 'What kinda solution?' he said thickly, through his mouthful. 'I don't want to hurt Mam, but –'

'Exactly. So hear me out, feller! As I was ridin', I remembered my Uncle Josh. You've heered me tellin' the twins 'bout their Uncle Josh?'

'The feller who owns the Wandina?' Mal asked. 'He's old, but he taught you lots . . . you told me when Mam and I first come to the Magellan.'

'That's him. Did I ever tell you how old Josh actually is?'

'Nope. But old, you said.'

'Too right. He's eighty-two. He's spry, mind, but he's gettin' so he can't manage the place no more. He'd ha' been all right but one of his musterers went walkabout at the start of the dry and his head stockman was gored by a bull in the wet and hasn't come out of hospital yet. When he does – if he does – there's no sayin' he'll go back to the Wandina.'

'So?' Mal said. He felt sorry for the old chap but didn't see that it had anything to do with him, unless Royce meant that he'd let them down by his walkabout as much as the musterer had?

'So Uncle Josh could use a responsible stand-in head stockman.'

'Oh!'

'Well, you'd be paid, so you'd have money in your pocket. I've always added extra money to your mother's wage-packet because of the work you did, but I knew that weren't fair . . . you'd be paid right by me, too, now, if you decide to come back to the Magellan.'

He looked sideways at Mal and they both grinned, then laughed aloud. It was a fact that sons of station owners got everything they needed – or everything their parents thought they needed – bought for them, but rarely handled cash. It was a sore point with many lads other than Mal.

'What d'you think? Could you live with that? Me payin' you a proper wage, I mean. Only Mal, I think of you as my successor, you know. You an' the twins. 'Cept they may not take to the life like you have. What d'you say? Us? Or Uncle Josh?'

'Or the road,' Mal reminded him, but his heart wasn't in it. The thought of being a head stockman, even on a temporary basis, was heady stuff. He'd shared the job with Jim many a time, at a muster you were your own boss more or less, but to be officially in charge . . .

Royce ate the last of his own bread and cheese and stuffed the greaseproof paper which Kath had wrapped round it back in his saddlebag. Then he turned towards his stepson once more.

'Don't talk through your hat, Mal,' he said kindly. 'This is a chance for you and you know it. The Wandina's a bonza station but it's slippin'. If you bring it back up again it'll be the sort of experience I couldn't give you, not on the Magellan. Gonna grab it wi' both hands?'

There could be only one answer to that and Mal knew it. He could feel a grin beginning.

'Aw, but Roy, would he want me? I'm only just eighteen, I ain't related . . .'

'You're my stepson and I'll vouch for you,' Royce said. 'You'll come back from time to time, feller? Your mother – she'll miss you, but not so bad if she knows where you are and what you're doin'. If you keep in touch.'

'Whenever I can I'll come on over,' Mal said eagerly. He was afire with enthusiasm now, not caring at all if he showed it. 'When do I go? How far is it? Can I borrow Sandy . . . or buy him? I'll pay you for him with my first wages.'

'You can take Sandy as a present,' Royce said calmly. 'I told your mother I might not be home tonight. If you're game, we'll ride on over right away. We'll have to sleep out a coupla nights – got a bedroll?'

'Nope. Never thought,' Mal muttered. Some adventurer he was turning out to be! 'Well, if we went back to the Magellan . . .'

'Good on you,' Royce said at once. 'Say goodbye to Kath and the kids, the hands, your pals . . . make it official. Tell you what, we'll say you an' me rode into Mungana to telegraph to Uncle Josh that you were coming. How's that sound?'

'Far-fetched,' Mal said, but he grinned as he spoke. 'Reckon they'll all ha' guessed. But it don't matter.' He gave a subdued whoop and kicked his horse into a gallop. 'I'm movin' on!' he shouted. 'I'm movin' on!'

A week later, it was all settled. Royce and Mal rode over to the Wandina – it took two days – and Mal met Josh Walenski for the first time and as Royce had anticipated, they got along just fine.

Uncle Josh was a thin spider of a man with a small, merry face, long, thin arms and legs and almost no hair. But despite his years and his hard life – for he had run the station alone since his early twenties, when he had first come to the outback – he was still able to ride his horses, help with his musters and keep his finger on the pulse of the Wandina.

But for how long? The question vexed him, but as he said, it had to be faced. Now that he was over eighty he could not go on, could not continue to raise, rear and eventually sell the thousands of cattle which passed through the Wandina every year, not unless he had proper help. 'If only Gumbo hadn't gone walkabout . . . or if old Wally was here,' he said sadly when the three of them settled down to a meal that first evening. 'But without them things are gettin' out of hand. The men do as they're told but they can't always see danger . . . and I don't get the best men, not now Mrs Forbes has passed on. It's always the same, they came for the good tucker and good livin' standards, and the women came for the clothes an' the house-things. Now Mrs Forbes ain't here, the tucker ain't so good an' the clothes are store-bought rubbish. Tain't the same, see?'

Mal saw all too clearly. Good workers could pick and choose, and they picked the stations where they were well looked after, where the food was good and varied and the clothing decent. They didn't mind hard work, but they wanted a decent leisure time, and the women liked schooling for the kids and decent clothing, too.

Royce had explained to Mal earlier what the set-up had been at the Wandina. Mrs Forbes, who had been his uncle's cook and housekeeper for many, many years, had just about kept the place running. Everyone thought the pair would marry, but they never had and so far as anyone knew, there had never been anything between them but friendship and the trust which old friends feel one for another. Mrs Forbes's death, earlier in the year, had been a great blow and since then the men had done their best to feed themselves, run the homestead and see to the stock, though Maisie, one of the aboriginal woman, worked in the house now.

'Maisie's a good girl, but her bread ain't up to much and she forgets what she's doin' half-way through cookin' and jest wanders off,' Uncle Josh said. He turned to Mal. 'Any ideas, young feller? I dessay you like your tucker?'

'I do,' Mal said fervently, with happy memories of Kath's cooking and of the beautiful garden they'd made at the Magellan coming immediately to mind. 'I've been watchin' my ma since I was small, I think I can make bread, stews and so on. Mebbe I could teach this Maisie a bit?'

This was greeted with great enthusiasm, though when Maisie was told to take the new head stockman round the garden her eyes saucered. She was a plump, lively woman, married to Colly, one of the hands, but it soon transpired, neither an inspired cook nor a gardener. The aboriginals hunted and harvested the rivers and the bush but they neither sowed nor ploughed. It was not necessary, they thought, when nature had such bounty available to them.

'As for a garden, we ain't got one,' she told Mal frankly, leading him out across the yard to where he had assumed the garden would be. 'Look at it, cobber! You can't call that a garden, nor it ain't been one since the old lady died.'

The garden, Mal saw with lively dismay, was worse than a wilderness, worse than the bush because the ground, rich with manure and with the good alluvial mud of the river, had simply *roared* into fertility and, when untended, had then gone back to nature with a vengeance.

'We'll plough it in,' Mal said at last. 'It's the only way – I don't think there's a man or woman born who could do anything else with that lot. And we need greenstuffs. What have you been eatin'?'

'Pigweed, mostly,' Maisie said. 'That's all right if you cook it well. And once or twice I done fought my way in an' dug sweet taters.'

Mal knew that pigweed was a sort of wild spinach and agreed that it would have to do for the time being, but he longed for the moment when the garden was a garden once more, and also for the moment when Maisie could cook. If only he had been able to get his mother to come over for a few weeks and give Maisie lessons – but it was impossible. Royce needed Kath; without her the Magellan garden, too, would speedily return to nature.

But it was a challenge; that was all you could say.

'We could mebbe spare someone to cook a bit, help clear the ground, set some seed,' Royce said at last, when the problem had been chewed over for a couple of evenings. It was not all that had been chewed over. Maisie's beef stew could not be eaten by anyone not blessed with their own strong teeth and the strange root crop which she had dug up and cooked was stringy and tough. Uncle Josh, uncomplaining, had sopped a hefty slice of doughy bread in the gravy and eaten that, but for a man used to filling his belly twice a day it didn't seem much.

'Gosh Roy, that 'ud be real grand,' Mal said when Royce made his suggestion. 'But what will Mam say?'

'Your mother will be delighted to know that you're eating properly,' Royce said. 'But you've gotta get goin' on the garden, feller! Once the wet comes . . .'

He had no need to finish the sentence. The Wandina was close to the Mitchell River and the alluvial mud which was so rich and good was not spread across the flats by fairies but by floods. Once the wet came no one would be doing much gardening.

'The houseboys cut the corn and thresh it and then it goes off to be milled and we get the flour back,' Uncle Josh told Mal. 'Cattle feed stays here, of course. We need more stores, we're 'most down to bare essentials.'

'Can Maisie order up?' Mal said with a trace of anxiety. He had seen his mother ordering but had no idea of quantities, he only knew one ordered a great deal. 'Uncle Josh, d'you know what we need?'

'I ain't too sure, but Mrs Forbes kept a book,' Uncle Josh said. 'You'll be takin' over her room, young feller, you can read it all up when we go off to our beds.'

And that was what Mal did and discovered, to his pleasure, that Mrs Forbes had not only kept 'a book', she had also kept a diary. Recipes, tips, blow-by-blow accounts of mustering tucker, clothing, general needs including medication, filled the large pile of five-year diaries in the long bottom drawer of her clothes chest. Mal felt a bit mean reading them but speedily realised that without them he would be lost – and with them, he stood a good chance of finding out just how to run this place.

So he and Josh discussed money, agreed what both thought was a fair wage for a beginner, and then Mal waved his stepfather off with heartfelt thanks and many messages for his mother and the twins, and turned back into the house with a sigh of pleasure. Now to get down to the essentials of running a station!

A week later Mal and Bas, the most experienced of the stockmen, decided they would have to have a cattle muster next day. A small part of the garden had been cleared, Mal had made bread and done his best to pass on his knowledge to Maisie, and had despatched his first order, courtesy of Mrs Forbes's little book, to the nearest town. It was July, and the dry was getting to everything. The creeks had mostly dried up, dust rose in stifling clouds whenever you crossed a river bed and cattle, as Mal well knew, don't have the sense to find water for themselves as the wild animals do. The men would have to ride out, round them up from wherever they had wandered, and drive them towards a water hole, or a creek, or the banks of a river. Once the beasts had been taken to water they'd stay by it for a little but then they'd wander off to find better grass and you'd be out after them again, cursing every bullock that ever lived, persuading them back to water.

Mustering could take weeks – would take weeks – and during that time, Uncle Josh would be coping alone at the homestead. But the men shouldn't be asked to do a muster without a leader, not when they'd been used to Wally and Gumbo showing the way. If I stay at home they'll never accept me as the new boss, Mal told himself. Perhaps I'll ride out with them this time, let them do most of the guesswork, see how they get on, and then next time, let them go alone.

He put it to Uncle Josh, who was not certain what would be best.

'I'd ha' gone myself, once,' he said. 'But when you're my age, three or four weeks lyin' on the ground plays merry hell with your bones. No, I'll stay behind, keep an eye on things. Maisie says you want the garden ploughin' in.'

'It's got to be done,' Mal said grimly. 'Trouble is, Uncle Josh, there's everythin' wants doin' and not enough of us to do it. But we'll get shipshape in time.'

And then next morning, when they were taking their swags out to the horses and preparing for the camp, they had a surprise. A figure rode in and swung down out of the saddle in the mustering yard. It was Soljer, grinning from ear to ear, his swag on the saddle before him.

'I've come to work wi' you, Boss,' he said to Mal. 'Mr Malone said it was okay and your mammy said she'd feel safer if we were together. Anythin' I can do?'

'Bloody hell, Soljer, you're a gift from the gods,' Mal gasped. 'I want to get the garden cleared – Maisie'll show you where it is – before the wet so I can get seeds planted, and there's fruit trees between the river an' the garden which need waterin' terrible bad. And Maisie can't cook . . . we're off on a muster. Can you stay and give Uncle Josh a hand here?'

Soljer agreed to stay, Uncle Josh welcomed him with open arms, and Mal rode out with the Wandina hands mounted on the best nags the station could provide and with a half-caste called Arthur bringing up the rear with the spare horses and all the camping gear.

It was a hot, dry day. As they trotted down the long, sandy track which led, eventually, to civilisation, Mal suddenly realised that he was completely happy for the first time since his mother had married Royce. In fact, he thought it went back further than that. He'd not known contentment like this since young Petey died. Mal had never forgotten his little brother nor the manner of his dying and he still had the nightmares, but had learned, even in his sleep, to control them. He never shouted out, or he didn't think he did since the men who shared his bunkhouse had not complained. And besides, he was getting harder. Since Bill's death he had realised that he would have to make his own way in life, for though Kath supported him, she was a mere female, not a member of the superior sex. So a nightmare was just a fantasy, nothing to be afraid of. If it upset him, he kicked it brusquely to the back of his mind and told himself that he was a Man, wasn't he, and Men weren't scared by shadows.

It was odd, Mal reflected now, feeling the sun burning down and glad of the shade of his broad-brimmed hat, that he'd had to wait until now to get contentment back. After Bill had died, life had been so tough for Kath and himself that the struggle to survive had simply eaten up every hour that came. School could not be relished, nor could games, food was sparse, clothing always hand-me-downs from the most unlikely sources, his mother always tired, always worried.

When they went to the station at Cooktown life had become easier, but only until the lady of the house started to make a fuss because Kath was prettier than she, and younger, livelier.

161

Desperately dismayed, Kath and Mal had searched the papers and eventually struck gold and once they had moved to the Magellan life became not only easier but more fun, as well. Royce did not want his twin sons brought up to think that work was the only thing that mattered. For the first time for years, Mal found himself engaged in pursuits which were enjoyable and which didn't necessarily fill his stomach or bring in money. He swam in the river, fished, went out rabbit shooting, or 'roo shooting, if the 'roos were taking what Royce considered was more than their fair share of the available grass. He played a peculiar sort of football with his cobbers on the river flats in the dry, and built tree-houses, fished for baby crocs and then teased the hands' women by tipping the little creatures, snapping and wheezing, into their humpies and laughing as the women jumped on stools and screamed to the men to 'Get 'em out, get 'em out!'

But right from the start he had known Royce was keen on his mother, even if she hadn't known herself, and it had spoiled things for him. First it was Bill and me, then for a bit it was Petey and me, but both those things got spoiled, Mal thought. Then it was Mam and me, until Royce came along. Can't I have anyone of my own?

And now, suddenly, he realised that it didn't matter. He was a head stockman, in charge of the other hands, in time he would be running the station, others would consult him, ask his advice. It was more than he had dreamed of, more than he had any right to expect . . . and wasn't it good? He thought of schoolmates in Melbourne, Sydney, and in all the small towns where he and his parents had roosted uneasily, waiting for the inevitable moment when Bill would lose yet another job. So many people he'd known over the years, and he'd lost touch with all of them so he couldn't write and say 'Look at me – I've made it, fellers!'

Still. He could be happy, could feel the warm glow of contentment. That would do for now.

Seven

There was a swing-seat in the garden of the Old House and Tess and Cherie were sitting on it, swinging gently. They were in league right now, and very nice it is too, Tess thought, to have someone unequivocally on my side.

After her adventure with Andy, her father had been very definitely on her side for quite a long time. He had taken her away from boarding school and turned her into a day-girl again despite Marianne's vehement opposition, but it only lasted a term, and it had been Tess who had asked to go back to boarding again.

'It's easier if Marianne and I don't see too much of each other,' she had explained to Peter. 'She can just about get through the summer hols if I steer clear most of the time. But non-stop me every evening . . . Daddy, it isn't fair on any of us. I get defensive and you get nervy and Marianne gets . . . well, worse. I'd rather go back to boarding, honest.'

Peter had been glad to agree, and since he telephoned her either from the office or when Marianne was out of the way almost every evening during term-time she no longer felt that she had been dismissed. Well, not by Peter, at any rate, and she didn't mind in the least being dismissed by Marianne.

But she missed Andy. They had spent that glorious summer holiday together, even though their enthusiasm for detective work had palled when they saw the size and complexity of the archives through which, they supposed, they must plod to discover where Leonora was buried.

'We'll try again at Christmas, when the weather isn't so good,'

Andy had said, but a couple of days into the Christmas holiday he was recalled to Paris by his parents. And ever since then he'd gone straight to whichever embassy his parents were posted to when the holidays started, and returned to school without visiting Norfolk. He and Tess had exchanged letters and the odd card, but hadn't met since that first wonderful summer.

'He's old enough to be interesting now, to his mother and father,' Tess had said rather bitterly to Janet the last time a letter had arrived for her with a foreign postmark. 'Still, I like his letters. They make me laugh.' She and Janet were friends again, since Janet was now working behind the counter in Sainsbury's on Gentleman's Walk and was too tired to search Violet out when she got home at night. She was downright glad to meet up with Tess again, for Tess had caught up with Janet so far as interests went and could happily talk about film stars, plays, the Royal family, and anything else which struck them as worth investigation. Though Janet had never really known Andy she appreciated that Tess liked him and was glad to discuss the chances of his returning to Barton, if only because it meant she could, in return, tell Tess about Bertie, who was on the bacon slicer at work and who could be ever so cheeky and suggestive when he felt like it.

So one way and another, Tess thought now, gently rocking the swing seat with one sandalled foot, things weren't so bad. She was happy at school and had several good friends, though she still didn't invite people home. Peter appreciated that if she did, life would become difficult for them all, and he loved her more than ever, Tess thought indulgently, for not making an issue of it.

She never made an issue of anything if she could help it. It only made things difficult in the end and she saw how often Marianne shot herself in the foot in her efforts to have everything her own way, instead of accepting a reasonable compromise now and then.

Tess was beginning to suspect that Peter no longer loved Marianne in the old way. She thought that Cherie had noticed it too, and was certain that Marianne herself had not the foggiest notion – her self-esteem would not allow her to suspect such a thing. But Marianne's capriciousness, which had apparently been quite attractive years ago, no longer seemed to amuse Peter quite so much. Sometimes it made him downright cross. And then

Cherie's Awful Discovery – the capitals were Cherie's and not Tess's – had partly explained the temper tantrums and the sudden violent crying fits.

Cherie, poking around in an embroidery bag in Marianne's room searching for embroidery silks to finish off the traycloth she was making, had discovered a copy of her mother's birth certificate. It proved, embarrassingly, that Marianne was not saying farewell to her twenties, as she tearfully – and frequently – claimed.

'Why did she lie, Tessie?' Cherie asked plaintively when she had shown her sister the documentary evidence. 'Why did she pretend to Daddy and us that she was born in 1906? She's almost as old as Daddy, isn't she?'

'No, love, she isn't. Daddy's five years older than she is. As for pretending, I don't understand it at all. It isn't as if she were really old.'

'Thirty-seven is old,' Cherie said positively. 'None of my friends at school have old mothers.'

'Mrs Thrower's older than that,' Tess said after some thought. 'But it doesn't really matter, Cherie. People's ages aren't important. We'd better forget it, pretend we don't know . . . let her get away with it.'

'All right,' Cherie agreed, after thinking it over. 'She can be so horrible though, Tessie! She told me this morning I was an ugly little thing, all teeth and kneecaps!'

She sounded so injured that Tess had to laugh, and then to hug her to take the woeful expression off her face.

'Cherie, don't worry! It's just because you've got your second teeth and your face doesn't fit them yet. As for knees . . . have you seen the colts down in Mr Rope's long pasture?'

'Ye-es . . . oh, they're all knees too, d'you mean? But aren't they *pretty*, Tess, with that velvety stuff on them and their knobbly foreheads? I'd love one for my own.'

'Well, we can go and fuss them,' Tess pointed out. At seventeen she had already realised that life's various pleasures do not have to be owned to be enjoyed. 'But what I meant was that the fillies will grow into beautiful, elegant mares, just as you'll grow into a pretty girl with a lovely figure one day.'

'*Will* I?' Cherie said, fluttering her lashes and stroking her skirt down over her knees in a manner which would have befitted an eighteen-year-old, but which looked oddly foreign on a child of eight. 'Oh, I hope I do!'

'You will, truly. Marianne's pretty and Dad's got a very handsome sort of face,' Tess pointed out. 'And now do stop thinking about how you look, Cherie, and concentrate on your French verbs.'

Marianne talked French to them both but she didn't have the patience to repeat a remark until they understood, so neither child had picked up the language to any great extent. And now Cherie was boarding at Tess's school – at the tender age of eight – and Marianne nagged if she wasn't in the first three when French exam time came around. Cherie was a weekly boarder at present so she had weekends at home but the truth is, Tess thought now, that Marianne likes babies but she doesn't much like girls, and Cherie's shot up and got awfully *aware* just lately. She's not a tomboy, like me, she's always prinking and preening. Just like Marianne, in fact, only Marianne suddenly doesn't see that as an advantage: she sees it, quite simply, as competition. So Cherie has to mind her ps and qs and walk round Marianne instead of straight across, as she had in the old days.

'Another ten days and we'll be back in school,' Cherie said suddenly. 'I won't mind, will you, Tessie? I don't like the water, boats make me afraid, there are wasps in the wood . . . I shan't mind going back to school.'

Tess laughed. 'I shan't mind much, either. I *do* like the water, and the boat, and the woods, but nothing's much fun without someone to share it and Jan's too busy being gainfully employed to enjoy mucking about. And there's no one else of my age around here.'

'You went eel-trapping with Mr Thrower,' Cherie said; her voice sounded dangerously close to a whine. 'What about that, then? You left me to 'muse myself.'

'It was fun, but Mr Thrower won't see seventeen again,' Tess told her little sister. 'You'd have hated it – the eels have rows of sharp little teeth and they didn't half lash about in the bottom of the boat. It was perilous, I'm telling you. And on the way back I saw an adder. It was lying on the bark of an ancient old willow tree, it was so well camouflaged you wouldn't believe . . . but you don't like snakes much either, do you?'

Cherie shuddered. 'Ugh, eels, snakes . . . I hate wrigglies or ticklies or slimies or flutteries I do.'

'Very comprehensive,' Tess said drily. 'Well, tomorrow I'm catching the bus into the city. I'm meeting Freddy and we're going round the shops. You can come if you want, but it'll be a long day.'

'Freddy? I don't like boys,' Cherie said. She was definitely whining now. 'Must you meet him? Can't we two go round the shops? I'll be ever so good, dear Tess, truly I will, I won't be any trouble at all.'

'Freddy, dear little noodle, is short for Frederica and she's a girl, my age, in my class. I don't think she'll be thrilled if I take you, but I'm prepared to risk it if you really want to go.'

'No, not with two of you,' Cherie said rather sulkily. 'You'll walk ahead and laugh about things I don't understand and tell me to shut up and stop whining.'

Tess had to laugh because it set out Cherie's intentions so clearly; if she came and they talked she would whine. She had an awful lot in common with her maman, poor little thing!

'Right, I'll go off with Freddy then. And I'll bring you back a present – what would you like?'

'Hair ribbons – bright red, please, or a very pale blue,' Cherie said promptly. She did not even have to think, Tess realised. 'And a matching hair-slide, if you can afford two things.'

'Right,' Tess said. 'I'll make a note. And now, chick, we'd better go in and start making the tea or Marianne will hit the roof.' She jumped off the swing seat and eyed the distance between it and the back door measuringly. 'Race you to the kitchen,' she ended.

'You'll win, you always do,' Cherie moaned. 'Can I have three yards' start?'

'All right,' Tess said good-naturedly. 'Go on, run . . . I'll catch you up.'

Cherie, with a triumphant squeal, broke into a gallop but Tess drew level and overhauled her long before they reached the back door.

'You've got longer legs, it isn't *fair*,' Cherie panted, arriving a second or so later, very pink in the face. 'Will you come home when you've finished shopping with that – that person?'

'Of course. Come on, you get the bread and butter out and lay the table whilst I slice.'

'Freddy! Cooee, I'm over here! Oh drat that girl, she's deaf as a post!' Tess ran across the bus station and hurled herself at tall, red-haired Freddy Knox, nearly knocking her friend off her feet. Freddy gasped, then shook a reproving finger at Tess.

'Good Lord, girl, what are you trying to do? You nearly had me over . . . when did your bus get in? I was watching your stop like a hawk.'

'Didn't come by bus. My father brought me and dropped me off at the bottom of Surrey Street,' Tess said. 'Come on, where shall we go first? Dad gave me half a crown, so I've got some something to spend for a change.'

Freddy was a new friend, because she and her family had only recently returned to Norfolk after a dozen or so years living in the south of England. The Knoxes had lived in Eastbourne and Freddy and her brothers had gone to school there, whilst her father commuted to the city every day. However, Mr Knox had recently become the senior partner in a Norwich firm of solicitors, so the family had bought a house in a local village and Freddy had become a pupil at the Norwich High School. Freddy's elder brother, she had told Tess proudly, was at Cambridge, reading law. Ashley was *extremely* clever, Freddy said, and was expected to follow in his father's footsteps.

But now, standing on the pavement in Surrey Street, Freddy seized Tess's arm and spoke urgently. 'Nice to have money to spend but look, Tess, would you mind most awfully if we changed our plans? Only my mama's sister, Auntie Phoebe, is having a baby and she's just been whipped into the nursing home so my mama has promised to go round and look after Auntie Vera's two little boys. They're four and six and a real handful so Mother promised she'd keep them in their own home . . . which leaves our house empty. It wouldn't matter, but we've got the men coming in today to empty the septic tank – pooh, pooh! – so someone really should be at home. Oh Tess, would you mind awfully scrubbing the shopping trip, and coming over to our place instead? I've got money for the bus fares and everything, and before she rushed off Mother told Ella – Mrs Brett, who works for us – to make us a really good luncheon . . . what do you think? You can ring your mother and tell her what's happened when we get home. Only otherwise I'll have to love you and leave you . . . oh Tess, do come!'

'Oh!' Tess said doubtfully, rather overwhelmed by such a rush of words. 'I don't mind at all, in fact I'd love it, but I did tell you I don't go to other people's houses because my stepmother's French and doesn't like entertaining in return. Oh Freddy, why didn't you just cancel me? We could have gone shopping another day.'

'We tried, but you'd already left,' Freddy said frankly. 'Mother told your stepmama what had happened and asked if you could come home with me and Mrs Delamere seemed to think it would be all right for you to come back to ours. As for a return visit, it doesn't matter a hoot. My dear father would say that was foreigners for you! Do, do come, dear Tess, we'll have a lovely day, really we will. And having two of us there would help my mama enormously, because my guess is she'll be stuck at Auntie's place for ages, and I don't see why you shouldn't stay for a few days, if your father agrees. We could have marvellous fun, you know.'

'I'm sure he wouldn't let me stay over, because of not being able to ask you back,' Tess said gloomily, but Freddy said not to be such a defeatist, and did Tess know that Freddy's mother and Tess's father had known each other once, years ago?

'No, he's never said,' Tess said, much struck by this gratuitous information. 'But then Daddy hardly ever talks about his past – because my stepmother's his second wife, you know. But he lived in Brundall for a time – is that near you?'

'Very near,' Freddy said, taking Tess's arm. 'Look, we can catch the Seven, it leaves in five minutes, and be back and ringing your father before you know it. Your stepmama made it clear that his word is law. Oh come on, Tess, be a sport!'

'Oh, all right then, I'd love to come,' Tess said, surrendering.

'Isn't it a small world though – fancy our parents knowing each other!'

'Yes, it's odd,' Freddy agreed. They reached the bus stop where the Number Seven was revving its engine impatiently. 'Jump on!'

Without giving herself time to think, Tessa jumped aboard and followed her friend down the aisle to an empty front seat. Sinking on to the shiny red leatherette, she said rather breathlessly, 'Where do you live, Freddy? I've never thought to ask!'

'Blofield,' Freddy said. 'How odd you don't know, because I know where you live. Barton Turf, isn't it?'

Tess stared at her. Where had she heard that name before? Blofield . . . it had some sort of significance, she knew it did. But just where she'd heard it before she couldn't . . .

Inside her head, all of a sudden, she could hear her father's voice. *She lived in a small village called Blofield on the road between Norwich and Yarmouth.* Of course, that was it – Leonora had lived in Blofield! She and Andy had talked about tracing her mother but he'd not come back to the area, and there had seemed little point in trying to detect alone. But now she was to visit Leonora's home village officially, perhaps she could stay there for several days! She was bound to be able to find out something in that time. But Freddy was looking quizzical; she had been silent too long. Tess hurried into speech.

'Blofield – yes, that is near Brundall, I remember now. Umm, yes, we live near Barton Turf . . . we're quite a way outside the village, though. I don't know Blofield at all – is it a pretty village? And what's Brundall like?'

Freddy chuckled and settled herself more comfortably in her seat. 'Brundall's all right – the river's there, which makes it rather special. Ash and I bike down there sometimes to snoop round and look at the boats. Blofield's pretty ordinary, but we like it. I hope you will, too. Oh, I say, do you still have relatives living in Brundall? If so, you could visit them.'

'I don't think so. My grandparents moved to Horning years ago – they're both dead, now – and Dad's only brother lives on Unthank Road, in the city. But there must be people who remember him, I suppose. It's a pity about the relatives; I'd like to have some to visit.'

'I should think not having them would be quite an advantage,' Freddy said frankly. 'Some of my uncles and cousins . . . honestly, they're dreadful! But I suppose I wouldn't like not having them, if you see what I mean. Having been away for so long, it's quite fun having relations popping in. We've only been back nine months, but every time I go into the village post office or walk past the bus stop, someone says "Mornin' – you'll be Sally's girl. Settlin' in?" Sally's my mother's name,' she added.

'I'd like that,' Tess said, trying not to sound wistful. 'Uncle Phil's twelve years older than Daddy and his children are much older than me. We hardly ever see them, in fact. Do you like Blofield, then?'

'We love it. Daddy says the village is unpretentious and Mummy says the house runs itself, which means we have a lady from the village – Mrs Brett – who comes in twice each day, mornings to clean, late afternoons to cook dinner. And in the school hols Mum expects what she calls "co-operation" and I call slavery from her only daughter . . . and more practical help from Ashley, when he's at home, of course.'

Tess laughed. 'Marianne doesn't like housework much, either, but she's got Cherie and me to help her in the hols. She really loves cooking, though, so Mrs Thrower comes in most days for a couple of hours and does all the really hard things, like windows and scrubbing, and Marianne cooks.'

'Good for Marianne,' Freddy said. 'Well, I'll take you round the village as soon as the tank emptiers have been. We'll be able to explore properly, especially if your parents say you can stay for a bit. Do try to persuade them, Tess! Why, you might discover a long-lost cousin of about our age living in Brundall, which would be very nice for me. No one else from our school lives really near, so I've got no one to do things with.'

'I'll do my best to stay for a while,' Tess promised, meaning it. She would lie, deceive, anything, but she meant to stay with Freddy and find out as much as she could whilst she had the chance. 'How do you get about? I've got a bike and a boat, but then we're slap-bang on the Broad. What river is Brundall on?'

'It's the Yare. And we have a boat, too. Dad and Ashley sail an International Star – I'm going to have a go one of these days I

171

keep telling them. But I've got a fat little row-boat. If we have time – that is, if your father will let you stay – we could go out in her. She's called *Scottie*, after Scott Fitzgerald, of course. I say, Tess, can you sail? Perhaps you could teach me.'

'I can, a bit,' Tess said. 'A boy called Barry Saunders taught me. But I've not sailed for ages. He got a much bigger yacht and a girlfriend . . . she crews for him . . . and they don't sail on Barton any more. Too tame.'

'Lovely,' Freddy said vaguely. Ahead of them a woman was reading a paper, the headlines big enough to read even from a distance. 'Someone's flown the Atlantic – a woman . . . can you see?'

'Beryl something,' Tess said. Her interest in current affairs was minimal. 'I didn't know anyone was trying to do that . . . hasn't someone done it already?'

'Oh, Tess, of course they have! But isn't this the other way round or something? There was an announcement on the News this morning, I think . . . or was it last night? Anyway, she's clearly done it – another blow for women's rights!'

'Yes, I suppose so,' Tess said. She cleared her throat. 'Umm, you know your mother knew my father, Freddy? I wonder if she ever met my mother?'

'Why? Was your mother local, too?' Freddy asked. 'No reason why not, of course. Ask her, anyway. She'd love to tell you her life story, my mum's like that.'

'Right,' Tess said, and decided not to elaborate. Take it slowly and gently, she advised herself. That way no one will get suspicious. 'I say, Freddy, why can't your brother supervise the tank emptiers?'

'He would, but he's gone to London for the day. He'll be home tonight, though, so if you can stay over we might persuade him to take us out for a run tomorrow. He drives the car, lucky blighter.'

'Lovely,' Tess said. But a nasty thought had just struck her. 'Oh gosh, how can I possibly stay over? I don't have any clothes or peejays or anything . . . toothbrush, flannel, that sort of thing. Oh dear, and I really did think we might get away with it.'

'Fool!' Freddy said affectionately. 'I told you, Ashley can drive,

Mum planned to get him to run us over to Barton this evening to pick up your things. Won't that do?'

'Well, yes, of course. If only, if *only* they'll agree!'

'If they refuse you, I'll get my mama to have a word with them,' Freddy said briskly. 'And now let's talk about something different. You know Alex Matthias? Well, Biddy Andrews told me . . .'

The burning subject of staying over was put to one side and Tess pushed her excitement over her detecting role to the back of her mind. The two girls made themselves comfortable, paid their fares, and settled down to a good gossip.

Because Peter had given her a lift that morning and intended to pick her up again at the same spot that evening, Tess knew it would be all right to ring him rather than Marianne. And anyway, Peter would always have the last word. Even so, she rang with a degree of trepidation. Suppose he said 'no', or told her to okay it with Marianne?

But to her great relief, her father was delighted to hear from her, and relieved, too, since it transpired that there was an emergency on in the Delamere household.

'We've had a telegram from France, love,' he said. 'Odd that you rang, I was just wondering how on earth I could get hold of you before this evening. Marianne's sister and brother-in-law have been injured in a motor accident – we don't know how badly, just that they're alive but in hospital – and we have to go to France at once. Marianne's arranging it through Thomas Cook . . . we're going to take Cherie, but we rather hoped you might go home and close the house up for us, then follow on a later boat. You're seventeen, after all – old enough to travel alone. We'd meet you off the ferry, of course,' he added quickly.

'Actually, Daddy, I rang to tell you that I'm not in the city at all, I'm at Frederica Knox's house,' Tess said. 'We had to come back because her mother's been called away for a couple of hours and the men are coming to empty the septic tank. Freddy's mother asked if I could stay for a few days . . . a week, even, because she's going to be down at her sister's quite a bit. Apparently Mrs Knox's sister has gone into a maternity home to have a baby.'

'Oh! And you'd like to stay? Rather than coming to France, even?'

'Much rather,' Tess said quickly. She had been to France once to visit Marianne's relatives and had felt bored and out of place. What was more, she found Marianne's boastfulness hard to take, particularly as it verged on the untruthful. 'Of course I'll go home and lock up and so on, but if I could come back here and stay with the Knoxes it would be easier all round.'

She waited for her father to remind her that she could not stay with friends because that would mean a reciprocal visit, but Peter raised no such objection; indeed, he said in a relieved tone of voice that if the Knox family really did not mind it would seem the perfect solution.

'I'll handle Marianne,' he finished. 'You're too grown up to be told you can't have a friend to stay. It's your home as much as ours, chick. But what about pyjamas and things?'

Tess explained that Freddy had a brother who would run them over to Barton in the car that evening and help her both to lock up the house as well as to pack some clothing and toiletries. Her father was enthusiastic – he had already phoned Mrs Thrower to explain the situation – and Tess began to nurse real hopes of a reciprocal visit. Marianne could do it easily because she occasionally had large dinner parties for a dozen or so friends and acquaintances and sailed through them, presenting her guests with exquisite food and wine and obviously enjoying her role as hostess. But from what her father had said it didn't really matter whether Daddy talked Marianne round or not. I'll tell Marianne nicely but firmly that I intend to have my friend to stay since she was kind enough to put up with me for a week, and Marianne will have to put a good face on it, she decided. Daddy's right, I really can't let her rule my life the way she did when I was younger – I'm a sixth former, studying for my Higher, not a kid she can push around.

'So that's arranged, then, I'll stay with Freddy,' she said into the receiver. 'Come to think of it, Daddy, if you have to stay longer than a week Freddy and I could move back into the Old House – or I could ask Janet to stay. I know you wouldn't like me to be there alone,' she added conscientiously, though she wouldn't have minded it herself.

'Well, we'll see,' Peter said now. 'Sure the Knoxes won't mind? It's awfully good of them, do tell Mrs Knox so when you have a chance.'

'She's not here now, but I will, when she gets home,' Tess said quickly. It had been on the tip of her tongue to remark, brightly, that Mrs Knox had known Peter years ago, but discretion stopped her short. She realised that, since she had not known herself where the Knoxes lived, Peter was unlikely to realise that she was staying in Blofield. Why should he even suspect it? She had said nothing to alert him to the fact and anyway there was no reason for telling him. She could stay where she liked.

'Fine, darling.' Peter sounded distracted, Tess guessed that he was already beginning to think about France, the journey, where they would stay and so on. 'Oh, one thing – we may want to get in touch with you; what's your address? And telephone number, of course.'

Blast, Tess thought crossly, that's torn it. She glanced down at the telephone. *Brundall 29* was written upon it. Telephone exchanges, she knew, were often shared between a group of villages.

'Oh, the telephone number is Brundall 29,' she said glibly, therefore. 'And the address is *c/o Knox, The Turrets, The Street.*'

'Got that. I lived in Brundall once,' Peter said. 'You've got Marianne's sister's address, haven't you? I don't believe they're on the telephone, which is a nuisance, but if you need us you can telegraph.'

'I don't have the address here, but it'll be at home,' Tess said, so Peter told her to fetch pencil and paper and dictated it to her.

'Thanks, Daddy,' Tess said. 'If I need you I'll get in touch. Will you telephone when you get back to England?'

'I'll telephone tomorrow evening, and each evening after that,' Peter said. 'Just to make sure you're all right, sweetheart. Now is there anything else?'

'No, we've settled everything,' Tess said, crossing her fingers. Her father hated writing letters, he would telephone if he possibly could. And anyway, the postman, seeing the name Knox

175

and the address, would only assume that someone had confused Brundall with Blofield.

'Right then, darling. Take care of yourself and have a lovely time. God bless.'

Peter rang off and Tess replaced the receiver and went through the hall and into the small, cosy kitchen where Freddy was sitting with her bottom on one chair and her feet on another, reading the newspaper. She chucked the paper on to the table when her friend appeared, however, and got to her feet.

'All sereno? Are you staying? Oh marvellous, Tess, I couldn't be more thrilled, and Mummy will be pleased, too. I say, you're a bit red about the gills, though. Was there trouble?'

'No-oo, because it really suited my parents to have me stay here. The fact is, Marianne's sister and brother-in-law have been in a motor accident, they're in hospital, and so of course Marianne and Daddy are going to hare off to France. They're taking Cherie with them, thank goodness, and they would have taken me, but they're hoping to leave at once so they wanted me to stay behind to close up the house and so on.'

'Fancy missing a trip to France and not minding! But honestly, Tess, we'll have a much better time here. We'll do all sorts of things. Promise.'

'I know it,' Tess assured her friend. 'I'm not particularly keen on my step-relatives. They're all howling snobs, like Marianne. You can't do anything unless it's the "done thing". Daddy knows how I feel, though we don't talk about it. He said to thank you very much, incidentally.'

'It's a pleasure,' Freddy said buoyantly. 'Tomorrow we'll explore, then. We're house-sitting today, of course – hope the tank emptiers aren't too late – but after that we can take a mooch around. As you say, we might set eyes on a relative or two. What was your mother's maiden name, incidentally? Because she moved away after they married, of course.'

'I actually don't know,' Tess said, rather embarrassed. 'Still, folk will surely remember Delamere? It isn't that common.'

'True. Right then, I'll show you round.'

The day continued pleasantly. Freddy took Tess all round the house and introduced her to Mr Brett, who did the garden. He was married to Mrs Brett, who cleaned and cooked, and told the girls pleasantly that he'd skin 'em alive if he caught them pickin' his apples afore they was ripe.

'Norfolk people do say what they think, don't they?' Freddy said, when they got indoors. 'And now it's time for luncheon – Mrs Brett's left us something on a tray. It's in the pantry – let's have a snoop.'

The pantry was the large, walk-in kind, and there was a refrigerator, the first one Tess had seen. It nearly stopped her heart though by suddenly starting to make a peculiar whirring noise which, Freddy said, was just the motor cutting in. Tess said yes, of course, and was glad that so far, Marianne had not managed to get Peter to have them put 'on the electric' and was thus unable to inflict a refrigerator on them.

'Let's take a look,' Freddy said, having carried a cloth-covered tray out of the pantry, plonking it down in the middle of the kitchen table. The kitchen was square, with a red tiled floor, a huge cream-coloured Aga stove, a dresser which reached the ceiling and a great many pot plants. The kitchen table was, predictably, wood and well-scrubbed, and the chairs were ladder-backed. And when Freddy whipped the cloth off the tray she revealed just the sort of food Tess felt like on a warm, early September day. Cold chicken and ham, lots of salad, a pat of butter and a large cottage loaf.

'There's lemonade to drink and peaches or plums for afterwards,' Freddy said, having fetched out a big bottle and a basket of fruit from the refrigerator. 'Mum told Mrs Brett to do enough for three but Ash won't be back – hooray! Tuck in, Tess!'

Tess tucked in, and when they had finished their meal the tank emptiers arrived and did their work. When they left Freddy took Tess on a short tour of the village, including the village shop and the school, mercifully closed for the holidays still. Then they made their way home and shortly after they arrived back at the house, which was large and modern, with a huge garden, Mrs Knox drifted into the kitchen where the girls were podding peas for dinner and sat herself down on the edge of the kitchen table. She was tall and slender with hair even redder, if anything, than

177

Freddy's and long, scarlet-painted nails of which she seemed rather proud, for she kept eyeing them, polishing them with the other palm and generally cosseting them.

'Hello, Tess, I'm Freddy's mother,' she introduced herself. 'Ashley's just garaging the car – he picked me up from Strumpshaw on his way home. Now are you able to stay with us for a while? Freddy said she'd get you to ask your parents.'

'Yes, my father was delighted, thank you very much indeed,' Tess said conscientiously. 'Actually, your invitation couldn't have come at a better time, because my parents have had to rush off to France, and I'd much rather be with Freddy than over there.'

'Really? Well, you *are* unusual,' Mrs Knox said, widening her large grey-green eyes a little. 'Still, I suppose the whole of France isn't like Paris, or the south. Did Mrs Brett leave you a nice luncheon?'

'It was lovely, thanks,' Tess said, whilst Freddy rushed out of the back door and could be heard telling her brother triumphantly that her friend Tess would be staying and would much appreciate a lift to fetch her things later.

Ashley came in just as Mrs Knox was describing the dreadful things her small nephews had done in their mother's absence. He was tall, with reddy-brown hair and eyes and what Tess supposed, rather doubtfully, were classic features – a straight nose and a firm chin – definitely good-looking anyway. He came across the kitchen and grinned at Tess, revealing square white teeth.

'Hello; you'll be Sprat's little pal. I'm Ashley Knox, her big brother. Sprat tells me you're staying over?'

'That's right,' Tess said guardedly. She thought she had seldom seen a handsomer young man – he must be twenty if he's a day she thought, awed, or possibly more. But she wasn't sure if she liked him. He was looking at her in a measuring sort of way which disturbed her. However, having stared, he turned away to lope into the pantry.

'Any grub I can have right now, Ma?' he called over his shoulder. 'I'm absolutely famished and I'll bet the kids are too; it's a long while since lunch.'

'There's bread and cheese, I think,' his mother said, having given the matter a moment's thought. 'And apples, of course.'

Ashley groaned but found the loaf and delved inside the refrigerator, returning to the kitchen with a doorstep of bread and a great chunk of cheese which would have taken Tess a week to eat.

'Ta, Ma,' he said. 'What's for dinner?'

After some discussion it was agreed that Ashley should take Tess back to Deeping Lane before dinner.

'It'll be lighter, easier to get your stuff packed. And you'll probably want to have a word with your neighbours, explain what's going on,' Ashley said. His mother, flapping a hand at them, had told them to sort out what was best and gone up to her room, leaving the three of them sitting round the kitchen table devouring bread and cheese. 'I'll just nip upstairs and tell Mother we're off so she knows what's happening.'

He left the room and Freddy yawned, stretched, and then smiled across at Tess.

'What does your mother do before dinner? Mine has a hot bath with lots of bath oil floating on the top, and then she'll come out and puff talcum all over the place and put on a négligé. Then she'll go to her room and do things to her hair and her face, put on a clean, cool gown, and appear like a lady, ten minutes before the meal's served. And believe me, the meal will be served spot on seven-thirty, because my father comes back from the city extremely hungry and Mummy likes a leisurely dinner.

'So if we go to your house and take longer than we expect we can pick up fish and chips on the way back – there's a shop in the village, but we can probably get some on the road between Barton and Blofield.'

'If your mother doesn't like housework, and you're at school still, why don't you have a full-time maid?' Tess asked Freddy as the two of them walked round to where Ashley was waiting in the car. 'If you had a proper housekeeper she could cook the meals as well.'

Freddy shrugged. 'We used to have a maid, but none of us liked it much, and Mrs Brett's a wonderful cook and a very good cleaner, too. The only snag is the washing up, which the family have to do, and things like ironing, only Mummy says she's getting someone in to do a couple of hours each afternoon whilst Ash and I are home. And clearing the table and washing up aren't at all bad, in fact. We take it in turns, me and Ash one night, Mummy and Father the next, so we do get evenings off.'

'And your parents play fair and do their share?' Tess asked, and was then embarrassed by her incredulous tone. But Mrs Knox did not look like a lady who would take kindly to clearing tables and washing up – certainly Marianne never lifted a finger when she had two daughters home, though it did occur to Tess, for the first time, that maybe, during the term, her stepmother was forced to wash up after dinner.

'Play fair? Yes, of course they do. What a bad example it would be for us if they didn't! Ah, now if we both sit in the back Ashley will moan that he isn't a chauffeur – you can sit in the front.'

'No indeed; I wouldn't know what to say to him. He's your brother, you sit in the front,' Tess said, thoroughly alarmed. It was all very well thinking Ashley Knox good-looking, but trying to talk to him for a whole half-hour was more punishment than pleasure.

They reached the car, a sporty looking model with its hood rolled down. Ashley leaned over and opened the passenger door.

'Hop in,' he said briskly. 'If we get a move on we could be home before they start dinner. Otherwise it's whatever's left and you know what a hog Father can be!'

He was looking at Freddy as he spoke and she, taking advantage of Tess's momentary hesitation, nipped into the back seat, leaving Tess no choice but to get into the front passenger seat.

'There you are, then, Ash . . . amuse Tess,' she said, adding quietly, for Tess's benefit alone, 'Don't be a goose; once we get going you won't be able to hear yourself think, let alone converse with my brother!'

And this was true, to an extent. Besides, Ashley simply drove, concentrating on the road ahead so that Tess was able to sneak occasional glances at his profile without his noticing.

He *was* good-looking, she concluded after a few miles had passed. Not only was he the possessor of that nice straight nose, but his eyelashes were dark despite his hair having that reddish tinge and the freckles which she could now see, being closer to him, added to his charms.

The car slowed as Ashley left the wider roads and entered the network of lanes which led to the Broad. It was beautiful down here; peaceful. Tess, who had felt very tense because she was sitting beside a strange young man, began to relax. When he turned to her she got ready to give him instructions . . . take the right fork, then at the junction . . . etc., but it wasn't instructions which he was looking for.

'Know me again?'

'I beg your pardon?' Tess said in a small chilly voice. Oh damn, he had noticed her eyes on him, then.

'I asked if you'd know me again? You've been giving me the once-over for the past twenty minutes. I'm not blind you know! Have you never realised men can see out of the corners of their eyes?'

It was said lightly, but there was enough malice in his tone to bring heat sweeping across Tess's face. She said dismissively: 'If I glanced at you it was because I was waiting for you to ask me the way. I'm sorry if I embarrassed you.'

He laughed softly and she saw his eyes flick to the rear-view mirror, then he put his hand out and caught hers, which were lying quietly in her blue gingham lap. He squeezed briefly, then returned his hand to the wheel once more.

'You didn't embarrass me; it's rather nice for a fellow to know a girl likes to look at him. Is it left at the next junction?'

'Yes, left. And – and don't jump to conclusions,' Tess said, amazed at her own temerity. If Ashley had been a real gentleman, she thought crossly, he would not have embarrassed her by admitting he'd noticed her watching him. Not that I was, she added. Well, not much, anyway. 'I told you why I was looking at you.'

'And I don't believe you,' Ashley said equably. 'How old are you? Seventeen? And you've no brothers of your own, Sprat told me. I expect you're dying to know all about me, really, you're just too inhibited by your upbringing to ask.'

'My stepmother's French,' Tess said wildly. 'The French don't believe in inhibitions.'

This was wildly, totally untrue, but it sounded good. Ashley shot her an astonished look. The look said: *she can fight her corner! Good, she's got spirit!* and Tess found the look as infuriating as she had found his words. Who the hell was Ashley Knox to pat her on the head because she answered him back? Deliberately, she turned in her seat and faced Freddy.

'You all right in the back?' she shouted above the wind of their going. 'You can sit in front on the way back; fair's fair, after all.'

Freddy, curled up on the back seat watching the passing scene, blinked and looked across at her. 'Why? Aren't you happy there?'

Before Tess could reply, however, Ashley was speaking again.

'Tess, is this your road coming up? Quick, do I turn right or do I go straight?'

'Turn right,' Tess snapped. 'We're about a mile down Deeping Lane, you can't miss it. You'll pass a tied cottage, then quite a bit of country, then it's the Old House.'

'Got you,' Ashley said. He looked sideways as he drove. 'Nice farmland.'

He was calling a truce. Tess said non-committally: 'Very nice. Mr Rope grows mostly wheat and barley, but some oats and quite a lot of hay and root crops. I didn't know you were interested in farming.'

It was a mistake.

'You don't know anything about me,' Ashley remarked. 'But if you behave yourself, you soon will. Want to come to the flicks with me?'

'No thank you,' Tess said promptly. He gave her an astonished glance, then returned his eyes to the road.

'Why not? I'm an *extremely* eligible bachelor, you know. All your little school friends will be mad with jealousy.'

'Why not? Because, as you say, I don't know you. And I don't know that I want to know you, either.'

'Oh, come on, tell the truth! I fascinate you, you know I do.'

Tess thought it polite this time to say nothing and presently was able to tell Ashley that the house coming up on his right was the Old House, and since the gates were open she would be obliged if he would drive up to the front door.

Without a word Ashley obeyed and drew the car to a halt, with only a minimal scattering of gravel, right outside the oak front door. 'Ladies, we've arrived,' he said, jumping out and running round to open the passenger door, only Tess, still simmering, had already done so. 'Now what? Do you have a key?'

'Yes, but to the back door,' Tess said quickly. She did not have a key of any description but guessed that the back-door key would be under the milk churn where it was usually kept. 'You stay here and I'll come through and open up.'

She ran round to the back door, found the key, unlocked, and stepped into the kitchen. She closed the back door behind her and glanced around. My God, the mess! Marianne must have had the telegram between breakfast and luncheon; she had simply abandoned the place with a pile of dirty dishes on one wooden draining board and some more washed up but not wiped dry on the other. And on the kitchen table were a pile of vegetables, various pans, a bag of flour, another of sugar, a square of cooking margarine . . . clearly dinner preparations had been under way. It was almost frightening, as Miss Havisham's kitchen must have been, to see the place so obviously deserted. What was more, despite the homely muddle she was aware of a coldness, a remoteness, about the place, as though the house had been empty for months, perhaps even years. But her friend and Ashley were waiting outside, no time to stand here pondering. She ran across the kitchen, through the hall, and over to the front door. She unlocked it, her fingers trembling slightly on the enormous iron key, and pulled it open. Freddy's placid face and Ashley's sardonic one met her gaze.

'Good-oh,' Freddy said. She came into the hallway and looked around her. 'I say, this is rather nice! What do we do first?'

'Well, I'm awfully sorry but I think I'll have to wash up,' Tess said apologetically. 'Marianne must have left in a great rush – just come and look at the kitchen.'

They followed her and stood in the doorway, gazing.

'It isn't like Marianne,' Tess said defensively. 'She's usually most awfully neat and methodical, the telegram must have put her in quite a state . . . it won't take me long to clear away.'

'We'll do it whilst you pack.' The remark came simultaneously from the two Knoxes. 'It won't take more than ten minutes,'

Freddy added. 'Particularly if you'll come down and put away, because we don't know where anything goes.'

'Right. Thanks,' Tess said. 'I'll be quick.'

As soon as Tess left the kitchen, Ashley and Freddy began to clear the table and sort out the washing up.

'It's an odd house, wouldn't you say? I mean the family must be fairly well-heeled to send the kids to your school, and they board, don't they? But it's nowhere near as big as our place and it's kind of cottagey, too.'

Ashley kept his voice down but Freddy turned on him anyway.

'Hush, do! It's a really nice house, and the Broad comes right up to the end of their orchard. Mr Delamere's an accountant, he's the second partner in a firm of six. He bought the house when there was only him and Tess though, and now he doesn't want to move. Tess told me.'

Ashley sniffed and took a plate out of the plate rack. 'This isn't *clean*,' he said accusingly. 'There's egg or something on it still. You can't wash up properly in cold water, Freddy. Let me heat a kettle on the Aga.'

'It's probably out,' Freddy said. 'But you can try. Only don't be so damned critical, Ash. You upset people.'

'I don't. Well, if you mean you're upset because you handed me a dirty plate to dry up then I suppose you're right. What did you mean?'

'I meant you upset Tess. I don't know what you were saying to her, I couldn't hear a word for the wind, but she went very pink. Look, she's my best friend – the only friend I've got, really – and I don't want her put off coming back to ours. Right?'

'I haven't put her off,' Ashley said promptly. 'She likes me, even if she doesn't know it yet.'

'And you told her so, I suppose? I can't imagine why you think the way to make friends is to – Oh, there is hot water in this kettle – hooray! I'll just use this lot and then put the kettle on again. I wonder why Mrs Delamere didn't get her woman to come in for a few hours and clean through, though? Tess told me a Mrs Thrower comes in each day.' Freddy chuckled. 'Tess's mama is no keener on housework than ours, it seems.'

184

'Probably never thought. If you'd had a motor accident, Sprat, I can't say I'd worry much about a few dishes.'

Freddy turned from the sink, eyes very wide, and patted her brother's arm with a soapy hand. 'Wonders will never cease – that's the nicest thing you've ever said to me, Ashley Knox! You know I'm ever so fond of you, but you're so touchy and sarky, I never really know where I am.'

'That, my dear Sprat, is the effect I strive to acquire. Mystery is what brings women flocking to me, hadn't you realised? I've decided to have a gay old time with lots and lots of beautiful women whilst I'm young and gorgeous, then marry and settle down when I'm old and played out, say when I'm thirty.' He looped his tea-towel round his sister's neck and tugged her gently away from the sink, causing her to giggle and flick at him with the washing-up cloth. 'And I'm going to start with your little friend Tess,' he added.

'But Ash, women don't flock to you,' Freddy said, returning to the sink. 'As for Tess, she's not a woman. She's still at school, like me. Oh don't, *don't* do anything to spoil our friendship, there's a dear.'

'It will be all the stronger . . . say, Sprat, you've got a bit of a crush on Keith Arden, haven't you? You know – old 'Keefie keefie, got no teefie'.'

'It is *not* a crush. I admire Keith very much, he's – he's clever, a tremendous tennis player, he's generous, he's a first-class yachtsman . . .'

'And he's very pretty-pretty, or he would be if he had teeth,' her unfeeling brother said smartly. 'So why don't –'

'There you go again! Always sarky, never finding out the good in people, only being cruel . . . and anyway, he's got lovely, even white teeth . . . and they *don't* stick out, which is more than you can say for some people's teeth!'

'All right, all right, his teeth are perfect, like the rest of him. And I wasn't going to say they stuck out because they don't, of course. They go in a bit like teeny little weasel teeth . . . hitting me never solves anything, Sprat, because I'm bigger than you and can, if I choose, hit a lot harder.'

'You're a nasty swine, Ashley Knox!' Freddy shrieked, windmilling her fists like a whirling dervish whilst Ashley held her easily at arm's length. 'Just shut your evil gob and let me get on with this damned washing up!'

'Look, I was only going to suggest . . .'

'I don't want to hear. I *won't* hear!' Freddy dived into the sink and began to clatter plates and sing a hymn very loudly and rather tunelessly. Ashley raised his voice.

'I was going to suggest a *foursome*, brainless one! Keith and I are good friends, if you'd like to go out with him and bring Tess . . .'

'I'm not listening,' Freddy said loudly. 'Onward Christian so-o-o-oldiers . . .'

'You are. You heard every word. Do you want to get your hands on Keith's beautiful body or don't you? He likes you, he told me so.'

Freddy stopped singing. 'Likes me? How do you know?' she said suspiciously. 'I didn't think he knew I existed!'

'Well, he does. Now come on; do you want to make up a foursome with Tess, me and Keith or don't you?'

'We-ell, but suppose Keith fell for Tess? She's most awfully pretty, all that beautiful, shining black hair and those big blue eyes. Her skin's lovely, too. She doesn't go dirty brown like I do, she goes a lovely golden colour.'

'She won't fall for Keith. Not with me around,' Ashley said complacently. 'Hush, I hear her fairy footsteps on the stairs. Are you on?'

'We-ell . . .'

'Yes or no, Sprat? We've got to move fast, whilst her people are away and she's under our roof.'

'Yes, all right then! Definitely yes,' Freddy gabbled just as the door opened and Tess came into the kitchen, lugging a large black bag.

'Yes what?' she said. 'I'm packed, so we can leave as soon as I've tidied the stuff away in here. Oh, I say, you have been busy – it's beginning to look quite respectable!'

'Yes, we've done pretty well,' Ashley said, looking round the tidy kitchen. 'Can we walk down to the Broad before we go home, though? We've missed dinner, so there's no point in hurrying.'

'Sure,' Tess said. 'Follow me!'

Eight

Tess stood under the lychgate outside Blofield parish church, listening to the steady tap of the rain on the leaves of the great lime trees which lined the road and looking into the churchyard. It was much bigger than she had anticipated, and for a moment her heart failed her. What was she doing here, gazing out over that great expanse of gravestones, grass and trees, preparing to search the whole area for one grave . . . and she didn't even know what sort of stone was above it, how it would be marked!

But she was beginning to believe that of all the places he might have chosen, her father would have wanted her mother to be buried here. After all, Leonora had spent most of her short life here in Blofield; it had been the place where she and Peter had met and fallen in love. They had married here, despite the fact that Leonora's parents had not liked the match. Tess and Andy had concentrated on Walcott when they visited the Record Office, they had not even thought of Blofield, but now circumstances had made Tess consider it, and she was quietly confident that she would find Leonara's grave here, if she looked.

So she had told Freddy that she was going to search for her mother's grave, and her friend had offered to accompany her, but the Knoxes were so busy! Mrs Knox had gone off to keep an eye on her wicked nephews, Ashley had disappeared as soon as breakfast was over, and when it began to rain, Freddy had looked almost pleased.

'I know it's awful for you, but it's a real blessing for me,' she declared. 'I'm in the middle of making myself a new dress, so rain will give me the chance to finish it. We'll do something later, Tess,' she added, 'but rain like that is a bit off-putting, wouldn't you say? And you could do some sewing as well if you like, or potter round the house, or read my books. You could listen to the wireless . . . whatever you like.'

Normally, Tess would have jumped at the chance to spend a rainy morning reading her friend's books, but right now she was in an agony of impatience to get to the graveyard before something happened to prevent her search. If her father knew what she was doing he would be upset, but he didn't know . . . and I *must* find the grave, Tess told herself. It's important to me – she was my mother, after all.

So she saw Freddy settled over her dressmaking, donned her oilskins, pushed her hair under the hood, and set off.

And here she stood now, under the slight shelter of the lychgate, staring out across the churchyard. There was a long gravel path bisecting it, with the church itself on the left surrounded by what looked like very old gravestones, and the newer graves to the right. Tess imagined her mother would have been buried on the right-hand side of the graveyard, but she would have to examine both . . . and the rain was coming down like stair-rods, flattening the long grass round the edges, bouncing off the headstones, gurgling down the sides of the gravel path.

Still. No one said detection was easy, she reminded herself. So get going, Tess Delamere!

Accordingly, she retreated into the hood of her oilskin as a tortoise retreats into its shell, deserted the lychgate, and began to walk down the gravel path, examining the gravestones on either side of her as she went. She found a good few local names, including a Francis Delamere who had died at the age of eighty-eight in 1904. A grandparent? Possibly. She trudged further. More gravestones. Opposite the church she looked across and realised the enormity of her task. It's the rain, she thought despairingly. You can't look at a stone from a few yards away and read what's engraved on it, you have to be really close, nose to nose almost, before you can make out a word. It will take me weeks at this rate!

It was tempting to give up, to go back to the Knox house and curl up in a chair with a good book. But that meant the very first obstacle had beaten her – she didn't fancy writing to Andy and telling him that!

So she heaved a sigh, reached the end of the gravel path, and turned back, climbing the steep grassy bank on to the church side. She would do all the really old graves as quickly as she could, and hope that the rain would stop before she started on the newer side. Meanwhile, it was interesting, and gave her a good deal of satisfaction, to see the name Delamere on another tombstone. It helped to dispel the horrid feeling she sometimes had that she had been born at the age of three, when her father took her to the Old House and Deeping Lane.

It wasn't all that bad either, once she got going. Of course she got steadily colder as the rain seeped past her oilskins and penetrated her grey cardigan, her cotton dress, her vest, but she kept moving, which helped to warm her up a bit, and though her hands speedily went blue with cold, her feet were snug in thick socks and her sturdy wellington boots.

Some of the graves were really old, too. Tess thought them fascinating and found herself lingering over the more ancient ones, imagining what their lives must have been like in an era before motor cars, trains, telephones, wishing she might have known something about Eleanor Meadowes, who had grown up during the Regency, or little Laetitia Suffling, who had died, much mourned, at the age of six, in the mid-nineteenth century. She finished the left-hand side of the churchyard, then went down to the end, where the woods began without so much as a hedge or a fence to show where the churchyard ended, and started on the right-hand side.

This was harder work, because some of the deaths were recent enough to make her feel uncomfortably like a voyeur, if that was the word. One who snooped, who stared through the lighted windows of quiet country homes and observed the unselfconscious actions of the people within. These dead could not, she felt confusedly, have got far on their path through purgatory towards the heavenly gates. They must be seeing her, watching her as she read epitaphs, pulled aside long grass, spied on their last resting places.

What was more, instead of clearing, the rain was growing heavier and a dullness was creeping over the scene as the clouds overhead grew blacker and blacker. It looks as though a storm's brewing, Tess thought, and was tempted all over again to give up. But she'd covered a good deal of ground already, she might as well continue. I can't get much wetter, she reminded herself as the rain continued to patter on her oilskins.

Doggedly, as the sky darkened, she continued to search.

'Where's your pal, Sprat? It's such a bloody miserable day that I thought the flicks this afternoon might cheer us all up. What d'you say? I asked Keith, he's going to ring me if he can get away.'

Freddy looked up. She was sitting in her mother's small drawing-room, with the sewing machine before her, carefully clicking her way along a seam, and she was getting extremely tired of it. It was all very well to want a new dress, to say she would make herself one, but the sheer hard work of it was almost more than she could stand. And even when she finished machining, she would have to hand-stitch all the hems – the sleeves, the neck, the skirt. But although she was glad to see Ashley's face poking round the door, she didn't intend to say so. He was conceited enough as it was!

'She's sightseeing,' she snapped. 'Go away, Ash. I must finish this seam before luncheon.'

Ashley promptly came right into the room and shut the door behind him. 'It's only half past eleven,' he pointed out. 'You've at least an hour before lunch. And why can't you ever simply answer a straight question? I asked if you'd like to come to the flicks with Keith and me after lunch – that means at about two o'clock. Surely you'll have done in here by then?'

'Not if you don't leave me alone I shan't,' Freddy growled. Why could Ashley never see that his cool assumption that he knew what was best for everyone simply made people want to contradict him?

'But do you want to go?' Ashley persisted. 'I'll tell Keith yes, shall I? After all, I'll be paying – you can't afford to see Charlie Chaplin in *Modern Times* on your pocket-money I don't suppose.'

'Oh! I'd love to see that,' Freddy said, but she didn't take her eyes off her seam. Slowly, slowly, carefully, carefully . . .

'Right, that's it, then. Plans for this afternoon finally approved. Where did you say Tess was?'

190

'Sightseeing,' Freddy said briefly. 'She'll be back for luncheon.'
'Sightseeing? In *Blofield*? Dammit, Sprat, there's nothing worth
seeing in the village. Come on, where is she?'
You never learn, brother, Freddy said inside her own head.
You've never really understood that the best way to put people's
backs up and make them annoyed with you is to talk in that
impatient, suffer-fools-gladly tone. Out loud she said, 'Oh, then I
must be mistaken. She must be sitting on that chair over there,
reading a book.'
'She's not there, I looked the moment . . . oh!' Ashley stared at
her, then gave a long-suffering sigh. 'Sarcasm does not become
you, Sprat. If you don't tell me where she is this moment I'll ring
Keith and cancel this afternoon. How about that, eh?'
'When will it occur to you, Ash, that I simply don't know where
she is?' Freddy said patiently. 'Not everyone's as devious as you,
you know. She went out to have a look around the village, that's
all I know. She'll be back quite soon I expect, we'll have plenty of
time to talk about the cinema.'
It wasn't all she knew of course, but she had no intention of
telling Ashley that he might find Tess snooping round the churchyard. She was pretty sure Tess wouldn't want anyone else to
know what she was doing. It's a private sort of thing, meeting
one's mother for the first time, Freddy thought. Perhaps it's even
more private when one of you is dead. So she smiled sweetly up
at Ashley and suggested that he might like to make them both a
nice hot cup of coffee, since Mrs Brett didn't take kindly to extra
tasks during her working hours.
'Okey-dokey,' agreed Ashley, suddenly amenable. 'Shan't be
long.'
He disappeared and Freddy thankfully returned her full attention to her sewing. And when, presently, she reached the end of
the seam and carefully knotted the cotton and then snipped it
free, she had stopped thinking about Ashley at all. Her mind was
full of the new dress and whether it would be humanly possible
to wear it to the cinema that afternoon.

'Only three more to go,' Tess told herself at last, cupping her
frozen hands and blowing gently into the blue palms. 'Wouldn't

you know it – why did I start at the top end, for goodness sake? I might have guessed it would be one of the last I reached.'

But it wasn't. She examined Ruby Cotman, spinster of this Parish, who had died the previous year aged ninety-three, and Joseph John Charlesworth, who had died at the age of twenty-five, almost twenty years earlier. Then she went to the last gravestone, her heart thundering uncomfortably. This was it! It looked very new and well-tended, though . . .

She leaned over the stone and read the words engraved on it.

'In memory of Matthew Meadowes, killed at the Battle of the Somme, 1916, and of his wife, Ethel Mary, who died in April, 1925. Sadly missed.'

Wrong again, Tess thought. I wish I knew my mother's maiden name though, then I'd be able to identify my relatives. But I'll ask the Knoxes later; they might know. And now, what next?

She looked around her. Here, the churchyard became a meadow, and a little further down, a wood with great, dripping trees, brambles, nettles and drooping rosebay willow herb; a wilderness. And et . . . and yet . . .

With her oilskins swishing wetly against her legs, Tess pushed her way through the long, wild grass. She half closed her eyes and began to pray; let me find your grave, Mummy! I can't remember you, Daddy hardly ever talked about you even before Marianne, but it means so much to me to find your grave!

Truly alone now, moving far from the neatly labelled dead, Tess searched on amongst the tall, unruly grasses, the brambles, the encroaching trees.

It was a small grave, just a rounded hump, with no footstone and only a small headstone. It was almost completely hidden, but Tess, who had found it by not looking, just trusting, tore at the grasses until she could see the stone clearly. It didn't say much.

'Leonora. 10th April 1900 – 30th April 1922. Unforgettable, unforgotten.'

Tess crouched down in the long grass and put her hand on the headstone. Despite the fact that the name Delamere did not appear, she knew at once that she had found her mother's grave. Peter had loved her so much, had missed her so horribly. So much that he had caused to be written, on her tombstone, the words before her: unforgettable, unforgotten. Yet he couldn't have thought much of her last resting place since he had clearly neither visited her grave nor got anyone else to take care of it. And because of this, and his freely expressed wish that she should not pry, he had made it almost impossible for Leonora's daughter to do anything about it, either.

It was odd, though. If she had relatives here, why didn't they tend poor Leonora's grave? And – and why was she so far from the rest of the dead, pushed away down here, as though they were ashamed of her?

Tess hunched herself down inside her oilskins and concentrated. She put the tips of all her cold fingers on the headstone, closed her eyes tightly, and let her mind roam free. Come to me, Mummy, she cried in the hollow ringing blackness behind her eyelids. Tell me why Daddy is so strange about you, why your own parents didn't insist that you be buried amongst other people . . . try to tell me all the secrets, reasons, hidden truths, that my father should have told me!

Into the silence little sounds crept. A breeze touched the grasses and rain plopped off a broad grass-blade and ran down its neighbour. An insect clicked, buzzed. A bird cried, then another. In the nearby woods a chiff-chaff sang his monotonous little song and a wren whirred as it went about its business. Tess could feel calm begin to invade her mind, she felt sure that any moment now . . .

She must have gone down to the church, because there's nothing else of interest in the village, Ashley decided, setting out from the house two minutes after promising to make his sister a cup of coffee. He had donned his own oilskins and felt comfortably warm with the rain beating on the hood. He wondered if Tess might have stopped to take a look at the library, but it wasn't exactly an historic building. Now the church is old as old, and some of the brasses are said to be unique, he reminded himself. Yet, it'll be the church. Funny, because she didn't strike me as the sort to go praying all over the place, but then you don't expect girls as stunning as that one to do anything, much.

He'd been astounded by Sprat's little friend and that was the truth. He was used to her bringing friends home – she had done so constantly in Eastbourne – but as soon as he set eyes on Tess he had known she was different; special. Of course with her looks most men would be interested in her, but for him, at any rate, it wasn't just her looks. There was something very attractive in the way she held herself, the way she moved – straight-backed but graceful, like a dancer. And she had the nicest voice he thought he had ever heard, soft and musical with a laugh in it even when she was serious. He started to think about her black and glossy hair, the dark blue of her eyes, the tilt of her mouth, then stopped himself. No point. She was a stunner and he intended to sit next to her in the flicks this afternoon; further than that he was not prepared to let his thoughts go. Not yet.

He loped down the Street as far as the Turnpike, looked right towards the Globe and then left towards the King's Head. No sign of her, not that he had expected one. He crossed the main road, deserted and traffic-free in the rain, and dived down Stock's Lane. There wasn't a soul about, but no one enjoyed being out in rain like this – he would have preferred to be indoors himself, but his errand was more important than a wetting.

He turned left into Church Road and walked briskly along under the dripping limes, then dived under the lychgate and entered the churchyard. He cast a quick glance around, but did not expect to see anyone. She would be inside, of course.

It was a big church and since his family worshipped there every Sunday, Ashley knew it well. The Sunday school corner, the choir stalls, the altar, the pews. He went in cautiously, on tiptoe, just in case she was kneeling reverently, having a quiet pray, but there was no one in the pews, by the altar, looking up at the stained-glass windows. He moved slowly up the aisle towards the grave-stones with their ancient brasses; scholars came here sometimes, to do rubbings of the brasses and take them back to their pupils as an example of early whatever-it-was.

No one knelt on the tiles nor rubbed away at the brasses. Puzzled, he let his glance wander further. There were hiding places – the vestry, for one – but why should she want to hide? She wouldn't, of course. If she fancied a look in the vestry though, she might be there still.

He looked; she wasn't. He thought of the bell-tower. He knew how to get up there since he had gone with the vicar on a tour of the church when they'd first moved into the village. He went through the vestry and pulled open the small wooden door in the corner which hid the spiral stone stairs. He climbed them quickly, nimbly, sure that she must be up here. The bells were very old, probably very interesting. And on a clear day the view from the roof was remarkable, though the vicar would not approve of strangers climbing up to it in case they managed to fall over the crenellations and broke their silly necks on the ground far, far below. And of course it wasn't a clear day. But nevertheless, if anyone was interested in churches . . .

He reached the ringing chamber and looked around with only moderate interest. The ropes were down, the sallies dangling invitingly. Ashley considered giving a quick tug – he could be down again and half-way home before anyone came to investigate. But it would have been childish, a kid's trick, so he ignored the temptation and went back through the door on to the stone stair. Bell chamber next, with the great bells hanging silent, waiting for Sunday. She would be in there, peering into their vast brazen mouths, probably making notes the way girls were so fond of doing.

He opened the door and knew at once by something in the dusty silence that no one had been into the bell chamber before him. Pity. He rather fancied pouncing on her, telling her off for being up here, giving her a consoling cuddle . . .

He crossed the bell chamber, giving the nearest bell an admonitory tap with his knuckle. It was a light tap but a deep, hollow tone answered him, making him jump. Who would have thought a little tap like that could result in such a noise? Who would have thought the old man to have had so much blood in him? They'd done *Macbeth* last term . . . wasn't it unlucky to quote *Macbeth*, or was that just on the stage?

He went to the foot of the ladder which led to the roof, then climbed it. Outside, the leads were an inch or more deep in water and the rain still lashed down. The roof was empty. Ashley climbed up and cursed under his breath. She wasn't here, either – what the devil was she playing at? Or had Freddy been wrong?

Was Tess visiting someone she knew in the village? The girl had been born and bred in Norfolk, she'd seldom been out of it from what he could make out, it was likely enough, surely, that she would know someone in the neighbourhood, visit them on a rainy morning when the friend with whom she was staying had other fish to fry?

He turned disconsolately back to the ladder, then saw the reason for the flooding on the roof. Right across the middle of the tower ran a gully which, in its turn, ran into another gully which encircled the tower. A bird had made a nest out of great many twigs, mosses, lumps of clay, and the nest was blocking one of the gullies. Best clear it out of the way before the water gets any deeper, Ashley decided, feeling virtuous, because if I don't, by Sunday the water could get down into the bell chamber and cause all sorts of havoc.

He dug out the old nest, which wasn't easy with bare, wet hands, and carried it over to the parapet. No one was about, he would drop it over the edge and see it splat on to the gravel far, far below.

He held the remains of the nest at arm's length for a moment, then let go and watched, with some satisfaction, as it plummeted earthwards. He bent and picked up the rest of the muck and rubbish and threw that more prosaically over the parapet, and turned to go down the ladder. But just as he turned a flicker of movement caught his eye. Hello, Ashley said to himself, so there is someone – or something – in the churchyard after all. What is it – a dog? A fox, perhaps?

He stared out across the greens and greys and saw, in the long, wild grass only a yard or two from the woodland, that something was crouched down there. Something . . . no, it was definitely someone . . . wearing faded, beige-coloured oilskins.

Tess! He had found her! But what on earth was she doing? Had she collapsed, was she ill? He was seeing her from an odd angle, of course, but he was pretty sure she was sitting down on the ground amongst all that wet grass and not doing anything at all.

He ran over to the ladder, jumped on to it, closed the trapdoor carefully behind him, and then began the descent. He hoped she hadn't wrung her ankle or something, but if she had he would carry her home . . . the thought made his heart beat faster in delighted anticipation. He wanted so badly to hold her in his arms and if she'd sprained her ankle, hurt herself somehow, it would be the perfect excuse! But if she was all right and just sitting there for some reason he could not yet fathom, then he had best make all speed, or she might have got up and moved away by the time he left the church.

The thought lent wings to his feet. He hurtled down the ladder, then down the spiral stair, across the church . . . out into the rainy morning.

'Hello-ello-ello! Whatever are you doing, Tess Delamere? You must be soaked!'

Ashley's voice brought Tess out of her silent communion with horrible suddenness and a pounding heart. She jumped a foot, she knew she did, and was furious when he cackled with laughter. But she already knew him well enough to try to cover her fright and discomposure.

'Oh hello, Ashley. Is luncheon ready? I'm afraid I don't have a watch so the time has rather slipped away.' She scrambled to her feet. 'Sorry, I hope I haven't put anyone out.'

'No. It isn't time for luncheon.' He squatted down, clearly intent on seeing what she had been up to. 'What a very odd place to commune with nature, my dear Tess!'

'I wasn't communing with anything,' Tess said stiffly. 'Just sitting down for a moment.'

'Sitting down? On wet grass in the pouring rain in a churchyard?' Ashley cackled again. 'For no reason? Oh, I doubt that, I really do.'

He really is pretty horrible; I wonder how Freddy puts up with him, Tess thought, straightening her clothing, which had got somewhat crushed from her crouching position. But she did not intend to tell him anything, not if she could help it, so she made no reply but simply stood there, with the rain running down the inside of her oilskins as well as the outside, patiently waiting for him to move. But instead of heading out of the churchyard he came over to her and tilted her chin with one finger, staring down into her eyes with a very odd look on his face.

'You've been crying,' he said. And for once he spoke gently, as though he cared, and the finger which traced the tears down her cheek was gentle, too. And then, just as Tess was beginning to think that Ashley wasn't so bad after all, he looked behind her and began to nod his head and look smug again.

'Oh, I *see*. You've found the grave of our local bad girl and you've been crying because she's all by herself out here; is that right?'

Tess said nothing. She just stared.

'Well, young Leonora Meadowes was a suicide, you see,' Ashley said. 'She killed herself, that's why she's all by herself out here. But first she had a baby out of wedlock, by some fellow who got himself killed. So her parents threw her out, said they never wanted to see her face again. Then she married some poor sucker who fell for her and was willing to take the child on, and after a year or two I suppose she got bored with him and the kid and killed herself, like I said.' His voice changed abruptly from its rather salacious note to alarm. 'What's the matter? Where are you going?'

Tess had been frozen with shock, breathless with it, but suddenly she became galvanised; she had to get away from that hateful voice, that sneering face! She set off across the graveyard, stumbling through the wild, wet grass.

'I'm going home,' she shouted over her shoulder, her voice wobbly with tears. 'Home to the Old House. Tell Freddy I'm sorry, I c-can't stay.'

She ran. Through the wet grass, past the big old church, over the wet gravel. Ashley caught up with her under the lychgate and grabbed her, refused to let go even when she kicked and fought like a wildcat. He was white, his reddish-brown eyes round, scared.

'Tess, I'm sorry, but it doesn't matter, it isn't important! She was just a silly girl a long time ago ... everyone knows the story, I didn't think you'd mind. I've – I've made a fool of myself, but I do like you so much ... please don't hate me, I didn't mean ... didn't realise ...'

'She was my *mother*,' Tess screamed at him, suddenly too furious to care what anyone thought. 'And that poor sucker was my *father,* damn your eyes! And I didn't know *anything* until you told me and I'll hate you for as long as I live and I won't, I won't, stay under the same roof as you, I don't care how rude everyone thinks me!'

'Your *mother?*' Leonora was your *mother?* B-but you're called Delamere, she was a Meadowes, everyone knows that, so she can't be . . .'

Tess slapped his face hard. He rocked back on his heels, looking stunned. She slapped his face again, twice, the slaps cracking like pistol shots.

'Her married name was Delamere,' she shrieked. 'Women take their husbands' names when they marry, or didn't you know that? You poor ignorant bloody snob, didn't you know even that? And now let go of me or I'll claw your bloody eyes out!'

He hung on. Grimly. Still frightened by what he had done. She saw the fear in his eyes, naked and ashamed. She tried to wrestle herself free but he wouldn't let go and he kept imploring her to forgive him, to let him make it up to her.

'I didn't know, honestly,' he said, his voice cracking with sincerity. 'I swear on the bible that I didn't know. Let me . . .'

'No! No, no, *no!*' Tess shouted. She wasn't crying any more, she was too angry. 'If you don't let me go I'll kill you!'

'Look, you can't walk back to your home and there's no one there anyway . . . Please, Tess, listen to me! If I promise . . .'

She jerked herself out of his grip then and ran. Away from the road, and civilisation and people. Wildly, without thinking, she tore through the churchyard and into the trees, hearing Ashley crashing through the wet undergrowth behind her. The shock of what she had been told was still hovering, it was safest to feel anger and rage, but somewhere, in the back of her mind, a little voice was saying: *Your mother was a bad girl and your father isn't your father at all! You're a bastard, that's what your father didn't want to have to tell you – and your mother was a loose woman who didn't love you one bit – she couldn't have loved you or she'd never have killed herself. Why, she must have hated you – she died rather than stay with you!*

'Tess? Stop, will you – you'll hurt yourself! Look, it's not such a . . . Oh, my God!'

She had half turned to see how close he was and must, she realised afterwards, have run slap-bang into a tree. She reeled back, then felt the ground come up and crush dead leaves, undergrowth, wet grass, against her unresisting face. She screamed, then a heavy weight landed in the middle of her back and someone's arms went round her in a tight hug.

'My God, Tess, have I hurt you? I was so close behind that I couldn't stop myself . . . Oh my darling, *how* I love you! Please, please love me a little!'

The fall had knocked all the breath out of her and addled her wits; she could not remember what she had been doing, who this person was. She said unsteadily, 'What's happened? Where am I?' and then the speaker began to kiss her. Soft kisses trembled across the nape of her neck, moved round to the side of her face, across her chin . . . up to her unresisting mouth.

She had never been kissed before; her father's kisses were not like this! And the hands which turned her to face him were gentle, careful of her. Suddenly all the misery and horror of the last twenty minutes resurfaced and she remembered everything – the visit to the graveyard, Ashley's words, her subsequent flight. She gave a small sob, but the kissing continued, and the gentle handling, and she was past flight, past fight, too. She sighed and looked into the face so near her own, at the tangle of hair beaded with raindrops and the wet, tanned skin. She would have to face up to what he had told her, and now seemed like a good time to start.

'Ash? I hated you. I didn't know, you see. No one told me . . . just that she was dead, not that she . . .'

'It's probably just a story they tell in the village,' Ashley said. He had been lying half on top of her, now he removed his weight from her and rolled her into his arms, cuddling her wet, oilskinned figure against his chest. 'I've always been a stupid, insensitive pig but believe me, I'd never have said a word if I'd known – if I'd known you were Leonora's daughter. And your father . . . I know what I said, but it was just my stupidness . . . your father stood by her and was a real brick. I hope I'll meet him one day.'

'He's not my father,' Tess said steadily. 'He's a wonderful person, and he's been better than any real father could have been, but . . . he can't be my father. You said the man who was my father d-d-died.'

She was shaking now, with cold and shock, her voice trembling with it.

'Does it matter?' Ashley put his cold, wet face against hers and made a sweet, purring sound. 'Mr Delamere must have adopted you, I suppose. If he isn't your real father, of course. But I've never heard anyone say who – who Leonora's chap was, so it could have been your dad.'

'I don't know and I don't suppose I ever shall,' Tess said wearily. 'I'll have to think about things, but I can't face it quite yet, and until I do, I'm going to put it right out of my mind and forget I know.' She gently freed herself from Ashley's arms and stood up, then gave a muffled sob. 'Oh Ash, what do you suppose we looked like, the pair of us? Soaked to the skin, still in our oilies, and lashing around in the long grass, kissing and crying! What on earth will people think?'

'Doesn't matter because no one saw,' Ashley said, getting to his feet as well. Tess saw that he was red in the face but that his eyes were peaceful. 'I'll forget it too, then. I wish I'd kept my big mouth shut, but . . . That reminds me, I never said what I came down to the churchyard to say, either. Me and a friend of mine, Keith, thought it might be fun to go to the flicks this afternoon – you and Freddy, me and him. The new Charlie Chaplin film's showing at the Haymarket – *Modern Times*, it's called. What d'you think?'

'Can't afford it,' Tess said briefly. 'Sorry.'

'No, idiot, it's our treat, Keith's and mine.'

'Oh. Well, we'll ask Freddy, shall we?'

'Right. I expect she'll say "yes", especially if she's finished that wretched dress. And Tess – you've been a sport, honest. I promise you I won't say anything about what happened here to anyone if you won't. I'm really ashamed of myself. I behaved so badly . . .'

'I won't say a word,' Tess said tiredly. 'I just want to forget it for now. But later . . . oh, later I'm going to have a lot of sorting out to do.'

In bed that night, when the cinema trip and the fish and chip supper at Deacons were just memories, Tess fought to come to terms with what Ashley had told her. Oddly, her hatred of him, her disgust, had evaporated as though it had never been. It was not his fault that he had, unknowingly, told her the truth, and heaven knew he had said he was sorry in every way he knew how. She remembered that she hadn't liked him much before he'd told her those dreadful things in the churchyard but now, after the kisses and the huggings, she realised that Ashley was quite a complex person and that the sneery way he behaved sometimes was some sort of defence. She had talked it over with Freddy before Freddy had fallen asleep, and Freddy had assured her that Ashley, though he could be sarcastic and tactless, even cruel, was also often generous and kind. Tess trusted Freddy's judgement, but had no intention of getting too involved with Freddy's brother. He knew too much.

She wondered what she should say to Peter, when he and Marianne and Cherie came home. Should she tell him she knew what had happened to her mother? But it wasn't quite true; she knew that Peter had married Leonora and brought up Leonora's child as his own, but she didn't know who her real father was. She supposed it must be the boy who had been killed, but she didn't know for sure. And had Leonora committed suicide, or was that just spiteful village gossip? Tess had lived in a small village for long enough to realise that it really did exist. People would believe what they wanted to believe and deny the truth if it pleased them to do so. So it was quite possible, then, that Leonora's boat had come to pieces just as Peter had said. If only – oh, if *only* he hadn't lied!

On thinking it over, she was shocked to find that her own illegitimacy mattered deeply to her. Now and then, when she least expected it, the words *I'm a bastard* would enter her mind and each time they did, she felt a stab of pain. And what Peter had said about her maternal grandparents' attitude hurt, too. I was only a child but she wouldn't see me, didn't want to know me, Tess thought. It would have been awfully nice to have a granny, all lavender water and lace caps and those mittens with the fingers out, who would feed me with sugar almonds and tell me stories about when she was a girl. She might have told me about Leonora, too, made the whole thing easier to bear. But she couldn't have been a very nice woman, to throw her daughter out like that and never have her back, not even after she married.

She understood now why she had seen so little of her paternal grandparents, too, in fact she found their attitude much easier to understand than that of Leonora's parents. Why should they welcome a child who was no blood relative into their family? They had retired to a cottage in Ilfracombe, North Devon, when she had been quite small and though Peter wrote to them and they wrote back, it had not been suggested that visits might be exchanged. *Indeed, I know Marianne's family better than I know the Delameres,* Tess realised with a slight pang. *And I don't like the Duprés one bit!*

There was Uncle Phil, of course, and the cousins. She didn't see much of them, but they exchanged visits from time to time. Auntie May was always very sweet to her and the cousins were friendly, though they were older than she, already working, living away from home.

But of course they aren't my cousins, and Uncle Phil and Auntie May aren't related to me either, Tess found herself thinking. A dreadful coldness began to seep into her mind. In one blow she had lost everything – identity, parents, relatives. *And if her mother had killed herself, that was the worst pain of all, because it must mean, it had to mean, that she hadn't loved the young Tess. Not even enough to bring me up,* Tess mourned now. *She must have loved Daddy, because he's such a wonderful person, so it must have been having me that pushed her into doing what she did. Dear God, she must have hated having a daughter!*

But balanced against that was Peter's love, which had been strong enough to take on someone else's baby. It was impossible to doubt the depth of his love, which was a warming thought. But other thoughts, cold ones, crowded in thick and fast. *Marianne hates me. I tried to get her to like me but it never did work and she hates me. Cherie doesn't care much one way or the other, she just likes a quiet life. And Andy hasn't been back and we were good friends – I thought we were, anyway.*

What about Janet, though? Janet was still very much her friend, and Mrs Thrower's warmth and affection were always there.

When Tess behaved badly Mrs Thrower mobbed her as she did her own kids, but forgiveness was always there at the end of the day, warm arms and a motherly hug would welcome her the next time she called round.

Am I bad or good? Tess asked herself, tossing and turning in her bed in the guest room at the Blofield house. Ashley likes me, he kissed and cuddled me beautifully – but suppose he likes me because he thinks I'm a loose woman, like my mother? Suppose he thinks I'll 'come across' as they say in books? Alarmingly, it occurred to her that girls were not supposed to enjoy being kissed and cuddled by boys they scarcely knew. Was it a sign of loose morals to enjoy such things? Girls at school talked about kisses and more as though it was all wonderful, wicked, daring. But if my mother got into trouble then I should be especially careful not to do the same, Tess told herself. Oh, how I wish I'd never found that poor, strange little grave, all by itself in the long grass! I thought I wanted to know the truth – but the truth hurts like a knife twisting in an open wound so that I can hardly bear it.

At midnight she heard the grandfather clock strike twelve times, then she slept, waking at two a.m. when the life force is at a low ebb and unhappiness hovers behind one's sleepless shoulder. She sat up and looked across the room at the lighter patch which was the window and thought: *I'm a different person. Like Pandora in the Greek legend I opened the box and all the troubles of the world flew out and buzzed around my ears. The carefree, inquisitive Tess of yesterday has gone for ever, and quite a different person has come in her place.*

Presently, she slept again, only to wake an hour later. This time the thought leapt straight into her mind: *How will I face Daddy, knowing what I do?* It wasn't as if she could talk it over with a friend, tell Mrs Thrower, ask Freddy's opinion. That would be cruelly unfair to her father, a real betrayal. He had moved from Blofield to Barton to try to keep clear of gossip and conjecture, she must be careful not to let him down, to give away a secret which was more his than hers.

She had sat up on the thought, but now she lay slowly down again. She was alone, she had always been alone, therefore her problems would have to be solved by her alone.

She was trying hard to go back to sleep when another thought hit her, so hard that she sat up like a jack-in-the-box.

Andy! He had known there was a mystery four years ago, when they were both kids. They hadn't met since, but they'd written, she knew his address, didn't she? She could even telephone if she was desperate. And to confide in Andy wouldn't be disloyal because he was far away, either in boarding school or in Paris or Rome or wherever his work had taken Andy's father.

Yes, Andy was the answer. Immensely reassured, Tess lay down again. How could she have thought she was alone? She had a loving father and good friends – Mrs Thrower, Janet . . . and Andy. It would be such a help to talk to Andy, tell him what she had discovered, discuss with him what her next move should be. Her eyelids were drooping, her problems no longer seemed insoluble. Andy would help, explain, tell her what to do.

Soon, she slept.

The dream, when it came, was different; worse. The beach no longer seemed a safe and gentle place for a child to play, it was lit with a strange, dangerous yellowish light. The very sea seemed antagonistic, the waves menaced her, rolling in topped with foam which seemed, to her childish dream-eyes, like angry tiger-claws, arched to pounce.

She did not do as she usually did and go down to the tideline, therefore, but kept well up the beach. And looking out to sea saw, for the first time, the boat. Small, seeming black in the lurid light, it crawled up the wave crests and swooped giddyingly into the troughs and though she had no recollection of why she should be seeing a boat it frightened her, brought the breath sobbing into her throat.

She turned to the long pool beside the breakwater and as soon as she did so the sun came out from behind the clouds and shone on the dark golden hump of the sand, on the little shells, the occasional gleam of a wet pebble, a strand of dark-red weed. She forgot the angry sea, the little cockleshell of a boat, her fears. This was her place, where she had most wanted to be! She sat down and took off her shoes and socks, then glanced behind her.

The boy was coming, hurrying. He would spoil it all, boss

her about, tell her what to do! She jumped to her feet and the shoes and socks plummeted into the water. Oh, she was in trouble now! The shoes were brand new, she shouldn't have been wearing them on the beach!

The boy reached her, snatched her up . . . and she saw that the sky was lurid once more, the light horrible. She struggled to get down, she pointed to her shoes, moving to the tide's whim far below the surface, and then she saw . . . she saw . . .

Before her eyes the scene began to shift and blur, to tilt and dance crazily even as she opened her mouth and screamed and screamed . . .

The screams woke her. She sat up, trembling violently, and realised someone had their arms round her, someone's face was close to hers.

'Hush, hush, my love, it was just a nightmare, only a nightmare. Do hush, or you'll have the whole family awake!'

She had difficulty orientating herself. The room was grey, the light coming in through the window strangely subdued . . . but there were no trees outside her window, she looked straight out on to the silvered surface of the Broad! What on earth was happening? Was she still dreaming? She twisted in the arms that held her; a man's arms, trying to look into his face with eyes that were still unfocused, sleep-filled.

'Daddy?' She knew as she said the word that it couldn't be Peter. The feel of the arms around her was all wrong, and the smell, too. But she knew it was a man, and in the confusion of sleep only just banished she could not think of anyone else who could come to her in the night. 'Did I wake you?'

Someone laughed softly and nuzzled her neck with his mouth.

'Idiot! It's me, Ashley. I heard you shout so I came through.'

'Oh,' Tess said vaguely. 'Sorry.' Of course, she was at Freddy's house, in Blofield, and Freddy's brother had come into her room when he heard her scream. She frowned. 'But your room is the other side of the house; you couldn't have heard me,' she said with certainty. 'Freddy's right next door . . . I didn't disturb her.'

'Freddy sleeps like the dead . . . and keep your voice down, sweetheart, or you'll have Mum and Dad down on us like a ton of bricks. What on earth were you dreaming about? You shrieked like a steam train going into a tunnel.'

He was lying on her bed! Tess squiggled her arms free of him and gave him a shove. 'Get off! How dare you come into my room in the night! If you don't go at once I'll scream a lot louder than that!'

He swung his legs off the bed and sat up. 'Don't get in a fuss,' he said. 'A lot happened to you today, I was afraid you might sleep badly. I dossed down in the green room, next door to you. Aren't you glad I woke you?'

'You didn't. I always wake then,' Tess said frostily. 'And what do you mean . . .'

Her voice faded away. Recollection of the day's events, cold as a bucket of iced water tipped over the head, flooded her.

'What do you mean, you always wake then?' Ashley's voice was indulgent, amused. 'Do you often have nightmares?'

'Not often. Sometimes. Do buzz off, Ash, I'm all right now. And don't doss down in the green room on my account. I'm all right as soon as I wake up.'

He shrugged. His face was a white blur in the greyness of the night. Then, unexpectedly, he stood up, turned round, bent, and kissed her very gently on her unprepared mouth. She couldn't help the little gasp she gave, nor the way her heart began to hammer. It doesn't mean a thing, she told herself severely, snuggling defensively under the covers again. It was how everyone felt when someone who was almost a stranger kissed you.

'Good-night, darling Tess,' Ashley murmured. 'See you in the morning.'

'Good-night,' Tess said, making her voice as cool and remote as possible. Just who did Ashley Knox think he was? She liked Freddy very much, was sure she would like her parents once she got to know them, but her brother was a different matter, a different kettle of fish. It wasn't just what he had said about her mother and about Peter, it was something about Ashley . . . she didn't think he was very trustable, if there was such a word, nor did she want the sort of relationship with him which he seemed to imply when he called her darling, sweetheart.

Still, she needn't stay if things got difficult. Two days ago I really wanted a boyfriend, she realised sleepily. But now I'm not at all sure. It's such a *complication*, it makes things so difficult. He had put his arm round her in the pictures in front of Freddy and that Keith person . . . in front of a whole cinema full of people, come to that. And he'd kept sort of snuggling . . . it wasn't until she got really fed up and bit the hand which was stroking along the line of her jaw, at the same time pinching his intrusive other hand with all her might, that he got the message and withdrew a little.

'He isn't terribly sensitive,' Freddy had said apologetically when they were getting ready for bed, sharing the bathroom and giggling together. 'But he really does like you, Tess. I've never known him fall so heavily for a girl before, honest.'

'Well, I haven't fallen for him,' Tess had said briskly, spreading paste on her toothbrush. 'He's your brother and very nice, I'm sure, but to be honest, Freddy, I scarcely know him and I don't like being . . . oh, taken for granted, I suppose.'

'I'll warn him to back off a bit, then,' Freddy agreed. 'Because I do want you to come and stay again, I don't want you put off!'

But she couldn't have warned him before they went off to bed, there had been neither the time nor the opportunity. So he had sneaked into the room next to hers and curled up on the bed . . . spying on me, Tess thought, and felt the heat rise in her cheeks. How could he – how dared he! What was the world coming to when a girl couldn't even have a nightmare in peace?

She was almost asleep again when a most unwelcome thought struck her. Suppose Ashley thought *Like mother like daughter*? Suppose he assumed that because Leonora had conceived a child out of wedlock then Leonora's daughter would be prepared to – to –

The thought was so horrid that it brought her eyes wide, had her struggling into a sitting position once again. Could he have somehow assumed . . . But then she remembered that he had been far too interested in her before the churchyard episode. Ashley, she supposed, was simply chancing his arm. Some would, some wouldn't, and he wasn't sure yet into which category each girl fell.

She lay down again. I'm behaving like a yo-yo on a string, she thought crossly. If I keep lying down and sitting up every time something occurs to me I'll never go back to sleep. She tried to think soothing thoughts, to remember Andy in patched grey shorts and a checked shirt, with his glasses gleaming, telling her that they would find out about her mother. Little did he know! But just remembering that long-ago summer was soothing and might have worked had it not suddenly occurred to her that there was one dilemma which she simply had to meet head on. When the Delameres returned from France she would have to face Peter, and try to behave naturally, because she did not think she could ever tell him all she knew.

With a sigh, she rolled over and sat up on one elbow. Right! Sleep was out of the question; she would spend the rest of the night deciding exactly what she would say to Andy when she rang him next morning.

Waking was odd; she felt fuzzy in the head and her mouth tasted horrid, as though she was recovering from a long illness. She had felt like this, she remembered, after a bad bout of measles when she was seven.

But she was a guest in the Knoxes' house so she got up, washed, dressed and made her way downstairs. Breakfast was being prepared by Mrs Knox in the kitchen whilst Mr Knox was upstairs.

'He's having his bath,' Mrs Knox said. Tess, who had only just emerged from the bathroom herself, realised this must mean there were two bathrooms and, from the casual way Mrs Knox spoke, that a daily bath was a normal routine for her husband. Despite herself, she was impressed. As one who now queued up for a weekly bath – if she was lucky – the thought of bypassing all that lengthy flannel business was enviable . . . how clean all the Knoxes must be!

'You're early,' Mrs Knox went on affably, shaking the grill pan so that the kidneys spluttered and spat. 'I'm afraid Freddy and Ash won't be up for at least an hour. They're lazy little beasts in the school hols. Want your brekker now?'

'Well, if it isn't too much bother,' Tess said. She had a healthy appetite and breakfast, for her, was a seven-thirty affair at the latest. 'Just tea and toast will be fine, though. Then – then I thought I might go for a stroll in the village, if you don't need me for anything.'

'Tea and toast, and you a growing girl? Nonsense, you'll have kidneys, bacon and scrambled egg like the rest of us,' Mrs Knox said briskly. 'Ah, here he comes. Be a darling, Tess, and cut a round of bread off that loaf and shove it in the toaster; Mr Knox likes toast with his scrambled egg.'

When breakfast was finished Mr Knox went out to his car and Tess washed up the dishes and then ventured out into the sunny morning. She had her purse in the pocket of her flowered cotton dress and was really looking forward to talking to Andy after so long. Of course she didn't know where he was, but she had plenty of change and she knew Lady Salter's number by heart; his great-aunt was bound to have his telephone number or if not, at least his address. Directory enquiries would do the trick.

There was a red telephone box outside the post office, Tess had noticed it the previous day. She went into its odd-smelling interior, lifted the receiver, set out her pennies, sixpenny bits and shillings on the shelf below the little mirror, and picked up the receiver. Now it had come to the point she discovered she was nervous, but nothing venture, nothing win, she reminded herself and, when the operator spoke, asked for Lady Salter's number.

Distantly, she heard the telephone bell, then an elderly – and crotchety – voice spoke in her ear.

'Hello? Who's that?'

Tess pressed Button A with trembling fingers and said, 'Lady Salter?'

'That's right. Whom am I addressing?'

'Oh, it's Tess Delamere, Lady Salter, I'm trying to get in touch with – with your great-nephew, Herbert Anderson. Can you tell me where he is, please?'

There was a very long pause. Tess, conscious of her pennies clicking away, tried to be patient, but it was hard going.

'Herbert? My daughter's second boy, d'you mean?'

'Yes, that's right. He stayed with you one summer four years ago – do you remember, Lady Salter? I'm Tess Delamere, he and I were very friendly that summer. I rather want to get in touch . . .'

'Not possible.'

'Isn't he on the telephone, then? I know he's probably abroad but I thought if he was in an embassy they might be on the telephone and . . .'

'No, no, not possible,' Lady Salter repeated impatiently. 'The boy's gone.'

'Gone? Left home, d'you mean? Then perhaps if I could telephone his parents they could . . .'

Lady Salter interrupted again; testily, this time.

'My dear Miss Delamere, when I say gone' – she pronounced it *gawn* – 'I mean gone. He's with friends; they're touring India in a bullock cart and hope to do most of the Middle East before returning home in a year's time. I dare say they won't be anywhere near a telephone for the next six months. Thank you for calling.'

And down went her receiver so sharply that Tess's ear buzzed.

'But Lady Salter . . .' she began, then, realising the futility of it: 'You nasty old woman, a fat lot you care!' She put her own receiver on to its hook and turned disconsolately away. Andy was unreachable. Now what should she do?

It was a fine October afternoon with a stiff breeze blowing across the face of the Broad. Through the trees, which no longer carried their summer burden of rich and glossy leaves, Peter could see the sails of three or four small craft as they tacked and turned across the Broad, avoiding the buoys, shallow water, mud banks.

Peter and his wife were sitting on the small terrace which he had made between the house and the long back lawn. When she came back from France Marianne had insisted on buying a long pink-and-orange swing seat with a striped awning and flowery cushions. Peter had thought it a foolish and frivolous purchase, but now he was not so sure. They had used it all through the autumn and he guessed that it would be brought out again in the spring. It smiled at them as they worked around the house, and beckoned. Come out and laze, it said, and quite often in the past eight weeks since they had returned from France, Peter and Marianne had answered the call. Tea on the terrace, which had been a dream rather than a reality, was now taken out here whenever the weather was fine, and Tess and Janet spent time out here too, swinging and chatting, knowing they were tolerated outside whereas, within doors, Marianne would have complained every time they laughed.

So now Marianne lounged back against the cushions, swinging the seat with one foot whilst Peter sat and frowned into space. Finally he jerked his head at the sailing dinghies and spoke.

'She's changed. We were away ten days, almost no time, yet when we came home she was different. Look at her now!'

'She's the cat's mother,' Marianne said amiably. 'Do you refer to Cherie, or to Tess?'

Peter raised his eyes to heaven. 'Is Cherie sailing out there? Did Cherie stay in England for ten days whilst we swanned off to France? Has she changed?'

'Sarcasm is the lowest form of wit,' Marianne informed him. 'Do I take it, then, that you mean Tess has changed? I've not noticed.'

'No. You wouldn't. You don't notice Tess much at all, do you, Marianne?'

'Not much,' Marianne admitted, and Peter was unable to stop a small grin playing about his mouth. One of the things he continued to love about Marianne – and they were getting fewer every day – was her ability to speak the whole truth even when it did her no credit. 'But still waters run deep, and Tess doesn't tell me much. Besides, she's almost a woman. I do not like women.'

'You didn't like her when she was only a kid,' Peter started to stay, then stopped, shaking his head at himself. No point in stating the obvious and besides, Tess was clearly a kid no longer. She was a very attractive young woman, young men were beginning to buzz round her like bees round a honeypot, and Peter did not like it. He particularly did not like Ashley Knox and that was strange, because Ashley was, he supposed, the type of young man most parents would encourage gladly. He was at university studying law, his father was a prominent and successful lawyer with a very large firm indeed, and Ashley's sister was one of Tess's closest school friends.

So why don't I like him? Peter mused, staring across at the little sails outlined against the sun-silvered Broad until his eyes watered. Why don't I trust him? Why do I have to fight a horrible urge to tell him to get his filthy paws off my darling girl and leave her for someone more worthy?

'You don't like the Knox boy,' Marianne said, and Peter stared at her, convinced for a moment that she had read his mind. 'So why should you expect me to like Tess? You're jealous, and so am I.'

'Jealous? Me? Of my own *daughter*? That's a very unpleasant suggestion, Marianne. Very unpleasant and totally untrue. I simply don't trust young Knox to – to do the right thing by her.'

'He's a delicious young man and she's lucky to have caught his interest,' Marianne said flatly. 'I take it they're sailing this afternoon?'

'Yes. Practising. He's running her over to Oulton tomorrow to compete in some race or other.' Peter yawned and stretched, then leaned forward to peer into the teapot on the low white table by his knees. 'I wonder if this will run to another cup?'

He tested the pot, but it was cool, so he got to his feet and headed for the kitchen. 'Just going to make new tea,' he called over his shoulder. 'Shan't be a mo.'

Inside, busying himself with filling the kettle, he could have kicked himself for mentioning Tess. It brought out the bitch in Marianne, there was no doubt of that. And no one, seeing them together, could help making comparisons. Tess with her clear, pale skin, the gleam of health on her hair, the perfect teeth, the slender, long-legged figure. And Marianne. She was growing plump, rather saggy, her skin showing big pores around nose and chin, lines which came from her frequent bouts of peevishness running horizontally across her forehead, vertically between nose and mouth.

Yet I still love a good many things about her, Peter reminded himself. She can be loving, generous, amusing . . .

But not to Tess. Never to Tess.

He put the half-filled kettle over the hob and went and stood by the window, his original worry returning. They had gone off to France leaving a sweet-tempered, pretty young girl. They had returned to find a rather remote young woman. For the first week, she had kept looking at him whenever she thought he wasn't looking at her. Speculatively. What was worse, when he became worried and went to her room, sat on the end of her bed, reached for her hands to ask her what was the matter, she had snatched them away as if he was poison and coloured hotly.

'Don't,' she had mumbled. 'I'm not a baby any more. I'm all right, I can deal with Marianne.'

For once, he hadn't been going to ask her to 'deal with Marianne'. He had said quietly, 'Sweetheart, what's wrong?' and quite uncharacteristically she had burst into tears and repeated, in a muffled voice, that he must leave her alone.

Her grief was noisy and he was afraid Marianne might march in and make things worse, make a scene, shout, scream, have hysterics. She had done all of those things in her time, especially if she thought Peter was paying too much attention to his elder daughter, and he felt, instinctively, that Tess couldn't cope with that now no matter how grown-up and capable she felt herself to be. So he had patted her timidly on the shoulder, tried to ignore her growl of 'Don't *pat* me, I'm not a *dog*,' and left her.

Later, he had returned to the subject; outside this time, when the two of them were picking apples in the orchard, with one up the tree and the other on the ground to receive the fruit. It had been gusty, sunny, a wonderful day for apple picking, and they had both been in a friendly, relaxed mood.

'Tess, love, you've not been quite yourself since we got home from France,' Peter had said, as he took the ripe fruit from her hands and placed it tenderly in the big wheeled wicker basket. 'Did anything happen whilst we were away?'

She had shrugged carelessly, but avoided his eyes. 'No. I don't think so. I enjoyed myself tremendously though – the Knoxes were awfully kind to me.'

'Good, good. You must ask Freddy to come and stay here for a week or so then. In the spring, perhaps.'

'I will. Oh . . . one thing did happen, Daddy.'

She handed him down a huge, rosy-cheeked cooker. Play it cool, old man, or she'll never confide in you again, he commanded himself, whilst awful possibilities reared their ugly heads. Was she going to tell him someone had made a pass at her? That she had been . . . hurt, or interfered with in some way? But he kept his voice level, friendly, did not allow it to rise in panic.

'Oh? What was that, love?'

'I wanted to contact Andy – you know, Herbert Anderson – so I rang Lady Salter to get details, and she told me Andy's off with a crowd of friends touring India in a bullock cart. She said they're returning via the Middle East and wouldn't be near a telephone for six months. Isn't he lucky, Daddy? But I wish he'd told me. I really do miss Andy.'

The relief was so great he would have sworn it was tangible, a physical thing. It brought a big, foolish smile to his face, a sparkle, he was sure, to his eyes. He beamed up at her. 'You never know what you'll be doing, pet, once you've taken your Higher, next year. I suppose Andy's having a year off before going into one of the embassies, like his father. Would you think?'

'I don't know, Lady S didn't say.' She sighed. 'I do miss him,' she repeated.

Afterwards, of course, there were moments when Peter wondered whether she had simply told him about Andy's great adventure to put him off the scent, so that he would stop worrying about the change in her. But gradually he was beginning to accept that his open-faced, trustful little daughter had gone for good. In her place was a watchful, guarded stranger. Oh, he loved the stranger, admired the unusual beauty which was beginning to blossom (so like, so very like, Leonora!), but there were times when he would have given almost everything he possessed to have his little girl back.

The kettle boiled and Peter made fresh tea and carried the pot out to where Marianne lounged on the swing-seat. He poured tea into two cups, added milk, handed one to his wife who took it with a murmur of thanks, sipped, then put the cup down and lay back again. Presently, her breathing steadied and deepened. She slept.

Peter got up, careful not to jerk the seat, and made his way across the wide lawn, through the trees and down to where the Broad began with a gradual marshiness, then tall reeds, then the deepening water. The boats were returning to the staithe now, their practice presumably over for the day. He could pick out his daughter's dark head anywhere . . . he grinned to himself as that puppy helped her out of the boat and tried to hug her and got shoved sharply away. Good for you, old girl, he thought approvingly. Don't let the little bugger get too close. I know what boys are like – I should do, I was one, a million years ago.

It made him remember, that little cameo of a scene, the lithe and lovely girl stepping out of the boat, pushing the handsome boy aside, turning back to the boat, gathering up an armful of possessions . . .

Leonora. She had died young so she would always be young to him. Unforgettable, unforgotten, a lass unparallel'd. Who had said that – a lass unparallel'd? The first words were from Rupert Brook's poem about the Old Vicarage, Grantchester . . . the next bit? Not me, I'm not clever enough, Peter thought humbly. Shakespeare, probably. He seemed to say most things well. And that just about put Leonora in a nutshell – a lass unparallel'd. God, he had loved her! He could still remember the twist of pain in his gut, the ache which was so bad that he could scarcely sleep or eat, when someone had told him she'd taken a shine to Ziggy Freeman, was going with him.

Though there were worse pains; unrequited love had been an agony for a young and impressionable boy in his late teens, but losing her to death! To see all that brightness and beauty brought to nought, to know they would never touch, kiss, laugh together again! He dared not think of it lest he resurrect the terrible emptiness of those first few months, the moments when he, too, hovered on the brink, knowing that nothing would ever compare with what he and Leonora had had.

The child had kept him going, of course. But all that came later. It had started when beautiful Leonora had fallen in love with Ziggy Freeman. She was the loveliest girl, Ziggy the handsomest, most eligible young man in their circle. They had been so exultantly happy and so right for each other, so deeply, dramatically in love. So Leonora and Ziggy made their plans, but never had a chance to carry them out; tragedy struck. Ziggy, hurrying back to Norwich after a successful job application and riding his motor cycle too fast on a wet road surface, skidded on a sharp bend, fought to control his machine, and met an oak tree head on. Poor Ziggy, tall, flamboyant, head over heels in love with Leonora, full of enthusiasm for his new, well-paid job. He should have taken her up the aisle, bought her a little house, spent a happy lifetime with her. Instead, he gasped out his life alone on a wet, cloud-reflecting road whilst blood pumped steadily out of a great hole in his neck.

Leonora's parents had disapproved of Ziggy so their daughter had moved into the city, into a bedsit, so that they could see one another without constant arguments, but she came back to the village for the funeral. Peter saw her in a back pew, crying as a child cries, with gulps and sobs and big tears, totally bereft. And when the service was over and the congregation had gone their separate ways he had followed her to the bus stop on the turnpike and reminded her that he had always loved her, that nothing would give him more pleasure than to be allowed to take care of her.

'I love you, Leo and I'd make sure you were never lonely,' he had told her tenderly, holding her small hands in his and looking earnestly down into her tear-drenched countenance. 'I can't ever take Ziggy's place I know, but we could have a good life, sweetheart. I promise you that.'

He had done his best. He had never faltered in his love for her, he had quite simply adored their little girl, but he had never known, for certain, how Leonora felt about him. Oh, he thought she loved him, but he had learned that there are many degrees of love. The wild passion of first love which she had known with Ziggy would never – could never – be repeated. Was what they had enough? He had thought it was until that dreadful telephone call, the maid's voice, distraught, almost inaudible through her sobs.

'Come at once, sir . . . there's been an accident!'

He had known, then. Oh, not that she was dead, but that she must be badly hurt. If it had been the child Leonora would have telephoned herself. He had driven like a madman, arriving home in Walcott to be told first that she was lost at sea, that the little boat had overturned . . . then that they had found her body.

The sea had been rough, the wind strong, but not enough to capsize a boat, surely? Leonora had been fit and well, not a brilliant oarswoman, perhaps, but someone had seen her rowing steadily along the coast. An old man, up on the cliffs poaching rabbits, claimed he had seen her stand up in the boat, then jump into the water. Deliberately. So the old parson had only agreed to bury her in the churchyard if she was away from the other graves. Down near the trees, where no one ever went.

He hadn't cared. Wherever that bright and beautiful spirit had gone, it didn't linger in a graveyard, mourning her separation from the other dead. Besides, he had other worries. His failure to make her happy paled into insignificance beside the bringing up of their little girl, how he should behave now that he was on his own, whether it would be right to leave their home, move on to where they weren't known . . . these things occupied him, kept him from despair.

But now, standing on the margin of the Broad watching as his daughter and her companion pulled the boat out, dealt with the sails, the mast, their gear, he could still remember every line of Leonora's profile, every fluid movement. Leonora, so like Tess. When Tess reached up for the mast, one long, lovely line, pain, raw as salt in a wound, stabbed him. Ziggy gone, Leonora gone . . . but he had survived and was, he reminded himself briskly, turning back towards the terrace, a damned lucky fellow. He was happy, Marianne was a good wife in many ways, Tess and Cherie good daughters. His home was much loved, he was successful at work and could still play a brisk game of squash, a punishing round of golf. Whilst Leonora . . .

Tears formed in his eyes and he stared at the house and the terrace as though through water. God, he missed her!

Nine

Uncle Josh had been old when Mal first took over as head stock-man at the Wandina, but he didn't get ill until he got bit by the red-back spider – if it was a red-back – and it wasn't until he got bit by the red-back that Mal discovered the disadvantages of illness in the wet.

Wally had come back from hospital within a couple of months of Mal arriving, but he was crippled and there was no hope of any further recovery, the doctors said. Fortunately, Wally was the sort of man who took everything philosophically. He limped into the kitchen at Wandina that first evening, grinned at Mal, said, 'G'day; you the new head stockman?' and then slumped into a chair.

'G'day. You'll be Wally,' Mal said carefully. Wally was tall and broad, even though he limped. 'I ain't took your job, you know. It's just that Uncle Josh needed a temporary replacement . . .'

'Came to say you ain't a temp'rary replacement no more,' Wally interrupted. 'This 'un . . .' He slapped his right leg, which was shorter than the left and drawn up in an awkward manner, the knee pointing always inwards. '. . . This 'un won't work no more, not ever. The docs say it's crook for good. I'll never ride another muster. Right?'

'What'll you do?' Mal said, horrified by the other man's words. 'If you can't ride . . .'

'I can cook, sew, mend harness, tack up, mebbe even shoe a horse,' Wally said. 'I ain't never tried to shoe a horse, but if the smith'll learn me . . .'

'You can cook?' Mal's voice rose to an adolescent squeak from sheer excitement. He was so sick of trying to cook, trying to jam some ideas other than bully beef and sweet potatoes boiled to mush into Maisie's head . . . He cleared his throat and dropped his voice into his boots. 'You say you can *cook*? Oh boy, oh boy, oh *boy!*'

From that moment on, they'd got on great, just great. Wally wasn't just any cook, he was superb. He read up recipes and followed them to the letter, spent hours 'figurin' out' as he called it why a dish had not turned out quite as planned, and took an enthusiastic interest both in the ordering of supplies, which was a nightmare for Mal, and in the growing of their garden, though he could not do much in the way of heavy digging or planting out.

Uncle Josh paid him a good wage and his keep, so that was all right, and though occasionally Wally watched them going off on a muster and then got roaring drunk, he was always sober again by the time Mal and the hands rode home and Uncle Josh just chuckled and said it wasn't a *serious* binge, just a 'poor bloody Wally' one.

In the two years which had elapsed since Mal had left the Magellan, he had been home twice, and found to his surprise that he had thoroughly enjoyed both visits. Royce and Kath were patently happy and the new baby, Susie, was a plump and chuckling armful who was adored by everyone on the station, especially the twins.

'We earn good money lookin' after her, Mal,' Bart told him. 'We takes her out in the tug-cart an' sit her on the swing . . . and Mum counts the hours we do and Dad pays us at the end of the week.'

It made Mal chuckle, but he admired his mother's planning. She had got herself two happy little boys who were doing just as she wished and thinking themselves lucky to be doing it.

And now that he was away from the Magellan, he got on very much better with Royce. Royce said he was much missed, which is always good to hear, and then the two of them discussed the running of their separate stations and Mal unashamedly picked Royce's brains and Royce said he was going to take on several of Mal's ideas.

But getting back to the Wandina was best. Until Josh trod on the red-back, that was.

They had had a good Christmas. The hands loved the wet because they couldn't do anywhere near as much work with the river swollen and every creek a torrent and they loved Christmas because of the presents, the food and the fun and games. That year, Uncle Josh had got store-bought presents for them, putting in a big order in November and then being very secretive over six packing cases and not allowing anyone else near them.

Excitement reached fever pitch on Christmas Eve and spilled over into wild revels on Christmas Day. Then things quieted down a trifle, what with the wet and all.

Mal decided afterwards that the red-back – if that's what it was – must have come in from the wet, because the day Uncle Josh was taken bad the rain was coming down like great steel rods, sizzling and bouncing on the baked earth, making clouds of steam rise up from the tops of banks and the ridges of the plough. They had had a good breakfast, starting with porridge, going on with fried potatoes, bacon and eggs and finishing up with a good deal of bread and butter spread thick with marmalade. Wally made the nicest marmalade Mal had ever tasted. He made it from their own fruit but instead of using just oranges he used lemons too and a few limes, and it was so good that Kath, presented with a tub last winter, in the dry, had actually asked Wally for his recipe.

Uncle Josh was pottering round as usual in an old pair of carpet slippers, with his reading glasses on his nose in case he saw something he fancied reading. There had been a storm of alarming ferocity in the night and when Mal looked out of the window at about three a.m. it was like trying to look through a waterfall, so he wasn't surprised to find three angry scorpions in the bathtub that morning and that was a sure sign that the migration had begun. He had warned Uncle Josh to look out, but they all knew there was a lot of luck involved with creepies. There were just so many of them around the house and outbuildings once the wet got going.

Mal still wasn't truly used to it – the migration. Kath called it that. She said that the moment the wet started every living creepy-crawly – and that included snakes, scorpions and spiders – would be fighting for a place in a nice dry house or store, so everyone had to look out. She also said that nothing bites you for fun, only if it believes you're threatening its life, but no one seemed to have told the creepies this interesting fact. Mal had been stung by a scorpion within a month of arriving at the Magellan, and only prompt action by Royce, who had cut the wound, sucked out the poison and doused it with meths, had saved him from what Royce had called 'a nasty experience'.

And when it rained the way it had last night damage was nearly always done. The Wandina owned four boats, two quite large and two very small, and because of the way the river had risen they would now be bobbing about in midstream – if their anchor ropes hadn't snapped, that was. So Mal was getting ready to go out and most of the hands were doing the same. He would round up the fowls and feed them and all the rest of the livestock which was kept close to the house – the pig-pens might well be awash – and then check as best he might on the horses and those of the herd close enough to the homestead to be checked. And whilst he got ready to go Maisie was washing up, Wally was mending harness and the cook-boy, Toulu, was peeling potatoes.

Uncle Josh's yell brought them all running, but at first they couldn't find him. He didn't seem to be in the sitting-room, they knew he wasn't in the kitchen, the verandah was no place to sit in the wet . . .

'Him in he bedroom,' Maisie gasped out. 'On the floor . . . him look bad!'

He didn't just look bad, he looked very strange, but that was because his face and neck had swollen and gone a sort of bluish pink. He was also deeply unconscious.

'He's been bit,' Wally said. 'Snake? Scorpy?'

They scanned the room but could see nothing. 'Red-back,' Mal decided. They were small, almost impossible to see in a crowded little room like this. 'Find the punctures.'

When Mal first arrived at the Wandina Uncle Josh had been old but big. Now, without Mal really noticing, he had become even older, thin and rather frail. It took no strength to lift him up and carry him out of the dark little room into the bright, noisy kitchen.

Maisie did it before either of the men could stop her. She laid him on the big, scrubbed wooden table and before anyone could say anything, she had his shirt off and was examining his skinny, bony chest for signs of puncture marks. There were none.

'It'll be on his face or neck, where the swellin' is,' Mal gasped, and grabbed the old man's head, turning it sideways. 'Look, all of you!'

They looked, but could find no puncture marks.

'If it was a red-back there won't be much of a mark to notice,' Wally said. 'But there's a flush round the bite, so they say.'

'Your Colly was bit last year, Mais,' Mal said suddenly, struck by the recollection of Colly's embittered remarks – and yells – at the time. 'What did the wound look like? Was there a flush round it?'

Maisie snorted. 'Colly him too black to see some li'l mark,' she said scornfully. 'Him say . . . "It hurt there, fool woman, there!", so I made the cut where he say.'

'Well, I'm not cuttin' at random,' Mal said uneasily. 'But somethin' ought to be done; I don't like the look of him at all, he's goin' bluer by the minute.'

It was Wally who thought of pressing . . . and it did the trick. He began by pressing lightly with his careful cook's hands all round Josh's neck, moving up and up until a pressure behind the old man's right ear brought a strangled shriek from Josh.

'Found it!' 'That's got 'un!' 'Now you're talkin'!' came from three mouths simultaneously. Mal reached out for a sharp kitchen knife, Wally bent the old man's long, withered ear carefully forward and Maisie lit a candle from the kitchen stove and held it above the table.

'There!' Mal said. He pressed the blade into the flesh and felt the hard lump where the venom had entered. Uncle Josh groaned, loud and deep, then gave a short, barking cry . . . and blood spurted as Wally did his best to press out the venom.

'We'll have to get him to a hospital though,' Mal said, carefully laying down the knife. 'The first blood was black, but this looks red again – is that a good sign, Mais?'

Maisie shrugged. 'Dunno. Best get the Boss to the 'ospital, like you done say. Him old. Poison go deeper when him old.'

'Right. Wally, I'll have to take Soljer and some of the other fellers, because of the rivers. Can you cope? You give the orders, they'll do as they're told. If you see anything needs doin', get it done. Right?'

'Right,' Wally said quickly. 'You'll want tucker; I'll do that. And a swag. Mais, pack their swags. You'll take him on a waggon?'

'Nope. River's too high,' Mal said. He didn't even have to think about it. After two years of living in this particular part of the country he knew that it would be boat and horses, with Uncle Josh propped up in a sort of hammock held between two of the steadiest mounts. 'Get the fellers to tack up would you, Wally?'

After that all was bustle, and in less time than he had imagined the little procession was all ready to set out for the river, with Uncle Josh, unconscious still but looking no worse, in a canvas sling between Mal and Soljer's mounts.

'I hope to God we're doing the right thing,' Mal had said privately to Wally just before they left. 'Suppose we make him worse?'

'If you can reach the Saundersfoot homestead there's women there who know a thing or two,' Wally advised. 'One of them, old lady Saundersfoot, was a nurse. Or you might leave him there and go and fetch a doc to him. It don't matter which way you do it, s'long as he's brung round all right.'

'Right,' Mal said. 'You do your best, Wally. I'll be back as soon as I can.'

And now they were on their way at last. What'll I do if he dies before we get to Saundersfoot, though? Mal worried. It was a big responsibility, taking the old man away from his home in conditions like these. It was very hot, but the clouds overhead were black and so low they seemed to press on the tops of the trees which grew on the river banks. There's going to be a storm presently, Mal thought, and then what'll we do?

They reached the river, which had risen so that the black mud flats where the Wandina maize would later be planted were under water. The boats were in what looked like midstream and it was only by straining his eyes that Mal could see the further bank, or rather the line where water and land met, for the river had flooded equally on both sides. The boats were pulling at their mooring chains though, so Mal dismounted, told Soljer to take charge of both mounts and the stretcher between them, took off his tall boots and shed hat and coat, and waded into the strong-flowing, muddy water. It wasn't pleasant, his feet sank into the rich mud, but the current's tug was only medium strong. He turned back to the silent watchers on the bank.

'Rupert, can you swim out to the boats with me, help bring them inshore?'

Rupert was twenty or so, with a happy disposition and a good deal of natural intelligence. What was more, though most of the men swam well without thinking about it, Rupert was their champion. Unusually, he was well over six feet in height and muscular with it. He had come across the Wandina a couple of years ago when he was on walkabout, and had stayed when asked to do so. He must have been mustering for years despite his youth, Mal thought, and he certainly seemed to enjoy his work. He was naturally athletic, a born horseman as canny in the saddle as Mal himself, and extremely strong.

'Sure, Boss. Now?'

For answer, Mal waded further into the flood and Rupert splashed in after him. Together, they continued until the water reached their waists, then launched themselves into deep water. They swam strongly out to the boats and Rupert seized the moor-ing chain of one of the larger ones, but Mal, bobbing up beside him, shook his head.

'No, Rupe, we'll leave them till we get back. For now, we'll take the little one. I just want to get Uncle Josh and the stretcher over without soaking them, that's all, and everyone else will have to swim the horses.'

'Right on, Boss,' Rupert said, immediately transferring himself to the smaller boat. 'Ready?'

Together, they swam ashore, heaving the boat behind them, cursing as they came into the shallows and the mud sucked at them.

'Bring the stretcher out here, Soljer,' Mal shouted. 'Johnny, you take the other end. Gently now, don't tip it – the mud's quite deep.'

They grinned but carried the stretcher and its occupant with gentle care across the flooded mud-flats, depositing their burden gently in the boat.

'Soljer, you're the smallest and lightest. Get in with Uncle Josh in case something goes wrong.' He raised his voice, addressing the men still on the river bank. 'Bring the horses over when we're ashore, not before – all right? No heroics, just get ashore in one piece. Toulu – most of the fellers will swim beside their horses, but you're light and you've got the spare nags, so you ride: understand? Put the tucker in the boat first though – we don't want that gettin' wet if a horse stumbles.'

'Yessir,' Toulu said. The cook's boy was eleven or twelve, a cheerful, wide-eyed youngster whose mother had handed him over to work in the house three years previously and had then gone off and hadn't been seen since. But Toulu didn't seem bothered.

'Her'll come back,' he had said cheerfully when Mal had first asked how long Mollie would be away. 'Her knows I'm doin' well here with you, Boss.'

Having settled everything to his satisfaction, Mal splashed back to the boat and he and Rupert pushed it with great care across the width of the river and hauled it out on the further shore. All that time Uncle Josh had lain deathly still, not moving, though Mal fancied that the awful blue at lips and ear-lobes was beginning to fade.

The horses and the men came ashore, the tucker was unloaded and put back on the spare horses, and when the men had wrung out the clothing which had got soaked they remounted and set off once again.

'We'll take it gently, but I'd like to get to the Saundersfoot place before the storm starts,' Mal said, looking apprehensively up at the lowering sky. 'If it rains, that hammock will hold the water, which isn't good.'

'We could cut drain holes,' Rupert suggested, riding up along-side. 'Or wrap him in canvas, Boss. But best t'ing is to hurry, I reckon.'

'I dare not joggle him about too much,' Mal said. A long time ago he had heard a doctor giving a lecture on poison bites and he had said to keep the patient as still as possible so the venom did not travel any faster than it needed. You can't put a tourniquet round a feller's neck to stop the bad blood, the doc had explained, but you can keep him still.

'Right, Boss,' Rupert said when Mal had explained about the lecture. 'How's about if someone rides ahead, tells the folk at Saundersfoot we're comin'?'

'Good idea; then perhaps someone could ride out to us,' Mal said, very relieved. 'Will you go, Rupert?'

But Rupert, it transpired, had never visited the homestead before and though he was sure of finding it, could not be sure of his welcome.

'Tom go,' he suggested. 'Everyone know Tom.'

The men laughed. Old Tom had worked for Uncle Josh since he was ten and had lived at the Wandina all his life.

'Yeah, right. Tom, can you ride ahead?'

The man needed no second bidding. He disappeared into the bush, head down, elbows out, the horse seeming as glad to be moving fast as Tom was.

'He'll be there in a few hours,' Mal said, much relieved. 'Careful with the stretcher, Soljer. We don't want Uncle Josh worse hurt.'

The storm caught them no more than a mile further on, and it was a bad one. It turned day to night, for a start, and brought thunder and lightning as well as torrential rain.

'I know it ain't safe under the trees, but sure as hell we'll be struck if we stay in the open,' Mal shouted. 'Rupert, what's best?'

He had been out in plenty of storms in the wet before, but not with a sick man. Rupert, he guessed, would have more of an idea what to do for the best than he.

'Build platform and make shelter,' Rupert bawled back above the crash of the thunder, the howling of the wind. 'One foot off ground be high enough . . . come on, fellers.'

Everyone worked fast. They got the horses well under the trees, hobbled them, then began to build a number of platforms. They selected groups of young trees, cut them off a foot from the ground with their small axes, stripped them of bark, then used the trunks for the platforms and the stripped-off bark, bent into a half-circle, as roofs and walls all in one.

'There you are, Boss,' Rupert said proudly as the storm roared overhead and lightning lit up the scene like day one minute, plunging it back to night the next. 'Best get some sleep. This storm's stayin' around for a while. The ladies won't come out in it.'

'They wouldn't find us, not while the rain continues and it's so dark,' Mal said. 'Right. Make the best of it. Oh, what about the mozzies?'

'We'll light smoke fires,' Rupert said. He grinned. 'Plenty wet leaves for that.'

There were. Mal did his best to see that Uncle Josh was comfortable but it was impossible to know how the old man felt. One of the men used the fire to heat up some soup which they'd brought with them, then Mal dribbled a bit of it into Uncle Josh's mouth. After that, because the storm still raged, they lay down and, against all the odds, slept.

Morning came and the sun rose on the dripping tropical forest. Great, leathery leaves and gnarled trunks steamed until a white mist hung about them, in which every sound came crystal clear on the still air. Mal and Rupert lit a fire and made food, roused their companions, and ate soup and some bread. Uncle Josh neither ate nor drank; he moved, muttered, but did not seem to know who he was or where.

'Good job,' Mal said grimly as he and Soljer mounted their horses and picked up the stretcher once more. 'We've a ways to go yet.'

He was right. Presently the rain began again as they forded two more creeks, swollen into torrents by the downpour, and then met the river itself. It was an awesome sight. It charged down from the upper reaches with a sound like a hundred express trains and one glance at the flurry of white water being thrown feet into the air at every obstruction was enough to confirm they could never cross it safely.

'What happened to Tom, though?' Mal wondered aloud, looking at the terrifying water raging past. 'Did he try to cross here? If so, he's a goner for sure.'

'He won't have tried, Boss,' Soljer assured him. 'Tom wise, not stupid. He'll walk upstream, lookin' for good way across.'

'Then we'll follow suit,' Mal decided. He had given Uncle Josh more soup that morning and though the old man could not be said to have woken his throat had worked when it felt the liquid and he had swallowed. Rupert said it was a good sign, which had cheered Mal considerably. 'Come on!'

They went on upstream, but though they continued doggedly for four hours, they found nowhere suitable for crossing.

'Maybe last night the river weren't so high an' Tom got across,' Toulu suggested. 'We see him soon, eh?'

But they didn't. They made camp because the rain stopped as suddenly as it had started and a watery sun began to shine, making the jungle steam once more, but though they ate again – bread and cheese this time, since Mal decided they ought to save the soup for Uncle Josh – they did not linger. Rupert said he remembered another homestead up this way, though he did not know the people well and did not think they numbered a nurse amongst them, but nevertheless they would surely be willing to help.

'A boat, Boss,' he said. 'If they've got a boat we could mebbe get across.'

'Right,' Mal said. 'You lead, Rupe.'

Before nightfall they began to see signs of jungle clearance, and quite soon after that a domestic hen wandered out on to the path in front of them, squawked, and scuttled back into cover. Rupert turned on his horse and grinned triumphantly at Mal.

'Not far now, Boss,' he said. 'Ten minutes, no more.'

And sure enough, in less than ten minutes they found themselves walking up a short driveway between post and rail fencing and into a familiar yard. The homestead was built of corrugated iron and timber, like the Wandina, but it looked pleasanter all round. It was surrounded by trees for a start, cultivated trees, and there was a pretty flower-garden, though because of the recent heavy rain everything looked a bit battered. There were gingham curtains at the windows, and white nets, and someone had painted the corrugated iron roof red and the doors and window frames green.

'Where is it? Who are they?' Mal hissed at Rupert, but the other man just shrugged his shoulders.

'Dunno, Boss. But they've seen us – they're a-comin'.'

And sure enough seconds later the door was flung open and a pretty girl with skin which was the colour of milky coffee and odd, pinky-fawn hair came out on to the verandah, smiling at them.

'Welcome!' she said. 'You brung the sick feller? Your black feller come yesterday, late, and we lent him the boat. He ain't back yet . . . river's still powerful high.' She held out a slim hand. 'I'm Coffee Allinson. You'll be Uncle Josh's head stockman, I don't reckon I can remember your name. Come in an' bring Uncle Josh an' my mother will take a look at him whiles I mek you a cup o' coffee.'

'I'm Mal Chandler,' Mal said awkwardly as the men carrying the stretcher filed past them and into the house. The flood of words and the prettiness of the girl had completely floored him, and that weird hair! He hadn't seen any women except the aboriginals since he'd last visited his mother, and she, he thought, was not a woman as such – not to her son, anyway. This girl, on the other hand, was all woman! But he held out his hand and took her slim fingers in his, trying to act cool and collected. 'How d'you do, Miss Allinson. Tom got through, then? Is he bringin' a doctor? I don't fancy the river crossin' with a sick man aboard and that's the truth.' The rest of the men had followed the stretcher into the house, leaving Mal and Miss Allinson alone on the verandah. He half turned to follow them, then turned back. 'Tom got here all right then?' he repeated.

'He come in, explained the situation, we lent him the boat, and he's not yet come back,' the girl said cheerfully. 'He's mebbe findin' it difficult to persuade Mrs Saundersfoot to get into the boat – she's pretty old an' wou'n't be too keen wi' the river that fierce. If so, reckon he'll go on to the railhead. There's a doctor there, sometimes. He does a weekly surgery . . . nice feller, name of Crompton.'

'Yeah, but would he come out to us?' Mal said doubtfully,

following her on to the verandah and then through the door into a pleasant living area. Uncle Josh was already laid out on the floor on his stretcher. He looked sick unto death, Mal thought apprehensively. 'Umm . . . could you fetch your mother, Ma'am? Only Uncle Josh ain't too bright.'

Miss Allinson went to the door and shouted, then told her guests to get out of their wet clothes.

'No sense in sittin' around soaked,' she said. 'I'll have them things over the stove in the kitchen an' dry before you can say knife. As for Doc Crompton, sure he'll come back – if he's at Manguna, that is. Hey, Maybelle!'

A muffled shout from outside answered her.

'Coffee an' cakes for our guests,' the girl shouted, then turned to Mal. 'I dare say you'd rather have beer, but coffee's better for you. Ah, Mother, this here's the sick feller we was told to expect. Can you take a look at him now?'

A tall, raw-boned woman stood in the doorway. She had very blonde, very straight hair which she wore tied in a sort of horse-tail at the back and she was wearing a yellow shirt, tan breeches and long black riding boots. Mal thought approvingly that she was a handsome, sensible kind of woman and watched as she strode into the room, glanced briefly at the men, and then went over to the stretcher. She knelt on the floor, took Uncle Josh's pulse, felt for his heart, examined the site of the injury and then rolled back his eyelid and peered at his eyeball.

'Hmm,' she said at length, in a strong German accent. 'I'll get him a dose. But he's a strong old man, sure he is. He'll come through.'

Mal could have kissed her. Relief flooded him and he smiled stupidly at her.

'He will? Oh, thank God, Ma'am!'

She smiled then, a brief, understanding smile. 'Yes, someone acted promptly, there's not much venom left in his system by the look of him. No more purple round his eyes, his lips, a bit of colour coming when you press on his cheek . . .' She demon-strated. 'If the crittur had bit you, young man, you'd have been riding a muster the next day, but an old man has to take things easier.'

'Thank you, Mrs Allinson,' Mal said fervently. 'Old Tom's gone for the doc, but I don't know if they'll get back, not until the river falls a bit.'

'No matter. Coffee, go fetch the dose, then later he will wake and eat. A few days under my care and you'll be able to take him back to his homestead.' She glanced towards the door which immediately opened. A smiling woman entered with a tray upon which were several mugs, a tall jug and a big platter of home-made biscuits. 'Here's the coffee my daughter promised you.'

Mal, taking the cup she presently proffered, looked around the room but the girl had disappeared. She must have obeyed her mother pretty promptly, whilst they were giving all their atten-tion to Uncle Josh, he supposed. But no sooner had he begun to sip his coffee than the door opened again and the pink-haired girl reappeared with a bottle full of dark-red, evil-looking physic in one hand and a spoon in the other.

'Here it is, Mother,' she said cheerfully. 'You meant this?'

'That's the stuff; good girl, Coffee,' Mrs Allinson said. 'You give him a couple of spoonfuls while I hold his head.'

Between them, mother and daughter dosed the old man so effectively that only a tiny drop ran down his chin, then the daughter put a sofa cushion under his head, the mother turned the frail old body on to its side, and they sat down on the sofa.

'There!' Mrs Allinson said briskly. 'Now! Go to the bunkhouse with my men and strip off. You'll have dry stuff in your swags?'

'If they ain't got soaked,' Mal said rather gloomily, but he need not have worried. His bed-roll was dampish but the clean shirt and breeches rolled up inside were dry, if rather creased. And presently he had the satisfaction of coming back into the living area, dressed in clean clothes, to find Uncle Josh conscious, though weakly, still.

'I'll do, now I'm bein' took care of,' the old man said faintly, when Mal sat down beside the stretcher and told him how much better he looked. 'You want to go back, feller? Leave me here? I'm in good hands.'

'But what about the station?' Mal asked. 'The Wandina's your home, Uncle Josh.'

'Oh aye, I know it. As soon as I'm stronger . . .'

'Do the Allinsons mind?'

Uncle Josh grinned faintly. 'Mind? To have a handsome feller like me as a payin' guest, an' them a lonely widder woman an' a spinster? Course they don't mind! 'Sides, soon as I'm fit . . .'

'All right, Uncle Josh,' Mal said. 'We'll wait for Tom and go home as soon as he arrives. He'll be back here in the morning, no doubt.'

They stayed four days and nights but Tom didn't come and Mal began to get restive. Coffee Allinson was a pleasant, competent young woman, but he thought she was forward, wanting to get him alone all the time. She was twenty-one years old, scarcely knew any men save the ones who worked for her mother – her father had died when she was ten – yet it seemed to Mal that she was experienced beyond her years. Once, she had caught him on his way out to the bunkhouse and had pressed him into the corner where the kitchen and the verandah met and kissed him. He still went hot all over when he thought how she had kissed him . . . she had opened her mouth and virtually tried to *eat* him, embarrassing him so much that for a whole day he had been unable to look her in the eye. I'm twenty-five this year, he thought, but even so I wouldn't do that to a girl I wasn't even engaged to . . . I wouldn't do it to a girl I wasn't *married* to, come to that. But Coffee had done it without a qualm, and had laughed afterwards, and patted his cheek . . . But he hadn't been a stock-man for so long without realising that Coffee was looking for a mate, even if she didn't know it. Only he didn't want to be that mate, pretty though she might be. I don't want to marry someone just because she's the first girl I've ever really known, he told himself defensively. Besides, I don't really know her at all, and the Bartok Range is a long way from the Wandina.

She caught him again, inevitably. Down by the river, searching the heaving, tumbling waters for some sign of the boat and Tom. It was early morning, yet it was hot and languorous already, the sun still hidden in the early mist but the heat promising a fine day. Mal was standing on the bank under the trees, staring out, when a soft hand closed over his and a voice said in his ear:

233

'Well, Mal Chandler, down here already, before you've had your breakfast? Want a swim? I'll come in with you, if you do.'

He looked down at her, wanting to be frank, to tell her to go away, but totally inhibited by the fact that one was never rude to a woman.

'No, I ain't swimmin',' he said gruffly. 'If you want a dip I'll make myself scarce.'

She laughed softly, then pressed herself against him. He could feel the shape of her, the soft mounds of her bosom, the thrust of her stomach, the taut length of her thighs. He swallowed uneasily, ashamed of the physical response which her shameless closeness provoked in him. I'm no better'n a ruttin' steer, he thought miserably. And I don't even like the girl above half!

'Mal? You wanna touch me? Put your arms round me – I won't holler out, I promise.'

He stood there, rigid, unmoving and extremely uncomfortable. Would it be an insult to Coffee to turn down advances so blatant? He did not think that nice girls ever behaved in such a way – perhaps she was not a nice girl? But her mother was respectable, and Coffee was only twenty-one. But whilst he pondered, Coffee was not simply standing still. She was pressing against him and her fingers were tracing little circles in the palm of his hand. He meant to push her away but once his hands were on her it wasn't so easy; without at all meaning to do so, he grabbed her by the soft flesh of her upper arms and, suddenly furious with himself and with her, he tugged her closer still, squashing her breasts against his hard chest, pushing his knee between her legs, breathing hard as he did so. If she wants it, he thought with a viciousness foreign to his nature, she can bloody well have it – then see how she feels!

'Mal? Oh Mal, at last! Take me, take me!'

They fell against a tree, then on to the ground, Coffee rolling over on impact so that she ended up beneath him. He tore at the flimsy shirt she wore, and breasts like small, golden-brown melons came into view. He sighed, gazing at them. They were sweetly feminine, enticing, the chocolate nipples standing out as though imploring his attention, and as he watched he saw her skin gooseflesh as she curved her back, thrusting her breasts clear of the constraining cotton.

Heart beating nineteen to the dozen, he touched a breast, brushing the nipple with the palm of his hand. Coffee groaned and drew his hand down, tearing open her side-fastening skirt. She wore no drawers beneath it and she had his hand in an iron grip, forcing it lower, lower. Scarcely knowing what he was doing, he began to caress the bare and supple flesh, then, as she began to whimper and move, he touched the division of her thighs and gave a whimper of his own. He mustn't – he'd be in deep trouble! If she said she'd not been willing he could be accused of rape. In any event, they'd make him marry her and he really didn't want to do that!

He took his hand away as though she was red-hot and pulled her skirt across. He realised afterwards that she thought he meant to undress himself the better to pleasure her, because she didn't drag him back when he moved away but lay there, on the long, wet grass, smiling up at him, her lids half down over her eyes, her mouth open, the tongue just showing, touching her lower lip.

Mal stood up. He turned away from her, intending to return at a run to the house, then turned back. He couldn't leave her lying on the ground with that look on her face! Suppose someone came by?

He reached down and caught hold of her hands, pulling her to her feet. Her breasts bounced as he did so and he was forced to look away, swallowing. Oh my God oh my God oh my God, why did you make me this way and then give me a conscience which tells me such things are wrong?

'No!' he said forcefully. 'No, Coffee. It ain't right. Come on, there's no sign of Tom, we'd best get back to the homestead.'

She couldn't believe he didn't intend to go on with whatever it was he had so nearly started. She stared, then put a hand over her mouth. Her eyes, big and dark-brown, widened.

'Mal? What's wrong? Don't you like me?'

'Sure I like you, Coffee, but . . . I don't know you all that well, do I? You've not met many young fellers and I've not met many girls. Right?'

'What's that got to do with it? I bloody well want you, Mal

Chandler! What d'you mean workin' me up like that and then droppin' me flat? There's words for fellers like you, Mal.'

She hissed the last sentence, outrage in every syllable, but Mal couldn't help himself; he laughed.

'Words like "gentleman", d'you mean? Come on, Coffee, you know we mustn't. We ain't wed, nor engaged, nor nothin'.'

She began to use words which he did not think women knew; words he scarcely knew himself. He tried to hush her, but her voice rose to an angry shriek so he broke and ran, not looking behind him until he was well clear of the river and then only checking to make sure she wasn't following.

She wasn't. Mal took a deep breath and wiped sweat off his forehead. What a helluva thing – what a weird, pink-haired girl she was, and how lucky he had been to escape from her toils before he'd done something he would later regret. He had been running, but he slowed to a walk, then a saunter. He shouldn't have left her flat, like that, and in such a foul temper! But he wasn't going back, not he – she would have to find someone else to tease and tickle into wrongdoing.

Having made up his mind, Mal strode back to the homestead. The sooner I'm out of here the better, he told himself. That Coffee ain't no little lady, that's for sure, and she's quite capable of telling her mother I misbehaved down by the river so must be persuaded to marry her.

He wondered how he would face her, too. But he was lucky. Rupert was waiting for him up by the verandah.

'Boss? We goin' to wait another day for Tom? Only there's work to be done back at the Wandina and we ain't doin' much good here.'

'We're leavin' now,' Mal said at once. 'I've checked, and there's no sign of Tom, nor of the boat. My swag's ready. We'll live on the country goin' home. There's plenty of game in the bush.'

'Right, I'll tell the hands,' Rupert said, immediately accepting what Mal had said and not arguing, like some would. 'You goin' to tell Miz Allinson and Uncle Josh?'

'Yup. You saddle up.'

And thus it was that they left the Bartok Range before Coffee Allinson had gathered her wits enough to come up from the river and tell her tale, or do whatever all that bad language had indicated.

'You'll be all right, Uncle Josh?' Mal asked anxiously, his swag slung over Sandy's withers, his saddle-bags laden with the bread, cheese and cakes which Mrs Allinson had pressed upon him. 'Send a message when you're ready to come home.'

'I'll do that, boy,' Uncle Josh said. 'I'm gettin' stronger by the day . . .'t won't be long now before I'm ridin' home.'

Mal thoroughly enjoyed the journey from the Bartok Range to the Wandina. The weather stayed clear and sunny, and though it was hot, it wasn't that damp, oppressive heat of the week before and without the worry of a sick man, even the hands felt in a holiday mood.

'We'll have a big corroboree when we get back,' Mal said jubilantly. 'To celebrate Uncle Josh bein' all right and our journey bein' successful. There'll be plenty of food an' plenty of root beer.'

'Good on you, Boss,' Rupert said, whilst Soljer, riding just behind them, gave a subdued cheer. 'We celebratin' anythin' else?' he slanted a sideways glance at Mal which spoke volumes.

Mal grinned. 'What d'you mean, Rupe? I don't know what you mean.'

'She was good cook,' Soljer remarked. 'Woman make homestead good place. She plant garden, make curtings, all sorts. Mrs Kath made the Magellan good place.'

'Yeah, but it's got to be the right woman,' Mal said. 'Just any woman may not be the right one.'

Rupert nodded sagely. 'She like you, Boss, but you din't like her,' he said. 'No good, that.'

'True. You'll have the last word on that, Rupe old son. Hey, where'll we make camp tonight? By the river? We could build a platform in a tree, save a lot of work.'

The men agreed and when evening began to come on they turned off their track and went down to the river bank. There they chopped trees, made a platform in a tree, stretched the bark, and lit their smoke-fires. Only then did they get out their tucker and decide what they would eat that evening.

'Fresh meat good,' Soljer said. 'You make dampers, Boss, me an' Johnny go hunting.'

Mal agreed and watched the two men melt into the bush, their hunting boomerangs in their hands, and presently they returned with a wallaby which they had killed and skinned.

'Good eatin' on this,' Johnny said, squatting by the fire they had built and holding out a joint on a sharpened stick. 'We got any bread, Boss?'

They had bread and also a bag of mustard powder of which Mal was very fond. Presently, when the meat was almost cooked, he went down to the river for some water to make up the mustard. The sun was setting and the river, turbulent still, looked like a river of flame. Mal was standing looking at the flame and blue of the water and wishing he had the ability to paint when he noticed something else. Loose timber, several sizeable planks of it.

'Rupe, come an' fish this wood out,' he shouted. 'It'll save us cuttin' any more trees down . . . come on, give me a hand!'

The men came running and they all waded into the water to fetch back the planks, which had caught, temporarily, in the back-eddy caused by a particularly stubborn old tree which the flood had not yet managed to uproot.

'There's somethin' else, caught in the roots,' Johnny said breathlessly, as the four of them – for Toulu had been left to cook the wallaby meat – wrestled the planks out on to the bank. 'Here, give me . . . aargh!'

'What is it?' Mal splashed forward, wet to the waist, and peered at the curled-up object in the lee of the great tree. 'Oh, my God!'

It was a body. And when they reached the bank and laid the bloated corpse close to their fire, all Mal's worst fears were confirmed. It was old Tom.

The dream had never left him, but that night, as they lay on the platform in the tree, it came back as badly and painfully as it had in the first few weeks after Petey's death. All over again Mal, Bill and Petey traversed the long tongue of rock, took their places, made their preparations. Petey grew bored, the storm got steadily worse, the sea rose and rose . . . and Mal, screaming, saw his small brother's tiny corpse dragged off the rocks and curled into the curve of a great green breaker.

Only tonight it wasn't only Petey who was seized and smothered by the sea. It was old Tom. And the guilt which had never quite left Mal over Petey's death – for had he not stood by and watched his brother drown, his father overcome? – came back again tenfold. He had sent old Tom ahead of them to find a way across the torrent and Tom had taken the boat as he had meant him to do. Whether he had even reached the further shore was doubtful, for when he had left the Bartok Range the weather had still been at its worst. So once again, Mal had allowed someone else to do the dirty work. First Bill, then Tom. Both dead.

But Bill had survived his rescue attempt, had lived to be a hero for his valiant effort to save his small son. Kath had stuck by Bill because she knew what losing Petey had done to her husband. What did I do? Mal thought, waking, wet-haired, the sweat pouring off him in a steady stream. I did precisely nothing. I let my father struggle in the water, I sent old Tom off to do what I didn't fancy.

The night was stuffily warm, though there was a slight breeze from the river, but Mal sat up. He didn't fancy going back to sleep and dreaming again. Old Tom's reproachful eyes rolled in his dead head now whenever Mal so much as closed his eyes. The corroboree would be a funeral . . . and someone would have to tell old Tom's wife, Nita, and his brother, Colly.

It wasn't a good thought and of course it made sleeping an impossibility, so after another twenty minutes or so of fruitless worrying and wakefulness, Mal decided he would get up and check the smoke-fires and make sure that the body had not been disturbed. He creaked to his feet and stepped carefully over Rupe's sleeping figure . . . only Rupe wasn't asleep. He nearly gave Mal a heart attack by sitting up and addressing him.

'You awright, Boss?' he said in a hissing whisper. 'You dream awful bad, I shook you 'wake jest now. It waren't your fault Old Tom drown. He knew boats an' rivers. His time had come.'

'I should have gone myself,' Mal whispered wretchedly. 'Or kept him with us so that we could all go together.'

Rupert shook his head. 'No, Boss. Tom knew the way to

Saundersfoot Station, you din't. But don' forget, Uncle Josh needed you, not us fellers. You done right. Tom won't ghost you.'

'I'm not afraid of that, it's just that I feel bad because I told him to go. But you're right, what happened wasn't my fault,' Mal said, and to his surprise his guilt was lessening already. Rupert was sensible; he, Mal, could not possibly have left Uncle Josh and swanned off ahead of the others to see if he could fetch help. And Tom was good with boats, at ease with the river. And though they called him 'old Tom' he wasn't that old, probably no more than thirty-five – in the prime of life, in fact.

Except that he's dead, Mal's conscience reminded him miserably. You had the men in your charge and one of them is dead. Just how do you explain that?

But he knew he was simply blaming himself for something he could not possibly have avoided. So he climbed down the tree, put more damp undergrowth on the smoke-fires, checked that Tom's corpse still lay in the hammock slung, now, between two trees, and then climbed up to the platform once more. He got back into his bedroll, then looked towards the eastern horizon. Very soon now the light would begin to strengthen; it was scarcely worth trying to sleep . . .

Moments later, he slumbered, and continued to do so dreamlessly until morning.

Mal had not known quite how old Tom's corpse would be treated, waterlogged as it was, and afterwards he was advised by Wally that if such a thing ever happened again, he should bury the body and not bring it back, but because he didn't know, he became, for a month, a part of the mourning process.

It included many corroborees, enactments of old Tom's last wild ride down the river, his overturning in the boat, the destruction of his craft and his eventual death. And of course, though it was the wet, the temperature was well over a hundred degrees Fahrenheit and humid, too. The smell of poor old Tom gently rotting got into Mal's nostrils and seemed to permeate every corner of the Station and despite himself, Mal was thoroughly relieved when at last Tom was buried.

In March, with Tom's corpse gone, the weather gradually

began to improve. The storms eased and though rain fell, it was softer, warmer rain. April came, but Uncle Josh still did not send the message that he was coming home. So in May, with considerable trepidation, Mal visited the Bartok Range.

He was warmly greeted by Mrs Allinson and Uncle Josh. Coffee kept out of the way for a bit, then came through into the living area, very demure in a white lawn dress with pale-green embroidery round the neck and sleeves, her pink hair tied back with a piece of green satin ribbon. She offered tea, biscuits and slices of rich fruit cake and then sat on a low stool staring at Mal whilst Mrs Allinson told him that Uncle Josh was making a very good recovery and would probably be returning to the Wandina in June, when the boggy low ground, near the river, would have begun to dry out.

'You'll be musterin' then,' she added. 'So you'll be off all day and Uncle Josh will be able to oversee life at the homestead in your absence.'

It sounded reasonable and Uncle Josh certainly looked well. He was far less frail, and he had been making bits and pieces of furniture for the Allinsons. Two neat stools, a small round table and what he described as a clothes chest which, he said with a twinkle, was especially for Coffee to put her trousseau in.

'Are you gettin' wed then, Miss Allinson?' Mal asked politely. If she was, what a relief! He would no longer need to feel bad about her if she was getting married.

'Hear him!' Uncle Josh said, wheezing with laughter. 'Don't worry, young feller, Miss Coffee won't be wed for a whiles yet. These things take time.'

Mal said he was sure they did and swiftly changed the subject. He wanted to know whether they should plant an extra two or three tons of maize, because the mares had foaled well and the calves out on the wonderful after-rains grass were making up nicely. Mal had it in mind, he told Uncle Josh, to increase the size of the herd this year.

'You're a good hand with the horses, I grant you that. Royce says so, and he was always horse mad, but have you broken any brumbies yet, this year?' Uncle Josh said. 'If you're goin' to do that you'd best plant more maize. The brumby mares will have their foals at heel by now, you can get good stock that way.'

Mal disagreed, but did not say so. They could argue it out later. He thought Royce's attitude to horses was the right one – breed your own, breed from the best, and you wouldn't go far wrong. You could pick a pretty foal out of a herd of wild horses and find when it grew up it was vicious, lazy, anything. You had no blood lines to guide you, there was no way you could look back and say, *Of course, the mare was always quick to pick a fight as a filly,* or *The stallion that sired this one had an independent streak.* But there you were; Royce thought for the future, Uncle Josh still sometimes just thought for cheapness or convenience.

Wally, still cooking for the Station, was delighted with the amount of fresh food being brought in each day from the bush. They did not need to bring a killer in from the herd for its beef when there were wild duck, geese, wild pigs and even the barramundi fish waiting to be cooked and eaten. Meals were large, delicious and varied. Wally made huge fruit cakes, covered them in marzipan and then iced them thickly to keep them fresh. He wrapped them in greaseproof paper and packed them away in sealed tins and they would be brought out, throughout the year, whenever someone had something to celebrate.

'Make 'em rich an' they'll stay good longer,' he instructed Mal, limping contentedly around his kitchen. 'My, won't we have a corroboree when Mr Josh gets back!'

'Sounds more like women than cakes; make 'em rich and they stay good longer,' Mal said, grinning. 'But before we can have a corroboree, there's work to be done. We're cuttin' the rice grass tomorrow.'

'Fat lot you know about women,' Wally pointed out. 'You've less idea than Mrs Quilter's cat. But I'll give a hand with the rice grass if you like.' Mal knew the older man liked cooking all right, but he enjoyed doing what he would have called 'man's work', when he was able to handle it, and he enjoyed being back with the other stockmen, too. 'Tell you what, Boss, I'll drive the cutter.'

Rice grass was wild, but it made excellent hay. It had to be cut just as the seed formed, before the ground was properly dry, and it meant going away from the homestead to the swampy, boggy country where it flourished. It would be a day out, and a nice day, too, and Mal told Wally that, provided he made the men's tucker first, they would be glad of his help.

'That'll be bonza,' Wally said. 'I'll pack the tucker tonight, then we can be out by dawn.'

June arrived, and on the Wandina Mal set the men to ploughing the mud-flats down by the river and sowing the maize first and then their vegetable seeds. Wally threw himself into such pursuits with the utmost pleasure, enjoying an activity which meant he could be active but did not need to straddle a horse, and even Toulu, the cook-boy, helped. The tiny children, lower lips stuck out, would weed between the rows once the vegetables were established, for directly after the wet everything grew like wild-fire on the mud-flats. Indeed, everything grew like wildfire everywhere . . . Mal's garden, modelled on Kath's, flowered mag-nificently and in the orchard the branches were bowed low with the weight of the young fruit.

And it was time for the first muster. The cattle, sleek and fat from the rains and the abundant grass, were everywhere. They would have to be rounded up, counted and physicked if they needed it, the calves would be branded and then they would be taken to water. A muster can take around four weeks and the first one after the wet was usually a fairly lengthy business so Mal went round checking every single thing.

'Tucker?' he said to Wally, who would be accompanying them as cook. It left Maisie doing her worst on the station, but with the men away that didn't matter much. 'How much salt beef? Is it well dried out?'

'Sure, Boss,' Wally said in a slightly aggrieved tone. 'I been dryin' out the beef ever since the maize went in – the kitchen was like an oven yesterday. And I've packed all the other stuff – flour, tea, sugar, rice, seasonings, treacle. We shan't go short.'

'Tobacco? Matches?'

Mal never forgot his first muster, when he had failed to bring any matches. It didn't matter that much since every aboriginal new how to make fire with two sticks and some dry leaves and twigs, but it riled him that he had forgotten something like that and he'd been well teased about it, too.

'Sure, Boss. Some of them dried plums, an' all, and some spare clothing, and a roll of canvas.'

Mal nodded. You never knew when you might need a roll of canvas. It could come in useful for a thousand things, from bringing a wounded man home in comfort to patching torn trousers.

'Right. Then we're off at first light tomorrow.'

'We'll be ready, Boss,' Wally said. He meant it, too. When Mal came into the yard at first light Wally would be before him and so would most of the men. 'Bed now, though. Last night on a mattress for a while, eh?'

'That's it,' Mal agreed. 'And Uncle Josh will be home some time this month . . . I shan't be sorry. I love the work, but it's better when Uncle Josh is here to tell me how he wants things done. Even if that does include breaking in a few brumbies.'

'Now's the time for that,' Wally pointed out. 'You want the foals young.'

'I do. But we'll tackle that after the muster.'

It was a fair muster. Johnny Byall discovered he had been sharing his bedroll with a taipan, a deadly poisonous snake, but since neither bit the other, as the men said, it was just a good story to tell round the campfire. They rounded up a number of cattle, were delighted with the condition both of the beasts themselves and of their new calves, and lost a horse when the animal brushed against a stinging tree in a particularly bad and thick part of the bush and broke its neck as it panicked and tried to escape the pain of its stings.

It was always hard to tell if one had suffered from the attention of duffers, the thieves who came silently on to your Station, branded your cattle with their own mark, and then drove them away, but Mal did not think so. He had a fair idea of how many head they should have and so far, nothing seemed amiss.

Indeed, after four weeks of sleeping rough and eating, at least in part, off the country, though with plenty of tea to drink and dampers and salt beef to make the diet more solid, he found himself oddly reluctant to turn for home. He was riding a tall, raw-boned grey called Puff, a gelding who liked to lead, but for some reason he felt compelled to hold the animal back. I'm being stupid, he told himself. If Uncle Josh is back then life at the Wandina will be easier for all of us. But despite these brave words the nearer he got to the Wandina, the deeper grew his unease.

It was not just him, either. Rupert, riding up beside him, turned his face up to the blue and cloudless sky.

'Sometime trouble come from clear sky,' he said unexpectedly. 'I have bad feeling . . . yet it's been good muster. Mebbe Mr Josh still crook?'

'You've got indigestion from too much salt beef and too many dampers,' Mal said. 'I'm the same. I feel kinda heavy. Or mebbe it's just that no one wants a good muster to end.'

Rupert gave him an astonished glance and Mal had to laugh. Musters were grand, but you didn't sleep soft, you ate whatever was going, you rode hard and small injuries made themselves felt – cuts across your palms, softened by the months of hanging round the homestead during the wet, blisters, gashes and bruises caused by the awkwardness of the calves, the aggression of the cows, the antipathy of some of the bulls. So even if you enjoyed a muster, it was a good feel to return to the homestead with the job well done.

'All right, all right, I'm talkin' through my hat. It'll be bonza when we get home, see if it ain't!'

They reached the slip rails round the home paddocks when it was still evening, though in June the nights seem long. Their small company had brought a killer back, a 500-lb bullock which was lame in its off-fore. Two of the hands saw it into the yard, but Mal had seen the lantern light coming from the homestead – not from the kitchen, but from the living area. Uncle Josh was home, then, his conviction had been well-founded. He slid off Puff and threw the reins to Soljer.

'I'll come out in a minute; I'm just goin' to tell Uncle Josh we're back,' he said. 'Get Puff's tack off as soon as you've done your own mount.'

Soljer nodded and led the two animals off, and Mal strode up the steps, across the verandah and into the living area. Uncle Josh

245

sat in his favourite chair, tamping tobacco into his pipe; he raised a hand in greeting as he saw Mal.

'Heared you comin',' he said cheerfully. 'Near as dammit come to meet you, but decided against it. The lad'll be here soon enough, I said to myself. Then we can have a jaw about what's been goin' on.'

'I guessed you'd hear us, what with the killer bellowin' an' all,' Mal admitted. He squatted on the floor, stockman fashion. 'You're lookin' better, Uncle Josh. How d'you feel?'

'I'm grand. Mind, I had good nursin' – I'm havin' it still, come to that. Guess who's come to help keep house while I'm poorly, boy? Ah, here she is!'

Mal turned his head.

Standing behind him, smiling sweetly, with her pinky-fawn hair piled up on top of her head and a big white apron hiding her dress, was Coffee Allinson.

Ten

War

It was a Sunday morning in late September and Tess was string-ing beans in the kitchen and thinking about going upstairs to get ready for morning service when the telephone rang. She waited for a moment, but the bell continued to sound steadily, *tring tring, tring tring,* so she slid off the stool on which she was perched and went, knife still in hand, across the kitchen and through the hall to the foot of the stairs. The telephone was on the little table to one side of the banister and Tess snatched the receiver off its hook rather crossly. Why did Marianne never answer the telephone when there was the remotest chance that someone else would do it for her? Why did Cherie never dash into the hall to grab it, as she had done when she was younger? For that matter, why did Peter, lying in the garden reading the Sunday papers, not hurry in, because it was usually for him? But no, each of them assumed that Tess would answer it, even though it was her turn to prepare Sunday lunch – and she had, of course.

'Hello!' Tess snapped into the receiver, not bothering to give her number. She felt like telling the caller pretty tartly that there was a war on and he – or she – should be restricting calls to essential ones only. And there was no such thing as an essential call on a Sunday morning, not when one member of the family was an accountant and the only other working person, Tess herself, was on the staff of the Castle Museum.

Tess had been working at the museum for two years now and loved the job, but she did think that Marianne might make Cherie pull her weight a bit more. She was twelve now, quite old enough

247

to lend a hand so that she, Tess, might have a day off from time to time.

'Tess? Is that you? My word, you sound in a bate! Who's knocked you off your donkey, then?'

The voice was young, male, teasing. Tess scowled at the banister. She did so hate people who assumed you would know their voice – she hadn't a clue who the caller was.

'Who's speaking?' she said sharply, not allowing her tone to mellow at all. 'I'm afraid I don't . . .'

'Of course you do!' The voice sounded offended now, disproportionately so. 'How many fellows know you well enough to ring you first thing on a Sunday morning? It's me – Ashley!'

'Good Lord, Ash! It's been years . . . what do you want?'

'How bloody uncouth you are,' Ashley said crossly. 'Years, indeed! Well, it might be a year or two, I suppose . . . and come to think of it, after our last encounter it's a miracle I'm ringing you at all. I should still be offended. Well, I am, actually, but I've decided to forgive you, because . . . because I have. Now. I'm home on leave. When can we meet?'

Tess gasped. The cheek of the fellow! They had quarrelled bitterly over his negligence as skipper of his Yare and Bure One Design, after he had forgotten to shout 'gybe ho!' when he was going about with the result that his crew – Tess – had suddenly found herself whacked across the head by the boom and knocked straight into the water.

He hadn't apologised; he was Ashley Knox, the superior, and when he reached overboard and scooped her out of the water he had been laughing, saying she'd have a black eye in the morning, that she should have guessed he intended to go about, God knew she'd been crewing for him long enough to be able to anticipate most of his moves by now!

And as if that wasn't bad enough, when they got back to the clubhouse and everyone asked how she had ended up in the drink Ashley had told them unconcernedly that he'd forgotten to shout because he was watching the little blonde with the big tits who had been crewing for Charlie Jackson.

'If you want to watch her, get her to crew for you,' Tess had said coldly. 'I'm sure she'll be delighted. Especially when she's chucked into the water by a careless, selfish skipper.'

'Don't be daft,' Ashley said. He had looped an arm round her waist and tugged her close, maddening her once again by his easy assumption that he could charm his way out of any situation. 'You know it's you I love, sweetie-pie. I dare say you don't have tremendous ti . . .'

'Let go of me!' Tess knew her face was red, knew that half the clubhouse – the male half – was watching the disagreement with prurient interest. The men, ever hopeful, always assumed that if a girl crewed for a fellow then she did other things for him, too. Several of them had hung round her, intimating that if she ever grew tired of Ashley Knox there were others who would be delighted to sail with her. And Tess was quite bright enough to know, too, that the women, who had been openly astonished by Ashley's preference, would be hugging themselves with glee at this sign of a rift in the lute. Ashley might be boastful and big-headed – well, he was – but he was a first-rate yachtsman and a very eligible *parti*.

'Honey-lamb, I'm sorry, your tits are just . . .'

By now, Tess had been blazing, both with humiliation and with rage. She knew, dammit, that her slight breasts couldn't compete with Miss Big Tits, but she also knew that Ashley was now playing to the gallery and it was too bad of him. He pretended to love her, he pretended that he never looked at other women, but he never really considered her at all. It was self, self, self all the way with Ashley. So she faced him across the club room and spoke with chilly distinctness.

'Ashley I'm going. I won't ask you to take me home, I'd sooner walk. And don't come bothering me again, please. Find another crew.'

He had pursued her, pleaded with her, ordered her . . . and finally had tried to manhandle her into his car. She had slapped his face – it had been a wonderful, liberating sensation – and stalked off, ringing Peter from the nearest telephone box, almost incoherent with tears and temper, to beg a lift home.

And that hadn't been the end of it, either. Ashley had turned up outside her place of work, inside it, at the bus stop. Tess was working as assistant to the curator of the Castle Museum and loving every minute of the job but she couldn't shake Ashley off entirely. At the time of the big break-up he had been down from University, working in his father's law firm as a junior, no doubt being as much of a nuisance to Mr Knox as he was to Tess. So naturally whenever he had time off he turned up in Deeping Lane, on the Broad, in the city – wherever Tess was, in fact.

'Tess? You are a very odd girl – you don't sound at all pleased to hear from me after all this while.'

'How very perceptive of you,' Tess said appreciatively. You had to admire his cheek if nothing else, but she remembered Ashley well enough to realise that she had best put a stop to this once and for all. 'I was just thinking, Ash, how relieved I was when you went off and joined the Air Force. At least you stopped making a nuisance of yourself – I mean I could go outside the door without seeing you hovering somewhere. Indeed, ever since your departure I've had a very pleasant social life. Hasn't Freddy told you? I've got another boyfriend and I'm sure you've got another girl, as well.'

It should have been a sufficient snub to have Ashley getting off the phone as fast as he decently could, but his skin could be thick as elephant hide at times.

'You've got around a bit, Freddy did tell me that, and I've done the same, of course,' Ashley said equably. 'Nothing picks up bits of fluff quicker than an Air Force uniform.'

'Good. Then why should we want to meet?'

This caused Ashley to heave a deep, impatient sigh. 'For God's sweet sake, Tess, as if you didn't know! We're made for each other, you and I, why try to deny what's so patently obvious? Of *course* you've been out with other fellows when I'm not within reach, of *course* I've been out with other girls for the same reason. But now I'm home. What about this afternoon? I've got a car, I could pick you up after lunch.'

Tess looked through the kitchen doorway. Outside, the sun still shone, the breeze was gentle. She had no real plans for the afternoon – she had meant to go for a stroll around, pick Janet up, discuss with her friend what they should do if their respective places of work were closed down for the duration. If she could only consider Ash as a friend! But she couldn't. He wouldn't let her. Everything had to be done his way and he wanted a girlfriend, someone to cuddle in the back of a car, to canoodle with in the flicks, to boast about back at his Air Force station. Friendship, so far as Ashley was concerned, was a non-relationship, between her and him at any rate. So it had really better be a firm 'No, thank you'.

'Or before lunch, if you're free,' Ashley said whilst Tess was still considering how to turn him down nicely. 'Or this evening? Tomorrow? Do stop playing hard to get!'

'I'm not, I'm thinking,' Tess said truthfully. 'The trouble with you, Ash, is that if we meet you'll start trying to back me into a corner again. I know you, remember.'

'I shan't,' Ashley protested. 'I've changed. Honest.'

Tess snorted. 'Fat chance! Look, I tell you what, why don't you bring Freddy and we'll make up a foursome. We could go down to the seaside if you like – Sea Palling, I love Sea Palling.'

'A foursome? Who's the other fellow, then? Freddy's rather keen on Malty – George Maltson, you know. He's all right I suppose, but he's a brown job so we don't have a lot in common. And I don't think he's around at the moment . . . but I could ask, I suppose, if you're set on it. If you don't trust yourself alone with me.'

'I trust myself totally, it's you I don't trust,' Tess said acidly. 'And I wasn't thinking of Malty, I was thinking of a chap called Ted Bovis. He and I have been seeing quite a bit of each other . . .'

She got no further. An explosion caused her to snatch the receiver away from her ear and hold it at arm's length whilst Ashley told her what he thought of *that* idea. It wasn't much.

'All right, all right,' she conceded, her voice trembling with laughter, when the shouts had died away to mutters. 'Better to leave it for now, then, Ash. Perhaps we'll meet in the city, some time. Bye!'

She put the receiver down on his furious yelp and walked away from the instrument, which promptly began to ring. And continued to do so whilst Tess sat in the kitchen and strung the rest of the beans. Marianne came to the head of the stairs and called down to Tess to 'Answer that wretched thing or I shall go

251

mad!' and Peter came reluctantly in from the garden, very pink and puffy from too much sun, and tried to pick up the receiver, only Tess shouted to him to leave it.

'It's a fault on the line, the exchange will deal with it,' she called. 'I've scraped the potatoes, Daddy, d'you think I've done enough?'

Peter came and peered into the big saucepan and presently the telephone stopped ringing and Tess heaved a huge sigh of relief and continued with her preparations.

'Aren't you coming to church?' Marianne said presently, appearing in the kitchen doorway looking mint-cool in a pale-green shantung suit and matching hat with delicate white strap-sandals on her feet. 'You should change if you mean to accompany us.'

But Tess assured Marianne that she had not yet made the York-shire pudding, and that they had run out of horseradish, so she would miss morning service and go to the evening one, instead.

'I'll dig a root of horseradish and grate it,' she said. 'Daddy adores horseradish with beef, don't you, Daddy? And then I'll do the table and so on. All you'll have to do when you get back from church is sit down and eat.'

Afterwards, she wondered why she hadn't gone with the family, because she must have realised there would only be one reason for Ashley no longer trying to ring her. Sometimes she wondered about herself – could Ashley be right? Did she really love him, want him? It seemed unlikely, but on the other hand, why hadn't she gone to church? She should have realised he would get into his car and come over to Barton if she continued to ignore the telephone.

Ashley slammed the phone down and thought about the roast chicken his mother had promised him, and the crunchy roast potatoes, cooked just as he liked them, and the peas and beans, the rich chicken gravy, the chocolate pudding to follow. Or he could grab a sandwich and go and visit Tess.

He stared at the telephone, then picked up the receiver and tried once more to reach the Old House. No reply. Had they gone to church? But it was too early, they didn't have to leave yet, unless they were walking, which seemed unlikely. She's sitting by the telephone, Ashley thought balefully, deliberately not answering, deliberately keeping me on tenterhooks. What's the matter with the wretched girl? Why can't she simply admit that she's as crazy about me as I am about her, and then we could both be happy?

But for some reason she seemed obtuse on this one issue. And indeed, after the break-up, he had decided that she didn't deserve him. Stupid girl, to make an issue out of being knocked into the water once – just once – because he'd not been concentrating. It was almost unbelievable, but she'd gone on refusing to see him even after he'd rung and told her he wouldn't be in Norfolk long.

'I've joined the Air Force,' he said. 'And they're sending me to a training centre abroad somewhere. Come on, let's have a coffee together before I go.'

'No, thanks,' she had said. No thanks! You'd have thought she'd have wanted to forget their differences, to part friends, but not Tess! You had to admire her in a way, though, because she did stick to her guns. She had decided that they needed time apart and she was sticking to it.

So he had gone abroad, and he'd had a damned good time and increased his experience of women tenfold. Well, it would be truer to say he had *got* some experience of women, because apart from Tess – and she thought kissing dangerous – he hadn't had many girlfriends before he joined the Air Force. He had gone to Rhodesia though and undergone training, first on fighters and then on the big, unwieldy bombers, and he had been sent back as soon as war was declared, flying one of the aircraft he would presently fly in anger, against the Nazis.

He hadn't written to Tess from Rhodesia because he had still been annoyed with her. Fancy refusing to meet to say goodbye! But the moment he felt Norfolk soil beneath his feet once more he'd remembered everything about her, all the little things which he had conveniently forgotten whilst he assiduously courted Lorraine, Marcia, pretty, flirtatious Ruby. Her skin which was so much whiter than anyone else's, her hair which was so much darker. True black, her hair gleamed like satin whether it was pushed behind her small ears, falling across her face, or screening her smiles or tears. Then there was the tilt of her mouth, the small, jutting chin, the straight back, the long, slim legs . . . Tess Delamere. His Tess.

Standing in the sunny living-room watching the telephone wasn't going to do much for their relationship, though. Would she ring? Would she pick up the receiver if he telephoned again? He took the receiver off the hook and asked the operator for Tess's number. The phone rang out and rang out. No one answered.

She knows I'll go over there if she won't talk to me on the phone, Ashley told himself, abruptly slamming the receiver back on to its hook and turning towards the hallway. I might as well go now. And if she's in church then I'll wait until she comes out.

Driving along the sunny summery lanes with the branches meeting overhead, he wondered fleetingly why he did it. Why he continued to chase Tess, when there were other girls as pretty, with better figures. He was, after all, a tit man. All of his crew were tit men. So long as the tits were big enough they would put up with other things. He blinked as the road wound and the sun caught him across the eyes. So far as he could recall, Tess's tits were nothing out of the ordinary. Indeed, for all he knew they might be a couple of oranges, or possibly wodges of cotton wool stuffed into a brassiere, for Tess did not approve of petting.

'Keep your hands to yourself,' she was apt to say sharply. 'That's rude!'

He'd gone along with this peculiar viewpoint partly because he had believed her to be right and partly because he could see he'd lose her if he persisted. And, dammit, she was important to him, he could not imagine life without her. Sure, he'd been happy without her in Rhodesia, but in the back of his mind he had known it was just an interlude. He would go home, find her again, talk her round . . . and she would be his Tess once more.

And she, too, had been seeing other people since he left Norfolk. He hoped sincerely that she had slapped faces and kicked shins if anyone tried to get fresh with her, but at least she would now know that he wasn't some sex-crazed monster, that other young men really did expect a bit more than a couple of closed-mouth kisses at the end of an evening.

It was odd, he reflected, bowling along through the sunny

countryside, that he could want her more experienced yet feel a dreadful twist in his gut at the thought of any man other than himself laying a finger on her. I'll buy her a book about sex and things, he thought vaguely as he turned off the main road towards the Broad. I'll buy her a book and we can read it together. The thought brought a lump, but not to his throat, he thought, grinning guiltily. Ah, God, the thought of sitting next to Tess, their thighs touching, and reading a book about what he wanted so desperately to do to her! Come to that, the thought of seeing her in the flesh instead of just in his dreams! She would come to the door, smile at him, kiss him . . .

He roared down Deeping Lane, parked the car wildly askew outside on the verge, and charged at top speed up the short gravel path. He swerved round the house and banged briefly on the back door, then pushed it open.

She was whipping something in a round yellow bowl. Her glorious hair was tied on top of her head with what looked like a little scrag of string and she was completely enveloped in a big blue gingham overall. He registered that it hid her shape totally and was horrid, but then she raised a flushed face and started to speak and he was across the kitchen in one bound, round the table, and she was in his arms.

Unexpectedly, he wanted to cry. He felt tears of longing and relief flood his eyes. Oh, the feel of her, slender and supple in his arms, the fresh, youthful scent of her skin, the gloss of her hair as he laid his cheek on it . . .

She tried to push him away, wiggling desperately in his embrace. He turned her round so that they faced each other.

'Please, Tess, don't push me away, don't hurt me! I can't help loving you. You are so dear to me! Just let me hold you.'

She stopped trying to escape. She heaved a great sigh, and then she drooped her head on to his shoulder and relaxed. Her arms stole round his waist. It was the closest she had ever come to acceptance of his caresses and it was heady stuff but for once in his life, Ashley didn't take advantage of it. He simply stood there, cradling her in his arms, closing his eyes, letting his whole body relax. Love seemed to flow out of him, and suddenly it was enough to love her; it was no longer necessary that she should love him back.

She will, one day, he told himself, standing in the kitchen with his eyes closed and Tess warm against his chest. But until then, I have love enough for two. That will have to do, until she's older. She's still a baby, after all – I'm twenty-five. I mustn't hurry her; that's the way to lose her.

And he was careful to be the first one to move, to put her gently away from him and tell her that she had grown prettier than ever in his absence, to apologise for being such a brute on the telephone just now ... to ask her if she would finish whatever task she was engaged on and then come out with him, just for a quiet meal, or a walk – anything, so long as they could talk, be together.

'I'm making Sunday lunch,' she said. 'That was the Yorkshire pudding mix that you slopped on to the floor! Tell you what, Ash, why don't you stay here for lunch, sample my cooking? You know Daddy and Marianne will be pleased to see you after all this time. Yes, stay for lunch.'

He thanked her, said that would be lovely, and when she suggested it, went to and from the dining-room, laying the table. He felt peaceful, at ease, as though the embrace and Tess's sweetness had somehow damped the fire of longing for her, the feeling that she must acknowledge that they were made for each other.

Damped it for now, anyway.

'Can you go and dig a horseradish root, Ash? Only I've just remembered, I promised Daddy I would and I haven't done it yet.'

Tess and Ashley, between them, had finished off all the other preparations for Sunday lunch. The table was laid, the vegetables were simmering on the stove and from the oven, delicious roasting smells wafted forth.

'Sure,' Ashley said easily. 'Where does your horseradish grow? What does it look like?'

It made Tess laugh. He really had changed! Once, he would have gone out and searched and got crosser and crosser, but he wouldn't have admitted, to her, that he didn't know a horseradish plant when he saw one.

'The leaves are very long and broad, a bit like dock leaves,' she said. 'Look, it grows in the orchard . . . I'll show you. Bring a fork or something out of the shed as we pass.'

She went ahead of him, chattering. She had been horrified to see those tears, and the look in his eyes! Confident, bossy Ashley, actually pleading with her not to push him away, not to hurt him! It had changed things, of course. She really hadn't understood that Ashley had meant all the things he said. But if he'd meant them, why had he treated her so badly when they had gone out together? Being knocked into the Broad was just the last straw, but there had been plenty of straws before that! He had been silly at dances, trying to ping her suspenders whilst swaying lazily to the tune of the last waltz or sliding a hand under a shoulder strap and trying to slip it off her shoulder. God knew, she had told him crossly, that her straps slipped easily enough of their own accord without having to put up with his efforts as well! And then he'd been rude, often. Verbally rude sometimes, the other sort at other times. Cuddling was all right, it was fun and a comfort, but suddenly finding yourself having to repel insidiously seeking hands wasn't. She'd got hot and cross, bothered as much by the secret fear that Ashley might assume she was easy because her mother had got herself pregnant before marriage as by what he wanted to do, and that of course had made her twice as determined not to give an inch in the game which Ashley seemed intent on playing.

Of course she realised, now, that Ashley wasn't unusual; all young men seemed to try it on at least once. The main difference was that other young men took no for an answer. Some of them sulked, some of them went chasing off after someone a bit easier, but for the most part they took her strictures gracefully and stayed friends, whereas Ashley had become insulting and cross and had simply continued to try to break down her resistance.

But now, it seemed, Ashley had grown up and was going to be sensible. Reaching the shed he went in and came out with a garden fork, and when they got to the orchard and he had the horseradish pointed out to him, he dug obediently. He produced a couple of good big roots and carried them back to the kitchen, washed them, and watched as Tess, with watering eyes, grated them into a blue china bowl and then covered the horseradish with watered-down vinegar.

'There,' Tess said at last, carrying her booty through to the dining-room and standing the blue bowl in the middle of the table. 'It's worse than grating onions for making you cry, but it does go well with beef. Better than mustard. Oh, help, it's time the Yorkshire went in!'

She ran back to the kitchen, Ashley coming behind at a steadier pace, and grabbed the big tin out of the top of the oven. It was smoking and when she tipped the batter in, the fat hissed and spat and the batter puffed up round the edges as though it intended to become a pudding there and then.

'Won't be long now. I'll give the Yorkshire twenty minutes maximum,' Tess said, eyeing the big kitchen clock hanging on the wall above the door. 'Ashley, whatever will we do if there really is rationing? I can't imagine making a Sunday lunch without heaps of meat and fat to cook it in and lots of sugar and butter for the pudding. And Marianne's a real French cook, she can't start a meal without lashings of olive oil and lovely wine vinegar and stuff like that. Do you know, she buys special *flour* when she goes over to France, enough to last until her next visit? She doesn't like our flour for croissants and things like that.'

'You'll manage, just like everyone else will,' Ashley said. 'It's like the black-out; you've done the whole house, haven't you?'

'Yes, because Daddy explained about showing a chink of light and being bombed. He said that in the last lot a Hun pilot followed a train by the sparks from its smoke-stack until it reached a big city, he knew it was a big city because he saw lights – they weren't so fussy in the last lot, it appears – and he dropped his bombs and destroyed buildings and killed people. Daddy said Norfolk is in the front line more than any other part of the country because we're so far to the east, so he made Marianne do good, thick black-outs. We've got shutters, too, only they've got to be put up again. They were taken down before our time, but Daddy says they're in the shed all right, over at the back behind all the deck-chairs and things.'

'Well then, if you managed the black-out you'll manage cooking on rations,' Ashley said reasonably. 'Marianne's been spoilt –

we all have – but we'll all knuckle down to it if we have to. After the sinking of the *Athenia*, I think most people must have realised that there won't be much coming in from abroad, so it'll be English flour and no fancy olive oil, either. But you've got your orchard, the hens, a super vegetable patch . . .'

'You're right,' Tess said. 'I hear voices – they're on their way up the drive! Quick, Ash, chuck me that flour and I'll start making the gravy!'

The sun shone on the mirror-surface of the Broad and the breeze lifted a wing of Tess's gleaming hair and then dropped it so that it fell across her forehead. Tess pushed it behind her ear and squeaked as the willow branch, in which she and Ashley were sitting, creaked a protest.

'I wish I'd given the pudding a miss,' Tess said. 'This branch is groaning beneath my weight and yours – and my tummy's tight as a drum!'

'So's mine – you're a good cook,' Ashley said. 'That was one of the best roast beef lunches I've ever tasted, and Mrs Brett cooks a lovely roast, believe me. I was sad to miss my midday meal at home today, but I do believe yours was better.'

'Thank you,' Tess said. She shot him a round-eyed glance. 'Are you feeling quite well, Ash?'

'Why?'

'Well, that's a compliment, to tell me the meal was good, and you aren't lavish with compliments, as a rule. In fact apart from liking the odd dress or skirt or something, you've criticised more than you've praised.'

'Never!' Ashley said. He sounded disproportionately astonished, like a vicar falsely accused of swearing. 'I'm always telling you how clever you are and how pretty you look.'

Tess shook her head. So far, Ashley had not so much as held her hand. Things are improving, Tess told herself, and tried to ignore an uneasy suspicion that perhaps he simply did not find her attractive any more.

'No, you don't, Ash. The reason we broke up was because you said . . .' She felt her cheeks grow hot, but continued anyway. '. . . You said my – my chest wasn't as good as Stella Barlow's.'

Ashley chuckled. 'I was a fool. I was showing off, you see, trying to take everyone's mind off the fact that I'd knocked you into the 'oggin. Tess, it was two years ago! I've learned a thing or two in that time.'

'Oh. Good,' Tess said. 'So you like my cooking – what's the food like in the Air Force, then?'

'I'm in the officers' mess, and it's not too bad,' Ashley said. 'But it's not home cooking. I suppose you wouldn't like to come and sit this end with me? Then we could hold hands.'

'All right,' Tess said. 'But nothing more, please. I can't imagine anything worse than the pair of us ending up wrestling in the reed bed, which is feet deep in mud.'

'Then don't wrestle, give in gracefully,' Ashley said, and immediately looked stricken. 'I'm sorry, I'm sorry! I'll be good, I'll be good!'

Tess laughed and moved nearer, putting her chin on his shoulder. Immediately she became sharply aware of him; the smell of his hair and skin, the warmth of his shoulder against hers . . . and there was something else. The Ashley who had spent all their time together hotly fumbling at her clothing, perpetually trying his luck, had gone; he was a boy. The Ashley who put a gentle hand on her shoulder now was a man, and he knew . . . oh God, he knew . . . how to please her.

It was a stupid thought, but it had popped into her head and now she couldn't get rid of it. If she allowed him a little more licence, this Ashley would know how to give her pleasure without frightening or annoying her. So why didn't she . . .?

He turned her slowly into his chest and, with one arm round her, lifted her chin with the other hand. He said: 'Tess?' on a gentle note of interrogation and she said, 'Yes, Ash?' and did not try to jerk her chin free.

He came nearer gradually, slowly, as though she were a shy little bird who would be scared away by a quick movement. She saw his eyelids begin to lower over his full dark eyes, saw his nostrils flare a little . . . saw his mouth open to show the tip of his tongue. Then very gently, his mouth covered hers. For a second she wanted to laugh; it reminded her of a sea anemone swallowing a shrimp. And then she felt his tongue moving across her lips and excitement and a heavy longing, though for what she could not have said, stirred deep in her stomach. So this was the sort of kissing Janet had told her about – French kissing, she had called it. It was wicked, exciting, undoubtedly sinful . . . could you have a baby if a man did things like that with your mouth? She was not at all sure and meant to keep her own lips tightly sealed, so it was a surprise when they suddenly parted, pop, and Ashley's tongue invaded her mouth.

She tried to pull away, or she thought she did, but her body refused to obey her command, perhaps it recognised that it was in fact being given two commands, to go and to stay. She sat very still, eyes tightly closed, her hands resting lightly on Ashley's shoulders, as the kiss continued, both fascinated and repelled by what was happening to her, and when Ashley drew back she drew back too, though not quickly. She opened her eyes and closed her mouth. They stared at each other.

'Well?' Ashley said. 'Was it nice?'

Truthfulness came first. 'Yes,' she said. 'Odd, but rather nice. It – it couldn't give me a baby could it, Ash?'

She could see he was struggling not to laugh but he remained grave so she forgave him. He tilted her chin again though and gazed down into her eyes. 'Oh, Tess, no wonder I love you,' he said tenderly. 'No, you won't have a baby from a kiss. Nor will you have one if I put my hand on your breast, as I shall presently do.'

There he went again, ruining everything, making her feel silly, bringing the hot blood rushing to her cheeks. She said: 'You will do nothing of the sort, Ashley Knox, and if you try I shall give you a good, hard shove. Don't forget, the mud's a foot thick around here.'

'Fair enough,' Ashley said. 'You don't think you would like it, then? Me putting my hand . . .'

'No!' Tess yelped. She wriggled along the branch and thudded on to dry ground. Ashley began to follow her, so she jumped into the boat which was pulled into the reeds, making it rock precariously. 'Why can't you ever be nice for long? I'm going to take the boat out so you'd better get off home – and don't come round again because I won't see you!'

261

She reached for the oars just as Ashley thumped into the boat and grabbed her. She fell back, striking her head sharply on the rowlock. She gave a squeak of pain, then began to try to get to her feet again, only to find herself wrapped in Ashley's arms. She fought hard, but though he held her lightly, she could tell he did not intend to let her go. And he wasn't laughing, for once.

'Tess? Isn't it better to tell you what I'd like to do than to do it first and then apologise after? I'm only being frank, sweetheart, but if you don't want me to touch your br . . . to touch you, then I won't. Get it? I really won't.'

Tess stopped struggling. 'You kissed me without telling me what you were going to do,' she pointed out. 'You aren't consistent, Ash. You never were and I suppose you never will be and I'm sorry I started anything. We're better apart, you and I.'

'But you liked being kissed . . .'

'Yes, I liked it. But I don't like being poked and squeezed – understand? Men, honestly! You all think girls are like cows at market, standing there waiting for some fellow to feel around and decide if we're worth the price! I'm fed up with it – no, I tell a lie, I'm *bloody* fed up with it – and I won't stand for it. *Comprenez?*'

'Yes,' Ash said in a subdued tone. 'Sorry. Can we go back to kissing, please?'

'No,' Tess said crisply. The truth was, if he started kissing her like that again the chances were she'd scarcely notice if he slid his hand down the front of her brassiere – all the little hairs on her body stood on end at the thought – and that really would give him ideas.

'Oh. Right. Can I row you out on to the Broad, Miss Delamere?'

Tess, ruffled and hot and feeling like a bottle of gingerbeer which had been thoroughly shaken and was longing to pop its cork, said that he might row for a little if it would cool him down. Accordingly, Ashley rowed out across the Broad and Tess sat quietly in the stern, thinking hard. She had enjoyed Ashley's kisses but she didn't want him to go further. Why didn't she want him to go further? Because she was frightened? Because she feared pregnancy before marriage and a sullied name? But none of it made sense. The only thing which did was that nice girls, the sort of girl her father wanted her to be, did not indulge in what she had once heard referred to as 'promiscuous petting', and therefore she did not want Ashley – or anyone else – to start something which, for all she knew, she might not want them to stop.

Satisfied by this conclusion, she smiled across at Ashley. 'Tell me about the Air Force, Ash. What do you *do*, precisely? I know you fly huge great aeroplanes but that's about all I do know. And where will you be staying now you're back in England? Come on, tell me all about it and then I'll tell you what's been happening up at the Castle Museum.'

It was breakfast time, and Marianne was standing, or drooping rather, beside the Aga, scraping scrambled egg round the saucepan whilst Cherie watched slices of bread under the grill and Tess made coffee.

Breakfasts had once been happy affairs, Tess thought now, looking around the kitchen, and affairs with only three participants, what was more. For until war broke out, Marianne had been quite content for Peter, Tess and Cherie to get their own breakfast and see themselves off. So in those happy days they were able to take their time and please themselves. Usually, Tess cooked whatever breakfast they fancied, Peter masterminded the percolator and Cherie watched the slices of bread browning beneath the grill. They had eaten the food wandering around the kitchen or perched on the kitchen table, not bothering with plates or cutlery but folding bacon and a dripping fried egg between two slices of toast, or eating fried tomatoes and kidneys from a porringer, employing a spoon at most. Toast and marmalade was rarely eaten in the house but was devoured, as often as not, whilst sitting in the car motoring in to the city. As Peter said, it saved time, gave them something to do, and meant that they were never late. Though they did sometimes arrive at work – or, in Cherie's case, at school – somewhat sticky.

But war had, unfortunately, galvanised Marianne into unusual activity. She considered it her duty to get up, see her family off, and – presumably – go back to bed, and whether they liked it or not they were landed with it. The table had to be laid, food was eaten off plates, with knives and forks, and if they didn't have time to eat their toast and marmalade at the table then they didn't eat it at all. No one had dared grumble, but that didn't mean all three of them weren't watching eagerly for the first sign of weakness, for Marianne to say could they cope alone again, just this once. Then, how eagerly they would have sprung to her aid . . . and enjoyed their early mornings once more.

But right now, Marianne was turning creamy scrambled eggs to little bits of rubber to go with the bacon which, ignored in the pan for too long, was hard as nails and splintered whenever the cook poked blearily at it with her cooking slice.

'It's ready,' Marianne said suddenly, snatching the scrambled egg pan off the stove. 'Call your father, someone.'

Tess guessed that the scrambled eggs were now not only rubbery, they were burnt as well, but she went to the back door and shouted.

'Daddy! Brekker's up!'

Peter came ambling out of the cart-shed, where he garaged the car, with oil on his hands and a smear of it across his forehead. He acknowledged her shout with a wave and broke into a trot. 'Coming!' he called. 'Any post?'

'Yes. Two for you and one for me and another for Mr and Mrs. Do hurry, Daddy, the bacon . . . the bacon needs you!'

Peter grinned and came into the kitchen. He went straight to the sink, throwing the oily handkerchief down on the wooden draining board and then looking round vaguely for something.

'I'm a bit mucky; I've been filling the oil thing,' he said. 'Any soap about?'

'You should wash in the bathroom,' Marianne said reproachfully. She was still in her dressing-gown, unwashed, frowsty, her eyes all too obviously wanting to close once more. 'How can I see that the girls do as they're told when you come and wash in my sink? Go upstairs, Peter. There's plenty of soap upstairs.'

'No time,' Peter said. He reached for the Vim and sprinkled it on his palms, ignoring Marianne's squawk of protest. 'Shove my grub on a plate, there's a dear, I want to be in early this morning.'

Marianne grabbed a round of toast and tipped her rubbery scrambled egg into the middle of it, then clattered – and it did clatter – brittle fragments of bacon on to the plate. A blackened tomato-half and a round of soggy fried bread completed the meal.

'There you are,' she said. 'Cherie, I'll serve you next.'

'I'm just having toast thank you, Maman,' Cherie said with more haste than politeness. 'I don't like scrambled egg.'

'You do! Petite, it's your absolute favourite, don't you remember how you've always loved it?'

'Not when it's gone rubbery I don't,' Cherie stated. She was not a tactful child. 'And I *hate* burnt tomatoes.'

'Burnt? Oh well, tomatoes always go a little black . . . they're nicest then, really they are. Now come along, I won't have you going off to school hungry.'

'I'll have plenty of toast and marmalade, and some coffee,' Cherie said quickly. 'We have a cooked meal at school and you'll make something delicious for dinner, you always do.'

'Oh, very well. Tess?'

'I'll skip the eggs too,' Tess said. 'If Daddy wants to get away in good time then I'd sooner just have a bit of bacon and some tomatoes.'

'Oh, very well . . . Peter, do eat up! You say you want to get away early, so there's no point in sitting there staring at your plate.'

Tess took her plate and sat down opposite her father, then glanced up at him and immediately froze. He had opened his first letter and was reading it intently, brow furrowed, fork frozen half-way to his mouth.

'Daddy? Who's it from? Not the Ministry! What do they say?'

Tess knew that her father had been bombarding everyone he could think of with requests to be allowed to join up or do some useful war work. But he was too old for the armed forces and, despite his efforts, no ministry had yet seemed particularly anxious to acquire his services. But this letter . . . she leaned across the table.

'Daddy? Who's it from?'

Peter laid the letter down on the table. He looked dazed but happy.

'They want me!' he said, his voice higher than usual with emotion. 'It's the Navy – they want me for a shore job, in Portsmouth!

265

I've got to go down for an interview in two days' time. Gee whizz!'

'Oh, Daddy,' Tess said. 'I'm glad for you but sorry for us. Whatever will we do without you?'

'I shall not be without you,' Marianne said. She crossed the room and leaned on her husband's shoulder, reading the letter from there. 'It is *not* good, you are too old, I won't let you go!'

'They want me,' Peter said again. 'No question, old girl. But I'll get leaves, no doubt. I'll come home then.'

'How'll I get to school when you've gone?' Cherie whined. 'You always take me as far as the city – how'll I get in?'

'Bus,' Peter said shortly. 'Or train. Or bicycle, I suppose. You'll be all right, darling, you've got your health and strength. Or you could be a weekly boarder again, I suppose.'

Cherie had become a day pupil a couple of years earlier, when Tess had left school.

'I don't want to be a boarder, and the bus gets me there too late . . . oh I know, Tess can drive us,' Cherie said now. She returned to her toast and marmalade. 'That's all right then.'

'I won't have it!' Marianne said pettishly. 'Though I suppose, if you are to be away all week and only home weekends, Tess will be able to shop for me.'

'They're going to ration petrol,' Tess said rather maliciously. Her father had taught her to drive some months ago but Marianne had said it was unfeminine and unnecessary and had refused to travel in the car when Tess was at the wheel. 'I probably shan't have anything to drive with, and anyway, if Daddy means to come home every weekend he'll need the car himself. Besides, it won't hurt you to use the bus, Cherie. They'll have to make allowances at school; tell them there's a war on.'

'Stop arguing, girls,' Peter said. Unfairly, Tess thought. She wasn't arguing and the other two weren't so much arguing as chewing it all over, trying to see into the future. 'We'll have to get a move on, darling, or we'll all be in trouble. I'll take a couple of rounds of toast and marmalade, though. Tess, do me some, would you? Cherie, get your satchel and your hat and coat or you'll be bussing in this morning, never mind after I've left.'

'I've told you before, Peter, that breakfast is not a picnic and should not . . .' Marianne broke off. She stared across at Peter, her eyes filling with tears. 'Oh, my dearest, whatever will I do without you by my side? I truly, truly can't bear it!'

She meant it, Tess could tell, but Peter could tell too, and he had learned long ago how to handle Marianne. He came round the table and swept her up in his arms, then plonked one kiss on her nose and another on her mouth.

'No nonsense, my little French croissant,' he said gaily. 'I shan't be far away; if you're desperately lonely you can always catch a train down to Portsmouth, come and see me. And as I said, I'll be home whenever I can. Now be a darling and help your wretched daughters to get a move on, will you? Only I've got to beard old Harrison in his den with this letter' – he waved it under her nose – 'and he won't be best pleased if I'm late into the bargain.'

Cherie skidded back into the room at that point, her black felt hat at a rakish angle on the back of her head, her burberry on but not buttoned, her satchel unfastened and clinging grimly to one shoulder.

'I'm ready, Daddy,' she said breathlessly. 'I want toast and marmalade as well!'

'I've got some for all of us,' Tess assured her. 'Chuck my coat over, Cherie!'

'Where's my briefcase?' Peter demanded, brushing past Tess and nearly causing her to drop the pile of toast and marmalade sandwiches she was holding. 'Oh, God, it's in the study . . . Cherie . . .'

'Going,' Cherie said, plunging back into the hall. 'D'you want all the papers on the desk shovelled back in, Daddy?' she shrieked from the study.

'No, don't bother, just the pink forms,' Peter shouted back. He was wearing his coat and had his bowler in one hand. 'Come *on*, girls, don't keep me waiting all day!'

Cherie, flushed but triumphant, came back towing Peter's large, shabby briefcase behind her. 'There!' she said. 'Where's my toast?'

'It is like a madhouse,' moaned Marianne, but Tess could see she was wide awake for once, and quite enjoying the unusual fuss. 'This eating in the car – it is anarchy!'

Peter held open the back door for his daughters, then rushed past them and into the cart-shed. They heard the clatter of the engine being started, then the car came out with Peter at the wheel.

'Come on, get aboard,' he shouted. 'Where's my toast, Tess? Cherie, shove my briefcase out of the way and settle down. Marianne, where's my kiss?'

Marianne, giggling, ran forward and bent down by the driver's window, was kissed and retreated, still giggling, looking very pink and young.

'Toast,' Peter said, clicking his fingers, as soon as they were out of the short drive and making their way along the road. 'Wish I'd thought to bring some coffee, I never had time for a drink this morning.'

'Miss Bromwich will make you some as soon as you set foot in the office,' Tess reminded him. Miss Bromwich was Peter's elegant, middle-aged secretary and, as he continually told his daughters, a jewel of the first water. 'You've only got to ask.' She handed him the toast sandwich, then posted another over her shoulder to Cherie, on the back seat. She took a large bite of her own toast, then spoke through a full mouth. 'Dear Daddy, you should have struck over the toast weeks ago! I've really missed it.'

'Couldn't. Wouldn't have been fair,' Peter said equally thickly. 'I only did it today because of the letter. Now girls, no more talking, eat up! And when the toast's finished we'll discuss what you should do when I'm gone.'

Two days later Tess bussed into the city and then caught the bus back again. Cherie had gone home on an earlier one, so she had time, for once, to think without having to help with homework or listen to Cherie's school gossip.

Peter had gone for the interview with the Navy, but Tess was sure that it was just a formality; her father would get the job. They needed someone to train people to use signalling equipment and Peter had done precisely that in the last war. She was sure he would find himself doing it again before much longer.

So what should she do? She could, of course, stay at the Old House, but she could see that without Peter, Marianne would speedily make her life miserable beyond belief. It wasn't that Marianne was cruel or wicked, she told herself, simply very jealous indeed. She was even jealous over any sign of friendliness between Cherie and Tess, though her own relationship with her daughter was not a particularly warm one.

I could get a bed-sit in the city, Tess told herself. Or I could even live with Uncle Phil and Auntie May. They probably wouldn't mind too much, because the boys are off to the Forces so their rooms will be free. But she decided she would ring Ashley first and see what advice, if any, he had to offer.

Since Ashley's return he had become a regular visitor and despite their frequent quarrels, he was still very much her friend. He was stationed in Lincolnshire somewhere and seemed to be having a good time. He phoned her two or three times a week and when he had telephoned last had said he would be coming home for Christmas and hoped they might meet up.

So Tess sat on the bus and rehearsed what she would say to Ashley. That her father would be moving down south, to work for the Navy, and that she had decided to move too. She wanted his advice on whether to . . .

No! Suddenly, she knew quite well what she wanted to do, and it wasn't to have a bed-sit nor to live with her aunt and uncle in Unthank Road. She wanted a war job too, like Daddy and Ashley! She would join up!

Eleven

January 1940

It was bitterly cold. Outside the Old House snow lay thick, piled against the windows where the wind had carried it, drifting six feet deep along the lane so that even someone on a bicycle would have had difficulty making their way along it. But the worst of it was, Tess reflected, digging her way down the front path with her father's huge old coal shovel, that beneath the snow the ground was iron hard with frost. The wind might move the snow around as it gusted icily about her ears, but it was unable to bring about a thaw, and that meant winter was here to stay – for a while, at least.

It's a good thing I'm still here, she told herself as she dug, because if I weren't, Marianne and Cherie would just sit inside the Old House and slowly starve. Despite the fact that it was Saturday, and her day off, she had been first up today, as usual. Not that you could blame Cherie for lying in on such a morning – the snow had been bad now for over a week and the buses ran when they could, which wasn't often. Marianne, of course, no longer bothered to get up to cook breakfast. Why should she? Peter was not there to appreciate her sacrifice.

So when the postman abandoned his bicycle at the top of Deeping Lane and came down, swearing, with the mail, Tess grinned up at him and straightened her back, leaning on her shovel for a breather.

'Well, fancy meetin' you, Miss Delamere,' George Broxton said, grinning at her and resting his bag on the mound of snow she had thrown up to one side of the gatepost. 'You've been snowed in for quite a while, by the looks of it. Well, you're in luck, I've got through an' there's a letter for you. You've got nine days' post there, mostly for your ma, but I'd best not stand here gossipin'. This is the fust time I ha' got through, see, since the snow come down bad. Oh, and I've give you the Throwers' letters an' all, save my old legs, 'cos I know you'll be down there some time today. Cheerio!'

'Wouldn't you like a cuppa?' Tess asked, taking the letters. 'I'm going down to the Throwers all right, but I can make you some tea first.'

'I would, but I dussen't stop,' George said. He was old but hale and hearty, with a shock of white hair which pushed his postman's hat up at an odd angle in front, and a cheery though toothless grin. 'As I told you, that's the fust time I got down here since the snow so there's folk other than you waitin' for 'portant letters. Never mind, I'll hev that cuppa some other time.'

So Tess trudged up the path with the letters, took a cursory glance at them as she slung them on the hall table – there was a letter with a French stamp and another from Portsmouth with Peter's familiar handwriting on the envelope – then picked out the three letters addressed to the Throwers and the one addressed to herself and wrapped her scarf securely round her neck once more. She bellowed up to Marianne that the post had come and she was just off down to the Throwers with theirs and took off, shovel in hand, hoping that this unplanned excursion – for she had only intended to dig as far as the narrow cleared path down the middle of the road – would not mean that Cherie and Marianne would snuggle down and simply not get up until noon or after.

Despite working like a Trojan it took Tess the best part of twenty minutes to reach the Throwers' cottage, a journey which normally took less than five. She pegged away with the shovel though, because if she just pushed her way through she'd be soaked to the skin in seconds, and eventually arrived at the point where the Throwers must have cleared the snow earlier in the week. Of course it had snowed since, and drifted as well, but Podge and Dickie, being schoolboys, were at home still and must have been told to do some digging so that Mr Thrower could get into the village and Mrs Thrower could go off to work. No matter what the weather, Tess reminded herself, Mrs Thrower would find a way to reach her ladies; she had to, they needed the money. Bad weather meant the men couldn't garden or work on the farms or do the thousand and one other small jobs by which marshmen made a living, so the women had to work twice as hard when conditions were harsh.

Reaching the back door, Tess knocked on it, then pushed it open. Warmth rushed out, smoky, rather smelly warmth. You could tell, Tess thought, appreciatively sniffing as she entered the room, that the Throwers had been housebound for a while. She bade everyone good-morning, then took off her coat which had managed to get pretty wet despite her digging, and kicked off her wellingtons, leaving them outside the door.

'Well, well, an early bird today, Tess!' Mrs Thrower, pummelling dough, beamed at her visitor. 'Don't tell me that's started in to thaw!'

Mr Thrower was puffing on his pipe and staring sourly at the glowing stove and the boys were writing something in exercise books. Letters to elder brothers, Tess suspected. She had done her share of writing to friends in the Forces of late.

'No, it isn't thawing, I dug my way through because George asked me to bring your post down,' she said cheerfully. 'Nice to see you relaxing for once, Mr Thrower.'

'Relaxing?' Mr Thrower snorted, tapping his pipe out against the side of the stove. 'I casn't cut reed in this, and it's reed-cuttin' time, young 'oman. Where'd I stack the shooves, for a start-orf? And don't you say I could rick 'em up, because when the thaw come – if it come – the floods won't go round a rick, not bloomin' likely, they'll carry it orf down to the sea with 'em. Wha's more the Broad's fruz over, the marsh walls is thick wi' snow, since I in't a bloody eximo I casn't git no fish . . .'

'Well, the reeds'll wait,' Mrs Thrower said philosophically. 'I in't never known a marshman what din't grumble about the weather for reed cuttin', whether 'tis rain, hail or snow, like now. If there in't nothin' doin' outside, why don't you mend your bow nets?'

'I mended 'em Christmas,' Mr Thrower said. 'Chuck us the

post, gal Tess, an' I'll tek a look at it.' Tess handed over the letters and Mr Thrower got his tiny little spectacles out of the top pocket of his jacket and perched them on his nose. He slit both envelopes, then pulled out two sheets of pale-blue lined paper.

'One's from our Ned – he's in France, you know. And t'other's from Ozzie, on this here frigate, only they're ashore, seemingly. Ah, an' the last 'un's from our Bert.'

Having said this he handed the letters to Podge, who read them aloud whilst Tess opened her own letter, which turned out to be information leaflets on the armed services. So far, she had done nothing further about choosing which service to honour with an application to join, but she rather fancied the WRNS since Peter was with the Navy and hoped the leaflets might make up her mind for her.

'Well, there y'are,' Mr Thrower said at length, when the three short letters from the Thrower young had been read out and exclaimed over. 'And now, if it in't actually *peltin'* wi' snow, I'd best go an' git some hay in for Susan.'

Susan was the Throwers' latest acquisition, a house cow. She was a good-tempered little beast, with a fudge-coloured hide and a wide-ranging appetite. She would happily eat marsh-hay, reed or gladdon, which was the local name for bullrushes, and she had been known to take a meat sandwich out of your hand and be licking your fingers with her long, blackish-purple tongue before you'd even realised where your food had gone.

'Right you are, Dad,' Mrs Thrower said placidly. 'She's on high ground, in't she? It 'ud break my heart if anythin' happened to that little old cow.' She turned to Tess. 'Ate my bloomers off of the line last week,' she said. 'I writ to Janet an' she said the girls in her billet near on died laughin'. You ha'n't decided yet whether or not to join the WRNS, then?'

'Not yet,' Tess admitted. 'But I've got information leaflets and application forms now, that was what my letter was. So maybe I'll start filling the WRNS one in tonight.'

'Good for you, gal,' Mr Thrower said. He was struggling into his huge marshmen's boots and slinging his waterproof round his shoulders, slapping his sou'wester on his grizzled head – over his cap, Tess was amused to see. 'I like to see youngsters doin' their bit, same as what I did, in the last lot. Our Janet, she's doin' good, that I do know. Now, young Podge, get you off that sofy an' come alonga me. Teks two to move marsh hay.'

'You'll put in for the WRNS I reckon, young Tess,' Podge said, getting to his feet. He got his own jacket off the hook and struggled into it. It was quite a lot too small, Tess realised, and this made her see how Podge had grown. He must be getting on for six foot and he had shoulders like barn doors, yet he was only fifteen going on sixteen, and desperately anxious to get into the Forces. He had told Tess he would probably choose the Navy, though he had a sneaking desire to fly. 'Why don't you put in for the WAAF, Tess, like our Jan?'

'Oh, I dunno. I might still do just that. I don't much like the WRNS hats, to be honest, they're awful, worse than my old school hat. And black stockings can look really frumpy and they make your legs look thinner, which mine can't do with. But it would please Daddy, though in a way I'd quite like to be stationed in Norfolk, near all my friends and family, which would mean the WAAF – most of the WRNS are down in Hampshire or up in Scotland. And then with Janet and Freddy both being in the WAAF it makes me think that perhaps I'd be happier in the Air Force. So you can see why I can't make my mind up!'

Podge grinned and let himself out of the back door without further comment, shutting it firmly behind him, but Dickie, sitting by the fire knotting a length of net, made a rude noise.

'Fancy not bein' able to mek up your mind 'cos you din't like the hat, an' the stockin's made your legs look skinny,' he crowed. 'In't that jest like a gal?'

'Mind your manners, Dickie Thrower,' Tess said. 'Do I'll give you a ding acrost the lug.'

Dickie crowed again, then ducked as Tess made for him. Mrs Thrower was dividing her dough between half a dozen tins now, and she looked up and shook her head at both her son and her guest.

'Dickie, you're no gentleman, and you in't much better, Tess, talkin' rough like that. Now settle down, the pair of you. Read us what it say about the WRNS first, Tess, and then what it say about the WAAF, then we'll talk it over.'

But Tess had scarcely done more than take the leaflets out of the envelope when someone knocked hard on the door and the handle began to turn. Quickly, she stuffed the leaflets into her skirt pocket and went across to the door. Cherie stood there. Tess stared, registering that Cherie wore a blue woollen dressing-gown and wellington boots and that she looked terrified out of her mind, but before she could open her mouth to ask Cherie what she was doing, coming outside in weather like this in her night things, Cherie had grabbed hold of her with shaking hands.

'Oh Tess, I thought you'd be here,' she gabbled. 'Can you come home? Maman's having hysterics, it's awful, she just sort of screamed and threw herself on to the floor and kept biting at the tiles . . . I think she's gone mad. Do come – she won't even look at me and when I threw water over her – it said to do that some-where, I'm sure it did – she rolled her eyes right up until only the whites showed and screamed louder than ever.'

'Yes, of course I'll come . . .' Tess was beginning, when she found herself pushed to one side. Mrs Thrower, in print apron, faded skirt and slippers with holes in the toes, was going up the garden as fast as she could, disregarding the snow which her every step dislodged.

'Put Dickie's coat round the kid,' Mrs Thrower shouted back over her shoulder. 'She'll catch her bloomin' death, else. I'll see to Mrs Delamere.'

Tess plucked Dickie's coat off the hooks and forced Cherie's trembling arms into the sleeves, then buttoned it briskly and dragged her sister outside.

'At least you had the sense to put your wellies on,' she said reassuringly. 'Don't worry, love, we'll soon be there and Mrs Thrower will know what to do. We'll get your maman right in no time!'

'She's ill,' Cherie said. 'Ill or mad. I'm so frightened, Tess. Do let's hurry.'

'Sure,' Tess said. 'Give me your hand.' She grabbed her sister's small, cold paw and they set off up the lane at the best pace Tess could manage and presently they drew level with Mrs Thrower, whose speed had been slowed to a breathless plod by the depth of the snow and the harshness of the cold.

'Had Marianne opened the post, got bad news from France?' Tess suggested presently, as they battled onwards. She remembered the letter with the French stamp. She was truly grateful, now, that she had dug a path for herself earlier and not simply fought her way through. Now at least there was a path to follow, though in places the wind had already blown snow over her shovelling. 'She can't have behaved like that for nothing.'

'I don't know,' Cherie said breathlessly.

'You don't know? But surely . . .'

'I'd only just come down,' Cherie said. 'I heard a thump and then an awful scream, like vixens give in the spring. So I ran downstairs . . .' she broke off and a shudder shook her small frame.

'Don't worry, love,' Mrs Thrower put in, slowing her onward progress for a moment and addressing Cherie over her shoulder. 'Soon be there. Ah, the path's widened out here – take my arm, and your sister's . . . that's it, that's better. Now we shan't be long!'

And they were not long, considering the time it had taken Tess to traverse that same length of lane, earlier. It could not have been more than five minutes after they set out that Tess was throwing open the back door and shouting cheerfully: 'Marianne, we're back!'

There was no answer. No one came to the door or called out.

'She've gone upstairs,' Mrs Thrower said briskly. 'I'll go up. Cherie, put you that kettle on, we'll have a nice cuppa. Tess, poke the fire up and make a hot water bottle. Mrs Delamere's likely needin' a good warm through.'

Glad to be given a job, Cherie filled the big kettle and carried it over to the Aga, whilst Tess riddled the fire and put more coke on. She listened as she worked, for the reassurance of voices, but she heard none. Only the chilly moan of the wind, the rattle of the fuel falling on to the glowing coals, Cherie's gasping breath as she handled the heavy kettle.

Then the sounds of heavy footsteps descending the stairs. Tess raised her brows as Mrs Thrower came into the room.

'Is she up there?'

'No, not as I could see. She must ha' gone along the lane a ways, to the Rope place. She'll need a doctor, from the sound.'

'She'd have telephoned . . .' Tess began, then remembered. The wires had been down for forty-eight hours, dragged into useless loops by the weight of the snow. 'Oh, she couldn't, of course. Is her coat missing, then?'

'I'll look,' Cherie said. Her voice was squeaky but she was calmer here in her own home, with Mrs Thrower's comforting bulk and her sister's presence. 'Oh, d'you think she went out after us? If she went round by the Broad . . .'

'That'll likely be the answer,' Mrs Thrower said comfortably, but her eyes were deeply worried and she glanced at Tess as Cherie went out to search the hall cupboard for her mother's coat, and gave a slight shake of the head. She did not think that Marianne had gone searching for her daughters and had somehow managed to miss them. Nor, for that matter, did Tess. She ran into the hall and returned to the kitchen with the letters. Two had been opened, but the rest were still in their envelopes. The letter from Peter was a cheery account of a trip round a warship which, it seemed, he had very much enjoyed. The other was a note from Garlands, about a fashion show they were about to hold. Tess riffled quickly through the rest of the envelopes. The one with the French stamp was missing.

'Well?' Mrs Thrower said impatiently. 'Anythin' there to gi's a clue where she's gone?'

'No-oo. There's a letter from Daddy, very cheerful, and another from Garlands, about a fashion show on make do and mend, whatever that may mean. But – but I noticed one envelope particularly, with a foreign stamp; French. That's missing. Not there.'

'Dear Lor', bad news,' Mrs Thrower said at once. 'D'you reckon it sent her over the top, like?'

'Must have, I suppose,' Tess said rather doubtfully. 'Only where's she gone?'

'Best take a look outside,' Mrs Thrower said in a breathy whisper. 'Keep it quiet to the kid though, Tess. I reckon Mrs Delamere's gone off up to the Ropes' or to the Millers'. She might even have tried to get to the shop.'

'The *shop*? But why on earth would she want to do that?'

'To send a telegram, acourse,' Mrs Thrower said. 'To tell them Frenchies she were goin' to do what she could. Oh no, she couldn't send a telegram I suppose, wi' the war an' all. I wonder now, hev she left you and Cherie a note? So's you'd know where she'd gone, like?'

'No,' Tess said positively. 'We leave notes on the cork board, and there's nothing there.'

Mrs Thrower started to reply but was cut short by Cherie returning at a trot to the kitchen. 'All Maman's coats are hanging up in the understairs cupboard,' she announced. 'Where would she go without a coat, Tess? Unless someone called for her, Uncle Phil or someone?'

'That'll be it,' Mrs Thrower said before Tess could open her mouth. 'But we'll just tek a look round, in case. How about you gettin' us some breakfast, young lady? Tess an' me'll jest tek a look outside.'

'Right, Mrs Thrower,' Cherie said importantly. 'I do lovely scrambled eggs, don't I, Tess? And I'll make a pot of coffee. Maman likes coffee better than tea at breakfast.' Her composure faltered a little. 'Why would she go off and not tell us where?' she asked querulously. 'I'm frightened, Tess.'

'Don't worry, Cherie,' Tess said quickly. 'We've worked it out, Mrs Thrower and me. There was a letter from France, I noticed it when George gave me the post. It's missing, so Marianne must have it with her. Mrs Thrower thinks they've written to ask for help and Marianne's flown off down to the post office to send a telegram. Something like that, anyway. So we're just going to go down the road a bit, see if we can catch her up.'

'Oh, right,' Cherie said. 'I'll start cooking brekker right away, then. You'll be hungry when you get back and so will Maman.'

Despite what she had told Cherie, however, Tess was very worried. There wasn't a coat missing, which must mean that Marianne had left the house in a real rush, probably in skirt and jumper, with her ordinary walking shoes on. Not having been outside for days, she probably had no idea of how appalling conditions were, and not being interested in her neighbours' affairs, she might well not have realised that all the telephone wires were down in Barton, including the Millers' and the Ropes'. And her stepmother was no countrywoman, used to walking. It wasn't far to the village, but it would take forty minutes at least, and where the snow had drifted it was dangerously deep.

She confided her fears to Mrs Thrower, who said rather sharply that Mrs Delamere was far too fond of her own comfort to risk a wetting.

'But from what Cherie said she's gone a bit barmy,' Tess pointed out. 'She's awfully highly-strung, you know. And I suppose she's very fond of her parents, though she doesn't talk about them much.'

'Yes, well you stop jabberin' an' use the eyes God give you,' Mrs Thrower said irascibly. 'Now that *is* odd.'

Tracks, presumably Marianne's, led straight from the back door, across the long lawn, through the orchard, and down to the edge of the Broad. The oddness, Mrs Thrower pointed out, was that Marianne had skirted the cart-shed and gone round the potting shed and the summer house, heading straight for the Broad. She hadn't even deviated to where the boat's small bulk could be dimly seen through the frost-encrusted reeds. So why come down here at all? But they doggedly followed the footprints right down to the reedbeds, though there they were stymied. The ice was really thick and patchily sown with snow, but even as they watched the wind blew a great veil of snow across the ice, completely obliterating any footprints which might have been visible seconds before. And then, as though repenting of its kindness in stopping for a few hours, the storm began again, the flakes coming down so fast that they could barely see the outline of the house. If Marianne had decided to get to the village across the frozen Broad then her footprints were obliterated now.

'Only I can't see her doing that – it's far too dangerous,' Tess shouted as they slogged their way across the orchard and up the lawn once more. 'If she took a look at it and then retraced her steps though, which seems the obvious thing to do, why didn't we find her there when we got back? Unless she went round the house and out the front, of course.'

'We'd best check,' Mrs Thrower shouted. 'Our tracks lead down to the staithe – what about goin' up Deepin' Lane?'

They went back to the front gate and were immensely cheered to find definite tracks; Marianne had clearly gone to the Ropes' or the Millers'. But then Tess remembered that the postman had come down that way earlier and gone the same way, too. Marianne *could* have left the house, run down the drive and turned left outside the gate, but they would not be able to track her across the churned-up snow.

'We'll try the Ropes,' Mrs Thrower decided. 'Wish I'd got my coat . . . I'll borrow one of yours, gal Tess.'

'Right,' Tess said. 'You go back and grab my old burberry from the downstairs cloakroom, and a hat and a scarf or something. I'll start out.'

'That you will not! 'Tis treacherous weather, my woman. We'll go together or not at all.'

'What'll we tell Cherie?' Tess said uneasily as they approached the back door once more. 'The more I think of it the less certain I am that she'd have gone into the village on foot and without a coat. I'm getting scared, Mrs Thrower. Where on earth can she be?'

'Not far off, I dessay,' Mrs Thrower said, but Tess could hear the uncertainty in her voice. 'Dear God, what a day to clear orf on!'

But when they got back to the house they found Cherie both busy and happy. She was breaking eggs into a bowl with a prodigal hand and whisking them into a froth.

'Any luck? I knew she wouldn't be in the garden in this weather, but I did wonder about the cart-shed or the summer house,' Cherie said. 'She must have gone to send that telegram, I suppose. Don't be too long, eggs are nicest fresh.'

Outside once more, though now both stoutly booted and with their coats buttoned right up to the chin, the two women stared doubtfully at each other through the whirling flakes.

'Marianne doesn't care for the rector, not on a social level,' Tess said finally. 'But she quite likes the Ropes and the Millers. I know they're off the phone but she probably didn't; we'll try there first, shall we?'

They followed in George's footsteps and only took about fifteen minutes to reach the Ropes' pleasant farmhouse but they drew a blank there, as Tess had feared.

'Mrs Delamere? No, she hasn't been near nor by since the snow come down,' Mrs Rope said cheerfully. 'Do you want a cup of tea? I've just made one.'

They declined, both too desperately anxious, now, to stop.

'If you hear any word of her, come down to the Old House, would you?' Tess pleaded. 'We're most awfully worried, she seems to have disappeared!'

'Oh, she won't be far,' Mrs Rope said. 'Try the Millers'.'

They tried the Millers' and drew a blank there, then the rectory, then the shop, then the blacksmith's. No Marianne.

'We'll hev to get back to the child,' Mrs Thrower said at last. ''Sides, there in't nowhere else to search. Oh, when I see Mrs Delamere I aren't half goin' to give her a piece of my mind! Scarin' us like this.'

But they didn't see her.

By six o'clock that evening Tess had put Cherie to bed with a comforting hot water bottle and a drink of cocoa and was sitting at the kitchen table with her own hot drink beside her, wondering how she would ever sleep. Cherie had been remarkably good and sensible but it was easy to see the strain was telling on her. The child's face had been wan, her eyes red-rimmed, and she had insisted that Tess sat by her beside until she fell asleep. None of their searching and enquiries had helped at all. No one had seen hide nor hair of Marianne, she had disappeared completely.

'I'm trying to be sensible but I'm afraid,' Cherie said humbly, clutching Tess's hand as the older girl perched on the side of her bed. 'I know Maman isn't always very nice to you, Tess, but I do love her, and I want her very, very much.'

'She'll be back in the morning; bound to be,' Tess said soothingly. She was both angry with Marianne and frightened for her – what on earth had caused her stepmother simply to fly out of the house in the way she apparently had, leaving them all in disarray?

But now Cherie was in bed and asleep, so Tess had come downstairs to make her own hot drink and get herself a sandwich. She'd not eaten all day and suddenly realised she was ravenously hungry. If she did not eat she would never sleep, so she found a loaf, cut two slices, added cheese and pickle and was sitting down at the kitchen table, eating, when someone knocked at the door and then came in. It was Mr Thrower, with Podge beside him looking extremely uneasy.

Mr Thrower looked at her, then cleared his throat. He was dressed in his outdoor things including his great marsh boots and his brown, seamed face was creased with worry.

'No sign yet, gal?' he said gruffly.

'Nothing.'

'Right. I'd been havin' a word wi' Mrs Thrower and we both think Mrs Delamere may have gone down to Portsmouth. Gawd alone know how she got a lift outa all this here snow, but we reckon she may well have done just that. So I'm agoin' to take old Piggot and my cart and go into Hoveton, see if I can find a telephone what's workin', so I can ring your dad's place at Portsmouth. Only I don't know the number. Can you give it me, gal Tess?'

'Ye-es. But I'd rather ring myself, Mr Thrower. It – it's all a bit complicated and if Daddy hears it from anyone but me he's going to get in an awful state. Would you mind awfully if I came with you?' She smiled at Podge. 'I'm lighter than you, Podge, so Piggot won't object,' she added.

Mr Thrower smiled and Tess realised that he had been hoping she would offer. It would have been desperately hard for a man of so few words to have told the story, she realised.

'Well, I did wonder . . . Piggot's a sturdy little mule but the less weight the better, an' Podge here will stay with the littl'un. In bed, is she?'

'Yes, and asleep. Are you sure you don't mind, Podge?'

Podge shook his head. 'I don't mind,' he said gruffly. 'Warmer here than down at Staithe Cottage, an' all. If the young'un's asleep, can I borrow a book to read?'

'Sure, as many as you like,' Tess said. 'It's a good long way to Hoveton, though, Mr Thrower. Are you sure Piggot won't founder and land us in a snowdrift?'

'Naw! Mules are tough old birds. Wrap up warm, though. That's a wicked old night.'

*

282

Jogging along the snow-covered roads, now getting out to lead the mule, now climbing back into the cart and having a ride, Tess thought she would never forget that journey. By the time they set out the storm had cleared and stars twinkled frostily in the great black arch of the sky, whilst a round-faced moon lit up the smooth blanket of snow which covered the countryside as brightly as though it were day.

'Good job there in't no wind,' Mr Thrower said, when Tess remarked on how beautiful the fields looked in the moonlight. 'That 'ud finish us an' no error. Snow's so dry, see, an' the air's so blooda cold, that a wind could pick up the lot an' put it down anywhere, just about.'

'Well, we're making good time,' Tess said, consulting her wristwatch. 'Oh, I shouldn't have said that – we're stuck again.'

It was the wheels of the trap, caught in a hidden dip, but they dug themselves out and slogged on, with Piggot really putting his back into his work and pulling like a carthorse.

'Bin eatin' his head orf in the lean-to,' Mr Thrower said when Tess told Piggot that he was an excellent animal and worth his weight in gold. 'He need the exercise, an' he like it, an' all. Oh ah, there's wuss animals than mules.'

It took time, but they reached Hoveton at last. It was quite late by now, but Mr Thrower drove them straight to the public call box. Tess jumped down, went into the box, lifted the receiver and held it to her ear and was overjoyed to hear a comforting burr and not the dreadful silence of a disconnected line.

As soon as she had given the operator the number, Tess opened the door and poked her head round it, addressing Mr Thrower, who was standing at Piggot's head. 'It's working, I've laid my money out and it's ringing in Portsmouth. I can't wait to tell Daddy and hear what he has to say – I'm hoping he'll come home if she isn't in Portsmouth with him, and help us to run her to earth.'

'Course he will,' Mr Thrower said stoutly. 'But I reckon she'll be there be now, tuckin' into some supper, I dare say.'

But although she got through to the number she had been given, it transpired that there was no one present who could give her any information at all and because the line was so bad the impersonal voice at the other end advised her to try again the following morning, and whilst she was trying to explain that this might well be impossible, the connection was cut.

Crestfallen, Tess opened the door of the box, letting in a blast of the icy cold, and told Mr Thrower what had been said.

'What'll I do?' she asked helplessly. 'It's taken us such ages to get here, it seems awfully feeble simply to turn round and go home.'

'Ring your uncle,' Mr Thrower suggested. 'Tell him what's bin a-goin' on. Can't do no harm.'

'Good idea,' Tess said. She returned to the box and rang her aunt and uncle, who were horrified to hear that Marianne had disappeared, leaving her daughters cut off by the snow.

'I'll get in touch with your father's commanding officer tomorrow and see what can be done there,' Uncle Phil said, his voice sounding strong and very like her father's over the telephone. 'You go back home now and have a good night's sleep; Auntie May and I will be over first thing in the morning, if we have to walk every mile of the way. And don't worry, we'll find Marianne and get in touch with Peter and you'll be laughing at this in a day or two.'

Tess was grateful for his warm good sense and she and Mr Thrower drove home quite cheerfully, even though it took them almost twice as long as the drive out had done.

'Snow's stickier. Thaw's comin',' Mr Thrower said as they turned into Deeping Lane at last. 'You're a good'un, gal Tess. Wouldn't mind havin' you wi' me in a tight spot.'

'Ditto,' Tess said, immensely touched by his words. 'And thanks a million, Mr Thrower. No one could have been kinder. You and Mrs Thrower are the best friends anyone could have. Now come in for a nightcap whilst I check on Cherie.'

Mr Thrower agreed that a nightcap wouldn't come amiss and got stiffly down out of the cart, so she ushered him into the kitchen, greeted Podge, and poured Mr Thrower a stiff whisky and ginger wine, which he drank down enthusiastically, agreeing to have a second to 'keep the cold out', as he put it.

Tess, meanwhile, tiptoed up to take a look at Cherie, then went downstairs again and allowed Mr Thrower to add a spoonful of her father's brandy to her hot cocoa.

'That 'on't harm,' he said gruffly. 'Sleep well, an' tomorrer come an' tell us when you've spoke to your dad.'

Tess promised to do so, drank her drink, thanked Podge for his help, waved the two men off and went up to bed. She stood in her bedroom window for a moment, lazily taking off her damp clothes, for perspiration had popped from every conceivable pore as she and Mr Thrower had laboured to get the mule and cart – and themselves – back to Deeping Lane, and gazed out at the moonlit Broad. It looked extraordinarily beautiful, she thought, with the reeds and trees silvered by frost, the snow lying thick even on the ice, and the stars twinkling above.

She was so tired, in fact, that moving seemed far too difficult a task. She could have stood there for ever, gazing out at the drama of the Broad in the snow, but she forced herself to go back into the room, put on her pyjamas and climbed between the sheets. She lay for a while, too tired to sleep, but then she found herself sliding helplessly into slumber.

The Broad was black in her dream, black in the shadow of the reedbeds and white with snow elsewhere. She was rowing a little boat across the ice – it was easy, it slid along beautifully – with Andy in the bows. He was young again, because she had never known him any age other than twelve or thirteen, and he was laughing at her, teasing her.

'You never see what's under your nose, do you, Tess?' he asked at one point. 'You're hunting for that wretched stepmother of yours but you haven't looked in the most obvious place.'

'What's that?' Tess said idly. She had stopped rowing now, the oars had disappeared as they do in dreams, and she was leaning out of the boat, trying to gather some sweet rushes which grew just out of reach. The scent of them was summery and evocative and a tortoiseshell butterfly had perched amongst them. It was sunning itself, its wings at rest, quivering slightly as her fingers brushed against its perch.

'Why, under your nose – didn't you hear me?'

He pointed at the reeds and she glanced towards them . . . then froze. In the dark depths, something moved, something greenish-white and sinister . . . it looked like a hand . . . it was a hand!

She woke with a muffled shriek which was more terrifying than a full-blooded scream and lay for a moment, heart thumping, whilst perspiration trickled down between her breasts and the bed became, not a place of refuge, but a nest in which horrors might leap on her the moment she relaxed and closed her eyes. Accordingly, she sat up. Moonlight streamed through the window, so she probably hadn't been asleep for long.

What should she do? She could light her candle and read for a bit. Or she could prowl downstairs through the moonlit house and poke the Aga into life and make herself another hot drink. Only it was awfully chilly for night-walks. Perhaps if she cuddled down . . .

But the minute she did she remembered the dream, and Andy's voice sounded once more in her ears. *You never see what's under your nose, do you, Tess?*

She sat up and swung her legs out of bed. All right, Andy, she said tiredly, only there's no point in it, because we looked everywhere, this morning, and Cherie's been here with Podge ever since.

She pulled a jumper over her head, shoved her feet into slippers, and made for the landing.

You never see what's under your nose, do you, Tess?

With an impatient sigh, she crossed the landing and opened the door of her parents' room.

Marianne lay, curled up on one side, the covers cuddled well up. She was fast asleep, and from her slightly open mouth came a small, purring snore.

'She was in the *wardrobe*,' Cherie said. 'Curled up small, right at the back. I woke up, you see, and wondered whether she might have changed from her light stuff into a thick wool suit, so I went to the wardrobe and there she was. I was so surprised and scared when I saw her that I screamed, and it woke her up. She made whimpering noises and sort of snuffled and cried a bit, and said I was a bad girl to startle her so. I began to say she had been pretty bad herself, that everyone was searching for her, only she didn't take any notice. She just stood up, stretched, did a lot of muttering in French and then rolled into bed, in her clothes, mark you. So then I went to your room, Tess, only you weren't there, so I thought – I don't know why – that you must have realised Maman was safe and I went back to bed myself.'

'You didn't go downstairs, tell Podge?'

'How could I? It was the middle of the night,' Cherie said righteously. 'Anyway, I didn't know he was down there. I would have told you, of course, but as I said, you weren't in your room.'

'Oh, Cherie . . . and we've been dreadfully worried, I rang Daddy's place in Portsmouth . . . he's going to ring me back tomorrow. What on earth will he say?'

The two girls were whispering on the landing, and they must have woken Marianne for she called out sleepily, 'What is happening? It's the middle of the night, girls, get back to bed.'

Tess poked her head round the door. Marianne was sitting up, looking down at herself with considerable surprise. She looked up at Tess as she entered the room.

'I'm wearing a *dress*,' she said slowly. 'Why am I wearing a dress?'

'You were ill,' Tess said, at a loss for a better explanation. 'What's that in your hand, Marianne?'

Marianne looked down at the scrumpled bit of paper gripped in her fingers as though it might bite her. 'I don't . . .' she began, and then her puzzled look fled and an expression of deep and terrible sorrow took its place. 'I'd forgotten,' she said, and then, her voice rising, 'I'd forgotten, forgotten, forgotten! How could I forget such a thing, how could I sleep when I am so, so alone?'

'We're here, Maman,' Cherie said doubtfully, but Tess leaned forward and plucked the piece of paper from between her stepmother's fingers. She looked down at it, expecting to see French, and saw, instead, English words. Abruptly, cold and terrible dread began to trickle, like iced water, along her veins. She hadn't counted the envelopes, clearly there had been two missing, not just one. She smoothed the paper out and saw that it was a telegram. She read it at a glance and then, stumblingly, read aloud the few words on it.

I am sorry to have to tell you that at midnight last night your husband was knocked down on his way to his quarters by an unidentified vehicle. An ambulance was called immediately but he was dead on arrival at hospital. Letter follows.

Cherie sobbed, once, then spoke, her voice small, bewildered. 'Is that our daddy, Tess? Does it mean our daddy's been killed?'

'Yes,' Tess whispered through numb lips. 'It means our daddy's dead.'

For days Tess worked ceaselessly, doing all the things Marianne should have done. She and Peter's commanding officer arranged for the body to be brought back to Norfolk, she and the local undertaker made what funeral arrangements they could, though the body could not be buried in the little churchyard by the Broad until the frost allowed the grave to be dug. Then she and the vicar planned the service, and whereabouts in the graveyard her father would be buried.

The Throwers and her uncle and aunt offered to help but Tess, numbed by the tragedy, said she would rather do it herself. And then she simply kept her head down and worked as hard as she possibly could, because when she was frantically busy she did not have to think. Indeed, she found it best and easiest to push the reality of her father's death to the very back of her mind; to deny it, in fact. She told herself that her father was away, that was it, simply away! Later, when she could bear to do so, she would face what had happened to him, but whilst she had so much to do she would do it in a vacuum.

Nights would have been hard, but the doctor had given Marianne sleeping tablets. Shamelessly, Tess stole some and slumbered each night, though she woke pale and heavy-eyed, often with a thumping headache. But even a headache was better than lying awake all night, trying to make sense of it all. Peter had been making his way from his offices to his billet, but because of the black-out he had not seen the Army lorry approaching and the lorry had not seen him. It was such a wicked, stupid waste, and whenever Tess allowed herself to think about it she felt red rage, followed by a deep, black sorrow. He had been such a marvellous father, such a *good* person; even if he wasn't actually my father by blood, he never let it affect his love for me, Tess told herself. And he was a volunteer, he needn't have gone back to the Navy. So why had it happened? Why, why, why?

What was more, she knew she had braced herself for Marianne's death, for the horror of finding her stepmother's body, frozen stiff, somewhere out in the snow and ice. She had not even dreamed that it might be her father whose death she would be mourning. It had come as a bolt from the blue, and there were times when she railed against fate, which had pretended to be about to snatch Marianne and, whilst Tess was doing her damnedest to find her stepmother, had taken Peter, instead.

It is as though I had my back to him, Tess grieved to herself. As though I was so busy over Marianne that I couldn't spare time to think of Daddy. So he was killed.

She knew it wasn't so, of course. Peter had been killed before Marianne had gone missing. But true or not, that was how she saw it. A malignant fate, seeing her absorbed in Marianne, had done the unexpected and taken her father from her.

'He was killed outright, he wouldn't have known a thing,' Peter's commanding officer told Tess. He had tried to talk to Marianne, but as he told Tess afterwards, he could see her distress was so great that she wasn't really taking in what he said, so he had turned to Tess, doubtless thinking that because she was handling all the arrangements she was a calmer personality, less likely to weep all over him. 'What's more, Miss Delamere, he was very happy with us. He was an excellent teacher who enjoyed passing on his knowledge, and he loved feeling a part of the war effort. If it's any consolation, I believe he died a happy man.'

So when all the arranging was done and the funeral date fixed, Tess made herself look at her loss, and acknowledged that it would change her life. She had relied on Peter in a hundred ways, trusted him totally, confided in him as far as she was able. And having faced up to the loneliness which would be her lot with only a stepmother to support her, she also realised that, in a way, she had lost Leonora all over again. Peter had been the one source of information on her mother's past. Now he had gone, as Leonora had, without really telling Tess all that she longed to know about her earliest years.

But oddly enough, losing Peter seemed to have made Marianne

far less aggressive and difficult towards her stepdaughter. Indeed Marianne's grief, which took the form of endless tears and a good deal of sleep during daylight hours, also helped, in an odd sort of way, to give Tess strength. I always knew she loved him far more than he loved her, though I never believed her capable of very strong emotions, Tess thought. But I was wrong; she lived for him. All that jealousy and unpleasantness were because she was deathly afraid of losing him, and now that the worst has happened and he's lost to her – to us all – she sees me as an ally, someone else who loved him, instead of an enemy, someone who shared his love.

It was strange but pleasant for Tess to find Marianne touchingly grateful for all that she did and was doing, strange when Marianne asked her stepdaughter's advice, wept on her shoulder. But Tess feared that it wouldn't last. She'll revert to normal once the shock of her loss begins to lessen, she thought cynically, and I don't want to be around then. I remember how I used to tell Daddy that it was better for me to be in boarding school so Marianne and I had less time together. Well, it'll be true again. Just give her time.

But time was passing, the weather was easing at last and there were things to plan which would have distressed Marianne unbearably, so Tess took herself off to Staithe Cottage and the comforting and comfortable presence of Mrs Thrower. Together, they would plan the tea which they would serve after the funeral service, and discuss how they should let people know that a date had been agreed, since the notice in the *Eastern Daily Press* had simply stated that the funeral would take place 'shortly', meaning, of course, when the ground was sufficiently soft to enable a grave to be dug.

'I think another notice in the paper, giving the actual date, would be best,' Tess decided, sitting at the terrible old kitchen table scarred with knife marks where various Throwers had gutted fish, jointed game, chopped turnips. And carved initials from time to time, she saw, trying to find an unblemished bit of wood on which to rest her writing pad. 'What do you think, Mrs Thrower? I had thought of writing personal letters, but that way I'll miss all sorts of people who might like to pay their last respects. There are people in Blofield who may want to come; my mother came from there, and Daddy lived in Brundall when he was small.'

Tess had agonised over whether her father would want to be buried in Blofield, close to Leonora, but had decided that it was quite impossible. Too many explanations, too many people hurt – and how could she ever explain to Marianne, and Cherie?

'Right enough,' Mrs Thrower said. 'Your uncle might do that.'

'Yes, a notice in the *EDP* would be best; now I come to think of it there may be people from Walcott who still remember Daddy,' Tess said distractedly. 'I wouldn't want anyone to feel left out. We lived there, you know, when I was small, before my mother died.'

'That's awkward when a feller marry more than once,' Mrs Thrower said, as though she had been reading Tess's mind. 'I dare say he were powerful fond of your ma, an' all, 'cos he took his time remarryin'. But he've made his life here these past years. He'd not want to be taken away from us.'

'I'm sure you're right,' Tess said. 'I did wonder myself, actually, so it's a weight off my mind that you agree, because it isn't the sort of thing I could say to anyone else. Now, shall we plan the funeral tea, and begin to make a guess at how many we'll be catering for? They won't all come back, I don't suppose. Now. Sandwiches, of course . . .'

'Aye, we'll have salmon, ham an' egg for the fillin's,' Mrs Thrower said. 'Some o' them little round biscuits wi' bits an' pieces on top an' my shrimp boats; Mr Dela . . .' she stopped short and Tess saw a tear slide down her cheek, but then she rallied, brushing the tear away, smiling determinedly. 'Well there you are, my woman, I can't believe he've gone no more'n you can. Never thought I'd be cookin' this sort o' tea for your pa.'

'I know,' Tess said. 'Isn't it odd, Mrs Thrower, that not really believing it helps a lot at first, and then it begins to make it harder, not easier? There's a part of me that just won't believe it's happened, but then when something makes you face it, the hurt is as bad as it was at the beginning. Once the funeral's over, perhaps things will seem real and I can go back to – to living my life again, but now I keep expecting the door to open and Daddy's head to poke round it. I can absolutely *see* his grin, hear him saying, *fooled you that time – you thought I was dead, didn't you?* And half my

291

mind really does believe it's going to happen, whilst the other half . . .' her voice wobbled and she stopped speaking for a moment, then heaved a tremulous sigh and continued. 'The other half is sore and aching because it knows it won't ever happen, no matter how long I wait.'

Mrs Thrower heaved herself out of her chair, walked fatly round the table, and put her arms round Tess's thin shoulders. 'That's what funerals are for, lovie,' she said. 'You see the person you love committed to the earth, and there in't nothin' more final than that. An' you cry, my woman. You let all your grief out in a gurt flood of tears, and you're better for it. Acceptance, see? That's what a funeral does, it makes you accept that the person you love in't around no more, nor they won't be. That they've moved on, like. And then you realise that there's allus a part of a person in the place they loved, an' that helps an' all.'

'Right,' Tess said. Tears formed and welled over. 'Right, Mrs Thrower. I'll hang on to that.'

'That's my girl,' Mrs Thrower said, patting. 'Now here's a thought – Mrs Delamere's a fust-rate cook, she've telled me so over and over. How about if we get her to make some cakes an' that? Only that in't right to clutch your grief to yourself an' ignore everyone around you. Whass more that in't healthy. She in't even *tryin'* to git a holt on herself, act normal, and she's puttin' all the work on you an' young Cherie.'

'Perhaps French people always behave like that,' Tess said doubtfully. She had wondered, herself, whether Marianne had simply reverted to her roots over this matter, for even her accent had got heavier since she had been widowed. 'I know Greek and Italian peasants do that sort of wailing thing, and rend their garments, like in the bible. Not that she's rending her garments, but she doesn't bother to dress half the time and when she does, she wears stained blouses and jumpers with holes in. And she's got heaps and heaps of really nice clothes.'

Mrs Thrower sniffed. 'She in't a peasant, as she'd be the first to tell you,' she pointed out. 'She's downright *enjoyin'* her grief if you ask me. An' the kid's mortal upset by it – seein' her ma mekin' a spectacle of herself.'

'I know. But from what you've just told me, don't you think

that, after the funeral, she'll begin to come round a bit?' Tess said. 'Especially since I'll probably have to leave home quite soon. I'm going to do war work, I think it's even more important now that Daddy isn't – isn't around any more to help with the war effort. Surely she'll have to pull herself together then, or she and Cherie will starve.'

'You're probably right. But you won't be off for a bit, will you, an' Mrs Delamere need to pull her socks up soon, that's for sure, do she'll never get to the funeral. She'll mek some excuse or other and stay at home.'

Tess sighed. 'I'm not really sure what to do, Mrs Thrower. I can't say too much to Marianne or she rushes out of the room. But I can't simply stay at home keeping her up to the mark, I've got to do my bit, and perhaps when she realises, Marianne will start to pull herself together. Only . . . when it comes down to it, the services may turn me down, which would mean I'd be stuck with the situation at the Old House. Unless I went into munitions and had to live out, of course.'

'They won't turn you down, gal Tess, they'll grab you wi' both hands, a nice, clever young 'oman like you,' Mrs Thrower said robustly. 'I'm sorry for young Cherie, mind. She'll have her work cut out once you're gone. I dessay you've spoke to young Mr Ashley, have you? What did he say?'

Tess knew that Mrs Thrower rather liked Ashley, who teased her, got on well with her sons and flirted with Janet. She agreed he was demanding, but seemed to think this, whilst unacceptable in a woman, was natural in a man. He would make a good husband, she told Tess firmly, and no one could deny he was generous and good-natured. Tess, who thought his generosity generally had an end in view and his good nature broke down if you didn't laugh at his jokes, said she wasn't interested in a husband just yet and received an unbelieving stare: Mrs Thrower thought girls ought to be interested in husbands from the moment they could walk, the stare said.

'Oh, yes, Ashley knows,' Tess said now. 'He said he'd get leave for the funeral. He didn't say much else. We're quite good friends, Mrs Thrower, but we're not particularly close. He'd like us to be, but we row too much, have too many fights. I think we're best with some distance between us.' She hesitated, then picked up her pen again and bent over the paper. 'Daddy didn't like him much,' she muttered. 'He thought I ought to meet more fellows before I took any sort of plunge.'

'Mebbe your dad were right,' Mrs Thrower said magnanimously, overcoming, Tess knew, her feeling that Ashley Knox was an ideal match for Tess. 'Anyroad, if he come over for the funeral you can talk to him then. And our Janet'll come home too, if she possibly can. I told her to say it was her uncle; that'll fetch 'em!'

Tess giggled and finished her notice for the *EDP*, then put down her pen. 'Mrs Thrower, what a whopper! And you always told us lies were *never* necessary! What's your excuse, then?'

'That's nice to hear you laugh,' Mrs Thrower said. 'Don't feel guilty to laugh, gal, it don't mean you've forgot your dad for one moment, it mean you're facin' up to life the way that stepma of yours should. As for lyin', wars change things. You can lie in wartime, if that's necessary. Stands to reason; if it's all right to kill people lyin' can't be that bad.'

'Right, though I don't think you've got a leg to stand on, morally. I mean it isn't as if you were lying to the Germans, you're lying to Jan's commanding officer, whoever that may be.'

Mrs Thrower sniffed again. 'Get Mrs Delamere to make them little meringue things.' She wrote laboriously on her list. 'From what Jan say, her commandin' officer *is* a bloomin' Nazi. My heart alive, what a devil she do sound! Do this, do that, don't you look at no young fellers, where's your gas mask, straighten your stockin's . . . oh aye, she's a tartar, that one. If Jan don't lie she won't last long.'

'Good Lord, Mrs T, if you think that's the way to encourage me to go into the services . . .'

'Oh, you!' Mrs Thrower said affectionately. 'You're one of the quiet, sly ones, Tess Delamere. You go your own way when all's said and done.'

'Do I?'

'That you do. You won't have survived for long wi' Mrs Delamere, else. Now I'm makin' two lists, one for myself an' one for Mrs Delamere. I'll leave her all the fancy stuff. Right? An' you mek sure she do it, my woman!'

Twelve

The funeral went off better than Tess had expected. From somewhere Marianne suddenly found dignity and restraint, and though her tears flowed copiously during the touching and beautiful service in the ancient church of St Michael and All the Angels, she presided over the funeral tea like a normal, rational person, talked to her guests, and did not disgrace herself – or her daughters – by an embarrassing or ostentatious display of grief.

And Tess found that Mrs Thrower was right. Before the service she saw her father, now a pale, stern stranger, lying in his coffin; after the service she saw the coffin lowered into the earth, went forward, with Cherie, and threw a handful of soil into the grave, stepped back and suddenly realised that her father was not lying below the raw earth in the churchyard, neither was he in Portsmouth, carrying out his work. He had, quite simply, gone. To another place, Tess found herself thinking, and found the thought oddly comforting. To a better place? Perhaps. But she would not know that until her own time came.

It was not until the funeral was over and people began to file past her, outside the church, that she noticed Lady Salter. Very correct in a long black coat with a bunch of artificial violets on the lapel, she was walking slowly along, leaning on an ebony stick and turning her head to talk to the young man who walked beside her, head bent, listening. Tess had seen Lady Salter's estate manager a couple of times and thought it kind that he had accompanied his employer on her sad errand. When they drew near, Lady Salter turned to Tess and held out one thin, elegantly gloved hand.

'My dear! I'm sorrier than I can say . . . your father will be much missed.'

Tess thanked her for coming to the funeral and told her that tea would be held in the Old House.

'I'm sure you brought your car, but if not, a friend of mine is giving lifts,' she said tactfully. Ashley and his father had both offered help with transport, for the church of St Michael and All the Angels was some way from the village itself. 'My stepmother would be pleased to see you, Lady Salter.'

'I think, my dear, that I shall go straight home,' Lady Salter said. 'But perhaps my nephew might accompany you? I see you don't remember this young man,' she added. 'Well, it's been a long time. I hardly recognised him myself.'

Tess turned and stared at the young man. Taller than she, but not particularly tall, around five foot ten, she supposed. Dark hair worn rather long, dark eyes behind horn-rimmed spectacles . . . he smiled.

'Andy!' Tess almost whispered it. 'Oh, Andy . . . I can't believe it! You've no idea how . . .' she stopped short, remembering Lady Salter. 'I – I thought you were probably miles away,' she finished lamely.

'I was,' Andy said. He took her hand in his. 'Tess, I'm sorrier than I can say about your father. And I'd like to come over some time, talk about old times. I'll take my aunt home now, but I'm here for a few days . . . would tomorrow be all right?'

'It would be fine,' Tess said. 'See you then, Andy. Early?'

'Crack of dawn time,' Andy said. 'I'd row over, only the weather wouldn't allow it, so I'll walk. Nine o'clock too early?'

'Nine o'clock's fine. I've taken a couple of days off from work, so I won't be going into the city. Stay to lunch.'

'Thanks,' Andy said. He took his aunt's arm and the two of them began to move away. 'Until tomorrow, then.'

Ashley, who had been arranging lifts, came over to her, eyebrows raised. He waited until Lady Salter and Andy had left the churchyard, then addressed Tess.

'Who was that? Are they coming to the tea? They've got a car with a chauffeur, they might be persuaded to give lifts.'

'They aren't coming,' Tess said briefly. 'It's Lady Salter and her nephew. Nice of them to come to the funeral, really. They didn't know Daddy at all well.'

'Oh, right.' Ashley put a hand on her arm; it was a proprietorial hand but Tess did not move away. Ashley had been wonderfully supportive, had worked as hard as he possibly could to help her. He had talked to her boss about her having time off, had been very good both with Marianne and Cherie. She did not mean to snub him now, even though, she told herself, their friendship was just that, a friendship. Not the oddly named 'relationship' which, in Ashley's eyes, meant so much more. He had told her only the previous day that he wanted to shoulder her burdens, to help her, and she had been happy enough to accept the help then.

'So do I take it the old girl's the lady of the manor? Then who's the bloke? Her son?'

'Yes to the first, no to the second. He's just a nephew. Ash, is it all right if I walk back? Only I – I'd really like to be alone for a bit.'

'Sure it's all right,' Ashley said at once. 'Your mother will welcome the guests, and Cherie will help. And of course Mrs Thrower is at the house already, putting kettles on and setting out cakes.'

'I know,' Tess said. 'I feel so bad about that, Ash. Mrs Thrower was a far better friend to Daddy than most of the people at the funeral, and she loved him, too. But someone had to put the kettles on, she said.'

'Mrs Thrower is a practical Christian,' a voice behind them said, and Tess turned to see the rector smiling at them. 'She'll have said her own goodbye to your father and it will be heard whether she said it in church or in the kitchen, boiling kettles and making tea. I came over to remind you, Mr Knox, that you're giving old Mrs Fretwell a lift . . . she's waiting down by the lychgate.'

'Right away, Rector,' Ashley said. 'Off you go, Tess . . . by the way, Freddy was terribly sad that she couldn't come along and support you today, but she couldn't get leave.'

'It was nice of Freddy to try to come, and awfully good of your parents.' Tess said. 'I'll be off, then. See you presently, Ash.'

Tess set off at a good pace, for though the snow was thawing, it was still extremely cold. The church of St Michael and All the

Angels was at least a mile from the village, so she would have a chance to stretch her legs – it would be the first chance, furthermore, since they had heard of Peter's death. And it gave her time to think.

Naturally enough, Andy pretty well filled her thoughts. He had been a kid of thirteen when last she saw him, now he was . . . phew, getting on for twenty-two, since she would be twenty-one this coming year. She couldn't make up her mind how she felt about him, though. He was a stranger, of course, that was why. She had known a boy, now she was meeting the man – there was a world of difference.

Yet against all the odds she was filled with happiness because he had come back. It was dreadfully sad that it had taken her father's death to bring him to Barton once more, but at least he was back, and he and she had been such friends, had got on so well! He wasn't a bit like Ashley, who was so complex that he probably puzzled himself; Andy was straightforward. Sensible. He had taken her hand, he hadn't tried to sweep her into his arms or to embarrass her by pretending they still knew each other intimately, as they once had. She swung along, her boots making quick work of the melting snow, her cheeks warming with the speed of her going, and knew a sweet, uncertain happiness.

It seemed wrong to be happy with Peter only just buried, but she knew that her father would have been glad for her. He hadn't liked Ashley but he had liked Andy right from the start. He wouldn't expect her to leap into anyone's arms, but he would want, above everything, her happiness. 'If it makes you happy, darling,' had been a phrase often on his lips as she grew older and began to want more independence. And anyway, she didn't intend to make a big thing of Andy's return, she was simply hoping for a resumption of their pleasant, friendly relationship.

She reached Deeping Lane, turned down it, and presently crunched up the drive, which had been cleared earlier in the day of the last traces of snow. At the front door, which was open, she braced herself. Warmth, food . . . and strangers as well as friends must be faced now.

Tess went into the house.

*

Marianne was doing the honours as Tess slipped into the draw-ing-room. She was neat and smart and not, to her daughters' relief, weighed down with widow's weeds. She wore a black dress with a low waist and a pleated skirt and black high-heeled pumps. She had put Peter's pearls around her neck and the gold bracelet circling one wrist was the one he had bought her on their first trip to France together. Before they set off for the church she had told Tess, quite simply and sincerely, that she wanted to look her best for Peter's sake. Tess, swallowing hard, had given Marianne's hand a squeeze before she moved away.

Now, Tess thought that Cherie looked neat in her grey school skirt and cardigan, a cream blouse and a black band round one arm, and Tess herself was sombre in a charcoal-grey pleated skirt and a black cardigan. The men had mostly put on black ties though the younger ones, of course, wore uniform.

Our clothes say we're sad, Tess thought. But our faces say it much better. Poor little Cherie is red-eyed and quiet, Marianne is white, my uncle and aunt are drawn. What does my face say? Does it say that I've got no one, now? Uncle Phil is a good, kind man, but we share no blood. I'm not even related to Cherie, though we call ourselves sisters. Ah, but I've good friends – the Throwers, Freddy and Ash . . . and Andy.

'Tess?'

Ashley moved across and stood beside her, took her hand fleetingly, then offered her a plate laden with meringues.

'Oh . . . thanks.' She took one, bit into it. She thought, *How can I eat Marianne's meringues, when they were Daddy's favourites and he'll never have another one, never tease her again about her cooking making him fat?*

'Your guests are thinking about leaving, Tess,' Ashley said gently in her ear. 'When you've finished that, it might be politic to wander into the hall. You and Marianne ought to thank them for coming and so on.'

'Of course; thanks, Ash.' She moved over to stand beside her stepmother and people drifted over to them to offer thanks, sym-pathy, kindness. Ashley stood beside Tess, warm fingers holding her cold ones. He introduced her to her father's colleagues and workmates. He had been busy finding out who was who whilst she walked back from church. It was a thoughtful thing to have done, Tess realised, and realised, too, that Ashley was at his best in this sort of situation. He looked incredibly handsome in Air Force blue with his wings on his chest, and he was being gentle with Cherie, sensible with Marianne, and tender and loving to herself. She was grateful to him; at that moment she almost loved him. But she knew, ruefully, that it would pass. Ashley wouldn't be able to keep it up, all this charm. He'd start being clever-clever, sarky, rude . . . and in no time at all they'd be quarrelling.

The Knoxes were amongst the last of the guests to leave. When Tess thanked Mrs Knox for coming the older woman said that she had come for old times' sake. 'I knew your father a little and your mother rather better when we were young,' Mrs Knox said quietly. 'You mustn't hesitate to get in touch if you need help of any sort. Ashley's very fond of you – but I don't have to tell you that.'

'I'm very fond of Ashley . . . and of Freddy, too,' Tess said. 'But I think it's Marianne who may need support. She was very wrapped up in my father.'

Mrs Knox squeezed her hand. 'I'll keep in touch with her, if she'll allow me to do so,' she said. 'Poor little thing – dreadful to be widowed so young.'

'There's no good age for it,' Tess said, and felt her cheeks grow hot. How pert she had sounded! But Mrs Knox just smiled and repeated her offer and then Mr Knox hooted and she ran to climb into the passenger seat of her husband's smart car.

'Ash will help you to wash up,' she called out of the half-open window. And then she began to crank it shut because it was still very cold, though the thaw had set in. 'Tell him supper's at seven sharp.'

'I will,' Tess called back, and turned to her next departing guest.

Ashley stayed to supper, in the end, largely because Tess suddenly could not bear the thought of an evening spent without even the ghost of Peter in the Old House. She had taken Mrs Thrower's advice to acknowledge and come to terms with her loss not because she wanted to do so but because it had happened as the coffin was covered over. Daddy had gone and she knew she could no longer expect to come face to face with him coming out of his study or heading for the stairs. A line had been drawn under her childhood and the house, which had been so much hers and Daddy's, would be theirs no longer. She would go away and Marianne would gradually make it completely her own. And that was right, Tess acknowledged, it was what should happen, but that didn't make her like it. So if Ashley stayed, she would be less likely to spend the evening mourning over times past.

It was a good supper, too. Mrs Thrower and Marianne had both over-catered, suddenly terrified by the thought of hungry, disappointed guests. So the four of them sat down to egg and ham pie, home-made bread and pickles, followed by a wonderful apple pie with thick cream.

'You're a first-class cook, Mrs Delamere,' Ashley said, with his mouth full. 'Tess will miss all this delicious food, I can tell you. They don't spoil us in the Air Force, you know.'

'Miss my cooking? Why, for goodness sake? Oh, you mean rationing, of course. Well, Ashley, I dare say we'll be better off than some. The Throwers keep poultry and they sold us six good hens, and we've got a large and thriving vegetable garden and the orchard . . .' She broke off, staring from face to face. 'You did mean rationing, didn't you?'

Ashley, for once, seemed unwilling or unable to talk his way out of it. He gaped at Marianne, then cleared his throat and glanced appealingly at Tess.

'No, he didn't mean rationing, Marianne,' Tess said. 'He meant that I had applied to join the WAAF. But I've written to them, explaining that I don't feel I should leave home at this particular juncture and withdrawing my application for the time being. So things will go on as usual for a while, at least.'

'Yes, but . . . you won't go away at all now, will you? Not now, not with your father . . . gone. How could we possibly manage, Cherie and I? We neither of us drive, I rely on you completely, you know that. Peter wouldn't expect you to desert me, Tess.'

'No, and I won't leave yet. But eventually I may have no choice,' Tess said with a coolness she was far from feeling. The words *you selfish person!* hovered on the tip of her tongue but must never be spoken. 'I did apply, you see.'

'Oh, but if you tell them . . .'

'Marianne, I've told them, but joining one of the services would be war work! You cannot imagine, for one minute, that working up at the museum and looking after you and Cherie could be classified as such? As it is, if the museum tell the government that my work's not essential – and it isn't – I'll probably have to go into a factory, which I don't much fancy.'

'You wouldn't have to work in a factory, you could go on the land, and that would mean you could live at home,' Marianne argued, and Tess sighed. Her stepmother really was incredible – this was the woman who hadn't been able to wait to get rid of her before the war, four or five months ago. And now, because things had changed, Marianne was suddenly finding her resented step-child indispensible!

'Let's not discuss it,' Tess said tactfully, however. 'Remember, it may never happen. The war may be over before they call me up.' She leaned across the table and helped herself to another slice of pie. 'This is really good, especially with those delicious pickled onions.'

'I'd better have some too, or you won't let me kiss you good-night,' Ashley said, reaching for the pickle dish. Tess stiffened, but she knew, really, that he was only trying to change the subject. And presently, when the meal was eaten and the washing up done, Marianne took Cherie off to bed and Tess put on her coat and her wellingtons and went out into the chilly dark to see Ashley off.

'Your stepmama is quite a lady,' Ashley said as they stood beside his small sports model. 'She doesn't care, does she?'

'Care?'

'What people think, I meant. Most people cover their selfish-ness with a thick layer of some sort. She just comes out and says *I want, therefore I must have.*'

Tess laughed. 'Oh yes, I know what you mean. Daddy once said it was one of the things he really loved about Marianne – that she was never ashamed to show her faults and weaknesses to the whole world. Indeed, immediately after his death she showed her grief in a totally uninhibited way which I found . . . distasteful, I suppose. But later I believe I began to envy her. I couldn't gnash my teeth and rend my garments as she did because I'm far too cold and inhibited and British, so all the pain and the missing got scrunched up inside me, to fester in the dark.'

'But you're all right now,' Ashley said. 'I can see it in your face. You've got your lovely, peaceful look back.'

'*Peaceful*? What on earth does that mean? I suppose you mean blank and unintelligent,' Tess said indignantly. 'And yes, I am okay now, because Mrs Thrower had a talk to me. And in case I haven't already said it, thanks, Ash.'

'Thanks for what? Friends don't need to be thanked, old girl.'

'Well, thanks for coming this afternoon, for a start. I did appreciate it, honestly. It made things easier for me.'

'Good,' Ashley said briskly. 'Look, I understand how you feel about leaving here now, after what's happened, but you'd love the WAAF, kiddo! Freddy's in her element and I don't see why you should miss out. As for working on the land, no doubt Mr Rope would be glad of your help but it's a waste of your brains, girl. You could have gone to university – should have – but you settled for your Higher and the job at the museum because you didn't have the self-confidence to leave home. Don't shoot yourself in the foot twice, Tess!'

'What a lecture,' Tess said lightly. 'But it's no use nagging, Ash. I can't leave Marianne just now. Later, perhaps.'

'Oh, later!' Ashley looked all round him in the gloom of late afternoon, then seized her firmly in his arms. 'Darling Tess, I love you more than I've ever loved anyone . . . kissy kissy!'

'More than you love yourself?' Tess asked nastily. Ashley groaned, cast his eyes up, and then slowly lowered his mouth on to hers. The kiss went on longer than usual because Tess was ashamed of her sharpness, but she broke it first, because she felt sure that Marianne and Cherie were probably either watching avidly through the gap in the curtains or timing her on the kitchen clock.

'There! Wasn't that the loveliest, most delicious thing?' Ashley demanded as soon as he'd got his breath back. 'Lucky, lucky Tess

Delamere, to have the finest pilot officer in the Royal Air Force at her feet!'

'I knew you'd go back to normal soon,' Tess said resignedly, stepping back. 'Go on, start the car and whizz off, you conceited beast!'

But she spoke indulgently. He had been kind today, kinder than she perhaps deserved when you thought how often and how thoroughly she had kept him at arm's length.

'Okay, okay, keep your hair on,' Ashley said. 'I'll be over early tomorrow morning, to whisk you off somewhere nice. I'm on a forty-eight, I'll have you know.'

'Tomorrow? I'm busy tomorrow,' Tess said at once, feeling the guilty warmth rise to her cheeks. 'Come the following day.'

'No can do. I'll be back in Lincoln by then. See you in the morning, honey-sweet, and don't you go out before I arrive or I'll do something desperate.'

'I'm busy I said,' Tess shouted as Ashley began to swing the starting handle. The engine roared into life and he ran round and jumped in behind the wheel. 'I'm *busy*!' Tess shrieked, but Ashley pretended not to hear. He cupped a hand round his ear, then shouted, 'Cheery-bye, sweetie-pie,' and roared off into the night, hooting *parp parp de parp parp* on his horn as he rounded the bend.

Back in the warm living-room, Marianne was sitting by the fire, gazing into the flames. She jumped as Tess entered the room and turned her face away, but not before Tess had seen the tears which streaked it.

'I'm just off to bed,' Marianne said, her voice small and formal. 'Cherie is well away. You'd best go up now, Tess, if you're going out with Ashley tomorrow.'

Tess agreed that she really should go up, though she told Marianne, rather stiffly, that she had no intention of going anywhere with Ashley.

'I don't know what makes you think I am,' she said crossly. 'But I'm not – I told him I'm busy tomorrow and if he comes over he'll just have to go off again.'

Marianne looked surprised.

'Ashley asked me earlier if I could spare you tomorrow,' she said. 'He wanted to get you away from the place for a bit. I said I'd manage somehow.'

Tess laughed. 'How absurd, Marianne – "manage somehow" indeed! If I were back at work you'd manage, wouldn't you? Look, I'm very fond of Ash but he's too bossy by half. I'm not seeing him tomorrow because I've got an old friend visiting. Are you going up to bed, now? If so, I'll bring you up a hot drink when I come. What would you like?'

'Oh . . . cocoa, please. And don't wake me early, I'm going to have a lie-in.'

Tess bit back the words *You've had a lie-in every morning since Daddy died* and said, patiently, that she would get Cherie off to school before she went out herself. Marianne, half-way to the door, turned and frowned.

'Cherie can't go back to school yet; I can't manage without her,' she said. 'Please don't argue with me, Tess . . . I can't lose her, too.'

'Marianne, you aren't losing me – and you most certainly aren't losing Cherie,' Tess said impatiently. 'She has to go to school, but she'll be back on the four fifteen and I'll probably not be long after her.'

'You don't understand,' Marianne said. 'Who am I, Tess?'

'You're Marianne Delamere, Cherie's maman and my step-mama,' Tess said resignedly. 'I know you're a widow now, Marianne, but apart from that you haven't changed, you're still the same person you were.'

Marianne went across the room, opened the door, then turned to Tess, her mouth drooping.

'No, you are wrong; I'm not the same person. I am only half a person now,' she said, and the very fact that she spoke quietly and without emphasis made more of an impression on Tess. 'And the half that's been torn away hurts so much it scarcely seems worthwhile going on.'

Tess ran across the room and hugged her stepmother as hard as she could. Just for a moment she had seen into Marianne's mind and what she saw there frightened her. Marianne's loneliness and despair were all-encompassing. Her stepmother honestly felt that without Peter there was no point in her existence.

'Don't!' she said sharply. 'You've still got Cherie, and me for

305

what I'm worth, and you're young, Marianne! Daddy was special, but he wouldn't want you to sink into despair just because – because he wasn't around any more. Look, I've said I won't join the WAAF yet awhile and I won't, either. I'll talk to my boss at work and see about the Land Army, and if Mr Rope will have me, I'll be able to live at home . . . or if I have to live at the farm then at least I'll be able to get back here whenever I have free time. And no more despair, do you hear me?'

Marianne sighed and rested her head on Tess's shoulder for a moment, then with sudden decision she moved out of Tess's embrace and gave her a watery smile.

'You are a good girl,' she said. 'Nearly as good as your father thought you. I'll try to come to terms with things. Good-night, my dear. See you in the morning.'

'See you in the morning,' Tess echoed. She had seldom felt so mentally and physically exhausted. Her stepmother, she could see, was going to be a big problem and for Peter's sake she could not simply walk away from it. But she was too tired now to decide what best to do, and her boss at the museum would have to be consulted. Sadly, she saw her dreams of being a WAAF disappearing into the distance, but at least, if she stayed at home, she knew she would be doing what Peter wanted. And that would give her a good deal of satisfaction.

Wearily, she turned towards the pantry, to make her stepmother's cocoa.

Tess woke whilst it was still dark with a pleasant sense of anticipation, feeling happier than she had done for days. She lay for a moment, savouring it without knowing what she was anticipating or why. Could it be just because she was to have a day off work? No, of course not, she knew what it was – she was going to see Andy!

Seeing him yesterday had been a terrific shock. Yet he wasn't that different. Taller, with longer hair, but not that different. And older, of course. A man, in fact. A man who wore a dark suit instead of the holiday clothing of a thirteen-year-old boy – shorts, open-necked shirts, sandals.

If I'd looked at him properly I'd have known him anywhere

though, she told herself now, trying to forget that he hadn't registered with her until Lady Salter had said he was her nephew. Awful, not to recognise him on sight, but she'd expected the farm manager or someone of that sort to be accompanying Lady Salter. She'd simply had no idea that Andy was around. The last time she'd spoken to Lady Salter, at a regatta where that lady had been presenting the prizes, one of which Ashley and Tess had won, Lady Salter had told her that her nephew was working in France.

'In the embassy?' Tess had asked. 'He hasn't written to me for ages.'

'No, not the embassy,' Lady Salter had told her. 'I'm not quite sure what he does, though his father is very proud of him, he tells me. All I do know is that he speaks French so well he could be mistaken for a native.'

She had made it sound a disreputable sort of thing, as though the native in question wore a grass skirt and a ring through his nose.

'Oh,' Tess had said, rather taken aback. 'Well, perhaps we'll see him in Norfolk again, one of these days.'

Lady Salter had given her a sharp look, almost a knowing look, before saying drily: 'Who can say? Young people these days . . .' and wandering off in mid-sentence.

But now, lying in bed, Tess hugged herself. She had longed and longed to be able to confide in someone about how she had learned her mother's history after all her attempts, but she could not bear to be disloyal to Peter, and he hadn't wanted Leonora's story bruited abroad. But Andy was different. He didn't *judge* people, Tess decided, getting out of bed and bounding across the icy lino to seize her dressing-gown off the back of the door. Well, the old Andy hadn't, anyway. Ashley had been so horrible about Leonora that it had somehow managed to stay in Tess's mind, a muddy black mark, not against her mother, but against Ashley himself. She had forgiven those cruel, thoughtless jibes, but she couldn't forget them. And since then, she'd told nobody. It wasn't the sort of thing you could put in a letter, which was why she'd never told Andy, and most of the people who would have understood knew Peter.

But now . . . Tess went quietly into the bathroom, lit the lamp –

it was still dark outside – and then put a match to the geyser. When the chilly blue flames had turned to gold she began to run the hot water, and presently, climbed into the bath. She wasn't supposed to have a bath in the morning, let alone a decent, deep one, but it would warm her up and get her ready for the day ahead. On reflection she decided not to wake Cherie; it wouldn't hurt her to have another day off school, so she was quite surprised when, just as she stepped out of the tub and reached for a towel, the bathroom door opened and Cherie came into the room.

'A bath! Oh, bliss – is it still hot, Tess? Can I have it after you?'

'Hop in,' Tess said. 'Why so early, chick?'

Cherie opened her eyes very wide. 'I'm going back to school, of course! My bus leaves in forty-five minutes.'

'Oh! Well, that's fine, but your mother did say you could have another day or two off if you wanted.'

Cherie slung her pyjama top in the general direction of the hatstand which stood by the toilet seat, then stepped out of her trousers. She sniffed scornfully.

'Huh! I'm not staying here doing all the housework and being a little comfort, like in *Simple Susan*. Besides, I'll get behind. Daddy always worried if he thought we were getting behind.'

Tess, who agreed with her, said: 'But you won't get far behind in a day or two, so if you want . . .'

'I don't want, thanks,' Cherie said firmly. She climbed into the water and lay down, shuddering with pleasure. 'Oh, how absolutely wonderful! When I'm grown-up I'm going to marry a rich man and have a hot bath every single morning of my life!'

'Don't blame you,' Tess said, rubbing herself vigorously. 'I brought my clothes through because it's warmer in here than in my room. Want me to fetch yours?'

'Oh please, Tess,' Cherie said. She hooked her big toe round the tap. 'Shall I run a bit more hot? As it's two to a bath, I mean.'

'Better not, if you want to catch the early bus,' Tess advised. She pulled her thick jumper on, then sat down on the edge of the bath to don her thick lisle stockings. Standing up and performing the contortions necessary to do up her back suspenders, she added, 'You'll want your uniform, then?'

'Please. It's all laid out on my chair. Only I'll put another jumper on top before I add my coat. Miss Elgar said we might, she said she was sick of trying to teach little blue children who shivered all day.'

Tess chuckled. 'I can see her point. Right, shan't be two ticks.'

Tess and Cherie usually caught the same bus into the city. It didn't come down Deeping Lane just for them, it stopped on the main road, more or less on the corner, so they had a mile to walk, morning and night. Not that they minded or indeed thought twice about it; it was what they had always done as children and now, with petrol strictly rationed, they took it for granted that they would walk again.

However, it was quite a spooky walk in the dark, so Tess put on her coat when Cherie donned hers and the two of them walked companionably down the short drive together.

'I'll come to the bus stop and wait until the bus arrives,' Tess said. 'Unless someone we know is waiting for it too, in which case I'll come straight back and take Marianne a cuppa.'

'But she doesn't want to get up early, today,' Cherie said. 'Why not let her lie in?'

'Because I don't think it's good for her, all this idling about,' Tess said. 'Cherie, the funeral's over, Marianne should start picking up the threads now. And you don't do that flat on your back in bed.'

There had been a sharp frost in the night and all the slush had frozen into gleaming, icy ridges. Cherie slid and then stopped so abruptly that Tess cannoned into her.

'Dinner money! And I haven't got any cushies for the journey home, either.'

'Tell them that you'll bring your dinner money tomorrow,' Tess said. She delved in her pocket and found a threepenny bit. 'Here, take this. You can get some biscuits or something for the journey home.'

'Thanks, Tess,' Cherie said. She was hurrying now, her boots crunching on the frosted grass of the verge. 'What'll you do today? Shopping? Or just nannying Maman?'

'Neither,' Tess said. Above her head in the dark sky the moon was sliding down towards the horizon, the stars so pale, now, that you had to stare to see them. Dawn was appearing in the east, a paleness, grey fingers, pink-streaked, reaching out to the great firmament above. 'Neither, chick. Today I'm meeting an old friend.'

She saw Cherie on to the bus, then stared after the vehicle as it rumbled off down the road. Cherie, sitting on the back seat with two cronies from the next village, waved vigorously, then turned to hold her season ticket out to the conductor. The bus, despite the blacking out of its headlights, the dim blue bulbs within, still looked like Christmas compared with the darkly soggy fields, the leafless trees, and the flat grey line of the road.

It was getting lighter, though. By the time I get back to the Old House, morning will have arrived, Tess thought. And when morning arrives . . .

'Tess! Hang on a mo!'

The voice came from behind her. Tess turned and there was Andy, running. He was wearing a dark overcoat, open all the way down despite the cold, and a scarf which flapped like a wounded bird as he ran. She couldn't make out any more details in the semi-dark, but she beamed at him anyway.

'Andy! When you say crack of dawn you really mean it, don't you?'

He puffed up beside her, put a comradely arm round her shoulders, gave her a squeeze, let her go.

'Tess, I can't tell you how marvellous it is to see you after so long, and you haven't changed at all! I thought early was best, because we've got such a lot to talk about! Now let's start with what you're doing now. Not the services, I imagine?'

'No. I got a job at the Castle Museum when I passed my Higher. It's fascinating stuff, but it isn't war work. I'd meant to put in for the WAAF, but then Daddy died and so I've asked for a postponement whilst I sort things out here. Marianne wants me to join the Land Army and work for Mr Rope so I won't have to leave home.'

'Same old Marianne,' Andy said, putting Tess's own thoughts into words. He linked arms with her and set off down Deeping Lane. 'Best foot foremost, old girl, then we can get ourselves a spot of breakfast at your place and go off again. Now what was I saying? Oh yes, leaving home; everyone wants to leave home when they get to be twenty or so. And since I'm twenty-two, Tess, you must be twenty-one, which means you'll be pretty keen to leave home, I imagine.'

'Yes, I'll be twenty-one this summer,' Tess said. 'But as for the kcy of the door, I've not acquired that yet. Metaphorically speaking, of course. The war got in the way rather, with Daddy being the one to go off instead of me.'

'Hmm. Did you go to university?'

'No. I wanted to work for the Museum service and I thought I'd do better to go in there as a junior and work my way up. And I do love it, Andy. Only I can't pretend it's war work, which is why I was going to put in for the WAAF. And why I'm a bit disappointed that it doesn't look as though I'll ever wear that gorgeous uniform.'

'Gorgeous? Well, I don't know about that, but I'm in the same sort of boat myself. I'm not in uniform and not likely to be.'

'Why not? It can't be eyesight, surely? I know you're dreadfully short-sighted, Andy, but surely that doesn't debar you from serving in the forces?'

'No, though they wouldn't have me in a kite, or only as a passenger. I drive a car, you know. But I'm liaising between the French and English forces, and it's easier if I'm out of uniform so that neither side claims me, I imagine. It's awfully odd, I have a rank, quite a high one, on both sides of the Channel, but no uniform so far. It's a thankless task, but awfully good practice for later – you have to be *extremely* diplomatic when you're explaining to one army why the other one does things all skew-whiff!'

'And now you're on leave?'

'That's right. Because . . . but that isn't important. What I want to know is why you aren't married with a string of kiddies and a doting husband.'

'Hang on, I'm only twenty-one, not forty-one,' Tess said. She pinched his hand hard, then giggled when he sucked in his breath. 'Suppose I said no one wanted to marry me, Andy?'

Andy snorted. 'Suppose you said pigs had wings? You were a very appealing little kid, but now . . . well, I don't need to tell you,

I'm sure. Who was that awfully pleased-with-himself fellow you were talking to outside the church yesterday? Reddish hair and a pilot officer's uniform?'

'Oh, that was Ashley Knox. He's the brother of my friend Freddy – Frederica – Knox, who was at school with me. He's all right, but . . . Andy, why didn't you keep in touch? There have been times when I've really longed to tell you things, discuss them and so on. I did try once or twice, but it was sort of soulless, writing letters about things which were so – so difficult. Ash and Freddy are nice, but . . .'

'I wrote,' Andy protested. 'I wrote quite often at first.'

'Yes, at first. But then you went off to India without telling me and though I did write I never got a reply . . .'

'I never got a letter,' Andy said. 'It was all the moving around, I expect. The truth is I'm a rotten correspondent, old girl, and once Father had decided I was all right and could be useful I simply never came back to England, except for very short business trips. Why, my degree's a French one – I went to the Sorbonne, you know, instead of Cambridge. So until the war started, I didn't see my future here at all.'

'I did wonder if you got my letters,' Tess admitted. 'But all that's happened, and it's over. And since you're older than me, you could easily be the married one.'

'Well, I'm not,' Andy said. 'I've had one or two girlfriends, of course, mostly French, though . . . You?'

'No girlfriends at all, apart from Freddy and Jan,' Tess said, smirking. 'Oh, you meant boyfriends – why didn't you say? There's been no one serious. A fellow who works with me, Paul, took me out a couple of times, but mostly it's been Ashley.'

'I knew it,' Andy exploded. 'Do you *like* that type? All swagger and slang and bulging trousers?'

'Ashley isn't like that,' Tess said. 'He's all right really. But no, in fact I don't like that type. Ash is a good friend but I don't have the slightest intention of marrying him. Or anything.'

They reached the gates. Tess slipped through them, pulling Andy behind her.

'Here we are – I'll get us some breakfast. We've got hens now but they aren't laying particularly well at present. Still, there's oodles of bacon from Mrs Thrower's last autumn pig – d'you like bacon sandwiches?'

'They're prime,' Andy said. 'What about your stepmother? Will she mind? I can't wave Lady Salter in her face the way I used to, since she'll realise I'm only here on leave.'

'She's changed,' Tess said. She pushed open the back door and the pleasant, kitcheny warmth rushed out to meet them. 'Take your outdoor things off whilst I make the tea. Then I'll take a cup up to Marianne and get going on brekker. And as soon as we've eaten we'll get off out.'

'Out? Where? Why?' Andy said, obediently hanging his dark coat and his scarf up on the hooks behind the door. 'I thought you wanted to talk.'

'So I do. Outside, though,' Tess said firmly. 'Unless you want Marianne hanging on your every word, of course.'

They ate bacon sandwiches and drank tea, and then Andy put on his long, navy-blue overcoat and Tess put on her dark-brown one with the fur collar, and they set off, into the chilly and uninspiring morning.

'I told Marianne we'd be out for lunch,' Tess said rather guiltily. 'But in for an evening meal. It's too cold for a picnic, but I thought – I thought we might buy a pie each or something.'

'You do want us out of your house, don't you?' Andy said quizzically. 'Now I wonder why?'

'I've told you. Because of Marianne,' Tess said. She could not bring herself to admit that she thought Ashley would turn up on the doorstep and make them both uncomfortable. For one thing, it would give Andy the impression that Ashley was a person of some significance in her life and for another, it would make her seem such a ninny. 'Now, where shall we go?'

'The Broad isn't iced up any more but I don't fancy boating,' Andy said as they stood in Deeping Lane, looking up and down it. 'Shall we walk up to the bus stop and go into the city? Or we could walk to Stalham, I suppose.'

'We'll catch a bus into the city,' Tess decided. She was certain that Ashley would find them in Stalham without any trouble; Norwich would be a whole lot more difficult. She had no idea just what she expected Ash to do, except that it would be something embarrassing and unpleasant both for herself and for Andy. Ashley was so *proprietorial*, that was the trouble. He seemed to think he owned her.

The bus came and the two of them jumped aboard and went right down to the front, for it wasn't full by any means. Tess sat in the front seat against the window and Andy sat down beside her.

'What luxury, a bus not crammed with office workers,' she said, turning to Andy. 'The bus Cherie and I catch in the mornings . . . oh!'

'Why *Oh*?' Andy asked curiously. 'Got a pain?'

'No, I just remembered . . . something I'd forgotten,' Tess said confusedly. 'It doesn't matter . . . tell me what you did after that summer, the one you spent in Barton.' She did not think it necessary to explain that she had just seen Ashley, in his snarling sports car, driving in the opposite direction. He had not, she was sure, seen her, which was one blessing, anyway.

'School, then Russia, then school again,' Andy said. 'Now what I want to know is, did you ever discover about your mother and your dream and everything? You kept hinting mysteriously but you never actually came out with much.'

'No. Well, I wasn't any better than you at putting things down in writing. But I really have found out more than I bargained for, Andy. D'you mind if I don't tell you right away, though? I'll save it for when we're alone, later.'

'Being alone in the city isn't easy,' Andy said. He sounded rather disgruntled. 'We could go to the flicks, I suppose, but then you can't talk. People keep hushing you because they want to hear the film.'

'We could go to the museum,' Tess said brightly. 'There are rooms in the castle that hardly anyone goes in. What's today?'

'Tuesday. Why?'

'Wonderful. It's the only day we charge an admittance fee, which means that the place is like a tomb on Tuesdays. We'll go up, pay our bob or whatever, and settle ourselves comfortably in – in one of the picture galleries, or the bird room, or by the cases where the poor butterflies are pinned out, or amongst the mummies. Then we can talk all we like in complete privacy.'

She half expected Andy to object, but he nodded thoughtfully. 'Grand idea. But first we'll get ourselves a cup of coffee at Lyons. All right? And later, we'll go and have a hot meal somewhere. How about the Bell?'

'Oh well, we'll talk about a hot meal later,' Tess said guardedly. She had heard things about the Bell Hotel, and suspected that nice girls didn't go there. But she found it reassuring that Andy wanted to take her to the Bell *before* hearing about her mother because he had no idea that Leonora had been – well – unwise, so he certainly wasn't judging Tess by anyone's actions other than her own. Yet nothing I've done could possibly lead Andy to believe I'm that sort of girl, Tess reminded herself. Dear me, is it possible that boys simply hope that any girl they come across is that sort of girl? It seemed perfectly possible, judging from the things she heard Ashley – and others – say.

The bus drew in to Castle Meadow and the two of them got down. Andy tucked Tess's hand into the crook of his elbow and led her back across the wide road and down Davey Steps, through Davey Place and on to Gentleman's Walk. The market, looking oddly bare without the stalls, stretched before them, the city hall and the red-brick clock-tower gazing benignly down.

'In we go,' Andy said as they reached the imposing portals of the restaurant. 'It's quite empty . . . it'll give us a chance of a chat, Tess.'

And very soon, comfortably seated in a dark corner with a jug of hot water, a pot of coffee and a couple of improbable-looking cakes, Tess began.

'Well, I got friendly with Freddy Knox, one of the girls in my class at school, and she invited me back to her home whilst Daddy and Marianne were in France . . .'

By the time the coffee was finished and the cakes no more than a memory, the story was told, right down to the moment in the churchyard when she had fled, screaming abuse, from the hateful Ashley. Andy listened without comment but at the end of the recital he reached across the table and squeezed her hands.

'Oh, Tess! But in a way, didn't you find it rather reassuring? At least you knew the worst, you knew why your father wouldn't tell you much about your mother. He would have felt he was letting everyone down – you, Leonora, himself . . . even the fellow, whatsisname . . . Ziggy.'

Tess stared at him and then found herself beginning to smile.

'Andy, you are wonderful!' she said. 'I must be the stupidest, blindest person in the whole world, because I never saw it like that, not once! Of course you're absolutely right, it wasn't that Daddy didn't want to talk about my mother, it was because once he started he would have had to give too much away. Oh, *poor* Daddy!'

'That's it. And telling you that you weren't his little girl . . . well, it would have hurt both of you, wouldn't you say?'

'Yes,' breathed Tess. 'And I wouldn't have understood when I was small, either. I might have talked about it . . .'

'To the wrong people,' Andy agreed, nodding. 'Kids can be awfully cruel; your father didn't want you called names. But Tess, you don't *believe* your mother killed herself, do you?'

'I – I'm not sure,' Tess muttered, suddenly not wanting to meet Andy's straight, golden-brown gaze. 'Some old man who was on the beach thought she jumped . . . but that's pretty flimsy, really. To tell you the truth, that's the bit that hurts most – the idea that she didn't care for me enough to stay around.' She laughed uncertainly. 'Is that abominably selfish and conceited of me? I wouldn't have said it to many people, Andy, but I don't mind saying it to you; you know me so well!'

'It isn't selfish or conceited,' Andy said decidedly. 'It's just practical; all parents want to see their children grow up and I'm absolutely certain Leonora was no exception. And as for me knowing you well, after nine years it's a wonder that I know you at all! You must have changed, Tess – I'm sure I have!'

'No you haven't,' Tess protested. 'You're taller and you aren't thirteen any more, but you're the old Andy, really you are. Aren't I the old Tess?'

'Do you know, I believe you are?' Andy said. 'How lovely . . . my favourite little playmate has turned into my favourite young woman.'

'Don't be daft,' Tess said at once, feeling foolish. 'Anyway, now you know how far my investigations went. Just far enough to frighten me off.'

'What about Ziggy? Aren't you curious about him?'

Tess shook her head. 'No; how could I be? I've got – I had – the best father in the world, it would be disloyal to be interested in Ziggy. Why are you looking so disapproving, Andy?'

'Because denying facts seems to be your long suit! Look, you exist because of two people, Leonora and Ziggy. You've found out a bit about Leonora – it is only a bit, sweetie, even though it's a very dramatic bit – and nothing at all about Ziggy. Half of you is his, Tess, you should be a little interested. After all, it isn't as if the poor bloke went off and left Leonora to manage alone, he was killed! So follow through, girl! You won't feel at ease with yourself until you've discovered the full story, you know. That churchyard; was Ziggy buried there?'

'I don't know,' Tess muttered. She was plaiting the ends of her scarf into a cat's cradle which would, she thought guiltily looking down at it, take her hours to unravel. 'I was only looking for Leonora.' She looked hard at Andy. 'You don't think it's disloyal to Daddy to – to dig around a little?'

'I think you won't be truly at ease until you've got the whole story,' Andy said. 'You won't understand Leonora unless you make an attempt to understand Ziggy, and I believe when you do understand her, you'll know definitely that she didn't commit suicide, couldn't have done. And now, kiddo, let's make tracks for this museum of yours!'

On the bus going home it was as if the nine years apart had never happened, as if they had grown up together, lovingly, and were just beginning to settle into a new and better relationship. Sitting demurely on the back seat of the bus, with Tess squeezed into the window corner, they held hands and talked with their heads close together, discussing how they would spend the next couple of days before Andy had to go back to France.

'We should try the churchyard, see if we can find Ziggy's grave,' Andy said. 'And talk to the oldest inhabitant . . . school-masters, postmen, farm hands, anyone . . . and you see, we'll get your parents taped by the time I have to go back.'

'I don't believe we'll ever find the boy I dream about, though,' Tess said wistfully. 'I used to think he would have the answer to all my questions, particularly whether she fell or jumped out of the boat.'

'She wouldn't have jumped,' Andy said firmly. 'Banish that thought, sweetie. First thing tomorrow we'll go over to Blofield and start asking questions. I'll do it if you are afraid of breaking your cover.'

'Oh . . . Blofield! Well, yes . . . it might be awkward, though.'

'Why, for heaven's sake? Just because you stayed there a few years ago doesn't mean everyone will remember you! Anyway, it's a free country still, just about. You can go where you like!'

'Oh yes, but . . . the Knoxes, you know. They might think me very rude to visit their village and not them.'

'Knox, Knox,' Andy said. 'Now where have I heard that name before?'

Tess knew she ought to say that Ashley Knox was the bloke with the reddish hair who had been such a help at the funeral, but she couldn't bring herself to do it; Ashley was a friend, but compared to Andy a very recent one. In fact, you could say that Ashley was just an acquaintance, her friend's brother, she told herself. Why muddy the waters by bringing him into it?

'You've heard the name because Freddy Knox is my old school-friend,' she said patiently, therefore. 'And her parents and brother were at Daddy's funeral yesterday. Don't you think it might be better to leave the churchyard for the time being – I mean what about death certificates and things like that? We know Ziggy died some time between . . . hmm, hmm . . . well, say three to six months before my birth. Couldn't we . . .'

'Find the grave and we find the dates,' Andy insisted. 'Tell you what, the Globe does decent sandwiches, we'll go there and have some lunch. Sweetie, I'm only home for another couple of days, I want to get you sorted out before I leave.'

'Oh, all right,' Tess said, bowing to the inevitable. Besides, Ashley's leave finished this evening so there was a good chance that she might escape detection. Not that she cared what Ashley thought, only it could be awkward. 'Our stop coming up, Andy!'

They bundled off the bus into the chilly, windy darkness at the top of Deeping Lane. Andy, who had jumped off first in order to catch Tess, turned her neatly and put his arm around her waist and Tess was just laughing, telling him that he would do better to get out his torch, for it was a moonless night and their eyes were not yet used to the dark, when the rays of a flashlight shone full in her face and a voice spoke in her ear, frightening the life out of her.

'What's going on here? Let go of her at once – at once, d'you hear me?'

Andy was still fumbling for his own torch but, the first shock over, Tess knew all too well who had addressed her. Nemesis – or Ashley, rather.

'Shut up, Ash,' she said crossly. 'This is an old friend of mine – if you'll kindly shine your torch on your own face then I'll introduce you.'

'Old friend! With his bloody arm round your waist!' Ashley loomed up out of the dark and caught hold of Andy's coat collar in a far from friendly grip. 'I'll give the bugger old friend! Let go of her at once, you bounder!'

'Who is this, Tess?' Andy said. His voice was cold, insultingly so. 'If it's a friend of yours, tell him to stop making a complete ass of himself. Unless, of course, the pair of you are secretly married, I see no reason . . .'

Ashley swung out, a vicious punch which whizzed harmlessly past Andy's head as he ducked. Tess screamed, then swung her gas-mask case as hard as she could at Ashley's middle. It landed with a *wump* and Ashley grunted, then came on again, trying to grab Andy, trying to push Tess behind him . . . It was impossible to know just what he was trying to do, save that it was aggressive.

'Secretly married, is it? I'll give you secretly married . . . she's my girl, isn't she? We're going to be married, of course we are, so you can keep your filthy, thieving paws off her . . . go on, bugger off, go back to whatever slum you crawled out of!'

Tess couldn't believe it. This was Ashley the urbane, Ashley the sophisticate! He went for Andy again and she swung her gas mask harder, this time catching Ashley a resounding blow round the ear.

'Ouch!' Ashley grabbed for the gas-mask case, then seemed to decide that attack was not, perhaps, getting him very far. He abandoned Andy and seized Tess by one arm. 'Come along, my girl,' he said breathlessly. 'We don't want to hang around here, whilst this – this blighter tries it on. Let's get home.'

Tess tried to wrench herself free, but finding this impossible, she grabbed a handful of Ashley's hair. She tugged hard, Ashley released her arm and grabbed a handful of her hair and Andy suddenly started laughing.

'Dear God, what's all this about?' he said, between snorts. 'Who is this madman, Tess? We'll *all* go home, that'll be best.'

'Let – go – of – my – hair,' Tess said between gritted teeth. 'Or I'll never speak to you again. Ashley, do you hear me?'

It was difficult to see in the dark, with the torches swinging madly, but Tess fancied Ashley was shamed into letting her go. At any rate let her go he did, and he didn't try to grab her again as she set off along Deeping Lane at a cracking pace. Instead, he hurried along beside her, now and again snarling some expletive in Andy's direction but not attempting to lay hands on her.

They reached the Old House and Tess pushed open the back door and almost collapsed into the kitchen. Uninvited, Ashley followed. Andy was close behind.

Marianne was standing at the stove, stirring something in a large pan. Cherie was sitting at the kitchen table, probably doing her homework – at any rate she had books spread out and a pencil in one hand. Both looked round as the back door opened; two mouths fell open, two pairs of eyes rounded with astonishment.

'Hello . . . what on earth . . .?'

'This – this *person* got off the bus with your daughter, Mrs Delamere,' Ashley said. His hair hung over his forehead and his face was red and at some stage in the argument he had apparently trodden on his scarf, which was extremely muddy and hung round his neck by a whisker. 'I don't know what he's doing in your kitchen but he followed us . . .'

'Rubbish,' Tess said briskly. 'Ashley followed *us*, Marianne. We got off the bus and he started shouting – I really do believe he's taken leave of his senses at last. He was most abusive to Andy, he grabbed hold of me . . .'

'Am I or am I not in love with the girl, Mrs Delamere? I'm about to ask her to be my wife, I've hung around the house all day waiting for her, and then she comes off the bus with this . . . this wretched youth and shouts at me for daring to – to tell him he's not wanted!' Ashley swung round and glared at Andy, then addressed Tess in a softened tone. 'Darling, you know how I feel about you . . .'

'And you know how I feel about you,' Tess shouted, absolutely furious with Ashley and no longer wanting to hide it. 'You don't bloody well own me, you've never asked me to marry you in your life and if you did you'd get a dusty answer! And now, to paraphrase you, would you kindly *bugger off* and let me and my friend have our supper in peace?'

Cherie's gasp was one of sheer astonishment; Tess, who never swore, could guess what the younger girl was thinking but when she looked at her, Cherie's eyes were sparkling, her mouth smiled.

'Tess . . .' Marianne murmured, clearly as surprised as Cherie, but less amused. 'What is all this? Who . . .?'

'It's me, Mrs Delamere; Herbert Anderson. Remember?'

'Andy!' Marianne's smile was genuinely welcoming. 'How lovely to see you after so long. You really have grown up!'

'I remember you,' Cherie put in. 'You used to come over the Broad in a row-boat. You and Tess got lost once, Daddy had to get the car out and go searching . . . my, there was trouble!'

Andy grinned at her. 'Trouble is my middle name, apparently,' he said. He turned to Ashley. 'Look, old chap, I'm just a family friend. Why not come down off your high horse and shake hands?'

Ashley muttered something.

'What was that?' Andy asked. 'If you're imputing something awful from the fact that I put my arm round Tess to keep us together as we walked down the lane . . .'

'Ashley,' Tess said. 'Go home. You've got your car outside no doubt? Then get into it and . . . and go home. Otherwise I shan't be answerable for the consequences.'

Ashley, unfortunately, chose to sneer at this, though Tess could see that the sneer had a distinct wobble to it.

'Oh, yes? I suppose you'll never speak to me again? I suppose you'll quite happily forget our past relationship?'

He made it sound . . . well, he made it sound a good deal fonder than it had been. Tess took a deep breath.

'Go home,' she repeated. 'Tomorrow's another day. Say good-night to everyone and go home.'

'Right,' Ashley said defiantly. 'See you in the morning, then?'

'No. I've a previous engagement.' Tess swung the back door wide, then shut it again as cold air flooded in and Ashley made no move to go. She turned to her stepmother. 'Marianne, would you tell Ashley, please?'

'Ashley, Andy's known Tess for many years; they were child-hood – childhood friends,' Marianne said calmingly. 'I really do think you'd better go.'

'But my leave ends tonight,' Ashley said. He suddenly sounded very young and very miserable. 'I can't come back tomorrow, even if . . . if Tess would see me. I can't go, just like that.'

'Yes, you can, Ash,' Tess said. 'Good-night.'

Slowly and dramatically, Ashley turned to the back door, pulled it open and went through it. Everyone was beginning to breathe again when he turned back.

'Tess? Come and see me off? Let me explain?'

Tess would have said no, but Andy gave her a shove.

'Go on, or you'll still be here at midnight,' he muttered. 'You won't be long, it's freezing out there. I'll put the kettle on.'

So out into the darkness stomped Tess, in a terrible mood, longing to tell Ashley a thing or two. In silence they made their way to Ashley's sports car, then Ashley swung the handle and hastily got behind the wheel.

'Tess,' he shouted above the roar of the engine. 'You know I love you, don't you?'

'I know you say you do,' Tess said coldly.

'What?'

'*I know you say you do*,' Tess bellowed.

'Oh . . . well, I want to marry you.'

It was now Tess's turn.

'What?'

'*I want to marry you*.'

Evilly, Tess cupped a hand round her ear.

'What? Didn't quite catch . . .'

'I WANT TO BLOODY MARRY YOU!' Ashley bawled. Even in the semi-dark, Tess could see his face flushing with effort.

'That's very nice of you, Ash, but I'm afraid I don't want to marry anyone, not just yet. There's a war on, remember?'

'Nice? And what's the war got to do with it? If you mean I'm nice, why don't you just say "yes"?'

Tess was jolly sure that Ashley had heard every word, was simply using the roar of the engine as an excuse to mess her around. So she leaned into car until her mouth was only inches from Ashley's ear.

'NO! The answer's NO,' she shrieked. 'Good-night, Ash.'

And leaving him pinioned behind the wheel of the car, with the engine roaring, she hurried back to the house, slammed the kitchen door and locked it. Then she stood, head bent, listening. She heard the sound of the engine gradually lessening as Ashley drove up Deeping Lane, she even heard the gear-change as he turned out on to the major road. Then silence came back, just the sounds of the night – the wind in the trees, the sleepy chirp of a nesting bird – came softly to her ears.

Tess turned back into the kitchen. Cherie, Marianne and Andy were all looking at her; Cherie and Marianne with respect, Andy with interest.

Tess took a deep breath, gulped, and burst into tears.

Andy was the first to reach her.

'Too much emotion all at once,' he said, taking her hand and shaking it gently, and not attempting to put his arms round her, though Tess half hoped he would. 'I'm awfully sorry I seem to have sparked off such a row, but I'm sure you've calmed things down with – er – Ashley.' He turned to Marianne. 'Now, Mrs Delamere, Tess asked me back for a meal but I'm sure it would be best if I made myself scarce. I'll be here early tomorrow morning since Tess and I have an appointment in the city later.'

'Nonsense, Andy, you will stay and have supper with us,' Marianne said briskly, very much in her old manner. 'Tess, go up to your room, dear, and tidy yourself up a little – your face could do with a wash and your hair needs a comb. Cherie, you must have finished your homework by now, so you can lay the table. Now, Andy, do you like roast rabbit and onions?'

Andy was telling Marianne how very much he liked roast rabbit and onions as Tess trailed miserably out of the room. What an idiot she had made of herself, bursting into tears like that! It wasn't as if she regretted the scene with Ashley – well, she regretted that there has been a scene, but she did not regret the fact that Ashley had been told where he got off. The cheek of him, the assumption that she was, in some way, his property, his girl! He had been riding for a fall for many months – years – it was about time he learned the truth.

But what had Andy really thought? Did he believe that Ashley was an important part of her life? That they would marry, one day? The trouble was, Andy really was sophisticated, though he didn't appear so. He knew how to hide his feelings. Never once, in the entire encounter, had he seemed ruffled, either by the physical danger posed by Ashley's wild attempts to hit him nor the subtler danger of being reminded that he was neither as tall nor as handsome as Ashley himself.

Does he like me? Tess found herself wondering as she washed, changed and combed her hair. Or did he come down here for old times' sake and nothing more? If he likes me, is it just friendship? Or could it possibly be something warmer?

It wasn't until she was half-way down the stairs, looking as cool, calm and collected as she urgently desired to feel, that it occurred to her to question her own feelings. Did she want Andy to like her very much? Ashley said he loved her – did she love Andy? How could she love a boy she had last seen nine years ago, when he was a stripling of thirteen? How, for that matter, could he possibly love her?

Bloody Ashley, Tess thought, crossing the hall. He messes everything up! If he hadn't come bursting in making stupid remarks then Andy and I would simply be two old friends who'd met after a long time and enjoyed one another's company. What I'd better try to do – what I'd better jolly well succeed in doing – is pretend the Ashley scene never happened and pick up where Andy and I were when we got off the bus.

If that were possible, that was.

Thirteen

Spring 1943

'Well, Tess Delamere, you're a one and no mistake! I know tha's a year or two since we're met – I'm that sorry about your dad's death, by the way, which go to show how long it is – but Mr Collins from the post office were tellin' me that you're Land Army now – as I can see! He say you'd worked up at that there Castle Museum all through the Blitz and the moment that eased off, you went and worked in the country! Whass it like, being a Land Army girl, then? I've often thought of doin' it myself, tell the truth. More fun than the bleedin' munitions factory, I dessay.'

Tess looked up, startled by the flow of words, then moved over; she was sitting on the Number 5 bus and Ruby Southern, Janet's one-time crony, was lowering herself into the seat beside her, talking as she did so. Now, she settled in and then turned to Tess once more, her loud, laughing voice overriding Tess's attempts to answer her first question.

'Cor, I caught the bleedin' bus by the skin of my teeth, that I did! Nothin's simple any more, gal Tess – hev you noticed? I bin to city hall 'cos all our stuff, ration books, the lot, was in the house when it come down, last Sunday mornin', early. Good thing I din't come down an' all, but I were stayin' wi' me cousin Suzie at the time, an' George, of course, weren't around.' Ruby peered curiously at her companion from under a rather long fringe. 'Come to think of it, what are you doin' on this bus? Mr Collins, he say you'd been posted away.'

Tess laughed, though she sighed inwardly. She used bus journeys pleasantly as a rule, to think about her latest outing with

Ashley or to wonder about Andy; where he was, what he was doing. But small chance there was of quiet reflection with Ruby beside her. As for being posted away, it was true that she had worked for the past two years at a farm no more than six or seven miles from the Old House, but it wasn't exactly foreign parts, the way Ruby had made it sound. Today she and her employer, Jim Sugden, had attended the cattle market in the city. They'd sold six fatteners and bought two in-calf cows and then Mr Sugden had said that if she wanted an hour or two in the city and didn't mind coming home by bus . . .

Tess had jumped at the chance, because she wasn't on duty again until early morning, which meant she could spend the night at the Old House. But first she'd gone up to the museum to see all her friends on the staff there, then she'd done a bit of window shopping – not that there was much to buy, mind you – and finally she had caught the bus home, and no sooner had she settled herself into a window seat than Ruby had plumped down beside her. She had lost touch with most of the village girls once they moved away or wed, but she did know that Ruby had married a worker in the shoe industry and moved into the city . . . oh, years ago.

Now, Ruby grinned at Tess and settled herself more comfortably in her seat, pushing her laden basket down on to the floor between them and then unbuttoning her coat and taking a deep breath which she expelled in a long, low whistle.

'Phew! Aren't I glad I don't live at home no more! D'you live at home? Naw, course you can't, not since bein' posted. I bin livin' in St Gregory's Alley till we was hit, last week, but the place was destroyed completely so since there's only me now George's abroad, I've moved back in wi' my parents.' She sniffed. 'You oughter hear 'em! Do this, do that, don't answer back, pick up them dirty socks . . . you'd think I were five, not nigh on twenty-five, wi' my own hubby an' my own home. Or at least, my own bomb-site,' she added with grim humour.

'Oh Ruby, you don't change – well, not in some ways,' Tess said, turning to laugh at the older girl. She remembered Ruby as a plumpish fifteen-year-old who wore too much make-up, curled her dark hair into a frizz and never stopped talking. Now Ruby was quite slim, with her hair cut short and no make-up at all – but she still never used one word if fifteen would do. 'How many questions is that and in what order do you want them answered?' I stayed at the museum until it was fairly clear I wasn't all that necessary, then I applied for the Land Army and said I'd like to work for Mr Rope because he was near home. I thought I'd be able to live in Barton and keep my eye on my stepmother and Cherie, but in fact they sent me to Catfield, to the Sugden's place, Willow Tree Farm, and since they've got a bed for me, and we start early and finish late, I live in. But I go home whenever I've got time off, of course,' she added.

'Oh aye? Get on better with your stepma, do you? I 'member some spats when you was a kid.'

Tess chuckled. 'She's not so bad now. She quite likes me – and I'm awfully useful in my own quiet way. I can do the tax and explain things about Daddy's pension and manage points and coupons and so on. And I work hard in the garden, catch fish in the Broad in summer, look after the hens . . .'

'Got a feller?' Ruby asked, clearly bored by so much perfection, Tess thought ruefully. 'My George's in the bleedin' Army, he's in Burma . . . abroad, anyway. But I've got ever such a nice friend – he's a Yank, ever so generous. Only my mum think that ain't right, so we're havin' to meet on the sly, like.'

'I don't really have a fellow, just good friends,' Tess said rather guardedly. She had heard rumours about Ruby and Yanks and now she knew they were true; poor George! 'I'm friendly with Ashley Knox still – do you remember him? And with Andy Anderson, Lady Salter's nephew.'

'Ashley? Oh aye, I 'member *him*. Everyone were in love with him,' Ruby said. 'Ever so nice lookin', was Ashley. In the Air Force, in't he? Oh aye, I 'member Ashley right well.'

'Yes, he's RAF,' Tess said, nodding. 'He's doing rather well, he'll probably be a squadron leader one day, but he's a flight louie now . . . lieutenant, that is. He's up in Lincolnshire, flying fighters. We spend a good deal of time together when we've got leave. And Andy is Herbert Anderson, Lady Salter's nephew. He was around all one summer when we were young. Surely you remember him, Ruby? He was a skinny, dark-haired boy with specs, rather serious.'

'I remember him, too,' Ruby said, nodding. 'Sin him a coupla times a coupla years back, as I recall. Must ha' bin after he come back from Dunkirk. Weren't too good, from what I heered. Where's he now, then, eh?'

'Oh, in London, somewhere,' Tess said vaguely. 'I see him from time to time . . . but his job takes him away a lot.'

She saw Andy when he came home on leave, but the distance between them was growing, partly because of something Andy had said on one of his leaves as he and she, crouched over a wood fire in the living-room at the Old House, had been trying to roast chestnuts in the glowing embers.

'When the war's over I think I'll live in Greece,' Andy had said, trying to shield his face from the flames whilst fishing a dropped nut out of the ashes in the grate. 'It's a marvellous country and the people are fine. I love England, of course, but no one could deny that it's pretty cold and wet nine months out of the twelve. How do you fancy Greece?'

'Dunno; never been there,' Tess had said. 'I don't speak the language, though. I expect I'd be homesick.'

'I talk Greek well enough for both of us,' Andy said lazily, and squatted back on his haunches to peel the rescued nut. 'Don't tell me you want to hang around here, after the war? Athens . . . all that history . . . the wine-dark sea . . . you'd love it.'

'I don't think so,' Tess had said, and turned the talk in other directions. But it had made her think. She was very fond of Andy, but could she abandon her home, her way of life, her friends, and go away with him? Sun, sea and sky were all very well, but she knew that, for her, it wouldn't be enough. She would pine for England, cold and wet though it might be.

'What does the boy Andy *do*?' Ruby asked inquisitively now, and then, without waiting for an answer: 'Hev he proposed yet? Hev Ashley, come to that? My George, he think you're quite pretty.' She guffawed, nudging Tess with a sharp elbow. 'Dessay Bernie – he's the Yank – might agree, do I ever give him the chance to meet you.'

Tess blinked. 'It's kind of George to say that,' she said mildly.

'As a matter of fact, Ashley proposes quite regularly, but I don't suppose he means it. He, and Andy, who is in the army, incidentally, are rather busy fighting a war right now.'

'Don't stop folk marryin',' Ruby said complacently. 'Me and George did, for a start-off. Fellers want to marry when they're in danger. So they say. My Yank, now . . .'

She began to tell Tess intimate details about Colour Sergeant Bernie Nicolayvitch and Tess stopped listening. Ruby, she realised, would run on quite happily for hours without more than a murmur of confirmation from her companion. Instead of hearing about Bernie, therefore, Tess let her mind go back to Andy's last leave, which was some months ago. It had been on that leave that she had first begun to realise that you could be fond of someone – very fond – without necessarily wanting to spend the rest of your life with them alone. She still hadn't made up her mind that she *wouldn't* marry Andy one of these days, but a seed of doubt had undoubtedly been sown when he had declared his intention of living in Greece. Making a new life sounded wonderful until you actually took a long, hard look at it, and then it just sounded . . . lonely.

And since then, Tess remembered, jogging along in the bus with Ruby chattering endlessly about her Yank, she had seen Andy precisely twice. On the first occasion it had been a rush visit – he had had a forty-eight – in which they had discussed her work as a landgirl and whether, having seen that both Marianne and Cherie were settled, she might consider applying, once more, for the WAAF.

'You'd enjoy the WAAF, but I like to find you at home when I come back,' Andy said with his usual straightforwardness. 'You are such a comfort, old Tess.'

It wasn't exactly lover's talk, but Tess didn't mind that. 'But I want to help with the war effort, too,' she had protested. 'Marianne can manage without me now, I'm sure she can. Have you met Maurice?'

'No. Who's he? You don't mean Chevalier, I suppose?'

The two of them had been sitting in her boat on the Broad one mild day last autumn, having taken to the water to escape Cherie, who had a mountain-sized crush on Andy, and Frenchy, Lady

Salter's little mongrel, who insisted that Andy's one aim in life should be to throw sticks for him to retrieve. Not that Frenchy retrieved such sticks, oh dear me no! In the little dog's extremely mixed ancestry there lurked no sensible labradors or intelligent gun-dogs. To Frenchy's tiny mind, anything vaguely bone-shaped – and that included sticks – was clearly meant to be devoured. So Andy would throw a stick and Frenchy would eat it. Simple.

Tess giggled and leaned over to thump Andy good-naturedly on the shoulder. 'Chevalier! I should think not! No, Maurice Louviers. He's one of the Free French, working under de Gaulle.'

Andy sniffed. 'I don't know what those fellows do, but it doesn't seem to be much. Why?'

'He's Marianne's admirer, to put it no stronger. He's done her the world of good, honestly. She was actually ashamed of liking him, at first, because I found her in floods of tears one night, thinking she was being disloyal to Daddy. Only as I said, Daddy would be the first to tell her to live her life with zest. So Maurice is the reason I'm considering going a bit further than Willow Tree Farm. Marianne's capable again, truly she is. Much more independent. And if I did leave – when I leave – she won't have to live there all by herself. Well, she'd have Cherie of course, but you know what I mean. She could have Maurice on a – a much more permanent basis.'

'I see. So if Maurice is your stepmother's admirer, who is yours? Apart from my humble self, of course?'

'If you mean am I still seeing Ashley, yes I am,' Tess said with spirit. 'Why shouldn't I? You're both my friends, and Ashley's huge ego needs boosting from time to time. Flying is terribly hard on the nerves. Besides, to be frank, he's around and most of the time you aren't.'

She had waited expectantly to see if Andy would say his nerves needed help and his ego needed boosting and why didn't she save herself for him? He could even have explained that he would like to be around more but simply could not manage it just at present. Tess found herself hoping that Andy would suggest that they might cement their relationship in some way, but Andy never did what you expected. He just said he supposed she was right and changed the subject.

The second time she had seen him she had been talking seriously to Marianne on the subject of her hoard, because far from getting less and less, thanks to Maurice the hoard actually seemed to be growing. When the war had started, Marianne had taken over the big walk-in wardrobe in the spare room for every bit of storable food she could acquire. You couldn't accuse her of meanness, either, she did use the hoard, yet it never seemed to get any less.

'Buying on the black market isn't fair, Marianne, on the people who won't cheat and just have their proper rations. And it's not fair on others, either – those who can't afford to buy on the black market,' Tess had explained. 'You're such a good manager and a marvellous cook, surely you could manage on what we're allowed?'

But Marianne had just shrugged.

'Why should we go short, if we can afford these things and they are offered?' she asked reasonably. 'Before the war, people such as the Throwers did not buy fresh salmon; they couldn't afford it. We, on the other hand, did. Was this wrong? If it was not wrong, why is it wrong now?'

And in the middle of her garbled attempts to make Marianne see that hoarding did not help the war effort and really wasn't fair, there had been a quick tattoo on the back door and before either woman could go and answer it, the door had opened, and there was Andy.

As usual, he had turned up without any song and dance, wearing the uniform of a lieutenant this time – such a new and shiny uniform, however, that she was almost certain it was only worn for his leaves – and inviting her to have lunch with him in the city and then catch a bus out to Blofield.

'I fancy a stroll round the village, and perhaps a drink at the King's Head,' he said airily. 'What's more, there's a wonderful old church there, with some remarkable brasses, and old stained glass. I'd like to take a look. Will you come with me, Tess?'

Tess didn't have to be back at the farm until next day so she agreed to go with him. She then added, rather meanly, that she had been trying to persuade Marianne not to buy on the black market, but if she expected embarrassment or contrition from her stepmother she was to be disappointed.

'I am French, and Frenchwomen know the importance of feeding their families,' Marianne had said with great aplomb. 'Go off then, the two of you, and if you'll come to dinner with us tonight, Andy, we will have a wonderful beef stew, followed by my famous crêpes with lemon and sugar.'

'If you had a conscience, you'd have told her you wouldn't eat them,' Tess grumbled later, as she and Andy climbed aboard the bus for the city. 'That room is crammed, Andy, simply crammed. I don't think we could eat it all if we started now and guzzled for ten years.'

'Oh, well,' Andy said. 'We'll have a really mingy lunch. Will that satisfy your urge to be patriotic?'

It had made her laugh, and the trip to Blofield, even the sandwiches and weak lemonade which they ate sitting companionably on the churchyard wall, had been a bright spot at a time when such spots were rather rare. And they had found her real father's grave, or at least they assumed they had. A long and exhaustive search had left them scratching their heads – no gravestone had the right name or dates. And then they had spotted the old man. He might have been a verger, or a gravedigger, or just an old man who enjoyed pottering in the churchyard, but Andy went up to him and after the usual politenesses (what a cold summer it had been so far, how the war was going, whether it would end in the next couple of years) Andy had asked, 'We're trying to find a particular grave, but it doesn't seem to be marked. I wonder if you could tell us if a young man called Freeman, Ziggy Freeman, is buried here?'

The old man had led them straight to a small, undistinguished mound, with a cross at the head of it.

'There y'are; that's poor Ziggy,' he said. 'The Freemans din't have much money, an' they're a big fam'ly so they never got round to a stone. Ziggy was the youngest of seven, you know. A real limb, an' all. Grand lad, though, grand lad.' He heaved a sigh. 'Turble thing, bein' killed like that. Damned motor bikes, oughtn't to be allowed.'

'I wonder if you could tell us when he died and how old he

was?' Tess put in gently. 'He was a great friend of my mother's, she – she often spoke of him.'

'Oh aye? Well, let me think. He were a year older'n his sister Betty, an' she must be forty-two or three. Unless he were a year younger?' He looked from one to the other of them, his eyes bright with curiosity. 'That in't much use, I s'pose, but there'll be someone in the village who'll 'member better'n me. He's a sister livin' nearby . . . name of Yallop, as I recall. Why not ask her? She live down the Alley.'

'We'll do that next time we're in the village,' Andy said. 'We've both got to catch the next bus, though, or we'll be in trouble.'

They had to run to make it to the bus, but leapt aboard just as the conductor was about to ting the bell, and as they subsided breathlessly into a front seat, Andy said that on his very next leave he would come over to Barton and collect her and they would have a chat to Mrs Yallop.

So now, sitting in the bus beside Ruby and not listening to a word the older girl was saying, she thought again about Andy. When would he turn up next? The truth was that neither he nor she had the foggiest notion, and she was getting a bit tired of it. He was her dear friend, but he didn't seem to want to be anything more, and time was passing. She was twenty-three years old, Ashley still thought he owned her, and she had no idea whether Andy felt anything for her, apart from friendliness. Come to that, she didn't really know what she felt for him – what a problem! Yet here was Ruby, pleasing herself, not worrying about anyone else . . . I almost wish I could be like that, Tess thought, and then smiled to herself. She could be like that if she wanted, the truth was she didn't want, not yet, anyway.

And she would be seeing Ashley at the weekend if he wasn't flying, and they might go out somewhere, because he and several friends at the station shared his small sports car, using it sparingly but finding it more convenient than the buses. Ashley always wanted her to go back to Blofield with him, to have a meal with his parents, play tennis on their tennis lawn, go the village flicks, but she usually put him off. It was too definite, too serious. And if she didn't intend to marry him, and she really didn't think she would, then she shouldn't do things which gave him hope.

'So he say to me he say, "Are you sure you don't mind?" and of course I said I didn't, because I din't know what he were goin' to do, did I? And next thing, there was his hand down my blouse, an' me wrigglin' like a bleedin' eel, an' him grabbin' an' squeezin' . . .'

Tess stopped listening again. Ruby's anecdote surely could not still be about Bernie the Yank, not if it included hands down blouses, anyway! Perhaps, since Tess had tuned in, she had reverted to George and their pre-war honeymoon?

So instead of listening to Ruby, Tess thought about her mother and the small, sad little hump of Ziggy Freeman's grave. And about Andy, who knew her mother's strange history and understood how she felt about it. Because though no doubt, in this enlightened age, people would tell her it was of no consequence that she was illegitimate, that she had no claim to the man who called himself her father and thus to his family, she thought it did matter. She felt she had been sailing under false colours for most of her life – what would they have thought at school if they had known, or at work? Andy's parents and Lady Salter would probably be appalled, but she didn't think Andy minded. At any rate, he was interested in finding out more about Ziggy, more about her past, and on the only occasion when she had admitted her shame, he had told her bracingly not to be such an idiot.

'You are what you are, not what you're born,' he had said. 'So kindly don't feel sorry for yourself, because your father – and Peter *was* your father, even if he wasn't actually related to you by blood – loved you very much. That's what matters, after all.'

Ashley was pretty unaffected by it, too. He knew that Leonora had been pregnant when Peter had married her – indeed, he had told Tess so – but he still spent as much time in her company as he could. Although he had teased her and upset her often in the course of their friendship, it was never in connection with her dubious birth. Indeed, Tess honestly believed that Ashley had forgotten every word about it, and thinking it over she realised how Ashley had matured these past two or three years. He was much more sensible, hardly ever teased her in the rather cruel, thoughtless way of old, and took life altogether more seriously.

He didn't even look like the old Ashley; his hair was the same, although he darkened it by constant applications of Brylcreem, but his eyes weren't. They couldn't hold your gaze for long, they were restless, flitting from place to place, unable to settle. And his face was all planes and no curves, his mouth was held too tight so that lines ran from the corners of his lips to the outer curve of his nostrils. It sounded silly, too obvious, to say he had been a boy and was now a man, but that, Tess thought, was the truth of it.

'I'm a Battle of Britain pilot who got through it alive,' he had said to her once. 'Now I'm teaching kids who are scarcely out of nappies to fly planes, knowing they may only do a couple of ops in before they go for a burton. It makes you think. So when I go back to active duties, I'd like to be a married man with my own home. I'd like to have someone waiting for me when I come back from an op, someone who smiles just for me. Life is short, and this war has made me realise that one shouldn't waste a moment of it.'

He needed someone, really needed someone, but why did he have to pick on me? Tess wondered helplessly. I'd like to love him, but I don't think I can. Well, I do love him, in a way, but it isn't the way he wants. Or I don't think it is. I think, of the two of them, I like Andy best, though I don't believe for one moment that we love each other. Oh God, what a tangle it is!

'So then he tried . . . ooh, here's my stop!' Ruby jumped to her feet with much clutching at her light coat, much groping after her shopping basket. 'Well, Tess, nice to see you, hear all your news. Give my love to Janet, do you see her, an' her mum. Byee!'

She jumped off the bus, waved and set off, whilst Tess sat and smiled to herself. Much news she had told Ruby – much chance she'd had! But that was Ruby all over. Only interested in herself, when you got down to it. Some people, Tess concluded, simply enjoy the opportunities which a war gives without a single pang of conscience. Poor George, sitting in a Burmese jungle some- where whilst his wife carried on with anyone who would carry on with her. But he must have known when he married her that Ruby was a hot little piece. Presumably, he was willing to take a chance on her fidelity.

'Deeping Lane!' called the conductress, and Tess hastily jumped to her feet. She would go and see Marianne, and then walk back to Willow Tree Farm in time for evening milking. Mr Sugden wouldn't mind, so long as she wasn't late back.

It was April. Mal sat in the back of the liberty truck with a dozen other aircrew and waited for the WAAF driver to arrive. The truck wasn't supposed to leave for another twenty minutes, but you never knew. If you were lucky enough to be free you didn't hang around your hut or the mess, waiting for someone to ask you to do something. You made for the hills – in this case, the liberty truck.

Mal had been in England now for five whole weeks, and he was still awed by it. The smallness, the variety of accents of its people, the greenness. He had tried to tell the folk back home, particularly Kath, how beautiful it was, but he didn't think he'd succeeded. The trouble was, writing to Kath about all this was like trying to explain Sydney Harbour Bridge to someone from Mars. Kath was so far away, so involved in another life, and the Magellan and Queensland seemed like a dream he had dreamed in other, peaceful, times. He had loved Rhodesia, but it was a different world, he had told Kath it was an Aussie's idea of paradise. Beautiful people, wonderful food, and for the whites, an easy life. As for the countryside – well, he and his pals had taken a trip to see the Victoria Falls and that had summed up Rhodesia for him. The river Zambesi, on its 400-foot plunge, sends up a constant rainfall in reverse which is all scattered across one bank of the river. That bank, therefore, has for centuries been a tropical rain-forest, verdant, luxuriant, whereas the other bank is dry, its foliage that of the veldt. And that was how Rhodesia was; the whites were on the rain forest bank, the blacks on the harsh veldt. The white Rhodesians had been extremely hospitable to all the foreigners. Relaxed and friendly, they took their good life for granted and delighted in sharing it. Labour was cheap, the natives working harder than any white, so though the farmers owned huge tracts of land they didn't work at all, not by Australian standards. They organised, Mal and his friends had decided, and very well they did it. Only it wouldn't have worked in Queensland – and Mal had seen right from the start that it wouldn't have worked in

England, either. One was too huge and harsh for anyone to exist without hard physical work, the other too small.

Because for all his travelling – he's spent time in Egypt and South Africa as well as in Rhodesia – England wasn't like anything he had seen or imagined, and though Kath's parents had come from here, she had been born in Australia and had never set eyes on their native land. She longed to know about England and he had tried to explain the extraordinary greenness and the diminutive fields, the age-old buildings, but she had simply written back, puzzled, saying that there were old buildings in plenty of Melbourne, and Queensland was surely green enough for anyone, in the wet.

But England's greenness was gentle, its lushness tender, a far cry from the harsh landscapes of home. And there were so many different greens – hundreds. In the matter of greens, even Rhodesia could not compete. So Mal tried to explain, to give Kath an idea, a taste of England, but he guessed that he tried in vain. There were no words to express how beautiful it was, or no words that he could command, at any rate, and the words of the poets told Kath nothing. She wanted his words, his experiences, she said, and she asked, wistfully, how everyone was bearing up. Even in the outback they had heard about the bombing, the carnage caused by the Blitz, the shortages of life's essentials, and the way the British were fighting back, a tiny lion against the mighty German war machine.

'Them Yanks waited long enough before they come in,' she had written crossly back in the spring of 1942, when he had just arrived in Rhodesia. 'But it's just like last time, they don't make no move until someone rubs their noses in it. Self-interest, that's all they know, the Yanks.'

It embarrassed Mal when his mother wrote things like that, because he'd only just entered the actual war himself, in spite of being one of the first to volunteer. The trouble was he had taken to flying, found it easy, delighted in it, so when he got his wings he was told – not asked, told – that he would be instructing others for a while.

So he had missed everything, from the evacuation of Dunkirk through the Battle of Britain and the Blitz down to the more recent battle – Stalingrad, where the Russians had turned the tide of war so effectively that for the first time, even the most pessimistic were saying that there was hope for the Allies.

But all the while Britain had been suffering he had been doing his bit, instructing other men in the art of flying aircraft. He might have been there still but he had grown restless as the war continued and horror stories began to flow out of Germany and Japan. Concentration camps, torture, the dreaded SS and the stormtroopers entering Russia and killing, killing, killing. Not soldiers. Women and kids. Folk dragged from hospital beds and strung up on gallows ten, twenty at a time. And the sickening cruelties of the Japanese, the bombing of Britain until it seemed as though not a city would be left standing. He could no longer bear inaction whilst such deeds were being perpetrated by the hated enemy, so he had applied for active service and a posting to England.

It had taken time, of course. Everything took time. He had applied in the early autumn and it had been late spring of the following year before he had finally got his posting to a fighter station 'somewhere in England', the somewhere turning out to be Norfolk.

He was glad to be moving on, though he had enjoyed Rhodesia immensely. Despite being so near the equator, the fact that it was 4000 feet above sea-level meant that it was warm but pleasant all year round, never gaspingly hot like Queensland or terribly cold. And the girls, particularly, were so friendly, bronzed, open-faced and healthy! They had thronged round the aircrew, and all his shyness and diffidence with the opposite sex had disappeared under their delightful tuition. He began to enjoy female company, to be at ease with women, in a way which had not been possible in Queensland, where women were so rare.

He seldom thought or spoke of the reason for his flight from Australia any more, though it had haunted him for the first few months. Even now, he had never told anyone that he had fled from the too-eager attentions of Coffee Allinson, a girl five years his junior, who had decided she was going to marry him. From the moment that she had set foot on the Wandina, his fate had been sealed. She had made up her mind that it was Mal she wanted and so far as Coffee was concerned, what she wanted she got. She caused considerable resentment by pushing to one side the loyal staff and the good friends he had gathered round him so that she might always be on hand, and no one resented this more than Mal himself.

If she had been more intelligent she would have realised that her too-obvious pursuit embarrassed and annoyed him, but she was not intelligent. She was, however, the possessor of a very strong sex drive. Her needs and desires were an itch that she had to satisfy. So instead of taking it slowly and gently, instead of waiting for him to make a move, she followed him around the house, never losing an opportunity to cast her arms round his neck, her pink hair brushing against his chin, her firm, muscular body pressed against his. 'Come on, Mal, cuddle me,' she would croon. 'What's wrong with a quick cuddle, Mal? Ain't you human, feller? Don't you want me?'

The truth was he did want her, though not in the way she imagined. His need was on a shamefully basic level. He wanted her because she was so obviously available, so obviously panting for his touch. If she had been less eager, less pushy, he might have given in, gone to her. But because he resented her manipulation of him and feared her appetites, he had no difficulty in turning away from her, time after time.

But it ruined the Wandina for him, spoiled his good life. And unfortunately, Uncle Josh couldn't see it.

'She's a fine gal, boy,' he said several times, when Mal tried to persuade him to send Coffee packing. 'What's wrong with settlin' down young, eh? I made the mistake of puttin' it off, thinkin' next year would do, or the next, the next . . . and then it was too late and I was alone, with a station I couldn't handle and a staff who didn't have no confidence in theirselves or me. If you marry now you'll have kids quick an' before you're forty you'll have sons to teach an' train up.'

'I don't want sons yet,' Mal had said sulkily. 'I just want to be left alone to get on wi' my work, Uncle Josh. I don't want someone forcin' herself on me the way Coffee does.'

'You work hard,' Uncle Josh agreed. 'But a feller should play hard too, Mal. You won't never git nowhere if you don't play, now an' then.'

'Yeah ... but not with Coffee,' Mal insisted. 'I don't have no feelin' for her, Uncle Josh. And I don't believe she's got no feelin' for me. To be blunt, she just wants a man.'

'And you don't want a woman? I don't deny it ain't ideal boy, but there ain't much choice in the outback, not amongst women. You grab what you can get, you'll not regret it.'

The climax came when Coffee said she was pregnant, said the child was his. He was furious, outraged that she could lie over such a matter. He suspected that she was promiscuous, what was more, so when she told him she was pregnant he simply stared coldly at her and said that since he was not the father she had best cast her mind back and discover which of the men on the station she had been with over the course of the last four months.

Screams, shrieks, a thrown vase ... threats. She had been an innocent virgin before she met him, she hated him more than she had ever hated anyone, she would get one of the aborigines to point the bone at him, she had been humiliated beyond bearing, he knew very well he had fathered her child, how dared he deny her?

Mal expected Uncle Josh to support him on this, knowing as he did that Mal didn't want Coffee, but Uncle Josh wasn't interested in the truth. He said that Coffee might have done wrong but it was clear she loved Mal, clear that Mal had lain with her, so why not do the decent thing and marry the girl, then they could all sit back and enjoy a wedding first and then the baby, when it came?

'The baby won't bloody come, Uncle Josh,' Mal said, almost crying with frustration and rage. 'Not if it's mine it bloody won't. I've told you an' told you, she ain't my sort of girl and I've not touched her.'

The men knew it was true and sympathised. In fact it was Rupert who suggested he should cut and run.

'That woman, she dangerous,' he said one evening when he and Mal were in the home pasture, rubbing down the horses. 'She not give up till she git some poor feller, an' there ain't much choice around these parts. Why not go walkabout, Boss, till she move on? She won't hang about here when there's no feller to come on strong with.'

He went, of course. Went walkabout for six months, meaning to stay away a year, maybe, and ended up on an airstrip in Rhodesia, learning how to fly planes.

Wally and Soljer, between them, had taken over after he had fled. Rupert was immensely helpful too, and they all sent messages that it would soon be safe to return. Coffee, they thought, would move on once he was out of the way.

She didn't, though. Unbelievably, she married Uncle Josh.

The old man wrote, telling him of the wedding, pleading with him to return.

'With you gone, Mal, I needed someone to take care of me,' he wrote pathetically. 'She's a good gal – you could come home now, you'd have no more trouble, I swear it. You were right, there weren't no baby, but perhaps there will be, now.'

Mal, reading the letter, had snorted to himself. No more trouble, with young Coffee married to a man well over eighty, pushing up against him the moment Uncle Josh was out of sight, wheedling him to make love to her, to give her a baby which she would pass off as Josh's get, no doubt? He could just see it! But he didn't intend to say so, of course.

'I wish you both happy, but I can't come back to Wandina yet a while, Uncle Josh,' he had written back serenely. 'I'm serving my country, learning to fly so I can defend her. Mebbe I'll come back when it's all over.'

'Hey, where's the bleedin' driver, then? Someone go an' buck her ideas up or we'll not get any time in the city. How about you, Shorty? Go on, give a yell in their mess or whatever it is.'

The voice cut across Mal's day-dreams like a hot knife through butter and he blinked around him, as startled as a baby owl caught in a searchlight's beam. Where was he? He had seen the Wandina, Uncle Josh's sad face, Coffee's smug, predatory smile so clearly in his head that for a moment he could not reorientate himself. Then he recognised the canvas top of the liberty truck, the men around him, even the slanting sunshine outside, lighting up the grass, the distant trees . . .

'I'll go,' Mal said, getting to his feet whilst the man called

Shorty – who must be all of six and a half foot tall – protested that he was wedged into his place like a cork in a bottle. 'Where's the mess?'

They pointed it out to him and he began to walk across the concrete, then stopped as a WAAF came towards him, waving him back.

'It's all right, I'm on my way,' she said crisply. 'Got held up – sorry. But you know what officers can be . . . oh, sorry, sir!'

She sketched a salute, looking pointedly at the single stripe of a pilot officer on Mal's sleeve, then hurried round to the front of the truck whilst Mal climbed into the back and took his seat once more.

'All set?' the WAAF called over her shoulder. 'Hold tight then – Norwich, here we come!'

It was a beautiful city, even allowing for the bomb damage, which was everywhere. In narrow side-streets gaps in rows of terraced houses, in the city itself missing shops, boarded-off areas with danger notices, told their own story. When he had first seen damaged buildings, bomb craters, Mal had wondered why they didn't put such things right. Now he knew. There were too many of them and there simply weren't enough materials to rebuild, not whilst the whole nation, backs against the wall, was desperately fighting a war.

The liberty truck dropped them off at a place which they were told was called Castle Meadow, a wide and gracious street with a great castle built of light-grey stone on a grass-covered mound on one side, and ordinary shops and offices on the other.

'We pick you up on the Cattle Market; it's over there,' the driver said, waving a vague hand. 'Sort of behind the castle. Be back there by eleven-thirty, chaps, because if you miss the truck a taxi will cost you. Have a good time.'

Mal stood still for a moment, staring around him, then a hand plucked his sleeve. 'You want to come with us, Skip? We're going to a dance later, but first we thought we'd get us a meal. Lyons is on Gentleman's Walk – go down Davey Place and you'll come out on the Walk – it's pretty good. A change from the cookhouse, anyway.'

It was Percy Parrott, Mal's navigator, a small, dark, square man with satanic eyebrows which belied his easy-going, friendly personality.

'Sure; thanks, Perce,' Mal said at once. 'But I'd like to take a look at that castle; suppose you tell me how to find Lyons and I'll join you there in half an hour?'

'Yeah, sure,' Percy said. 'Come down from the castle, cross the wide road – it's called Castle Meadow – and dive down Davey Steps. That'll bring you out into Davey Place, which in its turn comes out on what they call Gentleman's Walk. Once you're there, you can't miss Lyons.' Percy turned to the rest of the crew. 'Split up, shall we? Get more done that way. The skipper wants a look at the castle – anyone else interested?'

But most of them had seen the castle many times before, for Mal was the only new boy in the crew. They had been flying together for some months, and Mal had only inherited his crew because the previous pilot had been seriously wounded on a raid earlier in the year, whilst Mal was still in Rhodesia.

'Random shot got him through the side of the neck, but he got us down all right,' the bomb aimer, Fred Milne, told Mal. 'He's still in hospital and they reckon he won't fly again when he gets out. The muscles of his neck have tightened on the side of the bullet hole so he's skew-whiff. Nice bloke, though. And a good pilot.'

He didn't say 'Hope you're as good', but it was there, in the long glance, the slightly cautious air with which they had treated him, at first.

But it had dissipated as soon as they'd flown with him. The raid hadn't been particularly successful, though they'd laid their eggs more or less on target, but he had shown his ability in weaving and ducking as they were chased by an ME 109 on their return flight across the channel. The hun had sprayed their wing with bullets, but Mal had managed to shake him off and had felt, not only his crew's relief, but their silent approbation as he brought the Lancaster smoothly in to land.

He had great faith in the Lanc – they all did. He had trained on other aircraft – Hurricanes first, then Manchesters, Wellingtons – but the Lancaster got his vote for ease in flying and instant response. And he soon began to have faith in his crew, too. They wouldn't let him down.

Indeed, soon they became good cobbers, all of them. Fred and Percy were stolid Brits with a daft sense of humour and a tremendous thirst for the thin, bitter beer which was all they seemed to brew in the pubs around the airfield. Geoff Webb, his engineer, was an Australian like himself, a tall man with a prominent adam's apple and large ears. He was the only member of the crew older than Mal, being twenty-eight years old, but he was first-rate at his job and an easy man with whom to get along.

The mid-upper gunner, Paul Medlicott, was a New Zealand farmer with a wife and twin sons back home and the rear gunner was Dave Betts, a Hebridean Scot with a sly sense of humour.

Lastly there was Sidney Clayton, the wireless operator. Young, with frizzy fair hair and freckles, he was only nervous around women and officers, he said. Once they were airborne he had no qualms and enjoyed his job, even seeming to get pleasure from teasing a response out of the sometimes fractious radio set.

So that was his crew, at this moment discovering the joys of freedom in the city. I'll just take a look at the castle, then I'll join them, Mal told himself, climbing a small path which led up to the top of the mound. This place must be old – but old!

They didn't charge admittance for the castle, which was also a museum, so he went in, of course. He wandered across a huge room which must once have been the castle keep. Now, Egyptian mummies and glass cases containing the burial goods from a hundred tombs thronged it, a far cry from the huge feasts, the dancing bears and the jesters of middle England who had once thronged this great room, Mal thought ruefully. Still, the Egyptian stuff was interesting, even to one who had actually climbed a pyramid, for Mal had done his share of sightseeing as he crossed half the world.

From the keep Mal made his way through galleries lined with pictures, rooms stuffed with stuffed birds, and the minutiae of some collector called Fitch who had acquired everything, from early books to fossils, pottery and Roman antiquities, and had then given them to the museum. Fascinated by the hoard, Mal slowed, examining everything, wondering about the donor. But he had to get a move on, or he would still be in here when the pubs shut! Accordingly, he began to walk faster.

It was in the Norfolk Room that he first noticed the girl. Slim, with dark hair tied up in a bunch on top of her head, she was wearing a light-coloured shirt, a short, practical-looking grey skirt, and brogues. He could only see her backview though, and that not distinctly, because the Norfolk Room was in darkness. It consisted of a number of brilliantly lit dioramas depicting the flora and fauna of the country actually in its characteristic habitats, or so it said on a notice near the door which Mal had studiously read whilst trying to get a better look at his companion, for they were, so far as he could tell, the only two people in this part of the museum. But now the girl had finished looking at whatever she was examining and was moving on, so Mal moved on as well; to Breydon Water, the notice said.

It was fascinating to see a whole scene set out before him, lifesize and life-style, too, for it was three-dimensional. There was the curve of the horizon, the reeds and flowers, the water, beautifully depicted by someone who knew how to paint, a punt, and seabirds – you expected to hear them cry, so real was the scene before him.

But even more than the dioramas, the girl herself fascinated him; he loved the way she walked, even the turn of her head seemed to hold a special significance, and she had moved one further down, so Mal followed, keeping well back. She might hurry ahead if she thought he was watching her. It was a lonely place, the Norfolk Room.

By a dint of only half reading the explanations of each scene, however, Mal kept up with the girl, though he never really saw her properly in the semi-darkness. But he thought she had dark eyes and he was sure that she was slightly built and of medium height and she carried herself beautifully, as he imagined a dancer would. Was she a dancer? She moved with such completely unselfconscious grace, surely she must have learned to do that?

But they had reached another scene now, an autumn one, with rabbits, a little hedgehog, the scarlet of hips and haws, the various browns and golds of autumn leaves. How did they do it? How could they preserve everything the way they did, as though it really were autumn and he was peeping through a window into a woodland scene?

Mal was peering, fascinated, when he realised that the girl seemed to have lost interest. He saw her glance at her wrist and then she began to walk quickly out of the Norfolk Room. He followed, naturally. He thought her beautiful and intriguing – he wanted to catch her up, talk to her, suggest that they might perhaps have a cup of tea together, at that place on the Walk the fellows had mentioned. And once she was out of this particular gallery she would be in daylight again and he could approach her without seeming in any way threatening.

The thing to do was not to hurry, though. I'll wait until she goes one way round a glass case and I'll go the other and stage a collision, Mal planned. It's easy enough to get talking, if you really set your mind to it.

He emerged from the Norfolk Room and looked hopefully around him. Nothing. No one. Where on earth could she have gone? The only door within easy reach was firmly shut and had *Staff Only* written, in gold letters, across it. Well, she obviously wasn't staff, for one thing she was far too pretty, for another thing far too young, and to clinch it, she was most unsuitably dressed. No, she must have realised he was following her and really hurried.

Mal didn't really notice the rest of the museum, he was too busy searching. But he didn't see so much as a wisp of dark hair disappearing round a corner and in the end he simply had to give up and make tracks for Gentleman's Walk and Lyons Restaurant.

They had a good meal in Lyons, Mal considered, when you took rationing and shortages into account. They ate fish cakes, reconstituted potato, tinned peas and bread and margarine, followed by an apricot sponge pudding in which you could taste the dried egg. And when they'd drunk all the tea in the pot they got to their feet and made for the outdoors once more.

'Dance starts in a few minutes; we'd better hurry,' Sidney said. Only one crew member was married but Fred and Geoff had girlfriends amongst the WAAFs at the station, though they were not 'steadies'. Both young men considered themselves free to dance and flirt with other girls, though they probably would not arrange to meet them again. Percy, Sid, both gunners and Mal, on the other hand, were still free as air – they needed to met someone, possibly the sort of girl who would take them home and welcome them into her circle. Mal missed the social side of life in Rhodesia and wanted the chance to get to know local families, so he had been looking forward to the dance.

That girl from the museum would have been bonza, Mal thought wistfully, as they jogged, elbow to elbow, along the pavement. If only I'd not been such a gallah, I'd have grabbed her while I had the chance, darkened room or no. I could have walked past her, pretended to go back, bumped into her . . .

But he hadn't, so he hurried on, wondering whether beer would be available at the dance; Lyons had not risen to anything other than tea or lemonade.

The dance hall, when they reached it, was imposing. At the entrance two huge plaster statues armed with clubs held up the roof of the portico. 'That's why it's called the Samson & Hercules,' Percy informed Mal. 'Wasn't it Hercules who held the world on his back?'

'Aye, and it were Samson who had his hair cut off an' all his strength ebbed away,' Sid pointed out. 'But these two've got long hair – they're pre-haircut, not post. Come on, let's get inside, see what the talent's like tonight.'

They were early, but the girls were earlier. They drifted in and out of the ladies' cloakroom on a tide of perfume and talc, smiling, calling to each other, eyeing the men. Mal's crew found a table, went to the bar, bought beer, returned to sit down as the orchestra filed in and began tuning up.

'I fancy that one,' Percy said presently, leaning over and speaking directly into Mal's ear. 'The one in the blue dress with the curls. A proper little cutie, isn't she? Fancy the friend, do you? Oh yes, I'm going to stroll over in her direction presently . . .'

The girl was blonde, small, giggly. Not my type, Mal thought. As for the friend – oh, no, I couldn't go along with that. Too like Coffee. She kept glancing across at them, smiling above their heads, tossing her pinky-brown curls, crossing and uncrossing solid, plump-calved legs, making sure she did so with the maximum of thigh showing.

'Are you sure you like those two?' he said to Percy presently. 'The dark girl's showing off too much and the other, she'll be doing the can-can on a table by the end of the evening. I'm for something quieter myself.'

'I don't want a quiet one, I want a willing one,' Percy said, unabashed. 'I don't have time for persuading, life's too short. Yes, the little blonde will do me nicely.'

'You'll do her nicely, you mean,' Sidney said. 'I want a really young, shy one who won't mind me being a bit young and shy myself.'

Raspberries were blown all round at this, since though Sidney was only nineteen he never showed any signs of his much talked-about shyness and indeed seemed, to Mal, to have a good deal of self-confidence for one so young.

'Never mind them, Sid, there's plenty of choice, you'll find someone who suits you,' Mal said now. 'Ah, band's starting! Go on, Perce, make your first masterly move while us beginners look on.'

Percy was half-way across the dance floor when another man reached the table ahead of him. The other man, taller, older, in Army uniform, with a neat little moustache and thin hair almost glued to his scalp, leaned over the blonde just as Percy ducked under his elbow and said, 'Can I have the pleasure of this dance, beautiful? I've always adored blondes with blue eyes.'

The blonde hesitated, glanced from one to the other, then stood up. Percy grabbed her and whisked her on to the floor whilst the brown job, as Mal was learning to call them, looked startled and fingered his moustache for a moment before turning to the girl sitting next to the blonde's now empty chair. He spoke, the girl got up, the brown job whirled her away, and other men began to cross the mysterious divide – men on one side, girls on the other – in order to claim dancing partners.

Presently, Mal found himself alone at the table. He drank the rest of his thin, warm beer, then stood up. He would get a refill whilst everyone was dancing and then find himself a partner for the next dance. The bar wouldn't be crowded now, with so many people on the floor.

He was wrong, though. The bar was crowded and he had to stand in a wild and indisciplined sort of queue, waiting with what patience he could muster until his turn came to be served.

It was while he was waiting to be served that he saw the girl. She was by herself, sitting at one of the small tables with a glass in front of her. She looked . . . familiar. It was not that she resembled someone he knew, it was more as though he really knew her, though how, he could not imagine. His first thought was the girl in the museum, of course, but this girl had shoulder-length, blue-black hair, straight and simple. The girl at the museum had had her hair pulled up into a bunch on top of her head. And this girl was wearing something grey and clinging, like smoke, and high-heeled shoes. No, it couldn't possibly be the girl at the museum. He went on looking at her though, puzzling about it. Where, where? He had been in England five weeks, she might have served him in a shop or sat next to him on a bus or train. She could have been in a queue before him or she might have been at the next table in a restaurant somewhere. She was slim and quite tall, though it was difficult to judge her height since she was sitting down, and she had the palest skin he had ever seen or imagined and shiny, blue-black hair, straight and simple, which fell forward like a blackbird's wing when she bent her head. He did not consider whether she was beautiful, she was just – familiar, he supposed. He stared so hard, in fact, that she looked up and, for a moment, their eyes met. Then she looked away, down at her hands once more, and he saw that there was colour in her cheeks.

I'll go over, apologise for staring, Mal thought. It was the familiarity which got to him, as though they knew one another and had done so for a long time.

He reached the bar, ordered another beer and, after some serious thought, a gin and orange. All girls drank gin and orange, didn't they? He would take it over to her, apologise for staring . . .

He was half-way to her table when a young man joined her. An extremely handsome young man in flight lieutenant's uniform, Mal saw, and disliked him on the spot. Six foot or more, curly, red-brown hair, a lean, piratical face full of danger and amusement. The stranger bent over the girl in the grey dress and kissed the top of her head, then took the seat beside her, picked up her hand, played with the fingers for a moment and then kissed her palm in a lingering sort of way, closing her fingers over the kiss as he moved his mouth away at last.

What a drongo, Mal thought scornfully. That girl can't like it – can she? You wouldn't find me kissing her hand when there were so many other places more fitted for kissing. Like lips. Oh God, did I say she wasn't beautiful? She's special, that's what she is, and she's gone and landed herself with a greaseball who kisses hands!

He carried the drinks over to another table, but nearer the girl in the grey dress this time. He didn't want to be caught staring though, so he sat to one side, where he could watch her profile. She was talking to the young man now, laughing, telling him something, then listening with intent intelligence . . .

She knew Mal was watching. He didn't know why he was so sure, he just was. Her awareness of him crackled like electricity between them, he was sure his hair was standing on end, he felt twice as alive as he usually did. But she was with another man; all he could do was watch and wait. Still, in the nature of things the fellow would have to take a pee eventually and when he did . . .

Mal drank his beer, and was standing the empty glass down just as the greaseball stood up. He's going . . . I'll rush in . . . Mal thought, already half on his feet, his hand gripping the gin and orange. But the girl in the grey dress rose too; they were going on to the dance floor. And as soon as he saw her in motion Mal knew that it was the girl from the museum. The same wonderful, flowing walk, she held her head the same way . . . yes, it was definitely her!

He sat down, then jumped to his feet again, determined to make a move – any move – which would bring him to her attention. If I don't I'll lose her, he thought, his mouth drying up at the mere threat of such a thing. They'll go and sit somewhere else when the dance finishes and I'll lose sight of her – or they'll leave, or go for a walk . . . I'll lose her!

The nearest girl still unclaimed, sitting at a table alone, as he was, was extremely young and rather spotty, with a bush of dark, wiry hair. She was wearing a pink dress with little cap sleeves and she hadn't shaved her underarms; hair bushed out from her armpits as wirily as it did on her head. He crossed the space between them in a stride, slammed the gin down on her table and said, 'Like to dance?'

Colour flooded her face; less rose than beet, she was almost purple with a mixture of joy and embarrassment. She wasn't used to being asked to dance, Mal thought, and knew, shamingly, that his eye would have passed over her quickly, completely, had it not been for the girl in the grey dress. The spotty girl began to say yes, she would like to dance, but he had hauled her to her feet and on to the dance floor before she had got half-way through the sentence.

'All right? Off we go, then.'

He steered her on to the floor and began to pursue the greaseball through the canoodling, cuddling crowds. It was a waltz, he thought, or possibly a quickstep. Whichever, it didn't matter so long as . . .

'Sorry, cobber. Okay are you?'

He had trodden, heavily, on someone's shinily shod foot. The girl in his arms looked as though she might cry – what was the matter with her? He pulled her a bit closer and whirled her round, then pushed her through a small gap in the crowd, nearer the centre of the floor. If they could reach the centre he could pin the greaseball down and follow him, dog his footsteps.

He found the greaseball and the girl in the grey dress and calmed down a bit. He shovelled his partner into the group, wishing he'd chosen someone lighter on her feet. This girl weighed a ton and didn't move with him, he had to keep shoving her along as though he was a gardener and she a wheelbarrow. Still. The greaseball and the girl in the grey dress were only separated from them now by two other couples. He had better not get closer. She had been aware of him at the table, if she noticed him on the dance floor, realised he was following her, gave him the brush-off . . .

But she wouldn't. That marvellous feeling had to be a shared sensation, he could not have been the only one conscious of it. Once she got rid of the greaseball they could . . . they could . . .

What could they do? Dance? Well, why not? This was a dance, wasn't it? Though with a ton of perspiring partner now uncomfortably draped across his chest dancing was the last thing on his mind.

For some moments he had been hearing a voice, buzzing away dully, like a mosquito, on the periphery of his consciousness. Now, as the music drew to a close and people began to move off the floor, he listened to it, feeling vaguely guilty. It was his partner, trying to act normally, to make friends.

'Whass your name, bor?' she was saying. 'I'm Ethel Wicks. I live down Magdalen Street – thass not far from here.'

'Oh . . . sorry.' He held her away from him, shook her solemnly by the hand. 'I'm Malcolm Chandler, Mal to my friends.'

'Hello, Mal. How d'you do?' Obedient now, to his hand on her elbow, she moved back to the table she had just vacated and sat down heavily. He sat down too; he could see the girl in the grey dress better from here. She was fanning herself with her hand, laughing at something her companion had said, looking up at him . . .

She knows I'm looking at her, Mal told himself. Her cheeks are stained with the slightest of slight flushes, that's because she knows I'm looking at her. Ah God, how can I get away from Ethel Wicks without being bloody rude? Do I want to get away from her, though? The chaps are right the other side of the room, I don't want to go over there, I'd rather sit here and listen to Ethel wittering on whilst I watch the girl in the grey dress, the way she moves, the dimple that springs up in one cheek when she smiles . . .

'. . . Wouldn't mind a drink myself.'

That was Ethel, sounding wistful. Quickly, he handed her the gin and orange. 'Here . . . I bought that for you – I thought it would be an introduction – only then the music started and I asked you to dance instead. I'll go and get myself another beer, though – shan't be a tick.'

The bar was impossible, the uniforms wall to wall. But he wedged himself amongst them and watched and presently the greaseball added himself on to the outside of the scrum. A chance! He could go over to her table, ask her to dance . . . the music had just struck up again . . . all while the greaseball was fighting his way to the bar.

But Ethel would see him. Mal was not a cruel person and he had seen her incredulous joy when he had approached her, had recognised it as the pleasure of a perpetual wallflower suddenly plucked, danced with, talked to, made beautiful, perhaps by a little attention. And he'd lied to her, told her the drink had been intended for her whilst all along . . .

But even so he left the crowd round the bar and walked towards the girl in the grey dress. He dared not lose this opportunity, he just dared not. She watched him coming towards her, her eyes very large and dark in her pale face. He smiled at her but she did not smile back, not with her mouth. Her eyes smile, he thought, and felt dizzy. Ah God, if I touch her hand the electricity which sparkles and splutters between us will probably burn!

He reached the table and bent over her. For the first time but not, he was sure, the last, the smell of her skin and hair was in his nostrils, turning him drunk with the pleasure, the *rightness*, of it. 'Excuse me, what's your name? I'm sorry . . . where do you live? I want . . . I thought at first I knew you and then I realised you were in the museum this afternoon, in the Norfolk Room. I tried to catch up with you but you disappeared. I want to . . . if we could meet . . . That fellow, the flight louie, he isn't . . . I'm sorry . . .'

He was stammering like a ten-year-old, all his calm, his certainties, suddenly gone, leaving him tongue-tied, stupid. But she was smiling now, and it was the most beautiful smile in the world, a tilted, three-cornered smile which creased her eyes into long, shining slits and showed small white teeth between lips which were red by nature, not artifice.

'I'm Tess Delamere,' she said, quick and soft, beneath her breath. 'I'm a landgirl on a farm not far from Norwich – Catfield, the place is called. The fellow's Ashley Knox, he's an old friend . . . Oh Lor', he's coming back! Look, can I phone you?'

'Yes! Tomorrow . . . any time. My station's not far from Norwich, either.' He gave her his number, drunk with success. He had known it wasn't going to be difficult, all it had needed was courage. 'It's the officers' mess, someone will fetch me if I'm not around. I'm night flying. Lancs.'

'Oh... Ashley's a pilot too, but he's stationed in Lincolnshire . . . I'm sorry, I didn't ask you what your name was?'

A voice spoke behind them. A disgruntled voice. The tall flight louie whose name, it appeared, was Ashley was standing by the table, empty-handed.

'Well, bugger me, I go to the bar for a drink and when I come back some bloody Aussie is trying to pinch my girl! Piss off, you, the lady's not for rough colonial boys to play with.'

It was the greaseball, but he hadn't guessed that there was anything between Mal and the girl in the grey dress – Tess. The greaseball's words sounded offensive but he was only joking. Mal had heard enough English jokes in the past five weeks to know this was one of them. He turned, giving the greaseball his most placid, easy-going grin.

'Sorry, I didn't realise the lady had a partner for this next dance . . . I'd best be getting back to my crew.'

'Oh Ashley, how silly you are,' the girl named Tess said resignedly. 'And where's my drink?'

'I told you, the bar's impossible. Well, no, I didn't tell you, but it is. I waited and waited and whilst I was trying to decide what to get you if they didn't have sherry or port some scum of a brown job shoved in front of me. So if you really want a drink, sugar plum, we'd better get out of here, go to a pub and get one in a civilised fashion. What d'you say?'

He had actually forgotten Mal, had sat himself down and recaptured Tess's hands. Tess began to reply, to say that she had come dancing and she would jolly well stay and dance, but Mal judged it was time to make his next move.

'What are you drinking? Bitter?' he said. 'Let me get them in . . . Ethel!'

Ethel, sitting staring, heard her name and came lumbering over. She smiled awkwardly at Tess – she had rather a sweet smile, Mal thought, or was it the reflective glow of Tess's smile which made everyone else look prettier, better?

'Yes, Mal? You did mean me to come over, didn't you?'

'That's right. Look, I'm going to get some drinks, you sit here whilst I fight my way back to the bar. What're you drinking, dear?'

She was so happy that the beet red came flooding back. She giggled breathlessly, cast a triumphant, half-frightened glance at Tess and said boldly, 'I do love gingerbeer.'

'Right. Two bitters, one gingerbeer . . .' he glanced at Tess, remembering just in time that he wasn't supposed to know her name. 'What d'you fancy?'

'Tess will have a dry sherry,' Ashley said. 'It's very good of you . . . shall I come and give you a hand?'

'I won't, I'll have a gingerbeer, the same as – as Ethel,' Tess said. Mal was fairly sure she had only said it to annoy the Ashley bloke, but he just nodded down at her, then turned and grinned at Ashley.

'Easy; two bitters, two gingers,' Mal said. 'No need for anyone to help, my navigator's been waiting ages, I'll ask him to get them in for us, then we shan't have too long to wait. Bye for now.'

He went off, flushed with triumph. He knew her name, he knew she was a landgirl, working in Norfolk. Knew that she and greaseball Ashley weren't married or engaged or anything like that – if they had been, Ashley would have said, because it was plain as the nose on your face that he regarded Tess as his own property. And girls, Mal thought wisely, did not much care for that.

Reaching the bar he wondered, as he made a long arm and asked Percy, in a loud shout, to enlarge his order by a couple of bitters and two gingerbeers, just what was between those two, Ashley and Tess. More than she wanted and not as much as he did was as far as guesswork would take him. But he'd find out; already a plan for the evening was forming. Percy, old in the ways of queue jumping, simply nodded at the addition to his order and presently fought his way out of the crush once more with a lurching tray laden with booze.

'Found yourself a bit of stuff?' he asked breathlessly. 'Why so many?'

'What, drinks? Oh, because my bit of stuff has a feller in tow, so I've had to throw dust in their eyes.' Mal took the tray and Percy removed one of the beers from it, and a small glass full of red liquid. 'I take it that's for the cute little blonde?'

Percy pulled a face. 'Not exactly. She found someone with more stripes and a bigger wallet – well, that's what I tell myself. I'm with another one; older and not so blonde, but you should see the tits on her – and feel them! She bounced me round the floor on 'em, I tell you no lie. Can't wait to get her outside, later.'

'You're a dirty old man,' Mal said appreciatively. 'Are we going to share a taxi back to base or shall we quit at eleven-thirty?'

'My God, you must be smitten if you're considering a taxi! We'll catch the truck or walk, and I don't mean to walk. I'll keep my eye on you, we'll all go out at eleven and have a snog round the back of the Royal Hotel, then it's a run for the liberty truck and snoring in our beds by midnight.'

'I'm not snogging with a load of fellers,' Mal said. 'Oh, you mean girls, do you? Didn't sound like it.'

Chuckling, he made his way back to their table with the drinks and handed them round. Tess took hers and their fingers touched; lightning shot along Mal's arm and tingled its way down to his toes. He glanced uneasily at Ashley but the other man was immersed in his beer, totally unaware. Thank God lightning doesn't show, Mal thought, then looked at Tess. Faint rose was flushing her cheeks again. I knew we must both feel it, Mal told himself triumphantly. Ah God, the greaseball's going to dance with her again . . . heave ho, Ethel!

They left the dance hall soon after eleven and walked under the stars, arm in arm with the girls they had met, round to the Cattle Market where the liberty trucks were lined up, waiting for them. Ashley and Tess had disappeared in a smashing little sports car – Mal had felt envy, but no unease. He was sure, certain sure, that Tess and he were right for each other. They would meet again, and soon.

On the way back to the trucks Ethel hung heavily on Mal's arm, chattering in what at times he took to be a foreign tongue, but was only her thick Norwich accent. She reversed 'ooh' and 'oh' so that soup became soap and soap, soup. She said 'Git you a mauve on, bor', when she meant him to speed up a bit and 'hare' when she meant 'here'. She asked him where he came from and sighed with happiness when he told her Australia.

'I've got an uncle there,' she said. 'I wonder if his voice is funny, like what yours is?'

'Probably,' Mal said. 'How old are you, Ethel?'

'Seventeen come July,' Ethel said. 'Why?'

'Oh, I just wondered. I'm a lot older than you. I'm twenty-seven. I'm the oldest in my aircrew apart from Geoff, who's already twenty-eight.'

'It don't matter,' Ethel said. 'I like older men.' She clutched his arm tighter. 'Will you come home wi' me, one o' these nights? To meet my mum, I mean, an' hev some grub?'

'It's very kind of you, Ethel, but I don't think . . .'

His voice trailed into silence. Ethel sighed deeply.

'It's all right, I didn't think you would,' she said. 'I in't your type really am I? You was just lonely, a long way from home? Is that it?'

'It's not so simple as that, but . . . yes, I was lonely. And it's been a lovely evening, you've made me very happy. Honest. Only I am a lot older than you and . . .'

'You don't hev to explain,' Ethel said. 'You say I ha' made you happy – you're done more'n that for me, bor. You're broke my duck.'

'Pardon?'

'You're broke my duck. I in't never been axed to dance afore, though I bin goin' to the dances time out o' mind. And you din't just dance one dance, you danced wi' me *all evenin'*, you bought me drinks, you interdooced me to your friends. . .' She sighed luxuriously. 'Wait till the girls in Woollys hear tell of it.'

'You're a very lovely young girl,' Mal said, conscious of the debt he owed this plain, plump child with the spotty face and the frizzy mop. Without her, he might never have managed to meet Tess. 'Just you have confidence and smile at people in future, though. I tell you, Ethel, I was nearly put off because you just sat there, not smiling. And you've a very pretty smile, it changes your whole face.'

He wondered whether a hint about pink not being everyone's

colour might go down all right, but decided against it. She probably only had the one dance dress.

'I will smile, Mal. And thanks.'

They had reached the Cattle Market and in the shadow of the waiting trucks people were embracing. Mal pulled Ethel into his arms and hugged her, then kissed her with gentleness and affection. She shivered in his arms, hugging him back, and when he put her away from him he saw tears shining on her short, stubby lashes.

'Ethel? I'm sorry, didn't you like being kissed?'

'Oh, *yes*, I liked it all right,' Ethel said. 'Another first, Mal!'

'Well, it won't be the last, I'm sure.' Mal gave her a squeeze, then turned and climbed into the truck. He sat down on the hard metal seat, then leaned out for one more word. 'Don't forget, honey – smile!'

'I won't forget,' Ethel said, She waved jauntily, turning away to retrace her steps, for she lived past the Samson & Hercules in the other direction. 'Thanks again, bor.'

'Was *that* your date?' Percy asked incredulously, clambering into the truck and subsiding on the seat by Mal. 'That fat girl?'

'Well, not entirely. And it's only puppy fat, she'll soon lose it when she gets a bit older. She's not seventeen until July.'

'Cradle snatcher,' Geoff said smugly. 'What d'you mean by not entirely, anyway?'

'I was in a foursome,' Mal explained. 'With another chap, Ashley something or other, and another girl. Tess. I'm hoping to see her again,' he added.

'Does Ashley something or other know you've frozen on to his date?' Percy asked. 'Bet he doesn't. Bet he'd break both your Aussie legs if he had an inkling.'

'He doesn't own her,' Mal said. 'Oh, by the way, how went it with the enormous tits?'

'Grand. Apart from bloody nearly smothering in 'em . . .'

'Wha-at? Boasting again . . . unless she was a tall girl' . . . 'Where did you find enough dark for that sort of carry on?' . . . 'Don't listen to him, all he got was a smack in the kisser I dare say . . .'

The remarks came from half a dozen throats. Mal laughed and

sat back on his uncomfortable seat as the truck lurched into motion and his navigator began to defend himself. When would she ring? When could they meet?

All the way home in the car, with Ashley going on about his hopes of being returned to active service quite soon, Tess sat beside him, hummed a hum every time he stopped for breath, and dreamed. She simply could not start discussing Ashley's plans for the future, because they contained her, and she, who had puzzled for so long because she seems a little in love with Ashley and quite a lot in love with Andy, could suddenly see just what her feelings really were.

Sisterly, that was it. What she felt for dear Ash and darling Andy was simply a deep and sisterly affection, but she had not recognised it as such until this very evening, when Mal had entered her life.

Mal. Was it short for Malcolm, what was his surname, why, in God's name, did he affect her like – oh, like a lightning strike? When he had passed her her drink and their hands had touched – dear God, the wonderful, exciting tingle that had torn through her, from the top of her head to the tips of her toes! He meant more to her, after a couple of hours in which they had only looked covertly at one another, exchanged the occasional smile, than either Ash or Andy, both of whom she had known for years.

She hadn't seen him at all in the Castle Museum, though she had been aware that someone else was also in the Norfolk Room with her. But she was intent on getting in to see her old colleagues, that was all she had been thinking about, really. No, she had first noticed him staring at her when Ashley had gone to the bar for their drinks. She had seen a sturdy, dark-haired young man in Australian Air Force uniform, sitting at an adjoining table with his dark eyes fixed on her face. She had looked away, kept her eyes down, glanced across the dance floor, but she had felt his eyes on her as though he was touching her physically, sending a warmness, a glow, tingling through her body.

She hadn't danced with him, and apart from those few tense sentences when he had come to her table before Ashley's return, she had scarcely spoken to him. Ashley had rattled on, the Australian had answered, once or twice the fat little girl with the spots had shyly whispered a few words . . . but she, Tess, had kept her mouth shut. Afraid to open it? Afraid to give away how she felt? She didn't know, she had simply felt that it wasn't necessary to talk. All her energies were concentrated on thoughts of the moment, which must surely come, when they met without the restrictions caused by Ashley and little Ethel.

'So what do you want to do tomorrow, poppet? I'll call for you and bring you back to Blofield for lunch – mother is longing to see you again – but after that I'm at your disposal – as ever. How about a run down to the coast? We could go to Yarmouth, there's always a bit of beach where you can walk without being blown sky-high. A different town can be fun, anyway.'

Tess dragged herself back to the present, to the car rushing through the darkness, to the wind tugging her hair, to Ashley's voice, self-assured, amused, asking the inevitable question; what shall we do tomorrow? She had wondered, when she first accepted his invitation to spend the following day with his people, whether she might do a bit more detecting, but suddenly it no longer seemed important. If she had been with Andy it might have been different, but the truth was, all she could think about was the Australian and the slow stir of excitement in the pit of her stomach whenever their eyes met. Was this what the girls called love? If so, it was an emotion which she knew she had never experienced before. But perhaps it was just . . . well, perhaps it wasn't love, anyway. She found she did not want to name the other emotion which the girls had talked about.

'So what'll we do?' Ashley asked, an edge of impatience in his voice. 'I wanted you to come back tonight, to stay over, but you wouldn't, so I've got to traipse out to Barton . . .'

'I'm milking in the morning,' Tess said. 'It wasn't *wouldn't*, Ashley, it was *couldn't*.'

'You mean if you weren't milking you'd have come?'

There was a short silence whilst Tess struggled with her conscience. Finally, she giggled. 'Oh damn you, Ash, I probably wouldn't have stayed over, because it would make you think . . . it would lead you to expect . . .'

'I am *not* an idiot, Tess,' Ashley said. 'But I begin to suspect that you are. Spending the weekend with my people wouldn't mean anything, except that it would be easier for me to take you out if I didn't have to use precious petrol driving all the way to Barton and back. Besides, you adore me, you know you do. When the war's over . . .'

Tess sighed at this blatant self-deception. Whenever he could, Ashley tried to use their long friendship as a sign of her undying love for him – why, this very evening he had tried to discourage Mal from talking to her! *Some bloody Aussie is trying to pinch my girl . . . Piss off, you, the lady's not for rough colonials to play with.* If that wasn't laying claim she didn't know what was. He seemed impervious to snubs, what was more. Telling him she didn't want to marry anyone whenever he proposed got her a deep, unbelieving sigh. Well, he would do well not to believe her next time she said it, Tess realised, because now she did want to marry someone. She wanted to marry the Australian bomber pilot, Mal whatever his name was. At least, she wanted to be with him, and what better way of being with someone was there than marrying?

Still, Ashley did have one big advantage. If he hadn't taken her to the Samson she would probably not have met Mal. Her heart nose-dived into her dancing shoes at the mere thought. She turned and smiled forgivingly at Ashley, but he was singing a nursery rhyme song about Old King Cole, only somehow the words had got twisted to fit the Air Force and were no longer concerned with the king's pipe, bowl or fiddlers three.

Tess sighed. Men! They were all little boys at heart, really – probably Mal was just as bad in his own way. Probably if Mal were in the car he would join in the chorus of the rude song Ashley was now belting out at the top of his voice.

Old King Cole was a merry old soul, and a merry old soul was he,
He called for his kites in the middle of the night,
And he called for his pilots three.
Every pilot was a very fine type and a very fine type was he,
'I don't give a f . . . damn,' said the pilot, merry merry men are we,
For there's none so rare as can compare with the boys of old Waddy!

'You're extremely rude and vulgar, and don't think I didn't hear what you nearly said instead of "damn",' Tess said severely, just

361

as Ashley screeched to a halt before Willow Tree Farm. 'Don't call for me too early; when I've done the damned cows and had my brekker I'll have to change out of my overalls.'

She went to get out of the car but Ashley leaned across her and calmly shut the door again, the fielded her against his chest.

'Kissy kissy,' he demanded. 'Pucker your pretty lips and prepare for the experience of a lifetime.'

He kissed her. After a moment he stopped kissing her and held her away from him, peering down at her in the moonlight.

'Hmm. About as exciting as kissing a pound of cod, I'd say,' he murmured. 'What's the matter, sweet Tess? Cross?'

'Oh, Ash, I'm tired of saying you should start trying to find a girl who appreciated you a bit more! I said if we went on going out it must be no strings; I told you I wanted your company and your friendship, not a lot of mauling.'

'Mauling! I was kissing you. Rather nicely, I thought. Only even the world's greatest lover needs a *leetle* encouragement and that, it seems, you were not prepared to give. And I thought you'd enjoyed our evening out.'

'I did!' Tess said remorsefully. 'I'm sorry, Ash. I think I'm just very tired.'

'Hmm. Try again?'

Tess remembered his sister's friendship, his mother's kindness, his own eagerness to help her in any way he could. She put her arms gently round him and this time, when he kissed her, she kissed him back, allowing her mouth to soften and her body to curve towards him.

'Better,' Ashley murmured. 'Tess . . . I fool around a lot, but I do love you, you know.'

'You don't, Ash,' Tess said quickly. 'You like me, as I like you, but love – well, I think love's something quite different. I don't think we've known one another long enough to fall in love.'

'Time has nothing to do with it. The moment I saw you I fell. Look at that Aussie bloke this evening – one look at you and he went head over heels. Oh yes, I noticed even if you didn't. For two pins he'd have tried to cut me out.'

He sounded indignant. Tess laughed, unable to help herself.

'As if he could, and you so wonderful! Look, I'd ask you in for a hot drink, but you've got a long drive, and . . .'

'Thanks, I'd love a drink. You go and get the cocoa on whilst I park the car deeper on the verge. I dare not leave it out in the road, last time I did that stupid old fart you call a copper rode into it in the dark and gave himself a black eye. My name was mud – and he fined me two bob!'

'Righty-ho,' Tess said, hopping out and heading for the front door. 'Don't be long; I'm tired if you aren't, and I've got an early start tomorrow.'

In the dimness she saw Ashley shake his head. 'Shan't be a tick. Tess . . .?'

'What? Do hurry up, Ash, I'm really quite cold.'

'Nothing. Tell you in a minute.'

Tess went into the hall and closed the front door gently behind her. She stole across to the kitchen and switched on the light, then began, hastily, to make two cups of cocoa. She had a nasty sort of feeling that a serious Ashley might be even more of a problem than a jokey one. But he came in presently, still cool from the night air, took off his jacket and hung it on the back of the door as though he owned the place, and then kissed her lightly on the nose and headed for the pantry.

'I want bickies,' he said from the depths, rummaging. 'Damn rationing, what I hate most is no nice little titbits to eat when you're hungry and it isn't mealtime. Aha, I knew Mrs Sugden would have a secret supply.'

'What have you found? Are you sure it isn't special, not to be touched?' Tess asked suspiciously. Marianne's pantry was always full of special food, not to be touched by wandering landgirls. 'Mrs Sugden's been good to me, I don't want to upset her.'

'No, it's all right, honest. She told me last time I came that she kept a tin labelled "Bits and Pieces" in the pantry, and this is it, see? She fills it with odds and ends for workers or her kids or anyone who happens by . . . oh boy oh boy oh boy, cheese straws! Bless her – wonder where she got the cheese from? Lovely, indigestible food, cheese straws. Oh, and under the first layer of greaseproof . . . yes, yes, *yes*! Shortbread, and oatcakes, too. Come on, if the cocoa's ready we'll have a midnight feast.'

The cocoa was soon made and Tess, thinking wistfully of her bed, sat down beside the kitchen table but Ashley refused to allow anything so sloppy.

'Midnight feasts are eaten in wicked luxury, either in your bedroom – me too, of course – or in the front parlour. Which?'

'The parlour, I suppose,' Tess said gloomily, following Ashley and the tin with a mug of steaming cocoa in each hand. She had no desire to find herself wrestling with Ashley on her bed. 'Only I really am tired, Ash, so don't let's play for *too* long.'

'Play? What d'you mean, girl? Well, never mind . . . come and sit on the couch, by me, so I can give you the odd cuddle.'

Tess heaved an exaggerated sigh and sat beside him, then at his behest, dipped her fingers into the tin of goodies and the pair of them were soon munching in companionable silence.

'Phew, that's better,' Ashley said at last. 'Aren't midnight feasts grand when you've been dancing half the night? I say, Tess, do you have nightmares?'

'Everyone does after cheese and oatcakes and things late at night,' Tess said accusingly. 'Especially other people's cheese and oatcakes. But drink your cocoa like a good boy and you may be lucky this time.'

'I don't mean cheese nightmares. I mean the other sort.'

'What other sort? The crocodile in the bath sort?'

'No,' Ashley said. 'The sort where you're in the pilot's seat and the kite bursts into flames and you can't get out, or you do manage to get out but your parachute doesn't open, or you can hear your chief screaming over the intercom and when you turn your head you can see that one of the bombs the chaps have sent down is heading back up towards you like a surfacing shark. That sort.'

He was shivering. Tiny shudders rippled through him, and his face had gone pale and grim, with no laughter in the dark eyes, no teasing smile on his lips. Tess was horrified. She'd heard all about the strain the aircrews were under, she'd seen with her own eyes some of them break down, coming back from ops, but it simply hadn't occurred to her that Ashley was frightened, too. He seemed so cocksure, so full of jokes and fun . . .

She turned to him and wrapped her arms round him as tightly

364

as she could. Then she kissed the side of his face with little, soft kisses, whilst murmuring that it was all right, everyone had those dreams, she'd heard dozens and dozens of aircrew say something very similar. Why, she had a fearful nightmare herself, the recurring sort, which had haunted her all through childhood, haunted her still.

'But I'm not a girl,' Ashley said at last through stiff lips. 'I've been back on active service ten days and I'm a full-grown bloody bloke, and yet there's times when I shake like a bloody blancmange and – and dammit, I *know* I'm going to die. I wasn't like it first time round, but I'm too knowing, now. No one could be so lucky that they did fifty ops and got put on to training, then went back on ops . . . oh Tess, if it weren't for you, waiting for me, I don't think I could go on.'

'Of course you could,' Tess crooned, cuddling. 'Of course you could, Ash dear. And you are lucky, and you're going to go on being lucky. Now you drive slowly and carefully back to Blofield and go to bed. We'll both forget all this in sleep.'

'Right. You're sure you can't come home with me? Only if you could, and if I had a real shocker and yelled out, you'd have my permission to come and jump into my bed and make me better; right?'

Tess laughed. 'Right. Come on, and put that tin down, eating late at night really encourages bad dreams.'

She went with Ashley out to the car, but just before he drove off he jumped out, put his arms round her and kissed her.

'I know you say you aren't in love with me, Tess, but you will be, one day, I'm sure of it,' he muttered against her hair. 'Don't go off with anyone else, please? I've loved you for an awfully long time, you know. Ever since I first saw you.'

'Oh come on, Ash, you surely can't believe in love at first . . . at first sight,' Tess finished slowly. She had just remembered Mal and the electric shock of his touch, his glance. Was that love at first sight? If so, how wonderful, how world-shaking, it was. And if Ashley really had fallen in love with her, how horribly he must suffer when she teased him, turned from him.

'It's true, love at first sight really does exist. Tess? Say you'll give me a chance, let me show you that I can be what you want, the sort of person you could be happy with for the rest of your life. Promise me you won't go with anyone else!'

'I can't make promises like that, Ash,' Tess said. 'I'm not experienced enough to know how I feel, even if you are. And now, dear sir, I'm going to bed.'

She went back into the farmhouse, locking the door firmly behind her, and presently, after a short wait, she heard Ashley's car roar off down the road.

Fourteen

Tess woke because she was having a nightmare; not the usual one but something new and different. She dreamed she was standing on an airfield looking up at a plane which was coming in to land, and she knew that Ashley was flying it, knew he was in trouble.

'He's lost his undercarriage,' someone near her whispered. 'And the rudder's gone. The pilot's got a bullet lodged in his hip and he's had his face cut up by flying glass. It'll need a hell of a lot to get him down in one piece.'

The plane came towards them, staggering, one wing too low, then passed them by, pulling itself up into the air again, clearly going to try another approach. And as it passed Tess saw Ashley, pale-faced and with horror in his eyes, staring at her through the perspex window. As she watched he leaned out and called to her, his voice beseeching.

'Tess, oh Tess! I won't die if you'll promise not to leave me, it'll be all right if you're there for me. Promise you won't leave me!'

And she had promised, shouting her vow to the great wheeling plane above her, and then she had woken up with tears streaming down her cheeks.

Now, she lay on her back, gazing up at the ceiling, recovering. What a truly horrible dream – it must have come about because Ashley had told her, last night, of his fears. Well, she was very sorry but she could not ruin her whole life for Ashley, who was a handsome and capable young man, well able to find himself a girlfriend other than her if he so wished. She had promised to ring Mal – well, she hadn't promised, exactly but she had said she would. And the deeply tanned, slow-spoken young Australian pilot officer meant something to her already, though she did not know quite what. He wasn't handsome, like Ashley, he was of a stocky rather than athletic build and would doubtless prove to be a very ordinary bloke. But for a few moments, last night, she had known such a strength of attraction towards him that she had felt as if she was one half of a magnet and he the other.

So I can't not telephone him just because of a dream, she told herself. I have to talk to him, to arrange a meeting. I can't just walk away from someone who could be so important to me.

Presently she fell asleep again and woke when her alarm clock shrilled. She got up at once, washed and dressed, guessing that the other landgirls, Molly and Susan, would still be fast asleep. But she was on milking with young Harold, so it behoved her to get a move on – Harold was fourteen, cheeky, wicked, but always on time for milking. He'd nag her something horrible if she was so much as five minutes late.

Tess grabbed herself a round of bread from the loaf and spread it with honey; thanks to Mrs Sugden, there was always plenty of food around. Then she stirred the fire, pulled the big old kettle – filled by one of the girls the previous evening – on to the hob and headed for the back door. Breakfast was eaten after milking, not before, but the bread and honey would stop her stomach from rumbling, she hoped.

She unbolted the kitchen door and pushed it open. A milky, misty morning met her eye, the sun still out of sight beyond the horizon, the pale-blue sky its harbinger. She inhaled deeply; there were lovely smells in the yard first thing in the morning, but before she could begin to analyse them Pup, the second of the Sugdens' two sheepdogs, came running across the yard and bounced all over her. He got the last of the bread and honey by default – Tess dropped it – and grinned gratefully up at her, licking his chops.

'Wasn't that nice?' Tess said. 'Come on, we've got work to do – where's young Harold?'

'Here,' young Harold growled, coming over the gate and swishing with his curved ash-stick at the mist which hung around him. 'Where's Minnie?'

Minnie, the older of the two sheepdogs, came out of the stable block. She was licking her lips too; Tess guessed she had been eating something a good deal less acceptable than bread and honey, but smoothed a hand over the dome of the old dog's head anyway.

'Morning, Min. Come on, the cows'll be at the gate by now. You coming, Harold, or will you get the parlour ready?'

'Jacob 'ull do it. He enjoy that better'n chasin' after the herd.' Harold, his hair in spikes all over his head, his working boots and trousers a size too large to allow for growth, clicked his fingers at the dogs, who promptly belted across the yard, heading for Moss Bank, the steep, downward-sloping pasture with its mossy banks on which silver birches and rowans mingled their branches. Further on, right at the end of the pasture, the brook had carved its way between the two meadows, creating, at one end of the field, an area of bog in which iris, burr-reeds and water forget-me-not flourished. The cows would have spent the night grazing on the rich new grass at the bottom of the meadow, but by now they would have made their way up the steep slope and would be milling hopefully around beside the mossy old gate, poaching the soft ground there into another, though less sightly, bog.

'Right. Come on then. Race you to the gate, Harold!'

Much later, work over for the day, Tess went up to her room and fetched her purse. The other girls were planning an evening of letter-writing and various other indoor activities but Tess said: 'Shan't be long!' and left without actually telling anyone where she was going.

It was to the public telephone box, of course. She had a good walk, two miles or more, but at last she came to the little glass and metal booth and slipped inside. The telephone number which Mal had given her was engraved on her memory; she picked up the receiver, repeated it to the operator, put her money into the hungry little slot at the top of the box and waited, finger poised hopefully over Button A.

After a good many rings a man answered, giving the name of the station and adding, rather crossly, 'Officers's Mess'.

It was only then that Tess realised she did not know the Australian's full name.

'Umm . . . can I speak to Mal, please? I'm afraid I can't remember his surname.'

'Mal? I'm sorry, Miss, what was his last name?'

'I can't remember,' Tess said again, feeling small. 'He's a pilot officer, he flies bombers – Lancasters. He did ask me to ring.'

'Sorry, I don't know anyone called Mal,' the voice said. And put the receiver down.

Tess stared at the instrument for a few moments, then slowly replaced her own receiver. Damn and confound it, she thought violently. Why on earth didn't I ask for his full name? I could have, easily. I could have worked the conversation round to it, instead of sitting there like an idiot, basking in his presence.

She considered ringing again, then decided not to bother. The same man would answer, without a doubt. She would leave it for a while and then try again. Perhaps if she left it until later she might have more luck? But if she didn't manage to get in touch with him, would he not ring her? Yes, of course he would, he had her name, all he needed to do was look in the telephone directory. Delamere was an unusual name, he would only find three or four, if he was really keen – and she knew he was – he would try them all and would come, at last, to Marianne.

Only Marianne was still a bit annoyed because she hadn't managed to get a job at Rope's, and live at home. And she didn't think Marianne would take kindly to strange Australians ringing up and asking for her stepdaughter, though she had no idea why she felt this to be so. Indeed, Marianne was quite fun now when she went home on leave, though she was still subject to terrible fits of melancholy.

Maurice had made all the difference, there was no doubt about that. He made Marianne feel young again and because she felt young she accepted Tess as simply another girl in whom she could confide. It's sad that it took Daddy's death to make the two of us friends, Tess thought now, but the truth is, once Daddy was out of the equation Marianne looked properly at me and decided I was quite nice, after all. And I dare say I looked at her differently, too. At any rate, I find her good company.

But right now, she had to decide whether to ring again in a few minutes, or hang around here for an hour or two, or go home and face the long walk back. She had more or less decided on the long walk back when something else occurred to her. Mal hadn't talked a lot about himself, but he had said he was on bombers, and British bombers, she knew, flew at night. It was only the Yanks who undertook daylight raids. Which could mean that she wouldn't find Mal in the officers' mess in the evenings at all.

I'm on early milking today, tomorrow and the next day, Tess told herself. What's to stop me coming down and telephoning instead of having breakfast? I can bring some grub with me – bread and honey – and eat it as I walk. And I'll probably speak to someone different at a different time of day – someone who's not so cross and impatient. And right now, so my walk isn't wasted, I'll ring Marianne and warn her that she may be getting a phone call.

She asked the girl on the exchange for the Barton number, then waited whilst the connection was made, deciding what she should say and wondering what Marianne would say in reply. She would tell her stepmother he was just a bloke she'd met at a dance and Marianne, who was extremely annoyed with Ashley right now, might well approve simply because Mal wasn't Ashley Knox.

Marianne was cross with Ashley because he had told her off for hoarding, that was the trouble.

'You've got enough food in that spare bedroom to feed an army,' he had said disapprovingly. 'If a bomb fell on the house you'd lose the lot. Why not hand it out to those in need?'

'How do you know what I've got in there?' Marianne had said, bristling. 'Can you see through walls?'

Ashley, who had hung out of Tess's bedroom window and waved a mirror around until he could see clearly into the spare room had said, mysteriously, that it was surprising what you could see from a low-flying Spitfire. Cherie and Tess had immediately got the giggles, but Marianne had gone quite white. She had said, 'I didn't know . . . it isn't as if I've told any lies or anything,' and had then rushed out of the room. To check her hoard and pull the curtains, Ashley said wickedly.

'She'll be a lot more careful when she undresses now,' Cherie

371

crowed, clapping her hands. 'And she'll stop having baths altogether!'

'You're a cruel pair,' Tess had said. But she had laughed too, because Marianne's attitude had been funny. And later, when Marianne realised that Ashley had been teasing her, she had been very cross with him.

'He isn't welcome here, coming to pry and spy,' she had said. 'You tell him, Tess, that he's no gentleman. It's not nice to say the things he did.'

'He was joking, Marianne,' Tess said gently. 'He never thought you'd believe him.'

'Why should I not believe him? I still don't know how he knew . . . unless you told him.'

'I said he couldn't sleep in the spare room because it was where you kept your extra bits and pieces of food,' Tess said, not wholly truthfully. She had actually used the words 'wicked hoard'. 'I expect he looked out of my bedroom window. You can see things sometimes, if the spare room window's open.'

That sent Marianne rushing off again, to investigate, and when she came back, flushed and breathless, it was to say that Tess was right, it was possible to see into the spare room as she had said, that Ashley was a horrid young man, and that Cherie must stop laughing or she would get a smack.

At this point in Tess's thoughts, however, the telephone receiver was picked up and Marianne cooed "Ello?' into the receiver. She always sounded extra specially French on the telephone.

'Marianne, it's me, Tess. I've only got fourpence, so I can't talk for long, but I've met a young Australian bomber pilot, called Mal. I think he may telephone me, only the farm isn't on the phone so he'll ring the Old House. If he does, could you take a message, please?'

'Ye-es,' Marianne purred. 'A young man who is not Ashley is always welcome here. What was his name again?'

'Pilot Officer Mal something-or-other of the Australian Air Force,' Tess said, speaking slowly and carefully. 'I'm free on Thursday afternoon and Friday morning, and if you could give him my address at the Sugdens', then he could perhaps come and find me there.'

'Why don't you ring him?' Marianne said plaintively. 'Suppose I am out? Maurice is coming at the weekend, we may go out. He often takes me out.'

'I keep ringing, but I can't get hold of him,' Tess said. 'Please, Marianne. If he rings, give him my address. And could you tell Cherie as well, please?'

'Very well,' Marianne said. Suspiciously. 'This young man . . .'

'Oh, oh, the pips!' Tess squeaked. 'Sorry . . . goodbye . . . see you next weekend!'

Mal returned to his station in a daze and tumbled into bed happier than he had been for a long time. Tess, Tess, Tess, he kept thinking. Soon we'll talk without that Ashley chap listening, meet each other on equal terms. Why, we might hold hands, maybe even kiss!

He waited for a telephone call all day but nothing came, and he was flying that night. He went into the briefing meeting, returned to his quarters, put on warm clothing, for it was always cold at altitude, and planned what he would say when she rang. He went along to the mess but though he looked on the cork board there was no message for him and though he asked one or two people, no one had taken a telephone call for him.

The briefing was for a sortie to Munchen-Gladbach and as they neared the target, Mal became aware that because of Tess, his feelings had all turned around. Usually at this point the fear and the excitement pounding through his head made him think of the very things he most dreaded. He imagined the horrible plunge to earth, the fearsome smash, the darkness. Then he saw pictures of his mother, reading the dreaded telegram, telling his small half-brothers that he wouldn't be coming home any more . . . he saw the homestead, the cattle, the men, tacking up for a round-up. The bush in the wet flashed before his eyes, the river in spate, the great crocs which could, and did, take the unwary whether it be man or beast. And all this went on whilst the kite droned onwards, the men went about their business of keeping them on course, dodging enemy aircraft and avoiding flak.

But tonight he saw none of those things. Tonight he saw Tess, holding the receiver as she telephoned the mess, smiling, small white teeth biting her lower lip, fingers playing an imaginary tune on the phone book whilst she waited.

It was cheerful, delightful, to be anticipating something good for a change, something positive. And the raid went well, because he rather thought they'd laid their eggs, in RAF parlance, around the right place at around the right time. Through the smoke and din, with flak bursting constantly just below them, to the right, to the left, they kept steadily on course and when they were over-flying England again, with eleven out of the dozen kites which had taken off five or six hours earlier, Mal felt reasonably satisfied with the night's work. And the kite which had been shot had been over northern France by then and he had personally seen the parachutes flower and had circled, watching their slow journey to earth, ready to fire if anyone attacked them.

Going down over France, furthermore, might mean you could get home. If you ditched over Germany it was prisoner of war camp for the duration. *For you, gentlemen, the war is over,* the Jerries were supposed to say, in true Music Hall fashion. Perhaps they really did. I hope to God I never find out, Mal thought, as he droned on towards Norfolk – and Tess – with the eastern horizon beginning to pale towards dawn. I've done ten ops now, so I'm a third of the way through my tour. And . . .

'There's the city, skip,' Percy said into his intercom. 'Not long now. Wonder what's for brekker?'

'Cold porridge and leathery toast if you're lucky, sport,' Geoff said. 'And if you ain't lucky it'll be cold *burnt* porridge and leathery toast.' His Australian idea of a good start to the day had received a rude awakening the first time he'd walked into the cookhouse after a raid; even their ordinary breakfast wasn't too marvellous, but at four a.m. on a cold winter's morning with a skeleton staff of weary, white-faced WAAFs yawning behind their hands the food was abysmal.

Still. After breakfast I can ring Tess, Mal told himself, stretching his legs one at a time, whilst making his hands into fists and then starfishing them inside his big leather gauntlets. He always tried to keep his limbs moving, otherwise, when he landed, he crawled out of the cockpit like an arthritic crab. 'We could skip the early shift, grab a few hours, and then eat later,' he suggested out loud. 'Where have the sandwiches gone?'

'They were bleedin' stale,' Fred said. 'I shot the crusts out when we laid the eggs. They probably did more damage than the bombs; they were damn' nearly as hard.'

Subdued chuckles all round but just then Sidney began to flap his hand for silence as he started to talk to the tower. Mal saw the airfield lights looming up in the greyness and worked his fingers some more, preparing for the approach. And presently they were skimming the runway, touching, bouncing, touching again, slowing . . .

'Brekker next, fellers,' Percy announced as Mal brought his craft gently to a halt. 'Anyone prepared to put money on burnt porridge?'

Breakfast proved to be porridge – unburnt – toast, and dried egg. Not bad, not good. But Mal was hungry and ate everything on offer, filled up with several cups of hot tea, then went over to the officers' mess. It was empty at this hour, but he strolled across to the cork board, just in case. There were several messages, but there was one with his name on it. He leaned closer. It was signed by someone on another flight, someone he'd never heard of, but it had his name across the top.

'Mal,' the message read. '*Some girl rang, said she didn't know the rest of your name. I think she said her name was Tess, or possibly Jess. Better get in touch, popsies who like cantankerous Aussies don't grow on trees!*'

I wonder who told the bloke I was an Aussie, then, Mal thought, before he realised that, failing to remember his surname, Tess would almost certainly have said he was Australian. He stood before the cork board, reading the message over and over, whilst a huge grin bisected his face. She had got in touch, she hadn't simply gone her way, forgotten him. He had known she wasn't that sort of girl, but when a week had passed without a word it was only human to wonder – what a relief to know he had been right about her.

He unpinned the message from the board, folded it and put it into the pocket of his flying jacket. Pity she'd not left a telephone number, but she would ring again. Or he could ring her. He hadn't caught her surname but thought it was something like Delmar. Not that it mattered; she knew he was here now, and would undoubtedly try again.

He left the mess and went to his quarters. He had a tiny slip of a room off a long corridor of similar rooms and went in quietly, because others who had been on the raid were already in bed, closing the door gently behind him. He undressed wearily, longing for sleep now, and opened the window, then pulled down the black-out blind to keep the light out, not in. He climb into bed, then remembered the note, got out, fetched it, flattened it out on his coverlet and got back into bed once more.

He lay down, heaved the covers up, then tried to read the note, but it was impossible in the gloom. Not that it mattered, he realised, as he turned on his side. He knew it by heart.

Mal, some girl rang, said she didn't know the rest of your name. The words were engraved on his memory, saying them was like saying a familiar childhood prayer, a guarantee that . . . that . . .

Deeply and immediately, Mal slept.

'He hasn't rung,' Marianne said patiently, as soon as she heard Tess's voice on the phone. 'But I'm sure he will. You are not unattractive, Tess. Did you give him this number? I forgot to ask before.'

'No . . . but I thought he'd look it up in the book,' Tess said, grinning to herself over Marianne's choice of phrase. *You are not unattractive,* indeed! 'Surely he'll do that, Marianne?'

'Well, perhaps. But we are still in the telephone book as P. Delamere, and now that I think about it, there are two P. Delameres, your father and your Uncle Phil. Friends, of course, know that Phil lives in Norwich and we live in Barton, but for a young man who does not know us well, it might prove a stumbling block.'

'Oh well,' Tess said. 'I expect Uncle Phil will pass on the message that I live at Barton. So if you get a call, Marianne . . .'

'All right, I'll see that he knows where you're to be found,' Marianne said briskly. 'When will you be home next?'

'Umm . . . probably in about a week. Marianne, if – if he gets in touch, will it be all right to bring him back with me? He's an Aussie, so he won't have parents or anything to stay with on his leaves.'

'But Tess, you don't even know his surname! You don't really know him at all, yet you're suggesting that he come here, to your home . . .'

'I'll know him by then,' Tess said. 'I'll be bringing him home when I next come if he's free. Bye, Marianne. Love to Cherie.'

Having got her message across to her stepmother, Tess waited for twenty-four hours and then decided that the onus of getting in touch would probably be on her. She went into the village and entered the box, asked for the number, clattered a respectable number of pennies into the box, and waited. After a couple of rings the receiver in the officers' mess was snatched up. Tess pressed Button A and spoke.

'Oh, hello, it's Tess Delamere speaking, I'd like a word with Pilot Officer Chandler if he's around,' she said politely. 'I'm in a call box, though, so if he isn't near a telephone perhaps I could leave a message?'

'No need, Miss. Mal . . . it's for you!'

Tess heard the phone clatter down, then it was picked up – and all at once she was shy, so shy that she was rendered speechless. She stared at the mouthpiece, then gingerly applied the earpiece to her ear.

'Hullo? Malcolm Chandler speaking.'

The voice she had longed to hear sounded different, the accent more pronounced. Was it him, or had she somehow got hold of the wrong bloke?

'It's Tess Delamere,' she said bleakly. 'I don't . . .'

'Tess!' Suddenly his voice was just right, she could hear his delight clearly across the miles. 'Oh, Tess! I thought . . . I thought . . .'

'So did I,' Tess admitted. 'I've rung ever so many times but you've not been around and now I'm in a box in the village and it's my dinner hour so we'd better be quick. My boss is cutting the wheat and he hates it if we're late, so . . .'

377

'Your boss? Cutting *wheat*?'

He sounded bemused, the slow Australian drawl sharpened a little by surprise.

'Yes, my boss, he's a farmer. I'm a landgirl, didn't I say? The Sugdens are very nice, but you know what farming's like – no, you probably don't – only the weather has to be right and . . .'

'Oh, my word,' Mal said. 'If anyone knows about farming, it's me. Listen, where are you? Can we meet?'

'That would be lovely,' Tess said. She hadn't known quite how to say it, but Mal had – straight out, no holds barred. 'I live in a little village called Barton, and I work at Catfield, which is the next village along. The farm isn't on the telephone, unfortunately, but I go home sometimes, so I'll give you my home telephone number and you can ring there.'

'Not on the phone? What's your address?'

'It's care of the Sugdens, Willow Tree Farm, Catfield.'

'Grand. I'm glad you got in touch, Tess, I was scared I'd never see you again.'

'Me too,' Tess said shyly. 'Do you have leave coming up?'

'Bound to. I've not taken any yet. You?'

'Yes, I get a forty-eight quite often. I start a forty-eight in three days' time.'

'Good on you. We'll meet then. All right?'

'Very all right,' Tess said, and even as she spoke she realised that they had passed over the commonplace preliminaries of a relationship as though they were totally unnecessary. It was usual, she knew, to get to know a fellow before letting him have such details as your address and home telephone number. In fact, it was not done for a girl to give such information to a total stranger. But how could she think of him as a stranger, after what they'd shared? If they had shared anything, that was. She had felt all sorts of extraordinary feelings whenever he looked at her, but who could say whether it had been the same for him? Perhaps he would think her forward, pursuing a young man she'd met once, giving him her telephone number so that he might ring her. What if he didn't want to ring, anyway? But he did, of course, since he had suggested meeting in three days' time.

'Thank God you rang again,' he said fervently, now. 'I thought your last name was Delmar – I rang ten of them. Imagine!'

She laughed. It was easy to laugh, now.

'I can imagine, but I've got to go. Where shall we meet? In Norwich? Or you could come over to the farm, if you don't mind buses and things.'

'No. Not the farm, somewhere quiet, where we can talk. I've got some leave due, I'll take it. When and how?'

Out of the corner of her eye, Tess saw a movement. Someone was standing outside the telephone booth, face almost pressed to the glass. It was young Harold; he'd split on her unless she was specially nice to him, and he was obviously longing to use the telephone. Of course Mr Sugden couldn't dictate what she did in her dinner hour, but she knew, really, that she should have stayed in the harvest field. What was more, her pennies were running out.

'Can't stop, there's someone I know waiting for the phone, quick! Where? When?'

'Right. Ten hundred hours, Friday. Where?'

'Oh, oh, I can't think . . . oh the pips, I've not got . . . Where? I know, the GPO on Prince of Wales Road.'

She was about to add under the portico not inside the building when they were cut off. Tess put down the receiver and erupted from the box. She screamed over her shoulder, 'Sorry, Harold, I tried to hurry,' as she rescued her bicycle from the hedge and struggled aboard. Harold grinned at her, then shot into the box in his turn and Tess cycled off down the road in the direction of the farm.

Back at the harvest field it was generally assumed that she'd gone back to the farm for some purpose and had had her food there. Tess, unfed, scarcely noticed. With stars in her eyes she toiled over the sheaves, sucked her sore fingers and dreamed of Friday morning at ten.

Tess arrived at nine-forty-five, and stood self-consciously in front of the huge building, with the eyes of the world upon her, or so she felt. The vast bustling conglomeration of roads which met at this point was always busy, so she had a good look round before taking up her position. She could see no one in RAF uniform, however, so assumed she had arrived first, and stood against one of the pillars which held up the portico, feeling both small and conspicuous. She had caught the workers' bus into the city which meant she had been here an hour already and was growing increasingly nervous.

The meeting place, which had seemed eminently sensible when she had suggested it, began to seem the height of idiocy once she was back at the farm. She was suddenly sure that something would go wrong, she even suspected that the GPO might no longer be on Prince of Wales Road or that it might be bombed out of existence before Friday. Her friends scoffed at such wild and unfounded fears, but as Tess said, you never knew with Hitler; he could easily send a bomber over to bop the General Post Office just to destroy her day out.

However, she had arrived early and the GPO had survived any attempts to remove it; at least it was still there, looming vast and important, with the Shire Hall on the corner, the Agricultural Hall next to it, and the GPO last in line.

Mal hadn't arrived, though. If Tess checked once that he hadn't misunderstood her meaning and was waiting inside, she checked a dozen times. And then she wondered whether he was waiting outside Shire Hall, or the Agricultural Hall, the Royal Hotel . . . they were all on this particular stretch of road, he could easily have misunderstood, the pips had gone whilst she was still talking . . .

Then she remembered that he would be travelling through a city which was strange to him, or fairly strange. She didn't know how long he'd been in England. And he'd probably be coming by bus and buses are always late, and sometimes leave gets cancelled . . .

She hadn't asked him what time his bus got in, or even whether he was coming by bus. She had simply hoped that he had heard before they were cut off.

Now, Tess glanced at her wrist-watch. It wasn't ten o'clock and wouldn't be for another ten minutes, and already, she was convinced, people were staring at her, thinking that she was some poor kid whose boyfriend had stood her up. She wasn't wearing uniform, but had opted for a navy-blue skirt, a blue cotton blouse and her pearl-grey mackintosh, worn casually unbuttoned. It wasn't raining, which was practically a miracle, but she still felt damned conspicuous, waiting here. He didn't have a car, she was fairly sure of that, so surely he would be coming by bus? If she walked up to Surrey Street, what was more, it would give her something to do and she would not feel so self-conscious once she was moving.

She was half a dozen yards from the pillar when it occurred to her that the easiest thing in the world would be to miss one another like this. And it still wasn't ten o'clock! What's the matter with you, you silly thing, he said ten hundred hours and he meant ten hundred hours, she told herself fiercely. Just get back to that pillar and lean against it, casual-like, and bloody *wait*!

She watched the hands of her watch creep round to ten . . . to one minute past . . . and decided to walk a little way along the pavement towards the Cattle Market. The liberty trucks came in there, she knew, if he'd managed to catch a liberty truck . . .

She turned and ran straight into someone. She stopped, gave a breathless giggle, started to apologise . . . and recognised him.

'Oh, it's you! Gosh! I was just . . . I thought I'd have a bit of a walk around, go up to the Cattle Market . . . I know the buses come in there . . . the trucks, I mean . . . and then I wondered if I'd recognise you . . . we've only met that once . . .'

'I'd know you anywhere,' Mal said. He said it matter of factly, as though he was just stating the obvious. 'Come along.' He took her arm, turned her towards Castle Meadow.

'Where are we going?' Tess said. Not uneasily, because the touch of his hand on her arm was strangely, lovingly, familiar. They had not danced together at the Samson, but she felt she knew what it would have been like, had they done so.

'Ever heard of a place called Stokesby? There's someone doing decent food there; a little pub. Riverside place, I'm told.'

'Oh! But Stokesby's miles from anywhere, isn't it? I bet there isn't a bus to get me back to the Old House tonight!'

Tess did not like to say she had intended to invite him to go home with her, just in case. She did not know in case of what. It simply seemed wrong to invite someone home within moments of meeting them.

He looked down at her. His eyes were quiet. It occurred to her that he was a peaceful person, that in his company she, too, would feel peaceful. It was a good feeling.

'We'll get a taxi. I've got enough money.'

After a second of stunned silence, Tess laughed. 'All the way from Stokesby to Barton? Honestly, Mal, it'll take every last penny. Why don't we catch a bus to Wroxham, if you want the river? There are several pubs there which do meals.'

He laughed too, looking relieved as well as amused.

'No, honestly, I've worked it all out. We can get a bus from the pub into the city, and from there we'll get a taxi to Barton. I really think you'll like this Stokesby place. One of the fellers told me about it, said it was a bonza place. You'd better ring your mother, tell her you won't be home till the late, though.'

'I have a stepmother, actually. I call her Marianne,' Tess said carefully as they drew nearer to the bus station. 'I'll ring her from this pub, if that's possible. Or I suppose there's a public call box in the village. How do we get to Stokesby?'

'Well, we've missed the bus which goes all the way, but we can ride to Acle and walk the rest of the way. Or we can hire a carrier, or a taxi, even, if you don't fancy walking. But it isn't terribly far.'

'I like walking,' Tess said. 'We'll want the number 7, I suppose.'

'Yeah . . . there it is! Run!'

They ran, climbed aboard, managed to get seats together, sank into them, Tess suddenly self-conscious. What would they talk about for a whole day? This bus journey would be hard enough!

It wasn't hard at all. For a start, Mal took her hand and this sent Tess into such a dizzying spiral of delight that talking did not seem at all necessary. And then, when he did turn to her, the conversation was natural, inevitable.

'Tell me about where you live, your family and so on. Unless you'd rather I told you, first?'

'Well, my father was killed in the first few months of the war and my stepmother lives with my stepsister, Cherie, in our family home,' Tess began, and found the rest was easy. Describing Peter, the Old House, Cherie, Marianne even, was fun when she was describing them to Mal. She said, wistfully, that she wished Mal could have met Peter and realised she meant it. He hadn't liked Ashley, he hadn't ever met the adult Andy, but she knew that anyone with an ounce of sense would love Mal, and her father had been, above everything, a sensible man.

'We've got a lot in common,' Mal said as they climbed down off the bus. 'You've got a stepmother. I've got a stepfather. You've got a stepsister, I've got two stepbrothers. Wonder if there's anything else? Well, we'll find out over the course of today, I dare say.'

'Probably,' Tess agreed. Privately, she thought that her early years were still a mystery to her, so they were unlikely to find any other points of similarity. 'Is that the turning?'

'Must be. Come on, best foot forward!'

They had barely begun to cross the marshes, however, with their pools of water blue in the warm May sunshine, when Tess stopped short. She had thought of something.

'I'm not really dressed for going on the river, Mal. I mean a skirt and high-heeled shoes aren't ideal. I'm most awfully sorry, I just thought you'd want to stay in the city, you see.'

'Doesn't matter,' Mal said. 'Tell you what . . . wellingtons!'

'Eh?'

'They don't cost a lot and village shops often stock 'em. Or plimsolls. Or you might borrow something from the landlady. The fellers say she's a good sort.'

'Well, that's all right then,' Tess said, falling into step beside him once more. 'Tell me, Mal, why do the fellers come all the way out here?'

She glanced at him as she spoke and thought his colour rose a little, but he shrugged. 'Dunno. Quiet, good food . . . that sort of thing.'

Tess laughed softly.

'And the landlady who's a *good sort*? Do – do they bring girls out here?'

Mal nodded, avoiding her eye, and then turned and grinned sheepishly at her. 'Yeah, you've got it. But I wouldn't do that; it's too soon. You're safe, Tess. I could tell at a glance you weren't that kind of sheila.'

'No, I – I don't think I am,' Tess said. 'You know I've never thought of these marshes as beautiful, but they really are. Look at that!'

They were crossing a small, hump-backed stone bridge which crossed a deep dyke, overhung with hazels and margined with thick, tasselled reeds. Two mallards paddled along in the centre of the dyke, followed by a convoy of tiny dark-brown ducklings. In the foreground groups of cattle grazed, and on the horizon a disembodied sail, very white against the blue of the sky, moved smoothly along on the unseen river.

'It's like a picture I saw in a shop in the city,' Mal said. 'I wanted to buy it for Kath . . . my mother . . . but it was too expensive – fifteen quid!'

'It was probably painted by someone important,' Tess said wisely. 'My father used to buy paintings occasionally, you get used to the prices. Now we'd better step out or we'll arrive after the bar's closed – and I am thirsty.'

Mal seized her hand and squeezed it and Tess, responding, thought she had seldom felt such happiness. This was a wonderful place, she would always love it; the marshes, the blue arc of the sky, the reflecting pools of water. There was a quiet which she had never known rivalled, and a salty freshness on the breeze which blew steadily enough to sway the reeds which lined each pool. She thought, *I'll remember this moment for the rest of my life,* and was grateful to Mal for his wisdom. Spending a day in Norwich would not have been the same.

They reached the village at last and slowed. It was a pretty, old-fashioned place with a shop, a cluster of cottages and a village green surrounded by chestnut and oak trees in pale new leaf. They bought a cheap pair of plimsolls from the shopkeeper, who explained that they had belonged to his own daughter, but she had outgrown them, and then headed for the river. The shopkeeper had told them that the pub was just a few yards further along the road, though he spoke in an accent so broad that Tess realised Mal was totally at sea. However, being naturally polite, he thanked the old man and they left the shop, unashamedly hand in hand.

'Did he say we were nearly there?' he asked plaintively when they were out of earshot. 'I guess he must have, but . . .'

'You didn't understand a word of it,' Tess said, giggling as she led the way down to the river bank. 'That's what I call a real Norfolk accent.'

'Oh? It could've been Scandinavian for all I could make out,' Mal admitted. He looked around him, at the broad and placid river Bure, and at the marshes, stretching as far as the eye could see. 'Not many trees about, are there?'

'Not many. Probably there'll be a few around farmhouses, but they don't seem to have planted trees round the pub, apart from that apple tree.' She glanced appreciatively at the Ferry Inn, which was whitewashed and tiled and pleasant, and not more than ten or a dozen feet from the river itself. 'Where's the front door?'

'There. Come on, let's go and ask if the landlady can get us a bite to eat.'

Together, with diffidence, they crossed the threshold and entered a bar parlour, black-beamed and still smelling of food and, more faintly, of beer. A large woman, polishing brass, looked up and smiled at them.

'Can I help you?'

'We'd like a bite to eat, and then later on we'd like to hire a boat,' Mal said. 'The fellers said you hired boats.'

The landlady put down her cloth and went behind the bar. 'We do indeed. Now what 'ud you like to drink? I'm on my own, daytimes, so you can take a seat and enjoy your drinks whilst I rustle up some grub.'

It was a day out of time, stolen from the war, a day at peace. They sat in the bow window with the sun pouring in on them and Mal drank beer and Tess drank lemonade shandy and they both ate the sandwiches which Mrs Figgis, the landlady, made with a prodigal hand.

'Cheese and pickle, home-cured ham and egg and cress,' Tess said with awe, examining the contents of the big blue china plate which Mrs Figgis set down before them. 'Pre-war food! Where do we start?'

'On the ham,' Mal said gloatingly. 'I've not seen real food like this since I left Australia – no, not since I left the Wandina.'

'Where's that?' Tess said, through a ham sandwich. 'Oh, isn't this *good*?'

Mal took another huge bite, chewed and swallowed before he spoke.

'The Wandina's the cattle station I worked on before I left Queensland and went south. My mother and stepfather live in Queensland, too, but they've got a different cattle station, the Magellan. Ma's the best cook you ever met, except that our cook on the Wandina was getting to be pretty damn good by the time I left.'

'I see,' Tess said, helping herself to egg and cress. 'Do you know, Mal, that's the most you've ever said to me since we first met? Did I gabble, coming over?'

Mal considered this seriously, then took a pull at his beer.

'Nope. You just told me about your family and the Old House. Nothing about yourself, really.'

'I didn't? But it seemed as though I talked and talked. Anyway, no one can talk and eat this wonderful food. Can you pass me a cheese one this time, please?'

When they had eaten they set off for a walk along the river bank. The bank was higher than the river, presumably to assist in keeping the river in its place and the water-meadows dry, though Tess doubted that the highest banks could prevail against the winter floods when they came.

'It's your turn to talk now,' she told Mal as they walked. 'Tell me all about yourself and your family, where you live and how you run a cattle station.'

Mal talked in his slow, considered way and watched her as he did so. Such a lively, beautiful face she had, he even loved the way her eyebrows grew, and the faint golden freckles across the white skin of her small nose.

She was the girl he wanted to spend the rest of his life with, he had known it the moment he set eyes on her, he couldn't get over that. All those girls in Rhodesia, all the ones back home, had been sweeties, but not one of them had stirred him as Tess had. Yet she was black-haired and he preferred blondes. She was very slim and he liked buxom girls. She was pale-skinned and he liked bronzed beauties.

But even saying that, there were a million things he loved about her. Her shyness, the way a flush crept over her face when he teased or touched her. She had a sort of delicacy – other girls, he concluded, were like roses and arum lilies, but his Tess was a wild flower, a primrose rather than a rose, a lily of the valley rather than the other sort.

She had told him about her home and her family, father, step-mother and stepsister. About her beloved father, who had been killed in the early days of the war and about someone called Mrs Thrower, who lived down the road and helped with the chores. She had told him about her job in the museum, and how she had gone into the Land Army so that she could still be near her stepmother and sister. He had wondered aloud how she managed the work and she had said, flushing brightly this time, that she was stronger than she looked and that it was often more knack than strength, lifting and carrying on the farm.

Now it was his turn. He told her about leaving the Magellan and going to the Wandina, about Uncle Josh and the hands, about Coffee and her mother. He tried to explain the fascination of the outback, the weirdness of the wildlife, the extremes of the seasons, when during the dry season great areas of bush would simply burst into flames and during the wet would be many feet under a roaring torrent of flood water.

'That's it,' he said at last. 'Now you know all there is to know about me.'

She smiled. Sceptically.

'I don't think so,' she said quietly. 'I don't think I know all about you by a long chalk. But it'll do for now.'

He stared at her. He hadn't said a word about his real father, the sort of life he had led prior to his mother marrying Royce, nor about Petey.

'You, too?' he said. 'You, too?'

She didn't ask what he meant, widen her eyes, pretend surprise. She said quite simply, 'Yes, me too. Half remembered, half forgotten. The things which made me what I am, I suppose.'

He nodded. 'Too right. But we've plenty of time to talk, now. We'll talk in the boat, then again whilst we eat our dinner, on the bus going home, in the taxi, outside your front door . . .'

'Oh, the boat – can you row?'

He grinned. 'You soon learn, in the wet. You?'

'You soon learn if you live by the Broad. Shall we take it in turns to row, then? We could get further than on foot.'

'Right. We'd best turn back now, I suppose, or we won't have time to row much further than we've walked!'

He turned her round and she stopped short, then hugged him, giving him a quick, embarrassed kiss on the chin. He caught her and held her, looking down into her face, wondering whether he should kiss her properly, deciding against it. For now.

'Oh thanks, Mal, for this lovely day – and you're right, we'd better start back.'

The boats were pulled up on the bank a bit further along from the pub. An old man took their money, pointed out the best boat, helped them launch it. Whilst they were settling themselves, Mrs Figgis came out of the pub with an elderly basket which she handed down to them.

'A foo scones,' she said briefly. 'An' some of my farmhouse fruit-cake. Have a bit of a picnic tea, 'cos I'm plannin' dinner for seven. That's roast duck tonight.'

They thanked her and took the basket aboard, then Mal leaned out of the boat and stroked the head of the old golden retriever which had followed the landlady out on to the grass. The dog wagged a slow tail and then waddled after his mistress, nose uplifted the better to smell the roast duck.

Mal chuckled. 'That old feller knows a good thing when he smells it,' he said. 'But that smell means grub for us, not for him. Are you comfortable, Tess? Off we go, then.'

The day had started out fine and bright, with seagulls crying faintly overhead and the breeze smelling of the sea. But by the time they set out in the boat, talking desultorily as they did so, clouds were beginning to appear on the horizon and presently a light rain started to fall. Tess, who had been wondering whether Mal would presently stop rowing and kiss her, was annoyed with the rain, which somehow banished the thought of kissing as though it were a pastime only possible in fine weather.

'We're miles from the inn, we can't get back in time to eat our tea, so where shall we have our picnic?' she said, as the light drizzle turned into real rain and the wind began to get up. 'There are some willows ahead . . . shall we see if they'll give us some shelter?'

They reached the willows and drew into the bank. Mal tied up whilst Tess jumped ashore, the basket which Mrs Figgis had lent them clasped in her arms.

'Damn!' she said angrily, gazing out across the flatness of the marshes. 'Damn and damn and damn! Oh, Mal, I'm sorry I suggested boating, I should have remembered the weather always lets you down.'

'It wasn't your fault,' Mal said. 'What's that down there?'

The rain was falling fast now. Tess peered through the grey curtain of it at a hollow in the flatness. He was right, there was something – a farmhouse? Unlikely, with no surrounding fencing, no track leading to it.

'It could be a barn,' she said doubtfully. 'Shall we take a look? Only what about the boat?'

'No one's likely to steal it out here,' Mal pointed out. 'There isn't a soul for miles. Coming?'

He took the basket in one hand, then extended the other invitingly.

'Oh, all right. I can't get much wetter, I suppose,' Tess said rather gloomily. She had been so delighted that Mal appreciated this lonely, marshy countryside and wanted him to take an impression of the beauty and calm away with him when he returned to his station. But no one could help the weather, and at least they would have the bright morning to remember. Accordingly, she took his hand but was soon forced to release it as the slope down which they were scrambling grew steeper. 'Goodness, how odd! It is a barn, right in the middle of nowhere, I don't suppose it's been used for years.'

They reached the barn and scurried inside. Dusty piles of marsh hay met their eyes, and implements so old that Tess was unsure of their use. But everything was bone-dry so clearly the place was weatherproof.

'Come on, at least we can eat with a roof of sorts over our heads,' Mal said, leading the way inside. 'Now look at that – a seat, specially for us.'

Someone, at some time, must have used this old place for a quiet smoke, or perhaps to eat, as they would. The seat was rough, rustic pine, but it held two nicely. They squeezed on to it and began to unwrap the food.

As they ate, Tess glanced around her. The barn was thatched with reed, quite professionally enough to keep out the rain, but the walls were made of split willow; you could see daylight all around, and the doorway had never boasted a door. The wind blew a little rain in, but not enough to inconvenience them. It was dim, but somehow cosy. Tess munched scones and then had a piece of cake. She was very happy.

'Just us,' Mal said at one point. 'All right?'

'Mm hmm, fine, thanks. Funny old picnic, though.'

'Maybe. Want another scone?'

But the picnic was finished before the rain, which still fell steadily. Tess got to her feet, went to the doorway, then came back.

'The sky's *black* towards Breydon Water,' she reported. 'It's no use sheltering and hoping, Mal. This weather's set in for a week, if you ask me.'

'Oh dear,' Mal said in an unconvincing voice. 'What'll we do, stuck in this barn, just the two of us?'

There was a laugh in his voice but something else, too, something which made Tess shiver all over, with excitement, apprehension . . .

'We'll have to go back to the boat and row back to Stokesby,' she said, however. 'No point in waiting for the rain to finish; of course we'll get drenched, but what's a little water between friends?'

'What indeed?' He stood up and put his arm about her, then lifted her off her feet and carried her, not back to the rustic seat but to a pile of marsh hay. He sat her down, then sat down beside her. A dried thistle insinuated itself briskly into the soft bit behind Tess's knee and Tess squawked and jumped. The fact that she landed in Mal's arms was neither here nor there, she told herself, explaining that she was being thistled and would he kindly . . . kindly . . .

He kindly kissed her and Tess, who had lost the thistle when she jumped, kissed him, too. And there, in the draughty old barn on the musty marsh hay, they kissed and cuddled and murmured each other's names and forgot the pouring rain, the chilly breeze, and the long row home.

But they couldn't ignore it for ever, and presently, warm and pink and wondering whether she had behaved badly or well when she stopped Mal from several delightful activities because, she thought, they were Going Too Far, Tess got to her feet.

'I love being cuddled, Mal,' she said frankly. 'But we've got to go, you know. The boat will be filling with water and the sooner we get back the sooner we can change into dry things and – and decide what to do this evening. Do come along!'

'I was enjoying it,' Mal protested, but he got to his feet too and began to brush hay out of Tess's hair and off her clothing, which nearly led to a resumption of those very activities which Tess thought so dangerous. 'And I've decided what I want to do this evening – I can do it here as well as there.'

'Oh, really? Roast duck, Pilot Officer Chandler, no doubt with all the trimmings!'

'I do think of other things besides food sometimes,' Mal said, but he went to the doorway and looked out, then looked back at her, grinning. 'Besides, I fancy there might be objections if we started cuddling in the Ferry bar, with half the village looking on. Of course, if we could ask Mrs Figgis to hire us a nice, dry bedroom . . .'

'What a suggestion!' Tess said in a combative tone, only she rather spoiled it by adding wistfully, 'Wouldn't it be nice, though? Only I expect Mrs Figgis would think we were up to something awful if we disappeared upstairs together.'

'What, in the middle of the afternoon?'

'Oh , yes. I forgot. And anyway we will have to get dry or we shan't enjoy her dinner. Let's get going, then.'

Hand in hand, they ran out into the rain, Mal carrying the now empty picnic basket. They reached the boat, which was rapidly filing with water, and emptied it, first by tipping it and then by baling furiously with the empty paint tin in the stern.

'I'll row,' Mal said, when this task had been accomplished. 'I don't think an oar each will work, somehow. I'm in a hurry.'

He bent to his task with a will and it wasn't nearly as long as Tess had expected before they were mooring their small craft at the pub's landing stage.

'Straight indoors, Tess,' Mal gasped as he and Tess ran across the soaking grass. 'Or should I say young drowned rat? You couldn't be wetter if you'd jumped in the river.'

They shot into the bar, where a young woman in her twenties was arranging glasses on a shelf above the counter. She had a cigarette apparently glued to her lower lip, since it remained there throughout the exchange which followed.

'Hello! My Gawd, you two bin a-swimmin', then?'

'No, boating,' Tess said. Water ran down her face and dripped on to the highly polished boards beneath her feet. 'I wonder, is there anywhere we could dry ourselves off a bit?'

The young woman considered.

'Don't see no harm,' she decided. 'Mrs Figgis isn't around, but she'd send you up I reckon. Bathroom's second door on the right at the top o' the stairs. There's towels laid out ready. An' dressin'-gowns. You go an' change, then bring your wet clothes down an' I'll dry 'em out in the kitchen, on the maiden.'

Tess hesitated, but Mal pushed her ahead of him across the bar to the stairs and then hustled her up them.

'Second door on the right,' he breathed into her ear. 'Don't worry, sweetheart, bathrooms aren't bedrooms.'

'Nor they are,' Tess agreed thankfully. She had felt quite guilty simply mounting the stairs, but Mal's remark put things in perspective. 'Who'll go first?'

'You.' Mal threw open the bathroom door and bundled her in, then followed her, closing and locking the door behind them. 'Now isn't this nice? A geyser with matches, so we can get hot water, and towels, and robes behind the door.' He smiled brightly at Tess. 'Well, love, what's holding you up? Start drying off.'

When Tess still hesitated he seized a towel and began to dry her hair, nearly rubbing her ears off in the process.

'Ouch!' Tess said wrathfully. She grabbed the towel from him and started to rub her face and neck more gently. 'I thought we were going to take turns, but if we aren't you just concentrate on drying yourself, Mal Chandler!'

He grinned but obeyed her and presently pulled off his jacket, tie and shirt, emerging rumple-headed but apparently unembarrassed by being half naked.

'I'm soaked to the skin,' he explained, seeing Tess's eyes widen. 'Don't worry, you won't see any more of me than you would if we were on the beach. Do the same, Tess – I'll turn my back, I'm a gent despite my accent – and wrap the towel round you.'

After a moment's hesitation, Tess obeyed, struggling out of her drenched outer clothing and somehow managing to get the towelling robe on without losing her dignity or revealing too much. Not that Mal would have known, since he had strolled over to the window and stood with his back to her, thoughtfully towelling himself across his broad shoulders.

And presently, clean and dried though with an armful of wet clothing each, they were ready to go downstairs once more.

'Give me a kiss before we go,' Mal said. He dropped his clothing across the side of the bath and pulled her into his arms. 'Oh, how lovely you feel, all soft and yielding without your clothes on.'

'That sounds very rude, and anyway, I'm not,' Tess said, pulling away. 'Not yielding, I mean. It isn't that I don't like all this, it's just . . . anyone might come in!'

'Door's still locked,' Mal mumbled against her neck. 'Oh, Tess, Tess, Tess!'

'I know. But come on, Mal, please. That woman will start to wonder why we're taking so long.'

'Right,' Mal said, clearly realising that she was serious. 'Incidentally, what did she mean when she said she'd put the wet clothes on the maiden? Don't say they have a servant who has nothing else to do but bend over the fire all day and dry out clothes?

Tess laughed. 'It's an old expression for a sort of wooden frame which stands in front of an open fire. You hang your clothes over the bars to dry,' she said. 'I expect she'll show it to us, then you'll know. We call ours a clothes-horse, but I've heard other people refer to a clothes-maiden.'

'Good; I didn't like the sound of it,' Mal said, as they re-entered the bar. 'Oh, she's gone. Which way's the kitchen?'

Despite their soaking, the two of them continued to enjoy their day. The girl, whose name was Eth, took them into the kitchen and left them to hang their clothing over the wooden airer, and when it was dry she despatched them, one at a time, back to the bathroom to dress. She might have meant them to go up together, of course, but Tess, who had felt warm and wonderful in Mal's arms, decided that it simply would not do to be alone with him again. He'll think the worse of me if I let him carry on, she told herself firmly. And I do want him to like me!

So when Eth brought their dried clothing through she took hers and then sent Mal ahead whilst she engaged Eth in conversation. And if she felt lonely upstairs in the big, old-fashioned bathroom whilst Mal, downstairs, cross-questioned Eth about the barn and its dusty marsh hay, she wasn't lonely for long and was buoyed up, in any case, by a sense of having behaved just as she ought.

The roast duck was wonderful, the apple pudding which followed it delicious, and they caught the last bus back to Norwich in very good charity both with the Ferry public house and with each other. They sat on the top deck of the bus, gazing out over the wet, moonlit countryside, for the rain had stopped earlier and now the stars pricked the dark velvet of a clear sky, and talked softly.

'You're sure your Mrs Thrower won't mind giving me a bed?' Mal asked as they queued for a taxi outside Thorpe Station, with a number of other people who had got off various buses and trains. 'I don't want to impose, but it's getting late for making other arrangements.'

'She'll be happy, honestly,' Tess assured him. 'She isn't on the telephone, but she's never let me down, not Mrs Thrower. It won't be much, but she's got ten sons, and only two of them are still at home, so you'll be sleeping in someone's bed.'

'Fine,' said Mal, and repeated the remark when Mrs Thrower, placidly accepting that Tess's friend would be grateful for a bed overnight, showed him a tiny room with an immense bed in it and bade him 'Mek yourself at home, my man'.

'Mrs Thrower, you're wonderful,' Tess said urgently when they returned to the kitchen and Mal had taken himself off to the 'little house' at the end of the garden. 'I wish I could have asked Marianne, but you know what she's like.'

'She'd not have refused you,' Mrs Thrower said. 'But I'm right glad to help, my woman, don't you think no more about it.'

'I know she'd have said yes,' Tess admitted. 'But she'd have thought it very odd, very forward. It's better this way.'

'Aye, you're right there,' Mrs Thrower said. 'He don't mind that we don't have no indoor lavvy?'

'No, they don't have an indoor toilet back in Australia, either,' Tess said. 'I – I like him awfully, Mrs Thrower. I've only known him a little while, but already I know he's special. Isn't it strange? I've known Ash for years and years and Andy even longer, but . . . oh, I can't explain.'

'You don't have to, dearie,' Mrs Thrower said, heaving the kettle off the hob and pouring boiling water into the teapot. 'You aren't the only woman on the planet what hev fallen in love, I 'member well what it were like.'

'Oh, then you really think . . . Oh, Mrs Thrower, I'm so happy!'

Tess awoke in her own bed next morning and could not, for a moment, understand the glow which filled her. She felt as she had felt as a child on Christmas morning, or on the first day of the holidays, when she and Daddy had been going somewhere special. She glanced across at the curtains and saw sunshine, and then remembered in a breathtaking flash. Mal was staying at Staithe Cottage, and she was in love!

She rushed over washing and dressing, and arrived downstairs as Cherie was making herself porridge. She beamed across at Tess, and waved a porridgy spoon.

'Hello, Tess. I didn't know you were home! Want some of this? I've made heaps, I thought I'd take a bowlful up to Maman, put her in a good mood because I'm going to be late home this evening. There's a rehearsal of *The Merchant of Venice* after class – did I tell you I was Portia? – and Sarah Threlfall's brother says he'll bring me home. He's gorgeous, in the sixth at the City of Norwich, Maman was really nice to him the last time he brought me home. He's got a motor bike.'

'No porridge thanks, and yes, you told me you were Portia and no, you've never mentioned whatsisname,' Tess said. She went across to the pantry and peered. 'Any eggs? A friend of mine spent the night at Mrs Thrower's, but he's coming here for brekker, I invited him.'

'Him? Ash, d'you mean?'

'No, not Ash. Another friend. His name's Malcolm Chandler, he's a bomber pilot and an Aussie. I'd like you to meet him, but if you can't you can't. He's only got a forty-eight, you see, the same as me.'

'Malcolm Chandler,' Cherie said slowly. 'You've never mentioned *him* before, Tess.'

'No, because I didn't meet him until quite recently, but now . . .' Tess broke off as there came a perfunctory knock on the back door, which then creaked open. She smiled. 'Mal? Wonderful, you'll just have time to say hello to Cherie – my sister – before she has to rush off to school.'

'Hel*lo*, Malcolm,' Cherie drawled. She pushed a wing of hair behind her ear and looked across at him, lowering her head and peering coyly through her thick, dark lashes. She also put her hands on her hips, drew in a deep breath, and made the most of her bosom, Tess saw disapprovingly. All of a sudden her sister had become very *femme fatale*, it seemed. 'So you're Tess's new friend!'

She made it sound as though friend was a synonym for something far warmer and less reputable, but Mal just laughed.

'Hi, Cherie. Nice to know you,' he said. 'And I'm Mal; I don't know why but whenever a woman calls me Malcolm it makes me feel I'm back in school.'

'I am in school,' Cherie said, suddenly abandoning her French film starlet pose and grinning engagingly up at him. 'It's hateful, and I'm jolly nearly old enough to leave, but Maman wants me to stay on, get myself a decent education.' She snorted. 'A fat lot of good an education is in wartime.'

'Mothers usually know what's best,' Mal said. 'Hey, is that porridge? I'm real fond of porridge; any chance of some?'

Marianne, alerted by her daughter, came down for breakfast so that she might meet Tess's friend, and Mal was nice to her, friendly, polite.

'I guess you don't meet many Australians, so I'm on my best behaviour,' he said when Marianne told him he hadn't eaten enough to keep a sparrow alive. 'I've heard all about your rations – come to that, we're rationed too, though not as meanly as civilians. I don't know how you've managed to produce such a wonderful breakfast, Mrs Delamere.'

'I'm a provident Frenchwoman, that's how,' Marianne said, twinkling at him. 'Tess disapproves, but you note she eats with a good appetite.'

'Well, the eggs came from our own hens, which is fair enough, but I daresay the bacon was the under-the-counter sort,' Tess said. 'Never mind, don't let's argue about hoarding now, Marianne. Mal and I are going to take the boat out on the Broad, if that's all right with you. It's a nice day, so I'll get some food and we can have a picnic.'

'And later, I shall prepare you a delicious dinner,' Marianne said, batting her eyelashes at Mal quite as vigorously as her daughter had done, earlier. 'For Maurice is coming over tonight, so we'll have two large men to feed, Tess. Do you play bridge, Mal?'

Mal admitted that he did not and Marianne, a recent convert, said that it might be fun to teach him.

'And Tess, of course,' she added rather as an afterthought. 'We could have a hand or two after dinner, before you have to catch your bus back. Tess will ride her bicycle over to Willow Tree Farm, as she always does, but it is quite possible that Maurice could give you a lift, Mal, since he has a motor car.'

Mal thanked his hostess politely and as soon as Tess had made their picnic the two of them escaped down to the Broad where

Tess waited until they were afloat before giving vent to the mirth which was consuming her.

'Mal, you should have seen your face when she asked you if you could play bridge – and when she said she'd teach you . . . but you've made a real impression on her, because she's never suggested teaching me bridge.'

'Your stepmother is a flirt; she wants to teach me bridge because I'm a feller and she likes fellers,' Mal said gloomily. 'I *hate* card games, always have. It's bad enough avoiding them in the mess when they want a fourth for whist or whatever it is, without having your mother land on me.'

'Don't worry, we'll be so late back that there won't be time for a game,' Tess said consolingly. 'I thought we'd row over to Catfield and then walk up to the farm. You could meet my friends and Mr and Mrs Sugden; they're awfully nice.'

'Oh, sure,' Mal said, brightening. He looked round the great, gleaming expanse of the Broad. 'But where'll we kiss?'

Tess, rowing, giggled rather breathlessly. 'We've come out to get to know each other and to have a picnic and see the sights, not to kiss,' she said. 'And incidentally, it isn't just because you're a young man that Marianne wants to teach you bridge because she's never tried to teach Ashley or Andy. You've obviously got hidden attractions.'

'What do you mean, hidden? Women fall for me all the time, hook line and sinker – you did it yourself! The fact is, darling, I'm a bloody fascinating bloke.'

'Yes, you are,' Tess said. 'But Ashley's attractive too, and so's Andy.'

'Oh? How come you won't be marrying them, then?'

Tess stopped rowing. They sat for a moment in complete silence whilst the heat slowly rose in Tess's face, then she said, 'What?'

'How come you won't be marrying Ashley or Andy?' Mal repeated gently. 'How come you're going to marry me, if they're so attractive?'

'You haven't asked me . . . you hardly know me and I hardly know you,' Tess said, gabbling a little. She felt sure she was red as a turkey cock, damn him! 'You shouldn't . . . it isn't fair to . . .'

She dug the oars into the water so hard that the boat almost lifted up and Mal said soothingly: 'Row for the shore, darling, it's easier to quarrel on dry land. Easier to kiss and make up, too.'

'I don't know why you're talking this way,' Tess muttered, rowing for the shore. 'Just because Marianne likes you, and Cherie, and the Throwers . . .'

She drove the boat into the reeds and Mal, on hands and knees, crawled the short distance which separated them and took her in his arms.

'Tess, I love you and I want to marry you,' he murmured with his mouth an inch from the crown of her head. 'War's a bitch, there's no time for all the gentle, beautiful things, like courtship. I want you desperately badly and that means marriage. Soon. As soon as we can arrange it in fact.'

Tess had been going to put him in his place, to tell him that she hadn't made up her mind that she wanted to marry at all, let alone one specific person, but his words took the wind out of her sails; there was a sort of desperate honesty in them, and it reflected an equally desperate honesty in her. She wanted him as badly as he wanted her, so what was the point in waiting, pretending? Any day now something could happen which would part them irrevocably and for ever. At least, if they married now, they could be properly together for whatever time there was.

She said as much, with her face muffled by his shirt, for he had removed his jacket and folded it up under his seat so that it didn't get messed up or wet.

'Then if we both want it, we'll go ahead,' Mal said. He began to kiss her, and for several moments Tess was completely carried away, no longer aware of her surroundings, the rocking of the boat, the possibility of being seen, condemned. His mouth and his hands were all that mattered, and they mattered supremely. The pleasure which was coursing through her body was a pleasure she could no longer deny – had the place been more private, she thought afterwards, she would have given herself to him un-reservedly, marriage or no marriage.

But the steady swish of oars heralded Mr Thrower, coming out to check his eel-traps, Tess supposed. She and Mal sat still as statues until he had passed, and then Mal picked up the oars.

'Right, we're getting married,' he said briskly. 'Let's go and talk to people and sign things and tell everyone. Oh my darling, waiting will be easy, now we know what we're waiting for!'

Fifteen

Mal went about his work on his first day back at the station walking on air. He had had a magical leave, they had gone ahead and done all they could towards getting married as soon as possible, and Marianne, charmed and delighted at the turn of events, or so she claimed, had suggested that they should have a large engagement party in ten days' time, because she and Maurice had decided that they would like to get married too.

'Many of our friends and most of Peter's relatives have never met Maurice,' she had said gaily. 'And of course none of them have met you, Mal. So we shall arrange this thing for all our sakes, and very good such a party will be. It will cheer us up and help us to forget the war for a little while.'

Tess and Mal had told each other the truth, too. The whole truth, which Mal, at least, had kept until now in his own mind and heart.

Tess began it. She told him about her dream and its terrible ending, and her painful fear that her mother might have committed suicide rather than remain with her small daughter. And Mal hugged her and said stoutly that he would never believe that anyone, far less a mother, would willingly leave her. And then he told her about Petey.

'That's awful, sweetheart; no wonder you have bad dreams too,' she had said when Mal had told her of the fateful fishing expedition which had ended so tragically. 'But at least you know Petey's death was an accident, that your father tried to save him.'

'No,' Mal said. 'No. That's the way I tell it, but that isn't really how it was. I suppose it's why I dream about it still, to this day. I've never told a living soul Tess, because it seemed so disloyal, but it didn't happen quite the way I said. My dad was an impatient man, you see. Petey stumbled over to him, leaning on the wind, to ask for the hundredth time if we could go home soon, and Dad gave Petey one hell of a push, I saw it with my own eyes. Petey staggered, then went backwards off the rocks and into the sea. He was a weak little feller. My dad killed Petey as surely as if he'd strangled the kid.'

Tess gasped, then she had leaned over and hugged him, muttering, with her mouth against the side of his neck, that terrible though it was it had happened, it was past, and that he must forget all about it, put it right out of his head.

'Your dad couldn't face what he'd done, that's why he started to drink so hard,' she said presently. 'And he lost everything through one moment of impatience: your love, your mother's love, and Petey. He did a terrible thing, but he never meant to hurt your brother, did he? And how he must have suffered!'

'Yeah, I suppose,' Mal said. He felt physically lighter, as though the knowledge, kept to himself for so long, had at last taken wing, left him. He took a deep breath and expelled it in a long whistle. 'Oh, Tess, I'm so glad I told you! It's – it's like putting down a heavy weight after years of having it on your shoulders. I guess I shan't dream that dream again.'

And I don't believe I ever will, Mal thought now, saluting the guard as he hurried past the perimeter gates. She's a wonderful girl, my Tess. He thought that as long as he lived he would never forget the look on her face, the sublime mingling of desire and innocence, when he had first taken her in his arms. And just before he left her to return to his station he had told her to continue the wedding arrangements so that they might marry as soon as possible.

And when this bloody, wicked war is over, his thoughts had continued, my little darling can come back to the Wandina with me . . .

The bubble had not burst at that, but it had lost some of its gloss. He had lied to her about the Wandina. So eager had he been to persuade her that marriage to him was not only right but inevitable, that he had exaggerated a little, given her to understand that Uncle Josh was a real uncle, that he, Mal, would return to the Wandina when the war was over and would, in the fullness of time, inherit the cattle station.

Still. He would own a third, or possibly a quarter, of the Magellan one day, when Royce fell off his perch. Only . . . only Royce was forty years younger than Uncle Josh and would last a good few years yet. By the time the Magellan was up for grabs, he, Mal, might well be in his fifties or sixties.

Not that it would matter to Tess. He knew that, really. She wasn't after his money or his property. She's after my body, he thought complacently, and I'm after hers . . . oh Tess, how shall I get through a whole week without you?

But he had to be sensible, he knew that. So he searched out his crew and they discussed their leave, had a hasty meal in the cookhouse and then, in the late afternoon, went with the others of their flight to the briefing room.

If all went well, he would see Tess again quite soon; the engagement party was to be held before long, so that he might meet her relatives and various friends. The two couples would announce their engagement – Mal was to accompany Tess into the city as soon as they both had a few hours free to buy a ring – set a date for the wedding and invite people to attend the ceremony. He meant to talk to his CO as soon as he could about married quarters, though he knew it was more likely that they would live off the station in lodgings in the nearest village.

But what bliss, to find Tess waiting for him when he came home, worn out and still buzzing with tension, after a sortie! It didn't matter what the lodgings were like, or where they were situated. Just to be together would be pleasure beyond belief. A place of my own again, he thought, striding towards the officers' mess. Because once we're married wherever we live will be our home, and I've not really had a home of my own since I was a kid. Oh, the Magellan felt like it, at times, and so did the Wandina, though somehow I always felt a bit of an outsider, tolerated rather than welcomed. But with Tess it'll be different. We're meant for each other . . . I'll tell her the truth about the Wandina just as soon as I get the chance, and she'll understand. Sometimes I don't even have to say the words, a glance is enough, so she'll know I didn't mean to deceive her.

He reached the mess and opened the door; noise hit him. Men talking and arguing, music from a wireless set, the occasional shout of laughter. Percy waved, shouted, Fred Milne stood up and lounged over towards him, talking as he came.

'Why the grin, Mal? Lost a farthin' and found a quid?'

Mal grinned too. 'Sort of. I'm getting married, fellers!'

When the party was over and Mal had been walked down to the bus and lovingly waved off, Tess returned to the house to help with the clearing up. Maurice had left earlier, very dapper in his uniform, swearing undying love but unable to get any more leave right now. Tess found Marianne and Cherie washing up in the kitchen with much clattering, whilst they rendered the latest popular song at the tops of their lungs. Marianne, who always sang flat and could not hold a tune for love nor money, adored to sing when she was happy.

'Here, let me give you a hand with that; it was my party, as well as yours, Marianne,' Tess said, seizing another tea-towel, but Marianne, standing at the sink with her best little black dress swathed in a huge wrap-around overall, said that she and Cherie were doing nicely, and would much prefer it if Tess would put away.

'Here goes then,' Tess said, picking up a pile of the best plates and tottering over to the Welsh dresser. 'What a lovely party it was – thank you, Marianne. The food was splendid, Mal couldn't believe his eyes when he saw the tea-table. Isn't he nice, Cherie? You like him, I know. What did you think Marianne?'

'Well, he's a great improvement on Ashley,' Marianne said. 'But he's no Adonis, my dear. He's nowhere near as handsome as my Maurice.'

She sounded complacent. Tess laughed.

'Oh Marianne, looks really aren't important! He's kind and gentle and amusing . . . Besides, he *is* handsome, in a quiet sort of way.'

'No, Tess, he is not handsome,' Marianne said positively. 'Your father was handsome, Maurice is handsome, even Ashley might be considered by some people to be handsome. But Malcolm is quite plain. He's charming, certainly, and reliable, and he's got marvellous white teeth, but handsome – no.'

'Well, I think he's very good-looking,' Tess said obstinately. She put the plates into the cupboard and shut the door on them. 'His face is so strong . . . his eyes are the brightest blue . . .'

Marianne, turning away from the sink, shook her head, but she was smiling. 'Now I know you're in love! He is certainly pleasant-looking, and he does have very blue eyes. I like him and approve of him and what's more important perhaps, I'm positive that Peter would have taken to him. I can't say more than that, can I?'

'Bless you, Marianne,' Tess said fervently, picking up another pile of plates. 'You couldn't have said anything which would please me more. Isn't his accent attractive? I could listen to his lovely, slow voice all day.'

'Now I *know* you're in love,' Cherie said, imitating her mother's earlier remark. 'An Aussie accent isn't lovely, it's a mixture between Birmingham and cockney. But I like him ever so much, Tess. I – I envy you. He's just right for you. He's – he's dependable and huggable.'

'That's it exactly, Cherie, you are a clever kid,' Tess said eagerly, sliding the plates on to the plate rack this time. 'You just feel you could lean back on Mal and he'd always be there to catch you. I know he isn't really handsome, like Ash, or sophisticated or anything like that, but he's most tremendously nice.'

'Why didn't Ash come to the party?' Cherie said curiously, standing cups in their places on the dresser. 'It wasn't as though it was just your party, Tess, he could have come for Maman and Maurice.'

'He was on standby,' Tess said patiently, not for the first time. 'Besides, he's always had such a – a proprietorial attitude towards me that perhaps he can't actually bring himself to admit I'm going to marry someone else.'

'He'll say it's just a phase you're going through,' Marianne said with some shrewdness. 'He won't give up until you're actually married, not that young man.'

After the excitement of the engagement party, it was odd to leave the beautiful sunshine for the blacked-out briefing room with the haze of cigarette smoke hanging above the lines of straight-backed chairs and the large map on the blackboard with their proposed route outlined in scarlet.

'Where is it this time, Skip?' Sidney hissed as they settled into their seats. Germany, sure, but where?'

'Hamburg,' Mal decided, squinting at the map. 'Well, it won't be the first time.'

'True. At least we know the way,' Fred said. 'You know the way to Hamburg, don't you, Perce?'

'And the way back,' Percy said. 'Hush, here come the big guns.'

The Station Commander and the Squadron Commander entered together, the little blonde WAAF who took shorthand notes slightly ahead of them. The buzz of muttered conversation died away. Notebooks were produced, everyone sat up straighter. The briefing began.

They took off at two minutes to midnight and reached the target area in good time, but after that, all hell was let loose. The flak was the heaviest Mal had ever known, the scarecrow flares – horrible inventions which looked, when they burst, exactly like a kite going down in flames – everywhere. They must have been amongst the last to arrive, since the flak and the bullets were flying and the sky was lit up with a demonic glare. The fighter defences hadn't picked them up on their way in to the target, perhaps because they had been one of the last kites to take off, but now they were here, it was clear that Hamburg, tonight, was a bad place to be. Mal didn't believe in safety in numbers – it was too easy to collide with another Lancaster if you were all milling around the target together, but he ordered everyone to keep a sharp look-out, conferred briefly with the bomb aimer and the navigator, and then put the kite as nearly over the target area as was possible in the circumstances.

'Bomb run starting,' he said presently over the intercom, when navigator and bomb aimer judged the time to be right. 'Okay, Perce?'

'Okay,' Percy called back.

'Fred?'

'Any minute, Skip . . . bombs away!'

The aircraft surged as the weight left it and Mal adjusted speed and turned away from the target. If it was the target – difficult to tell with the mass of enemy fire, flak and flares which were dancing below them, turning the night into hell.

'Turn starboard on to two-one-five degrees,' Percy said into his mike. 'Steady . . . what the hell was that?'

'Dunno,' Mal said. 'I felt her judder . . . anyone see anything?'

'Flak, Skip,' Geoff called from the turret. 'Caught us on the fuselage, near the wing. Doesn't seem to have done any real dam . . . oh well, there's quite a lot of cold air, but that's nothing.'

'Good,' Mal said. 'Eyes skinned, please. I want a quiet run home.'

They were an hour from the target when the rear gunner suddenly came to life. No one talked more than necessary on either a return trip or an outer – you could be picked up from radio transmissions – and Mal often teased Dave, the rear gunner, accusing him of falling asleep, though his position, with the firing point above his head, would not have made a snooze an easy matter. But his yell now had real urgency.

'There's a Junkers behind us, Skip – just over a thousand yards, I'd say.'

'Watch him, tell me when to weave,' Mal roared back. 'Geoff, Paul . . . keep your eyes skinned!'

'He's coming in!' Dave shouted. 'Go starboard, Skip . . . now port, now port!'

Mal, jinking desperately, heard Geoff chime in. 'Directly above us, Skip . . . lose altitude, perhaps . . .'

'Go port, port, *port*!' Paul, in the mid-upper shouted, and Mal realised, with considerable horror, that there must be more than one JU88 circling them.

Then he saw the plane, coming alongside, guns spitting, and saw a line of neatly drilled holes appear in the fuselage, shattering the perspex of his left-hand window and letting in what felt like iced water, though it was only wind.

'Paul, can you . . .?'

He heard the cannon roar, saw the Junker shudder, then Dave was shouting again.

'Starboard, Skip . . . starboard . . . get me round so I can get him!'

More fire, then another hit. The kite actually leaping . . . the Jerry appearing, disappearing . . . Paul saying 'Starboard, Skip, star . . .' his voice cut off suddenly, completely.

Mal shouted 'Percy? You there?'

'Just about, Skip. Where did Paul go?'

'Go port, Skip,' came from Geoff, obviously too busy watching the Jerry to wonder at his oppo's sudden silence. 'Now starboard!'

'Percy, see what's up with Paul,' Mal said as he manoeuvred the big plane into a violent fishtail motion. 'Everyone else all right?'

He thought he heard Sidney answer, knew Fred said he was still around, but then Geoff began shouting again and just as Percy reported, in a subdued voice, that Dave had been hit in the stomach and was unconscious, an explosion almost lifted them all off their feet. Light filled Mal's office, as the cockpit was usually called, and one of his unvoiced fears – that, in the event of trouble he would be unable to get out of his pilot's seat – was promptly proved groundless. He was out, a mighty roaring wind was tearing at him, and there was a terrible, excruciating pain in his right shoulder. He was falling, falling, head over heels, the noise was tremendous, yet above it he could hear someone screaming at him.

'Pull the ripcord, you prize pratt, pull the bloody ripcord!'

It seemed a pretty pointless exercise. Something hit him across the shoulders and for a moment he thought he had fainted from the pain. He fumbled for the ripcord, couldn't find it, felt a terrible, tremendous blow on his head and lost consciousness.

They all liked Mal, the girls, Mr and Mrs Sugden, the farm workers. They told Tess she was a lucky girl and advised a register office wedding because it would be quicker than going through all the business of a church ceremony.

'I will, if it's quicker,' Tess said. 'I don't want any more delays, not now I know what I do want.'

'Wish I was getting married,' Susan said. Her boyfriend was an

American, who flew in one of the big Liberator aircraft as a nose-gunner. His name was Benny Kertzer and he had been rather evasive about marriage. Susan sometimes came down in the morning red-eyed, because she had managed to convince herself, during the long watches of the night, that he was married with six kids.

'Oh, your turn will come, Sue,' Tess said cheerfully. 'Anyway, I'm not married yet. Which reminds me, if I'm going to a register office I really should telephone Marianne and tell her. She'll be pleased. Probably.'

'Why?' Molly asked. The three girls were cleaning out the cow-sheds, wielding shovels, large brooms and buckets of water.

'Because she and Maurice have decided on a register office. I think she'll feel that we're both marrying in the same sort of way, if you understand me. And of course she's so delighted that I'm not marrying Ashley that she'd be pleased about most things.'

The girls laughed, though Molly said wistfully that she wouldn't mind any sort of wedding, personally. Molly's boy-friend was a brown job, out in the Far East. They would marry when the war was over, not before, because he wouldn't be home until then. I am so lucky, Tess told herself, pushing a huge pile of dung along on her shovel. Most other people have to know some-one for months or years before they marry. But me and Mal . . . oh, he's such a marvellous person, I am so very lucky!

'Why not phone your stepmother now, in our brekker break?' Susan said presently, when the sheds were immaculate and they were heading across the yard towards the kitchen. 'If she's book-ing the register office for herself she might as well do it for you and Mal, too. It'll save time and the Sugdens won't mind, if you go on your bicycle and hurry.'

'Good idea,' Tess said. 'Tell them I shan't be long, would you? What's next anyway?'

'Stables,' Molly said briefly.

'Oh, right. I rather enjoy mucking out the stables,' Tess said, going into the cart-shed to fetch her bicycle. 'See you soon, then.'

'Marianne! I'm home, but I can't stop long. I'm on milking first thing, so I've just rushed over to have a quick word.' Tess stopped short half-way across the kitchen, realising that the person she had been addressing was Cherie and not Marianne, as she had supposed. 'What's up, kiddo? Where's Marianne?'

'On the telephone,' Cherie said. 'I thought it might be for me, but Maman beat me to it because she's waiting for a call from Maurice. I'll tell her you're here, though.' And before Tess could stop her she had hurled the kitchen door open, poked her head round it and shouted: 'Tess is back, Maman!' before clapping the door shut again.

'You are so noisy, Cherie,' Tess groaned, slumping down on a chair. 'Make a pot of tea, there's a love, and get out the bickies. I missed high tea because I wanted to come over tonight, see how the wedding arrangements are going.'

'Oh, right,' Cherie said. 'Maman made shortbread earlier; would you like some?'

'Would I! I wouldn't mind a sandwich, either – got any cheese?'

Cherie shrugged and sighed, looking very Gallic. 'Who knows? But I'll have a ferret around if . . .'

The door opened. Marianne stood in the doorway. She stared at Tess as if she was an apparition.

'Tess! I thought Cherie said . . . you're wanted on the phone, dear.'

Tess got up off her chair. 'Is it Mal?' she asked eagerly. 'If so, he'll ask about the wedding arrangements – what am I to tell him, Marianne? Did you manage to get a date for us?'

'No, it's not . . . it's someone else. An officer, I think. Come along, he's holding on but you know what the exchange is like.'

'Oh. Right,' Tess said. She bounced across the hall and picked up the receiver from where it lay on the half-moon table. 'Hello? Tess Delamere speaking.'

'Squadron Leader Matthews here, Miss Delamere. 'Ummm . . . was that your mother I spoke to just now?'

Mystified, Tess confirmed that it was.

'I see. Good, good. Because I'm afraid I have some rather worrying news for you.'

Tess opened her mouth but no sound came out. Her heart, which had been leaping excitedly about in her chest, seemed suddenly stilled. The lamp had looked cheery and welcoming a few moments earlier but now it cast long and terrible shadows.

'Miss Delamere, I've just come across a letter amongst Pilot Officer Chandler's effects. It asks that, in the event of an emergency, we treat you as – as next of kin. As you know he's an Australian with no . . .'

'Is he dead?' The question was torn from her, she shrieked it, yet it came out in such a dry, husky little whisper that Squadron Leader Matthews had to ask her what she had said.

'Is he . . . is he . . .' Tess stammered, and found she could not complete the sentence. 'You said . . . his effects . . . isn't that . . .'

A hand touched her arm. Marianne's face was concerned, sorry. She had lugged a chair out of the kitchen and now she pushed Tess into it and moved a little way off. But the Squadron Leader's voice was still talking. Tess strove to listen with intelligence, to damp down the wild flames of panic which threatened to engulf her.

'. . . There was a big raid on Germany last night and several of our aircraft failed to return.'

He had a young voice. He didn't sound old enough to be saying what she thought he was trying to say.

'One of the missing aircraft was Delta four one ninah, piloted by Malcolm Chandler. Obviously it's too early to say what has happened to the crew, but another squadron member believes he saw parachutes, which should mean that though the kite crashed, the crew have survived. They were over open country, too, which is always a good sign.'

'I see.'

He must be used to hearing the shock, the pain. His voice dropped a tone, became warmer, more personal.

'Look, m'dear, I know it's a terrible thing but I promise you he's got a good chance! They think he went down over occupied France, better than Germany, and though it may be a while before we know for certain, we'll find out exactly what happened as soon as we can and let you know. Normally, this sort of thing's done by telegram or letter, but . . . well, the chaps told me you and Mal were getting hitched, I thought a personal call . . .'

'Thank you,' Tess whispered. 'Thank you.'

'That's all right. Now get your mother to make you a nice hot cup of tea and sit down for a while. And remember, where there's life there's hope.'

Tess muttered something incoherent and clattered the receiver back on to its rest. She stood up and all of a sudden the hall became very dark, with swirling patterns which she could just make out on the periphery of her vision. She felt herself sway and knew, with cold and clammy certainty, that she was about to faint. She tried to sit down again, heard the clatter as she collided with the chair, and suddenly someone was holding her in a comforting embrace. Mal? It couldn't be Mal, yet . . .

'Come on sweetie, you're all right really, it's just shock. Come on, try to stand up, don't keep crumpling like that or you'll have us both on the floor! Here put your arm round me and we'll pretend it's a three-legged race and get you into the kitchen like that. *That's* better, good girl, left, right, left, right . . .'

Automatically she obeyed the half-hectoring, half-coaxing voice. She walked falteringly into the warm, well-lit kitchen and saw Cherie's white, tear-stained face, Marianne's shocked and rigid features. And Ashley was holding her, steering her towards the soft old armchair which had been Daddy's favourite, once.

'Ash? Oh, God, Ash, it was Mal's squadron leader; he rang to tell me Mal's . . . Mal's . . .'

'Ditched. I know, that's why I came over,' Ashley said briefly. 'A friend of mine's marrying a WAAF on Mal's station. But ditching isn't the end of the world, sweetie. He's probably cursing and walking across France at this very moment. Come on now, give us a smile! Even if the worst has happened, you'll live!'

But do I want to? Tess thought and heard, with horror, her own voice, small and hollow, saying the words out loud. 'Do I want to?'

Everyone was understanding and marvellous, Tess thought, when she returned to Willow Tree Farm. Mr and Mrs Sugden did everything they could to take her mind off her troubles and the girls were towers of strength. And Ashley, who had been anything but sensitive to the feelings of others in the past, excelled himself. He was there for her, not as an importunate lover but as a

412

friend. He telephoned, dropped little notes, called for her and took her out for undemanding car rides, for walks, for boating trips on the Broad. And Tess herself, despite her fears, hadn't broken down or taken to her bed or done any of the things she was afraid of doing. Instead, she had stayed at home with Marianne and Cherie for two days, getting accustomed to what had happened to her, and then with deliberation and calm, she picked up the reins of her life and went back to work.

And she very soon came to a decision. Mal had ditched, but that didn't mean he had gone for a burton; indeed, his squadron leader had seemed to think there was a good chance that Mal was alive and well. If so, he would either get home or be taken prisoner, and whichever it was, they should hear in a month or six weeks, possibly even sooner. The French Resistance, who helped aircrew who had gone down over France to get back to Blighty, always made sure that the British authorities knew of an airman's survival as soon as was humanly possible and as soon as a man became a prisoner of war his fellow countrymen were informed.

So she would stop thinking of herself as destined to be alone for ever, stop mourning Mal as gone. She would resolutely look on the bright side, wait for him, plan for the moment they would be together again. She would throw herself not only into work but into play, too, because that, she was sure, would be how Mal would want her to behave. She went to the cinema with Molly and joined the other girls at the village hop on a Saturday night. She began to keep a diary, especially for Mal, so that if he was a POW she could write him the longest letter in the world, detailing all her doings.

She told herself that this behaviour would see her through, and did her very best to remain cheerful and positive.

Her fellow-workers admired the stand she was taking and weren't afraid to say so. Tess reminded them that she had lost her father already and did not intend to lose her lover, too . . . and it heartened her that she had accepted Peter's death, whereas she did not intend to accept Mal's. She told herself over and over that if Mal had died she would know, in some mysterious way, and ignored her bad days, when his death seemed a certainty. And it was true that there were good days, when she woke full of optimism, certain he lived, certain he would soon be in touch. Such days helped her to cope with the bad days.

But nevertheless she was waiting, every moment of every day. Every letter that thudded through the letter-box, every tinkle of the telephone bell, every footstep, might be the letter, the call, the person, who was going to give her news of Mal.

She grew thinner, but she remained bright-eyed, calm, optimistic. She told herself that she was being tested, that she would not be found wanting.

And she waited.

Tess had spent the weekend at home with Marianne and Cherie, helping them get ready for the wedding, for Marianne and Maurice were to tie the knot the following Tuesday. Marianne had suggested that, in view of Tess's loss, they should put the wedding off for a month or two, but Tess wouldn't hear of it.

'It's absurd, Marianne,' she told her stepmother. 'You go ahead – as soon as Mal gets home we'll get married, but until then I don't want the whole world to grind to a halt.'

So Marianne, clearly relieved, had continued with her preparations, which included a very elaborate wedding party to be held at the Old House after the brief ceremony, and since Maurice would move in to the Old House when he was in England, she had also had the master bedroom redecorated. Despite the shortage of such things as decorating materials she managed to acquire from somewhere a quantity of extremely pretty floral wallpaper and a great many tins of magnolia paint, and with Tess's help she transformed the bedroom into a bower which Maurice, with his toothbrush moustache and gleaming patent-leather hair, no doubt thought was a fitting setting for his Gallic charms.

'I'll be glad when they're married, because Maman won't be so interested in my every move once she's got Maurice under lock and key,' Cherie said rather morosely to Tess as the two of them cleaned and polished the dining-room, where the wedding breakfast was to be held. 'She doesn't realise that at fifteen a girl needs a life of her own.'

Tess snorted, and rubbed away at the great dark dining-table more enthusiastically than ever. 'You don't know how lucky you are, Cherie,' she said. 'When I was fifteen Marianne couldn't stand me. The mere sight of me set her hackles up, so I felt it wisest to live my own life as far away from her as possible! It's odd, really, how fond of one another we've grown over the years, when you think that we were sworn enemies when I was a kid.'

'Oh, she was jealous because Daddy doted on you,' Cherie said, flicking a desultory duster over the ornately carved dining chairs. 'Where are we to put the chairs on Tuesday, Tess? Only we've asked thirty people at least, so they won't be able to sit down, they've got to circulate, Maman says, between the two rooms. She's going to set out the dining-table with savouries and the kitchen table with the puds, and tell people to help themselves and keep moving on.'

'Anyone cried off yet?' Tess asked, giving the table a final rub and standing back to admire her handiwork. 'I keep hoping someone will say no because if it pours with rain I don't know where they'll all go, but I think Marianne's reputation as a provider of marvellous meals has gone before her. Last time I asked she'd had all acceptances.'

'Your Ashley has written to say he will if he can, and I suppose several servicemen have done the same,' Cherie volunteered. 'But there haven't been any firm refusals so far as I know.'

'And he isn't my Ashley,' Tess said sharply. 'Is Mrs Thrower coming in on the Tuesday?'

'Of course! She's invited to the wedding, though we all know she'll turn up in her pinny and work like stink,' Cherie said. 'I was dumbstruck when Maman said she'd invited her, but then I realised. I know you think she's a snob, Tess, but it's just because she's so French. She believes everyone should stay in their place.'

'Oh, sure. And what did you realise?'

'Why, Mrs Thrower's hens are *reliable*, Tess, which means she'll have a good few eggs to spare. And the Throwers always have milk to spare, and butter, because of Susan. And now Sally, of course.'

Susan had dropped a heifer calf two years ago and Sally, as they had christened her, was in milk, with a calf of her own at heel.

'Oh, I see,' Tess said, striving for a neutral tone. 'Yes, I suppose you can't very well hoard milk or eggs.'

Cherie giggled. 'I know you don't approve of the hoard, and nor do I, but you must admit, Tess, that it's come in useful. And d'you know what? Last night, when Maman was gloating over it and choosing what to take out, she said she wanted to save all the icing sugar, because you'd need it for your cake, when Mal gets back.'

'Did she really?' Tess said, really touched. 'That was kind . . . I only hope it will keep until the end of the war, because if Mal's a POW it might have to.'

'He'll be home before then,' Cherie said stoutly. 'Are you coming home again tomorrow, Tess? Only tomorrow is the big, great, enormous getting-ready day and we could do with all the help we can muster. Maman's letting me stay away from school so I can put things in and out of the oven and dismember chickens and things.'

'No, I can't come tomorrow, it's good of Mr Sugden to let me have my weekend off and then have the Tuesday as well,' Tess reminded her sister. 'But I'll work really hard and finish early so I can bike over after tea. Will that do?'

'Yes, that will be fine,' Cherie said at once. 'You are staying over on Tuesday night though, aren't you? Because I don't much fancy being all alone in the house whilst Maman and Maurice are honeymooning in London.'

'I thought you were staying with Mrs Thrower?' Tess said. 'She told me she was clearing the small bedroom for you.'

'Oh, she is. But she's lending that bedroom to a couple of Maurice's colleagues for the actual wedding night,' Cherie said. 'You are staying over, aren't you, Tess? Maman was sure you would.'

'Yes, of course I will,' Tess said readily. 'If I'm on milking I can swap with Molly or someone. Then we can have a lie-in.'

'I wonder if Maman and Maurice will have a lie-in?' Cherie said ruminatively. 'I still don't know very much about what happens on wedding nights, do you, Tess? I took a sneaky look at the sixth form Human Biology book last term but all those diagrams made me feel quite sick. If I've got it right, and I'm not at all sure that I have, it's a physical impossibility anyway, what people are supposed to do to each other.'

'I don't see what Human Biology has to do with a lie-in,' Tess said. 'Don't be nosy about other people's experiences, Cherie, you'll have your own soon enough.'

'Not if I don't marry I shan't. Not if I decide the whole thing is too ghastly for words.'

'You won't. You're far too fond of men,' Tess said. 'Come on, let's go and see if Marianne wants anything else done.'

By Sunday night both sisters were exhausted, but the house shone and a good deal of cooking – bread rolls, fruit cakes, pies and pasties – had been done. Marianne, terribly excited, with her hair tied up in a duster and her figure enveloped in a huge blue pinafore, declared that they were saints and advised Tess to cycle slowly home and have a good night's sleep.

'It can't have been easy for you, my dear, helping to plan someone else's wedding party,' she said as she stood at the gate waving Tess off. 'But your turn will come, and how happy we shall all be then! And don't think I've used even half my goodies for this wedding breakfast, because I've been careful to save enough for you!'

'Yes, Cherie told me,' Tess said. 'Thanks, Marianne. And take it easy tomorrow.'

'I shall,' her stepmother promised sunnily. 'Oh, how nice it will be to be married again, to have someone to lean on, to turn to for advice!'

'I'm sure it will,' Tess said rather hollowly. 'Good-night then, Marianne. See you on the great day!'

She cycled home to Willow Tree Farm, parked her bicycle with the others in the cart-shed and went straight to bed. Her diary, under her pillow, showed her that it was a month since Mal had ditched. She had heard nothing, but that did not, she told herself defiantly, filling in her day's doings in pencil, mean that news would not be coming soon.

Molly and Sue, who shared her attic room, had both been asleep when she got in, but as she blew out the candle Sue moved and spoke.

417

'Tess? Have a good day?'

'Very good, thanks,' Tess whispered. 'I'm jolly tired, though. See you in the morning.'

'Another lovely day! I do love May, I think it's my favourite month.'

Tess and Sue came out of the cowshed, having finished the milking, and headed for the kitchen. Indeed, Sue's hand was actually on the doorknob when someone shouted.

'Hey . . . either of you called Miss Delamere? I've got a telegram for her.'

The speaker was a small, rosy-cheeked telegram boy, who was picking his way across the yard and pushing a bicycle which looked a great deal too large for him.

Tess's heart jumped into her mouth. A telegram! It had to be from Mal, or about him, at any rate – it must be the long-awaited news! She did not allow herself to consider that it could be bad news, but suddenly she felt the blood drain from her face, felt her knees begin to buckle. She grabbed the nearest object for support – it was Sue – and said faintly: 'That's me – I'm Tess Delamere.'

'Bear up, honey,' Sue said urgently into her ear. 'Don't go fainting on me, you're too heavy and the cow muck hasn't been cleared yet. Imagine, falling face downwards into that lot.'

Tess gave a breathless little laugh, as she was meant to, and took the small yellow envelope the boy was holding out. She tore it open and spread out the single sheet, her hands shaking so much that at first she could not read the words printed on it. Sue, with an arm looped comfortingly round her shoulders, read it aloud.

'*There's been an accident at your house stop*,' she read. '*Come home stop Thrower.*'

'An accident?' Tess said stupidly. Waves of relief were breaking over her head, making her feel almost as dizzy and disorientated as had her fear of bad news about Mal. 'What sort of accident? I don't understand.'

'Nor me,' Sue admitted, frowning. 'Stop Thrower doing what?'

Tess laughed again a little more strongly. 'No, it just means come home at once and it's signed Thrower. Oh dear, I wonder

418

what's happened? The Sugdens won't be too pleased if I disappear when I've just had a free weekend and am taking tomorrow off for the wedding.'

Susan turned to the telegram boy, who had just noticed the manure clogging the soles of his boots and was picking at it with a piece of stick.

'Can you tell them she'll be home as soon as she can get? We can't be more definite than that until we've spoken to the Sugdens.'

'Don't matter,' the boy said indifferently. 'No one ha'n't paid for a reply.'

'Then buzz off,' Susan said. 'Why are you hanging about? I thought you were waiting for a reply, naturally.'

'I'm waiting 'cos some people tip me a bob, or a kick,' the boy said hopefully. 'That's a long way to cycle, out here.'

'Oh . . . well, we're in our working clothes, we don't carry money,' Sue was beginning when Tess dived a hand into the pocket of her overalls and produced a sixpenny piece.

'There you are,' she said. 'It's all I've got.'

'Ta,' the boy said. He turned his heavy bicycle round and set off once more across the yard. 'Hope no one's dead.'

'Nasty little bugger,' Susan said, leading her friend towards the kitchen door. 'I wonder what's happened, though? Is it your sister? Only if so, why didn't your mother telegram instead of the Thrower person? Oh, Tess suppose it is your mother – and she's getting married tomorrow!'

'Can't be; I was with them both last night, remember,' Tess said as they re-entered the kitchen. 'An accident could mean anything. If Marianne or Cherie had been hurt, surely Mrs Thrower would have said? No, it must be . . . well, an accident.'

But when Tess gave her employer the telegram, Mrs Sugden was in no doubt where Tess's loyalties lay. 'You've got to go home, my dear,' she said. 'I'll take you round to Barton in the car, I want a word with Mr Chapman about some more poultry corn.' She turned to Susan. 'Will you finish off making the breakfast, dear? And when Molly comes down tell her she can finish the yard. Harold's taking the cows out, I suppose?'

'That's right,' Susan said. She turned to Tess. 'You'll have some brekker before you go, won't you?'

'Yes, we might as . . . no, on second thoughts, telegrams aren't sent lightly by people like Mrs Thrower,' Mrs Sugden said, suddenly making up her mind. 'Run upstairs, dear, and slip out of those overalls and we'll leave at once. If there's nothing we can do then we can be back in half an hour or so.'

'Good luck, Tess,' Susan said as Tess began to run up the stairs. 'I'll make you a couple of bacon sandwiches, you and Mrs Sugden can eat them in the car. I do hope you find it's a false alarm, but if you need us, we'll come over as soon as we can, me and Moll.'

'Isn't everyone good?' Tess said as Mrs Sugden drove the old Morris along the quiet country lanes. 'It's most awfully kind of you to bring me home, Mrs Sugden, when you're so busy. But it's not far now, this is Deeping Lane and the house is just . . . my God!'

They had rounded the corner and the house should have stood before them, serene against the backdrop of the trees and the distant Broad. It stood there all right, but it was . . . lopsided. And there was something wrong with the roof. Even as they watched, a curl of smoke drifted lazily from the ragged, oddly darkened thatch.

'You've been bombed!' Mrs Sugden said, stopping the car with such a jolt that Tess bumped her nose on the windscreen. 'Oh my dear, you've been bombed! What are those people doing? Ought we to help?'

Tess jumped out of the car and ran towards the house with Mrs Sugden close on her heels. Now that she was nearer she could see that the upper windows were glassless and the thatch had been partially burned off. Various Throwers were bustling in and out carrying furniture, rugs, books, crockery. They cast these objects on the front lawn and returned at once to the house. Tess saw the familiar shapes of dining-room chairs which she had polished only yesterday; some were water darkened, some scorched, blackened. A smell of burning hung in the air, and another smell, which Tess could not identify.

'What on earth . . .?' Tess gasped. Dickie Thrower emerged

420

from the front door, tugging after him a feather mattress scorched all along one side. Tess went over to him and tugged his sleeve.

'Dickie, what's happened? Was it a bomb? And where's your mother?'

'Oh, Tess, in't it awful? There was a 'splosion, the thatch went alight . . . Mum's now a-comin', she's been in the back kitchen, tryin' to get the cookery books an' the pans an' that sorted.'

Tess went towards the house, only to be shouted back by Mr Thrower, who was on a ladder, clawing with a peculiar instrument at the still-smouldering thatch.

'Keep away, gal Tess,' he shouted. 'Bess won't be a minute. She'll tell you wha's been happenin'.'

And sure enough, presently Mrs Thrower came round the side of the house with an armful of cookery books and smiled wearily at Tess. She was streaked with dirt and her eyes were bloodshot, but her smile was a comfort.

'Well, I hope my telegram didn't scare you, my woman,' she said cheerfully. 'I knew you'd come as soon as you could. They've took Miz Delamere to hospital, young Cherie went with her. I din't see her but it's to be hoped she in't too bad. House is a rare mess, though. As for the spare room . . . well, words fail me.'

'Oh, Mrs Thrower, thanks for the telegram,' Tess said. 'But if it was a bomb . . .'

'It weren't no bomb,' Mrs Thrower said gently. 'I had a word wi' Cherie, an' from what she said they're both lucky to be alive, love. That seem your stepma went into the spare room late last night with a candle, to tek another look at what she're got in there. She wanted olive oil to fry something or other for that there weddin' party.'

'Oh, that bloody hoard!' Tess said. 'But why . . .?'

'Cherie told me she kept some petrol for Mr Maurice in big cans,' Mrs Thrower said. 'And that cookin' oil was in big cans, too. She reckon your stepma must have been openin' cans to check which was what, an' she knocked agin one of 'em, dropped the candle . . . an' it were petrol and went up with a whoosh. It blew the winders out, destroyed just about everything in the spare room an' your room, an' burnt half the roof off – the beams ha' gone as well as the thatch – before the neighbours could do a

421

thing. I come runnin', all of us did, Ropes an' all. The Ropes phoned the fire brigade an' the ambulance, but I were round the back cartin' water from the Broad when they got your stepma out. Cherie was downstairs, a-doin' of her homework, when it happened. She couldn't get up the stairs for the flames so she come rushin' out . . . our Podge gave an eye to her till the ambulance people come.'

'And – and Marianne? Is she much hurt?'

'I don't rightly know,' Mrs Thrower said. 'But my Reggie say she was outside the spare room, agin the banisters. Not conscious, I'd say. Anyway, the ambulance people took her off to Norwich right quick. So soon as it was light this mornin' – we're bin fightin' the fire an' tryin' to save what we could all night long – I telegrammed you. Ropes sent it,' she added conscientiously, 'but I writ it. I didn't want to fright you, but I wanted you home . . . an' you come, dear, thank God.'

'And by the sound of it she'd better go again,' Mrs Sugden said. She had been listening anxiously, standing close to Tess with a hand on her arm. 'I'll run her into the city at once – Mrs Delamere's at the Norfolk and Norwich, I take it? Burns are painful and frightening, even small ones. Tess's place is with her mother and her younger sister now.'

'Oh, thank you, Mrs Sugden, you are so kind,' Tess said gratefully. 'Poor Marianne – and poor little Cherie, having to cope alone all night! I wonder why she didn't ring me herself?'

'Too confused, I dare say,' Mrs Thrower said. 'I knew she were in good hands, do I'd have made my way to the city. And if we hadn't been here, my woman, I mek no bones about it, you wouldn't even have half a house! The fire brigade didn't arrive until the early hours – not their fault, they were at another fire - so it was Broadswater and Broadsmen what saved the Old House.'

'Thanks, Mrs Thrower,' Tess said. She hugged the older woman hard. 'And from the look of you, you could do with a rest. Go home and have a cup of tea and some breakfast; I bet you've not eaten this morning.'

Mrs Thrower's face was white, her eyes scarlet pits, but she returned Tess's hug heartily. 'I'm a tough old bird, it'll tek more'n

422

fightin' a fire an' missin' a breakfast to disturb me. Off with you now, my woman, an' remember, where there's life there's hope.'

All the way to the hospital Mrs Sugden chatted gently and cheerfully, but Tess's apprehension grew and grew and in the end she had to talk about what she would find when she reached the Norfolk and Norwich.

'Marianne was right in line when the explosion happened, by the sound of it,' she said as they entered the city suburbs. 'She must have been hanging over the petrol can or the candle wouldn't have dropped into it. Oh, Mrs Sugden, do you thinks she's alive still?'

Mrs Sugden shot a quick look at her, then changed down to turn a corner. 'I don't know, dear,' she said at last. 'But miracles have happened. Your friend said that Mrs Delamere was hurled out of the room by the explosion. Perhaps she may have escaped relatively lightly.'

'I pray she has,' Tess said. 'I *pray* she's all right. Tomorrow – tomorrow was to be her wedding day.'

Mrs Sugden accompanied Tess into the hospital but said she would not go up to the ward.

'I'll stay down here, in the entrance hall, until you're ready to leave,' she said. 'I know the authorities don't encourage too many visitors to ill patients and we don't yet know how ill your step-mother is. But don't worry, I'll wait.'

'I don't know how to thank you,' Tess said distractedly. 'Aren't they busy? I can't see Cherie anywhere, so I suppose she's still with Marianne.'

The hospital staff were very busy, but as soon as Tess said who she was an orderly was sent to take her to the Burns Unit, where she was put into a waiting room and told that someone would be with her presently.

Overawed by the smell of disinfectant and sickness, Tess perched on the edge of a chair and picked up an old pre-war magazine. She was leafing through the pages, her mind in a terrible state of apprehension, when the door shot open. Cherie stood framed in the doorway. She gave a convulsive sob and ran straight into Tess's arms.

423

'Oh Tess, I'm so glad you're here! I couldn't ring, I didn't have any money, and I knew I should be with Maman until she woke up. Tess, she's . . . she's . . . awfully ill and I think she hurts badly. She moans, sometimes.'

Tess winced and was beginning to question Cherie when a nurse, following at a more leisurely pace, came into the room in Cherie's wake. She smiled at Tess.

'Miss Delamere? Your mother is very poorly, very poorly indeed, but we're doing everything we can to help her. Your sister will tell you that she looks . . . rather poorly, but . . . would you like to see her?'

'Yes, please,' Tess said. The nurse looked uneasily from her to Cherie and back again.

'It's . . . rather upsetting. Your sister's told you?'

'Yes,' Tess said. 'It's all right, I know a bit about burns.'

'Oh, well that's all right then,' the nurse said, suddenly brisk. 'Come with me.'

They followed her down a long, bleak corridor and into a tiny, bleak room. There were two beds but only one was occupied. Tess looked at the figure on the bed and recoiled. Was *this* Marianne? This blackened, hairless creature, hung about with tubes and bottles, lying still as death under the covers, with her gash of a mouth open, revealing that she had a bloody gap where teeth had once been?

Tess stood very still, trying to see a resemblance between what lay on the bed and her lively, attractive stepmother. But before she could speak Cherie's hand crept into hers.

'She looks poorly, doesn't she, Tess?' the younger girl murmured. 'But that's just dirt and things . . . she'll be all right when they clean her up, won't she? Only . . . she knocked her poor teeth out, the doctor says he'll give her a nice lovely bright new set, so that'll be all right, won't it?'

'That'll be fine,' Tess whispered back . . . and the figure on the bed moaned, a cracked and terrible sound which made her flesh crawl. 'Oh poor, poor Marianne!'

'Oh yes, poor Maman, but her left hand is all right,' Cherie said eagerly. 'I held her hand for hours and hours, only the nurse said I should have something to eat because Maman didn't know I was holding her hand so I went to the canteen with her. Only, it was odd, Tess, but I couldn't eat anything at all, and you know how greedy I am as a rule. I had some milk, but not even a bite of bread.'

'Never mind, chick, we'll go together presently and you'll eat when you have me for company, I'm sure,' Tess said. 'Look, after we've eaten we'll have to leave the hospital for a bit. We'll have to give Uncle Phil and Auntie May a ring and ask if we can stay with them whilst Maman's in hospital, and then we'll go back to the Old House and pick up some night things, clean undies, shoes . . . that sort of thing.'

'Why? Can't we go home and come into the city each day, once Maman's better?' Cherie said, looking puzzled. 'I don't know Auntie May or Uncle Phil terribly well, I'd rather be at home.'

Tess remembered that Cherie hadn't seen the house in daylight, probably hadn't given the damage a thought. Her mother was all she cared about. Rightly, Tess thought, glancing cringingly at the figure on the bed. Oh poor, poor Marianne!

'Darling, the house is badly fire-damaged, we can't go back there for a bit. It's pretty crowded already at Willow Tree Farm but I'm sure the Sugdens will find a corner for you until – until the house is mended, but for now, just whilst Maman is so ill, we ought to be nearer. On call.'

'Oh. Right,' Cherie said, immediately seeing the force of the argument. 'I didn't realise the house was badly damaged, though I knew the thatch had gone, of course. I looked back when the ambulance drove us away and I could see it burning.'

Marianne moaned again and the nurse, who had been standing by the door, stepped forward.

'I think you ought to leave Mother for a while, dears,' she said in a low voice. 'She's on morphine, so she really doesn't know you're here. Just you go out and get some air and make your arrangements and come back at, say, seven this evening.'

'Right,' Tess said, immensely relieved to be leaving the room and the figure on the bed. 'Come on, Cherie, there really isn't anything we can do here. And Mrs Sugden's waiting in the entrance hall; she'll take us up to Uncle Phil's if we ask her to, I'm sure she will.'

Mrs Sugden got to her feet when she saw them approaching. She looked very anxious.

'My dears, how is she? What's happening?'

Tess gave her a watered-down account of Marianne's condition and Mrs Sugden took them out to the car and drove straight to their uncle's house on Unthank Road. Auntie May was home and greatly distressed to hear their news and agreed at once that the girls must move in and have the small back bedroom between them.

'Mrs Sugden, I'm ashamed to ask any more of you, but could you take us back now, to fetch our night-things?' Tess asked, but Auntie May said that it wasn't necessary.

'Heaven knows what sort of a state your stuff is in, from what you've said,' she pointed out. 'I'll kit them out for the next few days, Mrs Sugden, and we'll keep you informed, of course. Something may well happen to – to make their presence in the city no longer necessary.'

'She thinks Maman will die,' Cherie said, as she and Tess were washing for dinner in their aunt's bathroom. 'But she's wrong, isn't she, Tess? Maman won't die, she's going to get married!'

'Lord, does Maurice know?' Tess said, begging the question. She could not imagine that marriage would be an option for Marianne for a long, long while, if ever. 'I'd better get in touch with him. Do you have a telephone number or an address?'

Cherie did not. 'It's in the brown book, at the Old House,' she said. 'Maman knows it by heart, so she'll be able to tell us in a day or two, but not quite yet I don't suppose. Perhaps we could bus over to Barton tomorrow, and make a note of it?'

Tess said they might do that, but Uncle Phil, when he got home, knew the number and contacted Maurice for them.

'He's very upset. He's coming over to the hospital at seven, to visit her,' he said, returning from the hallway, where he had made his telephone call. He looked straight at Tess. 'I wonder, my dear, if that's wise?'

'I don't think it is,' Tess said immediately. 'She's on morphine so she won't know he's there and the sight of her is – is very distressing. But Cherie and I are going to visit at seven o'clock, the nurse asked us to, so we can tell him it's early days.'

'I'll walk down with you, and walk you home,' Uncle Phil said at once. 'If the staff allow, I'll have a word with her doctor, ask him what the prognosis is.'

'I'd be very grateful,' Tess said earnestly. 'I'm afraid Cherie and I will just be told to wait and see. They won't fob you off like that, I'm sure.'

'So am I,' her uncle said grimly. 'And now let me see you two girls eat a hearty dinner, because you're going to need all your strength over the next few days.'

For ten days Marianne's life hung in the balance, though Cherie, Tess was sure, never realised it for one moment. For Cherie, her Maman was going to get better; it was simply a matter of being patient.

And for those ten days, Tess and Cherie slept in Uncle Phil's spare room and spent every moment they could at the hospital. They told Maurice that it was too soon to visit, that Marianne wouldn't know him, that he would only distress himself, and he stayed away, but on the eleventh day, when Marianne had sat up and drunk weak tea through a straw, he visited with the girls.

Tess had been dreading his reaction, what he might say or do, but she had underestimated him. He cooed to Marianne, talking to her exclusively in French, kissing her hands, telling her that soon, very soon, she would be his own adorable little girl again, and then they would marry and live happily ever after and this – pooh, this – would be but a terrible episode which he would spend the rest of his life ensuring that she forgot.

'Does he mean it?' Tess asked Cherie as they walked homewards that night. 'Will he really wait?'

'Why not? She's going to be beautiful again,' Cherie said in her most sensible voice. 'She's going to have lovely new teeth, and her hair will grow, most of it, and she'll have nice new skin in the places where the burns are worst.'

'Ye-es, but it'll take months,' Tess pointed out cautiously. She had never told Cherie that her beloved maman would probably never look the same again, and she was desperately worried over what Marianne herself would feel when she saw herself in the mirror. To date, the staff had carefully kept all reflective objects out of her reach and since she was still bedbound and unable, as yet, to leave the life-giving machines which were attached to her by various tubes, she had no idea of the extent of her injuries. Well, the staff said she didn't know and Tess had to believe them, though sometimes she wondered. She had seen tears running down Marianne's scarred and puckered cheeks more than once, and she didn't think they had been caused just by the physical pain she was suffering.

'Now that Maman is sitting up and talking and taking nourishment, I suppose I ought to start school,' Cherie said, on the eleventh day. 'I can still go in and see her before classes each morning and after each evening. Sister says.'

Cherie got on very well with Sister Prentiss, who was hard on her nurses but kindness itself to her patients and their young relatives. Indeed, she spent hours talking to Marianne and Cherie when she wasn't on duty, telling her patient that she was going to recover completely and assuring her patient's child that although recovery might take a long time, it was going to be worth the wait.

'Modern medicine can perform miracles these days,' she said cheerfully, and brought a book of photographs to show how skin grafting was progressing. 'You wait, you'll be a lovely thing again!'

'Will her hair grow back?' Tess asked Sister Prentiss, who said that it might well do so, but that wigs, today, were so natural that real experts had been fooled.

'I know you think she looks pretty awful now,' she said privately to Tess at one point. 'But she's a strong and determined woman who has an overriding urge to marry. That will bring her recovery on faster than you might imagine. Mind over matter, my dear; mind over matter!'

'I'm glad,' Tess said sincerely. 'We haven't always seen eye to eye, but we're fond of one another now. And Maurice – he's not the drongo I thought him.'

Sister Prentiss cocked her head on one side. 'Drongo? That's an Australian expression.'

'Yes,' Tess admitted. 'I'm going to marry an Australian bomber pilot. He's been posted missing right now, they had to ditch over occupied France, so I'm waiting to hear whether he's a POW or – or whether he's making his way home. His friends saw parachutes, you see,' she ended.

'I see. Well, I shall pray for him,' Sister Prentiss said matter of factly. 'As I pray for your mother, my dear.'

'Thank you,' Tess said. 'I pray for them both, too.'

The weeks passed and spring turned into summer. There was no word from the Air Force concerning Mal's whereabouts and Marianne's progress seemed painfully slow. Tess, living at Willow Tree Farm and going into Norwich whenever she could to see Marianne and Cherie, thought that, awful though it was, the explosion at the Old House had at least stopped her fretting all the time over Mal. Seeing how calm and optimistic Cherie and Maurice were, she would have been ashamed to have been less so herself. So she talked cheerfully of getting married when Mal got home, and applauded Maurice's plans to take Marianne away somewhere to convalesce just as soon as she was well enough.

And she went out with Ashley.

'I know Mal's coming back,' she said to Sue and Molly as they worked in the fields, planting, hoeing, harvesting. 'But Ash says why should that stop me living a normal life in the meantime, and I believe he's right. He knows I'm – I'm spoken for, he's just being friendly.'

'That's right,' Sue said, and winked at Molly. Tess, intercepting the wink, sighed but said nothing. She could not spend all her time hospital visiting and working, it was safer, she felt, to go out with Ashley, who knew the status quo, rather than with some other young man who might have his hopes raised, only to be blighted at Mal's return. But when she said as much to the girls they obviously didn't understand.

'Do you think it's unfair of me then, to see Ash?' she asked bluntly, a few days later, when the girls were reading their letters over breakfast. 'Only I get very low-spirited, sometimes. No home any more – Mr Thrower says he'll do what he can, but building materials just aren't available – no parents or family. And Ash does understand, really he does.'

'Sure, love. You go out with anyone you want to,' Molly said.

'Ashley's a decent bloke, he won't try to take advantage of your loneliness.'

'He'll get a smack in the kisser if he tries,' Tess said briefly. She had been hoeing cabbages, now she straightened, a hand to the small of her back. 'Gosh, thank God for the end of the row! Is it time to break for grub yet?'

Sixteen

It was a beautiful blue and gold summer's day in August, and Tess was helping Ashley to strip the plum trees at the bottom of the orchard so that Mrs Knox might bottle some of the fruit and make jam with the rest. It was a busman's holiday in a way, since the girls at Willow Tree Farm had spent every spare moment for three weeks picking plums, but Tess didn't mind. Mrs Knox had pointed out the flocks of blackbirds and starlings attacking the plums; it would help a great deal in the coming winter if the fruit were picked before the birds and wasps ruined the crop. What was more, because she no longer had a home to go to when she was on leave Tess had been glad of the Knoxes' invitation to visit them whenever she was at a loose end. And at least, Tess thought ruefully now, picking plums gives Ashley and me something useful to do whilst we quarrel.

Not that Ashley was much interested in being useful, she quite realised that. He was on leave, having finished his third tour, and would be instructing for the next few months and felt he was doing well by his country. Three tours with only one bad landing (a tyre had burst) and one ditching in the North Sea (near enough to the shore to be picked up speedily), wasn't bad, he had told Tess complacently earlier in the day. He had added that she should realise he was a warrior from the war returning, so why didn't she do the decent thing and cast herself on his bosom and gratify all his desires?

'Because I'm spoken for,' Tess had said . . . and that, of course, was why they were quarrelling, though since she was barely allowed to open her mouth it was less a quarrel, she supposed, than a lecture. But perched high in the branches, handing down her basket whenever it was full of plums so that Ashley could arrange them in the tray, at least she was at liberty to pretend his more offensive remarks hadn't been said.

Because the truth was that Ashley, who had come to Barton on that dreadful morning and been such a comfort, simply refused to believe that Tess could be in love with a man she scarcely knew. The words, *a man who, for all you've heard of him since his ditching, might well be dead*, could never be spoken between them.

'You only met him once or twice,' he had protested at the time, as he drove Tess back to Willow Tree Farm to start work once more. 'I know you must still be in shock but Tess, my love, this isn't Marianne, nor your father, nor anyone you know really well. It's always sad when someone goes for a burton, but to make yourself ill . . .'

'We were going to be married,' Tess had said in the new, thin little voice which had seemed all she was able to produce at that time. 'We saw each other on and off for a couple of weeks, that was all, but it was enough. I – I *knew*, you see, and so did Mal. We belonged together. Why, the reason Marianne was in the spare room that day was because she was sorting out the food so that there would be some left for our wedding reception, when Mal came home. Didn't you know that was why . . .'

'Yes, all right,' Ashley said hastily as Tess's explanation stumbled to a halt. 'But what you felt couldn't have been more than a – a passing fancy, sweetie! Damn it all, you and I have known each other for years, but I've never managed to persuade you to spend a day away with me, let alone . . . Christ, sweetie, you can't call that thick Aussie exactly charming, or a sweet-talker . . .'

'I didn't have to be charmed, or sweet-talked,' Tess had said dully. 'I don't understand it myself, Ash. But it's the way things are.'

'Were,' Ashley corrected, then, at her involuntary wince, added in a lower tone, 'I'm sorry, darling Tess, I shouldn't have said that. But – but you get under my skin and I can't understand why you don't feel the way I feel and . . .'

'It doesn't matter,' Tess had said patiently. Soon she would be back at work and Ashley would be flying his fighter once more.

There was absolutely no point in trying to convince him. 'I don't want to talk about it anymore, Ash.'

But right now her basket was full, which meant a scramble down and an eye-to-eye confrontation with Ashley. As she climbed lower the birds clustering in the next tree rose uneasily, then settled again. 'I've not finished this one yet, my feathered friends,' Tess informed them, descending on to the lowest limb of the tree and handing her basket down to Ashley. 'You won't starve – but you won't get the whole crop, either!'

'Stop talking to the bloody birds and ignoring me,' Ashley said plaintively. 'Tess, you know I love you, don't you?'

'I know you think you do,' Tess said. 'Please, Ash, don't let's . . .'

'It's all right, I'm not making any demands, I'm just telling you,' Ashley said. 'I'd do anything for you, Tess, anything at all. So if there is something I could do . . .'

'Thanks, Ash,' Tess said, and turned her head and smiled, because what she really wanted from him was to be left alone, but she couldn't say that. If Ashley had been in her shoes of course he would have blurted it straight out, but she wasn't capable of that sort of cruelty, and had turned away to smile in case he realised what she was thinking.

'Anything at all,' Ashley continued, oblivious. 'Because life goes on, you know. It has to. I've seen dozens of good fellows buy it, and – and life goes on. D'you know what I mean? Only one day, sweetie, you'll need someone and . . . d'you know what I mean, dearest Tess?'

'Well, I do. But Mal's only missing, Ash. I have such odd dreams, but he – he's often in them. So I won't stop believing he's alive until – well, until there's no hope left, I suppose.'

'Oh! Right,' Ashley said. So far as he was concerned, his tone said, missing meant presumed dead and that was the end of it. He began to unload the plums on to the new tray, talking over his shoulder as he did so. 'I know you shouldn't give up hope and all that, but you must be practical. Don't just stop coming out with me because you feel you're being disloyal to whatsisname! Let me go on taking you around a bit, come to the flicks with me, to the village hop . . . you can't just stop living life because of a – a dream!'

'It's nice of you, Ash, but if I do that you know how it will be.'

'No, I don't. Besides, what's the harm of a bit of a kiss and a cuddle now and then? You might easily find you feel just like I do, underneath. Believe me, sweetheart, if you'd only give me a chance you'd find you loved me just as much as you think you love . . .'

Tess, half-way up the tree again, picked the nearest plum and hurled it viciously at Ashley. It caught him just behind the ear and burst, messily. Ashley swore, laughed, stood up and grabbed her ankle before she could get out of reach.

'You vixen! Who's to say that Aussie would want to marry you, if he knew what a hell-cat you can be?' He pulled on her ankle and Tess kicked out, landing a good wallop on his shoulder. 'Now now, no violence! My ear's fairly humming; come down and kiss it better!'

Tess reached for a higher branch, missed, overbalanced and crashed out of the tree, landing heavily on Ashley. Their mingled cries sent the thieving birds shooting skywards and brought a faint shriek from the direction of the house.

'Now you've done it,' Ashley said. He extricated himself from beneath Tess and then grabbed her and began kissing any bit he could reach. 'That's Mum,' he mumbled against her neck. 'She'll think we're killing each other . . . oh, oh, oh, *how* I love you, Tess!'

Tess struggled crossly away from him, then ostentatiously wiped her hands round her neck and the sides of her face where his kisses had landed. Ashley was outrageous, she thought, totally unable to keep his hands – or his kisses – to himself. And then she looked at his face and saw the raw pain that her gesture had caused, and for a moment she hated herself. She turned and gave him her hands, pulling him to his feet, then allowing him to retain her fingers in his.

'Ash, why do you behave this way?' she said despairingly. 'I'm awfully fond of you and I love staying with your parents at weekends, especially now that I've not got a home of my own to go to. But when you're home, I'm beginning to think twice about coming over. You keep nagging and nagging . . .'

'I know I do; but I'm nagging for my life,' Ashley said in a low voice, his eyes still full of pain. 'You expect me to understand how you feel, Tess – well, how about you understanding how I feel for a change? I can't imagine life without you, and that's the dreary truth. Can you imagine what that's like? To wake with an ache inside you because the girl you love thinks she's in love with someone else? To see you in my home, with *Don't touch, I'm spoken for* written all over you? I say I love you, but it's more than that. I know you'll say I'm exaggerating and being unfair, but I'm damned if I know how I'll ever manage to live without you!'

Tess stared up at him, appalled by his words. For once there was no sneer, no sarcastic grin, nothing but an Ashley she scarcely knew staring down at her, gripping her hands so hard that it hurt.

Then he released her and turned away to start picking up the fruit which they had knocked over as they fell.

'Well, now you know,' he said lightly. 'It's the cross I have to bear, as they say. Come on, give me a hand with these plums or Mum will think we're on strike.'

Mrs Knox was very understanding when Tess told her, with real regret, she thought she had better not spend any more weekends in Blofield.

'I'm so sorry, dear, I'll miss you more than I can say,' Mrs Knox said. The two women were in the kitchen and Mrs Knox was making a meat and potato pie – potato and onion predominating – and continued to work as she spoke. 'I do wish you and Ashley could have made a go of it, because I'm so fond of you, but Ashley's not easy, I'm the first one to admit that. He can be so sarky and strange, but underneath he's very loving. I had him all to myself once, when he'd been suffering from mumps and I took him away to recuperate. He must have missed his friends and his home, but he amused himself, and helped in the house, and never grumbled. In other words, he was sweet and thoughtful. However, that isn't the point. Tell me about this young Australian, because if you're sure . . .'

'I am,' Tess said miserably. 'The awful thing is that I'm truly fond of Ashley, but I'm not at all in love with him. He's been like a brother to me, and the truth is no one can fall in love just because they want to. For me, it has to be Mal. I can't explain why, because he isn't nearly as handsome as Ash, but . . .'

'You don't have to explain, Tess. Love, true love, really isn't logical or even sensible, I know that. Why, when I first met Arthur I was engaged to someone else, and in those days . . . but I mustn't run on. This young Australian, didn't Ashley tell me he was . . . was missing? Wasn't his aircraft shot down over Germany?'

'Yes, he's missing. But not dead; not even *presumed* dead,' Tess said wildly. 'He's alive, Mrs Knox, I know he is. Ash won't believe it, but he is!'

'Ash probably can't let himself believe it,' Mrs Knox said sadly. 'Oh, what a tangle it all is! If only . . . if only things were different.'

She did not have to say how different; it was in the wistful glance she cast at Tess, in the way she immediately began to attack her pastry.

'I know,' Tess said. 'But what I can't tell Ash, without hurting him dreadfully, is that even – even if the worst happened, I wouldn't – couldn't turn to him. Because I know, now, what it's like to be in love. There's nothing like it, is there, Mrs Knox? And I couldn't accept second-best, not even for Ash's sake.'

'Especially not for Ashley's sake,' his mother said gently. 'Because to marry one man while your heart belongs to another, whatever the circumstances, is a wrong and foolish thing to do. All right, my dear, I'll do my best to explain to Ashley. That's what you'd like me to do, isn't it?'

'If you could,' Tess said apologetically. 'I can't. I've tried, but I don't seem able to get it across.'

'No. Because . . . but you know all that, of course. And now, Tess, if you'll just hand me that milk-jug, I'll glaze the pastry and put this fellow into the oven. You'll stay for luncheon?'

Tess shoved her bicycle into the Throwers' old shed and cooeed, heard an answering hail from the garden, and padded off down the path towards the sound. In the flower-beds as she passed dahlias nodded their heavy heads and when she brushed against

436

them, the rich scent of chrysanthemum beds, just bursting into bloom, met her nostrils.

The Throwers' garden was always fruitful, but as September got into its stride it seemed to make its maximum effort. Now, runner beans swarmed up their poles and along the strings, the blossoms long gone, the beans hanging in splendid bunches, whilst on a lower level sprout plants were beginning to form their first nobbles and winter cabbage, swedes and turnips were bushing out nicely.

Tess found Mrs Thrower and Cherie in the potato patch. Mrs Thrower was digging up the big, dark-green plants and Cherie, on hands and knees, was grubbing for the potatoes lying in the rich soil, every size from whales to sprats, as Mrs Thrower used to say.

Tess was seized with a sharp sense of *déjà vu*; how often, as a child, she had done just what Cherie was doing now, rejoicing over every potato found, rooting anxiously through the crumbly soil, heedless of black hands, split fingernails, or cold, wet knees! How they had enjoyed themselves, she and Janet, competing to find the biggest spud in the world, then sharing it when November 5th came round and the Throwers lit the bonfire they had been preparing all summer long and baked their home-grown potatoes in the embers.

They couldn't light bonfires now, of course. You didn't light fires after dark in wartime, not unless you wanted to face a jolly great fine and run the risk of bringing the enemy bombers homing in on you. But regardless of bonfires, you only had to look at Cherie's face to see that she was blissfully happy.

Cherie had stayed with her uncle and aunt until Marianne had been well enough to manage with a couple of visits a week, and then one morning Mrs Thrower had visited Marianne in hospital and had a long and confidential chat. As a result of that chat she had caught another bus and come surging confidently into the house in Unthank Road. She had had a private word with Uncle Phil and had then come into the living-room, where Tess was doing the crossword and Cherie was knitting khaki squares, and told the child that she was needed at Staithe Cottage.

'Our Jan scarce ever git back now she's in Scotland,' she

explained. 'And there's a deal of work to be done gettin' the Old House half-way decent, an' there's the two gardens, my jobs . . . well, tha's more'n I can cope with, tell the truth. So I thought if you'd like to move in alonga us, Cherie, why not? You'd catch the same school bus, an' you could hev the little back bedroom with all your truck in it – you'd be snug as a bug in a rug, I reckon.'

Tess had been visiting her sister at the time and had known nothing of the plans Mrs Thrower was hatching, though she had been uneasily aware, for several seeks, that Cherie must be a fish out of water in her uncle's town house with its small garden so close to the city. Uncle Phil and Auntie May had never really liked Marianne, and though they were sincerely sorry for her now, they had never had a close relationship with Marianne's daughter. Tess had racked her brains for a compromise, but Mrs Sugden simply didn't have the room to give Cherie a permanent bed and the Old House was still open to the winds of heaven – and the rains, as well. It had seemed, to Tess, that poor Cherie had no choice but to remain with her aunt and uncle until her circumstances changed.

But sitting beside Cherie on the sofa and remembering the tiny back bedroom at the cottage and the well-water, the tin bath before the fire, the smoky oil lamps, Tess waited for a polite refusal from her sister. It did not come. Cherie cast down her knitting and stared across at Mrs Thrower, whilst colour stole into her cheeks and a trembling smile curved her lips.

'Oh, *could* I?' she said simply. 'I would like that so much, Mrs Thrower. But the back bedroom's Dickie's and Podge's, isn't it? Wouldn't they mind?'

'Nah, they'll move into the bigger room. And they'll be tickled pink to have someone else do the washin' up,' Mrs Thrower assured her. 'Why, you could come right here an' now, if you want.'

It had not previously occurred to Tess that Cherie was actively unhappy with her aunt and uncle, but now she acknowledged it was so. Cherie was a polite young girl but like most young girls she had a life of her own to live, and she had been cut off, in one stroke, from her friends, her family and her own home. Her tentative interest in boys had died as her anxiety for her mother grew, and Tess realised now that she herself had not given much time to her sister. She had been desperately busy with the Old House, applying to the authorities for building materials to get at least a semblance of order back in her home, working extra hours at Willow Tree Farm so that she might come into the city to hospital visit, and Mal's loss had gnawed at her ceaselessly. No wonder the poor kid was staring at Mrs Thrower as though she had suddenly grown wings and a halo!

'Oh, *could* I?' Cherie said again, looking, this time, at Tess. 'Would it be awfully rude, Tess? Uncle Phil and Auntie May are very kind, but . . .'

'There's a litter o' kittens at the Ropes', I've always fancied havin' a kitten,' Mrs Thrower mused. 'Wi' two of us to give an eye to it, I reckon we could manage. Why, my woman, if you come wi' me now you could have the choosin' of it. There's a ginger one, prettiest thing you ever did see, an' a grey – tha's pretty an' all – an' a couple o' tabbies.'

'I don't think it would be rude at all, poppet,' Tess said, watching Cherie's suddenly bright face. 'Poor love, I've been so busy that I hadn't thought how dull you must be finding it.'

'Not dull,' Cherie said quickly. 'Only a bit lonely, at times. Would you come to see me at weekends, Tess? When you're off work, I mean?'

'She'll come to stay, weekends,' Mrs Thrower said heartily. 'There's allus room for Tess in Staithe Cottage, do she hev to sleep on the floor! Now pop an' put a few things in a bag, Cherie, whiles I hev a word wi' your aunt. I've already talked to Mr Delamere, an' he thinks it's for the best, like.'

It had been settled as quickly as that, with Tess dividing her time, when she was off duty, between Marianne, the Knoxes and Staithe Cottage. And true to her promise, Mrs Thrower always managed to find her a bed, when she was able to stay over for a night or two.

'Hey, it's *Tess*!' Cherie exclaimed now, squatting back on her heels and rubbing a dirty hand across her pink and shining face. 'We're lifting the main crop – I've found millions, I'm having the biggest for tea tonight, baked, with a tiny bit of butter!'

'I bags the next biggest, then,' Tess said, entering into the spirit

439

of the thing and bending down to rescue a marble-sized spud which energetic forking had sent tumbling several feet away. She turned to Mrs Thrower. 'All right if I stay over, Mrs T? Only I'm off all day tomorrow.'

'Cor, we'll hev to find you a few extra jobs, then,' Mrs Thrower said, digging her fork deep into the loam and leaning across it to give Tess a hug. 'Lovely to hev you, my woman. An' that in't just spuds for tea, either – there's runner beans what me an' your sister picked earlier, an' a savoury meat roll what young Cherie say is the best she's ever tasted!'

'Meat? I bet it's sausage,' Tess teased, hefting the box of potatoes. 'Shall I take this into the shed?'

'That 'ud be a help,' Mrs Thrower acknowledged. 'And that in't sausage meat, either, Miss Clever! That's minced mutton.' She sighed and dug into the next plant. 'Last one, Cherie, then we'll go an' make ourselves a nice cuppa.'

When Tessa had stayed at Staithe Cottage earlier she had slept on the sofa with a couple of thin blankets thrown over her, but now the weather was growing chillier, so Mrs Thrower produced a sleeping bag which she had rescued from the Old House.

'Here you are, Tess,' she said, displaying her find. 'That'll keep you warmer than them thin old things you had last time. Awright for you, is it?'

'It used to be Daddy's,' Cherie remarked, stroking it. 'Lucky you, Tess – mind you, I do love my little bed in the back room. I don't think I'll swap.'

Tess looked affectionately at the sleeping bag; a relic of Peter's schooldays, it was worn and rather dirty but perfectly service-able, and she found she was really looking forward to snuggling up in it in the creaking, comfortable kitchen by the remains of the fire. She had had a tiring day on the farm, but she knew that the Throwers were early risers and therefore went to bed early, so she would not have long to wait. And sure enough, they ate their meal, Cherie growing competitive over the size of the potatoes and vowing she had personally dug all the big ones, washed and wiped up, listened to the last news on the wireless, and then Dickie, Podge and Cherie announced that they would take the dog for a walk whilst Mrs Thrower damped the fire down and Mr Thrower went out to throw a piece of scorched net curtain over his chrysanths, in case of frost.

'They'll sell come Sat'day, war or no war,' Mrs Thrower said placidly when Tess asked why they were still growing flowers. 'Folk need cheerin' up now an' then.'

The dog was a raggedy urchin of a creature, all legs and ears, which Podge had found wandering by the Broad, collarless, a couple of months back. They named him Fluster, loved him dearly, and walked him first thing in the morning and last thing at night.

'Do else he puddle,' Cherie said, in the vernacular. 'Auntie Bess don't like it when he puddle.'

Tess opened her mouth to correct her, then closed it again. Until Marianne had come along she herself had spoken in dialect at home and without it at school. Marianne had objected and she had changed, but Tess was no Marianne. Let the poor kid take on protective coloration if it makes her happier, she decided. And she is happy; no one could doubt it.

So she accompanied the three youngsters and the dog on a quick scamper up Deeping Lane, and was amused by the way Cherie bossed them about and frequently exchanged insults with Dickie, who was her own age, though she was more circumspect with Podge.

Tess couldn't help glancing at the Old House as she passed it, though. Gaunt in the moonlight, the glassless windows seemed to glare at her, the mangled thatch to reproach her. Almost four months had passed, but little had been done to repair any of the damage because it was impossible to do anything major as yet. No money, no building materials, no time. But when the reeds were cut in January, Mr Thrower was going to ask the various authorities for permission to retimber the roof and rethatch it. At least it would be a start.

Returning to the cottage, the four of them and Fluster ran up the garden path and burst into the kitchen, to find Mrs Thrower making up the sofa as a bed. She turned and beamed at them as they entered.

'Had a good run round, then? Now off with you lads, so Tess

441

can get herself into this here sleepin' bag, which baffle me.' She turned to Tess. 'Are you sure you can get inside of it, my woman?'

'I'm sure,' Tess said, whilst Cherie giggled. 'And don't you laugh, Cherie Delamere, or you'll find yourself sharing your bed!'

'I wouldn't mind,' Cherie asserted. 'If you didn't mind Ginny and Fluz sharing as well, of course.' She bent and plucked the kitten up from its perch on the hearth. 'Come on, Ginny, beddy-byes! Come on, Fluster, you've had your run, now you must settle down.'

'She need somethin' to cuddle,' Mrs Thrower said a little defensively when the boys and Cherie had clattered up the bare wooden stairs. 'You know me, I don't believe in treatin' animals like humans . . .'

'I remember the times you told the boys and Jan that you wouldn't feed a pet animal whilst there was a child in need,' Tess said. 'What happened to change your mind?'

'Oh, I'm a bit older 'n' wiser now,' Mrs Thrower said, pulling a fat pillow out of the side cupboard and placing it at the top of the sleeping bag. 'And Cherie, she need pets. Your stepma din't bring her up to show much . . . but you can cuddle a kitten or a dog without feelin' self-conscious. I in't a lot of good wi' words, Tess, but I reckon you an' my kids had suffin' poor Cherie don't – an' I don't mean parents, either.'

'Love,' Tess said, struggling out of her cardigan. 'Why not say it?'

'Oh, well, as to that . . . now come on, get undressed do it'll be mornin' before I see you squoze down in this here contraption.'

So whilst Mrs Thrower laid the breakfast table, Tess undressed and climbed nimbly into the sleeping bag, then squiggled on to the sofa.

'There you are!' she said, laying her head on the pillow with a sigh of satisfaction. 'Good-night, Auntie Bess; sweet dreams.'

Whether it was the moonlit walk, or the enormous supper, or simply being rather restricted by the sleeping bag Tess could not have said, but as soon as her lids closed she plunged straight into a dream. She was walking up the short drive to the Old House with the moon at the full shining down upon her, and the wind in

442

the trees making gentle music – she almost recognised the tune though it was too soft for positive identification. She got to the front door, but it was closed, and though she knocked and thought she heard someone moving within, no one came to let her in. Even in the dream this did not worry her, however. She simply set off round the side path towards the back door. I'll go inside and then we can talk, she found herself thinking. It's been a long time – we'll have such a lot to talk about!

Half-way to the back door, however, she was stopped short. She paused, puzzled, then tried to walk forward again, only to be prevented by what she realised was a vast glass wall, which reared, sky-high, from the house right down to the Broad. Perplexed, she retraced her steps, then turned and hurried forward once more. Again the glass stopped her.

Baffled and beginning to be a little afraid, she banged on the glass, which quivered and shivered and gave off a rather menacing, plangent note, and as she did so the back door opened and someone came out.

It was Mal! He was wearing a huge, off-white woollen sweater and stained and shabby trousers, clothing she had never seen on him before, but she would have recognised him anywhere, though she saw, with a small sense of shock, that he was limping as he hurried towards her.

'Mal! Oh Mal, you're all right! Oh, my darling . . .'

The glass wall stopped him, as it was stopping her. He stared, as she had, then walked back a few paces, turned . . . and ran at the wall. She screamed; she knew what would happen, saw him collide with the invisible barrier, stagger back, hands to his face, blood running . . .

And woke.

'Well, my woman? Hev a good night?'

Mrs Thrower had pulled back the kitchen curtains, riddled the fire, put the kettle on, and Tess had slumbered right through it. But now she sat up, rubbed her eyes and yawned.

'Fine, thanks. I had an odd dream very soon after I lay down which woke me up, but I went back to sleep quite quickly, and didn't wake again till just now. Oh, isn't it lovely to wake to a fire?

First one up at the farm has to do all the things you've just done. It makes me feel wickedly luxurious to lie here and watch the flames flickering!'

Mrs Thrower chuckled. 'Wickedly luxurious – what a one you are, Tess! Hens are layin' well – want scrambled egg on toast? Wi' fried tomatoes on the side?'

'Oh, please,' Tess said, heaving herself out of the sleeping bag. 'Can I have some water? I'll take it through to Cherie's room – bet she isn't up yet.'

'You'd be wrong, my woman,' Mrs Thrower said placidly, heaving the big iron kettle off the fire and pouring steaming water into a blue-and-white enamel basin. 'She's back at school, remember, wi' a bus to catch. She in't come through yet, but she won't be long.'

And indeed, when Tess, clothes clutched in one hand, the bowl of water in the other, shuffled into Cherie's tiny cupboard of a room, her sister was up, dressed and brushing her hair, peering at herself in the tiny round shaving mirror which Mr Thrower had hung on the wall as a concession to her femininity. She saw Tess's reflection as she came through the doorway and turned to smile at her.

'Morning, Tess! I've got double maths for the first two periods, would you believe? So Stella and I have bagged seats at the back and we're going to get on with our knitting whilst Miss Wicklow drones on. I mean, if I'm going to finish that baby's coat *ever*, I need to spend some time on it.'

The baby coat in question, made out of a carefully unravelled pink jumper which had once been Tess's pride and joy, had been under construction ever since war had been declared and was still far from finished.

'What about maths, though? From what I remember of your last report it isn't exactly your best subject,' Tess objected. 'Oughtn't you to concentrate on your sums, poppet?'

'No. I'm useless at maths and trying to teach me is a waste of time and effort, Miss Wicklow has said so many a time,' Cherie said with unimpaired cheerfulness. 'What are you doing today, Tess? Coming into the city? Staying with Auntie Bess?'

Tess stood her basin of water on the washstand, pulled off her

444

pyjamas and began to soap herself with Cherie's tiny sliver of pink soap. 'Dunno. I had a weird dream last night, I might . . . I might just walk up to the Old House and have a look around. If I come into the city, though, I'll meet you after school and we can come back together. How would that be?'

'Oh, wizard,' Cherie said, her face brightening. 'I'm ever so proud of you, you know, Tess. I tell everyone you're my sister!'

Tess laughed. 'I'm rather proud of you, too,' she said lightly. 'Now do get a move on, poppet, or you'll miss your bus.'

The Old House looked sad rather than frightening with the soft September sunshine lighting up its damaged façade. Tess walked quietly up the front path, then patted the rosy old bricks beside the front door.

'Poor old place,' she said softly. 'What a thing to happen after three hundred years! Never mind, as soon as we can we'll put you back in order again. You see, you'll be good as new.'

She was still standing there, her hand on the warm bricks, when the most extraordinary thing happened.

The telephone rang. Quite loudly and distinctly, as though it was the most natural thing in the world, the telephone bell tinkled out its message that someone was trying to get in touch.

Tess jumped for the front door, only to find it locked and, presumably, bolted. The phone rang on. With her heart banging so loudly that it almost deafened her, Tess tore round the side of the house, half expecting a glass wall to rear between her and the back door. But she reached it without obstruction and grabbed the handle. It turned, but when she pushed there was a moment's resistance before it creaked slowly open.

Tess dived across the room and up the short hall to where the telephone had once stood on its small, half-moon table, but even as she entered, the ringing stopped. And the table wasn't there, anyway, it was one of the many pieces of furniture now in the repository in Norwich.

I'm going mad, Tess told herself. The telephone wasn't ringing, it couldn't have been, it isn't even here! But she walked up the hallway to make completely sure, and when she had checked that neither the half-moon table nor the instrument itself were in the hall, she turned, about to retrace her steps, feeling frightened now as well as puzzled. First she had the oddest dream she had ever heard of, and now she was definitely hearing things. Unless, of course, it was a ghost, but whoever heard of a ghostly telephone?

She was walking back down towards the kitchen when the ringing started again. *Trrring-trrring, trrring-trrring.* And there was the telephone, sitting on the fourth stair from the bottom, covered in dust and dirt but definitely ringing. Tess dived for it and snatched the receiver up in mid-ring, then held it to her ear.

Nothing. Or . . . or was that breathing? She went cold, icicles of fear prickling up and down the nape of her neck. She was suddenly absolutely certain that there was someone on the other end of the line, simply breathing softly, waiting for her to make a move.

The receiver was half-way back to its rest when it occurred to Tess that the first thing one usually said on picking up a ringing telephone was 'Hello?' Perhaps the caller was waiting for her to speak! Hastily, she clapped the receiver to her ear and spoke into the mouthpiece.

'Hello? Er Barton 123 . . .'

'Issss thatttt Misss . . .' – a spluttering cut the weird, otherworldly voice off in mid-sentence.

'Yes,' Tess said baldly. The voice, since it had rung the Old House, must want to speak to either Cherie or herself. 'Who's speaking?'

'I'mmm frommm RAFFFF . . .' splutter, hiss, cackle, went the line. And then, almost miraculously, cleared for a moment. 'I believe you're a friend of Pilot Officer Chandler?'

'Yes! Oh, yes,' Tess said shakily. 'Have you . . . is there . . .?'

'He's in a POW camp in Germany,' the voice said matter of factly. 'I've been trying to ring you for the besttt parttt offff threeeee dayssss . . .'

The voice tailed off into unendurable crackling, which ended abruptly with a click and a buzz; they had been cut off. With wet and shaking hands, Tess replaced her receiver. She was dizzy with delight, faint with incredible, almost unendurable relief and happiness. She stared down at the dirty telephone for a moment, trembling like a leaf, then raced out of the back door, down the

446

path, along the lane and into Staithe Cottage, where Mrs Thrower was making bread and covering the kitchen with a light dusting of flour.

'Hello! What's eatin' you?' she said breezily as Tess began to splutter about her strange experience. 'Calm down my woman, do I'll never get the story outa you.'

'I answered the phone in the Old House . . . some chap was on the line . . . Mal's alive, he's alive . . . I always knew he was,' Tess stammered. 'Mal's *alive*, Auntie Bess, and a prisoner of war in Germany!'

'Well, in't that wonderful?' Mrs Thrower said cautiously, giving Tess a very odd look indeed. 'Sit you down, my woman, an' tell me about it. Tell you what, don't say nothin' for a moment, I'll make us a nice cuppa.' She turned to the kettle, saying over her shoulder as she did so: 'Meet the postman half-way, did you? Got a letter?'

'No, I *told* you, it was a t-t-telephone call,' Tess stuttered. 'At the Old House. I didn't know the phone was still connected, so it gave me ever such a fright when it first rang. But it's all right, Mrs Thrower, I'm not going mad, it happened! Oh *God*, I'm so happy!'

'A telephone call, at the Old House?' Mrs Thrower said incredulously. 'But the wires was all burned up, my love. You couldn't ha' heard the phone ring there!'

'I did,' Tess insisted. 'I spoke to some man from his station, honestly I did. He asked if I was a friend of Mal's and said he'd been trying to get in touch for three days, and then the phone went all funny and we got cut off. But it doesn't matter, because now I know Mal's safe.'

'Well, that's wonderful news,' Mrs Thrower said. She poured the tea and handed Tess a cup. 'Drink that, dearie; that'll make you feel more yourself.'

Tess took a sip, then put the cup down and rose to her feet. 'I don't know what you think, Mrs Thrower, but I promise you the telephone rang, I answered it, and the chap said Mal was safe and a prisoner of war in Germany. I'm not going to try to ring from the Old House, because I admit the line was awful, crackly and horrid, but I *am* going to bike into the village and phone from the public call box. I want the details, you see – where he is and how I can get in touch.' She put her arms round Mrs Thrower's plump shoulders and kissed the side of her face. 'Honestly, I'm not round the bend, I'm just . . . oh, just so *relieved*.'

'Oh, well tha's eased my mind,' Mrs Thrower said, doubt in every syllable. 'Off you go then – ride careful!'

'I will, Tess said blithely, and cycled off at top speed, singing as she went.

An hour later she cycled back, a good deal more slowly. When she reached the Old House she stopped outside and stood very still, staring. The house stared back. Tess looked up, to the spot where the telephone wire had once looped across the drive and into the house. It looped still. Well, of course it did, because she'd had a telephone conversation with a man from Mal's RAF station only an hour or so earlier. She really should go inside now, pick up the receiver and check that the phone was still working. But she did not. What was the point? She had rung station HQ, but though everyone had been perfectly polite, no one had admitted telephoning her.

Not that it matters, Tess told herself now, still staring at the Old House, because I *know* that Mal's alive. Perhaps I'm going a bit dotty, perhaps I imagined the telephone call because I need to know that he's all right officially, but unofficially, in my heart, I'm sure. That's enough – isn't it?

Back at Staithe Cottage, Mrs Thrower was very solicitous, especially when Tess had to admit that no one at Mal's Air Force station had apparently telephoned her.

'There, love, you know what you know,' she said comfortably. 'Want another round of bread and butter? I love it when it's fresh baked.'

'He's *alive*,' Tess told Cherie fiercely later that same evening, when they were walking Fluster past the Old House. 'Mrs Thrower thinks I went a bit mad or heard things or something, but I didn't, Cherie. I'm not an idiot, I really did speak to someone from the station. It must be someone who's – who's on ops, or on leave, but I did speak to someone. And I'm not a loony, either.'

'Why don't we go in and check the phone?' Cherie said. 'Only my torch is a bit glimmery; what's yours like?'

'It's good,' Tess decided, fishing it out of her pocket and flashing it quickly down at her feet. 'Come on, then. Why not?'

Together, hand in hand, with the dog roaming ahead, the two girls went round the back of the house and let themselves in. They clattered through into the hallway and then stood looking down at the telephone, squatting innocently on the fourth stair from the bottom. Fluster stared at it too, large ears cocked expectantly.

'It *looks* all right,' Cherie said after a moment. 'Go on, pick it up, see if it's connected.'

'I know it is,' Tess said. Her heart was beating so loudly that it was making her body vibrate. 'I told you, I spoke to . . .'

Abruptly, she snatched the receiver off its cradle and held it to her ear. After a moment, slowly, she handed it to Cherie.

There was no sound. Nothing. No clicks or buzzes or sounds of breathing. It was dead.

'Oh,' Cherie said slowly. 'Well, you said you were cut off, didn't you? It's just that it's still cut off, Tess, that's all.' She replaced the receiver almost reverently and took Tess's hand, carrying it to her face and rubbing it against her cheek. 'It's all right, Tess, I know you spoke to someone, you aren't going off your head, really.'

She turned away from the telephone, her torch describing an arch which included the hall floor and the inside of the heavy oak front door. Tess hissed in her breath and Cherie clutched her.

'What? What's the matter?' she said, her voice echoing round the empty house. 'I nearly died when you grabbed me, Tess – it was you, wasn't it?'

'Yes, you clown,' Tess said. 'Swing your torch round again, poppet. I thought I saw something when the light fell on the front door. There! See?'

Something square and white glimmered in the torchlight.

'It's a letter,' Cherie said, going slowly over to it. Fluster, nose cautiously extended, crept after her. 'Tess – it's addressed to you!' She bent and retrieved the envelope, then handed it to Tess. 'How odd! Well, I suppose it isn't all that odd, really. Perhaps the postman dropped it in the road and someone didn't realise the house was empty and shoved it through the letter-box.'

'Anything's possible,' Tess agreed. 'Come on, let's get back home, I want to read it and I don't intend to do so by torchlight. Where's Fluster?'

Fluster, hearing his name, came bounding out of the shadows causing both girls, already strung up, to give a shriek which made him bark, and that made them laugh and considerably eased the tension.

'What idiots we were,' Tess said as they made their way back to Staithe Cottage. 'I'm so sorry, Cherie darling, for acting daft. Never mind, we'll make a nice hot cup of cocoa and drink it and . . .'

'And read your letter,' Cherie interrupted. 'It wasn't handwriting you knew, was it?'

'I don't know, I scarcely noticed anything, really. Come on, race you to the cottage.'

They burst into the kitchen, to find it empty.

'Mr Thrower will have gone up to bed and Mrs T will be down the garden,' Tess said. She took off her mac and hung it behind the door and then fished the envelope out of the pocket. She examined the writing, which was strange to her, and then the postmark.

'It was posted yesterday,' she announced, and slit the envelope. 'Hello – it's from Mal's station!'

'What does it say? Oh, what does it say?' Cherie was demanding, when the back door opened and Mrs Thrower came back into the room. She was carrying a dark lantern and stood it down on the draining board before turning to the girls.

'Last visit, anyone?' she said. 'Lantern's all lit . . . off you go now.' She looked from one to the other. 'Wha's up, then? Cat got your tongues?'

Silently, Tess handed over the letter. Mrs Thrower frowned down at it.

'Wha's all this, then? *Dear Miss Delamere, it gives me much pleasure to inform you* . . .' she broke off with a little scream, then dropped the letter and threw her arms around Tess. 'Oh my dear,

450

in't that wonderful news? I'm that glad for you, Tess, I declare I could dance a jig!'

'What? What does the letter say? Tess, how can you be so irritating?' Cherie all but screamed. 'Read it to me . . . no, I'll read it for myself!'

Tess pulled herself out of Mrs Thrower's embrace and flung her arms, in her turn, round Cherie.

'It's confirmation!' she said in a high, breathless voice. 'He's a prisoner of war in Germany. They've sent me his prison number, his address, everything, so I can write letters, sends parcels . . . oh Cherie, the *relief*! Mal's alive, just like I said! I'm the happiest person in the whole world!'

Marianne had to be told, of course. She was no longer at the Norfolk and Norwich Hospital but at a special Burns Unit where they were doing their best to repair the damage done to her, so on her first day off after the letter's arrival Tess went, by train and bus, across the country to tell her stepmother the good news.

She reached the Unit and was taken into the Day Room for Marianne's ward, a pleasant, airy room with large french windows opening on to a terrace, around which dahlias bloomed. The room wasn't crowded but there were a couple of women knitting and a man listening to a wireless set so the two of them, after their initial greetings, got some privacy by carrying a couple of chairs out on to the terrace and basking in the autumn sunshine, whilst Tess showed Marianne the precious letter.

'What marvellous news, my dear, even though you've still got a long wait ahead of you before you meet again,' Marianne said, laying the sheet down on her lap. The brilliant dentist had given her an excellent set of false teeth which looked amazingly real, and she had a wig of softly waving hair which fell rather pleasingly across her scarred brow. Shad had come a long way from the blackened figure on the bed which had so horrified Tess months before.

And it wasn't only Marianne's looks that had changed. Suffering, Tess thought now, had left its mark on her character. Indeed, it had improved her greatly. Now, Marianne was patient, thoughtful and sensible. She read the books she was brought instead of thanking the donor prettily and then throwing them down in a corner. She listened to the wireless, not just the war news but other programmes. She laughed over comedies, cried over music, enjoyed plays, opera, all sorts. For the first time since Tess had known her, Marianne seemed able to appreciate points of view other than her own. The tragic accident had made her slow down, stop to consider, and as a result she even thought before she spoke, so that hurtful remarks, Tess assumed, were often swallowed unsaid. Even her lost beauty, which had once meant everything to her, was no longer paramount: Marianne had been heard to say that character was as important as looks, and to mean it, what was more.

'I'm glad you're pleased,' Tess said gently, now. 'Because I know you must have wondered whether I was doing the right thing. We'd only known each other for about a week, but I suppose loving someone is always a bit of a gamble, and with Mal it's a gamble well worth taking. And as for waiting – well, waiting when you know that he'll be coming back is sheer bliss compared with waiting and secretly wondering if you'll ever set eyes on him again.'

'I'm sure it is,' Marianne said. 'Sometimes I wonder if Maurice and I will ever marry, you know. But if we don't, I'll understand. He – he could do very much better. I'm not getting any younger.'

Tess laughed. 'Who is? But don't worry about it, Marianne. Take each day as it comes and enjoy each one as far as you possibly can. That's what I made up my mind to do, when I didn't know what was happening to Mal.'

'I do try,' Marianne said. 'Did I tell you, they say I can go home for a few months, whilst scar tissue grows. I've told Maurice and he says he'll take me up to Scotland, to a quiet little hotel he knows, or down to Cornwall. I said we couldn't stay away for months, and he said why not? He said Cherie could come with us and go to a local school . . . he was awfully kind, Tess. But . . .'

'But what?'

'He's being too damned *noble*,' Marianne said with a return of her old fretfulness. 'I feel like today's good cause, not like a much-loved fiancée. And I don't like it.'

Tess giggled. 'You go away with him,' she advised. 'After a

few weeks in each other's company, you may both decide that marriage would be a mistake. You've changed a lot Marianne – for the better, I might add. If Maurice has any sense he'll realise what a pearl he's got and hang on with both hands.'

It was Marianne's turn to giggle. 'Oh, Tess, you do me good! But what will Cherie say? She's at the end of her school life, she may well feel deprived and annoyed with us if we try to move her now.'

'I imagine she'll stay with the Throwers, given half a chance,' Tess said at once. 'She's awfully happy with them and although she'll take her school certificate next June to please you, she wants to leave school then. She wants to join the WAAF.'

'The uniform will suit her,' Marianne said. 'You wanted to join the WAAF once, didn't you, Tess? I stopped you from very selfish motives I'm afraid, and I'm ashamed to say I'm still very glad you didn't go off and leave us. Oh my dear, what would I have done without you?'

Tess felt tears form in her eyes; Marianne had remembered about her stepdaughter's longing to join the WAAF and wasn't ashamed to say that she appreciated Tess's sacrifice. It touched her deeply, but she couldn't let Marianne see it.

'Well, I shall get a vicarious thrill out of seeing Cherie in Air Force blue,' she said cheerfully. 'I did wonder whether to put in for the WAAF again now that you and Cherie are both settled, but I decided not to. I'm very lucky at Willow Tree Farm, the Sugdens are kind and appreciative and the girls are lovely, I couldn't ask for better friends. So I'll stay very happily where I am for the duration.' She got to her feet. 'It took me half a day to get here and it'll take me half a day to get back, so I had better be going, but is there a canteen or a dining-room where we might get a cup of tea before I leave? I'm parched.'

'You will have luncheon with me,' Marianne said firmly. 'No, don't shake your head, it's all arranged. Follow me – the dining-room is a good walk away and you will have to push my wheelchair.'

'Luncheon – lovely!' Tess said immediately. 'I thought it would be a sandwich on the station, this is luxury indeed. But what's this about a wheelchair?'

'Oh, it's only temporary, whilst my thigh heals,' Marianne said airily. 'They took a strip of skin off my thigh to make me a nice cheek, and it hasn't healed up as it ought. Walking far is painful, but it will clear up in a week or two. I have patience, now.'

She got to her feet and Tess bent over and kissed her, noticing for the first time that Marianne seemed to have shrunk.

'You're a very brave woman, and I love you,' she said quietly. 'I think Peter would have been tremendously proud.'

'Thank you, dear,' Marianne said composedly. She limped slowly back to her room and, sitting down on the bed to catch her breath, added: 'I love you too, you know. How nice it is to have such a daughter as you, Tess!'

Tess laughed. 'How nice it is to have such a mother as you, Marianne,' she echoed. 'And now, where's that wheelchair?'

Telling Marianne had been a pleasure, but telling Ashley was not. He was polite, but he could not hide his incredulity over her feelings.

'Of course I'm glad he's alive,' he said robustly. 'But dammit, girl, how can you know he's the right person for you? You knew him for a week, it might be years before he gets home, by then he could be in love with someone else! What you're suffering from isn't love, it's infatuation, it has to be. So don't try and wriggle out of our long friendship on the grounds that I'll spoil anything for this Malcolm fellow, because it won't wash. If you're sick of having me around, have the courage to say so!'

'I'm sick of having you around,' Tess said promptly.

'Oh, rubbish, you know you love me,' Ashley shouted indignantly. 'Or if you won't admit to that, at least admit you like me and enjoy having me around. You love it when we go for a spin, or to a dance, or when we visit old friends . . .'

'I know I do, but I'm just trying to tell you, friendship is fine, the other isn't.'

'The other? What's *the other* when it's at home?'

'Oh . . . lovership, I suppose,' Tess said, after a moment's thought. 'Ownership, too. Yes, that's it. No ownership, otherwise we'll call it a day, Ash.'

They had met on neutral ground, in Lyons café on the Walk, for high tea, but even so, they were quarrelling. At least, Tess wasn't, but Ashley's raised voice had already seized the attention of the people at adjoining tables. And he doesn't give a toss, Tess thought furiously. He doesn't regard other people as at all important. They can listen or not, it's no skin off his nose – but it jolly well is off mine. I don't like being the object of stares and smiles and you'd think, after goodness knows how many years of claiming he knows me as no one else does, he'd have cottoned on to that simple fact.

She said so. Ashley lowered his voice and then, infuriatingly, leaned across the table and kissed her full on the mouth. Tess drew back and slapped him – it rang out like a pistol shot – and Ashley said: 'Who's making an exhibition of themselves now, then?' and captured both her hands in his, smiling blandly when she shrieked at him, in a whisper, to let her go.

They made it up, of course. Ashley apologised abjectly, said he understood about the ownership bit, and behaved so beautifully in the cinema – the film was *Casablanca* – that Tess found it easy to forgive him, easy to believe that they could be friends after all.

He saw her on to her bus with a chaste kiss on the brow which made Tess giggle to herself; it had been the sort of kiss, she thought, that Archbishops or Popes bestow on an erring but still loved parishioner. But that was Ashley for you, and she knew that this time he would be good, because he understood, at last, that if he wasn't it was the end of what had been a pretty good friendship, by and large.

I'll miss being constantly badgered in a way, Tess mused to herself as the bus chugged slowly across Wroxham bridge and past Roys store. It was after ten o'clock and black as pitch outside, but the hump of the bridge was unmistakable and the bulk of Roys equally so. Indeed, from here on Tess would be on the alert so as not to miss her stop, because to find yourself a mile or two from your intended destination, just because you'd gone off into a dream and not remained alert, was a wartime hazard which she did not wish to face tonight.

But a glance round the bus reassured her on that score. The Ropes' eldest son, in his uniform, was sitting near the door. Good, company for half the walk, Tess thought with satisfaction, and

455

someone near enough to the door to watch out that the driver stops at the top of the lane. She relaxed back into her seat once more. She would spend the next ten or fifteen minutes thinking about Mal, since she seemed to have Ashley under control at last.

Seventeen

The relief which Tess had felt on hearing that Mal was a prisoner of war was destined to be short-lived, however. On a freezing cold January day in 1944 she had a brief letter from a young woman she had worked with at the Castle Museum. The girl had joined the WAAF but she and Tess had corresponded from time to time and now the young woman wrote to say that her brother had been killed in a POW camp.

He tried to escape, the letter said sadly. *He never could bear being cooped up. They caught him tunnelling under the wire and shot him.*

Tess had been stunned, shattered. She had telephoned Ashley and read the letter aloud in a trembling voice and he had assured her that Mal would be fine.

'He'll not be stupid enough to try for an escape bid, not this late in the game,' he said bracingly. 'From what you've told me, he seems to have settled in pretty well, by and large. Didn't you say they had amateur operatics and a drama group going? And that they're learning languages and stuff?'

'Oh, yes. Come to think of it, Mal talked about learning German – my God, Ash, do you think it's so that he can escape as well? D'you know, I can't imagine, now, why I was so complacent over his being taken prisoner. He could be killed easier, in a way, like a rat in a trap.'

Ashley chuckled. 'I like the simile, but I don't imagine Mal would! Don't be a little idiot, Tess. Worry about things when they happen, not if they happen. Make plans for the future, knit him gloves, anything which is sensible.'

'I know you're right, really,' Tess said resignedly. 'But Ash, I'm deathly scared and that's the truth.'

'Of course you are, you wouldn't be human if you weren't. But Tess darling, he's an independent sort of chap, Mal. He'll do the right thing, never you fret.'

'But Ash, remember he's an Aussie. He's used to the wide open spaces, to being free. Suppose he finds being imprisoned suffocating and decides that anything would be better that that?'

'Being shut up in the cockpit of an aircraft doesn't allow for displays of claustrophobia,' Ashley reminded her. 'Look, I've said before, he's a sensible bloke and he's got you to think of. He won't jeopardise your future together, I'm sure of it. He wants to get back to you, Tess! Look at it like that and before you know it you'll be together again.'

Ashley had never sounded so positive when speaking of Mal before, quite the reverse in fact. After a pause Tess said sulkily: 'But I thought you said I was just infatuated with Mal and he with me. Now you're saying he loves me so much that he'll stay in a prison camp rather than put himself in danger. You could equally well say he'd break out and run for it to be with me earlier.'

'Don't be so bloody-minded,' Ashley snapped. 'I'm not saying he's right to want to come back to you, especially since you seem determined to show me how nasty you can be, I'm telling you why he'll just sit on his arse and wait, the way you seem to want him to. Look, I know telling you that things are coming to a head over there, and that Mal will know it, doesn't mean you won't worry, but at least you may not worry so much.'

'Yes, I do see. Thanks, Ash. Sorry I was so horrible,' Tess said contritely. 'I'm just sick with worry and misery, to tell you the truth. I don't even seem able to think straight.'

'I know, sweetheart,' Ashley said, immediately comforting. 'I can see all too clearly what you're going through. You felt he was safe in the camp, simply sitting out the war and now, because of your friend's letter, you realise that there is a darker side to it. But there's no point in fruitless worrying, so stop it. Think about something else – the future, your work, me, anything – and face forward. Get it?'

'Yes. I'll be sensible and look to the future,' Tess said. 'Thanks, Ash, I couldn't ask for a better pal than you.'

'That's all right, sweetheart. And keep your pecker up, for Mal's sake if not for your own. How's Marianne?'

'She's very much better,' Tess said. 'She's going back in March for another operation to do something about her mouth, but she really is much better. I don't know whether she and Maurice really will marry, but they spend an awful lot of time together, and she's being sensible and optimistic, which is easier now that she's not in constant pain, she says.'

'Good, good,' Ashley said heartily. 'Tell you what, sweetheart, why don't you nip over to Blofield the next time you're free, and stay with my parents for a few days? They'd love to have you and it might do you good to get right away from Barton for a bit.'

'I might,' Tess said cautiously. 'They – they won't want to talk about the war, will they?'

'Oh, Tess, honestly!'

'Well . . . and Ash, what about the weather? If it's cold here, which it is, what'll it be like in Germany?'

'Cold as well, but from what I've heard the POWs have a good few tricks to keep warm and cheerful. Look, I must go . . . promise me to stop worrying and try to look on the bright side?'

'I promise I'll do my best,' Tess said. 'Sorry to be such a misery, Ash. It's the shock, I think. When I'd thought I'd faced everything I had to face and it was just a matter of waiting, someone suggested a possibility that – that wrecked my peace of mind. But you've made me see straighter, at any rate. I'll be okay.'

She rang off. She was in a public call box on Davey Place with a queue of people waiting patiently in the cold outside so she left the box immediately, smiling an apology at the queue. She pulled on her gloves, settled her hat more firmly on her head, and set off for the bus stop. She had three days off, because the frost was into the ground and accordingly farm work had eased up a bit. They couldn't plant or plough, the cows were all in and she, Susan and Molly had just finished whitewashing the insides of all the farm buildings, so Mr Sugden said she might as well have a few days off.

She had come into the city to try to buy some wool. Knitting was all the rage in weather like this, and Molly had just finished a blue woolly jumper which was as warm as it was pretty. Very envious, she and Susan had decided to emulate this feat of industry, and she had actually managed to buy some wool, though it was a rather uninspiring peachy-pink colour.

I wonder whether I might go out to Blofield now, Tess mused to herself, emerging at the top of Davey Place steps and regarding Castle Meadow, which seemed pretty bleak in the icy wind which swirled the dead leaves along in the gutters. If I just gave the Knoxes a ring . . .

She turned round abruptly, to hurry back to the telephone box she had just left, and collided with someone.

'Sorry,' they apologised in unison, and then exclaimed, equally in unison: 'It's you!'

'Yes, it's me,' Andy said. 'What a bit of luck, do you know I called in at Willow Tree Farm on my way to see Aunt Salter and they told me you were on three days' leave? I was going to pop in to the Throwers', because I knew the Old House had been burnt out, and Mrs Sugden told me you often went to Staithe Cottage. Only then some girl said you'd come into the city to buy knitting wool and mightn't be back till late. So I thought I'd come in myself and try to buy something unrationed for my tea and there you were – or rather, here you are!'

'Yes, here I am,' agreed Tess. 'What brings you to Norwich, Andy? It's been ages . . . well, years . . . since you were here last.'

'True enough. I've been abroad, but things are coming to a head over there, so they brought me back and I'm going to be deskbound for a bit. Working here and there, in London, Portsmouth . . . anywhere they can find room for me, I suspect. And that'll last until the summer, anyway.' He peered at her in the grey and cloudy afternoon light. 'What's up, love? You look a bit pale and peaky.'

'It's Mal, the chap I'm going to marry. Did I tell you I was going to marry an Aussie?'

'I don't recall it,' Andy said cautiously. 'It's been ages since we really talked Tess, and I – I don't always receive letters. Look, why don't we go along to the Scotch Tea-rooms and get ourselves some tea? Then we can talk in the warm.'

'So you see, I was feeling pretty depressed,' Tess said when she had brought Andy up to date with her affairs. 'Fancy you not knowing that Mal was a POW, or that Marianne had been badly burned in that explosion – I know you hardly ever answer my letters, but I did think they'd be saved for you.'

'Sometimes people don't know where I am, or they forward my letters but by the time they arrive I'm not there,' Andy said. 'I'm most awfully sorry about Mrs Delamere, Tess. What a dreadful thing to happen. I remember the hoard, of course – she got very cross when you called it that – and her French boyfriend, but that must have been in 'forty-two. I'm afraid Auntie hardly ever passes on what she would think of as "local gossip", though she told me about the Old House, of course. Dear me, you must have thought me a poor sort of friend not to write and offer my condolences. By the way, did you ever do any more digging around to find out about your real mother? Lord, what a pair of innocents we were – detecting away and never getting round really to *doing* anything!'

'It's my fault. I should have gone and visited Ziggy's sister, Mrs Whatsername,' Tess said. 'But at first I didn't want to go ahead by myself and then when the war came, and I found Mal, it simply didn't seem to matter.'

'And now?' Andy asked. He looked at her shrewdly. 'Now that you're killing time until Mal gets back? Wouldn't it be worth doing a bit of detecting now?'

'Do you know, I really ought to have a go,' Tess said slowly. 'Last time I talked to Ashley he said I should stop driving myself mad with fears that Mal would get shot trying to escape, and concentrate on the future, or on something which was really going to happen. I was wondering what to do over the next couple of days, so why not investigate a bit further? If Ziggy was my father, and I suppose he must have been, then I really would like to know more about him.'

'Good. Then we'll go visiting, shall we, find out what sort of a man he was? Someone must know, twenty years isn't that long a time.'

'Twenty-five years,' Tess corrected him. 'I'll be twenty-five in June.'

'Yes, all right, twenty-five,' Andy conceded. 'And so often, one

461

thing leads to another. You might start trying to find out about Ziggy, and end up finding out about your mother, as well. How she died, why your father was so secretive about his first marriage – that sort of thing.'

'Yes, I might,' Tess mused. She looked affectionately at Andy, taking in his spectacles, the way his hair bunched on the crown of his head, the gentle charm of him. 'Andy, you're one of the nicest people I know, you really don't change one bit. But how busy are you? I'd love to go detecting with you, but you're usually home for such a short time, and I wouldn't want to hog your company. How long will it be, this time, before you have to whizz off?'

Andy smiled back at her. 'I'm at your disposal for three days at least, then it's London again, I'm afraid. Look, we can make good use of the time and start tomorrow. Why don't we visit Mrs Whatsername – I know, it was Yallop, I remember because there's a fellow called Yallop in my platoon, he comes from Norfolk as well. We can easily find out where she lives, people in villages all know each other. In fact if you just said "Ziggy", someone would be bound to tell us his history. What about it, Tess? I bet Mrs Yallop would absolutely love to talk to you and me about times past. Old people love reminiscing; you should hear Aunt Hannah when she gets going!'

'Tomorrow sounds ideal,' Tess said, suddenly sure that Andy was right and visiting Mrs Yallop was a good thing to do. 'When shall we meet?'

On the bus joggling along towards Blofield, with Andy sitting beside her, a large bunch of chrysanthemums across his knees, Tess pondered on what they might discover, and asked herself why she had allowed Andy to talk her into investigating again, when she'd let sleeping dogs lie for so long. But the fact was, she knew, that she would have done anything which would take her mind off Mal and the possibility that he might be killed in some terrible way. What was more she also acknowledged, at last, that it had been a reluctance to upset the apple cart which had stopped her from questioning Peter years ago, when Ashley had first told her about her dead mother and the mysterious Ziggy. She hadn't wanted to hear, from Peter's own lips, that he wasn't her father.

I buried my head, like a stupid ostrich, and then Daddy was killed and I lost the chance of finding out the proper way, she told herself now. He would have told me the truth once I was old enough to understand, I'm sure he would. I convinced myself I didn't want to hurt or distress him, but was that really true? Wasn't it *me* that I didn't want to hurt or distress?

The bus rumbled to a halt and the conductor called 'King's Head!' Tess got to her feet and she and Andy jumped off the step, thanking the conductor as they did so.

'Shall we go to the churchyard first?' Andy said. 'So far as I can remember we cross the road at some point. Hey, mind, those aren't puddles, they're solid ice.'

'So they are,' Tess said, very nearly finding out the hard way and keeping her feet with difficulty. 'What'll we do in the churchyard, though? Looking at the graves isn't going to tell us a thing.'

'It's an excuse for going to see Mrs Yallop – we say we came over to put some flowers on your mother's grave, and got talking, and . . . well, you'll see when we beard the Yallop in her den.'

'Oh, so that's what the flowers are for,' Tess said. 'I thought it was a sweetener for Mrs Yallop.'

'Well, actually they are for her – old people appreciate a little gift. But putting flowers on a grave is an acceptable sort of thing to do,' Andy said. 'You should always try to do what's expected, then you don't take people by surprise. People hate being taken by surprise, it puts their backs up and when you want something from them, even information, you should try to start off on the right foot. Ah, there's a local. Let's see if he can tell us where Mrs Yallop lives.'

Tess followed Andy's eyes and saw an elderly man sprinkling a mixture of sand and salt on the pathway of his bungalow. When they drew level with him Andy leaned over the gate.

'Morning, sir. Nice morning.'

'Morning,' the old man said. He straightened, one hand on the small of his back. 'Bitter night. As hard a frost as we've had this year. Come off the 10.50, did you?'

463

'That's it,' Andy said. 'My friend nearly measured her length crossing the turnpike. She skidded on a frozen puddle.'

The old man laughed. 'Aye, when the ice is clear it's deceptive. Going to take a look at our parish church? It's a fine building. Don't miss the pews – the carvings are unique, y'know. There's two old fellers, some gargoyles – I call 'em gargoyles – and of course the poppyheads, real as you please. And the west window, and the brasses . . . yes, there's a great deal to see. There's a wall monument to Edward Paston and his family, they died at the time of Henry the Eighth, so they say. You won't be able to go up to the bell-tower, unless you'd like to wait a minute while I finish off this path and fetch a coat, but one of the bells was cast when William Shakespeare was a lad – think of that!'

'Goodness,' Tess said, since Andy seemed rather overcome by this rush of information. 'But we won't trouble you to take us up the tower because we're going to visit a – a friend of my mother's before we go back to the city. Her name's Yallop, but I'm afraid we don't know her address.'

'Oh aye, that'll be Betty Yallop, she lives in the Alley. It's the last cottage before the big house. You can't miss it. It's along the Street, on the right, just past the Post Office. D'you know the Swan public house? Well, that's just a tiddy bit further along, if you come opposite it, you've gone too far.'

He chuckled at his own joke and threw another handful of salt from the bag in his hand on to the pathway.

'Thanks very much,' Andy and Tess chorused just as the old man took a deep breath, no doubt to continue with his lecture on Blofield Parish church. 'Well, we'd best be getting along.'

They walked quickly down the road and went under the lychgate and along the mossy path to the great north door. 'We'd better go in, just in case he's watching. I wouldn't want to hurt his feelings,' Tess murmured. 'Just a quick visit, then we can cut up the Alley and back to the main village that way.'

'But she lives on the Alley, so why do we have to cut back to the main village?' Andy asked puzzled. 'That was what he said, wasn't it?'

'Well, yes, but the Alley is cut in two by the Turnpike road, and this end is more like a footpath, really, which goes from the church as far as the main road. When you cross over, the Alley starts again, and the houses are there. See?'

'Not really,' Andy said, examining the canopied monument to the Paston family. 'If it's that simple why did he come out with all that tarradiddle about the Swan and the post office and so on?'

'Because he thinks of it like that,' Tess said patiently. 'It's quicker for him, living on the corner of Stocks Lane, to go straight up, over the Turnpike and into the Street. It probably hasn't occurred to him that the Alley has two ends!'

'Oh, I see,' Andy said doubtfully. 'Right, we've been in here several minutes. Let's go.'

Mrs Yallop lived in a small, very old cottage built of crumbling, apricot-coloured bricks and surrounded by a tiny, overgrown garden. In order to get up the short path Ashley and Tess had to push their way through the crisply frosted veronica and hypericum bushes which overgrew the bricked pathway, whilst the beds were starred with the spears of frost-defying bulbs. The cottage and its garden were closely surrounded by ancient, leafless elms in which rooks and crows had nested in considerable numbers, and as Tess unlatched the gate the inhabitants overhead rose in a cloud, cawing and calling, swooping low to take a look at them, for all the world as though they considered the house and garden as much their property as their shaggy, swaying nests.

Reaching the green-painted front door Andy knocked, and Mrs Yallop answered the door so promptly that Tess suspected she had been watching them approach. She was a skinny, severe-looking woman with very clear blue eyes and thick grey hair cut in as vaguely nineteen-twenties bob. She stared at them.

'Yes? If it's insurance . . .'

Tess cleared her throat, then glanced appealingly at Andy. He rose to the occasion.

'Morning, Mrs Yallop. No, it's nothing to do with insurance, it's a personal matter. I'm Hubert Anderson and this is Tess Delamere. You don't know either of us, but you used to know Tess's mother, I believe – she was Leonora Meadowes before she married. She – Leonora that is – died when Tess was only three so she

465

can't remember much about her. We wondered whether you'd mind telling us a bit about her?'

'Leonora Meadowes? Yes, I call her to mind.' The blue eyes scanned Tess shrewdly. 'You've a look of her, I'll give you that. Pleased to meet you both, I'm sure. You'd best come in, then.'

The two of them followed the old lady into a narrow hallway and were shown into a small living-room with a low ceiling and a log fire – unlit – in the grate.

'Sit yourselves down,' Mrs Yallop said, indicating a chintz-covered sofa. 'I'll just put a match to the fire – I was just about to light it, I always do after breakfast. It's powerful cold, wouldn't you say?'

'Shall I light the fire?' Andy said diffidently. 'I don't need matches, I've got my lighter.' He produced it, and whirled the little wheel with his thumb until a flame shot up, blue and gold.

'Well, thank you,' Mrs Yallop said. 'It draws well, that fire, I don't ever have to persuade it. I shan't be a moment, I'll just put the kettle on.'

She headed for the doorway but Tess cleared her throat and she stopped short.

'Umm . . . we brought you some flowers. Would you like to take them now, and put them in water? She held out the armful of gold and bronze chrysanthemums. 'It's a bit of luck that your curtains are autumn colours,' she said chattily. 'These will look really lovely in that dark-green vase in the window.'

'I always have flowers indoors, fresh out of my garden,' Mrs Yallop said rather defensively, but as she held out her arms for the bouquet her face softened and she began to smile. 'Not that there's much around this time of year, even my snowdrops are thinking twice about showing colour in this frost. Of course when Hubby was alive he kept me going all through the winter with chrysanths, but I can't give 'em the attention they need. As for buying flowers . . . have you seen the price of 'em in the shops?' She hissed in her breath. 'I'll just get that tea, then we can talk.'

She went over to the little round table in the window and picked up the green vase, then left the room. Andy, who had been kneeling before the grate, sat back on his heels as the flames caught hold. 'There!' That'll be blazing in two minutes and I do

466

love a log fire.' He lowered his voice. 'Said flowers would go down well, didn't I?'

'Know-all,' Tess said equally softly. 'Should I have offered to help get the tea?'

'No, because if the kitchen's still untidy from breakfast she wouldn't like you to see,' Andy said. 'Come and sit down . . . I imagine the sofa's for visitors and that lovely old rocking chair with all the cushions is for the householder.'

They were barely seated, however, before a clatter announced the arrival of Mrs Yallop, with a small, highly polished trolley on which she had arranged all the paraphernalia of tea-making, a cake on a blue willow-patterned plate and the green vase, now filled with chrysanthemums.

'Here we are, all ready,' she said, bringing the trolley to a halt beside the rocking chair. 'Now who takes milk? Sugar?'

Tea poured and served – Tess declining cake, Andy accepting a large slice – Mrs Yallop looked across at Tess.

'Well, Miss, I knew your mother as a child because I taught at the village school as a pupil teacher for a bit, and she was in my class. Later, I didn't see so much of her.'

'Do you have any photographs?' Tess asked. 'I – I believe she was friendly with your brother, Ziggy, when she was young.'

'Ah, Ziggy,' Mrs Yallop's face softened as it had when she took the flowers. 'He was the youngest of us, the only boy. I brought him up, you could say. It was the way of things then, the eldest girl would take on the youngest child, and that was me and Ziggy. Yes, now you mention it of course Leonora and Ziggy were about the same age so they're probably in the same school groups. I wonder if I might find up a few photographs . . .'

She got carefully to her feet and went over to a bureau which stood against the wall, presently returning with a small cardboard box.

'Here we are! Ziggy at the village school – he's in the back row and Leonora is just in front of him, she's got a ribbon in her hair.'

For the first time, Tess looked hungrily at a photograph of her mother as a child and saw what Peter must have seen – the likeness to herself. Apart from the old-fashioned clothing and the fact that Leonora's hair was pinned back from her face, the

467

photo might have been of Tess when she was eight or nine. But it wasn't only at Leonora she was looking. Ziggy took the eye. He was a curly-headed boy with one stocking wrinkled down and a wicked grin. So far as she could judge she did not physically resemble him, but that was scarcely surprising since she was so like her mother.

'Ziggy was ten then, which would make your mother about the same,' Mrs Yallop said. 'And this one was taken when Ziggy first got his motor bike – you can see how proud he was of the wretched thing. I hated that motor bike, I knew it was dangerous, knew he'd do something rash, but you can't tell lads anything, they have to make their own mistakes. Why, if it hadn't been for that dratted bike . . . but there you are, it was all a long time ago.'

She held out the second photograph and Tess took it and saw that the naughty, lively boy had become a handsome, lively young man with a gleam in his eye and hair slicked back, though you could see it was going to curl again just as soon as the camera clicked and moved on.

'There's another school one somewhere . . . it's the class reunion one, if only I can find it. You see several of the children went from the village school into city schools – Ziggy got to the C.N.S. and your mother went to the High School – so they had this reunion each year. It must be here somewhere . . .'

A rattling on the front door knocker made her look up, frowning, and then get to her feet. She handed the box to Andy, who was nearest.

'Here, you have a look, Mr Anderson. That'll be the insurance man; never misses. I'll be as quick as I can.'

She rustled out of the room and Andy, who had been sitting at one end of the sofa whilst Tess sat at the other, moved up so that they could both look at the box's contents.

'Wedding photos . . . gosh, that must be Mrs Yallop at her wedding, she was a lot older than Ziggy, almost old enough to be his mother, I should think . . . yes, he's in the group photo, he looks about fourteen . . . and this one's of another wedding . . . a studio portrait of a *very* plain girl . . . two babies in the usual baby-pose . . . what's this?'

'Certificates,' Tess said, peering at the forms which Andy had pulled out from the bottom of the box. 'Births, marriages, deaths, that sort of thing. Oh!'

'Why "*oh*"?' Andy said. 'Whose is it?'

'Ziggy's. His name was Sigmund Freeman, incidentally, I've often wondered how he came by Ziggy, haven't you? Oh, Ash, isn't it sad? He was so young! He died in June, and he wasn't eighteen till August.'

'*Did* he? Does it occur to you, Tess . . .'

The door of the living-room opened and Mrs Yallop came in, closing a large black handbag. 'There you are, all paid up for another month. Did you find that photograph?'

'No, we didn't, I'm afraid, and we turned the box inside out,' Andy said cheerfully. 'Is there anything else you'd like to ask Mrs Yallop, Tess?' He turned to their hostess. 'Tess's father was killed at the beginning of the war, and no one else ever talks about Leonora,' he said. 'So you are her last hope, in a way.'

'I see. Well, I'll tell you all I can, but Leonora moved away from the village when she grew up, so I remember her best as a child, really. She had a difficult childhood, because Mr and Mrs Meadowes were elderly and didn't understand the young – I used to say they were born middle-aged, because that was how they behaved. Leonora wasn't allowed to take friends home and her parents didn't like her playing with other children – did you know your grandparents at all, Miss Delamere?'

'No, they disowned my mother before I was born, over some disagreement or other,' Tess said rather uncomfortably. Did this little old lady know that her beloved baby brother had fathered a child before he died? If she did not, then Tess did not intend to enlighten her.

'Oh, that!' Unexpectedly, Mrs Yallop chuckled. 'Well, that was typical of the Meadowes. They knew nothing about the young. Leonora had to be perfect, and when she wasn't, instead of laying the blame where it belonged, they hit out at the child. But there, it was all a long time ago.'

'And Leonora died young, didn't she?' Andy said gently. 'She's buried in the churchyard here. I suppose you don't know how she died?'

'Well, as to that . . . she was drowned, that I *do* know. But she wasn't living in the village, then, and I'm not a one to listen to gossip.'

'Ziggy died before her, didn't he?' Andy said, after a moment. 'Did Leonora go to his funeral?'

'Indeed she did! They were walking out ... that was the expression then, though I dare say it's put different, today ... but we didn't speak; I reckon we were both too upset for idle chat. And of course just before Christmas she got married and moved away, and I don't think we set eyes on each other from that day on.'

'I see,' Tess said. 'You mentioned gossip just now ...'

'That's right. Said I didn't attend to such things, and nor I do, nor did,' Mrs Yallop said roundly. 'No good ever came of listening to gossip.'

'Oh I agree. I just wondered ... you see I couldn't ask my father much, he hatred talking about my mother's death, but she's buried a bit away from the other graves, and I did wonder ... I mean ...'

'Oh, that! I always reckoned old Mr Meadowes had a hand in that,' Mrs Yallop said surprisingly. 'He was churchwarden, you know. Now if you'll pass that box over here a minute, I'll go through it one more time. I was *sure* I had another photograph in there somewhere.'

Outside the cottage in the chilly morning air, Andy took Tess's arm and turned her in the direction of the village.

'Shame there isn't somewhere for a cuppa, but the King's Head will be open, and it'll be a lot warmer than hanging around at the bus stop. Shall we compare notes?'

'What notes?' Tess said, falling into step beside him. 'She was nice, but not a lot of help, wouldn't you say?'

'Dear heaven, girl, don't you use those eyes of yours? Remember, you're a detective – surely you picked up the most blatant clue ever to stare Sherlock Anderson in the face?'

'No-oo. Everything she told us we'd either known or guessed. Hadn't we?'

'What about everything we *saw*?' Andy asked. 'Why, you actually commented – I can't believe you didn't realise the significance!'

'What? Andy, you are the most aggravating . . .'

They reached the King's Head and went inside. Andy settled Tess in a corner seat by the window and went to the bar. He came back with the drinks and set them down on a small table.

'The chap's going to do us some cheese and pickle sandwiches,' he said. 'It's fifteen minutes before the next bus so we'll have time to eat them if we're quick. Now, where was I?'

'Clues. Which I'm blowed if I saw.'

'Ziggy's death certificate,' Andy said quietly. 'The date, little bean-brain, the date!'

'Gosh, I don't think I noticed, but I can't see . . .'

'He died in June, Tess, *in June!*'

'So?'

'Your birthday's in June.'

'So?'

'Your birthday's in June.'

'So?' Tess said again. 'I don't see that that proves anything!'

'No? Well, I know folk say first babies are always late, but I don't remember anyone ever talking about a twelve-month pregnancy. So if Ziggy really was your father then your mother ought to have been in the record books.'

Tess felt her mouth drop open and dragged it closed. For a moment she just couldn't take it in, then she felt a huge smile spread across her face.

'Oh, Andy, then Daddy really *was* my father! But what was all the secrecy in aid of, then? Why did Daddy try to keep me in the dark about things?'

Andy shook his head sadly, then took both Tess's hands and stared into her eyes. 'For an intelligent girl, Tess, you're awfully slow, sometimes. Your parents were married just before Christmas according to Mrs Yallop. And you were born . . .'

'In June!' Tess squeaked. 'Oh, Andy, do you mean to tell me that all poor Daddy was trying to hide was that he and my mother had . . . had jumped the gun? Why on earth didn't he tell me? I wouldn't have thought any the less of them. What an idiot I am, though, never to have thought of looking at their marriage certificate. I've got it at the farm, somewhere, with all the other bits and pieces which Marianne and Cherie didn't want.'

'How is your little sister?' Andy said. 'Ah, here come our sandwiches. Eat up, Tess, we don't want to miss the bus!'

After their eventful morning in Blofield, Andy decided that a quiet visit to the flicks would be a good idea, so they went up to the flat which Marianne had leased until such time as she either married or moved back to the Old House, and arranged for Tess to spend the night in the spare bed in Cherie's room. Then they walked round to the Regent Cinema, on Prince of Wales Road, made their way into the circle, and sat down to watch the main feature. At least Andy may have watched, but Tess was totally unaware of what was happening on the screen. She kept her eyes fixed on the movements of the cast, but the screen could have been blank for all the impact the film made on her. Her mind was far away, buzzing with speculation, interest and excitement.

Peter was her father, which meant that Cherie was her real half-sister! What a fool I was to take everything Ashley said at face value, she told herself. And all Daddy was trying to hide was that I was conceived out of wedlock. Of course it's rather shocking, but it's nothing like I feared. Why, my parents were safely married by the time I was born, after all.

And she had worried and fretted about her mother, whether she had committed suicide or not, when suicide hadn't apparently even entered the equation. Now, what Mrs Yallop had said about Leonora's father being a churchwarden and having something to do with the position of the grave in the churchyard made sense! Leonora had been pregnant when she married and she had married a young man of whom her stern – and probably horrible – father disapproved. So he had used his influence to get the grave put away from the others, near the woods and wild grasses at the bottom of the churchyard. That was all there was to it, after all!

When the big picture was coming to an end Andy whispered: 'Want to sit through the second feature? It's a gangster thing.'

'No, I'd just as soon leave,' Tess whispered back. 'Do you know, Andy, I've not taken in anything about the big picture at all

472

because I've been mulling over what we've found out. I'm just so thankful, and so grateful to you for making me actually do something, instead of simply wailing and gnashing my teeth.'

'Just remind me; what made you think that Peter wasn't your father? Was it that dream, or something more concrete?'

Tess hesitated. She didn't want to get Ashley into Andy's bad books, but it had been he who had repeated the rumour as gospel truth, though he'd not known he was talking about her parents when he'd repeated the story. She thought about making something up, then remembered that, if it had not been for Andy, she would not know the truth, might never have known it.

'Well, it happened when I first found my mother's grave . . .'

'Shhh, shhhh,' came sibilantly from around them. Andy got to his feet.

'Come on, we'll go up to the café and have sausage and chips. Then we won't disturb people.'

They pushed past knees, stumbled darkly up the aisle, and made their way via the luxuriously carpeted stairs to the café.

'Now!' Andy said when they were seated, with cups of tea before them and their meal ordered. 'Tell me from the beginning.'

'So that was how it all came about,' Tess ended. 'Honestly, Ashley would never have said what he did if he'd known Leonora was my mother. And he believed it was true. As for the suicide bit, Daddy actually said that there had been some doubt because an old fellow on the beach saw my mother stand up in the boat.' She hesitated. 'I really think Daddy may have half believed it as well,' she finished unhappily.

'Yes, it's possible,' Andy said. 'But you've got to unbelieve it, Tess, really you have. There are no real grounds for thinking that Leonora killed herself, you know.'

'But there are, Andy,' Tess said urgently. 'The sea wasn't rough enough to overturn a sturdy little rowing boat, from what Daddy said. And no one seems to have doubted that Leonora stood up – I ask you, why on earth should a woman, alone in a small boat, stand up? Unless she meant to swim for the shore, which seems unlikely, to say the least!'

'She could have stood up for a thousand reasons,' Andy said

crossly. 'She could have seen something in the water, or on the beach . . . but I'm sure, I've always been sure, that she didn't mean to kill herself.'

'I hope you're right,' Tess said. 'I just wish we could prove it, though. If only I could remember a bit more about that boy, the one in my dream.'

'Oh, you and your dreams,' Andy said affectionately. 'The trouble with Walcott is that not a lot of those bungalows are occupied all year round. And now I suppose people aren't allowed to go wandering around there asking questions in case someone thinks they're German spies. But when the war's over you'll have to see if you can look into that side of the story.'

'I don't see how I can,' Tess said dubiously. 'I don't know anything about the boy except that he was in Walcott around the end of April 1922. And I imagine he was six or seven because he seemed very old to me.'

'Well, there you are, you've cut the field down already,' Andy pointed out. 'April isn't a month when school holidays happen, so he wasn't on holiday. He probably lived there; a fisherman's son? Something like that?'

'Ye-es, possibly. Only he was a bit bossy to be a fisherman's son – I mean they wouldn't bother with a kid not quite three, would they? Oh, thanks very much, that looks delicious.'

They waited until the waitress had left and then Tess reached for the vinegar bottle.

'I hadn't realised how hungry I was – sandwiches fill a gap but they don't really satisfy, like a hot meal. So you think that, after the war, I might find that chap?'

'I think you might. It's worth giving it a go, anyway. Because you're quite right, a seven-year-old boy notices all sorts of things. But in the meantime, Tess, be content with what you've suddenly gained – your father, your half-sister, and a reasonable explanation for why Leonora's buried further down the churchyard than most.'

'I am content,' Tess said thickly, through chips. 'Daddy was the best, and Cherie's turned out to be a darling. And think what a lot I'll have to tell Mal, when he gets home!'

'Yes, a real saga,' agreed Andy. 'And Tess, I was furious with

Ashley when you told me what he'd said about your parents, but . . . I shouldn't have been. Ashley's been a good friend to you, better than I have. Neither of us should blame him for what he said all those years ago.'

'I don't. I never did, really,' Tess said. 'For a start, I believed him, and now, even though I realise he was just repeating lies, it was scarcely his fault that I never checked up on what he'd said. And you're right, he has been a good friend, even though he irritates the hell out of me half the time. He's always there you see. And . . . and you and Mal aren't.'

Andy laughed. 'What an honour, being spoken of in the same breath as Mal! Can I just plead, in our defence, that Mal and I have been rather busy these past four or five years?'

'So has Ash,' Tess said. But he rings, writes, turns up on the doorstep and helps with the harvest or stands leaning against the cowshed wall and chatting whilst I finish the milking. I'm not saying he's a saint because he can be *such* a – a bugger, but he's good according to his lights.'

'He's in love,' Andy said, half to himself.

'No, he just thinks he is,' Tess said at once. 'Ashley's known me a long time.'

'So have I, dear Tess, and I'm extremely fond of you. But we're just tried and true friends, wouldn't you say?'

'I would. And I wish Ashley could be as sensible as you, Andy,' Tess said, spearing a very large chip. 'It would be a real relief, believe me.'

'Ah, but Ashley's in love, and a man in love isn't a sensible creature,' Andy said softly. 'Is there another cup of tea in that pot?'

Eighteen

'Come round then, Prince . . . atta boy!'

Susan was leading Prince and Pal patiently across the stubbled cornfield whilst Tess, Molly and a number of others raked the straw into piles so that yet more helpers could pitchfork the stacked straw on to the cart.

Just over a year had passed since the Normandy landings but though she had heard from Mal shortly after the camp had been taken over by the Allies, he was still not home. Knowing that the war was over, that he was almost certainly on his way back to her and was therefore not writing letters had been, Tess thought, hard to bear. But she was philosophical about it. One of the returned airmen had actually seen Mal at a reception centre and reported that he was fit, though thin. It was, once more, just a matter of waiting.

Furthermore, a good deal had happened during the past few months. The war in Europe had ended in May, with Germany's unconditional surrender, but although the German prisoner of war camps were all in allied hands, a number of POWs, Mal amongst them, had still not actually arrived back in England.

'It's because he's an Aussie, I imagine,' Tess explained to anyone who would listen. 'Someone from his station told me that they may well repatriate him to Australia, and then he'll have to make his way back to Blighty under his own steam.'

The demobilisation was slower and more ponderous than Tess had imagined it would be, too. Janet hadn't been demobilised, or demobbed as they were calling it, nor had Ashley, nor most of Tess's friends, and Tess herself had agreed to continue to work for

Mr Sugden until he had his full complement of farm hands back once more.

'It's a long business,' Ashley had explained. 'But once it begins to happen there'll be civilians thronging the streets again. I'm not sure how most of us will take to civvy street, either. It will seem pretty tame after the last few years, I suspect.'

And on the home front, things had been happening too. Marianne and Maurice had got married down in Devonshire, on a week's holiday, not telling anyone until after the event, and then Cherie and the happy couple had moved into a small house in Ipswich Road. Temporarily, Marianne said, until the Old House could be repaired and made fit for habitation once again, but she had been saying it for too long. Tess didn't believe her and didn't blame her for not wanting to live in Barton again. The house held too many memories for her, so how much worse it must be for Marianne, who had so nearly died there.

The house was thatched once more, thanks to Mr Thrower, who had somehow wheedled or begged – or possibly stolen – sufficient timber to replace the ruined rafters and had then used his reeds to replace the missing thatch. The spare room was still impossible to use, though the window was boarded up, keeping the worst of the weather out, but the other rooms were coming along. Tess's bedroom had four good walls and most of a ceiling, and downstairs, apart from walls, ceilings and floors being dirty and water- as well as fire-damaged, the place was sound.

When the war's over, Tess had told anyone who asked, we'll get the work put in hand and then we'll move back, but she knew it would take time. And now that the war was over, the shortages and the coupons and points just went on and on anyway. Marianne and Maurice were settled and they welcomed Tess in Ipswich Road at weekends. But Marianne knows, and I know, that I wouldn't ever want to live in the city full-time, Tess reminded herself. I'm a country girl, I couldn't be anything else, I wouldn't be happy. What's more, I can't imagine living anywhere but around here.

She looked appreciatively around her as the horses wheeled close to the hedge, scattering straw as they went. It was so beautiful, this supposedly dull Norfolk countryside! Rain had fallen earlier, but now the sun was peeping from behind the clouds and the atmosphere was warming up once more. Birds called, searched for food, took wing to sweep inquisitively low across the gold of the half-cut field. On every leaf in the hedge raindrops glittered like diamonds in the sun and the sky overhead burned a deep sapphire blue. Beneath her sturdy wellingtons the stubble steamed gently, and Tess knew she was beginning to steam gently herself. She loved harvesting, watching the combine harvester gobbling the tall, pale yellow crop, but the rain, when it fell earlier, had sneaked down inside her waterproof so though that garment now hung on a convenient hazel twig in the hedge, the shoulders of her jersey and the collar of her shirt were both extremely damp.

Straw was insidious what was more, it got everywhere, even inside your boots, and if you were careless when cleaning yourself up you'd be chasing grains in your clothing for days, and of course the rain meant mud – her wellingtons were knee deep in it. Still, she'd have a swill-down under the pump when they got back to the yard, and get out of these dungarees, and take off the neatly tied headscarf and hope to God she hadn't got straw particles in her hair. Ashley was coming over this evening to take her to a dance in the city and then to run her back to Staithe Cottage for her two days off; she didn't want him complaining that she had left his car looking like a stable.

Tess divided her time conscientiously between the Throwers and her stepmother, but secretly enjoyed her time with the Throwers more. She and Mrs Thrower always spent at least part of the time in the Old House or its garden and Tess loved seeing it gradually returning to its old self. And in May Janet had managed to get ten days' leave and had come home. The two of them had had a marvellous time, revisiting old haunts, talking over old times. And discussing new relationships, of course.

For Janet had a boyfriend, a serious one after a great many casual friends.

'I wondered if it was ever goin' to happen, an' then Stuey come along,' she said with infinite content as she and Tess had strolled around the Broad, arm in arm. 'He's in the Navy, he was in Scotland, wi' me, but his ship went off down south to get the troops over for D Day. Since then he's been either in Portsmouth or at sea so we've been parted. We're both waitin' and hopin', same as you and Mal.'

'What's he like, your Stuart?' Tess asked.

'Oh . . . medium height, reddish hair, green eyes, lots of freckles,' Janet said dreamily. 'Truth to tell, Tess, he in't as good-lookin' as some fellers I bin out with, but it in't good looks what matter, in the end. We – we seem to *fit*, somehow.'

'That's exactly how I feel about Mal,' Tess confessed. 'He's nowhere near as good-looking as Ashley Knox – remember Ashley? – and not as clever as Andy Anderson, either. But when we're together, nothing else matters but him.'

'And you've not been together for more'n two years,' Janet said. 'Ma said you'd only known each other for a week. In't love wonderful, Tess?'

'It is. And of course it isn't just when we're together that he's the only thing that matters, it's all the time,' Tess said. 'We're lucky, Jan.'

'Yes, I reckon so. But . . . that don't stop me prayin', old Tess. War's war, and . . .'

'I know, I know. When I first heard Mal was safe I was so relieved and happy that I went around singing and smiling all day. I was full of plans for what we'd do when he came home, after the war. Life seemed so bright! And then, of course, not that much later, I began to think. A friend of mine lost her brother, he was shot escaping from his camp, and of course I managed to convince myself that Mal would escape too. For a bit I was too terrified to think straight. And it put a stop to all my plans, wham, as if they'd been made by another person, in another life.'

'I'd ha' been the same,' Janet admitted. 'Poor old Tess! Though now, of course, with the whole shootin' match over, you'll be seein' him pretty soon.'

'I'm sure you're right. But I try hard not to think too much about it. I just put it out of my mind and get on with my life. And I'm going to do that now, too. I wonder what your mum's cooking for supper tonight?'

That had been last May, with Europe in a turmoil as the Allies overran it. Now it was almost August, the war was finally over, and still she hadn't heard. Tess followed the cart to the next pile of straw and began to fork it into the cart. Dear Janet, how lovely it had been to see her, and how nice to be able to talk about Mal non-stop to someone who understood! Though it had reminded her of the terrible dangers that Mal must have faced before he was finally put into the camp, and resurrected all the old, nagging worries that something awful might be happening to him now.

'You all right, Tess? I'd offer to change over, only I'm covered in horse dribble and sweat and there's no point in two of us getting like it.' Susan turned and grinned at Tess from her place by the horses' heads.

'It's all right, no point in both of us getting mucky. And we've only got another half-dozen loads, I'd say, and as soon as the straw's all carted we can go back to the farm and start cleaning up.'

The girls and the Clydesdales slogged on, Prince and Pal beginning to show definite signs of wear and tear after a long day's work in rain and sun. Both horses had white feathering on their mighty legs which was now matted with a rich mixture of clay and straw. Because Susan had done all the leading, it would be her job to groom the horses before she was finished tonight, but I'll give her a hand when we get back to the yard, Tess told herself; I've got to have a bath or a strip-down wash when I get in, I might as well be truly mucky.

But mucky or not, in a couple of hours she would be wearing her nicest dress and her smartest shoes, with her hair washed and tied on top of her head, wafting round the floor in Ashley's arms and – imagining that he was Mal.

She loved the dances, and told herself that she was allowing him to take her out at least partly for Ashley's own sake. Whilst he took her around, at least he was meeting other people. Tess had had great hopes of an old school friend, Lucy, at one time, but somehow Lucy's charms had failed to . . . well . . . to charm and Ashley had moved on, his heart intact.

Tonight would be especially good, Tess reminded herself, because Freddy was home, and would be introducing her fiancé, Flight Lieutenant Len Bulman, to all her friends. The happy couple were planning an early wedding and Tess had agreed to be a bridesmaid, though looking at herself now it was difficult to imagine such a bedraggled and filthy person decked out in primrose silk.

'Whoa, Prince,' Susan shouted, bringing Tess abruptly back to the present. 'Last one, Tess! Stow it tight or we'll be shedding all the way back to the yard, and Mr Sugden will send us out with rakes to clear the lane.'

Hastily, Tess bent to her work and by the time Prince and Pal were easing themselves and their burden through the gateway and on to the lane, she was able to glance back and see that the carriageway and hedgerows were clean.

'Someone's coming down the lane, I'll pull over,' Susan sang out presently. 'It's your Cherie, I think, Tess – she's got a feller with her.'

'That'll be her Sammy. Can you imagine, my little sister with a real, flesh-and-blood boyfriend? Of course she's sixteen, which is quite grown-up, but she's still in school so . . . oh my God, my God, my God!'

Tess pushed past the horses and began to run up the lane as hard as she could go, whilst her heart raced and she tried to make sense of what she saw. Cherie was beaming up at a thin young man with rumpled, rather over-long brown hair, an ordinary sort of face, ragged clothing . . .

'Mal! Oh Mal! Oh my love!'

He had seen her; he broke into a run as well and they leaped joyously into each other's arms, hugging, kissing, exclaiming, and Tess felt tears begin to run down her cheeks and saw that his eyes were brimming, too.

He held her back from him suddenly, and began to laugh.

'Oh, my word, Tess . . . you look like the straw man from *The Wizard of Oz*! You're absolutely coated with straw!'

'So are you, now,' Tess said guiltily. She scrubbed at her tear-stained face with her filthy hands. 'Oh, Mal, I'm so sorry, but it's a miracle – I've been so horribly worried when peace was declared and there was no word from you!'

'Came into the port of Liverpool yesterday, on board the *Arundel Castle*,' Mal said, putting his arm round her waist. 'It's been a long time, Tess. But long or short, you're still the prettiest sheila in the world. And you've not said a word to your sister . . . how about asking her how we come to be walking along together?'

'Cherie, I'm so sorry,' Tess said, craning round Mal to beam at her sister. 'Susan said you were with a bloke and I thought it was your boyfriend and then I saw – I saw – '

'He came to Staithe Cottage because he didn't know how else to get in touch with you and I happened to be spending the afternoon there,' Cherie explained. 'He didn't come to the farm because he thought you'd have finished landgirling – some hope! Your bloke has been hugged by total strangers this afternoon, haven't you, Mal? Mrs Thrower, Mr Thrower, Mrs Rope, Glenda and Charlie . . .'

'I enjoyed it,' Mal said in his slow voice. He grinned at Susan, standing pop-eyed by the side of the road between the two great Clydesdales. 'Hi Susan, I'm back!'

'Nice to see you home, Mal,' Susan said, holding out a hand and taking the one Mal was offering. 'Well, this *is* a turn up for the books! We'd better get back to Willow Tree, though, then Tess can clean up.' She looked Mal over. 'And you, too,' she added.

'I'm willing,' Mal said. 'C'mon, let's go. We've got a lot to talk about, Tess and me.'

In bed that night, Tess snuggled down and tried to think lovingly and optimistically of Mal and their future, but it was not easy. She had so longed and longed for Mal's return, yet when it happened, it had been, in a way, an anticlimax. Oh, it wasn't too bad whilst they were all there, Mal talked in a desultory sort of way about the prison camp, but he didn't want to talk about ditching the Lanc, nor what had happened in the months between that and being taken prisoner.

'You need building up, lad,' Mrs Sugden said. 'You're nothing but skin and bone – didn't they feed you?'

Mal said that they had, and added, reluctantly, that back in the spring he'd had a bad bout of flu, which had laid him pretty low. And then he refused apple pie, saying he'd eaten all his stomach could take, thanks very much.

He kept staring, too. First at her, then around the room, as though his eyes didn't believe what they saw. And he looked so totally different! I fell in love with his chunky reliability, his – his *solidness*, Tess thought. But now it's gone, he's stringy and a bit twitchy, and he starts sentences and doesn't finish them . . . he's shy, I do believe!

When he said he must go, he had to be back at his station so must catch the last bus, she had walked him down to the main road. Once they were alone, she had thought, everything would be all right. But it didn't work like that. Alone, they should have been totally relaxed. Instead, neither of them knew what to talk about. 'How's Ashley?' Mal had said at one point after a rather difficult silence, and Tess had had to bite her tongue to stop herself saying: *What does Ashley matter? It's us that matter, you and me, and all you can do is stare at me and mumble . . . or ask how Ashley is doing!*

'Ashley? Well, he was all right last weekend. He was supposed to be taking me dancing tonight, but something must have come up and stopped him. Why?'

'Oh, I dunno. I guess you've been seeing a lot of him, these past two years?'

'Quite a lot,' Tess said coolly. 'He's been a good friend.'

'Oh yeah, sure. I don't blame you, exactly . . . I wouldn't want . . . I didn't mean . . .'

'I know what you meant,' Tess had said. Still cool. 'Tell me, Mal, what are your plans? Will they demob you now you're back or will they want to keep you on for a bit?'

'I dunno,' Mal said miserably. 'I'm going to talk to my CO tomorrow.'

'I see. And after that?'

'Well, can we . . . I could come over . . . I guess I'll ask for some leave if they aren't going to boot me out at once.'

'Right. Only I'm working from eight till eight tomorrow.'

'Oh. Well . . . the next day?'

Why didn't he insist that I tell Mr Sugden to find someone else? Tess raged inwardly. Why is he mumbling and looking at me sideways all of a sudden? If this is a new Mal, I'm not sure I like him – I'm certain sure I don't understand him!

'I don't know about the next day, yet,' Tess said. 'I think I'd better contact Ashley, in fact. I'm quite worried about him, he's never let me down before.'

'Yeah, reliable sort of chap, Ashley,' Mal said. He said it in a mock English accent, which infuriated Tess. 'Well, no doubt he has his reasons.'

'I'll tell you when I see you next,' Tess said. She had striven for a light, teasing tone; it came out threatening. 'Oh, here comes the bus. Good-night, Mal.'

'Good-night,' he mumbled and turned away from her, but just as the bus came alongside he turned back, grabbed her, kissed her so inexpertly that he missed her mouth altogether and then jumped aboard the bus. 'I'll be in touch,' he roared. 'Tomorrow . . . if they let me have some . . .'

The rest of the sentence was lost in the clatter of the engine as the bus got into its stride. Tess had a last glimpse of him, straining to wave out of the back of the bus, of the conductor grabbing him, heaving him back from the step . . . and then darkness swallowed them up.

She had made her way home, entered the farm kitchen, and burst into tears. To the horrified enquiries as to what had happened, what was the matter, she had simply replied, snuffling, that Mal had changed, that she didn't understand him, that he wasn't the man she had known, and that she wished she were dead.

'You'll settle down,' Mrs Sugden said. 'It's just a matter of relearning each other. He'll be just the same, m'dear, once he's used to being back, but I saw him show the whites of his eyes a couple of times over tea. Take it slow and don't let anyone rush you. Now I wonder what's happened to Ashley?'

She did not have long to wonder since ten minutes after she spoke, Ashley walked in at the back door.

'Sorry, sorry, sorry,' he said as all eyes fixed themselves upon him. He put both hands up to shield himself from an imaginary barrage. 'The fan belt went. I had to walk miles and miles before I met a WAAF with a spare silk stocking. Tess, my darling, I know I've ruined your evening, but I'll make it up to you. I've got two tickets for a dinner dance next week – how about that, eh?'

Tess gave him a watery smile. 'Mal's come home,' she said.

There was a moment's silence during which you could have heard a pin drop. Then Ashley said: 'Well, that's nice,' and drew the tickets out of an inner pocket. 'Now here's a thing, I just happen to have two tickets for a dinner dance next week. Would you and Mal like them, Tess? As a present, of course. I don't have a use for them myself.'

'Oh, Ash,' Tess said helplessly, and the next thing she knew, she was in his arms, crying that she was sorry, she was really sorry . . .

'Don't take on so,' Ashley soothed, stroking her hair. 'It'll take some getting used to, old darling, but it's what you've been praying for this past two years. Look, take the tickets with my blessing. And do stop crying all over my best blues, there's a good girl!'

Tess laughed and pulled herself out of his arms. 'Oh Ash, you are a fool,' she said helplessly. 'I'm in an awful state, I was so excited, and then . . . and then . . .'

'She's still excited, that's the trouble,' Molly said sagely. 'We're all excited. But I'm for bed, I don't know about the rest of you.'

They all left them, eventually, even Mr and Mrs Sugden, who normally made it a rule never to leave a landgirl alone with a boy. But they sensed, Tess supposed, that the last thing on either her mind or Ashley's was canoodling.

'Talk about tact,' Ashley said, when they were alone in the kitchen. 'Poor old Tess, was it very difficult? Well, you shouldn't expect to run before you can walk, you know. You've got two years apart to bridge and that takes time. Want to talk about it?'

'No, not really. And thanks for being so understanding, Ash. You're a very nice person really, underneath.'

'I'm bloody nice on top, too,' Ashley said, grinning. 'Look, I'll have to go, I only came over to explain why I didn't pick you up as arranged. And remember, Mal or no Mal, I'm always there. Just pick up the phone and I'll come running.'

'I will. I'm so grateful – I don't know what I've done to deserve you,' Tess muttered, rubbing her tear-stained cheeks. 'Are you sure the car's all right now? Will you go home, or back to Lincolnshire?'

'Oh, home. I've got tomorrow off, so if you need me, it's the

Brundall number. Can I go now? You won't dissolve into tears again the moment my back's turned?'

Tess giggled. 'No, it's all right. I'm just all of a dither, I suppose. I – I somehow never really thought beyond the moment that we flew into each other's arms, but now I know there's more to it than that.'

'Yes, a great deal more. And you have to work at it,' Ashley said sternly. 'And I don't know why I'm talking to you like a Dutch uncle, when for two pins . . . but I don't happen to have two pins on me, so you're safe. Good-night, dear old Tess.'

He headed for the back door.

'Good-night, dear old Ash,' Tess said softly. 'And thanks for everything.'

'Ditto,' Ashley said, half-way out of the door. 'Be good.'

'I will,' Tess said with meaning. 'Drive carefully.'

She started across the kitchen, to wave him off as she always did, then stopped herself. It wasn't fair to either Ash or Mal, she thought confusedly. Better just go straight up to bed. Everything would look better in the morning.

Mal, sitting in the front seat of the almost empty bus, could have kicked himself for his ineptitude and stupidity. Fancy asking her about Ashley! Fancy acting like a tongue-tied kid, for that matter. But the truth was, he hadn't remembered how slender and cool she was, how white-skinned, how softly beautiful, and it had knocked him back. She's like a film star, he had thought wonderingly. There's no way a girl like that will marry me, come back to the Wandina, slog through the wet and sweat through the dry, bear my kids and cook for me, work beside me, sleep beside me.

It was strange, too, how two years of inadequate diet and very little exercise could change you, physically. Oh, they'd tried to keep fit, eaten whatever was offered, but back in March, when it was so bitterly cold, he'd gone down with some sort of influenza bug. He'd been really ill and for weeks and weeks afterwards he had been unable to keep food down.

Of course he'd struggled back; he was far better now, but he knew that Mrs Sugden was right when she said he needed building up. Only his stomach had shrunk – that was what the MO had said – and he just couldn't eat as he once had.

Outside the bus the dark countryside rumbled past, but when they reached the suburbs of the city he saw lights – wonderful to see lights at night, curtains pulled back so that the windows were like little glowing stages on which the actors and actresses moved, ignoring their silent audience.

He did not, in fact, have to go back to the station tonight, though he did have an appointment with his commanding officer next day, but he meant to go back because he didn't have much money and squandering it on a night in an hotel seemed pretty silly. He cursed the fact that he'd told Tess a lie, but he had suddenly realised that he couldn't take the strain of staying at the farm overnight, even if they did have a bed for him which he doubted. He wanted – needed – to be alone for a bit.

It was odd, he mused, getting off the bus at Castle Meadow and hurrying up to where the liberty trucks waited, that he should want to be alone. There was nothing quite so cramped and crowded as a POW camp, of course, but he had spent the last two years longing for Tess so why, when she was suddenly within his grasp, did he feel that he must get away from her?

He reached the liberty truck. The driver was snoozing behind the wheel, but he had said be back by twenty-three hundred hours so soon the fellows would start assembling. Mal climbed into the back and sat down on a small metal seat. She's in love with that fellow Ashley and I can't blame her, he thought miserably. I'll back off, leave her alone, then at least one of us will be happy. And tomorrow morning, if the CO says I can go back to Australia, I'll bloody well go! I'm not staying here to see my girl marry someone else.

The thought jolted him, brought him up short. What exactly do you mean, Malcolm Chandler? he asked himself severely. Do you want her or not? If it's not, then why in heaven's name shouldn't she marry Ashley, greaseball though he is? You want her happiness, you just said so.

I want the old Tess, the one I left behind me, Mal's inner self said after a moment's thought. I don't know this new one. This one's . . . different. I feel like I never met her before. Why, she was

487

smaller before, when I kissed this one I missed her mouth, I'd never have missed the old Tess's mouth. So she really has changed – she's different, she isn't the girl who wanted me as much as I wanted her.

Voices came floating across the Cattle Market. Men began to climb aboard the truck. Someone asked him how his date had gone and he mumbled that it was all right, thanks. The men around him talked about the dance they'd attended, the girls they'd met, what they intended to do next night. Mal listened and longed for the solitude of his small room, his Air Force issue bed. When I'm by myself I'll be able to work it out, he thought. I just need to be alone.

Mal was sitting in the mess next day, reading a paper, or pretending to read it, when the telephone rang and two minutes later his name was called.

'Chandler! For you – a girl.'

His heart beat loudly. Tess?

He picked up the receiver. 'Yes? Chandler speaking.'

'It's me. Tess. I – I wondered what your CO said?'

'I've got some leave,' he said. 'They're sending me back home in a few weeks. He said I can have some leave.'

The CO had told him to take himself off anywhere he liked because his demob would be through in a matter of days. He'd asked if Mal had any friends in England and had then said: 'What a question, there was a girl whose name you put down as next of kin in England – you're marrying, I understand?'

Mal had nodded, unable to risk speaking.

'Well, then! Stay with her people for a few days. You can ring me in, say, four days. I'll have definite news for you then, I hope.'

And now she was on the telephone, asking what his CO had said, which might be genuine interest . . . he wasn't sure. He wasn't sure of anything any more.

'Oh, wonderful!' she hesitated. 'Going to come and see me, then? Mal . . . we've got to try!'

It was a cry from the heart and it gave him courage. For a moment he felt confident, sure of himself. Like the old Mal, in fact.

'Sure. Come into the city tomorrow, meet me at ten. Outside the GPO. Tell Mrs Sugden you won't be back till late.'

She laughed. It was a happy, breathless laugh. 'Gosh, a day out – that sounds exciting. But you can come here, you know. Mrs Sugden says . . .'

He cut across her.

'That's kind, but . . . well, I'm a bit awkward with a lot of people right now. If it's just the two of us . . . we might find it easier, don't you think?'

'I don't know,' Tess said. She sounded doubtful. 'It wasn't easier the other night.'

'No. But we didn't give it much of a go, did we? A ten-minute walk up to the main road, a ten-minute wait for the bus? That's not much of a go.'

'You're right.' Her voice sounded light with relief. He realised he was smiling, that his heart was lifting. 'Right you are then, outside the GPO at ten. Where we met that first time, in fact.'

'Too right,' he said. 'I'll look forward to it.'

He put the receiver down and went slowly back to his chair. He knew she was right, they must try, and just for a moment, when she'd sounded so happy, he'd thought that it really might work. But now, picking up the newspaper again, he acknowledged that this might well be wishful thinking. The trouble was, times had changed and they had changed with them. They were two very different people from the bright-eyed young hopefuls who had planned a spring wedding two years ago.

'I'm meeting Mal in the city,' Tess said when Susan and Molly asked what she was going to do that day. 'We're having a day out. It should be fun.'

But the trouble was, she was dreadfully afraid it wouldn't be fun at all. It was raining, for a start. She didn't have a lot of civvy clothes, so she wore an old brown skirt, a checked blouse and her Land Army mac, with the inevitable scarf wrapped round her head. She checked herself in the mirror and thought she looked deadly dull, but there was no help for it. She was damned if she would wear her only decent dress to get soaked in the downpour

– she had borrowed an umbrella from Mrs Sugden but doubted that it would be much use, it was blowing a gale out there.

She was soaked by the time she reached the bus stop. Naturally. She was still wet when she got off the bus at Tombland and set off for the GPO. And this time, things were different because Mal had arrived before her. He was in uniform, standing against the very pillar she had leaned against, looking around him. Not as though he were searching for her, but simply idly scanning the people going by.

And then, when she was feet away from him, he turned away and began to walk rapidly along the pavement towards Castle Meadow. She had to run and grab hold of his arm.

'Mal, where are you going? Changed your mind?' She was panting, breathless. She felt angry, and also, at the same time, very sorry for him. What a business it was, meeting after a long parting!

'Oh . . . Tess!' he looked hunted, as though she'd caught him out in some immoral act. 'I thought I'd got the place wrong, I might have said the Corn Exchange or . . .'

'It isn't ten yet, I wasn't even late,' Tess said. She sounded injured, even to herself. 'Where are we going? It's a filthy day – just my luck to get leave on a day like this.'

'We're catching a bus, I'm afraid,' Mal said. 'I don't have a car, like Ashley; with me it's bus or shanks's pony.'

'I don't have a car either,' Tess said. 'What does it matter? Which bus, anyway?'

He was starting to speak when he suddenly grabbed her arm and began to tow her across the road. 'This one! Hurry, or we've forty minutes to wait! Come on, give it your best, Tess.'

They both ran and got the bus when it stopped at the traffic lights. Tess collapsed, giggling, into a seat.

'Oh, Mal, I'm soaked to the skin, out of breath, mud-splattered . . . and I was determined not to wear my best frock, because to ruin that would be the end, what with all the shortages and me needing all my coupons for something to wear to Freddy's wedding. And I did so want to look nice for you!'

He turned to stare. Then he smiled, and it was his old, slow smile. 'You'll do,' he said. 'As for rain, who cares about that? We're together, aren't we?'

Tess touched his hand timidly. Then, more boldly, took it in both hers. 'Yes, we're together,' she said. 'And we're going to have a wizard day, rain or no rain!'

Sitting close beside her on the bus, Mal kept stealing glances at her. She looked lovely, he thought, with her face wet with rain and that scarf soaked with it and raindrops trembling on her long lashes. But he couldn't tell her that, she'd think he was trying to outdo Ashley, so instead, he put an arm round her shoulders and drew her against his chest.

And it felt fine! It felt right, as natural as it had ever done and as different from the way he had felt the day before as could be. He squeezed her and then, highly daring, slid his hand down her arm and rested it gently against her side. He could feel the light, swift pitter-patter of her heart against his palm ... it made him start to breathe more quickly, brought a surge of desire in its train.

'Tess?'

'Yes, Mal?'

'Can you guess where we're going?'

'Blofield? Or Great Yarmouth? Only they won't let us go on the proper beach because they haven't dug out all the mines yet, I believe.'

He shook his head.

'Wrong and wrong. Stokesby.'

She turned to stare at him. 'Oh, but ... what'll we do there, Mal? It's still raining like stink, if you ask me it's set in for the day.'

Mal smiled at her and the hand which had been resting against her side tightened in a light squeeze.

'The rain won't matter. Trust me.'

'Well, all right then,' Tess said. 'We could play dominoes, I suppose. I saw a box last time we were there, on that shelf behind the bar.'

'Dominoes!' he said scornfully. He was feeling better with every minute that passed, more in command. They had been so happy in Stokesby, now they were going back there, to find whatever it was that had somehow gone missing in the years between. He kept on smiling.

They sat in the bow window, at the very table they had sat at two years earlier. Tess said: 'Why did you go to the bar and talk to Mrs Figgis whilst I was taking my wet things off in the toilet?'

'How do you know I did?'

'Because you were turning away as I came back, and Mrs Figgis took my coat and scarf and my wet stockings and said something about the forecast being better for tomorrow.'

'Whoops,' Mal said. 'Did she?'

'Yes, she did.' Tess tried to glare, but giggled instead. 'What's going on?'

'I told her we wanted a room for the night.'

Tess stared at him. 'A room? One, not two?'

'A room,' Mal confirmed. 'Why should we bother with two, when we've come away specially to be together?'

'But we're not – '

'Hush! I think she thinks we *are*.'

'I wonder where she got that idea?' Tess said. 'Could it have been something you said?'

'I wonder?' Mal said vaguely. 'I booked dinner for seven o'clock and said we'd come down and have a sandwich lunch at around one, like last time.'

'Come down?'

'Well, we've got to see our room, haven't we? And you might like a wash, or something.' He grinned at her. 'You might like to lie on the bed for a bit, relax. After all, there isn't much else to do here, as you've pointed out.'

'Mal, that wasn't what I said! Well, it was, but it wasn't what I *meant*. I meant we wouldn't be able to walk or boat in the rain, that's what I meant.'

'True. But there are other things one can do, as I said at the time.' He got to his feet and held out a hand. 'Coming? Mrs Figgis says it's left at the top of the stairs, the first door.'

'How can I? Suppose she asks to see our wedding lines or something? Mal, I'd be embarrassed out of my life ... I think we'd better have the sandwiches and go.'

'If that's what you really want . . .'

'It is. And anyway, I haven't got a nightie. Or a toothbrush. Or – or anything. What will she *think*?'

'She'll think we're in love,' Mal said softly. 'She'll think we want to be together and she'll be glad we feel at home here. Tess, look at me!'

Tess got to her feet and met his eyes with some difficulty.

'Love me, sweetheart?'

'Yes, of course, only I'm all mixed up and . . .'

Mal took her arm and gently drew her towards the stairs. 'Well, if that's all, I am about to unmix you. There's plenty of time before lunch. Come on, sweetie, up the wooden hill!'

They didn't make love that morning, though Tess thought that Mal had probably expected they would. Instead, they lay on the bed and talked and held each other. And slowly, the fears and strangenesses which had bound them began to unravel. Mal told Tess how he'd been ill and unable to eat, how he'd felt caged from the moment he had arrived at the POW camp.

'Lots of the fellers felt better, more secure, but I just felt . . . shut in,' he said. 'It was awful at first, I used to wake in the night thinking I was suffocating. I stayed sane, Tess, by fixing my mind on you. You were all that mattered, you were my past and my future. So when I got home and you seemed different – remote, beautiful, and very, very English – it . . . it kinda took the wind out of my sails.'

'You seemed different, too,' Tess told him. 'Not so sure of yourself, not so dependable somehow. You didn't seem . . . well, you didn't seem to like me very much.'

'Ho ho! I liked you *very* much, but I felt I couldn't get close to you any more. It was odd, as if – as if I'd forgotten the language.'

'The language of love,' Tess said dreamily. 'It's so easy to say, but so difficult, too. I love you, Mal.'

He snuggled a kiss into the side of her neck just below her ear. 'I love you, too, Tess. Shall we seal it with a kiss?'

'Why not?'

They kissed. Tess said: 'Why does that make my heart leap about I wonder?'

'Because of what comes next, I daresay,' Mal said. 'Oh, Tess!'

'Sandwiches come next. Lunch for two, Pilot Officer Chandler,' Tess said, suddenly brisk. 'Let's pretend this is our wedding day, Mal. Downstairs, our wedding breakfast awaits!'

'Spoil-sport,' Mal grumbled, getting off the bed. 'But I dare say you're right.'

They went down to the bar and had the sandwiches, beer and ginger cake which Mrs Figgis had prepared for them, then spent the afternoon walking.

'I didn't intend to be this athletic,' Mal grumbled, striding out along the tow-path with Tess tucked into his side. 'Or at least, not on these marshes, with the wind coming across them like a drawn sword.'

'Or a whetted knife, like in the Masefield poem,' Tess remarked. 'You said you didn't get enough exercise in the camp, so don't grumble about a brisk walk. It's better for you than lounging about indoors.'

'I didn't say I wanted to lounge about indoors, I wanted to be very athletic indeed,' Mal said, grinning down at her. 'All right, all right, you can force me out into this bitter wind now, but my turn will come.'

It did. They had their dinner, which was excellent, and went to bed. And, held close in Mal's loving arms, Tess discovered that there was an indoor game which was even more fun than striding across the Acle marshes.

'So this is what they make such a fuss about,' she remarked when they lay quiet at last. 'Dear, darling Mal, we *are* going to get married, aren't we? So that we can be together for always?'

'We are,' Mal said gently. 'Will you give up all this and come back to the Wandina with me? Even knowing that I'll just be the old feller's manager for a while, at least?'

Coffee had left Uncle Josh, going into town one morning in the pony-cart and sending an ill-written note to say she was moving on. Uncle Josh had written at once to Mal, begging him to return when the war was over and assuring him that the place would be his, when he himself passed on.

'Yes, of course I'll come with you,' Tess said without hesitation.

'That's how I first knew it was for real, Mal. When Andy said he wanted to live in Greece – sun and sea, you know – I knew I could never love him enough to leave England. But when you came along . . . oh, there was no question, no question at all. Whither thou goest, Mal Chandler, I goest also.'

'It's a harsh old life,' Mal said. 'Harder on a woman than on a man. There's no softness in the outback and precious few amenities, either. On the good side, though, Uncle Josh is a man of his word; he'll leave the place to us when he goes, so everything we do there will be for our own benefit, in the end. There is another option, of course; I could go for a job in the city, but I've never reckoned much to that.'

'You wouldn't consider staying here, getting work on a farm? Perhaps studying to be a farm manager, or trying to get the money together to buy a farm of your own?'

'For you, anything. But I don't think an English farm could ever mean what an outback cattle station means to me, and for the old feller's sake I'd like to go back. Look, say we give it a go on the Wandina for a couple of years and if you hate it, we think again. How's that?'

'It's very generous of you but there's no need, really,' Tess said sleeply. 'I meant what I said. My home, in future, will be where you are, Mal.'

'Oh, Tess, what have I done to deserve you?'

It rang a faint bell, but only a faint one. Tess sat up and put both arms round Mal, then squeezed him hard.

'Nothing, I'm a pearl beyond price. And now let's get to sleep. Tomorrow the weather's due to improve and we can *really* go for a walk!'

They married quietly, in the village church of St Michael and All the Angels. Cherie was a bridesmaid and Freddy matron of honour, for she had married a couple of months before. Marianne, very pink and pleased, gave the bride away and the reception was held at Willow Tree Farm because the Old House still wasn't habitable. The Knoxes came to the wedding, but Ashley was absent. He had gone up to London, his mother explained, for an interview.

'He isn't sure it's a good thing to work for his father,' she said, pulling a face at her large, quiet husband. 'So he's hoping to get some experience with a bigger firm which specialises in criminal law. I daresay he'll come home again after a year or two, but he's probably right. After the Air Force, practising in a provincial city is going to seem dull work for a bit.'

Tess was both glad and sorry that he hadn't come, but when she mentioned it to Freddy her friend said it was definitely for the best.

'He'll see you before you go off to Australia,' she assured Tess. 'He's taking your marriage pretty well, considering.'

'Considering what?' Tess said rather stiffly. 'I've spent the last God-knows-how-many years telling him that we weren't suited in any way for each other, so . . .'

'Considering that he's been in love with you ever since you met,' Freddy said frankly. 'Don't go all defensive on me, Tess, because I know better than anyone how obnoxious Ash can be, so I sympathise. When we were kids he made my life a misery, in fact when Mum took him off to the seaside to recuperate from mumps I was delighted to be left behind. But love's like mumps; once you've got it there isn't a lot you can do except to soldier on. It goes, in the end.'

'Oh, thanks. I'm an attack of mumps now! Well, I hope with all my heart that Ash recovers soon.'

'I'm sure he will,' Freddy said gaily. 'In fact, if you're changing trains in London he said he'd be on one or the other platform, to wish you luck.'

They were honeymooning in Wales, because the Sugdens had friends who owned a cottage in the Vale of Clwyd which they were willing to let. A week there was the Sugdens' wedding present to the happy couple, and after that they meant to go straight to Southampton to board their ship. Heading for Wales indeed meant that they would change trains in London and sure enough, when they reached Liverpool Street, Ashley was waiting for them.

'Tess, Mal! Congratulations! I hope you'll be very happy. I'm sorry I couldn't be with you for the ceremony, but it's a long way to go just for a few hours. And what's more . . .'

496

'I'll go and get our luggage,' Mal said, having silently shaken Ash by the hand. 'Shan't be a mo.'

'Nice chap,' Ashley said appreciatively. 'Giving me a chance to have a quiet word. Tess . . . there's something I want you to know. I'm getting married.'

'Wha-aat?' Tess couldn't help her amazement showing, but she hid a feeling rather close to dismay. Marrying? Ashley? But she supposed it was quite possible; he was an attractive man.

'That's rude, you make it sound as if no one in their right senses would have me,' Ashley said reproachfully. 'I'm not sure when it will be, probably not for a year to two, but . . . well, I just wanted you to know. So when you're sailing the ocean blue, arriving in Australia, sightseeing in Sydney, you'll know that your old friend is about to settle down as well.'

'That's lovely, Ash,' Tess said sincerely, trying to ignore the little knot of ice which had formed in the pit of her stomach. 'Who is she? Do I know her?'

'No, I don't think so. She's an actress, of all things, both beautiful and talented. Her name's Marie, though that isn't her stage name. Ah, here comes your husband, wheeling an extraordinary amount of luggage – this is a honeymoon, isn't it, not a house-move?'

'It's both, actually,' Tess said, laughing. 'We're not going back to Norfolk when we leave Wales, it wouldn't be worth it. We're going straight down to Southampton and taking ship for Australia.'

'Oh,' Ashley said blankly. 'Oh I see, I hadn't realised . . . then this really is goodbye?'

'That's right,' Tess said. More ice formed in her unreliable stomach. 'But I expect we'll come back from time to time, or you could come out to the Wandina, Ash! Yes, you must come, and bring your wife. But in the meantime, you – you'll write to me, won't you?'

'If you write to me.' Ashley shook Mal's hand again, told him to take care of Tess, and turned to go. Then turned back.

'Give me a kiss, Tess, for old times' sake.'

They kissed. Decorously. Then he put her away from him and touched the tip of her nose with a light finger. 'Daft thing . . . I wish you could meet my fiancée, you'd like her . . . but you must be off or you'll miss the train from Euston. Be good. And write.'

Tess watched him out of sight, then sighed and tucked her hand into Mal's arm. 'He's all right really, Ash,' she said. 'He came to tell me he's getting married, Mal – imagine that! She's an actress.'

'Good on him,' Mal said. 'Come on sweetheart, I've got a taxi waiting!'

Ashley went into the refreshment room after he'd left Tess and ordered a pint of beer. Then he sat at a small table which commanded a view of the taxi rank and watched her until she climbed into a cab. Then he watched the vehicle until it turned the corner and disappeared. Then, prosaically, he drank his beer.

He had done all he could for her. He had made her a present of complete freedom from him, he had invented a girlfriend, pretended a coming marriage, even given the girl a name, a career. Because of what he had done Tess would leave with nothing on her conscience, no guilt for a love she could not feel.

He had hoped, of course. Right up to the end, he had hoped that she might realise love like his only happened once in a lifetime. But she hadn't, she'd clung to Mal, and he hoped and believed she would be happy. Dear Tess, so mixed up and keen to do the right thing by everyone, she deserved happiness if anyone did. As for himself, he simply hoped that he would survive, perhaps to find happiness of his own one day.

He left the refreshment room and found it was raining. Charging along the pavement he stepped in a puddle and felt the water seep into his shoe with a certain savage satisfaction. He dug his hand into his mackintosh pocket and brought out a couple of squashed pontefract cakes. Ever since he'd been a kid he'd loved the things, though he'd stopped eating them once his parents had complained that he smelled of liquorice and was ruining his teeth. Defiantly, he crammed both the sweets in his mouth now, to give what comfort they could. He would go for a long, long walk, and by the time he got home perhaps the ache of knowing he would probably never see her again would have subsided a little.

Perhaps then, he could bend his mind to making his lies come true. Find a girl, marry her, be happy.

Perhaps.

Perhaps.

The honeymoon cottage was everything such a place should be, the countryside breathtakingly beautiful, the local people friendly. Mrs Lecky Williams, who owned the cottage and was the local farmer's wife, came in each morning, very early, and lit the fire and cleaned through. 'All part of the service, my love,' she told Tess when Tess thanked her. 'Goin'a long way off you are – want to leave a good impression we do!'

But even the nicest things come to an end, and when their week was over she and Mal set out on a slow little country bus on what was almost the last leg of their journey.

'Well, not quite the last leg; first we've got bus, train, ship, train, horse and cart,' Mal said, counting on his fingers. 'And then you'll see the Wandina. But it's better this way; you said your goodbyes a week ago, didn't you?'

'I did,' Tess admitted. 'Now I feel that I'm leaving the cottage behind, a lovely holiday home but nothing more. Yes, it's easier this way. There won't be any sense of personal loss when we sail away from Southampton.'

'That's good,' Mal said. 'A new life, Tess, that's how we've got to look at it.'

'It isn't a new life for you,' Tess pointed out. 'You were there for . . . what, your first twenty-five years.'

'More,' Mal said. 'But I've been away for seven years now, and I've had all sorts of experiences; I don't know how I'll settle down to cattle raising. It's not much like flying a Lanc, you know.'

'I expect you'll be happy as a pig in muck,' Tess told him. 'You liked it all right before, and it isn't *ordinary*, is it, like farming in England? I mean you cover such huge areas of ground, you're in the saddle for days at a time, you camp out in the bush at nights . . . I bet you can't wait!'

'Nor can you,' Mal said shrewdly. 'You should see your face – like a kid at Christmas.'

'Yes, well . . . I've never ridden a horse but I've always wanted

499

to. So let's not pretend we're not going to have fun, because we are.'

'Oh sweetheart!' Mal looped an arm round her waist and kissed her. 'You're everything I've always wanted! No regrets? No unfinished business?'

'No to both. I told you I found out that Daddy was my real father and not my stepfather, as I'd thought; that was wonderful, the best possible news. And I'm ninety-nine per cent certain that Leonora didn't kill herself, though I still don't really know how she died. As for regrets, I don't suppose, if I lived in Norfolk for the next fifty years, I'd ever find out any more about Leonora.'

'Unless you met the boy you dreamed about,' Mal said. 'If he exists, of course.'

'Even if he does exist, and I were to meet him, he might not be able to tell me much,' Tess pointed out. 'Anyway, I know as much as I've a right to expect. Oh, here comes the station! Off we get!'

'Coincidence is peculiar,' Tess mused a couple of nights later, as she and Mal lay squeezed together in the same bunk. Later she would get out and climb up to the top one, but for now, for what they described to themselves and each other as 'cuddles', they would share the lower of the two beds.

'Coincidences are always happening,' Mal said. 'What makes you say that?'

'Because I was talking to an old chap on deck, whilst you were practising your Australian crawl in the swimming pool, and he comes from Norfolk! Isn't that strange? Apparently he and his wife went out to Perth, in Australia, twenty years ago, and this is the first time he's visited England since then. And the first person he meets on board ship, going back to Perth, is me – a Norfolk dumpling, like him!'

'Oh my word,' Mal said. 'Why did he emigrate twenty years ago? Is he married?'

'No, he's a widower, she died a year ago. That's why he went ho . . . back, I mean. He had a great desire to see England again, he said, but he knows there's nothing for him there, now. All his kids are in Perth and doing well. So he just went for a three-month holiday. He told me he was a fisherman back in the old days, but he made a poor living at it, and then a cousin of his said he was off to the colonies, and the old chap – his name's Rolly Moss, incidentally – decided to go along as well. He said he'd never regretted it and nor did his missus, and when I said we were going to live in Queensland he said it's a hard life but it has rich rewards.' She chuckled. 'Rich rewards! As if there's gold in them thar hills!'

'There was, once. Didn't you know there was an Australian gold-rush, back in the 'nineties? You must introduce me to this Rolly character next time you spot him.'

But the next time Tess met up with Rolly, Mal was once more indulging in fitness pursuits, for he was determined to regain his muscle before they arrived in the land of his birth. 'It's all right for you, they aren't going to look at you and wonder what you've been doing to yourself,' he said when she teased him about it. 'No one's gonna believe I can be worn out after a day's work, or I can't take the round-ups.'

'Well, perish the thought that they might think less of you because you've lost condition fighting for your country,' Tess said sarcastically, but Mal merely told her to go away and let him lift weights, so she obeyed. And walked straight into Rolly, leaning against the rail and watching the tumbling water, already blue with a more tropical shade than any which Tess had seen before.

'Afternoon, Mr Moss,' Tess said politely. 'My husband's weight lifting, so I'm at a loose end. What are you watching?' She peered over the rail. 'Not flying fish!'

'No, just the sea,' the old man said. 'No flyin' fish yet – nor sharks and dolphins, neither. They'll come later.'

'Dolphins are interesting, but I don't much fancy the thought of sharks,' Tess said with a little shudder. 'Mal says you can't bathe in the sea up by Cairns except in the winter. He says there's stingers, sharks, seawater crocodiles, all sorts of horrid things in summer. So I don't think I'll be doing much sea-bathing, somehow.'

'Ah well, the sea's tricky in itself, whether it's tropical or icy cold,' the old man said. 'I remember well when I was young seein' a tragic drownin' off the coast where I fished. A beautiful young girl, it was . . . she were rowin' along the coast and I'd been ad-

501

mirin' the way she rowed, too, when all of a sudden up she jumped and began to wave and shout. Next thing, the boat turned sideways on to a wave and over she went, slap bang into the water, an' the boat, that reared up an' fell on her.'

'And she couldn't swim?' Tess said. 'Where were you? Why couldn't you reach her?'

'Could. Did,' the old man said. But she din't stand a chance, you know, the boat landed on her, forced her down. It were a good twenty minutes, half an hour perhaps, before I managed to git a hold of her.'

'Isn't that terrible? Oddly enough, though, my mother was drowned in a very similar incident,' Tess said slowly. 'Whereabouts on the coast did this happen, Mr Moss? Can you remember any more about it?'

He shook his head. 'Not a lot. Poor gal, what a way to go! I allus said to my missus, never you stand up in a boat my dear, no matter what the provocation. It's askin' for trouble, I telled her.'

'Where did this take place, did you say?'

Mr Moss shrugged. 'Somewhere along the coast; I were in my boat, see, checkin' crab pots. Soon as I saw her stand up I started to row over, but it were too late.' He shook his head sadly. 'Too bloody late,' he finished.

'And it was somewhere along the coast – would you say the North Norfolk coast?' Tess said craftily, but he was not to be deflected.

'Never you jump up in a boat, I tells folk. Not even for the sake of the one you love the most.'

'I don't see why anyone should jump up in a boat for the sake of the one they loved,' Tess objected, temporarily straying from the point herself. 'What makes you say that, Mr Moss?'

'Acos I knew *why* she jumped up, even though it were a foolish thing to do,' the old man said immediately. 'Plain as the nose on my face it were. I said so to the feller what came down and helped me to carry her ashore; not that he took any notice, old fool.'

'I'm not with you; why did she jump up?' Tess said. 'The beach was deserted, didn't you say?'

'Aye, it was deserted save for an old fool of a fisherman, the one I mentioned. But the sandhills above the beach, they weren't deserted. There were bungalows up there, with low walls separatin' them from the sea. An' this little kid, in a pink-striped frock, she were climbin' over one o' the walls. Not much more than a baby, she were. I could tell at a glance, *that* were why the gal jumped up. She were shoutin' to the baby to go back – beaches is dangerous places for babies by theirselves – and of course the boat, she tipped,' Mr Moss said simply. 'Sad, weren't it?'

Tess was staring at him. Tears had formed in her eyes but they did not fall.

'Sad? Yes, terribly said,' she said at last. 'Oh, that poor girl – so *that* was why she stood up in the boat! So *that* was what Daddy was trying to hide! It was my fault all the time . . . she wasn't trying to leave me, she was trying to save me!'

She told Mal, of course. Snuggled up in his arms, in the lower bunk, she told him everything that Mr Moss had told her.

'Isn't it strange though, Mal, that in order to find out how my mother really died I had to marry you and come all the way to Australia?' she said, when the tale was told. 'Mr Moss was only in England for three months, and in Norfolk for one of them. And he wasn't a Walcott man, so I could have asked and asked there and no one would have been any the wiser. He just happened to be checking crab pots off shore, and saw everything. Well, almost everything. He didn't see me go down to the breakwater and he didn't see the boy come interfering along and drag me off home.'

'If it happened,' Mal said gently. 'Oh, I don't mean what Mr Moss saw, that certainly happened just the way he told it. I mean you and the beach and the breakwater and whatever it was in the water, and the boy coming and picking you up . . . Don't you think it's likelier that the dream came out of all that happened afterwards? Hushed voices, talk of drowning, your father saying you must never be told . . . and perhaps the boy looked after you in the days directly following your mother's death, when everything was topsy-turvy and your father was too busy packing up and leaving the place, seeing to your mother's funeral and so on, to have much time for his little daughter?'

'I don't know,' Tess said drowsily. 'And I don't suppose it matters now. I've not had the dreams for years and years – not since I met you, in fact. All that matters is I understand it all, now.'

'And you aren't blaming yourself for Leonora's death?'

'It's a bit late to lay blame, wouldn't you say? But no, I'm certainly not blaming anyone, least of all myself. I was a very young child, mischievous certainly, but not bad. I know I said I killed my mother but that was over-dramatisation, to put it no stronger. Poor Leonora, she died for love, you could say.'

'What matters, to you, is that you know, now, that she didn't kill herself. Isn't that it?' Mal asked.

'That's it,' Tess said. 'If I have a baby I shall call it Leonora if it's a girl and Peter if it's a boy.'

'If you have a baby? If? Are you casting doubts on my abilities?'

Tess giggled. 'All right, when, then. Glory, I'm tired. Good-night, darling Mal.'

She struggled out of the bed and he caught her ankle as she swung herself on to the top bunk and kissed her soft little heel. 'Good-night, darling Tess.'

Tess lay on her back for a little, gazing up at the ceiling so close to her nose. The ship's motion was soothing, but she didn't want to go to sleep just yet. She wanted to savour her knowledge, hugging it to her bosom. Ever since she could remember, she had wanted to know who she was; the child of whom? Names meant little, it was the people behind the names she had longed to know.

And now, at last, she did know them. She could be proud of her father, who had died for his country, and of her mother, who had died trying to take care of her child. It was a pity she had never found the liquorice-eating boy, but it no longer mattered. What mattered was that Tess Chandler, who had been Tess Delamere until so recently, had found herself at last.

Tess turned on her side and closed her eyes and below her, Mal began, very softly, to snore.